THE PLUM IN THE GOLDEN VASE

PRINCETON LIBRARY OF ASIAN TRANSLATIONS

The Plum in the Golden Vase

or, CHIN P'ING MEI

VOLUME ONE: THE GATHERING

Translated by David Tod Roy

PRINCETON UNIVERSITY PRESS
PRINCETON, NEW JERSEY

Published by Princeton University Press, 41 William Street,
Princeton, New Jersey 08540
In the United Kingdom: Princeton University Press,
Chichester, West Sussex

Library of Congress Cataloging-in-Publication Data

Hsiao-hsiao-sheng.
[Chin P'ing Mei. English]
The plum in the golden vase, or, Chin P'ing Mei /
translated by David Tod Roy.
p. cm. — (Princeton library of Asian translations)
Includes bibliographical references and index.
Contents: v. 1. The gathering.
ISBN 0-691-06932-8
ISBN 0-691-01614-3 (pbk.)
I. Roy, David Tod, 1933– . II. Title. III. Series.
PL2698.H73C4713 1993
895.1'346—dc20 92-45054 CIP

The publication of this volume was made possible in part through
a grant from the National Endowment for the Humanities,
an independent federal agency, to which we would like
to express our deep appreciation

This book has been composed in Bitstream Electra

Princeton University Press books are printed
on acid-free paper and meet the guidelines for
permanence and durability of the Committee on
Production Guidelines for Book Longevity
of the Council on Library Resources

Printed in the United States of America by Princeton Academic Press

10 9 8 7 6 5 4 3

To all those students, friends, and colleagues

WHO PARTICIPATED WITH ME IN THE EXCITEMENT

OF EXPLORING THE WORLD OF THE *CHIN P'ING MEI*

OVER THE PAST QUARTER CENTURY

CONTENTS

LIST OF ILLUSTRATIONS

ACKNOWLEDGMENTS

TO MY PARENTS, Andrew Tod Roy and Margaret Crutchfield Roy, who served as Presbyterian missionaries in China and Hong Kong from 1930 to 1972, I owe my initial exposure to Chinese language and culture and my interest in Chinese literature.

It was not until the summer of 1949 when I was a sixteen-year-old schoolboy in Nanking that I began, at the insistence of my mother, the serious study of the Chinese language, together with my younger brother, James Stapleton Roy, who is now United States ambassador to China.

During the following decade I was fortunate to be able to study Chinese poetry with Frederick W. Mote; literary Chinese and Sinological method with Derk Bodde, Yang Lien-sheng, and Francis Woodman Cleaves; Chinese history with John King Fairbank; Chinese thought with Benjamin Schwartz; and Chinese literature with James Robert Hightower and David Hawkes. I was also lucky to have Harold L. Kahn and Lloyd Eastman as roommates; and Li-li Ch'en, Elling Eide, Philip A. Kuhn, and Nathan Sivin as fellow students. No one could have had a more distinguished roster of mentors or more stimulating and congenial classmates.

I first encountered Clement Egerton's translation of the *Chin P'ing Mei* in the library of the University of Nanking in 1949, and it was in the spring of 1950, not long before the outbreak of the Korean War, that I bought my first copy of the *Chin P'ing Mei tz'u-hua* in Fu-tzu Miao, an area full of secondhand bookstores and curio shops adjacent to the Confucian Temple in Nanking. While serving a two-year hitch in the Army Security Agency between 1954 and 1956, I bought my first copy of Chang Chu-p'o's edition of the *Chin P'ing Mei* on January 20, 1955, in the bookstore of the Confucian Temple in Tokyo. In view of the Confucian interpretation of the *Chin P'ing Mei* that I was to develop several decades later, it is a Nabokovian coincidence that the first two copies of the book that I acquired were purchased in the purlieus of Confucian Temples.

Over the years, as I read and reread the novel, and especially after I started to teach it at the University of Chicago in 1967, I began to think I saw things in it that had not been pointed out before, but I could not have contributed anything to the study of this tantalizingly enigmatic work if I had not been able to stand on the shoulders of such giants as the seventeenth-century critic Chang Chu-p'o (1670–98), and the twentieth-century scholars Wu Han, Yao Ling-hsi, Feng Yüan-chün, and Patrick Hanan, to name only the most important of them. Their work has not only provided an indispensable foundation but has been a constant source of inspiration to me. Like all students of Chinese fiction and drama, I have also benefited greatly from the pioneering publications of Cheng Chen-to, Sun K'ai-ti, Wu Hsiao-ling, James Crump, Cyril Birch, Hsü Shuo-fang, and C. T. Hsia.

My most consistent source of stimulation over the years, however, has been the work of such former students and present colleagues as Andrew H. Plaks, Daniel Overmyer, Paul V. Martinson, Martha Howard, Peter Li, Jean Mulligan, Katherine Carlitz, Gail King, Sally Church, David Rolston, Indira Satyendra, Amy McNair, Dale Hoiberg, Janet Lynn, and Charles Stone.

Successive curators of the East Asian Library at the University of Chicago, including T. H. Tsien, James Cheng, and Ma Tai-loi, himself a major contributor to scholarship on the *Chin P'ing Mei*, have provided invaluable help in keeping me abreast of the flow of current publications on this subject, a trickle that has recently turned into a flood.

Of those who have read all or part of the manuscript before publication and whose suggestions have helped to improve it in innumerable ways, I wish particularly to thank my friend and former colleague Lois Fusek, the first person to whom I showed the fruits of my labors as I proceeded, and to whose sensitive ear for stylistic niceties I owe the avoidance of many a blunder as well as the gift of many a felicitous emendation. Andrew H. Plaks, David Rolston, and my cousin Catherine Swatek have all read the translation from beginning to end together with the Chinese text and have been generous enough to share with me their detailed and invaluable critical reactions. Others who have read parts of the manuscript and offered suggestions for its improvement include Steven Black, Katherine Carlitz, Susan Daruvala, John C. Duggan, Magnus Fiskesjö, Harold L. Kahn, Matthew Krasowski, Robert A. LaFleur, Lin Chi-ch'eng, Lin Hsiu-ling, Amy Mayer, Robert H. Mazur, Andrea Paradis, Kenneth W. Phifer, Michael J. Puett, Alane Rollings, James St. André, Indira Satyendra, Edward Shaughnessy, Nathan Sivin, Laura Skosey, Charles Stone, Janelle Taylor, and Natalie Wainright.

To my wife, Barbara Chew Roy, who urged me to embark on this interminable task, and who has lent me her unwavering support over the years despite the extent to which this work has preoccupied me, I owe a particular debt of gratitude. Without her encouragement I would have had neither the temerity to undertake the task nor the stamina to continue it.

For indispensable technical advice and assistance concerning computers, printers, and word-processing programs I would like to thank René Pomerleau, my brother James Stapleton Roy, my colleague Ts'ai Fang-p'ei, and particularly Charles Stone.

The research that helped to make this work possible was materially assisted by a Grant for Research on Chinese Civilization from the American Council of Learned Societies in 1976–77. The first draft of the translation itself was supported by a grant from the Translation Program of the National Endowment for the Humanities in 1983–86. The Department of East

Asian Languages and Civilizations at the University of Chicago has also been generous in allowing me time to devote to this project. For all of the above assistance, without which this project could not have been contemplated, I am deeply grateful.

Needless to say, whatever infelicities and errors remain in the translation are solely my own.

INTRODUCTION[1]

THE *CHIN P'ING MEI* (The plum in the golden vase) is an enormous, complex, and sophisticated novel, surprisingly modern in its design, composed by an anonymous author during the second half of the sixteenth century and first published in 1618, or shortly thereafter. The title itself is a multiple pun that gives some indication of the intricacy as well as the ambiguity of the work it designates. It is made up of one character each from the names of three of the major female protagonists of the novel (P'an *Chin*-lien, Li *P'ing*-erh, and P'ang Ch'un-*mei*) that would literally mean *Gold Vase Plum*; it can be semantically construed as *The Plum in the Golden Vase,*[2] or *Plum Blossoms in a Golden Vase*; and it puns with three near homophones that might be rendered as *The Glamour of Entering the Vagina*. The seventeenth-century critic Chang Chu-p'o (1670–98), author of a famous commentary on the *Chin P'ing Mei*, has this to say about the title.

> The three characters of the title *Chin P'ing Mei* constitute a metaphor for the author's accomplishment. Although this book embodies so many of the beauties of spring,[3] every blossom and every petal of which cost the author the creative powers of spring itself to evoke, these beauties should be placed in a golden vase where they can diffuse their fragrance in a cultivated environment and adorn the desks of men of literary talent for all time. They must never be allowed to become the playthings of the rustic or the vulgar. Indeed, plum blossoms in a golden vase depend for their effect on the ability of human effort to enhance the handiwork of Heaven. In like manner, the literary quality of this book is such that it seems, in passage after passage, to have stolen the creative powers of nature itself.[4]

This is a perfectly possible way of interpreting the significance of the title. But there is a passage from a Sung dynasty (960–1279) poem that casts an altogether different light on the matter that is equally consistent with the concerns of the novel. This line from an anonymous poem on the subject of plum blossoms reads, "When displayed in a golden vase I fear they are vulgar."[5] Thus, even the title of this controversial novel poses something of an enigma.

LITERARY IMPORTANCE OF THE *CHIN P'ING MEI*

This work is a landmark in the development of narrative art, not only from a specifically Chinese perspective, but in a world-historical context. With the possible exceptions of *The Tale of Genji* (1010) and *Don Quixote* (1615), neither of which it resembles, but with both of which it can bear comparison, there is no earlier work of prose fiction of equal sophistication in world literature. Although its importance in the history of Chinese fiction has long been acknowledged, the comprehensiveness and seriousness of its indictment of the Chinese society of its time and the innovative quality of its experimental literary technique have not yet been adequately appreciated.

What are some of the reasons for this failure of understanding? On the one hand, its labyrinthine deployment of a bewildering variety of earlier material, ranging from canonical works and liturgical texts to the popular theater and song of the author's own day, and on the other hand its frequent and notorious resort to explicit descriptions of sexual activity, have combined to confuse the critical faculties of all but a few of its readers. As a result, I believe it is safe to say that it has suffered more from serious misinterpretation than any other work of comparable importance in the history of Chinese literature.

Misreadings

What are some of the significant misreadings to which the *Chin P'ing Mei* has been subjected? In roughly chronological order, it has been interpreted as a roman à clef, a work of pornography, a Buddhist morality play, an exercise in naturalism, or a novel of manners. It has also been dismissed by Professor C. T. Hsia of Columbia University, in what is probably the most widely read English-language essay on the subject, as a work of slipshod craftsmanship, characterized by "low culture and ordinary mentality." His essentially negative evaluation is epitomized in the flat statement that "One cannot expect a work to possess ideological or philosophical coherence when it manifests such obvious structural anarchy."[6]

Serious arguments can be made for each of the above readings of the *Chin P'ing Mei*—no one would dispute, for example, that it is, indeed, a novel of manners—and since these readings are not mutually exclusive there is room for considerable overlap between them. But I believe that none of them can be said to do it full justice, and that, far from being characterized by "structural anarchy," it possesses, in fact, the most finely wrought structure of any Chinese novel that has appeared before or since, with the sole exception of the great eighteenth-century masterpiece *Hung-lou meng* (The dream of the red chamber), which is demonstrably in its debt.[7] It is my contention that the *Chin P'ing Mei* is, indeed, possessed of "ideological or philosophical coherence," and that that coherence is provided by the particular brand of conservative orthodox Confucianism that is associated with the name of Hsün-tzu, the great Chinese philosopher of the third century B.C. The reading that is offered below is controversial, but it is put forward in the conviction that it accounts for more of the features of the text than any of the others.

Description

Before pursuing this line of interpretation any further, let me describe the *Chin P'ing Mei* a little more fully. It is a novel of 100 chapters, extending to 2,923 pages in the photo-facsimile of the original wood-block printing from which this translation is made,[8] of which all but chapters 53–57, which are by another hand or hands,[9] can be demonstrated, on the basis of internal evidence, to be the work of a single creative imagination.[10] Despite its selective reliance on a wide spectrum of earlier sources, including most notably the *Shui-hu chuan* (Outlaws of the marsh), from which the nucleus of its plot is derived, these sources are integrated into the design of the overall structure in a way that sets the *Chin P'ing Mei* apart from its predecessors among the great Chinese novels.[11] All of these either are the products of multiple authorship or represent the recasting of traditional bodies of material, and all of them are episodic in structure, whereas the *Chin P'ing Mei*, despite its length, has a tightly controlled unitary plot.

Andrew Plaks of Princeton University has pointed out that the four greatest of the sixteenth-century novels—the *San-kuo chih t'ung-su yen-i* (Romance of the Three Kingdoms), the *Shui-hu chuan*, the *Hsi-yu chi* (Journey to the west), and the *Chin P'ing Mei*—form a qualitative class by themselves, and that they are characterized not only by common structural features, but possibly by congruent authorial intentions.[12] Although I share this view in its general outlines, I believe that the "figural density," to use his term, of the text of the *Chin P'ing Mei* is so pronounced as to set it apart from the other works, at least in this respect. The book is replete with such rich intertextuality, so many internal and external allusions, resonances, and patterns of incremental repetition or replication, as to make it difficult, if not impossible, to apprehend fully on first reading. It is only on a second or third reading that the manifold functions of the individual components of the work begin to be perceived, as they contribute in their different, and sometimes dialogically[13] conflicting, ways to the achievement of a unified overall effect. In short, to be fully appreciated, the *Chin P'ing Mei* requires repeated close readings of the kind that we are accustomed to reserve for the works of the most difficult and demanding novelists in our own tradition, such as James Joyce or Vladimir Nabokov.

Paradoxically, it is, I believe, this very fact that accounts for one of the most misleading misapprehensions about the nature of the work, namely, that it is characterized by slipshod craftsmanship. It cannot be gainsaid that there are a number of loose ends, apparent false starts, and glaring internal discrepancies in the novel as we now have it. I believe that most, if not all, of these can be accounted for, however, if one adopts the hypothesis that it was a "work in progress,"[14] undergoing constant reworking and revision over a considerable period of time, and that the manuscript left the author's hands, under circumstances unknown, before he had quite settled on a definitive version. The very density and intricacy of "the figure in the carpet"[15] make it clear that the novel could not have been composed in any other way.

First Appearance

The first extant reference to the *Chin P'ing Mei*, which occurs in a letter from Yüan Hung-tao (1568–1610) to Tung Ch'i-ch'ang (1555–1636), indicates that a manuscript of the first part of the work was already in circulation among the members of a small coterie of avant-garde intellectuals as early as 1596. No prior mention of the text has been discovered. The novel in its entirety may not have been completed, however, until sometime after that date, possibly as late as 1606, the earliest date for which any reference to a complete manuscript is recorded.[16] Further revisions and/or editorial tampering with the text could also have occurred right up until 1618, the probable date of publication of the earliest printed edition that is extant.[17]

The A, B, and C Editions

In his study of the text of the *Chin P'ing Mei*, Patrick Hanan of Harvard University discriminates between three textual recensions of the novel, which he designates by the letters A, B, and C.[18] This is the A edition. The B edition is thought to date from the Ch'ung-chen reign period (1628–44),[19] and the C edition, which contains an elaborate commentary by Chang Chu-p'o (1670–98), includes a preface dated 1695.[20] The C edition eclipsed the two earlier versions in popularity during the remainder of the Ch'ing dynasty because of the quality of its commentary, but its text does not differ significantly from that of the B edition.

Unfortunately the B edition is an inferior recension of the text, published several decades after the author's time by an editor who not only completely rewrote the better part of the first chapter to suit his own ideas of how a novel should begin, but made significant alterations, including both deletions and additions, on every page of the remainder of the work. It is clear that this editor did not understand certain significant features of the author's technique, especially in the use of quoted material, for much of the poetry incorporated in the original edition is either deleted or replaced with new material that is often less relevant to the context. It is, however, precisely the subtle way in which the author uses poems, songs, snatches of dramatic dialogue, and other types of borrowed material as a form of running ironic commentary on the characters and action of the novel that makes this work unique. The inevitable effect of any tampering with this quoted material is to distort seriously the author's intentions and render the interpretation of his work that much more difficult.[21]

A complete, sparsely annotated translation of the A edition of the *Chin P'ing Mei* appeared in Japanese in 1962,[22] but until recently the only reasonably complete renderings into any European language were the four-volume translation of Clement Egerton, published under the title *The Golden Lotus* in 1939 and reissued in 1972,[23] and the six-volume German translation by the brothers Otto and Artur Kibat, published under the title *Djin Ping Meh: Schlehenblüten in goldener Vase* between 1967 and 1983.[24] The first of these contains no annotation and the second only a slim volume of notes. Both translations were made from a B or C edition. Neither Clement Egerton nor the brothers Kibat are to blame for their unfortunate choice of a text since the A edition was not available to them at the time they undertook their translations in the 1920s; it was only rediscovered in 1932. André Lévy's splendid, well-annotated French translation of 1985, entitled *Fleur en Fiole d'Or (Jin Ping Mei cihua)*,[25] is the first nearly complete translation into any European language to have been made from the A edition, but even this translation unaccountably follows the B and C editions in deleting, either in whole or in part, many of the longer song suites and other types of borrowed material included in the A edition.

Most scholars agree that the A edition is the earliest, and the closest to the work of the original author, and that his innovative rhetorical techniques are best represented by that version of the text. For this reason, in the translation that follows, the first of five projected volumes, I have chosen to translate everything that is included in the A edition, including the two prefaces, colophon, and eight lyrics that precede chapter 1. In addition I have provided in an appendix translations of the lyrics of songs, or song suites, that are only quoted in part, if they are available in other extant sources. I have also gone further than earlier commentators and annotators in attempting to identify the sources of quoted material. I do this because my own research has led me to the conclusion that a knowledge of these sources is germane to our understanding of the story itself, as well as the way in which the "implied author"[26] intends us to interpret it.

Nature of the Story

What kind of a story is it that the *Chin P'ing Mei* has to tell? At first glance it appears to be a tale of what Patrick Hanan has called the "folly and consequences" type,[27] fleshed out with an unprecedented amount of testamentary detail and presented, for the most part, through the medium of a "formal realism"[28] that observes no reticences. This description is accurate enough, so far as it goes, but it does not go far enough to account for all of the features of the text. These include apparent inconsistencies in point of view, occasionally blatant violations of probability, and frequent and abrupt shifts in the level of diction from the convincing mimetic evocation of reality to passages of parody or burlesque. Nor does such a description tell us very much about the probable intentions of the real or implied author, or the value system by which he intends the actions of his characters to be judged. Although the entire text of the novel can be drawn upon to substantiate the interpretation I am going to suggest, I believe that it is already adumbrated in the choice of the pseudonym that is assigned to the author in the preface to the earliest extant edition of the work. Let us consider this name for a few minutes to see what it can tell us.

Importance of the First Preface to the Novel

The pseudonymous author of the first preface to the *Chin P'ing Mei tz'u-hua* (Story of the plum in the golden vase) tells us that the work was written by a friend of his whom he refers to as Lan-ling Hsiao-hsiao Sheng, or the "Scoffing Scholar of Lan-ling." He also tells us that the book was intended by its author to be a serious moral critique of the age.[29] I believe that this preface has not received the critical attention that it deserves, and that it may provide us with a key that is essential to the correct interpretation of the novel.

On the basis of textual analysis, it appears likely that the writer of the preface may have been the author of the novel himself, or if not, at the very least a close associate of the author's who was thoroughly familiar not only with the contents of the novel but also with the rhetorical techniques of the author. As I point out in my annotation to this preface, he shows himself to be conversant with an enormous range of both classical and popular literature, and he interweaves quotations from both types of sources in a manner indistinguishable from that of the author. The degree of intertextuality between the preface and the novel as well as its sources is striking. Since the author of this preface is the only person who has ever claimed personal knowledge of the identity or intentions of the author of the *Chin P'ing Mei*, his testimony deserves to be taken seriously by all students of the novel.

SIGNIFICANCE OF THE SCOFFING SCHOLAR OF LAN-LING

What, then, is the significance of the pseudonym the Scoffing Scholar of Lan-ling? Because Lan-ling is an ancient name for a place in what is now Shantung Province, and because the novel is set in the Shantung area, it has generally been assumed that this pseudonym merely indicates that the author was a native of Shantung. However, there are problems with this interpretation. On the one hand, the assumption that the novel makes significant use of dialect peculiar to Shantung has never been properly documented,[30] and on the other hand, there is some reason to believe, on the basis of internal evidence, that the author of the novel need not have been a native of North China, and may not even have been very well informed about the local customs of that part of the country.[31] I believe that the assumption that the author was a native of Shantung, which does not tell us anything about how to interpret the novel in any case, is merely a red herring, and that the name the Scoffing Scholar of Lan-ling is, instead, intended to allude to Hsün-tzu, the great Confucian philosopher of the third century B.C.

In the brief biography of Hsün-tzu, which is found in the first and most important general history of China, the *Shih-chi* (Records of the historian) by Ssu-ma Ch'ien (145–c. 90 B.C.), we are told that late in his life he moved to the state of Ch'u where the Lord of Ch'un-shen, the prime minister of that state, appointed him to the post of magistrate of Lan-ling. After the assassination of the Lord of Ch'un-shen in 238 B.C. Hsün-tzu lost his post as magistrate but continued to reside in Lan-ling and was buried there after his death. Ssu-ma Ch'ien goes on to say:

> Hsün-tzu hated the corrupt governments of his day, the decadent states and evil princes who did not follow the way but gave their attention to magic and prayers and believed in omens and luck. The Confucian scholars of his day were petty and narrow-minded, while thinkers such as Chuang-tzu were wild and destructive of public morality. So Hsün-tzu expounded the advantages and disadvantages of practicing the Confucian, Mohist, and Taoist teachings. By the time of his death he had written tens of thousands of words.[32]

If Hsün-tzu was motivated to write by a desire to diagnose the evils of his age, as Ssu-ma Ch'ien suggests, and as the internal evidence of his works amply bears out, would not his example be an appropriate one for a similarly motivated author of a later age to invoke by his choice of a pseudonym?

But the place name Lan-ling is not the only element in this pseudonym that may be intended as an allusion to Hsün-tzu. Why did he choose to designate himself the *Scoffing* Scholar of Lan-ling? In Liu Hsiang's (79–8 B.C.) preface to his recension of Hsün-tzu's works, which contains the only other early biography of Hsün-tzu, we find the following statement: "Su Ch'in and Chang I endeavored to persuade the feudal lords with their false doctrines, and thereby attained great prominence. But Hsün-tzu retired and *scoffed* at them, saying, 'He who does not advance himself by espousing such doctrines will also escape destruction for so doing.'"[33]

Su Ch'in (fl. early third century B.C.) and Chang I (fl. late fourth century B.C.), the most famous itinerant politicians of the Warring States period (475–221 B.C.), are the archetypical examples in Chinese lore of statesmen whose amoral arguments are designed to appeal only to the self-interest of the rulers to whom they are addressed. I suggest, therefore, that the pseudonym the Scoffing Scholar of Lan-ling is intended to evoke the image of Hsün-tzu, the ancient magistrate of Lan-ling, who scoffed contemptuously at the amoral status-seekers of his day, and who was motivated by his hatred of what they stood for to write the book that has made him, along with Confucius (551–479 B.C.) and Mencius (c. 372–c. 289 B.C.), one of the three most important figures in the history of orthodox Confucianism.

Hsün-tzu's Philosophy as a Key to the Novel

If this hypothesis about the significance of the pseudonym the Scoffing Scholar of Lan-ling has any merit, it may enable us to develop a more satisfactory interpretation of the *Chin P'ing Mei*. A number of scholars, including Paul Martinson,[34] Andrew Plaks,[35] Peter Rushton,[36] and Katherine Carlitz,[37] have already suggested that the value system of the implied author of the *Chin P'ing Mei* is closer to that of Neo-Confucianism than it is to either Buddhism or Taoism. But Neo-Confucianism, in any of its various manifestations, is a far cry from the form of Confucianism championed by Hsün-tzu. Not only does it incorporate in barely disguised form many features of Buddhist and Taoist thought, but it explicitly repudiates the most fundamental proposition of Hsün-tzu's moral philosophy, namely, that human nature is evil, and at the same time it reveals a penchant for types of metaphysical and cosmological speculation that Hsün-tzu specifically condemns. My reading of the novel has persuaded me that the implied author adheres to an uncompromising version of Hsün-tzu's particular brand of orthodox Confucianism, and that the basic viewpoint he wishes to express is, therefore, not only antagonistic to Buddhism and Taoism, but less than friendly toward Neo-Confucianism, the dominant intellectual system of his day.

Hsün-tzu is most famous for his enunciation of the doctrine that, although everyone has the capacity for goodness, human nature is basically evil and, if allowed to find expression without the conscious molding and restraint of ritual, is certain to lead the individual disastrously astray. That the implied author of the *Chin P'ing Mei* endorses this view should be apparent to even the most superficial reader, but he also makes it quite explicit by quoting in four different places in his novel, including the first chapter, a line that reads "In this world the heart of man alone remains vile."[38]

Hsün-tzu attacks Mencius by name for his doctrine that human nature is basically good and clearly rejects his contention that "A great man is one who retains the heart of a new-born babe."[39] Hsün-tzu's position is unequivocal. He says:

> Those who are good at discussing antiquity must demonstrate the validity of what they say in terms of modern times; those who are good at discussing Heaven must show proofs from the human world. In discussions of all kinds, men value what is in accord with the facts and what can be proved to be valid. Hence if a man sits on his mat propounding some theory, he should be able to stand right up and put it into practice, and show that it can be extended over a wide area with equal validity. Now Mencius states that man's nature is good, but this is neither in accord with the facts, nor can it be proved to be valid. One may sit down and propound such a theory, but he cannot stand up and put it into practice, nor can he extend it over a wide area with any success at all. How, then, could it be anything but erroneous?[40]

It is clear from Hsün-tzu's remarks, both here and elsewhere, that he regarded Mencius as a well-meaning but soft-headed thinker whose position on human nature could not provide a viable foundation for a sound system of moral philosophy. Since the Mencian position on human nature was formally endorsed by both the Ch'eng-Chu and the Lu-Wang schools of Neo-Confucianism, which were prevalent in the sixteenth century, I believe that the implied author of the *Chin P'ing Mei* would have taken exception to them on this as well as other grounds.

It has been suggested that the *Chin P'ing Mei* may have been influenced by the iconoclastic and individualistic ideas of the T'ai-chou school of Neo-Confucianism, an outgrowth of the philosophy of Wang Yang-ming (1472–1529), and by the thought of Li Chih (1527–1602) in particular, the best-known exponent of this school. I believe that Li Chih's emphasis on the *t'ung-hsin*, or "childlike mind," and his assertion, in the words of Theodore de Bary, "that man's nature is originally pure and one should follow wherever it spontaneously leads,"[41] would have been anathema to the implied author of the *Chin P'ing Mei*.

As I read the *Chin P'ing Mei*, it is consciously intended to be, among other things, a frontal attack on just such views as these. In their place the author would surely have endorsed the following statement of Hsün-tzu:

> Now let someone try doing away with the authority of the ruler, ignoring the transforming power of ritual principles, rejecting the order that comes from laws and standards, and dispensing with the restrictive power of punishments, and then watch and see how the people of the world treat each other. He will find that the powerful impose upon the weak, and rob them, the many terrorize the few and extort from them, and in no time the whole world will be given up to chaos and mutual destruction.[42]

Hsün-tzu not only asserts that human nature is basically evil, but also reiterates the traditional Confucian view that the force of moral example moves downward from the apex of the social pyramid, and that if the leaders of society, from the ruler and his officials at the top to the heads of every individual household in the empire, do not exercise their moral responsibility to cultivate their own virtue and set a good example for their family members, colleagues, and subordinates, the inevitable result will be the collapse of the social order.

Though Hsün-tzu repeats these views on human nature and the force of moral example again and again, he offers no more to substantiate them than an already hackneyed set of allusions to the careers of the rulers of antiquity. He thereby violates his own precept that "Those who are good at discussing antiquity must demonstrate the validity of what they say in terms of modern times; those who are good at discussing Heaven must show proofs from the human world."

I believe that the implied author of the *Chin P'ing Mei* was an adherent of Hsün-tzu's philosophy in its entirety, and that he must have felt that it could be used to good purpose in diagnosing the ills of his own day. In so doing, however, he accepted the challenge of the philosopher to demonstrate the validity of his theory in terms of modern times and the human world. If I may resurrect an old critical chestnut, he chose to "show" the truth of Hsün-tzu's theory rather than merely "telling" it.[43] By so doing he succeeded, perhaps for the first time in the history of Chinese literature, in clothing these abstract and ancient bones in "all too human"[44] flesh.

By deliberately choosing to focus his attention on the quotidian minutiae in the household of an ordinary upwardly mobile individual from the midrange of the social pyramid, and periodically reminding his readers of the analogical relationship between this microcosm and the society as a whole,[45] he created a far more effective picture of the self-destructiveness of a society in the process of moral disintegration than he could have done if he had chosen instead, as most of his predecessors did, to depict the stereotypical acts of the emperor and his ministers at court. No more devastatingly convincing indictment of a morally bankrupt society has ever been penned.

THE *CHIN P'ING MEI* AND *BLEAK HOUSE*

The analogies between the methods utilized by the author of the *Chin P'ing Mei* in framing his indictment of sixteenth-century Chinese society and those employed by Charles Dickens in his most famous critique of Victorian society are so striking that I cannot resist quoting a few excerpts from J. Hillis Miller's introduction to a recent edition of *Bleak House*. To an uncanny extent, much of what Miller has to say about the technique of this nineteenth-century English novel is equally true of the *Chin P'ing Mei*. To demonstrate this, I have simply substituted the appropriate Chinese references for their English equivalents in the following patchwork of quotations, while leaving the rest of his wording absolutely intact.

> In writing the *Chin P'ing Mei* the author constructed a model in little of Chinese society in his time. . . . The novel accurately reflects the social reality of the author's day. . . . The means of this mimesis is synecdoche. In the *Chin P'ing Mei* each character, scene, or situation stands for the innumerable other examples of a given type. . . . Nor is the reader left to identify the representative quality of these personages for himself. The narrator constantly calls the reader's attention to their ecumenical role. . . . The *Chin P'ing Mei* is a model of Chinese society in yet another way. The network of relations among the various characters is a miniature version of the interconnectedness of people in all levels of society. . . . In the emblematic quality of the characters and of their connections the *Chin P'ing Mei* is an interpretation of Chinese society. This is so in more than one sense. As a blueprint is an image in another form of the building for which it is the plan, so the *Chin P'ing Mei* transfers Chinese society into another realm, the realm of fictional language. The procedure of synecdochic transference, naming one thing in terms of another, is undertaken as a means of investigation. The author wants to define Chinese society exactly and to identify exactly the causes of its present state. As everyone knows, he finds Chinese society in a bad way. It is in a state dangerously close to ultimate disorder or decay. The energy which gave the social system its initial impetus seems about to run down. . . . With description goes explanation. The author wants to tell how things got as they are, to indict someone for the crime. . . . The novel as a whole is the narrator's report on what he has seen, but it can only be understood by means of a further interpretation—the reader's. The *Chin P'ing Mei* does not easily yield its meaning. . . . The narrator hides as much as he reveals. The habitual method of the novel is to present persons and scenes which are conspicuously enigmatic. The reader is invited in various ways to read

the signs, to decipher the mystery. . . . The narrator offers here and there examples of the proper way to read the book. He encourages the reader to consider the names, gestures and appearances of the characters as indications of some hidden truth about them. . . . The reader of the *Chin P'ing Mei* is confronted with a document which he must piece together, scrutinize, interrogate at every turn—in short, interpret—in order to understand. Perhaps the most obvious way in which he is led to do this is the presentation . . . of a series of disconnected places and personages. . . . Though the relations among these are withheld from the reader, he assumes that they will turn out to be connected. He makes this assumption according to his acceptance of a figure close to synecdoche, metonymy. Metonymy presupposes a similarity or causality between things presented as contiguous and thereby makes storytelling possible. The reader is encouraged to consider these contiguous items to be in one way or another analogous and to interrogate them for such analogies. Metaphor and metonymy together make up the deep grammatical armature by which the reader of the *Chin P'ing Mei* is led to make a whole out of discontinuous parts. . . . The novel must be understood according to correspondences within the text between one character and another, one scene and another, one figurative expression and another. . . . Once the reader has been alerted to look for such relationships he discovers that the novel is a complex fabric of recurrences. Characters, scenes, themes and metaphors return in proliferating resemblances. Each character serves as an emblem of other similar characters. Each is to be understood in terms of his reference to others like him. The reader is invited to perform a constant interpretative dance or lateral movement of cross-reference as he makes his way through the text. . . . Though many of the connections in this elaborate structure of analogies are made explicitly in the text, many are left for the reader to see for himself. . . . The basic structural principle of the *Chin P'ing Mei* . . . is "allegorical" in the strict sense. It speaks of one thing by speaking of another. . . . Everywhere in the *Chin P'ing Mei* the reader encounters examples of this technique of "pointing" whereby one thing stands for another, is a sign for another, indicates another, can be understood only in terms of another, or named only by the name of another. The reader must thread his way though the labyrinth of such connections in order to succeed in his interpretation and solve the mystery of the *Chin P'ing Mei*. . . . It is no accident that the names of so many characters in the novel are either openly metaphorical [Ying Po-chüeh (Sure to Sponge), Wu Tien-en (Devoid of Kindness), Ch'ang Shih-chieh (Forever Borrowing), Wen Pi-ku (Language Always Archaic)] or seem tantalizingly to contain some covert metaphor lying almost on the surface. . . . The novel . . . is made up of an incessant movement of reference in which each element leads to other elements in a constant displacement of meaning. . . . Most people in the novel live without understanding their plight. The novel, on the other hand, gives the reader the information necessary to understand why the characters suffer, and at the same time the power to understand that the novel is fiction rather than mimesis. The novel calls attention to its own procedures and confesses to its own rhetoric, not only, for example, in the onomastic system of metaphorical names already discussed, but also in the insistent metaphors of the style throughout.[46]

Although the critical observations above were written not about the *Chin P'ing Mei* but about *Bleak House*, I believe that they apply with equal force to the Chinese novel, which seems to have anticipated many of Dickens's techniques by two and a half centuries. I do not wish to push the similarities between the *Chin P'ing Mei* and *Bleak House* too far; after all, they are products of very different times and places, and they convey quite different impressions to their readers. Not only was the attitude of Dickens toward the society he criticized more ambivalent, but he was prevented by Victorian reticence from employing the explicit descriptions of sexual conduct for which the Chinese novel is notorious. Nevertheless, I find the congruity of certain literary techniques between the two works to be striking.

Hsün-tzu and the *Chin P'ing Mei*

But if the *Chin P'ing Mei* is, indeed, as complex and ambitious a work as I am claiming it to be, how does the hypothesis that it was consciously inspired, or ideologically informed, by the work of Hsün-tzu help to elucidate it? If this hypothesis still appears to be far-fetched, I would like to point out some of the significant features of the life and work of Hsün-tzu that seem to me to have analogues in the work of the author of the *Chin P'ing Mei*.

Diagnosis of Causes of Social Disintegration

Hsün-tzu witnessed during his lifetime the final demise of the Chou dynasty in 256 B.C., and although the date of his own death is not known, it is clear that he lived long enough to foresee the conquest of the entire Chinese cultural area by the state of Ch'in in 221 B.C., even if he did not see it with his own eyes. The action of the *Chin P'ing Mei* takes place between the years 1112 and 1127, during the reign of Emperor Hui-tsung (r. 1100–1125) of the Northern Sung dynasty (960–1127), and the novel describes the internal collapse of that regime, culminating in the conquest of North China by the alien Chin dynasty (1115–1234) in 1127. It is clear from internal evidence, as well as from the comments of his contemporaries, that although the author set his novel in the Sung dynasty, the conditions that he described in it were really those of his own day, that is, the reigns of the

Chia-ching and Wan-li emperors of the Ming dynasty, who were on the throne from 1521 to 1566 and from 1572 to 1620, respectively. These two emperors, who between them occupied the throne for nearly a century, were among the most irresponsible rulers in the history of imperial irresponsibility. To quote from the summations of their careers in the *Dictionary of Ming Biography*:

> In the early years of his long reign the [Chia-ching] emperor's attention was focused domestically on . . . [the debate over imperial rituals], and in the later years he turned to the cult of religious Taoism in a search for a life without death. Both concerns ruined many able officials, and wasted the energy and wealth of the empire. In foreign relations these years saw Mongol bands sweeping across the Great Wall almost at will, raiding and killing from the northwestern frontier to the Liaotung peninsula. Along the southeast coast the . . . [Japanese pirates] caused equal suffering and destruction, and erupted just as often. In spite of his concentration on selfish whims and the menace on his borders, . . . [the Chia-ching emperor] never let anyone usurp his power and authority. In his time the rich grew richer and the poor became impoverished, particularly in the lower Yangtze area. Wealth bred leisure, which demanded luxuries and entertainment; it also encouraged the development of theatre, art, literature, and printing. The political vigor of the empire, however, began to decline, and the house of Ming showed signs of senescence.[47]

> When the [Wan-li] emperor died in 1620, the far northeast frontier . . . had been overrun by Manchus; ruinous tax increases or extortions had driven large numbers of people into banditry or rebellion in all parts of the empire, and state coffers were . . . drained; posts in both central and provincial government agencies were vacant as often as not, and officials on duty were locked in partisan antagonisms that almost paralyzed the government; and for a quarter century the emperor had done his best to neglect affairs of state. Extravagance, corruption, and ineptitude had become so normal that post-Ming historians have consistently attributed the collapse of the dynasty in the 1640s to trends that developed in Wan-li times, specifically blaming the emperor himself.[48]

This is precisely the world that the author of the *Chin P'ing Mei* describes, and he must have felt a special affinity for the following quotations from Hsün-tzu:

> Every phenomenon that appears must have a cause. The glory or shame that come to a man are no more than the image of his virtue. Meat when it rots breeds worms; fish that is old and dry brings forth maggots. When a man is careless and lazy and forgets himself, that is when disaster occurs.[49]

> Therefore, if the affairs of government are in disorder, it is the fault of the prime minister. If the customs of the country are faulty, it is due to the error of the high

officials. And if the world is not unified and the feudal lords are rebellious, then the heavenly king is not the right man for the job.[50]

If a ruler is frivolous and coarse in his behavior, hesitant and suspicious in attending to affairs, selects men for office because they flatter and are glib, and in his treatment of the common people is rapacious and grasping, then he will soon find himself in peril. If a ruler is arrogant and cruel in his behavior, attends to affairs in an irrational and perverse manner, selects and promotes men who are insidious and full of hidden schemes, and in his treatment of the common people is quick to exploit their strength and endanger their lives but slow to reward their labors and accomplishments, loves to exact taxes and duties but neglects the state of agriculture, then he will surely face destruction.[51]

One of the major themes explored in the *Chin P'ing Mei*, as in the *Hsün-tzu*, is the consequences of failure to assume moral responsibility for one's own actions. This failure is seen to infect the social system from top to bottom, but it is failure at the top that is most reprehensible for it sets an example that encourages the members of the lower orders of society to follow suit. The statements of Hsün-tsu that I have just quoted read like a description of the character and fate, not only of an incompetent ruler, but of Hsi-men Ch'ing, the middle-class protagonist of the *Chin P'ing Mei*. As Katherine Carlitz has pointed out, he displays in his conduct virtually all of the characteristics that Arthur Wright has included in his paradigm of the stereotypical "bad last ruler."[52] Innumerable subtle clues planted in the narrative indicate that Hsi-men Ch'ing is intended to function as a surrogate, not only for the feckless Emperor Hui-tsung of the world ostensibly depicted in the novel, but also for the Chia-ching or Wan-li emperors of the author's own time.

It is no accident that the "six traitors," or six evil ministers, who are traditionally blamed for the fall of the Northern Sung dynasty[53] have their counterpart in Hsi-men Ch'ing's six wives. This particular emblematic correspondence has even richer meaning in terms of the concerns of the novel, however, for in popular Buddhism, as readers of the *Hsi-yu chi* (The journey to the west) will recall, the term "six traitors" is also used as a metaphor for the "six senses."[54]

Hsi-men Ch'ing's servants and employees, who pander to his tastes, assume no responsibility for their own actions and sedulously imitate the examples of immorality set for them by their master and his wives, function as surrogates for the eunuchs and lesser officials in the imperial administration.

Both Hsün-tzu and the implied author of the *Chin P'ing Mei* would surely have agreed that whenever persons such as those described in the novel, at either the macrocosmic or the microcosmic level, assume political power, aided by such ministers and abetted by such eunuchs and lesser officials, the result can only be disaster, whether the temporal setting be the last decades of the Warring States period or the final years of the Northern Sung or Ming dynasties.

Choice of Popular Literary Form to Disseminate Ideas

Chapter 25 of the *Hsün-tzu* is entitled "Ch'eng-hsiang," which is thought to be the name of an ancient variety of work song or chantey. The chapter contains three compositions by Hsün-tzu in this genre, which was of popular origin and which has been described as a remote ancestor of the *ku-tz'u*, or drum song, a type of oral literature that flourished during the Ming and Ch'ing dynasties and is still performed today. In these three works Hsün-tzu employs this form, borrowed from the popular literature of his day, to express his despair over the disorder of his own times, to diagnose the causes of this disorder, to trace its historical antecedents, and to prescribe the remedies necessary for its cure. Tu Kuo-hsiang, an authority on the intellectual history of ancient China, has described this chapter as an epitome of Hsün-tzu's thought and has suggested that he chose to avail himself of this popular literary form in order to gain wider dissemination for his ideas.[55]

I submit that the author of the *Chin P'ing Mei*, who certainly shared Hsün-tzu's despair over the disorder of his day, and who seems to have agreed with his diagnosis of its causes, may also have seen an affinity between Hsün-tzu's use of a popular literary form to epitomize his ideas and his own choice of the long vernacular novel, a popular literary form of his own day, as a vehicle for his critique of late Ming society.

Importance of Formal Structure

Hsün-tzu was the most systematic of the ancient Chinese philosophers, and he chose to present his doctrine to the public in the form of a series of self-contained essays, each of which constitutes a coherent exposition of a particular aspect of his thought. As Burton Watson has pointed out, "Hsün-tzu's work represents the most complete and well-ordered philosophical system of the early period. It is so well ordered and integrated, in fact, that one scarcely knows where to begin in describing it, since each part fits into and locks with all the others."[56]

Although the specific forms they employed are completely different, Hsün-tzu's contribution to the formal development of philosophical discourse finds an analogue in the contribution of the author of the *Chin P'ing Mei* to the formal development of the novel.

Summary of the Plot

The *Chin P'ing Mei* is the first Chinese novel with a unitary plot, characterized by a symmetrical structure in which all the constituent parts are successfully subordinated to the effect of the whole. The work consists of one hundred chapters, which may be divided up as follows.

In the first twenty chapters the major characters are introduced and assembled one by one in Hsi-men Ch'ing's household, which serves as the setting for the main action of the novel. This action takes place in the middle sixty chapters, during the first thirty of which Hsi-men Ch'ing enjoys a rapid rise in socioeconomic status. In this segment of the novel his unremitting pursuit of his own gratification in the sexual, economic, and political spheres seems to be attended by every kind of success for which he seeks. He obtains an official post in the judicial system by presenting lavish gifts to Ts'ai Ching, the most powerful minister at court, and simultaneously gains a son and heir who is the product of a pseudo-incestuous liaison with Li P'ing-erh, the widow of his sworn brother, whom he has taken into his own household against the wishes of his legitimate wife. His gross favoritism toward Li P'ing-erh alienates the other members of his household, but he remains oblivious to this danger in the throes of an infatuation that gradually develops into a deep and genuine emotional attachment.

At exactly the midpoint of the novel, however, in chapters 49 and 50, he unwittingly sets the seal of destruction upon himself and everything he values by his acquisition of a powerful aphrodisiac from a mysterious Indian monk, who is presented to us, without comment, as the personification of a penis, and by his insistence on trying out this aphrodisiac on the unwilling person of his favorite wife while she is in her menstrual period, an act that is both a tyrannical exercise of power and the violation of a ritual taboo.

During the next thirty chapters Hsi-men Ch'ing's star appears to continue in the ascendant, but the seeds of self-destruction that he planted in the first half of the book bear fruit in the death of his son, the death of his favorite wife, and finally his own death in chapter 79, described in memorably gruesome detail, from an overdose of the aphrodisiac he had acquired at the midpoint of the novel, exactly thirty chapters earlier.

In the last twenty chapters Hsi-men Ch'ing's household disintegrates as its members disperse to meet the individual fates that they have prepared for themselves by their acts in the earlier part of the book. In the last chapter, Hsi-men Ch'ing's new son and heir, born to him by his neglected legitimate wife at the very moment of his own death, is spirited away into a life of celibacy by a mysterious Buddhist monk who is, as it were, the mirror image of the monk who had appeared to him in chapter 49 in the guise of a personified penis, and from whom he had obtained the aphrodisiac by means of which he encompassed his self-destruction. Thus, at the end of the novel he has been replaced not by his own son and heir, but by his former servant, Tai-an, as much a rascal as himself, upon whom his surviving legitimate wife is forced to depend. His ancestral line, or dynasty, may be said to have come to its irrevocable end.

Some critics have suggested that the novel ends on a positive note of redemption since the entrance of Hsi-men Ch'ing's son into a life of religious devotion may serve to atone for the sins of his father.[57] I do not believe that this interpretation can be sustained by a careful reading of the text. First, Hsi-men Ch'ing's son is named Hsiao-ko, which means Filial Son, and yet by entering the celibate life of the Buddhist clergy he violates the cardinal duty of a filial son, which is to perpetuate the family line and thereby make possible the continuation of the ancestral sacrifices. This sort of irony is one of the most commonly used devices of the author. Second, the survival of Hsi-men Ch'ing's son as a celibate monk, and thus only half a man in the traditional Chinese view, coincides temporally with the survival of Emperor Hui-tsung's son Kao-tsung (r. 1127–62), the founder of the Southern Sung dynasty (1127–1279), which is only half a dynasty, because it governs but a part of the Chinese cultural world. Third, just as it is a Buddhist monk who spirits Hsiao-ko away into a celibate life, so it is Buddhism that emasculates Hsün-tzu's hard-headed brand of orthodox Confucianism by transforming it into the hybridized and metaphysical Neo-Confucianism, which received its definitive formulation at the hands of Chu Hsi (1130–1200) during the lifetime of the same Emperor Kao-tsung (1107–87).

Incidentally, the historical Kao-tsung abdicated his throne in 1162, which, although it takes place outside the time frame of the novel, may be thought of as an act analogous to Hsiao-ko's abdication of his familial responsibilities. No less authoritative a commentator than the Ch'ien-lung emperor of the Ch'ing dynasty (r. 1735–95) declared in an edict, as paraphrased by Harold Kahn, that "Sung Kao-tsung, far from being an exemplar, was a weakling and a fool. Having relinquished any interest or involvement in the pressing affairs of state (notably, it was implied, the reconquest of the north), Kao-tsung . . . had abdicated his responsibility as well as his power."[58] It so happens that Hsün-tzu was virtually alone among ancient Chinese philosophers in condemning the ideal of voluntary abdication as exemplified by the legends about the sage emperors Yao and Shun.[59] For all of these reasons, and more, I do not believe that the ending of the novel is intended to strike anything but a somber note.[60]

The author's concern with the creation of an intricate fictional structure is far greater than this brief outline of the plot of the *Chin P'ing Mei* would suggest. Not only is each of the one hundred chapters composed of two or more episodes that serve to illuminate each other either by analogy or by contrast,[61] but the novel can also be seen to be built out of ten-chapter units that reveal a characteristic internal structure of their own. Each unit tends to develop a particular narrative or thematic line through the early chapters, to be interrupted by the introduction of a significant twist or new development, usually in the seventh chapter, and to culminate in a climax in the ninth chapter. These repetitive configurations, recurring at ten-chapter intervals, have the effect of producing a subliminal wavelike pattern that underlies and reinforces the overall structure as outlined above.

The plot of the *Chin P'ing Mei* may thus be described as a perfectly symmetrical attempt to demonstrate in unprecedentedly circumstantial detail the thesis enunciated by Hsün-tzu when he says: "In the world those who obey the dictates of ritual will achieve order; those who turn against them will suffer disorder. Those who obey them will win safety; those who turn against them will court danger. Those who obey them will be preserved; those who turn against them will be lost."[62]

I believe that the author of the *Chin P'ing Mei* may have seen Hsün-tzu's imposition of a formal order on the presentation of his thought as analogous to his own imposition of a formal order on the telling of his story. In any case, from a strictly formalistic point of view, both achievements were virtually without precedent and have seldom, if ever, been surpassed within the Chinese cultural context.

Ironic Setting and the Rectification of Names

The very choice of a setting for the novel may have been intended as an ironic commentary on the action, which derives its force from one of the major principles enunciated by Hsün-tzu. The episode involving Hsi-men Ch'ing and P'an Chin-lien that forms the nucleus of the plot of the *Chin P'ing Mei* is borrowed from the *Shui-hu chuan*;[63] but in that work it takes place in the district town of Yang-ku, whereas in the *Chin P'ing Mei* the scene of the action has been shifted to the district town of Ch'ing-ho. Since the other features of the original episode are copied almost verbatim, it is apparent that this change of locale must reflect a conscious choice on the part of the author of the *Chin P'ing Mei*. What is the significance of this alteration?

First of all it needs to be pointed out that the supposed small-town provincial setting of the novel is itself one of the author's feats of legerdemain. The real model underlying the description of the locale in which the events of the novel take place is neither Yang-ku nor Ch'ing-ho, nor any of the other sites in Shantung Province that have been proposed, but the city of Peking, which served as the capital of the Ming empire from 1421 to 1644. Wu Hsiao-ling has demonstrated that at least fifty-six of the place names and institutional names mentioned in the novel correspond to places and institutions in sixteenth-century Peking. Many are peculiar to it and are not known to have existed anywhere else.[64] This is, of course, completely consistent with the author's rhetorical strategy of using the microcosm of a household in a provincial town to suggest subliminally the macrocosm of the empire and its administrative nerve center in the capital city. But why did he settle on Ch'ing-ho as the name of his microcosmic world?

The name Ch'ing-ho means "Clear River." It is an ancient Chinese idea that the waters of the Yellow River will run clear only if a true sage is on the throne. The explanation for this belief is clearly stated in chapter 12 of the *Hsün-tzu*, entitled "The Way of the Ruler," where one reads: "The ruler is the source of order. The officials maintain the regulations; the ruler nurtures the source. If the water of the source is clear, the lower reaches of the stream will be clear. If the water of the source is muddy, the lower reaches of the stream will be muddy."[65]

The dire consequences that will inevitably ensue, in Hsün-tzu's view, if a society is impure at its source are precisely those described in the world of the *Chin P'ing Mei*. Hsün-tzu is famous for his insistence on the need for the "rectification of names" and on the dangers inherent in any situation in which names become divorced from realities.[66] What better way could there be to illustrate Hsün-tzu's doctrine on the rectification of names than to create in the household of Hsi-men Ch'ing a microcosm of an utterly corrupt society and to locate it in a place the very name of which implies the beneficent effects of good government?

There may even be a further irony implied by the author's choice of Ch'ing-ho as the setting for his novel. According to Hsieh Chao-che (1567–1624), who was one of the first persons to express his admiration for the *Chin P'ing Mei* while it was still circulating only in manuscript,[67] and who also served as an official in the very area in which the novel is set, Ch'ing-ho is located on a site that was known in ancient times as Pei-ch'iu, or "Mound of Cowrie Shells."[68] Since cowrie shells were used as currency in ancient times, the original name might be rendered colloquially as "Money Pile," a name that accurately reflects the values of the world of Hsi-men Ch'ing, where money is all powerful. But this unsavory reality has been disguised by the imposition of the high-sounding name Clear River, which implies a society in which the most powerful force is not money but the moral example of a sage ruler. This gross discrepancy between name and reality, the dangers of which are given their classic exposition by Hsün-tzu, is a major motif of the *Chin P'ing Mei*, and the choice of Ch'ing-ho as its setting is unlikely to have been fortuitous.

Sexual Description and Criticizing by Indirection

Chapter 26 of the *Hsün-tzu* is entitled "*Fu*," or "Rhapsodies," the same word that was later used to designate the literary genre of that name. It consists of a series of elaborate riddles in a kind of rhyming parallel prose, which are, in fact, sustained exercises in double entendre.[69] The original purpose of these exercises is not easy to ascertain, and various theories have been put forward, but the prevailing traditional view has always been that they are didactic in intent. For example, the postscript to the section on *shih* (poetry) and *fu* (rhapsodies) in the "Essay on Literature" in the *Han-shu* (History of the Former Han dynasty), by Pan Ku (32–92), says: "The great Confucianist Hsün-tzu, and the Ch'u official Ch'ü Yüan, when they encountered slander, and mourned about their country, both made *fu* in order to criticize by indirection."[70]

The author of the *Chin P'ing Mei* also makes frequent use of the device of sustained double entendre, and in most such passages the thinly disguised imagery evoked is sexual. Since the *Chin P'ing Mei* has often been misread as a work intended to celebrate the pleasures of sex, these passages have usually been either appreciated as adventitious jeux d'esprit or criticized for their incongruence with the air of verisimilitude that is alleged to characterize the bulk of the work. An example of a passage that has drawn such criticism[71] occurs in chapter 80, after the death of Hsi-men Ch'ing, when a group of his sycophantic and self-serving friends gather in his household to express their condolences and present a funeral eulogy that turns out, on careful reading, to be a thinly disguised description of the male genitalia.[72]

I believe that it was never any part of the author's intent to celebrate the pleasures of sex and that the sexual acts that he explicitly describes, and which have won the novel such notoriety, are intended, in fact, to express in the most powerful metaphor available to him the author's contempt for the sort of persons who indulge in them. The spheres of sexual, economic, and political aggrandizement are symbolically correlated in the novel in such a way that the calculated shock value of the sexual descriptions spills over into the other realms and colors the reader's response to them.

It is an essential part of the author's rhetorical strategy deliberately to awaken the latent sensuality of his readers by inducing them to empathize with the sensual experiences of his characters, only to shift unexpectedly from a realistic mode into one of mock-heroic or burlesque. The effect of this technique, which is used throughout the novel so repeatedly as to create a pattern, is to bring readers up short and remind them that, to the extent that they have allowed themselves to empathize with the events that they have just experienced vicariously, they have shown themselves to be, at least potentially, capable of the same, or similar, acts. This technique is, therefore, evidence not of the author's failure to maintain a consistent tone, but rather of his constant endeavor to provoke self-reflection on the part of readers by carefully modulated manipulations of their distance from the events described in the text. This is, in short, a significant feature of the author's overall design, in both senses of the word. As Robert Scholes has said:

> When we become aware of design in reading, so that one part of a story reminds us of parts we have read earlier, we are actually involved in a movement counter to our progress from beginning to end. Plot wants to move us along; design wants to delay our movement, to make us pause and "see." The counteraction of these two forces is one of the things which enriches our experience of fiction.[73]

Far from wishing the reader to remain mesmerized by the mimetic evocation of reality, the author of the *Chin P'ing Mei* wants to make readers periodically stop to evaluate not only the events and characters in the text, but themselves and their own reactions to them. As Alfred Appel says of *Lolita*, another novel of innovative technique and problematic subject matter, "Nabokov is able to have it both ways, involving the reader on the one hand in a deeply moving yet outrageously comic story, rich in verisimilitude, and on the other engaging him in a game made possible by the interlacings of verbal figurations which undermine the novel's realistic base and distance the reader from its dappled surface, which then assumes the aspect of a gameboard."[74] Passages such as this parodic eulogy thus serve to alert readers to the fact that in the estimation of the implied author not only Hsi-men Ch'ing but anyone who empathizes with him is in danger of becoming nothing but a prick, in that he has allowed his libido to aggrandize itself at the expense of his other faculties. Thus, the rhetorical trick of sustained double entendre is used in the *Chin P'ing Mei*, as it is in the *Hsün-tzu*, as but another form of the traditional device of criticizing by indirection.

Economic and Sexual Analogies

Even Hsün-tzu's economic theory may be reflected in the *Chin P'ing Mei*. In the chapter entitled "The Regulations of a King," Hsün-tzu says:

> A king enriches his people, a dictator enriches his soldiers, a state that is barely managing to survive enriches its high officers, and a doomed state enriches only its coffers and stuffs its storehouses. But if its coffers are heaped up and its storehouses full, while its people are impoverished, this is what is called to overflow at the top but dry up at the bottom. Such a state will be unable to protect itself at home and unable to fight its enemies abroad, and its downfall and destruction can be looked for at any moment.[75]

> These are the king's laws. . . . Goods and grain shall be allowed to circulate freely, so that there is no hindrance or stagnation in distribution; they shall be transported from one place to another as the need may arise, so that the entire region within the four seas becomes like one family.[76]

In chapter 49 of the *Chin P'ing Mei* the censor Tseng Hsiao-hsü (1049–1127), the only incorruptible official portrayed in the entire novel, submits a memorial to the throne protesting the economic policies of Ts'ai Ching (1046–1126), the venal prime minister. In this memorial he states: "The wealth of the empire should be allowed to circulate freely. To seize the economic resources of the people and accumulate them in the capital is not, I fear, the way to attain a just administration. . . . I have heard it said that if the people's resources are exhausted, who will there be to protect the country for you?"[77]

Ts'ai Ching is, of course, the name of an actual historical figure, but he is made to order for the purposes of the author of the *Chin P'ing Mei*, for his name happens to pun with the words for money and semen. An equation between these two significant entities is suggested in innumerable subtle ways throughout the novel. This symbolic correlation is hinted at as early as chapter 6, where one finds a poem describing Hsi-men Ch'ing's sexual intercourse with P'an Chin-lien, the last couplet of which reads:

> When pleasure reaches its height passions are
> intense, and feelings know no bounds;
> As the mouth of the "divine turtle"
> disgorges its "silvery stream."[78]

The term "divine turtle" is a standard euphemism for the penis. The expression "silvery stream" in the context of this poem refers unmistakably to semen, but it also puns with another compound that means "copper cash." Taking the pun into consideration, this line could, therefore, be rendered, "The eye of the urethra disgorges copper cash, or filthy lucre." The possibility of this interpretation is reinforced by the following line of prose, which tells us that before going home Hsi-men Ch'ing "left behind a few pieces of loose silver." The verb that I have rendered as "left behind" puns with another meaning "to dribble" and thus serves to introduce the subliminal impression that Hsi-men Ch'ing made his departure after having "dribbled a few pieces of loose silver."[79] If this were an isolated instance, it might be argued that I am reading too much into the text, but the fact is that the author uses devices of this kind so frequently that the text calls out for this sort of interpretation.

What is the significance of this symbolic interchangeability of money and semen? It is not that the author of the *Chin P'ing Mei* wishes to condemn sexuality per se, any more than he would condemn economic or political activities in themselves, but that he wishes to call attention to the dangers of excess and immoderation in all spheres of human activity. For this purpose the explicit description of immoderate sexual activity serves him as a particularly potent metaphor. In the course of the novel, sexual aggrandizement and economic and political aggrandizement are shown to go hand in hand as symptoms of the same malaise. As Katherine Carlitz has put it:

> Sexual conduct is seen as one aspect of a system of human relationships whose various elements must be properly restrained and balanced; immoderate sexual activity is destructive both of the individual self and of this fabric of social relations. In this it functions exactly like the drives for wealth and power, which when taken to extremes of avarice and tyranny also damage the canonized interdependent human relationships. Since immoderate drives for or exercise of sex, wealth, and power are equivalent in outcome, one of them may suggest another without necessarily standing for it—that is to say, none of these three drives merely symbolizes one of the others; rather, they are inextricably linked throughout the book, in part by the image of the bad last ruler.[80]

One of the major themes of the *Chin P'ing Mei* is that if the resources of the human body are not adequately distributed, but are constantly being drawn upon to replenish the supply of semen in the testicles, because it is being prodigally wasted, the result will be death for the individual. The same thing is true of the fiscal resources of the state. If they must be concentrated in the capital to replenish the prodigal expenditures of the ruler, this will drain the rest of the country of its resources, and the result will be the collapse or demise of the state. As Hsün-tzu colorfully puts it, "This is what is called to overflow at the top but dry up at the bottom." It is no accident that Tseng Hsiao-hsü's futile protest against Ts'ai Ching's irresponsible fiscal policy takes place in the same chapter in which Hsi-men Ch'ing acquires the aphrodisiac that, exactly thirty chapters later, causes his bloated penis, of which he has become the personification, to literally "overflow at the top but dry up at the bottom."[81]

I could go on and on in this vein, but I think that I have said enough already to indicate why I think that the probable allusion to Hsün-tzu in the pseudonym the Scoffing Scholar of Lan-ling may serve as a valuable key to the meaning of the *Chin P'ing Mei*. If my hypothesis is correct, it follows, as I have already stated, that the moral value system by which the author intended the actions in his work of fiction to be judged is that of a conservative brand of orthodox Confucianism. Far from being a manifestation of the syncretism, free thinking, and hedonism of the late Ming period, as some critics have suggested, the *Chin P'ing Mei* was written as a reaction against them.

Fallacy of Assumption that Human Nature Is Good

I believe that the author of this masterpiece wished to demonstrate the fallaciousness of the complacent assumption that human nature is basically good, and to reassert by negative example the need for unremitting conscious, rational, and hence, necessarily, artificial activity, molded and restrained by ritual and directed toward the goals of self-cultivation, on the one hand, and social amelioration, on the other. Nothing could have appeared more misguided to him than the suggestion that man should give in to the "claims of . . . the instinctive self," to use C. T. Hsia's phrase,[82] or feel free to "do his own thing." His attitude toward human culture is instead, like that of Hsün-tzu, remarkably similar to that expressed by Sigmund Freud in his essay entitled *Civilization and Its Discontents*.[83] It is an ironic coincidence that both the author of the *Chin P'ing Mei* and Freud have been popularly misunderstood to endorse precisely those permissive attitudes that they most severely condemned.

Author's Need to Disguise His Intentions

The question remains, however, in view of the all too common misinterpretations of the novel, why the author of the *Chin P'ing Mei* chose to express himself as elliptically as he did. I believe that his reasons for doing so were probably the same as those that led so many of his illustrious predecessors to adopt the device of criticizing by indirection. If he had explicitly stated his intention to criticize the condition of the society of his day, and by unmistakable implication to lay the blame for it squarely in the lap of the reigning emperor, his novel would have been regarded as seditious, and he would have placed not only his own life but the very existence of his work in jeopardy.

The last paragraph of the book of *Hsün-tzu*, which is from a part of the text believed to have been written by his disciples after his death, makes the following statement about him:

> Hsün-tzu found himself oppressed by a disordered age and threatened by severe punishments. Above there was no worthy ruler, and below he encountered the violent rule of Ch'in. Ritual and justice did not prevail, the moral example of the ruler was lacking, men of benevolence were forced into retirement, the world was dark, those who maintained proper standards of conduct were reviled, and the feudal lords were overturned. At such a time as this, the wise could not exercise their thoughts, the able could not administer, and the worthy could find no employment. When the ruler above is benighted and blind, worthy men will avoid him and refuse to accept office. Thus it was that Hsün-tzu who possessed the mind of a sage had to feign madness and play the fool in the eyes of the world. This is the meaning conveyed by the *Book of Songs* when it says:
>
> "Very clear-sighted was he and wise.
> He assured his own safety."[84]

Like Hsün-tzu, the author of the *Chin P'ing Mei* must have felt it necessary to disguise his intentions. So successful was the disguise he adopted that though his book achieved immediate notoriety, it has then and now, more often than not, been attacked, and not infrequently banned, as a work of pornography, or dismissed as a work that appeals only to vulgar or prurient tastes. Its true value has been appreciated only by those who have studied it with the care that its complexity demands. It is the desire to demonstrate this complexity, and to preserve, to the extent possible, the innovative rhetorical features of the most authentic edition, that has led me to undertake this new annotated translation.

Questions Concerning Authorship

On the controversial questions of whether the *Chin P'ing Mei* is the product of collective or individual authorship, whether it was written during the Chia-ching (1522–1566) or Wan-li (1573–1620) reign periods, and whether the author was any of the twenty or more individuals who have been proposed for the honor, I will be brief.[85]

As the reader who has read thus far will have inferred, I believe that, although the possibility of editorial tinkering by persons other than the author cannot be ruled out, a work of this kind could only be the product of a single, highly original mind.

The Chia-ching and Wan-li emperors were equally irresponsible rulers in their different ways, and either or both of them could have been drawn upon as models for the life-styles of Hsi-men Ch'ing or the Emperor Huitsung of the novel. I believe, however, that the weight of the evidence favors a Wan-li date of composition. There are historical figures referred to by name in the novel who did not become prominent before the Wan-li period and works of literature quoted in the novel, the extant editions of which do not antedate that time. But the most compelling reason, it seems to me, for preferring the later date is that a Chia-ching date of composition would not square with what we know of literary history. There is abundant evidence that the author of the *Chin P'ing Mei* was familiar, in one form or another, with the *San-kuo chih t'ung-su yen-i*, the *Shui-hu chuan*, and the *Hsi-yu chi*, but no evidence that the authors, or redactors, of any of these works were familiar with it. Nor is there any other work of comparable scope or sophistication reliably datable to the earlier period. It is hard to imagine that a work of such innovative technique, dealing with such controversial subject matter, with such unprecedented freedom, and which elicited such excited comment as soon as even a part of it was discovered in 1596, could have been in existence for a third of a century without attracting any attention.

I have proposed elsewhere that the author of the *Chin P'ing Mei* may have been T'ang Hsien-tsu (1550–1616), the leading playwright of his day and an all-around man of letters, who felt an affinity for Hsün-tzu, was known for his ability to write in a variety of different styles, was an aficionado of pastiche, and employed many of the rhetorical techniques of the novel in his five extant plays. The facts of his life, which is richly documented, and what is known about the prepublication history of the *Chin P'ing Mei* dovetail to a remarkable extent. Even if the author was someone else, he must have been a person with similar qualifications, that is, a member of the educated elite who was also profoundly familiar with the tradition of vernacular fiction and drama. I still think that T'ang Hsien-tsu is a more plausible candidate for the honor than any other who has been proposed, but since I have been unable to present any more than circumstantial evidence, and the case is not proven, I will say no more about it here.[86]

Bakhtin and the Rhetoric of the *Chin P'ing Mei*

Finally, let me revert once again to the rhetoric of the *Chin P'ing Mei* and how I have chosen to deal with it in my translation. The text of the novel is replete with verbatim quotations from every level of traditional discourse as well as parodies of the generic characteristics of many of them. These discourses and genres speak in different voices and represent divergent or conflicting points of view, which result in apparent antinomies of every kind. But the very pervasiveness of these antinomies has led me to conclude that in most cases they are an essential and deliberate part of the author's rhetorical strategy and not the result of mere carelessness or the imperfect melding of disparate materials. I believe that they are a manifestation of *heteroglossia*, and that they are intended to function *dialogically*, in the senses of those words expounded by the Russian critic M. M. Bakhtin in his book *The Dialogic Imagination*, from which I will quote a few key passages.

> The author participates in the novel (he is omnipresent in it) with *almost no direct language of his own*. The language of the novel is a *system* of languages that mutually and ideologically interanimate each other. . . . Therefore, there is no unitary language or style in the novel. But at the same time there does exist a center of language (a verbal-ideological center) for the novel. The author (as creator of the novelistic whole) cannot be found at any one of the novel's language levels: he is to be found at the center of organization where all levels intersect.[87]
>
> The novel can be defined as a diversity of social speech types (sometimes even diversity of languages) and a diversity of individual voices, artistically organized. The internal stratification of any single national language into social dialects, char-

acteristic group behavior, professional jargons, generic languages, languages of generations and age groups, tendentious languages, languages of the authorities, of various circles and of passing fashions, languages that serve the specific sociopolitical purposes of the day, even of the hour (each day has its own slogan, its own vocabulary, its own emphasis)—this internal stratification present in every language at any given moment of its historical existence is the indispensable prerequisite for the novel as a genre. The novel orchestrates all its themes, the totality of the world of objects and ideas depicted and expressed in it, by means of the social diversity of speech types . . . and by the differing individual voices that flourish under such conditions. Authorial speech, the speeches of narrators, inserted genres, the speech of characters are merely those fundamental compositional unities with whose help heteroglossia . . . can enter the novel; each of them permits a multiplicity of social voices and a wide variety of their links and interrelationships (always more or less dialogized). These distinctive links and interrelationships between utterances and languages, this movement of the theme through different languages and speech types, its dispersion into the rivulets and droplets of social heteroglossia, its dialogization—this is the basic distinguishing feature of the stylistics of the novel.[88]

The compositional forms for appropriating and organizing heteroglossia in the novel . . . are extremely heterogeneous in their variety of generic types. . . . The so-called comic novel makes available a form for appropriating and organizing heteroglossia that is both externally very vivid and at the same time historically profound: its classic representatives in England were Fielding, Smollet, Sterne, Dickens, Thackeray and others. . . .

In the English comic novel we find a comic-parodic re-processing of almost all the levels of literary language, both conversational and written that were current at the time. Almost every novel we mentioned above as being a classic representative of this generic type is an encyclopedia of all strata and forms of literary language: depending on the subject being represented, the story-line parodically reproduces first the forms of parliamentary eloquence, then the eloquence of the court, or particular forms of parliamentary protocol, or court protocol, or forms used by reporters in newspaper articles, or the dry business language of the City, or the dealings of speculators, or the pedantic speech of scholars, or the high epic style, or Biblical style, or the style of the hypocritical moral sermon or finally the way one or another concrete and socially determined personality, the subject of the story, happens to speak.[89]

A stylistic analysis of the novel cannot be productive outside a profound understanding of heteroglossia, and understanding of the dialogue of languages as it exists in a given era. But in order to understand such dialogue, or even to become aware initially that a dialogue is going on at all, mere knowledge of the linguistic and stylistic profile of the languages involved will be insufficient: what is needed is a profound understanding of each language's socio-ideological meaning and an

> exact knowledge of the social distribution and ordering of all the other ideological voices of the era.[90]

Although Bakhtin was writing about a certain kind of European novel in the above quotations, I believe that, just as in the case of the excerpts from J. Hillis Miller's introduction to *Bleak House,* his insights may also be applicable to some Chinese works of fiction, and to the *Chin P'ing Mei* in particular. Whether or not the above-mentioned antinomies in the *Chin P'ing Mei* are ultimately susceptible of resolution, I believe that the author of the novel hoped that his readers would attempt to resolve them, and that this endeavor would result in an enhanced, rather than a diminished, appreciation of his artistry. In fact, I would go so far as to say that it is precisely in the struggle to reconcile these antinomies that the meaning of the work resides.

Creative Use of Traditional Formulaic Material

One of the unique features of the technique of this extraordinary novel is the author's interweaving of the lyrics of the actual popular songs of his day with the interior monologue or spoken dialogue of certain of his characters. The spoken or unspoken thoughts of the characters are also often expressed in a complex mosaic of borrowed language, comprising proverbial sayings, catch phrases, stock epithets and couplets, quotations from earlier poetry and song, and formulaic language of all kinds inherited from the literary tale as well as traditional vernacular fiction and drama. Each of these different voices would have been familiar to the author's contemporaries and would have instantly summoned to mind a rich variety of connotations and generic expectations that are, unfortunately, largely lost on the modern reader, even in China.

This feature of the text makes it extremely difficult to translate, but I have tried to convey some idea of it by certain arbitrary conventions of my own. I have indented all examples of poetry or song to set them off from the surrounding prose. But I have also indented further most, if not all, examples of proverbial sayings, stock couplets, formulaic language, and descriptive parallel prose. Although this feature of my translation may seem annoyingly strange at first, I hope it will have the effect of defamiliarization, highlighting this phenomenon, and alerting the reader to the subtle counterpoint of different linguistic voices in the original.

The use the author makes of all this borrowed conventional material is neither careless nor accidental. One of the major themes of the narrative is the fatal consequences of self-deception. In passage after passage, beginning as early as the first chapter, P'an Chin-lien, whom the reader soon discovers to be a ruthless and depraved adulteress and murderer, is shown to identify herself almost completely with the personae of the sentimental popular lyrics that she sings, both to herself and to others. This is, therefore, on the one hand an economical and aesthetically effective way of demonstrating both the form and extent of P'an Chin-lien's self-deception, and on the other hand a telling exposure of the inadequacy of such traditional stereotypes to convey the complexity and problematic quality of human reality. The way in which the author of the *Chin P'ing Mei* exploits this kind of conventional material for his own unconventional ends is unprecedented in the history of Chinese fiction, but is reminiscent of the practice of some contemporary Western writers who have experimented with similar effects. Dennis Potter, for example, in his 1981 TV drama *Pennies from Heaven* uses popular songs from the 1940s, sung and mimed by the characters themselves at appropriate moments in the action, as an inventive and ironic means of commenting on the narrative in much the same way that sixteenth-century popular songs are used in the *Chin P'ing Mei*.[91]

The author does not introduce all his innovative effects at once; in fact, the first twenty chapters of the novel are in some ways the least representative. Much of the first ten chapters, especially those parts of chapters 1–6 and 8–10 that deal with the story of Wu Sung's relations with P'an Chin-lien and Hsi-men Ch'ing, are taken, with relatively little alteration, from chapters 23–27 of the *Shui-hu ch'üan-chuan*. The reader who is interested in such comparisons should read these sections of the *Chin P'ing Mei* together with Sidney Shapiro's translation of those chapters in *Outlaws of the Marsh*. This relationship between the two texts is well known, but the extent to which the author of the *Chin P'ing Mei* also makes use of material from other parts of the *Shui-hu ch'üan-chuan* is something that needs to be emphasized. There is hardly a chapter in the earlier novel from which some narrative detail, proverbial saying, or passage of descriptive parallel prose or verse is not purloined, and these borrowings are woven into the fabric of the *Chin P'ing Mei* from one end to the other, but especially in the first twenty and last twenty chapters, which are also the closest to each other, and to the earlier work, in terms of narrative technique.

It would seem that the author may have wanted to lull his readers into thinking they were reading a type of fiction with which they were already familiar, and to lure them only gradually into the new fictional universe that his innovative techniques, thematic focus, and subject matter create as the narrative unfolds. The second decade of chapters, which focus on the introduction of Li P'ing-erh into Hsi-men Ch'ing's household, are structurally parallel to the first, which focus on the same aspect of P'an Chin-lien's story, but in the course of incremental repetition there is a perceptible richening of circumstantial detail and an increase in the incidence of song and of other new narrative elements, which become more and more prominent as the story proceeds. In the course of the middle sixty chapters, especially chapters 51–80, there is a crescendo effect as time slows down and the amount of circumstantial detail becomes almost suffocating, leading up to the climax of Hsi-men Ch'ing's death in chapter 79, immediately after which time speeds up and the narrative focus becomes more diffuse, as at the beginning of the novel. In view of the prominent role of sexual imagery in the novel and the immediate cause of Hsi-men Ch'ing's death, it is not surprising that this narrative shape itself should be subtly suggestive of the cycle of tumescence and detumescence.

Nature of Annotation

It is my conviction that if works such as *Ulysses* or *Lolita*, which were written in English in our own century, require extensive annotation in order to be properly understood, an artistically complex sixteenth-century Chinese novel such as the *Chin P'ing Mei* must also require extensive annotation if it is to be fully appreciated. Like *Ulysses* and *Lolita*, the *Chin P'ing Mei* contains thousands of unidentified allusions to, and quotations from, earlier works of literature. In my notes I have striven to identify either direct sources or earlier occurrences for as much of this material as possible. Where I believe that the author has borrowed from an identifiable source, I describe it as the proximate or ultimate source. In other cases, where the expressions occur ubiquitously in classical or vernacular literature and can be said to be in the public domain, I merely list a sampling of earlier occurrences in roughly chronological order, without implying that the author was borrowing from any one of them directly. It is my hope that the annotation will give the reader some notion of the rich intertextuality[92] of this novel and of the extraordinary breadth of the author's erudition.

Philosophy of Translation

As I have already pointed out, the text of the *Chin P'ing Mei* is characterized by an amazingly dense network of internal, as well as external, allusions, verbal repetitions, resonances, cross-references, and patterns of incremental repetition or replication. What Brian Boyd says of Vladimir Nabokov's practice in this regard is equally true of the *Chin P'ing Mei*.

> He transmutes a recurrent element sufficiently for the repetition to be overlooked, he casually discloses one piece of partial information and leaves it up to us to connect it with another apparently offhand fact, or he groups together stray details and repeats the random cluster much later in what appears to be a remote context. . . . In a book swarming with detail and abounding in obvious

> patterns these details are so slight and their repetition subjected to such transformation that no reader could even notice these matching clusters until a careful re-rereading. Even then they may be overlooked as mere incidental decoration—*until* we discover how they take their place in a larger design that insists on an urgent explanation.[93]

Since I believe that these repetitious elements are not fortuitous, but part of the author's conscious artistry, I have striven, to the extent possible, to render all such passages in exactly the same way whenever they occur or recur. Occasionally this may produce a slight awkwardness in the English, but I hope that the reader will put up with this flaw in order to better appreciate one of the salient features of the text.

This introduction is itself an example of the technique of composition employed by the author of the *Chin P'ing Mei*, in that it consists of a pastiche of passages from my own earlier publications on this subject interspersed with quotations from other sources. The only difference is that I hope I have acknowledged more openly my intellectual debts. In closing, I would like to appropriate the moving words of my sometime teacher, David Hawkes, the translator of *The Story of the Stone* (another title for *The Dream of the Red Chamber*), who closed the introduction to his great translation with this statement, which has been a source of inspiration to me over the years:

> My one abiding principle has been to translate *everything*—even puns. For although this is . . . an "unfinished" novel, it was written (and rewritten) by a great artist with his own lifeblood. I have therefore assumed that whatever I find in it is there for a purpose and must be dealt with somehow or other. I cannot pretend always to have done so successfully, but if I can convey to the reader even a fraction of the pleasure this Chinese novel has given me, I shall not have lived in vain.[94]

David Tod Roy
Hyde Park, Chicago, 1992

CAST OF CHARACTERS

THE FOLLOWING list includes all characters who appear in the novel, listed alphabetically by surname. All characters with dates in parentheses after their names are historical figures from the Sung dynasty. Characters who bear the names of historical figures from the Ming dynasty are identified in the notes.

An Ch'en, winner of first place in the *chin-shih* examinations but displaced in favor of Ts'ai Yün because he is the younger brother of the proscribed figure, An Tun; becomes a protégé of Ts'ai Ching and is patronized by Hsi-men Ch'ing, later rising to the rank of secretary of the Bureau of Irrigation and Transportation in the Ministry of Works; rewarded for his part in facilitating the notorious Flower and Rock Convoys and the construction of the Mount Ken Imperial Park.

An Ch'en's second wife.

An, Consort. See Liu, Consort.

An Tun (1042–1104), elder brother of An Ch'en, a high official whose name has been proscribed for his role in the partisan political conflicts of the late eleventh century.

An-t'ung, page boy of Aunt Yang.

An-t'ung, page boy of Miao T'ien-hsiu who is rescued by a fisherman and does his utmost to see justice done for the murder of his master.

An-t'ung, page boy of Wang Hsüan.

Apricot Hermitage, Layman of. See Wang Hsüan.

Autumn Chrysanthemum. See Ch'iu-chü.

Barefaced Adept, Taoist master from the Fire Dragon Monastery in the Obdurate Grotto of the Vacuous Mountains from whom Yang Kuang-yen acquires the art of lying.

Bean curd-selling crone who identifies the home of Commander Yüan in Potter's Alley to Hsi-men Ch'ing.

"Beanpole, The." See Hui-ch'ing.

Black-robed lictor on the staff of Ho Hsin.

Black-robed lictor who announces the arrival of Chang Pang-ch'ang and Ts'ai Yu to congratulate Chu Mien.

Black Whirlwind. See Li K'uei.

Brocade Tiger. See Yen Shun.

Busybody who directs Ch'iao Yün-ko to Dame Wang's teashop when he is looking for Hsi-men Ch'ing.

Cassia. See Li Kuei-chieh.

Chai Ch'ien, majordomo of Ts'ai Ching's household in the Eastern Capital.

Chai Ch'ien's wife.

Chai Ching-erh, Sutra Chai, proprietor of a sutra printing shop in Ch'ing-ho.

Chai, Sutra. See Chai Ching-erh.

Ch'ai Chin, Little Whirlwind, Little Lord Meng-ch'ang, direct descendant of Ch'ai Jung (921–59), emperor Shih-tsung (r. 954–59) of the Later Chou dynasty (951–60).

Ch'ai Huang-ch'eng, paternal uncle of Ch'ai Chin.

Ch'an Master Snow Cave. See P'u-ching.

Chang An, caretaker of Hsi-men Ch'ing's ancestral graveyard outside Ch'ing-ho.

Chang, Auntie, go-between who helps arrange Ch'en Ching-chi's marriage to Ko Ts'ui-p'ing.

Chang Ch'eng, a neighborhood head in Ch'ing-ho.

Chang Ch'ing, a criminal innkeeper with whom Wu Sung seeks refuge after the murder of P'an Chin-lien.

Chang Ch'ing's wife.

Chang Ch'uan-erh, a garrulous chair-bearer in Ch'ing-ho, partner of Wei Ts'ung-erh.

Chang the Fourth. See Chang Ju-i.

Chang the Fourth. See Chang Lung.

Chang Hao-wen, Chang the Importunate, Chang the Second, proprietor of a paper shop in Ch'ing-ho, acquaintance of Han Tao-kuo.

Chang Hsi-ch'un, a ballad singer maintained at one time as a mistress by Hsi-men Ch'ing.

Chang Hsi-ts'un, an acquaintance of Hsi-men Ch'ing's who invites him to his home for a birthday party.

Chang Hsiao-hsien, Hsiao Chang-hsien, Trifler Chang, "ball clubber" in Ch'ing-ho who plays the tout to Wang Ts'ai on his visits to the licensed quarter and upon whom Hsi-men Ch'ing turns the tables by abusing the judicial system at the behest of Lady Lin.

Chang the Importunate. See Chang Hao-wen.

Chang Ju-i, Chang the Fourth, wife of Hsiung Wang, employed in Hsi-men Ch'ing's household as a wet nurse for Kuan-ko and later for Hsiao-ko, sexual partner of Hsi-men Ch'ing after the death of Li P'ing-erh, finally married to Lai-hsing.

Chang Ju-i's mother.

Chang Ko (1068–1113), promoted to the post of vice-minister of the Ministry of Works for his part in facilitating the notorious Flower and Rock Convoys and the construction of the Mount Ken Imperial Park.

Chang Kuan, brother-in-law of Ch'en Hung and maternal uncle of Ch'en Ching-chi, militia commander of Ch'ing-ho.

Chang Kuan's sister. See Ch'en Hung's wife, née Chang.

Chang Kuan's wife.
Chang Lung, Chang the Fourth, maternal uncle of Meng Yü-lou's first husband Yang Tsung-hsi who unsuccessfully proposes that she remarry Shang Hsiao-t'ang and quarrels with Aunt Yang when she decides to marry Hsi-men Ch'ing instead.
Chang Lung, judicial commissioner of the Liang-Huai region.
Chang Lung's elder sister (Chang the Fourth's elder sister), mother of Yang Tsung-hsi and Yang Tsung-pao.
Chang Lung's wife (Chang the Fourth's wife).
Chang Mao-te, Chang the Second, nephew of Mr. Chang, the well-to-do merchant who first seduces P'an Chin-lien; a major rival of Hsi-men Ch'ing in the social world of Ch'ing-ho who, immediately after Hsi-men Ch'ing's death, bribes Cheng Chü-chung to intervene with Chu Mien and have him appointed to Hsi-men Ch'ing's former position as judicial commissioner so he can take over where Hsi-men Ch'ing left off.
Chang Mao-te's son, marries Eunuch Director Hsü's niece.
Chang Mei, professional actor of Hai-yen style drama.
Chang, Military Director-in-chief, official in Meng-chou.
Chang, Mr., a well-to-do merchant in Ch'ing-ho who first seduces P'an Chin-lien.
Chang, Mrs., wife of Mr. Chang, née Yü.
Chang, Old Mother, go-between who tries to sell two inexperienced country girls, Sheng-chin and Huo-pao, to P'ang Ch'un-mei.
Chang, Old Mother, proprietress of an inn next door to Auntie Hsüeh's residence.
Chang Pang-ch'ang (1081–1127), minister of rites, promoted to the position of grand guardian of the heir apparent for his part in facilitating the notorious Flower and Rock Convoys and the construction of the Mount Ken Imperial Park, puppet emperor of the short-lived state of Ch'u for thirty-two days in 1127.
Chang the Second. See Chang Hao-wen.
Chang the Second. See Chang Mao-te.
Chang Sheng, Street-skulking Rat, "knockabout" who, along with Lu Hua, shakes down Dr. Chiang Chu-shan at the behest of Hsi-men Ch'ing; later a servant in the household of Chou Hsiu, brother-in-law of Liu the Second; murders Ch'en Ching-chi when he overhears him plotting against him and is beaten to death by Chou Hsiu at the behest of P'ang Ch'un-mei.
Chang Sheng's reincarnation. See Kao family of the Ta-hsing Guard.
Chang Sheng's wife, née Liu, sister of Liu the Second.
Chang Shih-lien, Ch'en Hung's brother-in-law, related to Yang Chien by marriage, an official in the Eastern Capital.
Chang Shih-lien's wife, née Ch'en, Ch'en Hung's elder sister.

Chang Shu-yeh (1065–1127), prefect of Chi-chou in Shantung, later pacification commissioner of Shantung, responsible for the defeat of Sung Chiang and his acceptance of a government amnesty.
Chang Sung, Little. See Shu-t'ung.
Chang Ta (d. 1126), official who dies in the defense of T'ai-yüan against the invading Chin army.
Chang, Trifler. See Chang Hsiao-hsien.
Ch'ang, Cadger. See Ch'ang Shih-chieh.
Ch'ang the Second. See Ch'ang Shih-chieh.
Ch'ang Shih-chieh, Cadger Ch'ang, Ch'ang the Second, crony of Hsi-men Ch'ing, member of the brotherhood of ten.
Ch'ang Shih-chieh's wife.
Ch'ang Shih-chieh's wife's younger brother.
Ch'ang Yü, Commandant, officer rewarded for his part in facilitating the notorious Flower and Rock Convoys and the construction of the Mount Ken Imperial Park.
Chao, Auntie, go-between who sells Chin-erh to Wang Liu-erh.
Chao Chiao-erh, singing girl working out of My Own Tavern in Lin-ch'ing.
Chao, Dr. See Chao Lung-kang.
Chao Hung-tao, domestic clerk on the staff of Yang Chien.
Chao I (fl. early 12th century), Duke of Chia, twenty-sixth son of Emperor Hui-tsung by Consort Liu.
Chao K'ai (d. c. 1129), Prince of Yün, third son of emperor Hui-tsung by Consort Wang.
Chao, Lama, head priest of the Pao-ch'ing Lamasery outside the west gate of Ch'ing-ho.
Chao Lung-kang, Dr. Chao, Chao the Quack, incompetent specialist in female disorders called in to diagnose Li P'ing-erh's fatal illness.
Chao Lung-kang's grandfather.
Chao Lung-kang's father.
Chao No, investigation commissioner for Shantung.
Chao the Quack. See Chao Lung-kang.
Chao, Tailor, artisan patronized by Hsi-men Ch'ing.
Chao-ti, servant in the household of Han Tao-kuo and Wang Liu-erh.
Chao T'ing (fl. early 12th century), prefect of Hang-chou, promoted to the post of chief minister of the Court of Judicial Review.
Chao, Widow, wealthy landowner from whom Hsi-men Ch'ing buys a country estate adjacent to his ancestral graveyard.
Chao Yu-lan, battalion commander rewarded for his part in facilitating the notorious Flower and Rock Convoys and the construction of the Mount Ken Imperial Park.
Ch'e, Hogwash. See Ch'e Tan.
Ch'e Tan, Hogwash Ch'e, a dissolute young scamp upon whom Hsi-men Ch'ing turns the tables by abusing the judicial system.

Ch'e Tan's father, proprietor of a wineshop in Ch'ing-ho.
Ch'en An, servant in Ch'en Ching-chi's household.
Ch'en, Battalion Commander, resident on Main Street in Ch'ing-ho from whom Hsi-men Ch'ing declines to buy a coffin after the death of Li P'ing-erh.
Ch'en Cheng-hui (fl. early 12th century), son of Ch'en Kuan, surveillance vice-commissioner of education for Shantung.
Ch'en Ching-chi, secondary male protagonist of the novel, son of Ch'en Hung, husband of Hsi-men Ta-chieh, son-in-law of Hsi-men Ch'ing who carries on a running pseudo-incestuous affair with P'an Chin-lien that is consummated after the death of Hsi-men Ch'ing; falls out with Wu Yüeh-niang and is evicted from the household; drives Hsi-men Ta-chieh to suicide; attempts unsuccessfully to shake down Meng Yü-lou in Yen-chou; squanders his patrimony and is reduced to beggary; accepts charity from his father's friend the philanthropist Wang Hsüan, who induces him to become a monk with the Taoist appellation Tsung-mei, the junior disciple of Abbot Jen of the Yen-kung Temple in Lin-ch'ing; is admitted to the household of Chou Hsiu as a pretended cousin of P'ang Ch'un-mei who carries on an affair with him under her husband's nose; also has affairs with Feng Chin-pao and Han Ai-chieh, marries Ko Ts'ui-p'ing, and is murdered by Chang Sheng when he is overheard plotting against him.
Ch'en Ching-chi's grandfather, a salt merchant.
Ch'en Ching-chi's reincarnation. See Wang family of the Eastern Capital.
Ch'en, Dr., resident of Ch'ing-ho.
Ch'en, Dr.'s son, conceived as a result of a fertility potion provided by Nun Hsüeh.
Ch'en, Dr.'s wife, conceives a son in middle age after taking a fertility potion provided by Nun Hsüeh.
Ch'en Hung, wealthy dealer in pine resin, father of Ch'en Ching-chi, related by marriage to Yang Chien.
Ch'en Hung's elder sister, wife of Chang Shih-lien.
Ch'en Hung's wife, née Chang, sister of Chang Kuan, mother of Ch'en Ching-chi.
Ch'en Kuan (1057–1122), a prominent remonstrance official, father of Ch'en Cheng-hui.
Ch'en Liang-huai, national university student, son of Vice-Commissioner Ch'en, friend of Ting the Second.
Ch'en, Master, legal scribe who assists Wu Sung in drafting a formal complaint against Hsi-men Ch'ing.
Ch'en, Miss, daughter of the deceased Vice-Commissioner Ch'en whose assignation with Juan the Third results in his death.
Ch'en, Miss's maidservant.
Ch'en, Mistress. See Hsi-men Ta-chieh.

Ch'en the Second, proprietor of an inn at Ch'ing-chiang P'u at which Ch'en Ching-chi puts up on his way to Yen-chou.

Ch'en Ssu-chen, right provincial administration commissioner of Shantung.

Ch'en the Third, "cribber" in the licensed quarter of Lin-ch'ing.

Ch'en the Third, criminal boatman who, along with his partner Weng the Eighth, murders Miao T'ien-hsiu.

Ch'en Ting, servant in Ch'en Hung's household.

Ch'en Ting's wife.

Ch'en Tsung-mei. See Ch'en Ching-chi.

Ch'en Tsung-shan, ward-inspecting commandant of the Eastern Capital.

Ch'en Tung (1086–1127), national university student who submits a memorial to the throne impeaching the Six Traitors.

Ch'en, Vice-Commissioner, deceased father of Miss Ch'en.

Ch'en, Vice-Commissioner, father of Ch'en Liang-huai.

Ch'en, Vice-Commissioner's wife, née Chang, mother of Miss Ch'en.

Ch'en Wen-chao, prefect of Tung-p'ing.

Cheng Ai-hsiang, Cheng Kuan-yin, Goddess of Mercy Cheng, singing girl from the Star of Joy Bordello in Ch'ing-ho patronized by Hua Tzu-hsü, elder sister of Cheng Ai-yüeh.

Cheng Ai-yüeh, singing girl from the Star of Joy Bordello in Ch'ing-ho patronized by Wang Ts'ai and Hsi-men Ch'ing, younger sister of Cheng Ai-hsiang.

Cheng, Auntie, madam of the Star of Joy Bordello in Ch'ing-ho.

Cheng, Battalion Commander's family in the Eastern Capital into which Hua Tzu-hsü is reincarnated as a son.

Cheng Chi, servant in Hsi-men Ch'ing's household.

Cheng Chiao-erh, singing girl in Ch'ing-ho, niece of Cheng Ai-hsiang and Cheng Ai-yüeh.

Cheng Chin-pao. See Feng Chin-pao.

Cheng Ch'un, professional actor in Ch'ing-ho, younger brother of Cheng Feng, Cheng Ai-hsiang, and Cheng Ai-yüeh.

Cheng Chü-chung (1059–1123), military affairs commissioner, cousin of Consort Cheng, granted the title of grand guardian for his part in facilitating the notorious Flower and Rock Convoys and the construction of the Mount Ken Imperial Park, accepts a bribe of a thousand taels of silver from Chang Mao-te to intervene with Chu Mien and have him appointed to the position of judicial commissioner left vacant by the death of Hsi-men Ch'ing.

Cheng, Consort, (1081–1132), a consort of Emperor Hui-tsung, niece of Madame Ch'iao.

Cheng Feng, professional actor in Ch'ing-ho, elder brother of Cheng Ai Hsiang, Cheng Ai-yüeh, and Cheng Ch'un.

Cheng the Fifth, Auntie, madam of the Cheng Family Brothel in Lin-ch'ing.

Cheng the Fifth, Auntie's husband.

Cheng, Goddess of Mercy. See Cheng Ai-hsiang.
Cheng Kuan-yin. See Cheng Ai-hsiang.
Cheng, Third Sister, niece of Ch'iao Hung's wife, née Cheng, marries Wu K'ai's son Wu Shun-ch'en.
Cheng T'ien-shou, Palefaced Gentleman, third outlaw leader of the Ch'ing-feng Stronghold on Ch'ing-feng Mountain.
Cheng Wang. See Lai-wang.
Ch'eng-erh, younger daughter of Lai-hsing by Hui-hsiu.
Chi K'an, right administration vice commissioner of Shantung.
Chi-nan, old man from, who directs Wu Yüeh-niang to the Ling-pi Stockade in her dream.
Ch'i family brothel in Ch'ing-ho, madam of.
Ch'i Hsiang-erh, singing girl from the Ch'i family brothel in Ch'ing-ho.
Ch'i-t'ung, page boy in Hsi-men Ch'ing's household.
Chia, Duke of. See Chao I.
Chia Hsiang (fl. early 12th century), eunuch rewarded for his part in facilitating the notorious Flower and Rock Convoys and the construction of the Mount Ken Imperial Park.
Chia Hsiang's adopted son, granted the post of battalion vice commander of the Embroidered Uniform Guard by *yin* privilege as a reward for his father's part in facilitating the notorious Flower and Rock Convoys and the construction of the Mount Ken Imperial Park.
Chia Jen-ch'ing, False Feelings, neighbor of Hsi-men Ch'ing who intercedes unsuccessfully on Lai-wang's behalf.
Chia Lien, name to which Li Pang-yen alters Hsi-men Ch'ing's name on a bill of impeachment in return for a handsome bribe.
Chiang Chu-shan, Chiang Wen-hui, doctor who Li P'ing-erh marries on the rebound only to drive away ignominiously as soon as Hsi-men Ch'ing becomes available again.
Chiang Chu-shan's deceased first wife.
Chiang, Gate God. See Chiang Men-shen.
Chiang, Little, servant of Ch'en Ching-chi.
Chiang Men-shen, Gate God Chiang, elder brother of Chiang Yü-lan, gangster whose struggle with Shih En for control of the Happy Forest Tavern in Meng-chou results in his murder by Wu Sung.
Chiang Ts'ung, Sauce and Scallions, former husband of Sung Hui-lien, a cook in Ch'ing-ho who is stabbed to death in a brawl with a fellow cook over the division of their pay.
Chiang Ts'ung's assailant, convicted of a capital crime and executed as a result of Hsi-men Ch'ing's intervention.
Chiang Wen-hui. See Chiang Chu-shan.
Chiang Yü-lan, younger sister of Chiang Men-shen, concubine of Military Director-in-chief Chang of Meng-chou who assists her husband and brother in framing Wu Sung.

Ch'iao, distaff relative of the imperial family whose garden abuts on the back wall of Li P'ing-erh's house on Lion Street, assumes hereditary title of commander when Ch'iao the Fifth dies without issue.

Ch'iao Chang-chieh, infant daughter of Ch'iao Hung betrothed to Hsi-men Kuan-ko while both of them are still babes in arms.

Ch'iao, Consort (fl. early 12th century), a consort of Emperor Hui-tsung, related to Ch'iao the Fifth.

Ch'iao the Fifth, deceased distaff relative of the imperial family through Consort Ch'iao whose hereditary title of commander passes to another branch of the family when he dies without issue.

Ch'iao the Fifth's widow. See Ch'iao, Madame.

Ch'iao Hung, uncle of Ts'ui Pen, wealthy neighbor and business partner of Hsi-men Ch'ing whose daughter, Ch'iao Chang-chieh, is betrothed to Hsi-men Ch'ing's son Kuan-ko while they are still babes in arms.

Ch'iao Hung's concubine, mother of Ch'iao Chang-chieh.

Ch'iao Hung's elder sister, Ts'ui Pen's mother.

Ch'iao Hung's wife, née Cheng.

Ch'iao, Madame, Ch'iao the Fifth's widow, née Cheng, aunt of Ch'iao Hung's wife, née Cheng, and of Consort Cheng.

Ch'iao T'ung, servant in Ch'iao Hung's household.

Ch'iao T'ung's wife.

Ch'iao Yün-ko, Little Yün, young fruit peddler in Ch'ing-ho who helps Wu Chih catch Hsi-men Ch'ing and P'an Chin-lien in adultery.

Ch'iao Yün-ko's father, retired soldier dependent on his son.

Ch'ien Ch'eng, vice-magistrate of Ch'ing-ho district.

Ch'ien Ch'ing-ch'uan, traveling merchant entertained by Han Tao-kuo in Yang-chou.

Ch'ien Lao, clerk of the office of punishment in Ch'ing-ho.

Ch'ien Lung-yeh, secretary of the Ministry of Revenue in charge of collecting transit duties on shipping at the Lin-ch'ing customs house.

Ch'ien, Phlegm-fire. See Ch'ien T'an-huo.

Ch'ien T'an-huo, Phlegm-fire Ch'ien, Taoist healer called in to treat Hsi-men Kuan-ko.

Chih-yün, Abbot, head priest of Hsiang-kuo Temple in K'ai-feng visited by Hsi-men Ch'ing on his trip to the Eastern Capital.

Chin, Abbot, Taoist head priest of the Temple of the Eastern Peak on Mount T'ai.

Chin Ch'ien-erh, former maidservant in the household of Huang the Fourth's son purchased by P'ang Ch'un-mei as a servant for Ko Ts'ui-p'ing when she marries Ch'en Ching-chi.

Chin-erh, maidservant of Wang Liu-erh.

Chin-erh, singing girl in Longleg Lu's brothel on Butterfly Lane in Ch'ing-ho.

Chin-erh, singing girl working out of My Own Tavern in Lin-ch'ing.

Chin-erh's father, military patrolman whose horse is fatally injured in a fall and, for lack of replacement money, is forced to sell his daughter into domestic service.

Chin-kuei, employed in Chou Hsiu's household as a wet nurse for Chou Chin-ko.

Chin-lien. See P'an Chin-lien.

Chin-lien. See Sung Hui-lien.

Chin Ta-chieh, wife of Auntie Hsüeh's son Hsüeh Chi.

Chin-ts'ai, servant in the household of Han Tao-kuo and Wang Liu-erh.

Chin Tsung-ming, senior disciple of Abbot Jen of the Yen-kung Temple in Lin-ch'ing.

Ch'in-tsung, Emperor of the Sung dynasty (r. 1125–27), son of Emperor Hui-tsung who abdicated in his favor in 1125, taken into captivity together with his father by the Chin dynasty invaders in 1127.

Ch'in-t'ung, junior page boy in the household of Hua Tzu-hsü and Li P'ing-erh, originally named T'ien-fu but renamed when she marries into the household of Hsi-men Ch'ing.

Ch'in-t'ung, page boy of Meng Yü-lou who is seduced by P'an Chin-lien and driven out of the household when the affair is discovered.

Ch'in Yü-chih, singing girl in Ch'ing-ho patronized by Wang Ts'ai.

Ching-chi. See Ch'en Ching-chi.

Ching Chung, commander of the left battalion of the Ch'ing-ho Guard, later promoted to the post of military director-in-chief of Chi-chou, and finally to commander-general of the southeast and concurrently grain transport commander.

Ching Chung's daughter for whom he seeks a marriage alliance with Hsi-men Kuan-ko but is refused by Hsi-men Ch'ing.

Ching Chung's mother.

Ching Chung's wife.

Ch'iu-chü, Autumn Chrysanthemum, much abused junior maidservant of P'an Chin-lien.

Cho the Second. See Cho Tiu-erh.

Cho Tiu-erh, Cho the second, Toss-off Cho, unlicensed prostitute in Ch'ing-ho maintained as a mistress by Hsi-men Ch'ing and subsequently brought into his household as his Third Lady only to sicken and die soon thereafter.

Cho, Toss-off. See Cho Tiu-erh.

Chou, Censor, neighbor of Wu Yüeh-niang's when she was growing up, father of Miss Chou.

Chou Chin-ko, son of Chou Hsiu by P'ang Ch'un-mei the real father of which may have been Ch'en Ching-chi.

Chou Chung, senior servant in the household of Chou Hsiu, father of Chou Jen and Chou I.

Chou, Eunuch Director, resident of Ch'ing-ho whose invitation to a party Hsi-men Ch'ing declines not long before his death.

Chou Hsiao-erh, patron of Li Kuei-ch'ing and probably of Li Kuei-chieh also.

Chou Hsiu, commandant of the Regional Military Command, later appointed to other high military posts, colleague of Hsi-men Ch'ing after whose death he buys P'ang Ch'un-mei as a concubine and later promotes her to the position of principle wife when she bears him a son; commander-general of the Shantung region who leads the forces of Ch'ing-yen against the Chin invaders and dies at Kao-yang Pass of an arrow wound inflicted by the Chin commander Wan-yen Tsung-wang.

Chou Hsiu's first wife, blind in one eye, who dies not long after P'ang Ch'un-mei enters his household as a concubine.

Chou Hsiu's reincarnation, see Shen Shou-shan.

Chou Hsüan, cousin of Chou Hsiu's who looks after his affairs while he is at the front.

Chou I, servant in Chou Hsiu's household, son of Chou Chung and younger brother of Chou Jen, clandestine lover of P'ang Ch'un-mei who dies in the act of intercourse with him.

Chou I's paternal aunt with whom he seeks refuge after the death of P'ang Ch'un-mei.

Chou I's reincarnation. See Kao Liu-chu.

Chou Jen, servant in Chou Hsiu's household, son of Chou Chung and elder brother of Chou I.

Chou, Little, itinerant barber and masseur in Ch'ing-ho patronized by Hsi-men Ch'ing.

Chou, Miss, daughter of Censor Chou, neighbor of Wu Yüeh-niang's when she was growing up who broke her hymen by falling from a standing position onto the seat of a swing.

Chou, Ms., widowed second wife of Sung Te's father-in-law who commits adultery with him after her husband's death, for which Hsi-men Ch'ing sentences them both to death by strangulation.

Chou, Ms.'s maidservant.

Chou, Ms.'s mother.

Chou the Second, friend of Juan the Third.

Chou Shun, professional actor from Su-chou who specializes in playing female lead parts.

Chou Ts'ai, professional boy actor in Ch'ing-ho.

Chou Yü-chieh, daughter of Chou Hsiu by his concubine Sun Erh-niang.

Chu Ai-ai, Love, singing girl from Greenhorn Chu's brothel on Second Street in the licensed quarter of Ch'ing-ho, daughter of Greenhorn Chu.

Chu, Battalion Commander, resident of Ch'ing-ho, father of Miss Chu.

Chu, Battalion Commander's deceased wife, mother of Miss Chu.

Chu, Censor, resident of Ch'ing-ho, neighbor of Ch'iao Hung.

Chu, Censor's wife.

Chu family of the Eastern Capital, family into which Sung Hui-lien is reincarnated as a daughter.

Chu, Greenhorn, proprietor of a brothel on Second Street in the licensed quarter of Ch'ing-ho situated next door to the Verdant Spring Bordello of Auntie Li the Third.

Chu Jih-nien, Sticky Chu, Pockmarked Chu, crony of Hsi-men Ch'ing, member of the brotherhood of ten, plays the tout to Wang Ts'ai on his visits to the licensed quarter.

Chu Mien (1075–1126), defender-in-chief of the Embroidered Uniform Guard, an elite unit of the Imperial Bodyguard that performed secret police functions; relative of Li Ta-t'ien, the district magistrate of Ch'ing-ho; chief mover behind the notorious Flower and Rock Convoys and the construction of the Mount Ken Imperial Park, for which service to the throne he is promoted to a series of high posts; one of the Six Traitors impeached by Ch'en Tung.

Chu Mien's majordomo.

Chu Mien's son, granted the post of battalion commander of the Embroidered Uniform Guard by *yin* privilege as a reward for his father's part in facilitating the notorious Flower and Rock Convoys and the construction of the Mount Ken Imperial Park.

Chu, Miss, daughter of Battalion Commander Chu.

Chu, Pockmarked. See Chu Jih-nien.

Chu, Sticky. See Chu Jih-nien.

Ch'u-yün, daughter of a battalion commander of the Yang-chou Guard purchased by Miao Ch'ing to send as a gift to Hsi-men Ch'ing.

Ch'u-yün's father, battalion commander of the Yang-chou Guard.

Ch'un-hsiang, maidservant in the household of Han Tao-kuo and Wang Liu-erh.

Ch'un-hua, concubine of Ying Po-chüeh and mother of his younger son.

Ch'un-hung, page boy in Hsi-men Ch'ing's household.

Ch'un-mei. See P'ang Ch'un-mei.

Chung-ch'iu, junior maidservant in Hsi-men Ch'ing's household serving at various times Hsi-men Ta-chieh, Sun Hsüeh-o, and Wu Yüeh-niang.

Chung Kuei, policeman from outside the city wall of the Eastern Capital into whose family Hsi-men Ta-chieh is reincarnated as a daughter.

Ch'ung-hsi, maidservant purchased by Ch'en Ching-chi to serve Feng Chin-pao.

Ch'ung Shih-tao (1051–1126), general-in-chief of the Sung armies defending against the Chin invaders.

Ch'ü, Midwife, maternal aunt of Lai-wang in whose house on Polished Rice Lane outside the east gate of Ch'ing-ho Lai-wang and Sun Hsüeh-o seek refuge after absconding from the Hsi-men household.

Ch'ü T'ang, son of Midwife Ch'ü, cousin of Lai-wang.
Coal in the Snow. See P'an Chin-lien's cat.
Died-of-fright, Miss, wife of Yang Kuang-yen.
False Feelings. See Chia Jen-ch'ing.
Fan family of Hsü-chou, peasant family into which Wu Chih is reincarnated as a son.
Fan Hsün, battalion commander in the Ch'ing-ho Guard.
Fan, Hundred Customers. See Fan Pai-chia-nu.
Fan Kang, next-door neighbor of Ch'en Ching-chi in Ch'ing-ho.
Fan, Old Man, neighbor of the Hsieh Family Tavern in Lin-ch'ing.
Fan Pai-chia-nu, Hundred Customers Fan, singing girl from the Fan Family Brothel in Ch'ing-ho.
Fang Chen (fl. early 12th century), erudite of the Court of Imperial Sacrifices who reports that a brick in the Imperial Ancestral Temple is oozing blood.
Fang La (d. 1121), rebel who set up an independent regime in the Southeast that was suppressed by government troops in 1121.
Feng Chin-pao, Cheng Chin-pao, singing girl from the Feng Family Brothel in Lin-ch'ing purchased as a concubine by Ch'en Ching-chi, later resold to the brothel of Auntie Cheng the Fifth who changes her name to Cheng Chin-pao.
Feng Chin-pao's mother, madam of the Feng Family Brothel in Lin-ch'ing.
Feng, Consort (fl. mid 11th–early 12th centuries), Consort Tuan, consort of Emperor Jen-tsung (r. 1022–63) who resided in the palace for five reigns.
Feng Family Brothel's servant.
Feng Huai, son of Feng the Second, son-in-law of Pai the Fifth, dies of injuries sustained in an affray with Sun Wen-hsiang.
Feng, Old Mother, waiting woman in Li P'ing-erh's family since she was a child, continues in her service when she is a concubine of Privy Councilor Liang Shih-chieh, wife of Hua Tzu-hsü, wife of Chiang Chu-shan, and after she marries Hsi-men Ch'ing, supplementing her income by working as a go-between on the side.
Feng the Second, employee of Sun Ch'ing, father of Feng Huai.
Feng T'ing-hu, left assistant administration commissioner of Shantung.
Fifth Lady. See P'an Chin-lien.
First Lady. See Wu Yüeh-niang.
Fisherman who rescues An-t'ung and helps him to locate the boatmen who had murdered his master.
Flying Demon. See Hou Lin.
Fourth Lady. See Sun Hsüeh-o.
Fu-jung, maidservant of Lady Lin.
Fu, Manager. See Fu Ming.
Fu Ming, Fu the Second, Manager Fu, manager of Hsi-men Ch'ing's pharmaceutical shop, pawnshop, and other businesses.

Fu Ming's wife.
Fu the Second. See Fu Ming.
Fu T'ien-tse, battalion commander rewarded for his part in facilitating the notorious Flower and Rock Convoys and the construction of the Mount Ken Imperial Park.
Golden Lotus. See P'an Chin-lien.
Good Deed. See Yin Chih.
Hai-t'ang, concubine of Chou Hsiu much abused by P'ang Ch'un-mei.
Han Ai-chieh, daughter of Han Tao-kuo and Wang Liu-erh, niece of Han the Second, concubine of Chai Ch'ien, mistress of Ch'en Ching-chi to whom she remains faithful after his death, ending her life as a Buddhist nun.
Han, Auntie, wife of Mohammedan Han, mother of Han Hsiao-yü.
Han, Baldy, father of Han Tao-kuo and Han the Second.
Han, Brother-in-law. See Han Ming-ch'uan.
Han Chin-ch'uan, singing girl in Ch'ing-ho, elder sister of Han Yü-ch'uan, younger sister of Han Pi.
Han Hsiao-ch'ou, singing girl in Ch'ing-ho, niece of Han Chin-ch'uan and Han Yü-ch'uan.
Han Hsiao-yü, son of Mohammedan Han and Auntie Han.
Han Lü (fl. early 12th century), vice-minister of the Ministry of Revenue, vice-minister of the Ministry of Personnel, brother-in-law of Ts'ai Ching's youngest son, Ts'ai T'ao, grants Hsi-men Ch'ing favorable treatment for his speculations in the salt trade.
Han, Master, formerly a court painter attached to the Hsüan-ho Academy, called upon by Hsi-men Ch'ing to paint two posthumous portraits of Li P'ing-erh.
Han Ming-ch'uan, Brother-in-law Han, husband of Meng Yü-lou's elder sister who lives outside the city gate of Ch'ing-ho; friend of Dr. Jen Hou-ch'i.
Han Ming-ch'uan's wife, née Meng, Mrs. Han, elder sister of Meng Yü-lou.
Han, Mohammedan, husband of Auntie Han, father of Han Hsiao-yü, renter of a room on the street front of Hsi-men Ch'ing's property next door to that of Pen Ti-ch'uan and his wife, employed on the staff of the eunuch director in charge of the local Imperial Stables.
Han, Mrs. See Han Ming-ch'uan's wife, née Meng.
Han Pang-ch'i, prefect of Hsü-chou.
Han Pi, professional boy actor in Ch'ing-ho, elder brother of Han Chin-ch'uan and Han Yü-ch'uan.
Han, Posturer. See Han Tao-kuo.
Han the Second, Trickster Han, younger brother of Han Tao-kuo, "knock-about" and gambler in Ch'ing-ho who carries on an intermittent affair with his sister-in-law, Wang Liu-erh, whom he marries after the death of Han Tao-kuo.

Han Tao-kuo, Posturer Han, husband of Wang Liu-erh, son of Baldy Han, elder brother of Han the Second, father of Han Ai-chieh, manager of Hsi-men Ch'ing's silk store on Lion Street who absconds with a thousand taels of his property on hearing of his death, content to live off the sexual earnings of his wife and daughter.

Han Tao-kuo's paternal uncle, elder brother of Baldy Han.

Han, Trickster. See Han the Second.

Han Tso, boy actor in Ch'ing-ho.

Han Tsung-jen, domestic clerk on the staff of Yang Chien.

Han Wen-kuang, investigation commissioner for Shantung.

Han Yü-ch'uan, singing girl in Ch'ing-ho, younger sister of Han Chin-ch'uan and Han Pi.

Hao Hsien, Idler Hao, a dissolute young scamp upon whom Hsi-men Ch'ing turns the tables by abusing the judicial system.

Hao, Idler. See Hao Hsien.

Ho Ch'i-kao, left administration vice-commissioner of Shantung.

Ho Chin, assistant judicial commissioner of the Ch'ing-ho office of the Provincial Surveillance Commission, promoted to the post of commander of Hsin-p'ing Stockade and later to the post of judicial commissioner in the Huai-an office of the Provincial Surveillance Commission, thereby creating the vacancy filled by Hsi-men Ch'ing in return for the lavishness of his birthday presents to Ts'ai Ching.

Ho Chin-ch'an, singing girl from the Ho Family Bordello on Fourth Street in the licensed quarter of Ch'ing-ho.

Ho Ch'in, son of Ho the Ninth who succeeds to his position as head coroner's assistant of Ch'ing-ho.

Ho Ch'un-ch'üan, Dr. Ho, son of Old Man Ho, physician in Ch'ing-ho.

Ho, Dr. See Ho Ch'un-ch'üan.

Ho, Eunuch Director. See Ho Hsin.

Ho Hsin (fl. early 12th century), Eunuch Director Ho, attendant in the Yen-ning Palace, residence of Consort Feng, rewarded for his part in facilitating the notorious Flower and Rock Convoys and the construction of the Mount Ken Imperial Park, uncle of Ho Yung-shou, entertains Hsi-men Ch'ing on his visit to the Eastern Capital.

Ho-hua, maidservant of Chou Hsiu's concubine Sun Erh-niang.

Ho Liang-feng, younger brother of Magnate Ho.

Ho, Magnate, wealthy silk merchant from Hu-chou, elder brother of Ho Liang-feng, tries to buy P'an Chin-lien after the death of Hsi-men Ch'ing, patronizes Wang Liu-erh in Lin-ch'ing and takes her and Han Tao-kuo back to Hu-chou where they inherit his property.

Ho, Magnate's daughter.

Ho the Ninth, elder brother of Ho the Tenth, head coroner's assistant of Ch'ing-ho who accepts a bribe from Hsi-men Ch'ing to cover up the murder of Wu Chih.

Ho, Old Man, father of Ho Ch'un-ch'üan, aged physician in Ch'ing-ho.

Ho Pu-wei, clerk on the staff of the district magistrate of Ch'ing-ho, Li Ch'ang-ch'i, who assists his son Li Kung-pi in his courtship of Meng Yü-lou.

Ho the Tenth, younger brother of Ho the Ninth, let off the hook by Hsi-men Ch'ing when he is accused of fencing stolen goods.

Ho Yung-fu, nephew of Ho Hsin, younger brother of Ho Yung-shou.

Ho Yung-shou, nephew of Ho Hsin, elder brother of Ho Yung-fu, appointed to Hsi-men Ch'ing's former post as assistant judicial commissioner in the Ch'ing-ho office of the Provincial Surveillance Commission as a reward for Ho Hsin's part in facilitating the notorious Flower and Rock Convoys and the construction of the Mount Ken Imperial Park.

Ho Yung-shou's wife, née Lan, niece of Lan Ts'ung-hsi.

Hou Lin, Flying Demon, beggar boss in Ch'ing-ho who helps out Ch'en Ching-chi when he is reduced to beggary in return for his sexual favors.

Hou Meng (1054–1121), grand coordinator of Shantung, promoted to the post of chief minister of the Court of Imperial Sacrifices for his part in facilitating the notorious Flower and Rock Convoys and the construction of the Mount Ken Imperial Park.

Hsi-erh, page boy in the household of Chou Hsiu.

Hsi-men An. See Tai-an.

Hsi-men Ching-liang, Hsi-men Ch'ing's grandfather.

Hsi-men Ch'ing, principal male protagonist of the novel, father of Hsi-men Ta-chieh by his deceased first wife, née Ch'en, father of Hsi-men Kuan-ko by Li P'ing-erh, father of Hsi-men Hsiao-ko by Wu Yüeh-niang, decadent scion of a merchant family of some wealth from which he inherits a wholesale pharmaceutical business on the street in front of the district yamen of Ch'ing-ho, climbs in social status by means of a succession of corrupt sexual, economic, and political conquests only to die of sexual excess at the age of thirty-three.

Hsi-men Ch'ing's daughter. See Hsi-men Ta-chieh.

Hsi-men Ch'ing's first wife, née Ch'en, deceased mother of Hsi-men Ta-chieh.

Hsi-men Ch'ing's father. See Hsi-men Ta.

Hsi-men Ch'ing's grandfather. See Hsi-men Ching-liang.

Hsi-men Ch'ing's grandmother, née Li.

Hsi-men Ch'ing's mother, née Hsia.

Hsi-men Ch'ing's reincarnation. See Hsi-men Hsiao-ko and Shen Yüeh.

Hsi-men Ch'ing's sons. See Hsi-men Kuan-ko and Hsi-men Hsiao-ko.

Hsi-men Hsiao-ko, posthumous son of Hsi-men Ch'ing by Wu Yüeh-niang, born at the very moment of his death, betrothed while still a babe in arms to Yün Li-shou's daughter, claimed by the Buddhist monk P'u-ching to be the reincarnation of Hsi-men Ch'ing and spirited away by him at the end of the novel to become a celibate monk with the religious name Ming-wu.

Hsi-men Kuan-ko, son of Hsi-men Ch'ing by Li P'ing-erh, given the religious name Wu Ying-yüan by the Taoist priest Wu Tsung-che, betrothed while still a babe in arms to Ch'iao Chang-chieh, murdered by P'an Chin-lien out of jealousy of Li P'ing-erh.

Hsi-men Kuan-ko's reincarnation. See Wang family of Cheng-chou.

Hsi-men Ta, deceased father of Hsi-men Ch'ing whose business took him to many parts of China.

Hsi-men Ta-chieh, Mistress Ch'en, Hsi-men Ch'ing's daughter by his deceased first wife, née Ch'en, wife of Ch'en Ching-chi, so neglected and abused by her husband that she commits suicide.

Hsi-men Ta-chieh's reincarnation. See Chung Kuei.

Hsi-t'ung, page boy in the household of Wang Hsüan.

Hsiao-ko. See Hsi-men Hsiao-ko.

Hsia Ch'eng-en, son of Hsia Yen-ling, achieves status of military selectee by hiring a stand-in to take the qualifying examination for him.

Hsia-hua, junior maidservant of Li Chiao-erh who is caught trying to steal a gold bracelet.

Hsia Kung-chi, docket officer on the staff of the district yamen in Ch'ing-ho.

Hsia Shou, servant in the household of Hsia Yen-ling.

Hsia Yen-ling, judicial commissioner in the Ch'ing-ho office of the Provincial Surveillance Commission, colleague, superior, and rival of Hsi-men Ch'ing in his official career.

Hsia Yen-ling's son. See Hsia Ch'eng-en.

Hsia Yen-ling's wife.

Hsiang the Elder, deceased distaff relative of the imperial family through Empress Hsiang, consort of Emperor Shen-tsung (r. 1067-85), elder brother of Hsiang the fifth.

Hsiang, Empress, (1046–1101), consort of Emperor Shen-tsung (r. 1067–85).

Hsiang the Fifth, distaff relative of the imperial family through Empress Hsiang, consort of Emperor Shen-tsung (r. 1067–85), younger brother of Hsiang the Elder, sells part of his country estate outside Ch'ing-ho to Hsi-men Ch'ing.

Hsiao Chang-hsien. See Chang Hsiao-hsien.

Hsiao Ch'eng, resident of Oxhide Street and neighborhood head of the fourth neighborhood of the first subprecinct of Ch'ing-ho.

Hsiao-ko. See Hsi-men Hsiao-ko.

Hsiao-luan, junior maidservant of Meng Yü-lou.

Hsiao-yü, Little Jade, junior maidservant of Wu Yüeh-niang, married to Tai-an after Wu Yüeh-niang discovers them in flagrante delicto.

Hsiao-yüeh, Abbot, head priest of the Water Moon Monastery outside the south gate of Ch'ing-ho.

Hsieh En, assistant judicial commissioner of the Huai-ch'ing office of the Provincial Surveillance Commission.

Hsieh, Fatty. See Hsieh the Third.
Hsieh Hsi-ta, Tagalong Hsieh, crony of Hsi-men Ch'ing, member of the brotherhood of ten.
Hsieh Hsi-ta's father, deceased hereditary battalion commander in the Ch'ing-ho Guard.
Hsieh Hsi-ta's mother.
Hsieh Hsi-ta's wife, née Liu.
Hsieh Ju-huang, What a Whopper, acquaintance of Han Tao-kuo who punctures his balloon when he inflates his own importance.
Hsieh, Tagalong. See Hsieh Hsi-ta.
Hsieh the Third, Fatty Hsieh, manager of the Hsieh Family Tavern in Lin-ch'ing.
Hsin Hsing-tsung (fl. early 12th century), commander-general of the Ho-nan region who leads the forces of Chang-te against the Chin invaders.
Hsiu-ch'un, junior maidservant of Li P'ing-erh and later of Li Chiao-erh, finally becoming a novice nun under the tutelage of Nun Wang.
Hsiung Wang, husband of Chang Ju-i, soldier forced by his lack of means to sell his wife to Hsi-men Ch'ing as a wet nurse for Kuan-ko.
Hsiung Wang's son by Chang Ju-i.
Hsü, Assistant Administration Commissioner, of Yen-chou in Shantung.
Hsü-chou, old woman from, in whose house Han Ai-chieh encounters Han the Second.
Hsü, Eunuch Director, wealthy eunuch speculator and moneylender, resident of Halfside Street in the northern quarter of Ch'ing-ho, landlord of Crooked-head Sun and Aunt Yang, patron of Li Ming, original owner of Hsia Yen-ling's residential compound, major rival of Hsi-men Ch'ing in the social world of Ch'ing-ho whose niece marries Chang Mao-te's son.
Hsü, Eunuch Director's niece, marries Chang Mao-te's son.
Hsü Feng, prefect of Yen-chou in Chekiang who exposes Meng Yü-lou's and Li Kung-pi's attempt to frame Ch'en Ching-chi.
Hsü Feng's trusted henchman who disguises himself as a convict in order to elicit information from Ch'en Ching-chi.
Hsü Feng-hsiang, supervisor of the State Farm Battalion of the Ch'ing-ho Guard, one of the officials who comes to Hsi-men Ch'ing's residence to offer a sacrifice to the soul of Li P'ing-erh after her death.
Hsü the Fourth, shopkeeper outside the city wall of Ch'ing-ho who borrows money from Hsi-men Ch'ing.
Hsü Hsiang, battalion commander rewarded for his part in facilitating the notorious Flower and Rock Convoys and the construction of the Mount Ken Imperial Park.
Hsü, Master, yin-yang master of Ch'ing-ho.
Hsü Nan-ch'i, military officer in Ch'ing-ho promoted to the post of commander of the Hsin-p'ing Stockade.

Hsü, Prefect, prefect of Ch'ing-chou, patron of Shih Po-ts'ai, the corrupt Taoist head priest of the Temple of the Goddess of Iridescent Clouds on the summit of Mout T'ai.

Hsü, Prefect's daughter.

Hsü, Prefect's son.

Hsü, Prefect's wife.

Hsü Pu-yü, Reneger Hsü, moneylender in Ch'ing-ho from whom Wang Ts'ai tries to borrow three hundred taels of silver in order to purchase a position in the Military School.

Hsü, Reneger. See Hsü Pu-yü.

Hsü Shun, professional actor of Hai-yen style drama.

Hsü Sung, prefect of Tung-ch'ang in Shantung.

Hsü Sung's concubine.

Hsü Sung's concubine's father.

Hsü, Tailor, artisan with a shop across the street from Han Tao-kuo residence on Lion Street in Ch'ing-ho.

Hsü the Third, seller of date cakes in front of the district yamen in Ch'ing-ho.

Hsü Tsung-shun, junior disciple of Abbot Jen of the Yen-kung Temple in Lin-ch'ing.

Hsüeh, Auntie, go-between in Ch'ing-ho who also peddles costume jewelry, mother of Hsüeh Chi, sells P'ang Ch'un-mei into Hsi-men Ch'ing's household, represents Hsi-men Ch'ing in the betrothal of his daughter Hsi-men Ta-chieh to Ch'en Ching-chi, proposes his match with Meng Yü-lou, arranges resale of P'ang Ch'un-mei to Chou Hsiu after she is forced to leave the Hsi-men household by Wu Yüeh-niang, arranges match between Ch'en Ching-chi and Ko Ts'ui-p'ing after Hsi-men Ta-chieh's suicide.

Hsüeh, Auntie's husband.

Hsüeh Chi, son of Auntie Hsüeh, husband of Chin ta-chieh.

Hsüeh Chi's son by Chin Ta-chieh.

Hsüeh, Eunuch Director, supervisor of the imperial estates in the Ch'ing-ho region, despite his castration given to fondling and pinching the singing girls with whom he comes in contact.

Hsüeh Hsien-chung, official rewarded for his part in facilitating the notorious Flower and Rock Convoys and the construction of the Mount Ken Imperial Park.

Hsüeh, Nun, widow of a peddler of steamed wheat cakes living across the street from the Kuang-ch'eng Monastery in Ch'ing-ho who takes the tonsure after the death of her husband and becomes abbess of the Ksitigarbha Nunnery, defrocked for her complicity in the death of Juan the Third, later rector of the Lotus Blossom Nunnery in the southern quarter of Ch'ing-ho who provides first Wu Yüeh-niang and then P'an Chin-lien with fertility potions, frequently invited to recite Buddhist "precious scrolls" to Wu Yüeh-niang and her guests.

Hsüeh, Nun's deceased husband, peddler of steamed wheat cakes living across the street from the Kuang-ch'eng Monastery in Ch'ing-ho.

Hsüeh-o. See Sun Hsüeh-o.

Hsüeh Ts'un-erh, unlicensed prostitute in Longfoot Wu's brothel in the Southern Entertainment Quarter of Ch'ing-ho patronized by P'ing-an after he absconds from the Hsi-men household with jewelry stolen from the pawnshop.

Hu, Dr., Old Man Hu, Hu the Quack, physician who lives in Eunuch Director Liu's house on East Street in Ch'ing-ho in the rear courtyard of which Hsi-men Ch'ing hides in order to evade Wu Sung, treats Hua Tzu-hsü, Li P'ing-erh, and Hsi-men Ch'ing without success, prescribes abortifacient for P'an Chin-lien when she becomes pregnant by Ch'en Ching-chi.

Hu, Dr.'s maidservant.

Hu the Fourth, impeached as a relative or adherent of Yang Chien.

Hu Hsiu, employee of Han Tao-kuo who spies on Hsi-men Ch'ing's love-making with Wang Liu-erh, accompanies his employer on his buying expeditions to the south, and tells him what he thinks about his private life in a drunken tirade in Yang-chou.

Hu, Old Man. See Hu, Dr.

Hu the Quack. See Hu, Dr.

Hu Shih-wen (fl. early 12th century), related to Ts'ai Ching by marriage, corrupt prefect of Tung-p'ing in Shantung who participates with Hsi-men Ch'ing and Hsia Yen-ling in getting Miao Ch'ing off the hook for murdering his master Miao T'ien-hsiu.

Hu Ts'ao, professional actor from Su-chou who specializes in playing young male lead roles.

Hua the Elder. See Hua Tzu-yu.

Hua, Eunuch Director, uncle of Hua Tzu-yu, Hua Tzu-hsü, Hua Tzu-kuang, and Hua Tzu-hua and adoptive father of Hua Tzu-hsü, member of the Imperial Bodyguard and director of the Firewood Office in the Imperial Palace, later promoted to the position of grand defender of Kuang-nan from which post he retires on account of illness to take up residence in his native place, Ch'ing-ho; despite his castration engaged in pseudo-incestuous hanky-panky with his daughter-in-law, Li P'ing-erh.

Hua the Fourth. See Hua Tzu-hua.

Hua Ho-lu, assistant magistrate of Ch'ing-ho.

Hua, Mistress. See Li P'ing-erh.

Hua, Mrs. See Li P'ing-erh.

Hua, Nobody. See Hua Tzu-hsü.

Hua the Second. See Hua Tzu-hsü.

Hua the Third. See Hua Tzu-kuang.

Hua-t'ung, page boy in Hsi-men Ch'ing's household sodomized by Wen Pi-ku.

Hua Tzu-hsü, Hua the Second, Nobody Hua, nephew and adopted son of Eunuch Director Hua, husband of Li P'ing-erh, next-door neighbor of Hsi-men Ch'ing and member of the brotherhood of ten, patron of Wu Yin-erh and Cheng Ai-hsiang; cuckolded by Li P'ing-erh, who turns over much of his property to Hsi-men Ch'ing, he loses the rest in a lawsuit and dies of chagrin.

Hua Tzu-hsü's reincarnation. See Cheng, Battalion Commander's family in the Eastern Capital.

Hua Tzu-hua, Hua the Fourth, nephew of Eunuch Director Hua, brother of Hua Tzu-hsü.

Hua Tzu-hua's wife.

Hua Tzu-kuang, Hua the Third, nephew of Eunuch Director Hua, brother of Hua Tzu-hsü.

Hua Tzu-kuang's wife.

Hua Tzu-yu, Hua the Elder, nephew of Eunuch Director Hua, brother of Hua Tzu-hsü.

Hua Tzu-yu's wife.

Huai River region, merchant from, who employs Wang Ch'ao.

Huai River region, merchant from, who patronizes Li Kuei-ch'ing.

Huang An, military commander involved with T'an Chen in defense of the northern frontier against the Chin army.

Huang, Buddhist Superior, monk of the Pao-en Temple in Ch'ing-ho.

Huang Chia, prefect of Teng-chou in Shantung.

Huang Ching-ch'en (d. 1126), defender-in-chief of the Palace Command, eunuch rewarded for his part in facilitating the notorious Flower and Rock Convoys and the construction of the Mount Ken Imperial Park, uncle of Wang Ts'ai's wife, née Huang, lavishly entertained by Hsi-men Ch'ing at the request of Sung Ch'iao-nien.

Huang Ching-ch'en's adopted son, granted the post of battalion commander of the Embroidered Uniform Guard by *yin* privilege as a reward for his father's part in facilitating the notorious Flower and Rock Convoys and the construction of the Mount Ken Imperial Park.

Huang the Fourth, merchant contractor in Ch'ing-ho, partner of Li Chih, ends up in prison for misappropriation of funds.

Huang the Fourth's son.

Huang the Fourth's wife, née Sun, daughter of Sun Ch'ing.

Huang-lung Temple, abbot of, entertains Hsi-men Ch'ing and Ho Yung-shou en route to Ch'ing-ho from the Eastern Capital.

Huang, Master, fortune teller residing outside the Chen-wu Temple in the northern quarter of Ch'ing-ho.

Huang Mei, assistant prefect of K'ai-feng, maternal cousin of Miao T'ien-hsiu who invites him to visit him in the capital and appeals to Tseng Hsiao-hsü on his behalf after his murder.

Huang Ning, page boy in the household of Huang the Fourth.

Huang Pao-kuang (fl. early 12th century), secretary of the Ministry of Works in charge of the Imperial Brickyard in Ch'ing-ho, provincial graduate of the same year as Shang Hsiao-t'ang.
Huang, Perfect Man. See Huang Yüan-pai.
Huang Yü, foreman on the staff of Wang Fu.
Huang Yüan-pai, Perfect Man Huang, Taoist priest sent by the court to officiate at a seven-day rite of cosmic renewal on Mount T'ai, also officiates at a rite of purification for the salvation of the soul of Li P'ing-erh.
Hui-ch'ing, "The Beanpole," wife of Lai-chao, mother of Little Iron Rod.
Hui-hsiang, wife of Lai-pao, née Liu, mother of Seng-pao.
Hui-hsiang's elder sister.
Hui-hsiang's mother.
Hui-hsiang's younger brother. See Liu Ts'ang.
Hui-hsiu, wife of Lai-hsing, mother of Nien-erh and Ch'eng-erh.
Hui-lien. See Sung Hui-lien.
Hui-tsung, Emperor of the Sung dynasty (r. 1100–25), father of Emperor Ch'in-tsung in whose favor he abdicates in 1125, taken into captivity together with his son by the Chin invaders in 1127.
Hui-yüan, wife of Lai-chüeh.
Hung, Auntie, madam of the Hung Family Brothel in Ch'ing-ho.
Hung the Fourth, singing girl from the Hung Family Brothel in Ch'ing-ho.
Hung-hua Temple in Ch'ing-ho, monk from, whom Hsi-men Ch'ing frames and executes in place of Ho the Tenth.
Huo-pao, eleven-year-old country girl offered to P'ang Ch'un-mei as a maidservant but rejected for wetting her bed.
Huo-pao's parents.
Huo Ta-li, district magistrate of Ch'ing-ho who accepts Ch'en Ching-chi's bribe and lets him off the hook when accused of driving his wife, Hsi-men Ta-chieh, to suicide.
I Mien-tz'u, Ostensibly Benign, neighbor of Hsi-men Ch'ing who intercedes unsuccessfully on Lai-wang's behalf.
Imperial stables in Ch'ing-ho, eunuch director of, employer of Mohammedan Han.
Indian monk. See Monk, Indian.
Iron Fingernail. See Yang Kuang-yen.
Iron Rod. See Little Iron Rod.
Itinerant acrobat called in by Chou Hsiu to distract P'ang Ch'un-mei from her grief over the death of P'an Chin-lien.
Jade Flute. See Yü-hsiao.
Jade Lotus. See Pai Yü-lien.
Jen, Abbot, Taoist priest of the Yen-kung Temple in Lin-ch'ing to whom Wang Hsüan recommends Ch'en Ching-chi as a disciple; dies of shock when threatened with arrest in connection with the latter's whoremongering.

Jen, Abbot's acolyte.

Jen, Dr. See Jen Hou-ch'i.

Jen Hou-ch'i, Dr. Jen, physician in Ch'ing-ho who treats Li P'ing-erh and Hsi-men Ch'ing without success, friend of Han Ming-ch'uan.

Jen T'ing-kuei, assistant magistrate of Ch'ing-ho.

Ju-i. See Chang Ju-i.

Juan the Third, dies of excitement in the act of making love to Miss Ch'en in the Ksitigarbha Nunnery during an assignation arranged by Nun Hsüeh.

Juan the Third's parents.

Jui-yün. See Pen Chang-chieh.

Jung Chiao-erh, singing girl in Ch'ing-ho patronized by Wang Ts'ai.

Jung Hai, employee of Hsi-men Ch'ing who accompanies Ts'ui Pen on a buying trip to Hu-chou.

Kan Jun, resident of Stonebridge Alley in Ch'ing-ho, partner and manager of Hsi-men Ch'ing's silk dry goods store.

Kan Jun's wife.

Kan Lai-hsing. See Lai-hsing.

K'ang, Prince of. See Kao-tsung, Emperor.

Kao An, secondary majordomo of Ts'ai Ching's household in the Eastern Capital through whom Lai-pao gains access to Ts'ai Yu.

Kao Ch'iu (d. 1126), defender-in-chief of the Imperial Bodyguard, granted the title of grand guardian for his part in facilitating the notorious Flower and Rock Convoys and the construction of the Mount Ken Imperial Park; one of the Six Traitors impeached by Ch'en Tung.

Kao family from outside the city wall of the Eastern Capital, family into which Chou I is reincarnated as a son named Kao Liu-chu.

Kao family of the Ta-hsing Guard, family into which Chang Sheng is reincarnated as a son.

Kao Lien, cousin of Kao Ch'iu, prefect of T'ai-an, brother-in-law of Yin T'ien-hsi.

Kao Lien's wife, née Yin, elder sister of Yin T'ien-hsi.

Kao Liu-chu, son of the Kao family from outside the city wall of the Eastern Capital, reincarnation of Chou I.

Kao-tsung, emperor of the Southern Sung dynasty (r. 1127–62), ninth son of Emperor Hui-tsung, Prince of K'ang; declares himself emperor in 1127 when the Chin invaders take emperors Hui-tsung and Ch'in-tsung into captivity; abdicates in favor of Emperor Hsiao-tsung in 1162.

Ko Ts'ui-p'ing, wife of Ch'en Ching-chi in a marriage arranged by P'ang Ch'un-mei with whom he continues to carry on an intermittent affair; returns to her parents' family after Ch'en Ching-chi's death and the invasion by the Chin armies.

Ko Ts'ui-p'ing's father, wealthy silk dry goods dealer in Ch'ing-ho.

Ko Ts'ui-p'ing's mother.

Kou Tzu-hsiao, professional actor from Su-chou who specializes in playing male lead roles.

Ku, Silversmith, jeweler in Ch'ing-ho patronized by Li P'ing-erh and Hsi-men Ch'ing, employer of Lai-wang after he returns to Ch'ing-ho from exile in Hsü-chou.

Kuan, Busybody. See Kuan Shih-k'uan.

Kuan-ko. See Hsi-men Kuan-ko.

Kuan Shih-k'uan, Busybody Kuan, a dissolute young scamp upon whom Hsi-men Ch'ing turns the tables by abusing the judicial system.

Kuan-yin Nunnery, abbess of, superior of Nun Wang, frequent visitor in the Hsi-men household.

Kuang-yang, Commandery Prince of. See T'ung Kuan.

Kuei-chieh. See Li Kuei-chieh.

Kuei-ch'ing. See Li Kuei-ch'ing.

Kung Kuai (1057-1111), left provincial administration commissioner of Shantung.

K'ung, Auntie, go-between in Ch'ing-ho who represents Ch'iao Hung's family in arranging the betrothal of Ch'iao Chang-chieh to Hsi-men Kuan-ko.

K'ung family of the Eastern Capital, family into which P'ang Ch'un-mei is reincarnated as a daughter.

Kuo Shou-ch'ing, senior disciple of Shih Po-ts'ai, the corrupt Taoist head priest of the Temple of the Goddess of Iridescent Clouds on the summit of Mount T'ai.

Kuo Shou-li, junior disciple of Shih Po-ts'ai, the corrupt Taoist head priest of the Temple of the Goddess of Iridescent Clouds on the summit of Mount T'ai.

Kuo Yao-shih (d. after 1126), turncoat who accepts office under the Sung dynasty but goes over to the Chin side at a critical point and is instrumental in their conquest of North China.

La-mei, maidservant employed in the Wu Family Brothel in Ch'ing-ho.

Lai-an, servant in Hsi-men Ch'ing's household.

Lai-chao, Liu Chao, head servant in Hsi-men Ch'ing's household, husband of Hui-ch'ing, father of Little Iron Rod, helps Lai-wang to abscond with Sun Hsüeh-o.

Lai-chao's son. See Little Iron Rod.

Lai-chao's wife. See Hui-ch'ing.

Lai-chüeh, Lai-yu, husband of Hui-yüan, originally servant in the household of a distaff relative of the imperial family named Wang, loses his position on exposure of his wife's affair with her employer, recommended as a servant to Hsi-men Ch'ing by his friend Ying Pao, the son of Ying Po-chüeh.

Lai-chüeh's deceased parents.

Lai-chüeh's wife. See Hui-yüan.

Lai-hsing, Kan Lai-hsing, servant in Hsi-men Ch'ing's household, originally recruited by Hsi-men Ch'ing's father while traveling on business in Kan-chou, husband of Hui-hsiu, father of Nien-erh and Ch'eng-erh, helps to frame Lai-wang for attempted murder, married to Chang Ju-i after the death of Hui-hsiu.

Lai-pao, T'ang Pao, servant in Hsi-men Ch'ing's household often relied upon for important missions to the capital, husband of Hui-hsiang, father of Seng-pao, appointed to the post of commandant on the staff of the Prince of Yün in return for his part in delivering birthday presents from Hsi-men Ch'ing to Ts'ai Ching, embezzles Hsi-men Ch'ing's property after his death and makes unsuccessful sexual advances to Wu Yüeh-niang, ends up in prison for misappropriation of funds.

Lai-pao's son. See Seng-pao.

Lai-pao's wife. See Hui-hsiang.

Lai-ting, page boy in the household of Hua Tzu-yu.

Lai-ting, page boy in the household of Huang the Fourth.

Lai-ting, page boy in the household of Wu K'ai.

Lai-wang, Cheng Wang, native of Hsü-chou, servant in Hsi-men Ch'ing's household, husband of Sung Hui-lien, framed for attempted murder and driven out of the household in order to get him out of the way, carries on a clandestine affair with Sun Hsüeh-o before his exile and absconds with her when he returns to Ch'ing-ho after Hsi-men Ch'ing's death.

Lai-wang's first wife, dies of consumption.

Lai-wang's second wife. See Sung Hui-lien.

Lai-yu. See Lai-chüeh.

Lan-hsiang, senior maidservant of Meng Yü-lou.

Lan-hua, junior maidservant of P'ang Ch'un-mei after she becomes the wife of Chou Hsiu.

Lan-hua, elderly maidservant in the household of Wu K'ai.

Lan Ts'ung-hsi (fl. early 12th century), eunuch rewarded for his part in facilitating the notorious Flower and Rock Convoys and the construction of the Mount Ken Imperial Park, uncle of Ho Yung-shou's wife, née Lan.

Lan Ts'ung-hsi's adopted son, granted the post of battalion vice-commander of the Embroidered Uniform Guard by *yin* privilege as a reward for his father's part in facilitating the notorious Flower and Rock Convoys and the construction of the Mount Ken Imperial Park.

Lan Ts'ung-hsi's niece. See Ho Yung-shou's wife, née Lan.

Lang, Buddhist Superior, monk of the Pao-en Temple in Ch'ing-ho.

Lei Ch'i-yüan, assistant commissioner of the Shantung Military Defense Circuit.

Li An, retainer in the household of Chou Hsiu who saves P'ang Ch'un-mei's life when she is threatened by Chang Sheng and resists her blandishments when she tries to seduce him.

Li An's father, deceased elder brother of Li Kuei.

Li An's mother, persuades Li An to avoid entanglement with P'ang Ch'un-mei by seeking refuge with his uncle Li Kuei in Ch'ing-chou.

Li, Barestick. See Li Kung-pi.

Li Ch'ang-ch'i, father of Li Kung-pi, district magistrate of Ch'ing-ho and later assistant prefect of Yen-chou in Chekiang.

Li Ch'ang-ch'i's wife, mother of Li Kung-pi.

Li Chiao-erh, Hsi-men Ch'ing's Second Lady, originally a singing girl from the Verdant Spring Bordello in Ch'ing-ho, aunt of Li Kuei-ch'ing and Li Kuei-chieh, enemy of P'an Chin-lien, tight-fisted manager of Hsi-men Ch'ing's household finances, engages in hanky-panky with Wu the Second, begins pilfering Hsi-men Ch'ing's property while his corpse is still warm, ends up as Chang Mao-te's Second Lady.

Li Chih, Li the Third, father of Li Huo, merchant contractor in Ch'ing-ho, partner of Huang the Fourth, ends up dying in prison for misappropriation of funds.

Li Chin, servant in the household of Li Chih.

Li Chung-yu, servant on the domestic staff of Ts'ai Ching.

Li, Eunuch Director. See Li Yen.

Li family of the Eastern Capital, family into which P'an Chin-lien is reincarnated as a daughter.

Li Huo, son of Li Chih.

Li Kang (1083–1140), minister of war under Emperor Ch'in-tsung who directs the defense against the Chin invaders.

Li Kuei, Shantung Yaksha, uncle of Li An, military instructor from Ch'ing-chou patronized by Li Kung-pi.

Li Kuei-chieh, Cassia, daughter of Auntie Li the Third, niece of Li Chiao-erh and Li Ming, younger sister of Li Kuei-ch'ing, singing girl from the Verdant Spring Bordello on Second Street in the licensed quarter of Ch'ing-ho, deflowered by Hsi-men Ch'ing, who maintains her as his mistress for twenty taels a month, adopted daughter of Wu Yüeh-niang, betrays Hsi-men Ch'ing with Ting the Second, Wang Ts'ai, and others.

Li Kuei-chieh's fifth maternal aunt.

Li Kuei-ch'ing, daughter of Auntie Li the Third, niece of Li Chiao-erh and Li Ming, elder sister of Li Kuei-chieh, singing girl from the Verdant Spring Bordello on Second Street in the Licensed quarter of Ch'ing-ho.

Li K'uei, Black Whirlwind, bloodthirsty outlaw from Sung Chiang's band who massacres the household of Liang Shih-chieh and kills Yin T'ien-hsi.

Li Kung-pi, Bare Stick Li, only son of Li Ch'ang-ch'i, student at the Superior College of the National University, falls in love with Meng Yü-lou at first sight and arranges to marry her as his second wife, severely beaten by his father for his part in the abortive attempt to frame Ch'en Ching-chi, forced to return with his bride to his native place to resume his studies.

Li Kung-pi's deceased first wife.

Li Kung-pi's servant.

Li, Leaky. See Li Wai-ch'uan.

Li Ming, younger brother of Li Chiao-erh, uncle of Li Kuei-ch'ing and Li Kuei-chieh; actor and musician from the Verdant Spring Bordello on Second Street in the licensed quarter of Ch'ing-ho; employed by Hsi-men Ch'ing to teach Ch'un-mei, Yü-hsiao, Ying-ch'un, and Lan-hsiang to sing and play musical instruments; driven out of the house by Ch'un-mei for having the temerity to squeeze her hand during a lesson but allowed to return on many subsequent occasions; assists Li Chiao-erh, Li Kuei-ch'ing, and Li Kuei-chieh in despoiling Hsi-men Ch'ing's property after his death.

Li Pang-yen (d. 1130), minister of the right, grand academician of the Hall for Aid in Governance, and concurrently minister of rites, alters Hsi-men Ch'ing's name to Chia Lien on a bill of impeachment in return for a bribe of five hundred taels of silver, promoted to the ranks of pillar of state and grand preceptor of the heir apparent for his part in facilitating the notorious Flower and Rock Convoys and the construction of the Mount Ken Imperial Park, one of the Six Traitors impeached by Ch'en Tung.

Li P'ing-erh, Vase, Mrs. Hua, Mistress Hua, one of the three principal female protagonists of the novel, concubine of Liang Shih-chieh, wife of Hua Tzu-hsü, commits adultery with her husband's neighbor and sworn brother Hsi-men Ch'ing, wife of Dr. Chiang Chu-shan, Hsi-men Ch'ing's Sixth Lady, mother of Hsi-men Kuan-ko, dies of chronic hemorrhaging brought on by grief over the death of her son and Hsi-men Ch'ing's insistence on trying out his newly acquired aphrodisiac on her while she is in her menstrual period, commemorated in overly elaborate funeral observances that are prime examples of conspicuous consumption, haunts Hsi-men Ch'ing's dreams.

Li P'ing-erh's former incarnation. See Wang family of Pin-chou.

Li P'ing-erh's deceased parents.

Li P'ing-erh's reincarnation. See Yüan, Commander.

Li Ta-t'ien, district magistrate of Ch'ing-ho, relative of Chu Mien, appoints Wu Sung as police captain and later sends him to the Eastern Capital to stash his ill-gotten gains with his powerful relative, accepts Hsi-men Ch'ing's bribes to abuse the law in the cases of Wu Sung, Lai-wang, Sung Hui-lien, Miao T'ien-hsiu, and others.

Li the Third, seller of won-ton in front of the district yamen in Ch'ing-ho.

Li the Third. See Li Chih.

Li the Third, Auntie, madam of the Verdant Spring Bordello on Second Street in the licensed quarter of Ch'ing-ho, mother of Li Kuei-ch'ing and Li Kuei-chieh, partially paralyzed, prototypical procuress who milks her customers for all she can get.

Li, Vice-Minister, employer of Licentiate Shui.

Li Wai-ch'uan, Leaky Li, influence peddling lictor on the staff of the district yamen in Ch'ing-ho who is mistakenly killed by Wu Sung in his abortive attempt to wreak vengeance on Hsi-men Ch'ing for the murder of his elder brother Wu Chih.

Li Yen (d. 1126), Eunuch Director Li, entertains Miao Ch'ing in his residence behind the Forbidden City in the Eastern Capital, rewarded for his part in facilitating the notorious Flower and Rock Convoys and the construction of the Mount Ken Imperial Park, one of the Six Traitors impeached by Ch'en Tung.

Li Yen's adopted son, granted the post of battalion vice-commander of the Embroidered Uniform Guard by *yin* privilege as a reward for his father's part in facilitating the notorious Flower and Rock Convoys and the construction of the Mount Ken Imperial Park.

Liang, Privy Councilor. See Liang Shih-chieh.

Liang Shih-chieh, Privy Councilor Liang, regent of the Northern Capital at Ta-ming Prefecture in Hopei, son-in-law of Ts'ai Ching, first husband of Li P'ing-erh, forced to flee for his life when his entire household is slaughtered by Li K'uei.

Liang Shih-chieh's wife, née Ts'ai, daughter of Ts'ai Ching, extremely jealous woman who beats numbers of maidservants and concubines of her husband to death and buries them in the rear flower garden, forced to flee for her life when her entire household is slaughtered by Li K'uei.

Liang To, professional boy actor in Ch'ing-ho.

Liang Ying-lung, commandant of security for the Eastern Capital.

Lin Ch'eng-hsün, judicial commissioner in the Huai-ch'ing office of the Provincial Surveillance Commission.

Lin Hsiao-hung, younger sister of Lin Ts'ai-hung, singing girl in Yang-chou patronized by Lai-pao.

Lin, Lady, widow of Imperial Commissioner Wang I-hsüan, mother of Wang Ts'ai, former mistress of P'an Chin-lien who learns to play musical instruments and to sing as a servant in her household, carries on an adulterous affair with Hsi-men Ch'ing under the transparent pretext of asking him to superintend the morals of her profligate son.

Lin Ling-su (d. c. 1125), Perfect Man Lin, Taoist priest who gains an ascendancy over Emperor Hui-tsung for a time and is showered with high-sounding titles, rewarded for his part in facilitating the notorious Flower and Rock Convoys and the construction of the Mount Ken Imperial Park.

Lin, Perfect Man. See Lin Ling-su.

Lin Shu (d. c. 1126), minister of works rewarded with the title grand guardian of the heir apparent for his part in facilitating the notorious Flower and Rock Convoys and the construction of the Mount Ken Imperial Park.

Lin Ts'ai-hung, elder sister of Lin Hsiao-hung, singing girl in Yang-chou.

Ling, Master, fortune teller in Ch'ing-ho who interprets Meng Yü-lou's horoscope when she is about to marry Li Kung-pi.

Ling Yün-i, prefect of Yen-chou in Shantung.

Little Iron Rod, son of Lai-chao and his wife Hui-ch'ing.

Little Jade. See Hsiao-yü.

Little Whirlwind. See Ch'ai Chin.

Liu, Assistant Regional Commander, officer of the Hsi-hsia army who gives a horse to Chai Ch'ien, who in turn presents it to Hsi-men Ch'ing.

Liu Chao. See Lai-chao.

Liu Chü-chai, Dr., physician from Fen-chou in Shansi, friend of Ho Yung-shou who recommends him to Hsi-men Ch'ing when he is in extremis but whose treatment exacerbates his condition.

Liu, Company Commander, younger brother of Eunuch Director Liu, indicted for illicit use of imperial lumber in constructing a villa on a newly purchased estate at Wu-li Tien outside Ch'ing-ho, let off the hook by Hsi-men Ch'ing in response to a bribe proffered by Eunuch Director Liu.

Liu, Consort (1088–1121), Consort An, a favorite consort of Emperor Hui-tsung, mother of Chao I.

Liu, Dame, Stargazer Liu's wife, medical practitioner and shamaness frequently called upon by the women of Hsi-men Ch'ing's household.

Liu, Eunuch Director, elder brother of Company Commander Liu, manager of the Imperial Brickyard in Ch'ing-ho, resides on an estate outside the south gate of the city, intervenes with Hsi-men Ch'ing to get his younger brother off the hook when indicted for misappropriation of imperial lumber but supplies Hsi-men Ch'ing with bricks from the Imperial Brickyard for construction of his country estate.

Liu, Eunuch Director, landlord of Dr. Hu's house on East Street in Ch'ing-ho.

Liu, Eunuch Director, resides near Wine Vinegar Gate on the North Side of Ch'ing-ho, patron of Li Ming.

Liu Hui-hsiang. See Hui-hsiang.

Liu Kao, commander of An-p'ing Stockade, friend of Shih En who gives Wu Sung a hundred taels of silver and a letter of recommendation to him when he is sent there in military exile.

Liu, Mr., official serving in Huai-an who passed the *chin-shih* examinations the same year as Sung Ch'iao-nien.

Liu Pao, servant employed as a cook in Hsi-men Ch'ing's silk dry goods store.

Liu, School Official, native of Hang-chou, educational official in Ch'ing-ho who borrows money from Hsi-men Ch'ing.

Liu the Second, Turf-protecting Tiger, brother-in-law of Chang Sheng, proprietor of My Own Tavern west of the bridge in Lin-ch'ing, pimp and racketeer, boss of unlicensed prostitution in Lin-ch'ing, beaten to death by Chou Hsiu at the behest of P'ang Ch'un-mei after Chang Sheng's murder of Ch'en Ching-chi.

Liu the Second, Little, seller of ready-cooked food in front of the district yamen in Ch'ing-ho.

Liu Sheng, foreman on the domestic staff of Yang Chien.

Liu, Stargazer, husband of Dame Liu, blind fortune teller and necromancer who interprets P'an Chin-lien's horoscope, teaches her a method for working black magic on Hsi-men Ch'ing, and treats Hsi-men Kuan-ko ineffectually.

Liu the Third, servant of Company Commander Liu.

Liu Ts'ang, younger brother of Hui-hsiang, brother-in-law of Lai-pao with whom he cooperates in surreptitiously making off with eight hundred taels worth of Hsi-men Ch'ing's property after his death and using it to open a general store.

Liu Yen-ch'ing (1068–1127), commander-general of the Shensi region who leads the forces of Yen-sui against the Chin invaders.

Lo, Mohammedan, one of the "ball clubbers" patronized by Hsi-men Ch'ing.

Lo Ts'un-erh, singing girl of Ch'ing-ho patronized by Hsiang the Fifth.

Lo Wan-hsiang, prefect of Tung-p'ing.

Love. See Chu Ai-ai.

Lu Ch'ang-t'ui, Longleg Lu, madam of the brothel on Butterfly Lane in Ch'ing-ho where Chin-erh and Sai-erh work.

Lu Ch'ang-t'ui's husband.

Lu, Duke of. See Ts'ai Ching.

Lu Hu, clerical subofficial on the staff of Yang Chien.

Lu Hua, Snake-in-the-grass, "knockabout" who, along with Chang Sheng, shakes down Dr. Chiang Chu-shan at the behest of Hsi-men Ch'ing.

Lu, Longleg. See Lu Ch'ang-t'ui.

Lu Ping-i, Lu the Second, crony of Ch'en Ching-chi who suggests how he can recover his property from Yang Kuang-yen and goes into partnership with him as the manager of the Hsieh Family Tavern in Lin-ch'ing.

Lu the Second. See Lu Ping-i.

Lung-hsi, Duke of. See Wang Wei.

Lü Sai-erh, singing girl in Ch'ing-ho.

Ma Chen, professional boy actor in Ch'ing-ho.

Ma, Mrs., next-door neighbor of Ying Po-chüeh.

Man-t'ang, maidservant in the household of Li Kung-pi.

Mao-te, Princess (fl. early 12th century), fifth daughter of Emperor Hui-tsung, married to Ts'ai Ching's fourth son, Ts'ai T'iao.

Meng Ch'ang-ling (fl. early 12th century), eunuch rewarded for his part in facilitating the notorious Flower and Rock Convoys and the construction of the Mount Ken Imperial Park.

Meng Ch'ang-ling's adopted son, granted the post of battalion vice-commander of the Embroidered Uniform Guard by *yin* privilege as a reward for his father's part in facilitating the notorious Flower and Rock Convoys and the construction of the Mount Ken Imperial Park.

Meng-ch'ang, Little Lord. See Ch'ai Chin.
Meng the Elder, elder brother of Meng Yü-lou.
Meng the Elder's wife, Meng Yü-lou's sister-in-law.
Meng Jui, Meng the Second, younger brother of Meng Yü-lou, a traveling merchant constantly on the road.
Meng Jui's wife, Meng Yü-lou's sister-in-law.
Meng the Second. See Meng Jui.
Meng the Third. See Meng Yü-lou.
Meng Yü-lou, Tower of Jade, Meng the Third, one of the female protagonists of the novel, widow of the textile merchant Yang Tsung-hsi, Hsi-men Ch'ing's Third Lady, confidante of P'an Chin-lien, marries Li Kung-pi after the death of Hsi-men Ch'ing, forced to return with her husband to his native place in Hopei after their abortive attempt to frame Ch'en Ching-chi, bears a son to Li Kung-pi at the age of forty and lives to the age of sixty-seven.
Meng Yü-lou's elder brother. See Meng the Elder.
Meng Yü-lou's elder sister. See Han Ming-ch'uan's wife, née Meng.
Meng Yü-lou's son by Li Kung-pi.
Meng Yü-lou's younger brother. See Meng Jui.
Miao Ch'ing, servant of Miao T'ien-hsiu who conspires with the boatmen Ch'en the Third and Weng the Eighth to murder his master on a trip to the Eastern Capital, bribes Hsi-men Ch'ing to get him off the hook, and returns to Yang-chou where he assumes his former master's position in society and maintains relations with his benefactor Hsi-men Ch'ing.
Miao-ch'ü, teenage disciple of Nun Hsüeh.
Miao-feng, teenage disciple of Nun Hsüeh.
Miao Hsiu, servant in the household of Miao Ch'ing.
Miao Shih, servant in the household of Miao Ch'ing.
Miao T'ien-hsiu, a wealthy merchant of Yang-chou who is murdered by his servant Miao Ch'ing on a trip to the Eastern Capital.
Miao T'ien-hsiu's concubine. See Tiao the Seventh.
Miao T'ien-hsiu's daughter.
Miao T'ien-hsiu's wife, née Li.
Ming-wu. See Hsi-men Hsiao-ko.
Mirror polisher, elderly itinerant artisan in Ch'ing-ho who polishes mirrors for P'an Chin-lien, Meng Yü-lou, and P'ang Ch'un-mei and elicits their sympathy with a sob story.
Mirror polisher's deceased first wife.
Mirror polisher's second wife.
Mirror polisher's son.
Monk, Indian, foreign monk presented as the personification of a penis whom Hsi-men Ch'ing encounters in the Temple of Eternal Felicity and

from whom he obtains the aphrodisiac an overdose of which eventually kills him.

Moon Lady. See Wu Yüeh-niang.

Ni, Familiar. See Ni P'eng.

Ni, Licentiate. See Ni P'eng.

Ni P'eng, Familiar Ni, Licentiate Ni, tutor employed in the household of Hsia Yen-ling as a tutor for his son, Hsia Ch'eng-en, who recommends his fellow licentiate Wen Pi-ku to Hsi-men Ch'ing.

Nieh Liang-hu, schoolmate of Shang Hsiao-t'ang employed in his household as a tutor for his son who writes two congratulatory scrolls for Hsi-men Ch'ing.

Nieh, Tiptoe. See Nieh Yüeh.

Nieh Yüeh, Tiptoe Nieh, one of the "cribbers" in the licensed quarter of Ch'ing-ho who plays the tout to Wang Ts'ai on his visits to the licensed quarter and upon whom Hsi-men Ch'ing turns the tables by abusing the judicial system at the behest of Lady Lin.

Nieh Yüeh's wife.

Nien-erh, elder daughter of Lai-hsing by Hui-hsiu.

Nien-mo-ho. See Wan-yen Tsung-han.

Niu, Ms., singing girl in the Great Tavern on Lion Street who witnesses Wu Sung's fatal assault on Li Wai-ch'uan.

Old woman who tells the fortunes of Wu Yüeh-niang, Meng Yü-lou, and Li P'ing-erh with the aid of a turtle.

Opportune Rain. See Sung Chiang.

Ostensibly Benign. See I Mien-tz'u.

Pai, Baldy. See Pai T'u-tzu.

Pai the Fifth, Moneybags Pai, father-in-law of Feng Huai, notorious local tyrant and fence for stolen goods in the area west of the Grand Canal.

Pai the Fourth, silversmith in Ch'ing-ho, acquaintance of Han Tao-kuo.

Pai Lai-ch'iang, Scrounger Pai, crony of Hsi-men Ch'ing, member of the brotherhood of ten.

Pai Lai-ch'iang's wife.

Pai, Mohammedan. See Pai T'u-tzu.

Pai, Moneybags. See Pai the Fifth.

Pai, Scrounger. See Pai Lai-ch'iang.

Pai Shih-chung (d. 1127), right vice-minister of rites rewarded with the title grand guardian of the heir apparent for his part in facilitating the notorious Flower and Rock Convoys and the construction of the Mount Ken Imperial Park.

Pai T'u-tzu, Baldy Pai, Mohammedan Pai, "ball-clubber" in Ch'ing-ho who plays the tout to Wang Ts'ai on his visits to the licensed quarter and upon whom Hsi-men Ch'ing turns the tables by abusing the judicial system at the behest of Lady Lin.

Pai Yü-lien, Jade Lotus, maidservant purchased by Mrs. Chang at the same time as P'an Chin-lien who dies shortly thereafter.

Palace foreman who plays the role of master of ceremonies at the imperial audience in the Hall for the Veneration of Governance.

Palefaced Gentleman. See Cheng T'ien-shou.

Pan-erh, unlicensed prostitute in Longfoot Wu's brothel in the Southern Entertainment Quarter of Ch'ing-ho patronized by P'ing-an after he absconds from the Hsi-men household with jewelry stolen from the pawnshop.

P'an Chi, one of the officials from the Ch'ing-ho Guard who comes to Hsimen Ch'ing's residence to offer a sacrifice to the soul of Li P'ing-erh after her death.

P'an Chin-lien, Golden Lotus, P'an the Sixth, principal female protagonist of the novel, daughter of Tailor P'an from outside the South Gate of Ch'ing-ho who dies when she is only six years old; studies in a girls' school run by Licentiate Yü for three years where she learns to read and write; sold by her mother at the age of eight into the household of Imperial Commissioner Wang and Lady Lin where she is taught to play musical instruments and to sing; resold in her mid-teens, after the death of her master, into the household of Mr. Chang who deflowers her and then gives her as a bride to his tenant, Wu Sung's elder brother, the dwarf Wu Chih; paramour of Hsi-men Ch'ing who collaborates with her in poisoning her husband and subsequently makes her his Fifth Lady; seduces her husband's page boy Ch'in-t'ung for which he is driven out of the household; carries on a running affair with her son-in-law, Ch'en Ching-chi, which is consummated after the death of Hsi-men Ch'ing; responsible, directly or indirectly, for the suicide of Sung Hui-lien, the death of Hsimen Kuan-ko, and the demise of Hsi-men Ch'ing; aborts her son by Ch'en Ching-chi; is sold out of the household by Wu Yüeh-niang, purchased by Wu Sung, and disemboweled by the latter in revenge for the death of his elder brother Wu Chih.

P'an Chin-lien's cat, Coal in the Snow, Snow Lion, Snow Bandit, longhaired white cat with a black streak on its forehead that P'an Chin-lien trains to attack Hsi-men Kuan-ko with fatal consequences.

P'an Chin-lien's father. See P'an, Tailor.

P'an Chin-lien's maternal aunt, younger sister of old Mrs. P'an.

P'an Chin-lien's maternal aunt's daughter, adopted by old Mrs. P'an to look after her in her old age.

P'an Chin-lien's mother. See P'an, old Mrs.

P'an Chin-lien's reincarnation. See Li Family of the Eastern Capital.

P'an, Demon-catcher. See P'an, Taoist Master.

P'an family prostitution ring operating out of My Own Tavern in Lin-ch'ing, madam of.

P'an the fifth, white slaver, masquerading as a cotton merchant from Shantung, who operates a prostitution ring out of My Own Tavern in Lin-ch'ing, buys Sun Hsüeh-o from Auntie Hsüeh, and forces her to become a singing girl.

P'an the Fifth's deceased first wife.

P'an the Fifth's mother.

P'an, old Mrs., widow of Tailor P'an, mother of P'an Chin-lien, sends her daughter to Licentiate Yü's girls' school for three years, sells her into the household of Imperial Commissioner Wang and Lady Lin at the age of eight, resells her in her mid-teens into the household of Mr. Chang, frequent visitor in Hsi-men Ch'ing's household where she is maltreated by P'an Chin-lien who is ashamed of her low social status, adopts her younger sister's daughter to look after her in her old age, dies not long after the death of Hsi-men Ch'ing.

P'an the Sixth. See P'an Chin-lien.

P'an, Tailor, father of P'an Chin-lien, artisan from outside the South Gate of Ch'ing-ho who dies when P'an Chin-lien is only six years old.

P'an, Taoist Master, Demon-catcher P'an, Taoist exorcist from the Temple of the Five Peaks outside Ch'ing-ho who performs various rituals on Li P'ing-erh's behalf but concludes that nothing can save her.

P'an, Taoist Master's acolyte.

P'ang Ch'un-mei, Spring Plum Blossom, one of the three principal female protagonists of the novel, originally purchased by Hsi-men Ch'ing from Auntie Hsüeh for sixteen taels of silver as a maidservant for Wu Yüeh-niang, reassigned as senior maidservant to P'an Chin-lien when she enters the household, becomes her chief ally and confidante; from the time that her mistress allows her to share the sexual favors of Hsi-men Ch'ing she remains loyal to her right up to and even after her death; after the demise of Hsi-men Ch'ing aids and abets P'an Chin-lien's affair with Ch'en Ching-chi, the discovery of which leads to her dismissal from the household; purchased as a concubine by Chou Hsiu, she bears him a son and is promoted to the status of principal wife, thereby rising higher in social status than any of the ladies she had formerly served as maidservant; comes to Wu Yüeh-niang's assistance when she is threatened by Wu Tien-en and condescends to pay a visit to her former mistress and to witness at first hand the signs of her relative decline; carries on an intermittent affair with Ch'en Ching-chi under her husband's nose and, after Chou Hsiu's death, dies in the act of sexual intercourse with his servant Chou I.

P'ang Ch'un-mei's deceased father who dies while Ch'un-mei is still a child.

P'ang Ch'un-mei's deceased mother who dies a year after Ch'un-mei's birth.

P'ang Ch'un-mei's reincarnation. See K'ung family of the Eastern Capital.

P'ang Ch'un-mei's son. See Chou Chin-ko.

P'ang Hsüan, clerical subofficial on the staff of Yang Chien.

Pao, Dr., pediatric physician in Ch'ing-ho called in to treat Hsi-men Kuan-ko who declares the case to be hopeless.

Pao-en Temple in the Eastern Capital, monk from, tries unsuccessfully to warn Miao T'ien-hsiu against leaving home before his fatal trip to the Eastern Capital.

Pao, Ms., singing girl in the Great Tavern on Lion Street who witnesses Wu Sung's fatal assault on Li Wai-ch'uan.

Pen Chang-chieh, Jui-yün, daughter of Pen Ti-ch'uan and Yeh the Fifth, concubine of Hsia Yen-ling.

Pen the Fourth. See Pen Ti-ch'uan.

Pen, Scurry-about. See Pen Ti-ch'uan.

Pen Ti-ch'uan, Scurry-about Pen, Pen the Fourth, husband of Yeh the Fifth, father of Pen Chang-chieh, manager employed by Hsi-men Ch'ing in various capacities, member of the brotherhood of ten in which he replaces Hua Tzu-hsü after his death.

Pen Ti-ch'uan's daughter. See Pen Chang-chieh.

Pen Ti-ch'uan's wife. See Yeh the Fifth.

Pin-yang, Commandery Prince of. See Wang Ching-ch'ung.

P'ing-an, page boy in Hsi-men Ch'ing's household, absconds with jewelry stolen from the pawnshop after the death of Hsi-men Ch'ing, is caught, and allows himself to be coerced by the police chief Wu Tien-en into giving false testimony that Wu Yüeh-niang has been engaged in hanky-panky with Tai-an.

P'ing-erh. See Li P'ing-erh.

Prison guard on Chou Hsiu's staff.

Pu Chih-tao, No-account Pu, crony of Hsi-men Ch'ing, member of the brotherhood of ten whose place is taken after his death by Hua Tzu-hsü.

Pu, No-account. See Pu Chih-tao.

P'u-ching, Ch'an Master Snow Cave, mysterious Buddhist monk who provides Wu Yüeh-niang with a refuge in Snow Stream Cave on Mount T'ai when she is escaping attempted rape by Yin T'ien-hsi; at the end of the novel he conjures up a phantasmagoria in which all of the major protagonists describe themselves as being reborn in approximately the same social strata they had occupied in their previous incarnations; convinces Wu Yüeh-niang that her son Hsiao-ko is a reincarnation of Hsi-men Ch'ing and spirits him away into a life of Buddhist celibacy as his disciple.

Sai-erh, singing girl in Longleg Lu's brothel on Butterfly Lane in Ch'ing-ho.

Sauce and Scallions. See Chiang Ts'ung.

Second Lady. See Li Chiao-erh.

Seng-pao, son of Lai-pao and Hui-hsiang, betrothed to Wang Liu-erh's niece, the daughter of Butcher Wang and Sow Wang.

Servant from the household of Chou Hsiu who is sent to fetch P'ang Ch'un-mei with a lantern.
Servant in the inn at the foot of Mount T'ai where Wu Yüeh-niang and Wu K'ai spend the night on their pilgrimage.
Servant from the Verdant Spring Bordello who runs errands for Li Kuei-chieh.
Sha San, Yokel Sha, one of the "cribbers" and "ball clubbers" in Ch'ing-ho who plays the tout to Wang Ts'ai on his visits to the licensed quarter and upon whom Hsi-men Ch'ing turns the tables by abusing the judicial system at the behest of Lady Lin.
Sha, Yokel. See Sha San.
Shamaness brought to the Hsi-men household by Dame Liu to burn paper money and perform a shamanistic dance on behalf of the sick Hsi-men Kuan-ko.
Shang Hsiao-t'ang, Provincial Graduate Shang, son of Shang Liu-t'ang, widower in Ch'ing-ho whom Chang Lung proposes unsuccessfully as a match for Meng Yü-lou, provincial graduate of the same year as Huang Pao-kuang, assisted by Hsi-men Ch'ing when he sets out for the Eastern Capital to compete in the *chin-shih* examinations.
Shang Hsiao-t'ang's second wife.
Shang Hsiao-t'ang's son.
Shang Liu-t'ang, Prefectural Judge Shang, father of Shang Hsiao-t'ang, formerly served as district magistrate of Huang Pao-kuang's district and prefectural judge of Ch'eng-tu in Szechwan, resident of Main Street in Ch'ing-ho from whom both Li P'ing-erh's and Hsi-men Ch'ing's coffins are purchased.
Shang Liu-t'ang's deceased wife, mother of Shang Hsiao-t'ang.
Shang, Prefectural Judge. See Shang Liu-t'ang.
Shang, Provincial Graduate. See Shang Hsiao-t'ang.
Shantung Yaksha. See Li Kuei.
Shao Ch'ien, boy actor in Ch'ing-ho.
Shen, Brother-in-law, Mr. Shen, husband of Wu Yüeh-niang's elder sister.
Shen Ching, resident of the Eastern Capital, father of Shen Shou-shan.
Shen, Mr. See Shen, Brother-in-law.
Shen, Second Sister, blind professional singer in Ch'ing-ho recommended to Hsi-men Ch'ing by Wang Liu-erh but driven out of his household by P'ang Ch'un-mei when she refuses to sing for her.
Shen Shou-shan, second son of Shen Ching, reincarnation of Chou Hsiu.
Shen Ting, servant in the household of Brother-in-law Shen.
Shen T'ung, wealthy resident of the Eastern Capital, father of Shen Yüeh.
Shen Yüeh, second son of Shen T'ung, reincarnation of Hsi-men Ch'ing.
Sheng-chin, ten-year-old country girl offered to P'ang Ch'un-mei as a maidservant but rejected for befouling her bed.
Sheng-chin's parents.

Shih Cho-kuei, Plastromancer Shih, shaman in Ch'ing-ho who prognosticates about the sick Hsi-men Kuan-ko through interpreting the cracks produced by applying heat to notches on the surface of the plastron of a tortoise shell.

Shih En, son of the warden of the prison camp at Meng-chou who befriends the exiled Wu Sung, obtains his assistance in his struggle with Chiang Men-shen for control of the Happy Forest Tavern, and gives him a hundred taels of silver and a letter of recommendation to Liu Kao when he is transferred to the An-p'ing Stockade.

Shih, Plastromancer. See Shih Cho-kuei.

Shih Po-ts'ai, corrupt Taoist head priest of the Temple of the Goddess of Iridescent Clouds on the summit of Mount T'ai.

Short-legged Tiger. See Wang Ying.

Shu-t'ung, Little Chang Sung, native of Su-chou, page boy catamite and transvestite presented to Hsi-men Ch'ing by Li Ta-t'ien, placed in charge of Hsi-men Ch'ing's studio where he handles his correspondence and caters to his polymorphous sexual tastes, becomes intimate with Yü-hsiao and when discovered in flagrante delicto by P'an Chin-lien purloins enough of Hsi-men Ch'ing's property to make good his escape to his native place.

Shui, Licentiate, scholar of problematic morals unsuccessfully recommended to Hsi-men Ch'ing as a social secretary by Ying Po-chüeh; after Hsi-men Ch'ing's death he is engaged by the remaining members of the brotherhood of ten to compose a funeral eulogy for Hsi-men Ch'ing in which he compares him to the male genitalia.

Shui, Licentiate's father, friend of Ying Po-chüeh's father.

Shui, Licentiate's grandfather, friend of Ying Po-chüeh's grandfather.

Shui, Licentiate's two sons, die of smallpox.

Shui, Licentiate's wife, elopes to the Eastern Capital with her lover.

Sick beggar whom Ch'en Ching-chi keeps alive with the warmth of his body when he is working as a night watchman.

Silver. See Wu Yin-erh.

Singing boys, two boy singers sent under escort all the way to Hsi-men Ch'ing's home in Ch'ing-ho by his host, Miao Ch'ing, after he expresses admiration for their singing at a banquet in the residence of Li Yen in the Eastern Capital.

Six Traitors, Ts'ai Ching, T'ung Kuan, Li Pang-yen, Chu Mien, Kao Ch'iu, and Li Yen.

Sixth Lady. See Li P'ing-erh.

Snake-in-the-grass. See Lu Hua.

Snow Bandit. See P'an Chin-lien's cat.

Snow Cave, Ch'an Master. See P'u-ching.

Snow Lion. See P'an Chin-lien's cat.

Snow Moth. See Sun Hsüeh-o.
Southerner who deflowers Cheng Ai-yüeh.
Spring Plum Blossom. See P'ang Ch'un-mei.
Ssu Feng-i, battalion commander rewarded for his part in facilitating the notorious Flower and Rock Convoys and the construction of the Mount Ken Imperial Park.
Stand-hard. See Tao-chien.
Star of Joy Bordello in Ch'ing-ho, cook from.
Storehouseman in charge of the local storehouse in Yen-chou Prefecture in Chekiang.
Street-skulking Rat. See Chang Sheng.
Sun, Blabbermouth. See Sun T'ien-hua.
Sun Chi, next-door neighbor of Ch'en Ching-chi.
Sun Ch'ing, father-in-law of Huang the Fourth, father of Sun Wen-hsiang, employer of Feng the Second, merchant in Ch'ing-ho engaged in the cotton trade.
Sun Ch'ing's daughter. See Huang the Fourth's wife, née Sun.
Sun Ch'ing's son. See Sun Wen-hsiang.
Sun, Crooked-head, deceased husband of Aunt Yang.
Sun Erh-niang, concubine of Chou Hsiu, mother of Chou Yü-chieh.
Sun Erh-niang's maidservant.
Sun Erh-niang's maidservant's father.
Sun Hsüeh-o, Snow Moth, originally maidservant of Hsi-men Ch'ing's deceased first wife, née Ch'en, who enters his household as part of her dowry; Hsi-men Ch'ing's Fourth Lady but a second-class citizen among his womenfolk whose responsibility is the kitchen; enemy of P'an Chin-lien and P'ang Ch'un-mei; carries on a clandestine affair with Lai-wang with whom she absconds when he returns to Ch'ing-ho after Hsi-men Ch'ing's death; apprehended by the authorities and sold into Chou Hsiu's household at the behest of P'ang Ch'un-mei who abuses her, beats her, and sells her into prostitution in order to get her out of the way when she wishes to pass off Ch'en Ching-chi as her cousin; renamed as the singing girl, Yü-erh, working out of My Own Tavern in Lin-ch'ing, she becomes the kept mistress of Chang Sheng until his death when she commits suicide.
Sun Hsüeh-o's reincarnation. See Yao family from outside the Eastern Capital.
Sun Jung, commandant of justice for the two townships of the Eastern Capital.
Sun Kua-tsui. See Sun T'ien-hua.
Sun T'ien-hua, Sun Kua-tsui, Blabbermouth Sun, crony of Hsi-men Ch'ing, member of the brotherhood of ten, plays the tout to Wang Ts'ai on his visits to the licensed quarter.

Sun T'ien-hua's wife.

Sun Wen-hsiang, son of Sun Ch'ing, brother-in-law of Huang the Fourth, involved in an affray with Feng Huai who dies of his injuries half a month later.

Sung Chiang (fl. 1117–21), Opportune Rain, chivalrous bandit chieftan, leader of a band of thirty-six outlaws in Liang-shan Marsh whose slogan is to "Carry out the Way on Heaven's behalf," slayer of Yen P'o-hsi, rescues Wu Yüeh-niang when she is captured by the bandits of Ch'ing-feng Stronghold and Wang Ying wants to make her his wife, eventually surrenders to Chang Shu-yeh and accepts the offer of a government amnesty.

Sung Ch'iao-nien (1047–1113), father-in-law of Ts'ai Yu, father of Sung Sheng-ch'ung, protégé of Ts'ai Ching, appointed regional investigating censor of Shantung to replace Tseng Hsiao-hsü, entertained by Hsi-men Ch'ing who presents him periodically with lavish bribes in return for which he gets Miao Ch'ing off the hook and does him numerous other illicit favors, rewarded for his part in facilitating the notorious Flower and Rock Convoys and the construction of the Mount Ken Imperial Park.

Sung Hui-lien, Chin-lien, daughter of Sung Jen, formerly maidservant in the household of Assistant Prefect Ts'ai who takes sexual advantage of her; sacked for colluding with her mistress in a case of adultery; marries the cook Chiang Ts'ung who is stabbed to death in a brawl; second wife of Lai-wang; carries on a clandestine affair with Hsi-men Ch'ing that soon becomes public knowledge; after Lai-wang is framed for attempted murder and driven out of the household she suffers from remorse and commits suicide.

Sung Hui-lien's reincarnation. See Chu family of the Eastern Capital.

Sung Hui-lien's maternal aunt.

Sung Jen, father of Sung Hui-lien, coffin seller in Ch'ing-ho who accuses Hsi-men Ch'ing of driving his daughter to suicide but is given such a beating by the corrupt magistrate Li Ta-t'ien that he dies of his wounds.

Sung Sheng-ch'ung (fl. early 12th century), son of Sung Ch'iao-nien, elder brother of Ts'ai Yu's wife, née Sung, regional investigating censor of Shensi suborned into traducing Tseng Hsiao-hsü by Ts'ai Ching.

Sung Te, commits adultery with Ms. Chou, the widowed second wife of his father-in-law, for which Hsi-men Ch'ing sentences them both to death by strangulation.

Sung Te's father-in-law, deceased husband of Ms. Chou.

Sung Te's mother-in-law, deceased mother of Sung Te's wife.

Sung Te's wife.

Sung T'ui, eunuch rewarded for his part in facilitating the notorious Flower and Rock Convoys and the construction of the Mount Ken Imperial Park.

Ta T'ien-tao, prefect of Tung-ch'ang.

Tai-an, Hsi-men An, favorite page boy of Hsi-men Ch'ing and his sedulous understudy in the arts of roguery and dissimulation; manages to stay on the right side of everyone with the exception of Wu Yüeh-niang who periodically berates him for his duplicity; married to Hsiao-yü after the death of Hsi-men Ch'ing when Wu Yüeh-niang discovers them in flagrante delicto; remains with Wu Yüeh-niang and supports her in her old age in return for which he is given the name Hsi-men An and inherits what is left of Hsi-men Ch'ing's property and social position.

T'ai-tsung, emperor of the Chin dynasty (r. 1123–35).

T'an Chen (fl. early 12th century), eunuch military commander with the concurrent rank of censor-in-chief, appointed to replace T'ung Kuan in command of the defense of the northern frontier against the Chin army.

T'ang Pao. See Lai-pao.

Tao-chien, Stand-hard, abbot of the Temple of Eternal Felicity at Wu-li Yüan outside the South Gate of Ch'ing-ho.

T'ao, Crud-crawler, an elderly resident of Ch'ing-ho who is renowned for having sexually molested all three of his daughters-in-law.

T'ao-hua, maidservant in the Star of Joy Bordello in Ch'ing-ho.

T'ao, Old Mother, licensed go-between in Ch'ing-ho who represents Li Kung-pi in his courtship of Meng Yü-lou.

Temple of the Jade Emperor outside the East Gate of Ch'ing-ho, lector of.

Teng, Midwife, called in by Ying Po-chüeh when his concubine, Ch'un-hua, bears him a son.

Third Lady. See Cho Tiu-erh and Meng Yü-lou.

Three-inch Mulberry-bark Manikin. See Wu Chih.

Ti Ssu-pin, Turbid Ti, vice-magistrate of Yang-ku district who locates the corpse of Miao T'ien-hsiu after his murder by Miao Ch'ing.

Ti, Turbid. See Ti Ssu-pin.

Tiao the Seventh, concubine of Miao T'ien-hsiu, formerly a singing girl from a brothel on the Yang-chou docks, carries on an affair with her husband's servant, Miao Ch'ing, the discovery of which leads to the beating of Miao Ch'ing and the murder of Miao T'ien-hsiu in revenge.

T'ien Chiu-kao, battalion commander rewarded for his part in facilitating the notorious Flower and Rock Convoys and the construction of the Mount Ken Imperial Park.

T'ien-fu. See Ch'in-t'ung.

T'ien-hsi, senior page boy in the household of Hua Tzu-hsü and Li P'ing-erh who absconds with five taels of silver when his master takes to his sickbed and vanishes without a trace.

T'ien Hu, bandit chieftan active in the Hopei area.

Ting, Director, Wu K'ai's predecessor as director of the State Farm Battalion in Ch'ing-ho, cashiered for corruption by Hou Meng.

Ting, Mr., father of Ting the Second, silk merchant from Hang-chou.

Ting the Second, Ting Shuang-ch'iao, son of Mr. Ting, friend of Ch'en Liang-huai, a silk merchant from Hang-chou who patronizes Li Kuei-chieh while on a visit to Ch'ing-ho and hides under the bed when Hsi-men Ch'ing discovers their liaison and smashes up the Verdant Spring Bordello.

Ting Shuang-ch'iao. See Ting the Second.

Ting the Southerner, wine merchant in Ch'ing-ho from whom Hsi-men Ch'ing buys forty jugs of Ho-ch'ing wine on credit.

Tou Chien (d. 1127), superintendant of the Capital Training Divisions and capital security commissioner.

Tower of Jade. See Meng Yü-lou.

Ts'ai, Assistant Prefect, resident of Ch'ing-ho from whose household Sung Hui-lien is expelled for colluding with her mistress in a case of adultery.

Ts'ai, Assistant Prefect's wife.

Ts'ai Ching (1046–1126), father of Ts'ai Yu, Ts'ai T'iao, Ts'ai T'ao, and Ts'ai Hsiu, father-in-law of Liang Shih-chieh, left grand councilor, grand academician of the Hall for Veneration of Governance, grand preceptor, minister of personnel, Duke of Lu, most powerful minister at the court of Emperor Hui-tsung, impeached by Yü-wen Hsü-chung, patron and adoptive father of Ts'ai Yün and Hsi-men Ch'ing, first of the Six Traitors impeached by Ch'en Tung.

Ts'ai Ching's mansion in the Eastern Capital, gatekeepers of.

Ts'ai Ching's mansion in the Eastern Capital, page boy in.

Ts'ai Ching's wife.

Ts'ai family of Yen-chou in Shantung, family of which Hsi-men Hsiao-ko is alleged to have been a son in his previous incarnation.

Ts'ai Hsing (fl. early 12th century), son of Ts'ai Yu, appointed director of the Palace Administration as a reward for his father's part in facilitating the notorious Flower and Rock Convoys and the construction of the Mount Ken Imperial Park.

Ts'ai Hsiu, ninth son of Ts'ai Ching, prefect of Chiu-chiang.

Ts'ai, Midwife, presides over the deliveries of Li P'ing-erh's son, Hsi-men Kuan-ko, and Wu Yüeh-niang's son, Hsi-men Hsiao-ko.

Ts'ai T'ao (d. after 1147), fifth son of Ts'ai Ching.

Ts'ai T'iao (d. after 1137), fourth son of Ts'ai Ching, consort of Princess Mao-te.

Ts'ai Yu (1077–1126), eldest son of Ts'ai Ching, son-in-law of Sung Ch'iao-nien, brother-in-law of Sung Sheng-ch'ung, father of Ts'ai Hsing, academician of the Hall of Auspicious Harmony, minister of rites, superintendent of the Temple of Supreme Unity, rewarded with the title grand guardian of the heir apparent for his part in facilitating the notorious Flower and Rock Convoys and the construction of the Mount Ken Imperial Park, executed by order of Emperor Ch'in-tsung after the fall of Ts'ai Ching and his faction.

Ts'ai Yu's son. See Ts'ai Hsing.

Ts'ai Yu's wife, née Sung, daughter of Sung Ch'iao-nien, younger sister of Sung Sheng-ch'ung.

Ts'ai Yün, awarded first place in the *chin-shih* examinations in place of An Ch'en when the latter is displaced for being the younger brother of the proscribed An Tun, becomes a protégé and adopted son of Ts'ai Ching, appointed proofreader in the Palace Library, is patronized by Hsi-men Ch'ing; after being impeached by Ts'ao Ho he is appointed salt-control censor of the Liang-Huai region where his illicit favors to Hsi-men Ch'ing abet his profitable speculations in the salt trade.

Ts'ai Yün's mother.

Tsang Pu-hsi, docket officer on the staff of the district yamen in Ch'ing-ho.

Ts'ao Ho, censor who impeaches Ts'ai Yün and thirteen others from the Historiography Institute who had passed the *chin-shih* examinations in the same year.

Tseng Hsiao-hsü (1049–1127), son of Tseng Pu, regional investigating censor of Shantung, reopens the case of Miao T'ien-hsiu's murder at the request of Huang Mei and arrives at the truth only to have his memorial suppressed when Hsi-men Ch'ing and Hsia Yen-ling bribe Ts'ai Ching to intervene; submits a memorial to the throne criticizing the policies of Ts'ai Ching that so enrages the prime minister that he suborns his daughter-in-law's brother, Sung Sheng-ch'ung, into framing him on trumped up charges as a result of which he is deprived of his office and banished to the furthest southern extremity of the country.

Tseng Pu (1036–1107), father of Tseng Hsiao-hsü.

Tso Shun, professional boy actor in Ch'ing-ho.

Ts'ui-erh, maidservant of Sun Hsüeh-o.

Ts'ui-hua, junior maidservant of P'ang Ch'un-mei after she becomes the wife of Chou Hsiu.

Ts'ui Pen, nephew of Ch'iao Hung, husband of Big Sister Tuan, employee, manager, and partner in several of Hsi-men Ch'ing's enterprises.

Ts'ui Pen's mother, Ch'iao Hung's elder sister.

Ts'ui, Privy Councilor. See Ts'ui Shou-yü.

Ts'ui Shou-yü, Privy Councilor Ts'ui, relative of Hsia Yen-ling with whom he stays on his visit to the Eastern Capital.

Tsung-mei. See Ch'en Ching-chi.

Tsung-ming. See Chin Tsung-ming.

Tsung Tse (1059-1128), general-in-chief of the Southern Sung armies who retakes parts of Shantung and Hopei from the Chin invaders on behalf of Emperor Kao-tsung.

Tu the Third, maternal cousin of Ying Po-chüeh.

Tu the Third's page boy.

Tu the Third's wife.

Tu Tzu-ch'un, privy councilor under a previous reign living in retirement in the northern quarter of Ch'ing-ho, engaged by Hsi-men Ch'ing to indite the inscription on Li P'ing-erh's funeral banderole.

Tuan, Big Sister, wife of Ts'ui Pen.

Tuan, Big Sister's father.

Tuan, Consort. See Feng, Consort.

Tuan, Half-baked. See Tuan Mien.

Tuan Mien, Half-baked Tuan, one of the "cribbers" in the licensed quarter of Ch'ing-ho patronized by Hsi-men Ch'ing.

Tuan, Old Mother, waiting woman in Lady Lin's household whose residence in the rear of the compound is used as a rendezvous by her lovers.

Tung the Cat. See Tung Chin-erh.

Tung Chiao-erh, singing girl from the Tung Family Brothel on Second Street in the licensed quarter of Ch'ing-ho who spends the night with Ts'ai Yün at Hsi-men Ch'ing's behest.

Tung Chin-erh, Tung the Cat, singing girl from the Tung Family Brothel on Second Street in the licensed quarter of Ch'ing-ho, patronized by Chang Mao-te.

Tung Sheng, clerical subofficial on the staff of Wang Fu.

Tung Yü-hsien, singing girl from the Tung Family Brothel on Second Street in the licensed quarter of Ch'ing-ho.

T'ung Kuan (1054–1126), eunuch military officer beaten up by Wu Sung in a drunken brawl, uncle of T'ung T'ien-yin, military affairs commissioner, defender-in-chief of the Palace Command, Commandery Prince of Kuang-yang, one of the Six Traitors impeached by Ch'en Tung.

T'ung Kuan's nephew. See T'ung T'ien-yin.

T'ung, Prefectural Judge, prefectural judge of Tung-p'ing who conducts the preliminary hearing in the case of the affray between Feng Huai and Sun Wen-hsiang.

T'ung T'ien-yin, nephew of T'ung Kuan, commander of the guard, director of the Office of Herds in the Inner and Outer Imperial Demesnes of the Court of the Imperial Stud.

Turf-protecting Tiger. See Liu the Second.

Tutor employed in the household of Miao Ch'ing.

Tz'u-hui Temple, abbot of, recovers the corpse of the murdered Miao T'ien-hsiu and buries it on the bank of the river west of Ch'ing-ho where it is discovered by Ti Ssu-pin.

Vase. See Li P'ing-erh.

Waiter in My Own Tavern in Lin-ch'ing.

Wan-yen Tsung-han (1079–1136), Nien-mo-ho, nephew of Emperor T'ai-tsu (r. 1115–23) the founder of the Chin dynasty, commander of the Chin army that occupies K'ai-feng and takes Retired Emperor Hui-tsung and Emperor Ch'in-tsung into captivity.

Wan-yen Tsung-wang (d. 1127), Wo-li-pu, second son of Emperor T'ai-tsu (r. 1115–23) the founder of the Chin dynasty, associate commander of the Chin army that occupies K'ai-feng and takes Retired Emperor Hui-tsung and Emperor Ch'in-tsung into captivity, kills Chou Hsiu with an arrow through the throat.

Wang, Attendant, official on the staff of the Prince of Yün to whom Han Tao-kuo appeals through Hsi-men Ch'ing and Jen Hou-ch'i to be allowed to commute his hereditary corvée labor obligation to payments in money or goods.

Wang, Butcher, elder brother of Wang Liu-erh, husband of Sow Wang whose daughter is betrothed to Seng-pao.

Wang Ch'ao, son of Dame Wang, apprenticed to a merchant from the Huai River region from whom he steals a hundred taels entrusted to him for the purchase of stock, returns to Ch'ing-ho, and uses it as capital to buy two donkeys and set up a flour mill, becomes a casual lover of P'an Chin-lien while she is in Dame Wang's house awaiting purchase as a concubine.

Wang Chen, second son of Wang Hsüan, government student in the prefectural school.

Wang Ch'ien, eldest son of Wang Hsüan, hereditary battalion commander of the local Horse Pasturage Battalion of the Court of the Imperial Stud.

Wang Chin-ch'ing. See Wang Shen.

Wang Ching, younger brother of Wang Liu-erh, page boy employed in the household of Hsi-men Ch'ing as a replacement for Shu-t'ung after he absconds, sodomized by Hsi-men Ch'ing during his visit to the Eastern Capital, expelled from the household by Wu Yüeh-niang after the death of Hsi-men Ch'ing.

Wang Ching-ch'ung (d. 949), military commissioner of T'ai-yüan, Commandery Prince of Pin-yang, ancestor of Wang I-hsüan.

Wang Ch'ing, bandit chieftan active in the Huai-hsi area.

Wang Chu, elder brother of Wang Hsiang, professional boy actor in Ch'ing-ho.

Wang, Consort (d. 1117), a consort of Emperor Hui-tsung, mother of Chao K'ai, the Prince of Yün, related to Wang the Second.

Wang, Dame, mother of Wang Ch'ao, proprietress of a teahouse next door to Wu Chih's house on Amythest Street on the west side of the district yamen in Ch'ing-ho who is also active as a go-between and procuress; go-between who proposes the match between Hsi-men Ch'ing and Wu

Yüeh-niang; inventor of the elaborate scheme by which Hsi-men Ch'ing seduces P'an Chin-lien; suggests the poisoning of her next-door neighbor Wu Chih and helps P'an Chin-lien carry it out; intervenes on behalf of Ho the Tenth when he is accused of fencing stolen goods with the result that Hsi-men Ch'ing gets him off the hook and executes an innocent monk in his stead; after the death of Hsi-men Ch'ing, when Wu Yüeh-niang discovers P'an Chin-lien's affair with Ch'en Ching-chi, she expells her from the household and consigns her to Dame Wang, who entertains bids from Magnate Ho, Chang Mao-te, Ch'en Ching-chi, and Chou Hsiu before finally selling her to Wu Sung for a hundred taels of silver plus a five-tael brokerage fee; that same night she is decapitated by Wu Sung after he has disemboweled P'an Chin-lien.

Wang, Dame's deceased husband, father of Wang Ch'ao, dies when she is thirty-five.

Wang, Dame's son. See Wang Ch'ao.

Wang, distaff relative of the imperial family. See Wang the Second.

Wang family of Cheng-chou, family into which Hsi-men Kuan-ko is reincarnated as a son.

Wang family of the Eastern Capital, family into which Ch'en Ching-chi is reincarnated as a son.

Wang family of Pin-chou, family in which Li P'ing-erh is alleged to have been formerly incarnated as a son.

Wang the First, Auntie, madam of the Wang Family Brothel in Yang-chou.

Wang Fu (1079-1126), minister of war impeached by Yü-wen Hsü-chung.

Wang Fu's wife and children.

Wang Hai-feng. See Wang Ssu-feng.

Wang Han, servant in the household of Han Tao-kuo and Wang Liu-erh.

Wang Hsiang, younger brother of Wang Chu, professional boy actor in Ch'ing-ho.

Wang Hsien, employee of Hsi-men Ch'ing who accompanies Lai-pao on a buying trip to Nan-ching.

Wang Hsüan, Layman of Apricot Hermitage, father of Wang Ch'ien and Wang Chen, friend of Ch'en Hung, retired philanthropist who provides aid to Ch'en Ching-chi three times after he is reduced to beggary and who recommends him to Abbot Jen of the Yen-kung Temple in Lin-ch'ing.

Wang Hsüan's manager, in charge of a pawnshop on the street front of his residence.

Wang Huan (fl. early 12th century), commander-general of the Hopei region who leads the forces of Wei-po against the Chin invaders.

Wang I-hsüan, Imperial Commissioner Wang, descendant of Wang Ching-ch'ung, deceased husband of Lady Lin, father of Wang Ts'ai.

Wang I-hsüan's wife. See Lady Lin.

Wang I-hsüan's son. See Wang Ts'ai.

Wang, Imperial Commissioner. See Wang I-hsüan.

Wang K'uan, head of the mutual security unit for Ch'en Ching-chi's residence in Ch'ing-ho.

Wang Lien, henchman on the domestic staff of Wang Fu.

Wang Liu-erh, Wang the Sixth, one of the female protagonists of the novel, younger sister of Butcher Wang, elder sister of Wang Ching, wife of Han Tao-kuo, mother of Han Ai-chieh; paramour of her brother-in-law, Han the Second, whom she marries after her husband's death, of Hsi-men Ch'ing, to whose death from sexual exhaustion she is a major contributor, and of Magnate Ho, whose property in Hu-chou she inherits.

Wang Liu-erh's niece, daughter of Butcher Wang and Sow Wang, betrothed to Seng-pao, the son of Lai-pao and Hui-hsiang.

Wang Luan, proprietor of the Great Tavern on Lion Street in Ch'ing-ho who witnesses Wu Sung's fatal attack on Li Wai-ch'uan.

Wang, Nun, Buddhist nun from the Kuan-yin Nunnery in Ch'ing-ho which is patronized by Wu Yüeh-niang, frequently invited to recite Buddhist "precious scrolls" to Wu Yüeh-niang and her guests, recommends Nun Hsüeh to Wu Yüeh-niang who takes her fertility potion and conceives Hsi-men Hsiao-ko, later quarrels with Nun Hsüeh over the division of alms from Li P'ing-erh and Wu Yüeh-niang.

Wang, old Mrs., neighbor of Yün Li-shou in Chi-nan who appears in Wu Yüeh-niang's nightmare.

Wang, Old Sister, singing girl working out of My Own Tavern in Lin-ch'ing.

Wang Ping (d. 1126), commander-general of the Kuan-tung region who leads the forces of Fen-chiang against the Chin invaders.

Wang Po-ju, proprietor of an inn on the docks in Yang-chou recommended to Han Tao-kuo, Lai-pao, and Ts'ui Pen by Hsi-men Ch'ing as a good place to stay.

Wang Po-ju's father, friend of Hsi-men Ch'ing's father, Hsi-men Ta.

Wang Po-yen (1069–1141), right assistant administration commissioner of Shantung.

Wang the Second, distaff relative of the imperial family through Consort Wang, landlord of Wu Chih's residence on the west side of Amythest Street in Ch'ing-ho, purchaser of Eunuch Director Hua's mansion on Main Street in An-ch'ing ward of Ch'ing-ho, maintains a private troupe of twenty actors that he sometimes lends to Hsi-men Ch'ing to entertain his guests.

Wang Shen (c. 1048–c. 1103), Wang Chin-ch'ing, commandant-escort and director of the Court of the Imperial Clan, consort of the second daughter of Emperor Ying-tsung (r. 1063–67).

Wang Shih-ch'i, prefect of Ch'ing-chou in Shantung.

Wang the Sixth. See Wang Liu-erh.

Wang, Sow, wife of Butcher Wang whose daughter is betrothed to Seng-pao.

Wang Ssu-feng, Wang Hai-feng, salt merchant from Yang-chou who is set free from prison in Ts'ang-chou by Hou Meng, the grand coordinator of Shantung, as a result of Hsi-men Ch'ing's intervention with Ts'ai Ching.

Wang the Third. See Wang Ts'ai.

Wang Ts'ai (1078–1118), Wang the Third, feckless and dissolute third son of Wang I-hsüan and Lady Lin, married to the niece of Huang Ching-ch'en, tries unsuccessfully to borrow three hundred taels of silver from Hsü Pu-yü to purchase a position in the Military School, pawns his wife's possessions to pursue various singing girls in the licensed quarter including those patronized by Hsi-men Ch'ing, tricked into becoming the adopted son of Hsi-men Ch'ing during his intrigue with Lady Lin, continues his affair with Li Kuei-chieh after the death of Hsi-men Ch'ing.

Wang Ts'ai's wife, née Huang, niece of Huang Ching-ch'en.

Wang Tsu-tao (d. 1108), minister of personnel.

Wang Tung-ch'iao, traveling merchant entertained by Han Tao-kuo in Yang-chou.

Wang, Usher, official in the Court of State Ceremonial who offers the sixteen-year-old wife of his runaway retainer for sale as a maidservant through Old Mother Feng.

Wang, Usher's runaway retainer.

Wang, Usher's runaway retainer's wife.

Wang Wei, supreme commander of the Capital Training Divisions, Duke of Lung-hsi, granted the title of grand mentor for his part in facilitating the notorious Flower and Rock Convoys and the construction of the Mount Ken Imperial Park.

Wang Ying, Short-legged Tiger, second outlaw leader of the Ch'ing-feng Stronghold on Ch'ing-feng Mountain who wants to make Wu Yüeh-niang his wife when she is captured by his band but is prevented from doing so by Sung Chiang.

Wang Yu, commander of a training division rewarded for his part in facilitating the notorious Flower and Rock Convoys and the construction of the Mount Ken Imperial Park.

Wang Yü, subofficial functionary on the domestic staff of Ts'ai Ching deputed by Chai Ch'ien to carry a message of condolence to Hsi-men Ch'ing and a personal letter from Han Ai-chieh to Han Tao-kuo and Wang Liu-erh.

Wang Yü-chih, singing girl from the Wang Family Brothel in Yang-chou patronized by Han Tao-kuo.

Wei Ch'eng-hsün, battalion commander rewarded for his part in facilitating the notorious Flower and Rock Convoys and the construction of the Mount Ken Imperial Park.

Wei Ts'ung-erh, a taciturn chair-bearer in Ch'ing-ho, partner of Chang Ch'uan-erh.

Wen, Auntie, mother of Wen T'ang, go-between in Ch'ing-ho who represents Ch'en Ching-chi's family at the time of his betrothal to Hsi-men Ta-chieh, resident of Wang Family Alley on the South Side of town, active in promoting pilgrimages to Mount T'ai, patronized by Lady Lin for whom she acts as a procuress in her adulterous affairs including that with Hsi-men Ch'ing, involved with Auntie Hsüeh in arranging the betrothal between Chang Mao-te's son and Eunuch Director Hsü's niece.

Wen Ch'en, one of the officials from the Ch'ing-ho Guard who comes to Hsi-men Ch'ing's residence to offer a sacrifice to the soul of Li P'ing-erh after her death.

Wen Hsi, military director-in-chief of Yen-chou in Shantung.

Wen, Licentiate. See Wen Pi-ku.

Wen, Pedant. See Wen Pi-ku.

Wen Pi-ku, Warm-buttocks Wen, Pedant Wen, Licentiate Wen, pederast recommended to Hsi-men Ch'ing by his fellow licentiate Ni P'eng to be his social secretary, housed across the street from Hsi-men Ch'ing's residence in the property formerly belonging to Ch'iao Hung, divulges Hsi-men Ch'ing's private correspondence to Ni P'eng who shares it with Hsia Yen-ling, sodomizes Hua-t'ung against his will and is expelled from the Hsi-men household when his indiscretions are exposed.

Wen Pi-ku's mother-in-law.

Wen Pi-ku's wife.

Wen T'ang, son of Auntie Wen.

Wen T'ang's wife.

Wen, Warm-buttocks. See Wen Pi-ku.

Weng the Eighth, criminal boatman who, along with his partner Ch'en the Third, murders Miao T'ien-hsiu.

What a Whopper. See Hsieh Ju-huang.

Wo-li-pu. See Wan-yen Tsung-wang.

Wu, Abbot. See Wu Tsung-che.

Wu, Battalion Commander, father of Wu K'ai, Wu the Second, Wu Yüeh-niang's elder sister, and Wu Yüeh-niang, hereditary battalion commander of the Ch'ing-ho Left Guard.

Wu, Captain. See Wu Sung.

Wu Ch'ang-chiao, Longfoot Wu, madam of the brothel in the Southern Entertainment Quarter of Ch'ing-ho patronized by P'ing-an after he absconds from the Hsi-men household with jewelry stolen from the pawnshop.

Wu Ch'ang-chiao's husband.

Wu Chih, Wu the Elder, Three-inch Mulberry-bark Manikin, elder brother of Wu Sung, father of Ying-erh by his deceased first wife, husband of P'an

Chin-lien, simple-minded dwarf, native of Yang-ku district in Shantung who moves to the district town of Ch'ing-ho because of a famine and makes his living by peddling steamed wheat cakes on the street, cuckolded by P'an Chin-lien with his landlord, Mr. Chang, and then with Hsi-men Ch'ing, catches P'an Chin-lien and Hsi-men Ch'ing in flagrante delicto in Dame Wang's teahouse but suffers a near-fatal injury when Hsi-men Ch'ing kicks him in the solar plexus, poisoned by P'an Chin-lien with arsenic supplied by Hsi-men Ch'ing.

Wu Chih's daughter. See Ying-erh.

Wu Chih's deceased first wife, mother of Ying-erh.

Wu Chih's second wife. See P'an Chin-lien.

Wu the Elder. See Wu Chih.

Wu the Fourth, Auntie, madam of the Wu Family Bordello on the back alley in the licensed quarter of Ch'ing-ho.

Wu, Heartless. See Wu Tien-en.

Wu Hsün, secretary of the Bureau of Irrigation and Transportation in the Ministry of Works, rewarded for his part in facilitating the notorious Flower and Rock Convoys and the construction of the Mount Ken Imperial Park.

Wu Hui, younger brother of Wu Yin-erh, actor and musician from the Wu Family Bordello on the back alley in the licensed quarter of Ch'ing-ho.

Wu, Immortal. See Wu Shih.

Wu K'ai, eldest son of Battalion Commander Wu, elder brother of Wu the Second, Wu Yüeh-niang's elder sister, and Wu Yüeh-niang, father of Wu Shun-ch'en, brother-in-law of Hsi-men Ch'ing, inherits the position of battalion commander of the Ch'ing-ho Left Guard upon the death of his father, deputed to repair the local Charity Granary, promoted to the rank of assistant commander of the Ch'ing-ho Guard in charge of the local State Farm Battalion as a result of Hsi-men Ch'ing's influence with Sung Ch'iao-nien, accompanies Wu Yüeh-niang on her pilgrimage to Mount T'ai after the death of Hsi-men Ch'ing and is instrumental in rescuing her from attempted rape by Yin T'ien-hsi.

Wu K'ai's son. See Wu Shun-ch'en.

Wu K'ai's wife, Sister-in-law Wu, mother of Wu Shun-ch'en, sister-in-law of Hsi-men Ch'ing and a frequent guest in his household.

Wu, Longfoot. See Wu Ch'ang-chiao.

Wu the Second, second son of Battalion Commander Wu, younger brother of Wu K'ai, second elder brother of Wu Yüeh-niang, brother-in-law of Hsi-men Ch'ing and manager of his silk store on Lion Street; engages in hanky-panky with Li Chiao-erh for which he is denied access to the household by Wu Yüeh-niang when it is discovered after the death of Hsi-men Ch'ing although he continues to manage the silk store and later, along with Tai-an, the wholesale pharmaceutical business; accompanies

Wu Yüeh-niang, Tai-an, Hsiao-yü, and Hsi-men Hsiao-ko when they flee the invading Chin armies to seek refuge with Yün Li-shou in Chi-nan; ten days after the climactic encounter with P'u-ching in the Temple of Eternal Felicity and Wu Yüeh-niang's relinquishment of Hsi-men Hsiao-ko to a life of Buddhist celibacy he accompanies Wu Yüeh-niang, Tai-an, and Hsiao-yü back to their now truncated household in Ch'ing-ho.

Wu the Second. See Wu Sung.

Wu the Second's wife, wife of Wu Yüeh-niang's second elder brother.

Wu Shih, Immortal Wu, Taoist physiognomist introduced to Hsi-men Ch'ing by Chou Hsiu who accurately foretells his fortune and those of his wife and concubines as well as Hsi-men Ta-chieh and P'ang Ch'un-mei; when Hsi-men Ch'ing is on his deathbed he is called in again and reports that there is no hope for him.

Wu Shih's servant boy.

Wu Shun-ch'en, son of Wu K'ai, husband of Third Sister Cheng.

Wu, Sister-in-law. See Wu K'ai's wife.

Wu Sung, Wu the Second, Captain Wu, younger brother of Wu Chih, brother-in-law of P'an Chin-lien; impulsive and implacable exponent of the code of honor; becomes a fugitive from the law for beating up T'ung Kuan in a drunken brawl; slays a tiger in single-handed combat while on his way to visit his brother and is made police captain in Ch'ing-ho for this feat; rejects attempted seduction by P'an Chin-lien and tells her off in no uncertain terms; delivers Li Ta-t'ien's illicit gains from his magistracy to the safe keeping of Chu Mien in the Eastern Capital; returns to Ch'ing-ho and mistakenly kills Li Wai-ch'uan while seeking to avenge the murder of his brother; is sentenced to military exile in Meng-chou where he is befriended by Shih En and helps him in his struggle with Chiang Men-shen for control of the Happy Forest Tavern; is framed by Military Director-in-chief Chang with the help of his concubine, Chiang Yü-lan, the younger sister of Chiang Men-shen, in revenge for which he murders his two guards and the entire households of Military Director-in-chief Chang and Chiang Men-shen; sets out for An-p'ing Stockade with a hundred taels of silver and a letter of recommendation from Shih En but is enabled by a general amnesty to return to Ch'ing-ho where he buys P'an Chin-lien from Dame Wang for a hundred taels of silver and disembowels her to avenge the death of his brother; once more a fugitive he disguises himself as a Buddhist ascetic with the help of the criminal innkeepers Chang Ch'ing and his wife and goes to join Sung Chiang's band of outlaws in Liang-shan Marsh.

Wu-t'ai, Mount, monk from, who solicits alms from Wu Yüeh-niang for the repair of his temple.

Wu Tien-en, Heartless Wu, originally a Yin-yang master on the staff of the district yamen in Ch'ing-ho who has been removed from his post for cause; makes his living by hanging around in front of the yamen and acting as a guarantor for loans to local officials and functionaries; crony of Hsi-men Ch'ing; member of the brotherhood of ten; manager employed by Hsi-men Ch'ing in various of his enterprises; misrepresents himself as Hsi-men Ch'ing's brother-in-law and is appointed to the post of station master of the Ch'ing-ho Postal Relay Station in return for his part in delivering birthday presents from Hsi-men Ch'ing to Ts'ai Ching; receives an interest-free loan of one hundred taels from Hsi-men Ch'ing to help cover the expenses of assuming office; promoted to the position of police chief of a suburb of Ch'ing-ho after the death of Hsi-men Ch'ing he apprehends the runaway P'ing-an and coerces him into giving false testimony that Wu Yüeh-niang has been engaged in hanky-panky with Tai-an, but when Wu Yüeh-niang appeals to P'ang Ch'un-mei he is dragged before Chou Hsiu's higher court and thoroughly humiliated.

Wu Tsung-che, Abbot Wu, head priest of the Taoist Temple of the Jade Emperor outside the East Gate of Ch'ing-ho, presides over the elaborate Taoist ceremony at which Hsi-men Kuan-ko is made an infant Taoist priest with the religious name Wu Ying-yüan, later officiates at funeral observances for Li P'ing-erh and Hsi-men Ch'ing.

Wu Yin-erh, Silver, elder sister of Wu Hui, singing girl from the Wu Family Bordello on the back alley of the licensed quarter in Ch'ing-ho, sweetheart of Hua Tzu-hsü, adopted daughter of Li P'ing-erh.

Wu Ying-yüan. See Hsi-men Kuan-ko.

Wu Yüeh-niang, Moon Lady, one of the female protagonists of the novel, daughter of Battalion Commander Wu, younger sister of Wu K'ai, Wu the Second, and an elder sister; second wife and First Lady of Hsi-men Ch'ing who marries her after the death of his first wife, née Ch'en, in a match proposed by Dame Wang; stepmother of Hsi-men Ta-chieh, mother of Hsi-men Hsiao-ko; a pious, credulous, and conventional Buddhist laywoman who constantly invites Nun Wang and Nun Hsüeh to the household to recite "precious scrolls" on the themes of salvation, retribution, and reincarnation, who has good intentions but is generally ineffectual at household management and is not a good judge of character; colludes with Hsi-men Ch'ing in taking secret possession of Li P'ing-erh's ill-gotten property but quarrels with him over admitting her to the household; suffers a miscarriage but later takes Nun Hsüeh's fertility potion and conceives Hsi-men Hsiao-ko who is born at the very moment of Hsi-men Ch'ing's death; thoughtlessly betroths both Kuan-ko and Hsiao-ko to inappropriate partners while they are still babes in arms; makes a pilgrimage to Mount T'ai after Hsi-men Ch'ing's death and narrowly escapes an attempted rape by Yin T'ien-hsi and capture by the bandits on Ch'ing-feng Mountain; expels P'an Chin-lien, P'ang Ch'un-mei, and Ch'en Ching-chi from the household when she belatedly discovers their perfidy but is unable to cope effectively with the declining fortunes of the family; forced to seek the assistance of P'ang Ch'un-mei when she is threatened by Wu Tien-en she has no alternative but to accept the condescension of her former maidservant; while fleeing from the invading Chin armies to seek refuge with Yün Li-shou in Chi-nan she encounters P'u-ching and spends the night in the Temple of Eternal Felicity where she dreams that Yün Li-shou threatens her with rape if she refuses to marry him; still traumatized by this nightmare, she allows P'u-ching to persuade her that Hsiao-ko is the reincarnation of Hsi-men Ch'ing and relinquishes her teenage son to a life of Buddhist celibacy without so much as asking his opinion; on returning safely to Ch'ing-ho she adopts Tai-an as her husband's heir, renaming him Hsi-men An, and lives in reduced circumstances, presiding over a truncated household, until dying a natural death at the age of sixty-nine.

Wu Yüeh-niang's elder sister, wife of Brother-in-law Shen.

Yang, Aunt, widow of Crooked-head Sun, paternal aunt of Yang Tsung-hsi and Yang Tsung-pao, forceful advocate of Meng Yü-lou's remarriage to Hsi-men Ch'ing after the latter offers her a hundred taels of silver for her support, quarrels with Chang Lung when he tries to prevent this match.

Yang Chien (d. 1121), Commander Yang, eunuch military officer related to Ch'en Hung by marriage, commander in chief of the Imperial Guard in the Eastern Capital, bribed by Hsi-men Ch'ing to intervene on his behalf against Wu Sung and in favor of Hua Tzu-hsü, impeached by Yü-wen Hsü-chung, reported in a letter from Chai Ch'ien to Hsi-men Ch'ing to have died in prison in 1117.

Yang, Commander. See Yang Chien.

Yang the Elder. See Yang Kuang-yen.

Yang Erh-feng, second son of Yang Pu-lai and his wife, née Pai, younger brother of Yang Kuang-yen, a gambler and tough guy who scares off Ch'en Ching-chi when he tries to recover the half shipload of property that Yang Kuang-yen had stolen from him.

Yang Kuang-yen, Yang the Elder, Iron Fingernail, native of Nobottom ward in Carryoff village of Makebelieve district in Nonesuch subprefecture, son of Yang Pu-lai and his wife, née Pai, disciple of the Barefaced Adept from whom he acquires the art of lying, husband of Miss Died-of-fright, con man employed by Ch'en Ching-chi who absconds with half a shipload of his property while he is in Yen-chou trying to shake down Meng Yü-lou and invests it in the Hsieh Family Tavern in Lin-ch'ing only to lose everything when Ch'en Ching-chi sues him with the backing of Chou Hsiu and takes over ownership of the tavern.

Yang Kuang-yen's father. See Yang Pu-lai.

Yang Kuang-yen's mother, née Pai.

Yang Kuang-yen's page boy.

Yang Kuang-yen's wife. See Died-of-fright, Miss.

Yang, Poor-parent. See Yang Pu-lai.

Yang, Prefect. See Yang Shih.

Yang Pu-lai, Poor-parent Yang, father of Yang Kuang-yen and Yang Erh-feng, brother-in-law of Yao the Second.

Yang Sheng, factotum on the domestic staff of Yang Chien.

Yang Shih (1053–1135), Prefect Yang, prefect of K'ai-feng, protégé of Ts'ai Ching, agrees under pressure from Ts'ai Ching and Yang Chien to treat Hua Tzu-hsü leniently when he is sued over the division of Eunuch Director Hua's property by his brothers Hua Tzu-yu, Hua Tzu-kuang, and Hua Tzu-hua.

Yang T'ing-p'ei, battalion commander rewarded for his part in facilitating the notorious Flower and Rock Convoys and the construction of the Mount Ken Imperial Park.

Yang Tsung-hsi, deceased first husband of Meng Yü-lou, elder brother of Yang Tsung-pao, nephew on his father's side of Aunt Yang and on his mother's side of Chang Lung, textile merchant residing on Stinkwater Lane outside the South Gate of Ch'ing-ho.

Yang Tsung-hsi's maternal uncle. See Chang Lung.

Yang Tsung-hsi's mother. See Chang Lung's elder sister.

Yang Tsung-hsi's paternal aunt. See Yang, Aunt.

Yang Tsung-pao, younger brother of Yang Tsung-hsi, nephew on his father's side of Aunt Yang and on his mother's side of Chang Lung, brother-in-law of Meng Yü-lou.

Yang Wei-chung (1067–1132), commander-general of the Shansi region who leads the forces of Tse-lu against the Chin invaders.

Yao family from outside the Eastern Capital, poor family into which Sun Hsüeh-o is reincarnated as a daughter.

Yao the Second, brother-in-law of Yang Pu-lai, neighbor of Wu Chih to whom Wu Sung entrusts his orphaned niece Ying-erh when he is condemned to military exile in Meng-chou; gives Ying-erh back to Wu Sung when he returns to Ch'ing-ho five years later only to repossess her after the inquest on P'an Chin-lien's murder when Wu Sung once more becomes a fugitive; later arranges for her marriage.

Yeh the Ascetic, one-eyed illiterate Buddhist ascetic employed as a cook by Abbot Hsiao-yüeh of the Water Moon Monastery outside the South Gate of Ch'ing-ho, physiognomizes Ch'en Ching-chi when he is reduced to penury and working nearby as a day laborer.

Yeh Ch'ien, prefect of Lai-chou in Shantung.

Yeh the Fifth, wife of Pen Ti-ch'uan, mother of Pen Chang-chieh, originally a wet nurse who elopes with her fellow employee Pen Ti-ch'uan, carries on an intermittent affair with Tai-an while at the same time complaisantly accepting the sexual favors of Hsi-men Ch'ing.

Yen the Fourth, neighbor of Han Tao-kuo who informs him of Hsi-men Ch'ing's death when their boats pass each other on the Grand Canal at Lin-ch'ing.

Yen P'o-hsi, singing girl slain by Sung Chiang.

Yen Shun, Brocade Tiger, outlaw chieftan of the Ch'ing-feng Stronghold on Ch'ing-feng Mountain who is persuaded by Sung Chiang to let the captured Wu Yüeh-niang go rather than allowing Wang Ying to make her his wife.

Yin Chih, Good Deed, chief clerk in charge of the files in the Ch'ing-ho office of the Provincial Surveillance Commission who recognizes that Lai-wang has been framed by Hsi-men Ch'ing and manages to get his sentence reduced and to have him treated more leniently.

Yin Ching, vice-minister of the Ministry of Personnel.

Yin Ta-liang, regional investigating censor of Liang-che, rewarded for his part in facilitating the notorious Flower and Rock Convoys and the construction of the Mount Ken Imperial Park.

Yin T'ien-hsi, Year Star Yin, younger brother of Kao Lien's wife, née Yin, dissolute wastrel who takes advantage of his official connections to lord it over the Mount T'ai area with a gang of followers at his disposal, colludes with Shih Po-ts'ai, the corrupt head priest of the Temple of the Goddess of Iridescent Clouds on the summit of Mount T'ai, in attempting to rape Wu Yüeh-niang when she visits the temple on a pilgrimage after the death of Hsi-men Ch'ing; later killed at Sung Chiang's behest by the outlaw, Li K'uei.

Yin, Year Star. See Yin T'ien-hsi.

Ying, Beggar. See Ying Po-chüeh.

Ying-ch'un, disciple of Abbot Wu Tsung-che of the Temple of the Jade Emperor outside the East Gate of Ch'ing-ho.

Ying-ch'un, senior maidservant of Li P'ing-erh who after the death of Hsi-men Ch'ing agrees to be sent to the household of Chai Ch'ien in the Eastern Capital and is raped by Lai-pao on the way.

Ying the Elder, eldest son of the deceased silk merchant Master Ying, elder brother of Ying Po-chüeh, continues to operate his father's silk business in Ch'ing-ho.

Ying the Elder's wife.

Ying-erh, daughter of Wu Chih by his deceased first wife, niece of Wu Sung, much abused stepdaughter of P'an Chin-lien who turns her over to Dame Wang when she marries Hsi-men Ch'ing; repossessed by Wu Sung when he returns from the Eastern Capital after the death of her father; consigned to the care of his neighbor Yao the Second when he is condemned to military exile in Meng-chou after his first abortive attempt to avenge the murder of her father; taken back by Wu Sung on his return to Ch'ing-ho five years later and forced to witness his disembowelment of P'an Chin-lien and decapitation of Dame Wang; repossessed by Yao the Second after the inquest and provided by him with a husband.

Ying, Master, father of Ying the Elder and Ying Po-chüeh, deceased silk merchant of Ch'ing-ho.

Ying Pao, eldest son of Ying Po-chüeh, recommends his friend Lai-yu to Hsi-men Ch'ing who employs him as a servant and changes his name to Lai-chüeh.

Ying Po-chüeh, Ying the Second, Sponger Ying, Beggar Ying, son of the deceased silk merchant Master Ying, younger brother of Ying the Elder, father of Ying Pao and two daughters by his wife, née Tu, and a younger son by his concubine Ch'un-hua; having squandered his patrimony and fallen on hard times he has been reduced to squiring wealthy young rakes about the licensed quarters and living by his wits; boon companion and favorite crony of Hsi-men Ch'ing, member of the brotherhood of ten; a clever and amusing sycophant and opportunist he has the art to openly impose on Hsi-men Ch'ing and make him like it while he is alive and the gall to double-cross him without compunction as soon as he is dead.

Ying Po-chüeh's concubine. See Ch'un-hua.

Ying Po-chüeh's elder daughter, married with the financial assistance of Hsi-men Ch'ing.

Ying Po-chüeh's grandfather, friend of Licentiate Shui's grandfather.

Ying Po-chüeh's second daughter, after the death of her father she is proposed by Auntie Hsüeh as a match for Ch'en Ching-chi but turned down by P'ang Ch'un-mei for lack of a dowry.

Ying Po-chüeh's son by his concubine Ch'un-hua.

Ying Po-chüeh's wife, née Tu, mother of Ying Pao and two daughters.

Ying the Second. See Ying Po-chüeh.

Ying, Sponger. See Ying Po-chüeh.

Yu, Loafer. See Yu Shou.

Yu Shou, Loafer Yu, a dissolute young scamp upon whom Hsi-men Ch'ing turns the tables by abusing the judicial system.

Yung-ting, page boy in the household of Wang Ts'ai.

Yü, Big Sister, blind professional singer in Ch'ing-ho frequently invited into Hsi-men Ch'ing's household to entertain his womenfolk and their guests.

Yü Ch'un, Stupid Yü, one of the "cribbers" in the licensed quarter of Ch'ing-ho who plays the tout to Wang Ts'ai on his visits to the licensed quarter and upon whom Hsi-men Ch'ing turns the tables by abusing the judicial system at the behest of Lady Lin.

Yü-erh. See Sun Hsüeh-o.

Yü-hsiao, Jade Flute, senior maidservant of Wu Yüeh-niang, carries on an affair with Shu-t'ung the discovery of which by P'an Chin-lien leads him to abscond and return to his native Su-chou; after the death of Hsi-men

Ch'ing agrees to be sent to the household of Chai Ch'ien in the Eastern Capital and is raped by Lai-pao on the way.

Yü, Licentiate, master of a girls' school in his home in Ch'ing-ho where P'an Chin-lien studies for three years as a child.

Yü-lou. See Meng Yü-lou.

Yü Shen (d. 1132), minister of war who suppresses Tseng Hsiao-hsü's memorial impeaching Hsia Yen-ling and Hsi-men Ch'ing for malfeasance in the case of Miao Ch'ing, rewarded with the title grand guardian of the heir apparent for his part in facilitating the notorious Flower and Rock Convoys and the construction of the Mount Ken Imperial Park.

Yü, Stupid. See Yü Ch'un.

Yü-t'ang, employed in Chou Hsiu's household as a wet nurse for Chou Chin-ko.

Yü-tsan, concubine of Li Kung-pi, originally maidservant of his deceased first wife, who enters his household as part of her dowry, reacts jealously to his marriage with Meng Yü-lou and is beaten by him and sold out of the household.

Yü-wen, Censor. See Yü-wen Hsü-chung.

Yü-wen Hsü-chung (1079–1146), Censor Yü-wen, supervising secretary of the Office of Scrutiny for War who submits a memorial to the throne impeaching Ts'ai Ching, Wang Fu, and Yang Chien.

Yüan, Commander, resident of Potter's Alley in the Eastern Capital into whose family Li P'ing-erh is reincarnated as a daughter.

Yüan-hsiao, senior maidservant of Li Chiao-erh who is transferred to the service of Hsi-men Ta-chieh at the request of Ch'en Ching-chi after her former mistress leaves the household, accompanies her new mistress through her many vicissitudes while also putting up with the capricious treatment of Ch'en Ching-chi in whose service she dies after he is reduced to penury.

Yüan Yen, professional actor from Su-chou who specializes in playing subsidiary female roles.

Yüeh Ho-an, vice-magistrate of Ch'ing-ho.

Yüeh-kuei, concubine of Chou Hsiu much abused by P'ang Ch'un-mei.

Yüeh-niang. See Wu Yüeh-niang.

Yüeh the Third, next-door neighbor of Han Tao-kuo on Lion Street who fences Miao Ch'ing's stolen goods and suggests that he approach Hsi-men Ch'ing through Wang Liu-erh to get him off the hook for the murder of Miao T'ien-hsiu.

Yüeh the Third's wife, close friend of Wang Liu-erh who acts as an intermediary in Miao Ch'ing's approach to Hsi-men Ch'ing.

Yün, Assistant Regional Commander, elder brother of Yün Li-shou, hereditary military officer who dies at his post on the frontier.

Yün-ko. See Ch'iao Yün-ko.

Yün Li-shou, Welsher Yün, Yün the Second, younger brother of Assistant Regional Commander Yün, crony of Hsi-men Ch'ing, member of the brotherhood of ten, manager employed by Hsi-men Ch'ing in various of his enterprises, upon the death of his elder brother succeeds to his rank and the substantive post of vice-commander of the Ch'ing-ho Left Guard, later appointed stockade commander of Ling-pi Stockade at Chi-nan where Wu Yüeh-niang seeks refuge with him from the invading Chin armies but dreams that he attempts to rape her.

Yün Li-shou's daughter, betrothed while still a babe in arms to Hsi-men Hsiao-ko.

Yün Li-shou's wife, née Su, proposes a marriage alliance to Wu Yüeh-niang while they are both pregnant and formally betroths her daughter to Hsi-men Hsiao-ko after the death of Hsi-men Ch'ing.

Yün, Little. See Ch'iao Yün-ko.

Yün, Prince of. See Chao K'ai.

Yün the Second. See Yün Li-shou.

Yün, Welsher. See Yün Li-shou.

THE PLUM IN THE GOLDEN VASE

PREFACE TO THE *CHIN P'ING MEI TZ'U-HUA*[1]

I VENTURE to observe that in writing the *Chin P'ing Mei chuan* (The story of the plum in the golden vase) the Scoffing Scholar of Lan-ling[2] has focused his attention on the manners of the age, about which he has something significant to say. Of the seven feelings natural to mankind,[3] melancholy is the most intractable. For such men of superior wisdom as may occasionally appear in the natural course of evolution, the fogs and ice that melancholy engenders disperse and splinter of their own accord, so there is no need to speak of such as these. Even those of lesser endowment know how to dispel melancholy with the aid of reason so that it may be prevented from encumbering them. Among the many who fall short of this, however, who have been unable to achieve enlightenment in their hearts, and who do not have access to the riches of the classic tradition to alleviate their melancholy, those who escape its infection are few.

It is in consideration of this fact that my friend, the Scoffing Scholar, has poured the accumulated wisdom of a lifetime into the composition of this work, consisting of one hundred chapters in all. Its striking rhetoric, which appeals to every taste,[4] is designed to illuminate the cardinal human relationships, to discourage sexual promiscuity, to distinguish between the pure and the impure, to edify both the good and the ungood, and to expound the secrets of flourishing and decay, failure and success, through the inexorable working of karmic cause and effect, in such a way that they lie utterly revealed before the reader's eyes. From its beginning to its end the strands of the plot are as intricately articulated as the conduits of the circulatory system[5] and are like a myriad skeins of silk that flutter in the wind without ever becoming entangled. So enticingly are these effects accomplished that the reader may, perhaps, be beguiled into forgetting his melancholy with a smile.

It is scarcely to be denied that in this work the language encroaches on the vulgar and the atmosphere is redolent of rouge and powder.[6] But I would assert that such allegations miss the point. The first song in the *Shih-ching* (The book of songs)[7] has been characterized by Confucius as expressing "Pleasure that does not extend to wantonness and sorrow that does not lead to injury."[8] "Wealth and distinction are things that man desires,"[9] but few are able to attain them without resort to wantonness. Sorrow and resentment are sentiments that man dislikes, but few are able to experience them without injury to themselves.

I have surveyed such productions of fabulists of earlier times as Lu Ching-hui's *Chien-teng hsin-hua* (New wick-trimming tales),[10] Yüan Chen's *Ying-ying chuan* (Story of Ying-ying),[11] Chao Pi's *Hsiao-p'in chi* (Emulative frowns collection),[12] Lo Kuan-chung's *Shui-hu chuan* (Outlaws of the marsh),[13] Ch'iu Chün's *Chung-ch'ing li-chi* (A pleasing tale of passion),[14] Lu Mei-hu's *Huai-ch'un ya-chi* (Elegant vignettes of spring yearning),[15] and Chou Li's *Ping-chu ch'ing-t'an* (Pure conversations by candlelight),[16] as well as such later works as the *Ju-i chuan* (The story of Lord As You Like It)[17] and the *Yü-hu chi* (Tale of Chang Yü-hu).[18] Their diction is so demanding that readers are often unable to enjoy them and discard them before reaching the end.

As for this story, although it may be couched in the everyday language of the marketplace or the idle chatter of the boudoir, even a three-foot-tall lad can derive as much pleasure from it as he would if he were enabled to suck the nectar of Heaven or pluck the tusk of leviathan,[19] so easy is it for him to understand. Although it may not be the equal of the works of former days, its purport and its rhetoric are outstanding enough to make it worthy of consideration. In addition, with regard to the moral reformation of the age, the reproof of vice and encouragement of virtue, the purification of the mind and cleansing of the heart,[20] it cannot fail to make a small contribution.[21]

As for those events that take place in the bedchamber, everyone feels attracted to them, on the one hand, and repulsed by them, on the other. Of those who are not sages or worthies like Yao and Shun,[22] there are few who escape entanglement. It is on this account that even the best of those who have attained wealth and distinction allow their hearts to be swayed and their intentions to be deflected. Behold: how secluded are the high halls and spacious structures,[23] the cloudy windows and misty chambers;[24] how magnificent are the golden screens and embroidered bedding; how enticing are the clouds of hair tumbling in disarray,[25] the creamy texture of swelling breasts; how assiduous are the cavortings of the cock phoenix and his mates; how extravagant are the brocade garments and the rare repasts;[26] how devoted are the women of beauty and men of talent[27] as they descant upon the breeze and apostrophize the moon;[28] how abandoned are the fragrant tongues as the jadelike drops of saliva commingle; how reckless are the pair of jade wrists, tugging and retugging at the ropes, and the pair of golden lotuses, tossing and retossing on the swing.[29]

Surely this is happiness. Yet, when joy reaches its zenith, it gives birth to sorrow.[30] Occasions for separation will occur, bringing haggard countenances in their wake, for this is inevitable. The need to "Pluck a sprig of plum blossoms to entrust to a courier,"[31] or resort to a square of silk to be conveyed by a fish,[32] cannot then be avoided. Calamitous missteps and disruptive dislocations[33] will become inescapable. Sacrifice of life to blade and sword can no longer be prevented. For in the world of light there is the imperial law, in the world of darkness there are ghosts and spirits,[34] that cannot be evaded.[35] And as for the propositions that if you defile the wife and children of another your own wife and children will be defiled,[36] or that calamity is the result of accumulated misdeeds and good fortune the reward of virtue,[37] they may all be subsumed under the rubric of the workings of the cycle of retribution.

Thus, "Heaven has its spring, summer, autumn, and winter,"[38] just as "Man has his sorrows and joys, partings and reunions."[39] There is no reason to be surprised that this is so. As for those who act in accord with Heaven's seasons, in the long term their descendants will continue to prosper, and in the short term they will serenely enjoy their allotted days. As for those who act in defiance of Heaven's seasons, they will sacrifice life and reputation, for calamity will strike before they can turn on their heels.[40] Since no man in this world can escape the periodic revolutions of the times,[41] those who remain unscathed by cruel fate and untainted by disgrace are fortunate indeed. That is why I have observed that the Scoffing Scholar in writing this story has something significant to say.

Written by the Master of Delight[42]
in his studio in Bright Worthy Village

PREFACE TO THE *CHIN P'ING MEI*

THE *Chin P'ing Mei* is an obscene book. In praising it as highly as he did, Yüan Hung-tao was merely giving indirect expression to his own discontent, not bestowing his approbation on the *Chin P'ing Mei*.[1] Nevertheless, the author did have intentions of his own that were admonitory rather than hortatory. For example, many women play a role in the story, but the fact that the author chose to emphasize only the names of P'an Chin-lien, Li P'ing-erh, and Ch'un-mei by including them in his title is an instance of the type of historiography exemplified by the *T'ao-wu* of the State of Ch'u.[2] Thus, Chin-lien dies for her adultery, P'ing-erh dies for her burden of sins, and Ch'un-mei dies for her licentiousness, each of them coming to a more horrendous end than any of the other women. The author has availed himself of Hsi-men Ch'ing to depict the great villains of the world. He has availed himself of Ying Po-chüeh to depict the petty clowns[3] of the world. He has availed himself of all these wanton women to depict the female clowns and villains of the world. So effective is his delineation that we cannot but break into a sweat as we read. Thus, his intentions are admonitory rather than hortatory.

I have remarked that "He who reads the *Chin P'ing Mei* and responds with a feeling of compassion is a Bodhisattva; he who responds with a feeling of apprehension is a superior man; he who responds with a feeling of enjoyment is a petty person; and he who responds with a feeling of emulation is no better than a beast."

My friend Ch'u Hsiao-hsiu[4] once accompanied a young man to a banquet at which live entertainment was provided. When the point came in the play at which the Hegemon-King feasted at night the young man drooled with admiration, saying, "How can the life of a real man be anything but this?"

"The fact is," responded Hsiao-hsiu, "that it is only by way of contrast with the denouement at Wu-chiang that the dramatist has inserted this scene."[5]

Those present who overheard this remark sighed at the prescience of his comment. Only those who grasp the significance of this statement should be permitted to read the *Chin P'ing Mei*. Otherwise, Yüan Hung-tao may be accused of having been a flagrant instigator of venery. The people of this world must be exhorted not to follow in the footsteps of Hsi-men Ch'ing.

Casually indited en route to Su-chou by
The Pearl-juggler of Eastern Wu[6]
Last month of winter, 1617–18[7]

COLOPHON

THE STORY *of the Plum in the Golden Vase* is a fable created by a prominent figure of the Chia-ching reign period[1] whose satirical shafts were directed at contemporary targets. But is not the explicitness with which he exposes the uglier aspects of human life also consistent with the purpose of our former teacher, Confucius, in not deleting the airs of Cheng and Wei from the *Book of Songs*?[2] The way that, in incident after incident, he has taken pains to sow the seeds of karmic cause and effect shows that the author was also a man of great compassion.

Those who help to disseminate this book in the future will earn immeasurable merit. The ignorant go so far as to regard this as an obscene book. In so doing not only do they fail to comprehend the author's purpose but they also unjustly repudiate the intentions of those who would disseminate it. It is the purpose of this colophon to make this clear.

Written by Nien-kung[3]

FOUR LYRICS TO THE TUNE "BURNING INCENSE"[1]

ONE

Gardens of Paradise, Isles of the Blest,
The storied towers of Golden Valley,[2]
Are scarcely equal to a thatched cottage
  for pure seclusion.
Where wildflowers embroider the ground,
Is that not also elegant?
Appropriate to spring,
Appropriate to summer,
Appropriate to autumn.

Wine is mature, ready for straining,
Guests arrive, fit for retaining.
Here is no glory, here no disgrace,
  here no sorrow.
Step back and relax.
What reason for that?
Only, when tired to sleep,
When thirsty to drink,
When drunk to sing.

TWO

A short angled wall,
Low roughhewn windows,
A tiny pond, no bigger
  than a pimple.
Amid serried peaks,
By green waters,
There is a little wind,
There is a little moonlight,
There is a little coolness.

Life's ordinary needs fulfilled,
By bamboo table, on rattan couch,
Look to what lies before the eyes,
  the water's hue, the mountain's light.
If guests appear and there's no wine,
What's wrong with plain conversation?
Just, carefully brew the tea,
Gently warm the cup,
Fastidiously pour the water.

Three

Situated amid water and bamboo,
I love my cottage.[3]
Rocks lie clear beneath the stream,
  like randomly placed steps.
The design of my retreat is personal,
Along lines delicately wrought.
It is secluded,
It is elegant,
It is comfortable.

At ease, without restraint,
What is this like?
Leaning on the railing, I gaze into the water
  and watch the fish.
From breeze and blossoms, snow and moonlight,
I have wrested the freedom,
To burn some incense,
Make some comments,
Read some books.

Four

Sweep away the dust,
Conserve the moss,
Before the door, let the red leaves
  cover the steps.
The scene might be depicted in a painting,
But that it still continues to surprise,
With only a few boles of pine,
Few stalks of bamboo,
Few sprigs of plum.

Flowers and trees are so cultivated,
That they come into bloom one after another.
As for the events of the morrow,
  leave them to Heaven.
Let wealth and distinction,
Come when they will.
I'll simply go where I please,
Abide by my lot,
Unbutton my collar.

LYRICS ON THE FOUR VICES[4]

TO THE TUNE "PARTRIDGE SKY"

DRUNKENNESS

Wine depletes the spiritual resources
  and destroys the home;
It causes speech to become incoherent,
  makes conduct riotous.
Estrangement from family, loss of friends,
  derive therefrom;
Deeds of injustice and ingratitude
  are all its doing.

One ought not to imbibe,
From the flowing cup.
If you are able to obey this injunction,
  you cannot go wrong.
The foundering of all your undertakings
  may be traced to this.
From now on, when you entertain guests,
  serve them tea.

LUST

Do not become enamored of glossy black hair
  and beautiful complexions;
Cease to hanker after crimson powder
  and halcyon-feathered ornaments.
What ravages man's body and shortens his life
  are those bewitching figures;
Beauties capable of toppling kingdoms and cities
  are more alluring still.

Be not beguiled,
Husband your cinnabar fields.[5]
Those who are able to diminish their desires
  live longer years.
From this time on, abandon all thought
  of casual amours;
Within paper curtains decorated with plum blossoms
  sleep by yourself.[6]

Avarice

Money and silk, gold and pearls, may
pile up in your coffers;
But, unless they are gotten legitimately,
forgo their greedy acquisition.
Family and friends, honesty and integrity,
are often forfeited for gain;
Even the feelings that bind father and son
are sometimes sacrificed for profit.

Pull back your hand,
Restrain yourself,
Lest body and mind be fraught with care,
both day and night.
Your descendants, of course, will have
the fortunes that befit them;
On their behalf, you can spare yourself
anticipatory worry.[7]

Anger

Do not resort to violence or endeavor
to show off your prowess;
By brandishing fists, rolling up sleeves,
or displaying your spirit.
Once you let the flames of your temper
escape your control;
You will subsequently stew with anxiety
at the calamitous results.

Don't go overboard,
Avoid catastrophe;
Be advised, the best policy is to be
tolerant in all things.
When it is appropriate to let things go,
you should let them go;
When you can make allowances for people,
you should make allowances.[8]

Chapter 1

WU SUNG FIGHTS A TIGER ON CHING-YANG RIDGE; P'AN CHIN-LIEN DISDAINS HER MATE AND PLAYS THE COQUETTE

PROLOGUE[1]

THERE IS a lyric to the tune "Pleasing Eyes"[2] that goes:

The hero grips his "Hook of Wu,"
Eager to cut off ten thousand heads.
How is it that a heart forged out of iron and stone,
Can yet be melted by a flower?

Just take a look at Hsiang Yü and Liu Pang:[3]
Both cases are equally distressing.
They had only to meet with Yü-chi[4] and Lady Ch'i,[5]
For all their valor to come to naught.[6]

The subject of this lyric is the words *passion* and *beauty*, two concepts that are related to each other as substance is to function. Thus, when beauty bedazzles the eye, passion is born in the heart. Passion and beauty evoke each other; the heart and the eye are interdependent. This is a fact that, from ancient times until the present day, gentlemen of moral cultivation ought never to forget. As two men of the Chin dynasty once said, "It is people just like ourselves who are most affected by passion";[7] and "Beauty is like the lodestone which exerts its unseen pull on the needle even when obstacles intervene. If this be true even for nonsentient objects, how much the more must it be so for man, who must spend his days striving to survive in the realm of passion and beauty?"[8]

"The hero grips his 'Hook of Wu.' " Hook of Wu is the name of an ancient sword. In those days there were swords with names such as Kan-chiang, Mo-yeh, T'ai-o, Hook of Wu, Fish Gut, and Death's-head.[9] The lyric speaks of heroes with temperaments of iron and stone and the sort of heroic prowess that vaults across the heavens like a rainbow, who yet did not escape the fate of allowing their ambitions to be blunted by women. It then goes on to refer to the Hegemon-King of Western Ch'u, whose name was Hsiang

Chi, or Hsiang Yü. Because the First Emperor of the Ch'in dynasty[10] was so lacking in virtue that he:

Garrisoned the Five Ranges to the south,
Built the Great Wall to the north,
Filled in the sea to the east,
Constructed the O-pang Palace[11] in the west,
Swallowed up the Six States,
Buried the scholars alive, and
Burned the books,[12]

Hsiang Yü rose up in rebellion against him and was joined by the King of Han, whose name was Liu Chi, or Liu Pang. Liu Pang rolled up like a mat the territory in which the capital of the First Emperor had been located and thus put an end to the Ch'in dynasty. Later he and Hsiang Yü agreed to make the Hung Canal[13] a boundary line between their territories and divided the empire between them.

Now, in the course of their conflict, Hsiang Yü was able, with the help of plans provided by Fan Tseng,[14] to defeat the King of Han in seventy-two military engagements. But he was so infatuated with his favorite, Yü-chi, who possessed the kind of beauty that can topple kingdoms, that he took her with him on his campaigns so they could be together day and night. The result of this was that he was finally defeated by Liu Pang's general, Han Hsin,[15] and had to flee by night as far as Yin-ling, where the enemy troops caught up with him. Although Hsiang Yü was defeated, he might have sought help from the area east of the Yangtze River, but he could not bear to part with Yü-chi. Hearing the armies that surrounded him on all sides singing the songs of his homeland, the region of Ch'u, he realized that his situation was hopeless and expressed his sorrow in song:

My strength can uproot mountains,
My valor knows no peer;
But the times are against me,
And my steed will run no more.
My steed will run no more,
So what can I do?
Oh, Yü-chi, Yü-chi,
What is to be done?[16]

When he finished singing his face was streaked with tears.

"Your highness must be sacrificing important military considerations on my account," Yü-chi said to him.

"Not really," the Hegemon-King replied. "It's just that we can't bear to give each other up. Moreover, you're such a beauty that Liu Pang, who is a ruler addicted to wine and women, is sure to take you for himself if he should see you."

"I would rather die in an honest cause than compromise myself in order to save my life," Yü-chi wept.

Then, asking Hsiang Yü for his sword, she slit her throat and died. The Hegemon-King was so moved by her act that, when the time came, he followed suit by cutting his own throat.

A historian has composed a poem to commemorate this event:

Gone was the strength that could uproot mountains,
the dream of hegemony destroyed;
Laying aside his sword, he merely sang
that his steed would run no more.
As bright moonlight flooded the encampment
beneath the liquescent sky;
How could he bear to turn back his head
and bid Yü-chi farewell?[17]

Now the King of Han, Liu Pang, was originally no more than a neighborhood head in Ssu-shui. Yet, with his three-foot sword in hand, he slew the white snake[18] and rose in righteous revolt in the mountainous area between the districts of Mang and Tang. Three years later he destroyed the Ch'in dynasty, and in the fifth year of his reign destroyed the Ch'u, thereby winning the empire for himself and establishing the Han dynasty.[19] But he became infatuated with a woman whose maiden name was Ch'i.

Lady Ch'i gave birth to a son whose title was Prince Ju-i of Chao.[20] Because Empress Lü[21] was jealous of her and wished her no good, Lady Ch'i was extremely uneasy. One day when Emperor Kao-tsu[22] was ill and lay with his head in her lap, Lady Ch'i began to weep, saying, "After you have fulfilled your ten thousand years, on whom shall my son and I be able to rely?"

"That shouldn't be a problem," the emperor said. "When I hold court tomorrow I'll depose the heir apparent and set up your son in his stead. How would that be?"

Lady Ch'i dried her tears and thanked him for his favor.

When Empress Lü heard about this she summoned her husband's chief adviser, Chang Liang,[23] for a secret consultation. Chang Liang recommended that the Four Graybeards of Mount Shang be induced to come out of retirement and lend their support to the heir apparent.

One day the Four Graybeards appeared in court with the heir apparent. When Emperor Kao-tsu saw these four men with their snow-white hair and beards and imposing caps and gowns, he asked them who they were. They identified themselves as Master Tung-yüan, Ch'i-li Chi, Master Hsia-huang, and Master Lu-li. Greatly astonished, the emperor asked, "Why did you not choose to come when We offered you employment in the past, only to appear today in the company of our son?"

"The heir apparent is destined to be the preserver of what Your Majesty has established," the Four Graybeards replied.

Upon hearing this Emperor Kao-tsu felt dejected and upset. As the Four Graybeards were on their way out of the palace he summoned Lady Ch'i into his presence, pointed them out to her, and said, "I would have liked to replace the heir apparent, but these four men have lent him their support. Now that his wings are full-grown his position will prove difficult to shake."

Lady Ch'i wept inconsolably and the emperor extemporized a song to explain the situation:

The great swan soars aloft,
A thousand li in one flight.
Once his pinions are complete,
He can range the Four Seas.
He can range the Four Seas,
So what can we do?
Of what avail are stringed arrows,
Against a target that lies beyond their reach?[24]

The emperor finished his song and, in the end, did not make the Prince of Chao his heir apparent.

After the death of Emperor Kao-tsu, to rid herself of her apprehensions, Empress Lü had Prince Ju-i of Chao put to death with poisoned wine and so mutilated Lady Ch'i as to turn her into a "human pig."[25]

Poets have remarked, on reaching this point in their evaluations of these two rulers, that Liu Pang and Hsiang Yü were certainly heroes of their day and yet did not escape the fate of suffering their ambitions to be blunted by these two women.

Although the position of wife is superior to that of concubine, the calamity that befell Lady Ch'i was even crueler than that which befell Yü-chi. Thus it is that the way of a wife or concubine who wishes to serve her husband faithfully and yet keep her head and neck intact within her own windows is hard. With regard to these two rulers, is it not true that:

They had only to meet with Yü-chi and Lady Ch'i,
For all their valor to come to naught?

There is a poem that testifies to this:

The favorites of Liu Pang and Hsiang Yü
  are much to be pitied;
These heroes proved powerless
  to protect their beauties.
Yet even the site of Lady Ch'i's burial
  remains unknown;
She was less fortunate than Yü-chi,
  who has a tomb.[26]

Now why do you suppose your narrator is so preoccupied with explicating the two words *passion* and *beauty*?[27] It is because "Gentlemen who presume on their talents are lacking in virtue, and women who flaunt their beauty are dissolute. If only they were able to maintain the fullness of their gifts while taking care to avoid the overflow of excess, they could be upright men and virtuous women."[28] What need would they have then to fear the calamity of unnatural death?

This has always been so, in ancient as in modern times;
It is as true for the exalted as for the humble.

Now this book is an instance of a beautiful woman who is embodied in a tiger and engenders a tale of the passions. In it a licentious woman commits adultery with a decadent man-about-town:

Every evening devoted to the pursuit of pleasure;
Every morning an occasion for deluded dalliance.

But in the end she does not escape the fate of:

A corpse prostrate beneath the blade,
A bloodstained carcass in the Yellow Springs;[29]
Never again to don silk or satin,
No longer able to apply rouge or powder.

If we pause to reflect on these events, from whence do they arise?[30] And moreover, what does the death of such a woman matter anyway?

He who coveted her sent to perdition his
imposing six-foot body;
He who loved her squandered wealth enough
to splash against the sky.[31]
The prefecture of Tung-p'ing
was dumbfounded;
The district of Ch'ing-ho
was greatly disturbed.

If, in fact, you don't know to whose family this woman belonged, whose wife she was, by whom she was subsequently usurped, or at whose hands she died, truly:

The telling of this tale is enough to knock the peak
of Mount Hua askew;
Its revelation is sufficient to make
the Yellow River flow backward.[32]

. . . . .

The story goes that during the years of the Cheng-ho reign period[33] of Emperor Hui-tsung[34] of the Sung dynasty,[35] the emperor bestowed his trust and favor upon the four wicked ministers, Kao Ch'iu,[36] Yang Chien,[37] T'ung Kuan,[38] and Ts'ai Ching,[39] with the result that the empire was thrown into great disorder. The people were unable to pursue their vocations and the populace was in dire straits. On all sides bandits arose in swarms and baleful stars descended to earth to be incarnated in human form.[40] The glittering facade presented by the empire of the Great Sung dynasty was disrupted, and in four different places great bandit chieftains arose.

Who were these four great bandit chieftains?

In Shantung there was Sung Chiang,[41]
In Huai-hsi there was Wang Ch'ing.
In Hopei there was T'ien Hu.[42]
In Chiang-nan there was Fang La.[43]

All of them:

Disrupted subprefectures and pillaged districts,
Setting fires and killing people;
Assuming royal titles for themselves.

Among them Sung Chiang alone:

Carried out the Way on Heaven's behalf,[44] and
Devoted himself to the righting of injustice;

endeavoring to slay all the:

Venal officials, corrupt functionaries,
Evil magnates, and delinquent commoners

in the empire.

At that time, in Yang-ku district of Shantung Province, there was a man named Wu Chih who was the eldest sibling in his generation of the family. He had a younger brother, by the same mother, whose name was Wu Sung. This Wu Sung was:

More than six feet in stature, and
Broad-shouldered as they come.

From his youth he had cultivated his strength and become expert with the spear and quarterstaff. His brother, Wu the Elder, who was not quite three feet tall, was of a meek disposition and muddleheaded to a ridiculous degree. He was disposed to mind his own business and did not pick quarrels with anyone. Because of the hardship created by a famine in the locality, he decided that he would have to let his younger brother fend for himself, sold the house they had inherited from their forebears, and moved to the district town of Ch'ing-ho.

Now at the time that this occurred Wu Sung, because he had beaten up the military affairs commissioner, T'ung Kuan, in a drunken brawl, found himself:

Completely on his own.

He had been forced to become a fugitive and had sought refuge on the manor of the Little Whirlwind, Ch'ai Chin, which was located in the military prefecture of Heng-hai, in Ts'ang-chou. This Ch'ai Chin enjoyed patronizing the heroes and stout fellows of the world and was so:

Chivalrous by nature and open-handed with his wealth,

that people called him Little Lord Meng-ch'ang.[45] In fact, Master Ch'ai was a direct descendant of Ch'ai Jung, Emperor Shih-tsung of the Later Chou dynasty.[46]

When Ch'ai Chin saw what a fine fellow Wu Sung was, he offered him a place to stay on his manor. But who could have anticipated that Wu Sung would come down with a case of malaria that required him to recuperate on the premises for more than a year? Upon his recovery he bethought himself of his brother, Wu the Elder, bade farewell to his host, and set out for home.

After spending several days on the road, Wu Sung arrived on the border between Yang-ku and Ch'ing-ho districts. At that time there was a ridge of hills on the border of Shantung Province called Ching-yang Ridge, and in these hills there was a bulging-eyed, white-browed tiger who had eaten so many people that travelers along that route were few. The authorities had ordered the licensed hunters of the locality, on pain of being beaten, to capture this tiger by a fixed deadline. There were public notices posted on either side of the road warning traveling merchants to form into bands and cross over only between the hours of 9:00 A.M. and 3:00 P.M., and prohibiting them from crossing the ridge at any other time.

When Wu Sung heard about this he laughed out loud and stopped at an inn by the side of the road for a few bowls of wine to bolster his courage. Then, with his quarterstaff at the ready, he staggered off, proceeding straight up the ridge in large strides. Before he had gone so far as half a li he saw another public notice, stamped with an official seal, posted on the gate of a temple to the tutelary god of the mountain. When Wu Sung looked at this notice he saw that the message read as follows:

> There is a tiger on Ching-yang Ridge that has recently attacked many people. At present the responsible persons of the relevant subdistricts and the licensed hunters of the locality have been ordered to capture it by a fixed deadline, and the authorities have offered a reward of thirty taels of silver for its capture. If there should be any traveling merchants who wish to use this route, they should first form into bands and cross the ridge only between the hours of 9:00 A.M. and 3:00 P.M. Passage over the ridge is prohibited at all other times, and unaccompanied travelers are forbidden to cross even during daylight hours. Be it known that anyone who disregards these instructions proceeds at his own risk.

With a loud voice Wu Sung proclaimed, "What the hell is there to be afraid of anyway! I'll just go on up the ridge and see what kind of a tiger this is."

Wu Sung tucked his quarterstaff under his arm and proceeded to stride up the ridge. He looked back and saw that the sun was slowly setting behind the mountains. It was the tenth month when the days were short and the nights long, so it got dark early.

Wu Sung continued on his way for a while when he began to feel the effects of the wine. Looking into the distance he saw a tangled clump of trees. When he had made his way, at a fast clip, through this clump of trees he came upon a big, shiny, black rock, the shape of a reclining water buffalo. Propping his quarterstaff against the side of the rock, he laid himself down on top of it and prepared to take a nap.

Just at this juncture, out of the blue sky, a strong gust of wind suddenly arose. What was this wind like? Behold:

Devoid of shape and form, it insinuates itself
into men's breasts;
Throughout the four seasons, it has the power to
blow things into life.
Touching the ground, it swirls away
the yellow leaves;
Entering the mountains, it pushes out
the white clouds.[47]

It so happens that:

Clouds arise in response to dragons;
Winds arise in response to tigers.[48]

As this gust of wind passed by, the yellow leaves from the clump of tangled trees fell to the ground with a rustling noise and, with a sudden roar, out jumped a ferocious striped tiger, as big as a water buffalo, with bulging eyes and a white forehead.

When Wu Sung saw this he cried out, "Ai-ya!" rolled off the black rock, grabbed his quarterstaff, and made haste to put the rock between himself and his assailant. The tiger was both hungry and thirsty. Pawing the ground with its front claws, it stretched itself and gave first one lash and then another with its tail. Then it gave a roar, like a dry clap of thunder out of the blue, which made all the hills and ridges reverberate. Wu Sung's consternation had long since turned the wine in his stomach into cold sweat.

The telling is slow;
What happened was quick.

When Wu Sung saw the tiger pounce at him he dodged to one side so that the tiger overshot him.

It so happens that this ferocious tiger had a short neck so that it was not easy for it to turn its head and look behind itself. Planting its front paws on the ground, it stretched its trunk and made a swipe at Wu Sung with its hindquarters. Wu Sung managed to jump to one side. When the tiger saw that it had failed to sideswipe Wu Sung it gave a roar that shook the ridge. But Wu Sung once again evaded it by dodging to one side.

It so happens that when tigers attack people, if they fail to overcome them with a pounce, a sideswipe, or a lash of the tail, their powers are half exhausted. When Wu Sung saw that the tiger's strength was failing, he turned around, swung his quarterstaff aloft with both hands, and brought it down with all the strength at his command. But the only thing he heard was a loud report and a thrashing noise as the branch of a tree, with all its leaves, came tumbling down in front of him.

It so happens that he had not made contact with the tiger at all, but had hit the branch of a tree so hard that his quarterstaff had broken in two, and only half of it was left in his hand. Wu Sung was more than a little disconcerted by this. The tiger gave vent to its wrath with a roar and, lashing its tail back and forth in a show of might, pounced at Wu Sung once again. With one leap Wu Sung leapt back some ten paces. The tiger's pounce fell short and its forepaws came to rest right in front of him. Wu Sung threw what was left of his quarterstaff to one side and took advantage of the inertia of the tiger's leap by stepping forward, grabbing hold of the skin on the crown of the tiger's head with both hands, and pressing its head down with all his might.

The tiger tried to put up a fight but its strength was already failing. Wu Sung held on for all he was worth, not letting up to the slightest degree. Meanwhile, with his foot, he kicked viciously at the tiger's face and eyes. The tiger roared with pain and pawed so frantically that it heaped up two piles of brown dirt and dug a pit for itself. Wu Sung pressed its head down into the pit and, freeing his right hand, pummeled it with his fist, using all the strength at his command. In no time at all he had beaten the tiger to death. It lay on the ground like an embroidered bag, no longer able to move.

There is an ancient-style poem describing Wu Sung's fight with the tiger on Ching-yang Ridge that goes:

On top of Ching-yang Ridge the wind
  blows wildly;
For ten thousand li dark clouds obscure
  the sun's light.
Flaming above the length of the river, the
  crimson sun is red;
Spreading everywhere over the ground, the
  grass has all turned brown.
Catching the eye, a sunset glow hangs
  over the woods;
Assailing the inhabitants, a cold fog
  fills the firmament.
Suddenly the sound of a thunderclap
  is heard;
From the side of the hill out flies
  the king of the beasts.
With head held high, flaunting its might,
  it bares its teeth and claws;
The deer in the valley all flee
  out of its way.

The foxes and rabbits in the hills
  keep out of sight;
The deer and gibbons by the stream
  are startled into panic.
If Pien Chuang[49] had seen it, his souls
  would have fled;
If Li Ts'un-hsiao[50] had met it, he would
  have lost heart.
The strongman of Ch'ing-ho while still
  in his cups,
Suddenly encounters it on the top
  of the ridge.
Searching high and low for its prey
  the tiger is famished;
Chancing on Wu Sung it pounces at him
  with ferocity.
The tiger's pounce at the man is like
  the fall of a mountain;
The man's response to the tiger is like
  the collapse of a cliff.
The fall of his arm is like that of a
  cannonball;
Its claws and teeth gouge a pit out
  of the earth.
The blows of his fist and foot
  descend like rain;
His two hands are splattered
  with fresh blood.
The stench of raw flesh suffuses
  the forest;
Tufts of fur and whiskers lie scattered
  over the mountain.
Even close-up, its thousand-stone might
  appears intact;
Though, seen from afar, its eightfold majesty
  is diminished.
Its body lies in the underbrush, the pattern
  of its stripes faded;
Tightly closed, its two eyes will glitter
  no more.[51]

In less time than it would take to eat a meal, Wu Sung had so beaten this ferocious tiger with his fists and his feet that it was no longer able to move. Panting hard, he let go of the tiger and went looking for his broken quarterstaff, which had fallen by the side of a pine tree. He was afraid the tiger might not really be dead, so he hit it another ten blows or so with his stick. But the tiger had already breathed its last.

Wu Sung thought to himself, "I might as well take advantage of this stroke of luck and drag the tiger down to the foot of the ridge." But when he approached the pool of blood in which it was lying and tugged at the tiger with both hands, he couldn't get it to budge. It so happens that he had exhausted his strength, with the result that his hands and feet had turned to jelly.

Just as Wu Sung was sitting on the rock, resting, he heard a rustling noise in the underbrush on the slope of the hill.

> From his mouth no word was uttered, but
> In his heart he was alarmed.

"It's already dark! If another tiger were to jump out at me, how could I hope to overcome it?"

Before he had finished speaking, lo and behold, two tigers emerged into view on the slope below. Wu Sung cried out in consternation, "Ai-ya! This time I'm done for!"

Before his very eyes, these two tigers stood up in front of him. When Wu Sung gave a closer look he saw that they were two men, clothed in tiger skins, who were wearing tiger skulls on their heads and carrying five-pronged spears in their hands. No sooner did they come up to Wu Sung than they bowed their heads in homage, saying, "Strongman, are you a human or a god? You must have eaten the heart of an alligator, the liver of a leopard, and the leg of a lion, or be made out of gall! Otherwise, all by yourself, in the waning light, and without a weapon, how could you possibly have slain this man-eating tiger? We've been on the lookout here for a long time. Tell us the truth, strongman, what is your name?"

Wu Sung replied:

> "I neither alter my given name when abroad,
> Nor change my surname when at home.

I am a man of Yang-ku district, Wu Sung by name, and the second sibling in my generation of the family." Then he went on to ask, "And who are the two of you?"

"There is no reason for us to deceive you," the two men replied. "We are licensed hunters from this locality. Ever since this tiger appeared on the ridge it has come out every night and attacked lots of people. We hunters alone have lost seven or eight of our number, and there is no telling how many travelers have suffered the same fate. His honor, the district magistrate, ordered us licensed hunters to capture it by a fixed deadline. He offered a reward of thirty taels of silver if it were captured beforehand, but promised us a beating if the deadline expired. Unfortunately, the damned creature is so powerful that no one has dared to go near it. We have been lying in wait for it here, along with several tens of corvée laborers from the subdistrict, and have set up spring-bows with poisoned arrows at a safe distance. Then we saw you come striding up the ridge, as cool as you please, take on the tiger and dispatch it, in no time at all, with three blows of your fist and two kicks of your foot. How could you be so strong! We will truss up the tiger for you and then invite you to come down to the foot of the ridge with us, to the district yamen, so you can meet the magistrate and claim the reward."

At this point the corvée laborers from the subdistrict and the licensed hunters, some seventy or eighty men in all, set off, bearing the dead tiger at the head of the procession and carrying Wu Sung in an open litter behind. They headed straight for the compound of a prominent householder in the neighborhood. This householder and the village head came out to meet them. The tiger was carried into the main room of the house where all the community elders came to see it. They asked Wu Sung his name and he related the story of his conquest of the tiger. Everyone said, "He really is a hero and a stout fellow!" The hunters provided game for a feast and toasted Wu Sung until he was quite drunk. Then a guest room was prepared for him and he retired for the night.

Early the following morning the community elders went to the district yamen to report what had happened. At the same time a litter was prepared for the tiger and a gaily decorated sedan chair for Wu Sung in which he was escorted to the yamen in appropriate state. The magistrate of Ch'ing-ho district sent runners out to usher him into the courtroom. The people of the whole district, on hearing that a strongman had killed the tiger on Ching-yang Ridge and was being given a formal welcome, all came out to see the show. The entire district was in an uproar.

When Wu Sung arrived at the courtroom he got out of the sedan chair and the tiger was carried in and laid down in front of him. The district magistrate looked Wu Sung over and thought to himself, "If he weren't such a hefty fellow, how could he have overcome this fierce tiger?" Then he summoned him to come forward and Wu Sung, after having paid his respects, related the story of his conquest of the tiger from start to finish. The functionaries standing to either side were stupefied with amazement.

The magistrate offered him several cups of wine right in the courtroom and then presented him with the reward of thirty taels of silver that had been contributed by the prominent families of the district.

Wu Sung said respectfully, "It is only owing to Your Honor's benevolent deeds that I have had the accidental good fortune to kill this tiger. It is due to no merit of mine. How could I accept this reward? These thirty taels of silver ought to go to the licensed hunters who have suffered so much at your hands on account of this beast. Why not divide up the reward among them as a demonstration of Your Honor's graciousness and of my own public spirit?"

"If that's what you want," the magistrate said, "you may do as you wish." There and then Wu Sung proceeded to distribute the thirty taels of reward money to the licensed hunters, who went their way.

When the magistrate saw that Wu Sung was a man of virtue and integrity, and a stout fellow to boot, it occurred to him that he might be able to do something for him, so he said, "Even though you come from the district of Yang-ku rather than Ch'ing-ho, they are right next to each other. If I were to appoint you to the post of police captain here in Ch'ing-ho, with the responsibility for maintaining law and order throughout the jurisdiction, what would you think?"

Wu Sung knelt down and thanked him, saying, "If Your Honor should deign to raise me up in this way, I would be grateful to you for the rest of my life."

The magistrate ordered his clerk to take care of the necessary paperwork immediately, and he appointed Wu Sung to the post of police captain that very day. All the village heads and prominent householders of the district came to offer him their congratulations, and the celebrations attendant upon his appointment lasted for three days.

Wu Sung had intended to look up his elder brother in Yang-ku district and could hardly have foreseen that he would end up being appointed a captain in Ch'ing-ho. He was so delighted he could scarcely contain himself. The news of this event spread throughout the two districts that comprised the prefecture of Tung-p'ing so that the name of Wu Sung was known to everyone. There is a poem that testifies to this:

The martial prowess of the strongman hero
  was highly esteemed;
Risking his life he marched straight up
  Ching-yang Ridge.
Even though drunk he slew the tiger
  on the mountain;
From then on his renown spread to the
  four quarters.[52]

Let us put aside the story of Wu Sung for a moment and return to that of Wu the Elder. After parting company with his younger brother because of the hardship created by a famine in the locality, he had moved to Ch'ing-ho district where he rented a house on Amethyst Street. When people observed his meek disposition and unsightly appearance they gave him the nickname Three-inch Mulberry-bark Manikin, in vulgar allusion to his coarse exterior and cramped features. There were many who did not scruple to take advantage of his weakness and naïveté, but Wu the Elder did not respond with anger, merely endeavoring to keep out of their way.

Gentle reader take note:

In this world the heart of man alone
  remains vile.[53]
It despises the weak,
While fearing the wicked.
If it's too hard it's brittle;
If it's too soft it's no use.[54]

A poet of yore has left us some words of admonition that express this very well:

To the tune "Moon on the West River"

Flexibility is the root of success;
Adamancy is the womb of misfortune.
Not to vie or contend is to show true worth;
If I lose out now and then, what's the harm?

History is but a succession of spring dreams,
Though the red dust spawns a profusion of talents.
There is no need to scheme or contrive;
It is those who abide by their lot who survive.[55]

To resume our story, Wu the Elder made his living by shouldering his carrying pole and peddling steamed wheat cakes on the street all day. Unfortunately, his wife died, leaving behind a daughter, named Ying-erh, who was just eleven years old. Father and daughter lived together as best they could, but before half a year had gone by their resources were exhausted and they had to move into a storefront, on Main Street, belonging to a well-to-do merchant named Chang, where Wu the Elder continued to ply his trade.

The servants in Mr. Chang's household, seeing that Wu the Elder was an honest man, looked out for his interests and often patronized his steamed wheat cakes and sat around in his shop when they had nothing better to do. Wu the Elder was always so obliging that everyone was partial to him and spoke up vigorously on his behalf in the presence of their employer whenever the opportunity arose. As a result of these good offices Mr. Chang even went so far as to forgive him his rent.

Now this Mr. Chang had the equivalent of ten thousand strings of cash in capital and owned a hundred parcels of real estate. He was more than sixty years old and did not have so much as a foot or an inch's worth of progeny of either sex. His wife, whose maiden name was Yü, ruled the roost with an iron hand so that there was not so much as an attractive servant girl on the premises.

One day Mr. Chang struck himself ostentatiously on the breast and gave vent to a sigh.

"Your property and wealth are more than sufficient," his wife remarked. "Why on earth should you disturb your leisure with such a sigh?"

"Old as I am," her husband replied, "I still don't have any children. Even though I may be rich, what good does it do me?"

"If that's what's bothering you," said Mrs. Chang, "I'll have a go-between buy two servant girls for you. Once they've been taught to play and sing they ought to be able to look after you."

Mr. Chang was delighted by this and thanked his wife accordingly.[56]

Some time later Mrs. Chang actually engaged a go-between to buy two servant girls, one of whom was called P'an Chin-lien and the other Pai Yü-lien.

This P'an Chin-lien was the daughter of Tailor P'an whose shop was located outside the South Gate. She was the sixth sibling in her generation of the family. Because she had always been good-looking and possessed a pair of very small bound feet she was called Chin-lien, or Golden Lotus.[57] After the death of her father her mother was unable to make ends meet, and so, when Chin-lien was only eight years old, she sold her into the household of Imperial Commissioner Wang,[58] where she was taught to play musical instruments and to sing. She was adept at:

Painting her brows and making up her eyes,
Applying powder and putting on rouge,
Combing her hair into a chignon,
Wearing form-fitting gowns,
Putting on airs,
And making a spectacle of herself.[59]

Moreover, she was quick and clever by nature. Before she was fourteen she could draw phoenix designs and execute them in embroidery and perform on woodwind and string instruments, her favorite among which was the *p'i-p'a,* or balloon guitar.

Sometime later Imperial Commissioner Wang died and Chin-lien's mother succeeded in extricating her from the Wang household only to resell her to the Changs for thirty taels of silver. She and Pai Yü-lien entered the household together where they continued to improve their skills as musicians and singers. Chin-lien concentrated on the *p'i-p'a* and Yü-lien on the *cheng,* or psaltery. Yü-lien was also just fifteen and was the daughter of a family registered as professional musicians. Because she had always had a fair complexion she was called Yü-lien, or Jade Lotus.

The two of them shared the same bedroom. Initially the mistress of the household, Mrs. Chang, treated them very well, not requiring them to work in the kitchen or do any housework, and giving them presents of gold and silver jewelry with which to adorn themselves. Later Pai Yü-lien died unexpectedly, leaving Chin-lien all by herself.

She was now seventeen years old and had developed into a slender and curvaceous beauty with:

Cheeks like peach blossoms, and
Eyebrows like the crescent moon.

Mr. Chang had wished to take advantage of her for some time, but fear of his wife's temper had prevented him from making a move. One day when the mistress of the household was out of the way on a visit to a neighbor, Mr. Chang surreptitiously invited Chin-lien into his room and had his way with her. Truly:

The beautiful unblemished jade
will one day be destroyed.
How will the pearl ever
regain its former perfection?

Once Mr. Chang had had his way with Chin-lien, before he knew it he found himself afflicted with four or five ailments. Truly, what five ailments were these?

No. 1: his loins began to ache.
No. 2: his eyes began to tear.
No. 3: his ears began to grow deaf.
No. 4: his nose began to run.[60]
No. 5: his urine began to drip.

And there was still another ailment that doesn't even bear mentioning.

In broad daylight he dozed off, and
At night he couldn't stop sneezing.

When the mistress of the household got wind of what was going on behind her back she quarreled for several days with her husband and gave Chin-lien a terrible beating. Mr. Chang realized that he wouldn't be able to keep her any longer but determined, in spite of his wife, to provide her with a dowry and marry her off to an appropriate person. The servants in the household reminded him what an honorable man Wu the Elder was and pointed out that he was not only currently unmarried but also resided on the premises, which would make him a convenient choice. Mr. Chang had hopes of being able to continue his liaison with the young woman, and so, without demanding a candareen from Wu the Elder, he made him a present of her as his wife.

After Chin-lien and Wu the Elder were married, Mr. Chang made it a point to look after him. If he were short of capital for his trade in steamed wheat cakes, he would slip him five taels of silver to make up the deficiency. While Wu the Elder was out peddling his wares, Mr. Chang would wait until there was no one about and then steal into their room for an assignation with Chin-lien. Although Wu the Elder occasionally happened upon them in compromising circumstances, he did not dare to make a fuss about it.

Mornings and evenings succeeded one another, and this situation had prevailed for some time when Mr. Chang suddenly came down with a venereal chill and:

Alas and alack,

died. When the mistress of the household discovered what had been going on, without more ado she angrily ordered the servants to drive Chin-lien and Wu the Elder out of the house, so they no longer had a place to stay.

Scarcely aware of the implications of what had happened, Wu the Elder once more found a house on the west side of Amethyst Street, belonging to a distaff relative of the imperial family named Wang, in which he rented an inner and an outer room and continued to peddle his steamed wheat cakes as before.

It so happens that ever since Chin-lien had married Wu the Elder and had a chance to observe his guileless disposition and unsightly appearance she had taken a violent dislike to him and quarreled with him all the time. She resented what Mr. Chang had done to her and said to herself, "It's not as though there weren't another man in the whole wide world. Why did he have to marry me off to the likes of this?

If you tug him he won't move;
If you hit him he pulls back.

The only thing he can be counted on to do every day is to guzzle his wine. When you get right down to it, you could jab him with an awl without arousing him. What did I ever do in a previous incarnation to deserve such a fate? It's really intolerable."

Whenever there was no one around she used to play a song to the tune "Sheep on the Mountain Slope" that testifies to this:

How did it all begin?
I was mismatched to him.
I thought he was a real man.
Not that I want to boast,
But how can a crow be a match for a phoenix?
I'm like buried gold,
He's only bogus brass;
How can his luster compare with mine?
He's just a hunk of rough stone;
What right's he got to my mutton-fat jade body?
I'm like a magic mushroom growing out of the muck.[61]
But what can I do?
No matter what he does,
I'll never be satisfied.
Just listen to me:
How can a gold brick be laid
On such a mud foundation?

Gentle reader take note: Most of the women of this world, if they are blessed with good looks and natural intelligence, will turn out all right if they are only married to a decent man. But as for the likes of Wu the Elder, even the best woman in the world might find it hard to avoid repining. It has always been true that:

Women of beauty and men of talent
 are seldom matched;
Just when you're in the market for gold
 you can never find a seller.

Every day Wu the Elder shouldered his load of steamed wheat cakes and went out to peddle his wares, not returning until evening. His wife had little to occupy her other than the preparation of three daily meals. After eating she would make herself up and stand behind the bamboo blind that hung over the front door. From that vantage point she was in the habit of:

Provoking attention with her brows, and
Sending messages with her eyes.

Now this fact was not lost on a number of dissolute young scamps in the neighborhood who were seldom up to any good. When they saw the way that Wu the Elder's wife was:

Dolling herself up so slickly,
Engaging the breeze and disturbing the foliage,

they began to make riddling allusions to her in public and even to engage her in badinage with remarks like:

"How did a piece of fine mutton
End up in the mouth of such a dog?"[62]

Everyone knew that Wu the Elder was a man of meek disposition but not many were aware that he had such a mismatched wife in his house, who was both romantically inclined and clever, in fact, good at everything, but particularly adultery. There is a poem that testifies to this:

Chin-lien's beauty is certainly worthy
 of remark;
When she laughs her eyebrows rise up
 like spring peaks.
If she ever encounters a dashing
 young gentleman;
She will make an assignation with him
 without more ado.[63]

Every day, after she had seen Wu the Elder out the door, this woman would stand inside the blind, cracking melon seeds with her teeth, and revealing her tiny golden lotuses for all to see. Such conduct attracted the aforesaid young gentlemen, who gathered on her doorstep day after day, strumming guitars and ukuleles,[64] and giving voice to every indecent suggestion their fertile imaginations could invent. As a result, Wu the Elder came to feel that he could no longer continue to live on that part of Amethyst Street and wanted to move somewhere else.

When he raised this issue with his wife she said, "You lousy muddle-headed ignoramus! If you're content to rent such inadequate lodgings in somebody else's house, it's scarcely surprising that petty-minded people should abuse you. Why don't you get together a few taels of silver, look about for an appropriate place, and take out a mortgage on a house with at least a couple of rooms? If we lived in more presentable quarters nobody would take advantage of us. You're the man of the house, but you're always so much at a loss that I end up taking the brunt of things on your account."

"And where would I get the money for a mortgage?" Wu the Elder asked.

"Phooey!" his wife exclaimed. "What a nincompoop! You can sell my hairpins and combs to make up the sum. What's so difficult about that? They can always be replaced later on when we're better off than we are now."

Wu the Elder allowed himself to be persuaded by his wife. When he had scraped together something over ten taels of silver he took out a mortgage on a two-story house near the gate of the district yamen. It was quite cozy, with three rooms on the ground floor, an upstairs room in the front, and two little courtyards. After moving to this new address, on that part of Amethyst Street that ran along the west side of the district yamen,[65] Wu the Elder continued to peddle steamed wheat cakes as before.

One day as he was going along the street he heard the din of gongs and drums and noticed several contingents of soldiers with tasseled spears escorting a man in a gaily decorated sedan chair. Who should this turn out to be but his own younger brother, Wu Sung. Because Wu Sung had killed the tiger on Ching-yang Ridge the district magistrate had elevated him to the position of police captain, and the community elders were participating in the celebration of this event by accompanying him on the way to his lodgings.

When Wu the Elder caught sight of him he grasped hold of him with his hand and called out, "Younger Brother, now that you're a captain, haven't you any time for me?" Wu Sung turned around and saw that it was his elder brother.

Both of them were greatly delighted by their reunion, and Wu the Elder invited Wu Sung to his home where he ushered him to a seat in the upstairs room and called Chin-lien out to meet him. Then he said, "The man who killed the tiger on Ching-yang Ridge the other day is your brother-in-law. Now he has just been appointed to the post of police captain. He and I are brothers from the same womb."

The woman:

> Stepping forward and saluting him with folded hands,

said, "Many felicitations, Brother-in-law."

Wu Sung returned her salutation by kneeling down to kowtow, but the woman attempted to help him to his feet, saying, "Please rise, Brother-in-law. You'll be the death of me yet."

P'an Chin-lien Disdains Her Mate and Plays the Coquette

"Accept my salutation, Sister-in-law," said Wu Sung. The two of them dickered politely for a while and ended up kowtowing to each other before getting to their feet.

After a brief interval Wu the Elder's daughter served tea to the two of them. Wu Sung saw that the woman was extremely seductive and merely lowered his head. Before long Wu the Elder took it upon himself to provide food and drink for Wu Sung's entertainment and, leaving the two of them to their conversation, went downstairs to buy the necessary provisions. The woman was left upstairs all by herself to keep Wu Sung company.

Chin-lien looked at Wu Sung and saw that:

> His physique was awe-inspiring, and
> His appearance was imposing.

His body seemed to be possessed of boundless strength. Were this not so, how could he have overcome the tiger?

"They are brothers, born of the same mother," she thought to herself, "and yet one of them is so big and strong. If I'd been married to him I might have gotten by somehow or other. But look at that Three-inch Mulberry-bark Manikin of mine! He's only:

> Three parts human, and
> Seven parts ghoul.[66]

I must have been so plague-stricken in a previous incarnation that I'm still suffering the ill effects to this day. Wu Sung certainly looks manly enough to me. Why don't I see if I can get him to move in with us here? Who knows? This may turn out to be the very love-match I've been waiting for."

Making herself all smiles, the woman asked, "Brother-in-law, where are you staying right now, and who's looking after your meals?"

"I've just been appointed to the post of captain," Wu Sung said, "so I have to be on duty every day to await the orders of my superiors. For the sake of convenience I'm making do with lodgings right in front of the district yamen. Two local recruits are detailed every day to act as my orderlies and take care of my meals."

"Brother-in-law," the woman said, "why don't you move in with us here? It would save you the trouble of having to put up with the services of those orderlies from the yamen who probably aren't any too sanitary where food is concerned. It's more convenient if we all live under the same roof. Then, if you happen to want some soup or something, I can make it for you myself, and you'll know it's safe to eat."

"Thank you very much, Sister-in-law," said Wu Sung.

"You must have a wife somewhere," the woman went on. "Why don't you bring her along and introduce her to us?"

"I've never gotten married," said Wu Sung.

"How old are you, Brother-in-law?" the woman asked.

"I'm twenty-seven," said Wu Sung.

"It so happens that you're just three years older than I am," the woman said. "Where have you come from on this occasion, Brother-in-law?"

"I've been living in Ts'ang-chou for more than a year," Wu Sung said. "I thought my brother was still living in our old house and had no idea he had moved here."

"It's a long story,"

the woman said. "Ever since I married your elder brother, people have taken advantage of his good-heartedness. That's why we had to move here. If he were only a real man like you, Brother-in-law, who would dare to say him nay?"

"My brother has always minded his own business," said Wu Sung. "He doesn't allow himself to lose his temper the way I do."

"You've got it all backward," laughed the woman. "As the saying goes:

If you aren't tough enough,
You will never be secure.[67]

I've always been quick-tempered myself, and could never abide the sort of person who:

If you hit him three times won't turn around; but
If you hit him a fourth time goes into a spin."[68]

There is a poem that testifies to this:

Brother and sister-in-law happen to meet
like floating duckweed;
With a seductive air she insists on
flaunting her beauty.
In her heart she only wants him
to make love to her;
With deceptive words she sets out
to inveigle Wu Sung.[69]

It so happens that this woman was the sort who is forever protesting her own virtue.

Wu Sung said, "My brother is not a troublemaker, so you have nothing to worry about, Sister-in-law."

Before the two of them had finished speaking, Wu the Elder returned from his shopping expedition, laden with meat and vegetables, fruit and pastries. Putting these down in the kitchen he started up the stairs and called out, "My dear, why don't you come downstairs and fix these things for us?"

"Just see what an ignoramus he is!" the woman responded. "Here you are, Brother-in-law, with no one to entertain you, and he wants me to go downstairs and abandon you."

"Please don't inconvenience yourself on my account, Sister-in-law," said Wu Sung.

"Why don't you go next door and ask Godmother Wang if she could help out?" the woman demanded. "Can't you ever figure things out for yourself?"

Wu the Elder did as he was bidden and Dame Wang prepared everything very nicely, bringing it upstairs and setting it out on the table for them. The fare consisted of fish and meat, fruit and vegetables, sweetmeats, and the like. As soon as the wine was heated, Wu the Elder asked his wife to play the role of host, with Wu Sung sitting across from her, while he took a seat to one side. When the three of them had sat down at their places Wu the Elder took up the wine and poured a little for each of them.

Picking up her winecup the woman said, "Brother-in-law, don't take it amiss, but we've nothing to offer you. Please try a cup of this watery wine."

"Thank you, Sister-in-law," said Wu Sung. "Please don't talk that way any more."

Wu the Elder was so preoccupied with running up and down stairs to heat and pour the wine that he could hardly concern himself with what went on between them.

The woman gave Wu Sung:

Such a smile you could have plucked it off her face,[70]

while her mouth was full of nothing but "Brother-in-law this and Brother-in-law that." "Why don't you help yourself to the meat, or some fruit?" she asked, and she picked out the best tidbits and put them on his plate with her own chopsticks.

Now Wu Sung was a man of straightforward temperament and took this to be no more than his sister-in-law's cordiality. How could he have known that this woman had started her career as a serving maid and become adept at the art of playing up to others? He was quite unaware that in her heart she had designs on him. Wu the Elder, on the other hand, was too naïve to be any good at entertaining guests.

By the time the woman had downed a few cups of wine with Wu Sung she couldn't take her eyes off him. Wu Sung was embarrassed by the way she looked at him and merely lowered his head without responding to her. After they had been drinking for a while the wine ran out and he got up to go. Wu the Elder said, "If you haven't anything else to do, Brother, why not have another cup or two before you go?"

"I've troubled you enough," said Wu Sung. "I'll come and see you again, Brother and Sister-in-law."

When they had seen him downstairs and out the door the woman said, "Brother-in-law, be sure you don't forget to come and move in with us here. People will laugh at us if you don't. After all, you're blood brothers. It's not as though you were anyone else. Besides, if you can stick up for us, you'll actually be doing us a favor."

"Since you're so hospitable, Sister-in-law," said Wu Sung, "I'll get my things and move in this very evening."

"Brother-in-law," the woman said, "be sure you don't forget. I'll be waiting for you." Truly:

The natural beauty of the vista
  remains unseen;
In spring the peach blossoms bloom
  all by themselves.[71]

There is a poem that testifies to this:

How reprehensible is Chin-lien
  whose schemes are deep;
She conceals her wanton intent though
  her desires are in a tumult.
Wu Sung is steadfast and true,
  not easily tempted;
The shining integrity of his name is worth
  ten thousand pieces of gold.[72]

That day the woman outdid herself in her efforts to please him.

To resume our story, Wu Sung returned to the inn in front of the district yamen where he had been staying, collected his luggage and bedroll, got his orderlies to carry them for him, and led the way to his brother's house. When the woman saw him she was happier than she would have been if she had:

Discovered a piece of gold or a precious stone.[73]

Then she swept out a room and fixed it up nicely for him. Wu Sung sent the orderlies back to the yamen and slept that night at his brother's house.

The next day he arose early and the woman also got up hastily and heated water for him so he could wash his face. Wu Sung washed, combed his hair, put on his turban, and headed out the door to make the morning roll call at the yamen.

"Brother-in-law," the woman said, "after the roll call is over come back for something to eat as soon as you can. Don't go anywhere else for your meals."

Wu Sung assented and then went to the yamen to be in time for roll call. When he returned home after putting in a morning on duty he found that the woman had prepared a full-course meal. After the three of them had finished eating, the woman brought Wu Sung a cup of tea and served it to him with both hands.

"I'm really imposing on you, Sister-in-law," said Wu Sung. "It makes me:

Too uncomfortable to sleep or eat in peace.[74]

Tomorrow I'll have the yamen send an orderly over to help out."

"Brother-in-law," the woman retorted, "how can you make so much of it? Our own flesh and blood! It's not as though I were waiting on anyone else. It's true we've got this little chit, Ying-erh, but when I see the way she:

Picks up this and then picks up that,
Floundering about all over the place,

there's no way I can rely on her. And even if you arrange for an orderly, he won't be any too sanitary where food is concerned. I really can't abide people like that."

"If that's the way it is, Sister-in-law," said Wu Sung, "I guess I'll just have to impose on you."

There is a poem that testifies to this:

Wu Sung's demeanor is really
  awe-inspiring;
His sister-in-law's wantonness can
  not be checked.
She inveigles him into coming to live
  under the same roof;
In order to share the clouds and rain
  in a romantic affair.[75]

To make a long story short, after moving into his brother's home Wu Sung took out some silver and gave it to Wu the Elder in order to buy pastries, tea, and fruit to entertain the neighbors on either side. The neighbors, on their part, clubbed together to return the treat, and Wu the Elder, in due course, reciprocated. But no more of this.

After several days had gone by, Wu Sung presented his sister-in-law with a bolt of variegated satin to make a dress for herself.

With an ingratiating smile the woman said, "Brother-in-law, this will never do. But since you've already given it to me, I can't very well refuse, can I? I guess I'll just have to accept." And she bowed to him, saying, "Many felicitations."

From this time on Wu Sung lived in his brother's home. Wu the Elder continued to shoulder his load and go out into the streets to sell his steamed wheat cakes as before. Wu Sung went to the yamen every day to report for duty and no matter whether he:

Returned early or returned late,

the woman would:

Cook some soup or cook a meal,
As though nothing in Heaven or Earth could
  make her happier.

This only had the effect of making Wu Sung feel more uncomfortable.

From time to time the woman would try to arouse him with a suggestive comment, but Wu Sung was an adamantly straightforward man and did not rise to the bait.

When there is a story to tell it is long;
When there is no story to tell it is short.

Before anyone knew it more than a month had gone by. It was now the eleventh month and a strong north wind began to blow, day after day. In every quarter what should appear but:

Dense masses of dark clouds,
and all of a sudden:
Fluttering and swirling,
A skyful of auspicious snow came flying down.
Behold:

To the tune "Immortal at the River"

For ten thousand li dark clouds
are densely massed;
In midair the auspicious omen
ripples the blinds;
The petals of alabaster flowers
dance before the eaves.
It was at just such a time,
on the Shan River,
That Wang Hui-chih's boat,
was immersed.[76]

In an instant the towers and terraces
are weighted down;
Rivers and mountains are linked by
an expanse of silver;
Flying salt and scattered powder
fill the sky.
Such was the occasion when
Lü Meng-cheng,
In his dilapidated kiln, bemoaned
his penury.[77]

The snow continued to fall that day until the first watch and made everything look like:
A world decorated with silver;
A universe carved out of jade.

The next day Wu Sung reported to the yamen in time for the morning roll call, as usual, and had not yet returned home at noon. Wu the Elder had long since allowed himself to be hustled out of the house by his wife to ply his trade. Now she asked Dame Wang, next door, to buy her some meat and wine, and then went into Wu Sung's room and lit a brazier of charcoal.

"Today I'll give his cinders a real stirring," she thought to herself. "Never fear, he's bound to catch fire."

Cold as it was, the woman stood inside the hanging blind at the door, all by herself, until she caught sight of Wu Sung:
Trampling the scattered fragments of alabaster and jade,
as he made his way homeward through the snow.

The woman raised the blind to let him in and said with a smile, "Brother-in-law, you must be cold."

"Thanks for your concern, Sister-in-law," said Wu Sung.

He came in the door and took off his broad-brimmed felt hat. The woman reached out her hand to take it from him, but Wu Sung said, "Don't bother, Sister-in-law," and proceeded to brush off the snow and hang it on the wall himself. Then he unfastened his belt, took off his parrot-green silk jacket, and went into his room.

"I've been waiting for you all morning, Brother-in-law," the woman said. "Why didn't you come home for breakfast?"

"A friend of mine treated me to a meal this morning," said Wu Sung. "Just now another one invited me for a drink, but I couldn't be bothered, and came straight home."

"In that case, warm yourself at the fire, Brother-in-law," the woman said.

"That's just what I need," said Wu Sung, who proceeded to take off his waxed boots, change his socks, put on a pair of warm slippers, pull over a bench, and seat himself next to the brazier.

By this time the woman had already told Ying-erh to shut the front door and check to see that the back door was closed also. Then she put the wine on to heat, prepared a few dishes of food, brought them into his room, and laid them out on the table.

"Where is my brother?" Wu Sung asked.

"Your brother has gone out to peddle his wares as he does every day," said the woman, "but I'll share three cups with you, Brother-in-law."

"I'd just as soon wait till he gets home," said Wu Sung.

"Why should we wait for him?" the woman said.

Before she had finished speaking the little girl, Ying-erh, appeared with a flagon of warmed wine.

"You needn't have gone to so much trouble, Sister-in-law," said Wu Sung. "Let me do the honors."

The woman also pulled over a bench and sat down next to the brazier. The table was already set. Picking up a cup of wine and holding it out to him in her hand, she looked at Wu Sung and said, "Bottoms up, Brother-in-law."

Wu Sung took the cup of wine and:

> Drained it in one gulp.

The woman refilled it and said, "The weather's cold, Brother-in-law. Have another cup. It takes two to make a couple."

"Why don't you help yourself, Sister-in-law," said Wu Sung, but he took the cup of wine and again:

> Drained it in one gulp.

Wu Sung then poured a cupful of wine and offered it to the woman, who accepted and swallowed it. Picking up the flagon, she refilled the cup and put it in front of Wu Sung. Then and there:

Her creamy breasts slightly exposed, and
Her cloudy locks half askew,

the woman said to him with an ingratiating smile, "I've heard people say, Brother-in-law, that you're keeping a singing girl on the street in front of the district yamen. Is that true?"

"Sister-in-law, you shouldn't pay any attention to the nonsense people talk," said Wu Sung. "I've never been that sort of person."

"I don't believe you," the woman said. "I only fear that:

Your mouth is not in harmony with your heart."

"If you don't believe me, Sister-in-law," said Wu Sung, "just ask my brother and see what he says."

"Ai-ya!" the woman said, "why bring him into it? What does he know about anything? For him:

Life and death are but a drunken dream.[78]

If he knew the score he wouldn't be peddling steamed wheat cakes. Brother-in-law, have another drink."

By the time a few more rounds had been poured and drunk the woman had reached that state in which:

Three cups of wine in the stomach
ignite the flames of desire.
How could she hope to repress
the fire of lust in her heart?

But she merely continued her idle conversation.

Wu Sung was now 80 or 90 percent aware of what was going on, but he merely lowered his head without responding to her.

The woman got up and went to heat some more wine, leaving Wu Sung alone in the room. He picked up the fire tongs and started to poke up the fire in the brazier. After a while, when the wine had been heated, she came back into the room. Holding the flagon in one hand, she reached out with the other and gave Wu Sung a pinch on the shoulder, saying, "Brother-in-law, if that's all you've got on, you must be cold, aren't you?"

Wu Sung was already more than a little uncomfortable about the situation, but did not pay any attention to her. When the woman saw that he did not respond, she grabbed the fire tongs out of his hand and said, "Brother-in-law, you don't know how to stir up a flame. Let me show you how. It's got to be red-hot or it won't do any good."

Wu Sung had nearly reached the end of his fuse, but did not make any reply. Without noticing that he was upset, the woman dropped the fire-tongs and poured a cupful of wine. She took a sip from this herself, leaving the cup more than half full. Then, looking at Wu Sung, she said, "If you share my feelings, you'll drink the rest of my cup."

Wu Sung grabbed the cup away from her and threw its contents on the floor, saying, "Sister-in-law, how can you be so shameless!"

At the same time, he gave her a push with his hand that nearly knocked her over. Opening his eyes wide, Wu Sung said, "I'm the sort of man who:

> Stands erect between Heaven and Earth,[79]
> With teeth in his mouth and hair on his head.[80]

I'm not the sort of pig or dog who:

> Poses a threat to public morality,[81]

or violates the standards of human decency. Sister-in-law, this kind of shameless behavior must cease! From now on:

> If the wind so much as stirs a blade of grass,[82]
> My eyes may recognize you as my sister-in-law,
> But my fists won't recognize you.[83]

Let's have no more of this."

The woman's face turned bright red as she listened to this tirade. Calling in Ying-erh to clear the saucers, cups, and other utensils from the table, she muttered under her breath, "I was only kidding. It's hardly worth taking so seriously.

> You wouldn't know a favor if you saw one."

As soon as the table was cleared she retired to the kitchen. There is a poem that testifies to this:

> Chin-lien's disreputable schemes are
> all too wicked;
> Wanton and shameless, she knows no
> behavioral norms.
> Even at table she seeks the consolation
> of clouds and rain;
> Only to find herself subjected to the
> captain's reprimand.[84]

Not only did the woman discover that Wu Sung would not respond to her advances, but she got a good verbal drubbing for her pains.

Wu Sung remained in his room, still fuming, and thinking to himself. Before long it was five o'clock in the afternoon and Wu the Elder, with his carrying pole over his shoulder, made his way home through the snow. After pushing open the door and putting down his load he came into the room and saw that his wife's eyes were red with weeping.

"Who've you been quarreling with?" he asked.

"It's all your fault," the woman said. "You never stick up for yourself, and you allow other people to take advantage of me."

"Who would dare take advantage of you?" Wu the Elder demanded.

"You know perfectly well who it is," the woman replied. "It's really intolerable! That bastard, Wu the Second! When I saw him come home through the snow I went to the trouble of fixing some wine and food for him. Then, when he saw there was no one about, he tried to proposition me. Ying-erh saw it with her own eyes. I'm not making it up."

"My brother isn't that sort of person," stated Wu the Elder. "He's always been an honorable man. Keep your voice down! The neighbors will laugh at us if they hear you."

Leaving his wife where she was, Wu the Elder went into Wu Sung's room and said, "Brother, if you haven't had an afternoon snack yet, I'll have something to eat with you."

Wu Sung made no reply. Instead, after thinking for a while, he took off his silk slippers and pulled his waxed boots back onto his feet. Then he put on his jacket and his wide-brimmed felt hat, fastened his belt, and strode out the front door.

"Brother, where are you going?" Wu the Elder called after him, but Wu Sung made no reply and proceeded straight on his way.

Wu the Elder went back into the house to interrogate his wife. "He didn't even respond when I called to him," he said. "He just headed along the street toward the front gate of the district yamen. I really don't know what's the matter with him."

"You lousy muddleheaded worm!" his wife railed at him. "What's so hard to see about it? The bastard's so ashamed of himself he doesn't have the face to confront you, so he's walked out on you. I'll bet he sends someone to fetch his luggage and refuses to live here any longer. I wouldn't put it past you to urge him to stay!"

"If he moves out people will laugh at us," Wu the Elder said.

"You muddleheaded troll!" his wife cursed. "If he starts playing around with *me*, no one will laugh at us I suppose! Go stay with *him*, if that's what you want to do; but I'm not the kind of person to put up with this sort of thing. Just give me a writ of divorce and you can have him all to yourself!"

Wu the Elder scarcely dared open his mouth again in response to this tirade from his wife. The two of them were still going at it when who should appear but Wu Sung, with an orderly in tow, who walked right into the house with his carrying pole, picked up his luggage, and headed out the door.

Wu the Elder ran outside and called after him, "Brother, why are you moving out like this?"

"Don't ask, Brother," said Wu Sung. "If I tried to explain, it would only serve to publicize the problem. Just let me go my own way."

Wu the Elder didn't dare ask anything more about it and let Wu Sung do as he wished.

Inside the house his wife continued to rail away. "A fine thing it is, too! Just as they say:

> It's not easy to collect a debt from a relative.

All anybody knows is that you've got a younger brother who's been made a captain, and everyone assumes that he's supporting his brother and sister-in-law in fine style. What they don't know is that he's just a sponger. In fact:

He's a real quince:
Good to look at, but not fit to eat.[85]
Now that he's moved out, all I can say is:
Thanks be to Heaven and Earth;
At long last my enemy has been removed from my sight."[86]

When Wu the Elder heard his wife utter these imprecations he didn't know what to make of it, and remained in a state of mental perturbation. After Wu Sung moved back into his room in the inn in front of the district yamen, Wu the Elder continued to go out on the street and peddle his steamed wheat cakes as before. He wanted to look up his brother and have a talk with him, but his wife forbade him, in no uncertain terms, to have anything to do with him. For this reason Wu the Elder did not dare seek out Wu Sung.

There is a poem that testifies to this:

Chin-lien's dream of clouds and rain
did not materialize;
Who would believe that this evoked
hostility in her heart?
Thus did she contrive to get Wu Sung
out of the way;
And sow enmity between brothers
of the same flesh and blood.[87]

If you want to know the outcome of these events,
Pray consult the story related in the following chapter.

Chapter 2

BENEATH THE BLIND HSI-MEN CH'ING MEETS CHIN-LIEN; INSPIRED BY GREED DAME WANG SPEAKS OF ROMANCE

In making this match, the Old Man under the Moon[1]
has made a mistake;
Displaying her talents, P'an Chin-lien
flaunts her beauty.
Merely because she dreams of assignations
under the moon, beneath the stars;
She attracts the attentions of those
beyond the door, outside the screen.
Tempted by greed, Dame Wang employs
a crafty scheme;
Peddling his fruit, Yün-ko becomes
the object of rancor.[2]
How can she foresee that a later day
will bring domestic disaster;
That her blood will spatter the standing screen
and make the whole floor red?

THE STORY GOES that Wu Sung had no sooner moved out of his elder brother's house than, in a snap of the fingers, the snow stopped and the weather cleared. This state of affairs prevailed for more than ten days.

To resume our story, two years and more had elapsed since the district magistrate of Ch'ing-ho assumed office, and during that time he had been able to put away a tidy sum in gold and silver. It now occurred to him that he should find a trustworthy person to deliver these valuables into the hands of a relative in the Eastern Capital[3] for safekeeping. When he reported to the capital for an audience at the expiration of his three-year term they would come in handy in fixing things up with his superiors. The only problem was that the roads were infested with criminal elements so that he would have to find a fairly formidable person for the task. Suddenly he thought to himself, "That captain, Wu Sung, with his heroic combination of courage and strength, is the very man for the job."

The same day he called Wu Sung into the yamen to discuss this matter, saying, "I have a relative who is serving as an official in the Eastern Capital. His name is Chu Mien,[4] and he holds the post of defender-in-chief in the Palace Command. I'd like to send a consignment of presents to him, along with a letter asking after his health, but I'm afraid that the roads may not be safe. You're the only person I can trust with such a responsibility, and I hope you won't refuse on account of the hardships involved. When you return, of course, I'll see that you are amply rewarded."

"Your Honor has already done so much for me," responded Wu Sung, "that I could hardly refuse. Since you have a mission for me to perform, I'll set off at once. Actually, I've never been to the Eastern Capital, so Your Honor is only doing me another favor by giving me this chance to take in the sights of the big city."

The district magistrate was delighted and rewarded Wu Sung with three cups of wine, along with ten taels of silver for his traveling expenses. But no more of this.

To resume our story, after Wu Sung had received his instructions from the district magistrate, he walked out the gate of the yamen and went by his lodging place to pick up an orderly. Then he stopped on the street to buy a bottle of wine and some groceries and proceeded straight to his brother's house. Wu the Elder happened to come home at about the same time and when he found Wu Sung waiting for him on the doorstep, he invited him inside and instructed the orderly to go into the kitchen and start fixing the food.

The smoldering feelings of the lady of the house had not been completely extinguished. When she saw Wu Sung arrive, with wine and food in hand, she thought to herself, "That bastard must not be able to get me off his mind, otherwise why should he come back like this? He may well have found me too much for him after all. I'll have to feel him out gradually."

Hurrying upstairs to:

> Retouch her powdered face, and
> Recomb her cloudy locks,

she changed into a more attractive outfit and proceeded to the doorway to welcome Wu Sung.

Bowing as she spoke, the woman said, "Brother-in-law, I don't know what sort of misunderstanding could have arisen to keep you from paying us a visit for such a long time. I've been at my wit's end over it. Every day I've told your brother to go to the yamen to look for you and try to make it up some way, but when he comes home he says you're nowhere to be found. I'm certainly glad you've stopped by again today, but what did you have to go and waste your money like that for?"

"There's something I particularly want to tell my brother," said Wu Sung.

"In that case," said the woman, "please come upstairs and sit down."

After the three of them had ascended the stairs, Wu Sung insisted that his elder brother and his wife take the seats of honor, while he pulled up a stool and sat to one side. The orderly served the wine and brought up a hot meal to go with it.

Wu Sung urged his brother and sister-in-law to eat. As they did so the woman kept glancing at Wu Sung, but he paid no attention to anything but his wine. After several rounds of drinks, Wu Sung asked Ying-erh to bring a set of pledge cups and then told the orderly to fill one of them with wine.

Taking this cup in his hand, he looked at Wu the Elder and said, "My respects to you, Elder Brother. Earlier today His Honor, the district magistrate, commissioned me to carry out some business for him in the Eastern Capital that will require me to set out tomorrow. At the most I should be away for two or three months, and at the least I should be back in a month. There is something I have come here especially to tell you. You have always been of a meek disposition, and I fear that while I am away people may try to take advantage of you. If you normally sell ten trays of steamed wheat cakes in a day, starting tomorrow, make only five trays. Go out late and come back early, and don't stop to have a drink with anyone. Take down the blind and close the door as soon as you get home. That ought to put a stop to any idle chatter. If someone does try to take advantage of you, don't make an issue of it, but wait until I get back and let me handle it for you. If you're willing to do as I suggest, Elder Brother, drink this cup to the bottom."

Accepting the cup, Wu the Elder said, "Your suggestions are good, Brother. I'll do just as you say," and drained it to the bottom.

Wu Sung then filled another cup and said to the woman, "You are a clever person, Sister-in-law, so there's no need for me to say more than a few words. My brother is ingenuous by nature, and totally dependent on you where decisions are concerned. As the saying goes:

> Outer strength is no match for inner strength.[5]

If my sister-in-law does a good job of managing the household, what will my brother have to worry about? You must be familiar with the old saying:

> If the fence is secure dogs won't get in."[6]

No sooner did the woman hear these words than:

> A spot of red appeared beside each ear, and
> In an instant her whole face was purple.

Pointing her finger at Wu The Elder, she launched into a tirade of vituperation. "You muddleheaded creature! If you had anything to complain about, why did you have to go and spill it to someone else so he could take such a high tone with me?

> I may not wear a turban, but I'm a match
>   for any man;

I may be only a woman, but I'm a real
dingdong dame.
I can lift a man on my fist,
Carry a horse on my arm, and
Trample on anyone else's face.[7]

I'm not the sort of:

Blood-sucking tick that buries itself in the skin
so you can't dig it out.[8]

Ever since I've been married to Wu the Elder not even an ant has dared to come into the house. What's all this about dogs getting in if the fence isn't secure? You'd better lay off that:

Wild and nonsensical talk.

Every word of an accusation has got to have a basis in fact.

If you throw a brick into the air,
It will come down to earth every time."[9]

Wu Sung laughed and said, "If you take charge in that way, Sister-in-law, everything will be fine; just as long as:

Your heart and your mouth are in agreement,[10]

but not if:

Your heart is not in harmony with your mouth.

In any case, if that's the way it is, Sister-in-law, I'll remember everything you've said. Please drain this cup."

Pushing the winecup aside with one hand, the woman jumped up and started to run downstairs, but before she had gotten half way down she stopped and said, "Since you're so smart you must know the saying that:

An elder brother's wife is like a mother.[11]

When I first married Wu the Elder I didn't hear anything about a brother-in-law. Where do you think you come off anyway:

Acting like a relative whether you are one or not,[12]

and demanding to play the role of head of the family? It's just my luck to run into this kind of crap!"

She then proceeded the rest of the way down the stairs, crying as she went. There is a poem that testifies to this:

Good advice proves bitter to the taste,
as do words of admonition;
Chin-lien resents him for this
and throws a tantrum.
So mortified, herself, that she can
scarcely remain at table;
She arouses the anger of the hero,
young Wu the Second.[13]

The woman succeeded in putting on quite a scene. Wu the Elder and Wu Sung felt so uncomfortable that after a few more cups of wine they came downstairs and bade each other farewell with tears in their eyes.

"After you've gone, Brother," said Wu the Elder, "come back and see me as soon as you can."

"Brother," said Wu Sung, "it would be just as well if you didn't do any business at all, but just sat at home. I could send someone to provide you with living expenses."

And just before he left Wu Sung said to him again, "Brother, don't forget what I've told you. Be careful not to let anyone into your house."

"I understand," said Wu the Elder.

Wu Sung took leave of his brother and returned to his lodgings in front of the district yamen where he got together his luggage and the weapons he would need to protect himself on the trip. The next day he took charge of the district magistrate's consignment of presents, checked to see that the gold and silver were properly packed in saddlebags, obtained the waybill authorizing the shipment, and set off on his way to the Eastern Capital. But no more of this.

To resume our story, after Wu the Elder allowed himself to be admonished by his younger brother, Wu Sung, he had to put up with three or four days of unremitting abuse from his wife. There was nothing he could do but:

> Swallow his anger and keep his own counsel,[14]

letting her curse herself out. Meanwhile, he followed his brother's advice by making only half as many steamed wheat cakes as usual every day. After making his rounds he came home before evening and put down his carrying pole, took down the blind, and closed the front door behind him before proceeding any further into the house.

When his wife realized what he was doing she was furious and cursed him, saying, "You ignorant nincompoop! Who ever heard of:

> Locking the jailhouse door while the sun is
> high in the sky!

Our neighbors will laugh themselves silly over this futile attempt to keep out the ghosts. You'll do anything your brother says. A lot of good your own cock and balls do you! Aren't you ashamed to make such a laughingstock of yourself?"

"Let them laugh," said Wu the Elder. "My brother's advice is for our own good and ought to put a stop to any idle chatter."

"Phooey!" the woman said, spitting right in his face, "you stupid clod! You call yourself a man, yet you can't make up your mind about anything, but let yourself be manipulated by others."

"So what?" said Wu the Elder with a negative wave of the hand. "As far as I'm concerned, my brother's words are as immutable as if they were graven in bronze or stone."

It so happens that from the time that Wu Sung left town Wu the Elder went out late, came back early, and closed the front door as soon as he got home. His wife was:

So angry she scarcely cared whether she were
dead or alive,

and gave him a hard time about it more than once, but eventually she got used to it. From then on, around the time that Wu the Elder got home, she would take down the blind and close the front door herself. When Wu the Elder noticed this he was secretly pleased and thought to himself, "This way everything ought to be all right."

There is a poem that testifies to this:

Careful as he is to lock the door
and come home early;
There is so little love between them
they are separated by peaks.
Once her desires are aroused
they weave a tangled web;
Even if she were shut up in a cage
it would not avail.

Time flies like a white horse galloping past a crack;[15]
The sun and moon shoot back and forth like shuttles.
No sooner has the flowering plum blossomed
at winter's end;
Than warmer weather proclaims the
return of spring.

One day in the third month, when spring was at its most beautiful, Chin-lien dressed herself up alluringly and could hardly wait for Wu the Elder's departure before taking up her position behind the bamboo blind that hung over the front door. She had become accustomed to standing there until her husband was expected home and then taking down the blind and going inside to wait for him. But this particular day was one of those occasions on which:

Something was destined to happen.

Just as she was about to take down the blind a certain person happened to walk by.

Without coincidences there would be no stories;[16]
It is those who are predestined to do so who meet.

The woman was in the very act of reaching up to take down the blind with a forked stick when a gust of wind dislodged it from her grip so that it fell,

Neither correctly nor precisely,

but right onto the hat of the passerby. As she hastened to put on an ingrati-

Beneath the Blind Hsi-men Ch'ing Meets Chin-lien

ating smile she looked at him and saw that he was twenty-four or twenty-five years old and cut quite a dashing figure.

On his head he wears a tasseled hat,
Gold openwork hairpins, and
A pair of jade rings inlaid with gold;
On his long torso, a green silk jacket;
On his feet, fine-soled Ch'en-ch'iao[17] shoes, and
Pure cotton stockings;
On his trouser legs, jet drawnwork kneepads.
In his hand he sports a gold-flecked Szechwan fan,
Enhancing a face as handsome as young Chang's,[18]
A countenance as good-looking as P'an Yüeh's.[19]
A man after my own heart,
As romantic as can be,
Beneath the screen he tips a wink at me.

This man, on whose head the forked stick had fallen, stopped in his tracks and was about to make trouble; but when he looked around to see who was responsible he found, to his surprise, that it was a beautiful and seductive woman. Behold, she has:

Glossy, black, raven's feather tresses;
Dark, curved, new moon eyebrows;
Clear, cold, almond eyes;
Redolently fragrant cherry lips;
A straight, full, alabaster nose;
Thickly powdered red cheeks;
A handsome, silver salver face;
A light, lissome, flowerlike figure;
Slender, jade-white, scallion-shoot fingers;
A cuddlesome, willow waist;
A tender, pouting, dough-white tummy;
Tiny, turned-up, pointed feet;
Buxom breasts; and
Fresh, white legs.

And there is something else as well:

Tight and squeezy,
Red and wrinkly,
Pale and fresh,
Black and cushioned;
Who can tell what it might be?[20]

The beauties of this woman were such that he could not look his fill. And how is she adorned? Behold:

The glossy black chignon on her head is enclosed
  in a fret spangled with gold,
Setting off the fragrant clouds of her hair
  and studded all round with hairpins.
The spit curl at her temple is embellished with
  a double-headed flower;
A comb of aromatic wood holds her hair
  in place behind.
Her arched willow-leaf eyebrows would be
  hard to depict;
As would the pair of peach blossoms
  that grace her cheeks.
Her openwork pendant earrings are
  beyond praise;
A glimpse of her smooth creamy bosom is
  beyond price.
A pale blue homespun blouse, with wide sleeves
  and jacket to match,
Complements the embossed silk of her
  beige skirt.
A figured handkerchief dangles
  from the mouth of her sleeve;
A sachet of pomander hangs low
  at her waist.
The rows of frogs on her bodice
  are neatly fastened;
Her ankle leggings, concealed above,
  extend below.
The upturned points of her tiny golden lotuses
  are just visible;
With a pattern of mountain peaks embroidered
  on the tips of their toes,
Her raven-hued shoes, with high white satin heels,
  are made to order for tripping the fragrant dust;
Her red silk ankle leggings are figured with
  orioles among the flowers;
Whether walking or sitting, the breeze parts her
  skirts and reveals what lies below.
From her mouth the fragrance of orchid
  and musk is constantly wafted;
When her cherry lips open in a smile
  her face breaks into bloom.

The mere sight of her makes one's "ethereal and
material souls take flight";
Shown off to such advantage, she is a
beautiful, if heartless, lover.

No sooner did the man catch sight of her than:

His starch began to melt, and
His anger flew to Java,[21]

as the irate look on his face changed into a broad smile.

The woman knew that she was in the wrong and, folding her hands in front of her, bowed deeply in his direction as she said, "The wind blew it right out of my hand, sir, and it happened to land on you. Please don't hold it against me."

Adjusting his hat with one hand, the man made such a low bow that he almost scraped the ground, saying as he did so, "It doesn't matter at all! Please make yourself easy, miss."

This scene happened to be witnessed by Dame Wang, whose teahouse was situated next door. Breaking into a laugh, the old lady said, "And whatever induced you to walk under these particular eaves, sir? It serves you right."

"It's really my fault," the man replied with a smile. "I've put you out, I'm afraid. Don't hold it against me, miss."

"I do hope you won't take offense, sir," the woman said.

"How could I dream of such a thing?" the man responded with a smile, and he made another low bow, during which his mischievous eyes:

Long experienced in sizing up the flowers;
Adept at assessing romantic possibilities,

never left the woman's body. As he made his departure he glanced back seven or eight times before proceeding to swagger on his way, concealing his face with his fan. There is a poem that testifies to this:

In the cool breeze and genial weather
he has sauntered out for a stroll;
By chance, beneath the blind he encounters
a seductive beauty.
Merely because, "on the point of departure,
she gives him a meaningful glance";[22]
His desires are so aroused that he cannot
call it quits.[23]

The woman, for her part, had had a good look at the man and thought to herself, "He's dashing and romantic as well as soft-spoken, and he seems to be rather taken with me; but I don't even know his name, or where he lives.

If he didn't care for me he wouldn't have glanced back at me seven or eight times before going his way. Who knows? This may turn out to be the very love-match I've been waiting for."

She fixed her gaze upon the man until he was out of sight before taking down the blind, closing the front door, and going back inside.

Gentle reader take note: It is scarcely likely that such a person should not turn out to be a man of some property. It so happens that he was the decadent scion of a family of considerable wealth from whom he had inherited a wholesale pharmaceutical business located on the street that ran in front of the district yamen. He had been a dissolute young scamp since his youth and had acquired some skill in such martial arts as boxing and fencing with the quarterstaff. He also liked to gamble, and there was little he didn't know about backgammon, elephant chess, and the various word games played by breaking characters down into their component parts. Now that he had come into his inheritance and had money of his own to spend, he had gone into cahoots with the officials and functionaries in the district yamen where he played the role of influence peddler, intervening in public business on people's behalf, for a fee. For this reason everyone in the whole district was rather afraid of him.

This man bore the double surname, Hsi-men, and the single given name, Ch'ing. He was an only son, so people had been in the habit of calling him Master Hsi-men, but now that he had come into his inheritance and had money of his own to spend they referred to him as the Honorable Hsi-men. Both his father and his mother were dead, and he had no siblings.

His first wife had died some time ago, leaving behind her only a single daughter. Recently he had been formally remarried to the daughter of Battalion Commander Wu of the Ch'ing-ho Left Guard, but he was not above availing himself of the four or five serving maids in his establishment. Moreover he had carried on an affair with a girl named Li Chiao-erh from the licensed quarter for some time, and he had just arranged to take her into his household. On top of this he had also been maintaining an unlicensed prostitute called Cho the Second on South Street. This girl's professional name was Cho Tiu-erh, or Toss-off Cho, and he had now moved her into his household as well.

In fact, Hsi-men Ch'ing was a past master at:

> Toying with the breeze and dallying with the moonlight.

Whenever he established a liaison with a woman, even one of good family, he was wont to take her into his establishment; but if she should then fail to please him in any way, however slight, he would call in a go-between and dispose of her without more ado. It was said that he sometimes resorted to the services of such brokers as often as twenty times in a single month. As a result, no one dared cross him.

Now this Honorable Hsi-men, once he had caught sight of that woman beneath the blind, went home and thought to himself, "What a fine filly! I wonder how I could get hold of her."

Suddenly he bethought himself of Dame Wang, who kept the teahouse right next door to her home. "She can surely do:

Thus and thus, and
So and so,

and help me to pull this affair off successfully. If it costs me a few taels of silver to reward her for her pains, what does it matter?"

Thereupon, without even waiting to eat, he sauntered out onto the street again, made straight for Dame Wang's teahouse, slipped in unobtrusively, and took a seat inside the beaded portiere.

"That certainly was a fat bow you took just now, sir," said Dame Wang with a laugh.

"Godmother," said Hsi-men Ch'ing, "come here. There's something I want to ask you. Who does that filly next door belong to?"

"She is King Yama's[24] younger sister, the daughter of the General of the Five Ways,"[25] said Dame Wang. "What do you want to know about her for?"

"I'm serious," said Hsi-men Ch'ing. "Stop joking."

"How is it you don't recognize her, sir?" asked Dame Wang. "Her old man's the one who sells ready-cooked food in front of the district yamen."

"You don't mean to say she's the wife of Hsü the Third who sells date cakes!" exclaimed Hsi-men Ch'ing.

"Not him," said Dame Wang with a negative wave of her hand. "If it were him, they'd make a pair. Guess again, sir."

"She must be the wife of Li the Third who sells won-ton," said Hsi-men Ch'ing.

"Not him," said Dame Wang with another wave of her hand. "If it were him, they'd be well matched."

"You don't mean to say she's the wife of Little Liu the Second with the tattooed arms, do you?" said Hsi-men Ch'ing.

Dame Wang laughed uproariously and said, "Not him. If it were him, they'd make another pair. Guess again, sir."

"Godmother," said Hsi-men Ch'ing, "the truth of the matter is I can't guess who it is."

"In that case," said Dame Wang with a sardonic smile, "I'll tell you, sir," and she burst out laughing again. "The man whose lot it is to cover her is Wu the Elder, who peddles steamed wheat cakes on the street."

When Hsi-men Ch'ing heard this he stamped his feet and laughed.

"You don't mean to say he's the Wu the Elder, whom everyone calls the Three-inch Mulberry-bark Manikin, do you?"

"That's the man," said Dame Wang.

When Hsi-men Ch'ing heard this he groaned and said:

"How did a piece of fine mutton
End up in the mouth of such a dog?"

"It's the same old story," said Dame Wang. "It's always been true that:

The finest steed may be forced to carry
an unworthy rider;
The loveliest wife must often share her bed
with a clumsy clod.[26]

That's just the way the Old Man under the Moon arranges things."

"Godmother," said Hsi-men Ch'ing, "how much do I owe you in the way of tea money?"

"Not much," replied Dame Wang. "Let it go for a few days. It doesn't matter."

"Who is your son, Wang Ch'ao, working for these days?" asked Hsi-men Ch'ing.

"I don't even want to talk about it," said Dame Wang. "He's gone off with a merchant from the Huai River region and hasn't come home to this day. I don't know whether he's dead or alive."

"Why doesn't he come and work for me?" said Hsi-men Ch'ing. "He's a likely looking lad."

"If you saw fit to favor him in such a way, sir," said Dame Wang, "it would certainly be handsome of you."

"Wait till he gets home and we can talk about it again," said Hsi-men Ch'ing. When he had finished speaking he thanked her profusely, got up, and took his leave.

Before four hours had elapsed, however, he showed up again, slipping into a seat just inside the beaded portiere of Dame Wang's teahouse and directing his gaze at Wu the Elder's door. In a little while Dame Wang came out and said, "How about a damson punch, sir?"

"That would be great," said Hsi-men Ch'ing. "Make it good and sour."

Dame Wang prepared an order of damson punch and served it to him with both hands. When he had finished drinking it Hsi-men Ch'ing put the cup down and said, "Mother, you really know how to fix a damson. How many more have you got in the house?"

Dame Wang laughed. "I've been fixing up damsels all my life, but what would I want with one for myself?"

"It was damsons I asked about," said Hsi-men Ch'ing, laughing in turn, "but you're talking about damsels. There's quite a difference between the two."

"All I heard, sir, was something about fixing damsels," said Dame Wang, "so I thought you were talking about the way I fix them up."

"Godmother," said Hsi-men Ch'ing, "if you're as good as all that at making matches, how about fixing one up for me? If you come up with a good one, I'll see that you're amply rewarded."

"You've got to be kidding, sir," said Dame Wang. "If the lady of your house found out about it, I'm afraid my head's a bit too old to stand up to being boxed about the ears."

"My wife has a most accommodating disposition," said Hsi-men Ch'ing. "I've already got a number of bedmates at home. It's just that none of them really tickles my fancy. If you've got anything good to propose, there's no harm in bringing it up. Even someone who's been married before would be all right, as long as she tickles my fancy."

"There was one that looked pretty good just the other day," said Dame Wang, "but I'm afraid you wouldn't be interested, sir."

"If she's really a good prospect, and you can bring it off," said Hsi-men Ch'ing, "I'll reward you generously."

"She's as talented as she can be," said Dame Wang. "The only thing is she's a little along in years."

"It's always been true," said Hsi-men Ch'ing, "that:

> A mature beauty makes a worthy mate.[27]

Even if she's been around a year or two longer than one might wish, it doesn't matter. Just how old is she anyway?"

"The lady in question," said Dame Wang, "was born in the year of the pig, so, come New Year's Day, she'll be just ninety-two."

"What a crazy old crone you are," laughed Hsi-men Ch'ing. "The only thing you're really any good at is pulling people's legs." And when he was through laughing he got up and took his leave.

Gradually it grew dark, and Dame Wang had just lit her lamp and was about to close her door, when who should appear but Hsi-men Ch'ing. Once again he slipped inside the beaded portiere, pulled over a bench to sit on, and proceeded to gaze fixedly at Wu the Elder's door.

"How about a concord punch, sir?" asked Dame Wang.

"That would be great," said Hsi-men Ch'ing. "Make it good and sweet, Godmother."

Dame Wang promptly served him a cupful and Hsi-men Ch'ing drank it, but he continued sitting there until it was quite late before he stood up and said, "Put it on my bill, Godmother. I'll settle the whole account tomorrow."

"Don't worry about it," said Dame Wang. "Pray let the matter rest. Drop in again tomorrow and we can discuss it then."

Hsi-men Ch'ing laughed and took his leave, but when he got home he was:

> Too uncomfortable to sleep or eat in peace.

He couldn't get the woman off his mind. Of the events of that evening there is no more to tell.

Early the following morning, when Dame Wang opened her door and looked outside, she saw that Hsi-men Ch'ing was already there, pacing back and forth in the street. "This sucker is certainly impatient enough," she thought to herself. "Just watch me:

Stick some sugar candy on the tip of his nose
Where he can't quite get at it with his tongue.[28]

That bastard is always presuming on his connections in the yamen to take advantage of people. Now that he's fallen into my hands I might as well make him pay for his fun by lining my nest with a few strings of cash."

It so happens that this Dame Wang, the proprietress of the teahouse, was not the sort to abide by her lot. In fact, for years she had:

Played the procuress,
Made a living as a matchmaker,
Peddled human flesh,
Been a broker,
Meddled in midwifery,
Acted as accoucheur, and
Revealed a knack for every sort of knavery.

And she had yet another accomplishment that doesn't bear mentioning:

She could jab a needle through the chignon, and
Inject solder into the cranial cavity.

Truly, this old lady's skills were such as to evade easy detection. Behold:

When she starts to speak,
 she excels Lu Chia;[29]
When she opens her mouth,
 she surpasses Sui Ho.[30]
She relies on the lethal lips that persuaded
 the Six States;[31]
She depends on the trenchant tongue that won
 the dominions of Ch'i.[32]
The solitary male phoenix and its
 female counterpart,
Are in a trice transformed into
 a couple;
The lonely widow and
 bereft widower,
Are by a single speech induced to
 form a pair.
She knows how to inveigle the young lady
 locked behind triple gates,
Into a tryst with the immortal
 within his nine-tiered palace.
The Golden Lad who tends the incense within the halls
 of the Jade Emperor,[33]

She can drag hither
by the arm;
The Jade Maiden who transmits messages in the palace
of the Queen Mother of the West,[34]
She can embrace
around the waist.
She has but to put in motion
one of her crafty schemes,
In order to induce an arhat
to cosy up to a bhikshuni.
She has but to resort to
one of her devices,
In order to cause Devarāja Li[35]
to embrace Hārītī.[36]
Once exposed to her sweet suasions
and inviting arguments,
Even such a paragon as Feng Chih[37]
would start to get ideas;
When confronted with her winning words
and beguiling promises,
Even so chaste a goddess as Ma-ku[38]
would find her equanimity disturbed.
"Concealing the head of the matter
while revealing the tail,"[39]
She incites even the Weaving Maid[40]
to thoughts of love;
"Playing the role of intermediary
in passion's heats and chills,"[41]
She prevails upon Ch'ang-o[42] herself
to take a lover.[43]

Truly, this old lady was:

Adept at manipulating the breeze and the moonlight
to her own advantage;
Constantly to be seen in the law courts
as an instigator of quarrels.

The old lady had just opened for business and was engaged in getting her teakettles ready when she caught sight of Hsi-men Ch'ing. After pacing back and forth a few more times he slipped hurriedly inside the beaded portiere and proceeded to stare fixedly at the blind over Wu the Elder's door. Dame Wang pretended not to notice and continued to fan up the fire in her stove rather than coming out to take her customer's order.

"Godmother," called out Hsi-men Ch'ing, "make me two cups of tea."

"Oh, it's you, sir," responded Dame Wang. "Long time no see. Please have a seat."

In no time at all she brought two cups of strong tea and set them down on the table.

"Godmother," said Hsi-men Ch'ing, "come have a cup of tea with me."

"I'm not the one you're after," said Dame Wang with a laugh. "Why should I have a cup of tea with you?"

Hsi-men Ch'ing also laughed a while and then asked, "Godmother, what do your neighbors have for sale?"

"Their stock in trade," replied Dame Wang, "is fried doughballs, cured coney, stuffed patty-cake, baked buns, noodles with cockle sauce, and hot Schlag in cider."[44]

"Why you crazy old crone," laughed Hsi-men Ch'ing, "all you can do is joke."

"It's no joke," Dame Wang laughed back at him, "she's got an old man of her own."

"I'm serious," said Hsi-men Ch'ing. "If her husband can make good steamed wheat cakes, I'd like to buy forty or fifty of them to take home with me."

"If all you want to do is buy wheat cakes," said Dame Wang, "he'll be back in a while and you can buy them then. What need is there to pay a formal call?"

"You're right, Godmother," said Hsi-men Ch'ing, who then drank his tea, sat a little longer, stood up, and took his leave.

Sometime later, as Dame Wang was tending her teashop, she looked out with a sardonic eye only to see another vision of Hsi-men Ch'ing. He was pacing back and forth in front of the door. First he would head east, then turn around and go west, only to repeat the process again and again. This happened seven or eight times in a row. Finally he came right into the teashop.

"This must be my lucky day, sir," said Dame Wang. "It seems like ages since I saw you last."

Hsi-men Ch'ing started to laugh and then fumbled for a tael of silver, which he handed to Dame Wang with the words, "Godmother, why don't you take this for the time being to cover my tea money?"

"Why so much?" asked Dame Wang with a smile.

"Godmother," said Hsi-men Ch'ing, "if it's too much, keep the difference."

"I've got him," the old lady thought to herself. "This is one sucker who's going to get what's coming to him. I might as well take his money. It'll come in handy to pay the rent."

Then she said out loud, "You look a little thirsty to me, sir. How about a well-steeped cup of tea?"

"How'd you guess what I wanted, Godmother?" asked Hsi-men Ch'ing.

"What's so hard to guess about that?" said the old lady. "It's always been true that:

When someone comes in the door don't bother
to ask how he's doing;
One look at his face will suffice
to give you the answer.[45]

I've guessed the answers to a lot of stranger things than that in my day."

"There is something I've got on my mind," said Hsi-men Ch'ing. "If you can guess what it is, Godmother, I'll give you five taels of silver."

Dame Wang laughed. "There's no need for any:

Three conjectures and five guesses.

One conjecture will be quite enough for my guess to hit the bull's-eye. Come a little closer, sir, so I can whisper in your ear. The last two days:

Your footsteps have been fidgety, and
Your inquiries incessant.

Surely it's because you've got my next-door neighbor on your mind. How's that for a guess?"

Hsi-men Ch'ing began to laugh. "Godmother," he said, "truly:

In intelligence you rival Sui Ho;
In resourcefulness you outdo Lu Chia.

There's no reason for me to deceive you. I don't know why it is, but ever since I caught sight of her when she was taking down the blind the other day, it's been just as though she had stolen away my three ethereal and my seven material souls. Day and night I can't get her off my mind. When I'm at home I don't even feel like eating or drinking and am far too distracted to work. I wonder if there's anything you could do to help me out?"

Dame Wang gave a cynical laugh. "There's no reason for me to deceive you either, sir. I get a customer in my teashop about as often as the devil plays night watchman. Three years ago, when it snowed so heavily on the third day of the sixth month, I sold a cup of tea, but I haven't been able to make a go of it since. The only thing that keeps me going is the occasional odd job."

"And what, may I ask, do you mean, Godmother, by the occasional odd job?" demanded Hsi-men Ch'ing.

Dame Wang laughed. "When I was only thirty-five my old man kicked off and left me with this youngster, but without any means of livelihood. At first I tried my hand at matchmaking. Then I went round collecting people's old clothes to sell. I offered my services as an accoucheur and then as a midwife. When the occasion arises I dabble in pandering and procuring. I can also perform acupuncture, moxabustion, and other medical services. And, lastly, I treat the 'proper tea' of every customer as though it were my own."[46]

When Hsi-men Ch'ing heard this he burst into laughter. "I had no idea you were as talented as all that, Godmother. If you can actually pull this affair off for me, I'll give you ten taels of silver toward the cost of your coffin. All I want you to do is to arrange a meeting between this filly and myself."

This proposal elicited a hearty laugh from Dame Wang. There is a poem that testifies to this:

That wastrel, Hsi-men Ch'ing, had the
wildest ideas;
He was willing to go to any lengths to get
his way with a woman.
But it was the proprietress of the teahouse,
old Dame Wang;
Who engineered the tryst between the Goddess of
Witches' Mountain and King Hsiang.[47]

If you want to know the outcome of these events,
Pray consult the story related in the following chapter.

Chapter 3

DAME WANG PROPOSES A TEN-PART PLAN FOR "GARNERING THE GLOW"; HSI-MEN CH'ING FLIRTS WITH CHIN-LIEN IN THE TEAHOUSE

Beauty does not delude people, they
delude themselves;[1]
But if they become deluded they will
suffer the consequences.
Their vitality will be dissipated, their
countenances grow pale;
The marrow in their bones will dry up and
their strength will wane.
Those who engage in fornication find that
their families will break up;
Once venereal disease is contracted
it is difficult to cure.
As always, "A full stomach and warm body
give rise to disorder";[2]
Those for whom disaster is imminent
never seem to realize it.

THE STORY GOES that Hsi-men Ch'ing said to Dame Wang, "The only thing I'm interested in is a tryst with this filly."

"Godmother," he went on to say, "if you can really arrange this for me, I'll give you ten taels of silver."

"Listen to me, sir," said Dame Wang. "Generally speaking, the words 'garnering the glow' refer to a most difficult matter. Do you know what this term 'garnering the glow' means? It's just another way of referring to what is commonly known as an illicit affair. Now there are five prerequisites that must be possessed by anyone who wishes to consummate such an affair:

No. 1: He must have the looks of P'an Yüeh.
No. 2: He must have the member of a donkey.[3]
No. 3: He must have the wealth of Teng T'ung.[4]
No. 4: He must have youth, and the resilience of a
'needle in a wad of cotton.'[5]
No. 5: He must have leisure.

Dame Wang Proposes a Ten-part Plan for "Garnering the Glow"

Only if you possess all these prerequisites, which are known for short as 'looks, member, wealth, youth, and leisure,'[6] can you hope to consummate such an affair."

"To tell you the truth," said Hsi-men Ch'ing, "I happen to have all five. As for the first: although I may not be as handsome as P'an Yüeh, I can certainly pass muster. As for the second: in my younger days I frequented the streets and alleys of the licensed quarter and reared a 'turtle'[7] of prodigious size. As for the third: I've got a few strings of cash laid away. Although I may not be in the same league as Teng T'ung, I've got more than enough to get by. As for the fourth: I've got the youth and resilience to take anything she can dish out. She could hit me four hundred times without my giving her a blow in return. As for the fifth: I've got leisure to spare. If I didn't, how could I spend so much time over here? Godmother, if you can pull this off for me, I'll make it worth your while."

Hsi-men Ch'ing had now made his intentions explicit.

"Sir," said Dame Wang, "you say you've got all five prerequisites. I understand that. But there's still another problem that might get in the way and make success unlikely."

"Tell me," said Hsi-men Ch'ing, "what might get in the way?"

"Sir," said Dame Wang, "don't take it amiss if I speak bluntly. The hardest thing about this business of 'garnering the glow' is getting you to commit yourself to it 100 percent. Even if you're willing to spend whatever it takes to complete 99 percent of the task, something might still stand in the way of success. I know you've always been a bit tight, unwilling to fling your money about with abandon. This is the only problem that might get in the way."

"That's easy," said Hsi-men Ch'ing. "I'll just do whatever you tell me."

"If you're prepared to spend the money, sir," said Dame Wang, "I've got a splendid plan for getting you and this filly together. But I don't know if you'll be willing to go along with me or not."

"No matter what you say, I'll go along with it," said Hsi-men Ch'ing. "What is this splendid plan of yours?"

Dame Wang laughed. "It's already getting late today. Why don't you go home for the time being. Come and see me again in half a year, or three months time, and we can talk about it then."

"Godmother," entreated Hsi-men Ch'ing, "stop joking. You've got to help me pull this off.

Your kindness will be amply rewarded."

Dame Wang broke into raucous laughter. "You're getting carried away again, sir. Although this plan of mine may not be worthy of commemoration in the Temple of Prince Wu-ch'eng, the God of War,[8] it's certainly superior to that scheme of Sun Wu's which called for drilling the palace ladies.[9] The odds are eight or nine to one that you shall have her.

"Let me give you the lowdown on this filly's background. Although she's only of humble origin she's as clever as can be. She's an excellent musician and singer. And as for needlework and suchlike feminine accomplishments, the standard repertory of popular songs, backgammon and elephant chess, and so forth, there's very little she doesn't know about any of them. Her given name is Chin-lien and her maiden name is P'an. Her father was the Tailor P'an whose shop used to be located outside the South Gate. After his death she was sold into the household of Mr. Chang, the well-to-do merchant, where she learned to play musical instruments and sing. Later, because Mr. Chang was getting along in years, he released her from the terms of her contract and gave her to Wu the Elder as wife without demanding a candareen in return.

"That was several years ago. Now Wu the Elder is something of a simpleton. Every day he goes out early and comes home late and doesn't pay attention to anything but his business. Ordinarily this filly is not much given to gadding about. When I've got nothing better to do I often go over to her place to pass the time of day, and when she needs help with anything she asks me to take care of it for her. She addresses me as Godmother just as you do.

"The last few days Wu the Elder has been going out early. If you want to pursue this matter, sir, buy me a bolt of blue pongee and another of white, along with a bolt of white damask. I'll also need ten taels' worth of good-quality silk wadding. When you've brought all these things to me I'll go over and ask to borrow her calendar so I can get someone to pick out an auspicious day on which to engage a tailor to make them up for me. If she responds by picking out a lucky day but doesn't offer to do the work herself, then it'll be all over. But if she says, 'Let me do it for you':

As though nothing in Heaven or Earth could
make her happier,

and doesn't want me to hire a tailor, then one-tenth of this glow-game will have been achieved.

"If I am successful in inviting her to come over to my place to do the work, then two-tenths of this glow-game will have been achieved.

"If she does come over to my place to do the work, at noontime I'll prepare some wine and a snack and ask her to have lunch with me. If she says it's inconvenient and insists on taking the work home with her, then it'll be all over. But if she doesn't say anything and agrees to eat lunch with me, then three-tenths of this glow-game will have been achieved.

"On the following day you mustn't show up. But on the third day, around noon, dress yourself up appropriately and cough outside my door as a signal. Then call out, 'It's been days since I've set eyes on you, Godmother Wang. I've come to buy a cup of tea.' I'll come out and invite you to come in and sit down while you drink your tea. If she gets up and retires to her own home when she sees you, I can't very well physically restrain her, can I? It'll be all over. But if she sees you come in and makes no effort to withdraw, then four-tenths of this glow-game will have been achieved.

"When you sit down I'll say to the filly, 'This is the very gentleman who was kind enough to give these materials to me. I'm greatly indebted to him.' Then I'll proceed to sing your praises and you can wax extravagant on the subject of her needlework. If she pays no attention and refuses to respond, then it'll be all over. But if she responds by engaging you in conversation, then five-tenths of this glow-game will have been achieved.

"Then I'll say, 'It's really kind of this young lady to have volunteered her services on my behalf. I'm greatly indebted to both of you benefactors; to one for providing the money and the other for providing her skills. If I hadn't:

> Asked her a favor, as one trouper to another,[10]

there would scarcely be any reason for this young lady to grace us with her presence. Why don't you play the role of host, sir, and show this young lady how much her efforts are appreciated.' You then pull out some silver and ask me to buy whatever's needed. If she insists on leaving at this point, I can't very well physically restrain her, can I? It'll be all over. But if she makes no effort to withdraw, the situation will be promising, and six-tenths of this glow-game will have been achieved.

"Then I'll accept your money and on my way out the door I'll say to her, 'Be so good as to keep the gentleman company for a few minutes, young lady.' If she refuses and gets up and goes home instead, I can scarcely do anything to prevent her, can I? It'll be all over. But if she doesn't budge, everything will be fine, and seven-tenths of this glow-game will have been achieved.

"When I've bought the things I'll put them on the table and say, 'Young lady, why don't you set your work aside for a minute and have a cup of wine? It's a rare treat this gentleman has provided for us.' If she refuses to drink at the same table with you and goes home instead, it'll be all over. But if she only talks about leaving and doesn't budge, everything will be going fine, and eight-tenths of this glow-game will have been achieved.

"After she's had enough wine to feel it, and the conversation has started to warm up, I'll say the wine has run out and suggest once again that you buy some. You pull out more silver and ask me to get it for you, along with some delicacies to go with it. I'll put the latch on the door so that the two of you are locked inside the room together. If she gets all hot and bothered and tries to run home, it'll be all over. But if she lets me put the latch on the door without getting hot and bothered, then nine-tenths of this glow-game will have been achieved.

"Only one-tenth will then remain, but this last step is the hardest. There in the room, sir, you'll have to move in with the sweet talk, but whatever you do, avoid any rough stuff that might wreck the whole affair. In such a case you'd be strictly on your own as far as I'm concerned. You might proceed by brushing a pair of chopsticks off the table with your sleeve and then giving her foot a pinch when you stoop down to pick them up. If she kicks up a fuss, I'll have to come to her rescue, and it'll be all over. That will be the end of the matter. But if she doesn't make a peep, the last tenth of this glow-game will have been achieved, for she will have given her consent to your conquest. If this glow-game is carried to a successful conclusion, how will you thank me?"

When Hsi-men Ch'ing had heard her out he was delighted and exclaimed, "Godmother, this plan of yours may not earn you a place in the Ling-yen Pavilion,[11] but it's certainly a splendid, first-class scheme!"

"Whatever you do," said Dame Wang, "don't forget those ten taels of silver you promised me."

Hsi-men Ch'ing replied:

"Whenever one gets so much as a
  tangerine peel to eat;
One should never forget Tung-t'ing Lake[12]
  from whence it came.[13]

Godmother, how soon can this plan of yours be put into operation?"

"I should have something to report this very evening," said Dame Wang. "I'll go over soon and ask to borrow her calendar, before Wu the Elder gets home, and then start to work on her as best I can. You'd better get cracking and send someone over with the pongee, damask, and silk wadding before it's too late."

"Godmother," said Hsi-men Ch'ing, "if you can pull this off, how could I ever let you down?"

Thereupon he took his leave of Dame Wang, walked out through the teahouse, and went to buy the three bolts of pongee and damask and ten taels' worth of the best-quality silk wadding. When he got home he instructed his young body servant, named Tai-an, to wrap them up in a bundle and deliver them to Dame Wang's house, where she was only too pleased to accept them and send the lad on his way. Truly:

Unless the clouds and rain come together
  on Witch's Mountain;
King Hsiang of Ch'u will have erected
  his terrace in vain.[14]

There is a poem that testifies to this:

The two of them feel an affinity
  as sweet as honey;
The way Dame Wang brings them together
  is remarkable indeed.
She devises a ten-part plan for
  "garnering the glow";
To ensure that they will come together
  without fail.[15]

Dame Wang Insists on the Proposed Remuneration for Her Plan

When Dame Wang had received the pongee, damask, and silk wadding she opened her back door and went over to Wu the Elder's house. The woman greeted her, invited her upstairs, and offered her a seat.

"Young lady," said Dame Wang, "how is it you haven't been over to my place for a cup of tea the last few days?"

"It's just that I've been out of sorts lately," the woman replied, "and haven't felt like doing anything at all."

"If you've got a calendar in the house, young lady," said Dame Wang, "lend it to me so I can get someone to choose a good day for me to have some tailoring done."

"What sort of tailoring do you have in mind, Godmother?" the woman asked.

"It's just because I seem to be suffering from all:

Ten aches and nine pains,"

said Dame Wang. "I'm afraid I could end up:

High as the hills or deep as the sea,

at any moment, and my son isn't even here to take care of things if anything should happen to me."

"Why haven't I seen Little Brother around for such a long time?" the woman inquired.

"That rascal is out on the road, traveling with a merchant," said Dame Wang, "and I never hear a word from him. I can't help worrying about him from one day to the next."

"How old is Little Brother this year?" the woman asked.

"That rascal's already sixteen," replied Dame Wang.

"Why don't you find him a wife, Godmother?" the woman said, "so she could lend you a hand?"

"It's just as you say," responded Dame Wang, "I've got nobody to help out. Sooner or later, someplace or other, I'll have to find him one all right. But I'm not going to worry about that till he gets home.

"Right now the problem is that, day and night, if I'm not coughing I'm short of breath; and I hurt all over, just as if I'd been beaten to pieces, so I can't even get any sleep. I've been wanting for some time now to prepare my burial garments, just in case. Fortunately a certain well-to-do gentleman who often drops into my place for a cup of tea—a man who has noticed how reliable I am as a medical practitioner, employment agent, and matchmaker, and insists on patronizing me in matters great and small—has made me a gift of all the materials I need for a complete set of burial garments, enough pongee and damask for both exterior and lining, along with a quantity of fine silk wadding. They've been sitting at home for over a year now without my having the time to get them made up.

"This year I really feel I may not be able to hang on much longer; and since it happens to be an intercalary month[16] in which I've got a few days to spare, I thought I'd get this taken care of. But the tailor is giving me a hard time, claiming he's too busy right now to do it for me. I can't tell you what a hassle it's been."

On hearing this speech the woman smiled and said, "I don't know if I could do a satisfactory job, but if you're willing to risk it, I happen to have some spare time right now and could do it for you myself. What do you think, Godmother?"

When the old woman heard this she said with an ingratiating smile, "If you deign to do it with your own hands, young lady, I'll feel myself honored even in the grave. I've heard for a long time how good you are at needlework, but I haven't presumed to impose on you."

"It's nothing, Godmother," said the woman. "I've offered to do it, and I insist. Take the calendar along and get somebody to choose a lucky day so I can begin."

"Young lady," said Dame Wang, "there's no need to pretend with me. There can't be many words in the standard anthologies of poetry and drama that you can't read. What need is there to get someone else to consult the calendar?"

"I'm afraid I never received a proper education," demurred the woman with a faint smile.

"That's a fine way to talk!" said Dame Wang, as she picked up the calendar and handed it to her.

The woman took the calendar in her hand and examined it for a while. "Tomorrow is an unlucky day," she said, "and the day after tomorrow is bad too. The next good day for tailoring is not until the day after the day after tomorrow."

Dame Wang snatched the calendar away from her and hung it back on the wall, saying, "The fact that you're willing to do it for me, young lady, makes you my lucky star. What need is there to be particular about the date. I already asked someone to check for me and he reported that tomorrow is an unlucky day. But I, for one, see no reason to pay any attention to the taboo against doing tailoring on unlucky days."

"Actually," said the woman, "an unlucky day might be the most appropriate for making burial garments."

"As long as you're willing to do it," said Dame Wang, "I'll make so bold as to trouble you to come over to my place tomorrow."

"There's no need for that," said the woman. "It'll do just as well if you bring it over here for me to work on, won't it?"

"The fact of the matter is," said Dame Wang, "I want to see the way you go about it, but there's no one to tend the shop for me."

"In that case," said the woman, "I'll come over after breakfast tomorrow morning."

The old lady descended the stairs with:

A thousand thanks and ten thousand
expressions of gratitude.

That evening she reported what had happened to Hsi-men Ch'ing and reiterated that he was not to turn up until the third day. Of the events of that night there is no more to tell.

The next day, bright and early, Dame Wang tidied up her room, laid out the necessary needles and thread, got the tea things ready, and sat down to wait for her visitor.

To resume our story, when Wu the Elder had eaten breakfast, shouldered his carrying pole, and gone off to work, the woman hung the bamboo blind over the door, told Ying-erh to look after the house, and went over to Dame Wang's place by the back door. The old lady, as pleased as could be, invited her in and offered her a seat. Then she poured her a cup of strong tea, flavored with walnuts and pine seeds, wiped the table clean, and got out the three bolts of pongee and damask. The woman took her measurements, cut up the material, and began to sew.

As the old lady looked on she kept up an unbroken stream of flattering commentary. "What exquisite skill! I've lived for sixty or seventy years without ever seeing needlework as fine as this."

The woman continued sewing until noon, when Dame Wang prepared some food and wine, along with a serving of noodles, and asked her to lunch. Afterward she continued sewing for a while, until late afternoon, when she put her work aside and returned home.

Wu the Elder happened to come home about the same time, and the woman put the latch on the door and took down the blind. When Wu the Elder came into the room he noticed that his wife's face was a little red and asked her, "Where've you been?"

"Just over at Godmother Wang's next door," the woman replied. "She asked me to make up a set of burial garments for her. At noontime she prepared some food and wine in the way of a snack and asked me to lunch."

"It would have been better not to accept her hospitality," said Wu the Elder. "We may need to call on her for help some time. Even though she asked you to make up these burial garments for her, you could just as easily have come home for a snack. It's not worth it, putting her to all that trouble. If you go back there to continue working tomorrow, take a little money along so you can buy some food and wine and return the treat. As the saying goes:

A distant relative is no match for a close neighbor.[17]

We mustn't fall behind in our social obligations. If she won't let you return the treat, bring the work home with you and give it back to her when you're done."

There is a poem that testifies to this:

The machinations of the old matron
  are deep indeed;
But Wu the Elder is too ingenuous
  to catch their drift.
By supplying money to return the treat
  he rewards her betrayal;
And by so doing gives his wife away
  to another man.[18]

The woman agreed to go along with Wu the Elder's suggestion. Of the events of that evening there is no more to tell.

The next day, after breakfast, Wu the Elder had no sooner shouldered his carrying pole and gone out than Dame Wang slipped over to press her invitation. The woman accompanied her back to her room, got out the unfinished work, and continued to sew. Dame Wang hastened to pour the tea and had a cup with her. As it drew near midday the woman pulled three hundred cash out of her sleeve and said to Dame Wang, "Godmother, let me buy you a cup of wine."

"Ai-ya!" said Dame Wang. "Who ever heard of such a thing? I asked you here to do something as a favor to me, young lady. How could I consent to let you put up the money? I hope the fare I provided hasn't disagreed with you."

"It's just what my husband told me to do," said the woman. "He said that if you raised any objections I was to take the work home with me and return it to you when I was through."

When the old lady heard this she said, "Wu the Elder really knows how to do things right, doesn't he? If that's the way you want it, young lady, I guess I'll have to accept, at least for the time being."

The old lady was afraid of interrupting the proceedings. Adding some money of her own, she went out to buy food and wine of good quality, along with some unusual delicacies, and waited upon her assiduously.

Gentle reader take note: Nine out of ten of the women of this world, no matter how smart they are, prove susceptible to flattery.

The old lady prepared an enticing repast of food and wine and invited her guest to partake of it. Afterward the woman continued sewing for a while, until late afternoon, when she returned home with:

A thousand thanks and ten thousand
  expressions of gratitude.

To make a long story short, the third day, after breakfast, Dame Wang waited until she had seen Wu the Elder go out and then went to her back door and called out, "Young lady, may I make so bold?"

"I'm on my way," the woman responded from the second floor.

After they had greeted each other they repaired to Dame Wang's room, where she got out her work in order to go on with the sewing. Dame Wang made haste to pour the tea and they had a cup together, after which the woman continued to sew until it was nearly noon.

To resume our story, Hsi-men Ch'ing had hardly been able to wait for this day. Dressing himself up to befit the occasion, taking three or five taels of silver along with him, and sporting his gold-flecked Szechwan fan, he swaggered off in the direction of Amethyst Street.

When he arrived at the door of Dame Wang's teashop he coughed and called out, "Godmother Wang, why haven't I seen anything of you the last few days?"

Dame Wang caught on immediately and responded with the words, "Who is that calling after this old body?"

"It's me," said Hsi-men Ch'ing.

The old lady bustled out to see who it was and then said, with a laugh, "I had no idea who it could be, but it turns out to be you, sir. You've arrived in the nick of time. Come into my room and see who's here."

Taking hold of Hsi-men Ch'ing by the sleeve, with one tug she pulled him into the room where, addressing herself to the woman, she said, "This is the very gentleman who was kind enough to give these materials to me."

Hsi-men Ch'ing opened his eyes wide and took a good look at the woman.

> Her cloudy locks rose up like serried hills;
> Her fair countenance evoked an air of spring.

She was wearing a white linen blouse with a peach red skirt and a blue vest as she sat there in the room, working on her sewing. When she saw Hsi-men Ch'ing come in she lowered her head.

Hsi-men Ch'ing quickly stepped forward and made her a bow as he uttered a word of greeting. The woman put down her work and returned his salutation.

Dame Wang then said, "It was rare generosity on this gentleman's part to give me these bolts of pongee and damask. They've been sitting at home for over a year now without my having time to get them made up. I'm greatly indebted to this young lady, my next-door neighbor, who has volunteered her services in making them up for me. Her needlework is as regular as any turned out on a loom, it's so close and fine. Such a thing is rarely to be seen. Just come take a look at it, sir."

Hsi-men Ch'ing picked up the garments and made appreciative noises as he examined them.

"Where could this young lady have learned to do such needlework?" he exclaimed. "It looks just like the work of a goddess or immortal."

"Don't make fun of me, sir," the woman said with a smile.

Hsi-men Ch'ing Flirts with Chin-lien in the Teahouse

Hsi-men Ch'ing deliberately proceeded to inquire of Dame Wang, "Godmother, I hardly dare ask, but whose household does this young lady belong to?"

"Make a guess, sir," said Dame Wang.

"How could I hope to guess correctly?" said Hsi-men Ch'ing.

Dame Wang laughed out loud and said, "Please sit down, sir, and I'll tell you all about it."

Hsi-men Ch'ing sat down across the table from the woman and Dame Wang said, "Let me tell you, sir. Remember what happened to you when you were walking under the eaves here the other day? Well it served you right, sir."

"You mean to tell me she's the one whose forked stick fell on my hairnet[19] the other day as I passed by her door?" responded Hsi-men Ch'ing. "I still have no idea whose household she belongs to."

"I'm afraid I may have unintentionally shaken you up a bit the other day, sir," said the woman. "Please don't hold it against me." As she said this she stood up and made him a bow.

Hsi-men Ch'ing returned her salutation with alacrity and said, "How could I dream of such a thing?"

"This same lady," said Dame Wang, "is the wife of Wu the Elder who lives next door."

"So you're Wu the Elder's wife," said Hsi-men Ch'ing. "I know your husband only as a hardworking family man who plies his trade in the streets. He has never given offense to anyone, high or low. He knows how to make a living and has a good disposition. Truly, men such as he are not easily come by."

"True enough," said Dame Wang. "Ever since the young lady has been married to Wu the Elder she's been:

> Obedient to his every whim.

They really hit it off with each other."

"My husband is an utterly useless person," said the woman. "Don't make fun of me that way, sir."

"You're mistaken, young lady," said Hsi-men Ch'ing. "As the poet says:

> Flexibility is the root of success;
> Adamancy is the womb of misfortune.[20]

When one has a husband as irreproachable as yours, who:

> Though he possess ten thousand fathoms of water
> will not suffer a drop to escape;[21]
> And strives throughout his entire lifetime
> to set an example of integrity,

how could he be anything but an asset?"

For some time Dame Wang kept up a steady drumbeat of praise for Hsi-men Ch'ing.

Turning to the woman she said, "Young lady, do you know who this gentleman is?"

"No I don't," she replied.

"This gentleman," said Dame Wang, "is one of the more substantial citizens of the locality. Even His Honor, the district magistrate, consorts with him, and addresses him as the Honorable Hsi-men. He disposes of property worth tens of thousands of strings of cash and owns the wholesale pharmaceutical business on the street in front of the district yamen. In his home:

> The piles of money reach higher than the dipper,
> The stores of rotting rice suggest a granary.
> What is yellow is gold,
> What is white is silver,
> What are round are pearls,
> What sparkle are jewels.[22]

And he also possesses:

> Horns off the rhinoceros's head, and
> Tusks out of the elephant's mouth.[23]

In addition to which:

> He lends money to officials, and
> Is very well connected.

At the time of his present marriage I played the role of go-between. His wife is Battalion Commander Wu's daughter, who's just as clever as can be."

Then, turning to Hsi-men Ch'ing, she asked, "Sir, how is it you haven't dropped in to my place for a cup of tea for lo these many days?"

"It's all on account of my daughter," said Hsi-men Ch'ing. "She's just been betrothed to someone and I've been tied up for some time."

"Who has your young lady been betrothed to?" asked Dame Wang. "And why didn't you employ me as go-between?"

"She's betrothed to Ch'en Ching-chi,"[24] said Hsi-men Ch'ing, "the son of that Ch'en family that's related by marriage to Yang Chien, the commander in chief of the 800,000 imperial guards in the Eastern Capital. He's only sixteen years old and is still going to school. In any other circumstances we would have asked you to represent us, Godmother, but they took the initiative by sending a certain Auntie Wen to propose the match; so we countered by asking that Auntie Hsüeh who is constantly to be seen around our place peddling costume jewelry to be coguarantor, and we have consented to the terms. If you would like to come, Godmother, I'll send someone to invite you over, one day soon, when they present us with the ritual gift of tea."

The old lady laughed uproariously. "I was only kidding, sir. We go-betweens are a pretty bitchy bunch. When they were conducting the negotiations I was nowhere to be seen. Why should I be entitled to a share of the feast they have earned by their own efforts? As the saying goes:

> Fellow professionals can't abide each other.

It will be more appropriate if I wait until the bride has been carried over the threshold and then go pay a call on the third-day or fifth-day celebrations, with a present in hand, in hopes of getting a bite to eat. There's no point in antagonizing people."

The two of them carried on an animated dialogue for some time, in which the old lady pulled out all the stops in her exaggerated praise of Hsi-men Ch'ing. Meanwhile, the woman merely lowered her head and continued to sew. There is a poem that testifies to this:

It has always been the nature of women
  to be like water;
Behind their husbands' backs they betray them
  with other men.
In her heart Chin-lien hankers after
  Hsi-men Ch'ing;
Once her desires are aroused she can
  no longer control them.[25]

Hsi-men Ch'ing sensed that Chin-lien was well-disposed toward him and could hardly wait to begin coupling with her.

Dame Wang poured two cups of tea and served one to Hsi-men Ch'ing and one to the woman, saying, "Young lady, have a little tea with the gentleman."

By the time they had finished their tea they were already exchanging meaningful glances. Dame Wang looked at Hsi-men Ch'ing and stroked her cheek with a finger. Hsi-men Ch'ing understood that five-tenths of the glow-game had already been achieved. It's always been true that:

Romantic affairs are consummated over tea, and
Wine is the go-between of lust.[26]

"If you hadn't dropped by, sir," said Dame Wang, "I would not have presumed to visit your home in order to issue an invitation. In the first place:

This meeting was fated to occur;

and in the second place:

You've arrived in the nick of time.

As the saying goes:

One guest does not trouble two hosts.[27]

You have provided the money, sir, and this young lady has provided her skills. I'm greatly indebted to both of you benefactors. If I hadn't:

Asked her a favor, as one trouper to another,

there would scarcely be any reason for this young lady to grace us with her presence. Why don't you play the role of host, sir, by coming up with the silver to buy some food and wine, in order to show this young lady how much her efforts are appreciated?"

"How stupid of me not to have thought of it myself," said Hsi-men Ch'ing. "I've got some silver right here." He reached into his wallet, pulled out a lump of silver of about a tael's value, and gave it to Dame Wang to buy the food and wine with.

"There's no need to put the gentleman to all this trouble," said the woman, but, although she uttered the protest, she made no effort to withdraw.

Dame Wang accepted the money and on her way out the door said, "Be so good as to keep the gentleman company for a few minutes, young lady. I'll be right back."

"Don't bother, Godmother," said the woman, but she made no effort to withdraw.

By now both of them had the same idea in mind. Dame Wang went out the door, leaving them in the room together. Hsi-men Ch'ing couldn't take his eyes off the woman, and she, too, stole surreptitious glances at him. When she saw what a handsome figure he cut she was more than half inclined in his favor, but again she merely lowered her head and continued to sew.

Before long Dame Wang returned from her shopping expedition with a plump cooked goose, a roast duck, baked meats, salted fish, and other delicacies.

When she had put them out on platters and plates she arranged them on the table in her room and said to the woman, "Young lady, why don't you set your work aside for a minute and have a cup of wine?"

"You keep the gentleman company if you like," said the woman. "It's not proper for me to do so."

"But all this has been provided for the sole purpose of showing you how much your efforts are appreciated," the old lady protested. "How can you say such a thing?" And she proceeded to set the platters of food down right in front of her.

When the three of them had sat down at their places the wine was poured. Picking up a cup of wine and holding it out to her in his hand, Hsi-men Ch'ing addressed the woman with the words, "Please don't refuse me. Bottoms up."

The woman declined, saying, "You're very kind, sir, but I have so little capacity that I couldn't handle it."

"I know perfectly well you could swallow the ocean itself," said Dame Wang. "Please relax and have a cup or two."

There is a poem that testifies to this:

Since "Boys and girls are forbidden,
  to occupy the same mat";[28]
Flaunting one's beauty and inviting seduction
  have perennial appeal.

Not only did Cho Wen-chün, once upon a time,
elope with Ssu-ma Hsiang-ju;[29]
But, even today, a Hsi-men Ch'ing may enjoy
the favors of a Chin-lien.[30]

The woman took the cup of wine and saluted each of the others in turn.

Hsi-men Ch'ing picked up his chopsticks and said, "Godmother, do me the favor of urging the young lady to have something to eat."

Dame Wang picked out the best tidbits and put them on the woman's plate. After the third round of drinks the old lady went to heat some more wine.

"I hardly dare ask," said Hsi-men Ch'ing, "how old you are, young lady?"

"I'm twenty-four," the woman responded. "I was born in the year of the dragon, on the ninth day of the first month, at two o'clock in the morning."

"You're the same age as my wife, then," said Hsi-men Ch'ing. "She was also born in the year *wu-ch'en*,[31] the year of the dragon, but you're seven months older than she is. She was born on the fifteenth day of the eighth month, at midnight."

"How can you compare Heaven to Earth?" said the woman. "You'll be the death of me yet."

"This young lady is an intelligent person," interjected Dame Wang. "She's as clever as can be. It's no wonder her needlework's as good as it is. As for the works of the hundred schools, backgammon, elephant chess, and the various word games played by breaking characters down into their component parts, she's thoroughly versed in them all. She even writes a good hand."

"Where could one hope to find the like!" exclaimed Hsi-men Ch'ing. "Wu the Elder is a lucky man, indeed, to have this young lady as his wife."

"I wouldn't want to make invidious comparisons, sir," said Dame Wang, "but you've got quite a few ladies in your own household, and which one of them is a match for this young lady?"

"That's no more than the truth," said Hsi-men Ch'ing.

"It's a long story.
I guess it's just my bad luck not to have found a good one yet."

"Your first wife was all right, wasn't she, sir?" said Dame Wang.

"Don't talk to me about my first wife," said Hsi-men Ch'ing. "If she were still alive, things wouldn't be the way they are.

When the family lacks a ruler,
The household is topsy-turvy.[32]

I've got three, five, maybe seven bedmates around the place right now, but a lot of good it does me. All they can do is eat; none of them is willing to take charge of anything."

"If that's the way things are, sir," asked the woman, "how many years has it been since your first wife died?"

"I don't even like to talk about it," said Hsi-men Ch'ing. "My first wife's maiden name was Ch'en. Although she was only of humble origin, she was as clever as could be. She was always able to act on my behalf whenever the occasion arose. But now, unfortunately, she's dead. It happened more than three years ago. Since my remarriage, my second wife has been sick so much of the time she hasn't been able to take charge. As a result, everything in the household is:

All at sevens and eights.[33]

That's why I spend so much of my time out of the house. When I'm at home all I do is get upset."

"Sir," said Dame Wang, "don't take it amiss if I speak bluntly. Neither your first wife nor your present wife could match the needlework of Wu the Elder's lady, not to mention her looks."

"For that matter," said Hsi-men Ch'ing, "my first wife also lacked the romantic air of Wu the Elder's lady."

The old lady laughed. "Sir, what about that mistress you've been maintaining—the one who lives on East Street—why haven't you had me over for a cup of tea?"

"You must mean the ballad singer, Chang Hsi-ch'un," said Hsi-men Ch'ing. "When I realized she was nothing but a street musician I grew tired of her."

"Sir," said the old lady, "you've been carrying on with Li Chiao-erh, from the licensed quarter, for some time."

"As for her," said Hsi-men Ch'ing, "I've already taken her into my establishment. If she had been able to run the household, I would have made her my legitimate wife."

"You're on good terms with Cho the Second too," said Dame Wang.

"I've also taken Cho Tiu-erh into my establishment as my Number Three," said Hsi-men Ch'ing. "But recently she's come down with an indisposition that she doesn't seem able to shake."

"If I ever came across anyone who might tickle your fancy to the extent that Wu the Elder's lady does," inquired Dame Wang, "would you have any objection if I paid you a call to broach the subject?"

"Both my father and my mother are dead," said Hsi-men Ch'ing, "so I'm my own master. Who would dare to say me nay?"

"I'm only joking," said Dame Wang. "Where could I ever find anyone who tickled your fancy to that extent?"

"It's not that there's none to be had," said Hsi-men Ch'ing. "It's just that my meager matrimonial affinities have prevented me from encountering one."

The two of them had carried on an animated dialogue for some time when Dame Wang exclaimed, "Just when we're having such a good time, the wine has run out. Don't take it amiss, sir, if I seem to be ordering you about; but what would you think of buying another bottle of wine?"

Hsi-men Ch'ing pulled out the three or four taels of loose silver remaining in his wallet and gave them to Dame Wang, saying, "You take these and use them to buy more if we run out of anything. If it's too much, keep the difference."

The old lady thanked him and got up to go. When she glanced at Chin-lien she saw that she had reached that state in which:

Three cups of wine in the stomach
  ignite the flames of desire.

From the manner in which they were:

Talking back and forth,

it was obvious that by now both of them had the same idea in mind. The woman merely lowered her head, but didn't budge from her seat. Truly:

The natural beauty of the vista
  remains unseen;
In spring the peach blossoms bloom
  all by themselves.

There is a poem that testifies to this:

The messages conveyed by her eyes and brows
  have never ceased;
The love match is about to be consummated
  with a romantic partner.
In her greed for reward Dame Wang
  possesses no other skill;
Than flowery words and a cleverly
  specious tongue.

If you want to know the outcome of these events,
Pray consult the story related in the following chapter.

Chapter 4

THE HUSSY COMMITS ADULTERY BEHIND WU THE ELDER'S BACK; YÜN-KO IN HIS ANGER RAISES A RUMPUS IN THE TEASHOP

Wine and beauty frequently occasion
  the ruination of the state;
From of old, good looks have been the undoing
  of the loyal and the true.
The royal house of King Chou came to an end
  because of Ta-chi;[1]
The sacred altars of the state of Wu perished
  on account of Hsi-shih.[2]
Those who care only for the joys of youth,
  seeking pleasure where they may;
Remain oblivious to the disasters
  lurking beneath the powdered smile.[3]
Hsi-men Ch'ing allowed himself to become
  so enamored of Chin-lien's beauty;
That he abandoned the domestic doe
  to pursue the high-stepping hind.

THE STORY GOES that as Dame Wang started out the door with Hsi-men Ch'ing's money in hand she turned to the woman with an ingratiating smile and said, "I'm just popping out into the street to get a bottle of wine. Be so good as to keep the gentleman company for a few minutes, young lady. There's a little wine left in the pot, so if you run out you can pour another couple of cups and share them with the gentleman. I'm going to go all the way to East Street, where I can be sure of getting a bottle of the best quality, so I'll be gone quite a while."

On hearing this the woman said, "Godmother, don't go. I've already had enough wine. I don't need any more."

"Ai-ya!" Dame Wang exclaimed. "Young lady, it's not as though the gentleman were anyone else. If you haven't anything else to do, why not share a cup with him? What is there to be afraid of?"

Although the woman said, "I don't need any more," she sat where she was and didn't budge from her seat. Dame Wang put the latch on the door and fastened it with a piece of cord so that the two of them were locked inside the room together. Then she sat down on the curb and devoted herself to spinning thread in order to pass the time.

To resume our story, inside the room Hsi-men Ch'ing looked at the woman.

Her cloudy locks were half askew, and
Her creamy breasts slightly exposed.

On her powdered face the colors red and white formed a pleasing contrast. Picking up the pot, he continued to ply the woman with wine.

After a while, pretending to be hot, he took off his green silk jacket and said, "I wonder, young lady, if you would hang this over the bedrail of Godmother's bed for me?"

Nothing loath, the woman took it in her hand and disposed of it as directed. Hsi-men Ch'ing then deliberately brushed a pair of chopsticks off the table with his sleeve so that they fell to the floor. It is clear that:

This meeting was fated to occur,

for the chopsticks came to rest right beside the woman's feet. Hsi-men Ch'ing quickly stooped down to pick them up. Behold:

The up-turned points of her tiny golden lotuses,
Barely three inches long,
But half a span in length,
Peeked out beside the chopsticks.

Hsi-men Ch'ing ignored the chopsticks but gave a gentle pinch to the embroidered tip of her shoe.

The woman laughed out loud. "There's no need to beat around the bush, sir.

If you've got a mind to it,
I've got the will.[4]

Are you actually trying to seduce me?"

Hsi-men Ch'ing got down on his knees with the plea, "Young lady, make a happy man of me."

The woman then embraced Hsi-men Ch'ing, saying, "My only fear is that Godmother may come back and catch us in the act."

"It doesn't matter," said Hsi-men Ch'ing, "she's already in on it."

At this juncture, right there in Dame Wang's room, the two of them:

Took off their clothes, undid their girdles, and
Enjoyed each other on the same pillow.

Behold:

Their necks entwined, the mandarin ducks
sport in the water;
Their heads together, the phoenixes
thread the flowers.

The Hussy Commits Adultery behind Wu the Elder's Back

How joyous their delight as the growing branches
intertwine;
How sweet their pleasure as the lover's knot
is tied.
The one sticks tightly with his
ruby lips;
The other clings closely with her
powdered face.
Silk stockings in the air,
Two new moons rise above his shoulders;
Gold hairpins askew,
A black cloud piles up beside the pillow.
Swearing eternal fidelity,
He kneads her into a thousand shapes of compliance;
Bashful at the clouds and rain,
She submits with ten thousand forms of complaisance.
The pleasing cries of the oriole,
Are never absent from his ears;
Forever moist with sweet spittle,
She smiles as she sticks out her tongue.
Her willow waist droops with the weight
of teeming spring;
Her cherry mouth is slightly split
with panting breath.
As her starry eyes grow dim,
Tiny beads of sweat form on her fragrant jade body;
As her creamy breasts heave,
A stream of dewdrops drips into the heart of the peony.
Despite the fact that they are both well matched
and compatible;
How true it is that "Stolen delights always
taste the best."[5]

The two of them had just finished with the clouds and rain and were about to get dressed when they were interrupted by Dame Wang, who pushed open the door of the room and walked right in on them.

With a great show of consternation,
Clapping her hands and beating her palms,

she said, "A fine thing the two of you have been up to!"

Hsi-men Ch'ing and Chin-lien were both caught by surprise. The old woman then addressed herself to the latter, saying, "Fine! Just fine! I asked you over here to do a job for me, not to do a job on a man. When Wu the Elder finds out, I'm going to be implicated. I might as well tell him about it before anyone else does." Having said which, she turned around and started out the door.

The woman was thrown into such a panic by this that she caught hold of her by the skirt and got down on her knees with the plea, "Godmother, forgive us!"

"You'll both have to agree to one condition if there's to be any hope of that," said Dame Wang.

"Don't talk about one condition," said the woman. "If you were to impose ten conditions, Godmother, I'd agree to them."

"Every day from now on," said Dame Wang, "you must agree to keep Wu the Elder in the dark and never to disappoint this gentleman, no matter whether he calls for you early or late. Then and only then will I agree to call it quits. If you refuse to come even once I'll tell Wu the Elder all about it."

"I'll do whatever you say," the woman replied.

Dame Wang then said, "As for you, sir, there's no need for me to remind you. All ten parts of this glow-game have been carried to a successful conclusion, so you can't very well renege on what you promised me. If you show bad faith by going away and not coming back again, I'll also tell Wu the Elder all about it."

"Godmother," said Hsi-men Ch'ing, "you can relax. I won't go back on my word."

"There's no way of holding the two of you to your word," said Dame Wang, "unless you exchange tokens of some kind as mementoes of your feelings."

Hsi-men Ch'ing then pulled a silver hairpin with a gold head out of his own hair and inserted it into the woman's cloudy locks. Fearing that Wu the Elder might suspect something if he saw it, she pulled it out and put it in her sleeve, from which she drew out a handkerchief which she gave to Hsi-men Ch'ing, who also put it away out of sight.

The three of them drank another few cups of wine together, by which time it was late afternoon. The woman then got up and said, "It's about time for that bastard, Wu the Elder, to be getting back. I'd better go home."

She then took her leave of Dame Wang and Hsi-men Ch'ing and slipped into her own house through the back door. Once there, she barely had time to take down the blind over the front door before Wu the Elder came in.

To resume our story, Dame Wang looked at Hsi-men Ch'ing and said, "Now was that a good scheme, or wasn't it?"

"I'm greatly indebted to you, Godmother," said Hsi-men Ch'ing. "Truly:

> In intelligence you rival Sui Ho;
> In resourcefulness you outdo Lu Chia.

Not one woman out of ten could escape your designs."

"And did this filly live up to your expectations?" asked Dame Wang.

"Why:

> 'She's two under full four words'!"[6]

replied Hsi-men Ch'ing.

"She got her start in life as a privately owned singing girl," said the old lady. "There isn't much she doesn't know about anything. And it was all my doing that has:

> Cast you in the roles of man and wife, and
> Contrived to make you a couple.

Whatever you do, don't forget what you promised me."

"You really outdid yourself, Godmother," said Hsi-men Ch'ing. "When I get home I'll pick out an ingot of silver for you and bring it over myself.

> Whenever I promise anything,
> I never fail to deliver."

Dame Wang said:

> "My eyes are on the lookout for the flag of victory,
> My ears are always on the alert for good tidings.[7]

Just don't leave me in the predicament of:

> Trying to collect the fee for the professional mourners
> after the coffin has already been interred."[8]

Hsi-men Ch'ing replied:

> "Whenever one gets so much as a
> tangerine peel to eat;
> One should never forget Tung-t'ing Lake
> from whence it came."

Then, after checking to see that the coast was clear, he put on his eye shades, laughed, and departed. But no more of this.

The next day he returned to Dame Wang's shop and called for some tea. Dame Wang offered him a seat and hastened to pour out a cup for him. When he had finished his tea Hsi-men Ch'ing pulled a ten-tael ingot of silver out of his sleeve and handed it to Dame Wang.

Generally speaking, nothing moves the people of this world so much as money.

When the old lady's black eyes caught sight of this "snowflake" silver[9] she tucked it away:

> As though nothing in Heaven or Earth could
> make her happier,

and saluted Hsi-men Ch'ing with a double bow, saying, "Many thanks for your generosity, sir."

She then went on to say, "I haven't seen Wu the Elder go out yet. If you'll wait a minute, I'll step over there and ask to borrow a gourd dipper so I can see if he's still there."

And she proceeded to slip over to the woman's house by the back door. The woman was in the main room serving Wu the Elder his breakfast.

When she heard someone at the door she asked Ying-erh, "Who is it?"

"It's Granny Wang," Ying-erh replied. "She wants to borrow our gourd."

The woman hastened out to greet her, saying, "Godmother, the gourd's right here. You can have it whenever you want. Why don't you come in and sit down for a minute?"

"There's no one over there to tend the shop," said the old lady.

As she spoke she made a sign with her hand which the woman understood to mean that Hsi-men Ch'ing had come and was waiting for her.

As soon as her visitor had picked up the gourd dipper and gone out the door, the woman urged Wu the Elder to finish his breakfast, shoulder his carrying pole, and start on his way.

After going upstairs, redoing her makeup, and changing into an attractive new outfit, she said to Ying-erh, "I want you to look after the house for me. I'm just going over to your Granny Wang's place for a visit; I'll be back before long. If your daddy comes home, be sure to let me know. If you don't do as I say, you little wretch, I'll beat your bottom right off!"[10]

Ying-erh nodded her assent. But no more of this.

The woman went over to Dame Wang's teashop to keep her tryst with Hsi-men Ch'ing. Truly:

> The coupled halves of the peach stone
> serve to evoke a chuckle;
> Because inside, it will be found, lie
> yet another couple.[11]

There is a poem composed of double meanings that testifies to this:

> This gourd's a gourd, the mouth of which is small,
> the body large.
> When young, up in its breezy arbor,
> it's high-slung;
> But when it grows bigger, it becomes
> hard enough to bite.
> How could it have hung in there with Yen Hui,
> content with privation for principle's sake;[12]
> When all it wanted to do was bob about on the water
> in the spring breeze?
> When you really need it
> it falls down on the job;
> But whether you want it or not
> it's always hanging about;
> Until you feel you simply have to
> take it in hand.
> It contributes its stale share
> to the work of the stable;
> And is not infrequently called upon
> in the teahouse.

You may not want it any more than Hsü Yu did,[13]
but can scarcely do without it;
And from its dark interior you never know
what nostrum will come out.[14]

When Hsi-men Ch'ing saw the woman come in he felt:
Just as though she had fallen from Heaven.
The two of them sat down:
Shoulder to shoulder and thigh over thigh,
while Dame Wang served them a cup of tea.

"When you went home yesterday," the old lady inquired, "did Wu the Elder raise any questions?"

"He asked whether I had finished the work on your burial garments yet," the woman said. "I replied that the garments themselves were finished, but that I was still working on the shoes and stockings."

As soon as this problem had been disposed of the old lady made haste to provide some wine. She served it to them in her own room and they immediately fell to exchanging cups and enjoying themselves without restraint. Hsi-men Ch'ing examined the woman closely and she looked even more beautiful to him than the first time he had seen her. After a few drinks, the colors red and white formed a pleasing contrast on her powdered face, the temples of which were adorned with two long spit curls. Truly:
She was the equal of any immortal, and
Excelled even the goddess Ch'ang-o.
There is a song to the tune "Intoxicated in the East Wind" that testifies to this:

How provocative are the red and white tints
of her flesh;
How lovable is this delectable maid.
Trailing a silk skirt of halcyon hue,
Beneath the gathered sleeves of a gold-flecked
blouse;
In her joyous abandon her chignon has fallen askew.
She is the very picture of Ch'ang-o come down
from the moon;
The like of which you could not buy for a
thousand pieces of gold.[15]

Hsi-men Ch'ing couldn't say enough in her praise. Taking her onto his lap, he lifted her skirt far enough to catch a glimpse of her pair of tiny feet, enclosed in black satin shoes, just half a span in length. His heart was filled with delight. The two of them passed the same cup of wine back and forth between them and laughed and joked with each other.

The woman then asked Hsi-men Ch'ing, "How old are you?"

"I'm twenty-seven," he replied. "I was born in the year of the tiger on the twenty-eighth day of the seventh month, at midnight."

"How many ladies do you have in your household?" the woman asked.

"Aside from my wife," said Hsi-men Ch'ing, "I've got three or four other bedmates at home. It's just that none of them really tickles my fancy."

"And how many sons have you got?" the woman asked.

"All I have is a young daughter," said Hsi-men Ch'ing, "who's about to get married. I don't have any other children."

After they had laughed and joked with each other for a while, Hsi-men Ch'ing reached into his sleeve and pulled out a cylindrical silver pillbox that contained breath-sweetening lozenges[16] flavored with osmanthus. One at a time he proceeded to put these into the woman's mouth on the tip of his tongue. The two of them then fell to:

Hugging and embracing each other,
Like snakes darting out their tongues.
The sound of their sucking was audible.

Dame Wang was so preoccupied with serving food and pouring wine that she could hardly concern herself with what went on between them, and left them in her room to enjoy themselves as they pleased.

In a little while, when they had both had enough wine to:

Ignite the flames of desire,

Hsi-men Ch'ing's lustful thoughts got the better of him. Exposing the organ that lay between his loins, he induced the woman to manipulate it with her slender fingers.

It so happens that ever since his youth Hsi-men Ch'ing had frequented the streets and alleys of the licensed quarter and patronized the women who dwelt there. About the base of his member he wore a clasp that had been:

Beaten out of silver, and
Imbrued with drugs,

which had the effect of making that organ both large and long. It was:

Dark red, with black whiskers;
Straight standing, firm, and hard;

a fine object, indeed! There is a poem about its characteristics that testifies to this:

There is an object that has always been
about six inches long;
Sometimes it is soft and at other times
it is hard.
When soft, like a drunkard, it falls down
either to the east or the west;
When hard, like a mad monk, it runs amok
either above or below.

It makes it's living by traveling in and out
of virgin territory;
It makes its home beneath the navel in the
Province of the Loins.
It has two sons who always accompany it
wherever it goes;
In how many skirmishes, with how many beauties,
has it emerged the victor?

It was not long before the woman had taken off her clothes and Hsi-men Ch'ing discovered, by both visual and tactile means, that her mount of Venus had been depilated of its pubic hair. It was:

Pale and fragrant,
Plump to bursting,
Soft and yielding,
Red and wrinkly,
Tight and squeezy;
Beloved of thousands,
Craved by tens of thousands;
Who could tell what it might be?

There is a poem that testifies to this:

Warm and tight, fragrant and dry, it tastes
better than lotus root;
It knows how to be soft and yielding and to
make itself agreeable.
When happy, it sticks out its tongue, opens
its mouth, and smiles;
When tired, it collapses lazily into itself
and takes a nap.
The name of the place it makes its home
is Crotch County;
Its old garden is to be found beside the
sparsely wooded slopes.
If it should ever encounter a dashing
young gentleman;
It will engage him in battle, without a word,
on the slightest pretext.

To make a long story short, from that day on, the woman slipped over to Dame Wang's teashop every day to keep her tryst with Hsi-men Ch'ing.

Their feelings for each other were like lacquer;
The love in their hearts was like glue.

It has always been true that:

Good deeds seldom become known beyond the gate;
Bad deeds are quickly transmitted a thousand li.[17]

In less than half a month the whole neighborhood knew what was going on, with the sole exception of Wu the Elder, who remained in the dark. Truly:

The only thing he knew was that it was his duty
to abide by his lot;
What did he know about defending himself from
deceit or foul play?

There is a poem that testifies to this:

As always, "Good deeds seldom become known
beyond the gate";
Whereas bad deeds and evil talk are quickly
noised abroad.
How pitiful it is that Wu the Elder's
lawful wife;
Should surreptitiously become the consort
of Hsi-men Ch'ing.[18]

At this point the story divides into two. To resume our story, there was in the same district a certain youngster who was just fourteen or fifteen years old and whose surname was Ch'iao. Because he had been born in Yün-chou, where his father was serving in the army at the time, people referred to him by the nickname Yün-ko, or Little Yün. The only remaining member of his family was his father, who was now well advanced in years. The lad was clever by nature and managed to scrape a living by peddling fresh fruits in the wineshops that were clustered near the front gate of the district yamen. Hsi-men Ch'ing was one of his patrons and often gave him a little extra to help with his expenses.

One day he set out to look for Hsi-men Ch'ing with a basket of snow pears for sale. As he was going his rounds a certain busybody said to him, "Yün-ko, if that's who you're looking for, I can tell you a place where you'll be sure to find him."

"Thanks, Uncle," said Yün-ko. "If you help me find him I can pick up thirty or fifty cash toward the expenses of keeping my old father alive. You'll be doing a good deed."

"Listen to me," said the busybody. "Hsi-men Ch'ing is carrying on an affair with the wife of Wu the Elder, who sells steamed wheat cakes. Every day he can be found sitting around in Dame Wang's teashop on Amethyst Street. He's almost certainly there at this very moment. You're still just a kid, so even if you walk right in on him it won't make any difference."

On hearing this Yün-ko said, "Thanks for your help, Uncle."

The little monkey then picked up his basket and headed straight for Dame Wang's teashop in Amethyst Street. When he got there he found Dame Wang sitting on a short bench, spinning hemp thread.

Yün-ko put his basket down and bowed to Dame Wang with the words, "Greetings to you, Godmother."

"What brings you here, Yün-ko?" asked the old lady.

"I'm looking for the gentleman in order to pick up thirty or fifty cash toward the expenses of keeping my old father alive," said Yün-ko.

"What gentleman is that?" asked the old lady.

"You know perfectly well who I mean," said Yün-ko. "That's the one."

"He may be a gentleman," said the old lady, "but even gentlemen have names."

"I mean the one who has two characters in his surname," said Yün-ko.

"And what two characters might they be?" inquired the old lady.

"All you ever do is joke, Godmother," said Yün-ko. "I want to have a word with the Honorable Hsi-men."

As he said these words he proceeded to walk in toward the interior of the shop. The old lady grabbed hold of him with one hand and said, "Little monkey, where do you think you're going!

> In every house there are areas that are private,
> and areas that are public."

"If you'll just let me into your room," said Yün-ko, "I'll find him for you soon enough."

"You cocksucking little monkey!" Dame Wang cursed at him. "What would the Honorable Hsi-men be doing in my room?"

"Godmother," said Yün-ko:

> "Don't try to keep it all for yourself;
> Spare me a mouthful of leftover gravy.[19]

Do you think I don't know what's going on?"

"You little monkey!" cursed the old lady. "What do you know about anything!"

Yün-ko said, "You don't give much away do you? Truly:

> You do your chopping in a wooden ladle
> with a horseshoe blade:[20]
> Not one drop escapes;
> Not even half a drop ever hits the floor.

If you make me tell the whole story, I fear our brother who sells steamed wheat cakes may kick up a fuss."

When the old lady heard these words, which struck her right on her sore spot, she was enraged and shouted, "You cocksucking little monkey! You think you can come farting around my place, do you!"

"If I'm a little monkey," said Yün-ko, "you're nothing but a procuress, a pandering old bitch!"

Yün-ko in His Anger Raises a Rumpus in the Teashop

The old lady tightened her grip on Yün-ko and gave him a couple of sharp raps on the head with her knuckles.

"Who do you think you're hitting!" Yün-ko yelled at her.

"You lousy mother-fucking little monkey!" the old lady cursed. "If you raise your voice again I'll drive you out of here with a couple of good boxes on the ear!"

"You lousy old bloodsucker!" responded Yün-ko. "You think you can start a fight with me over nothing, do you!"

Pushing him before her with one hand around his neck, and rapping him on the head as hard as she could with the knuckles of her other hand, the old lady drove him right out into the street and threw his basket of snow pears after him. The snow pears went rolling hither and yon all over the street.

The old lady had been too much for the little monkey to handle. Cursing and crying and scurrying all over the street after his pears, he pointed at Dame Wang's teashop and unleashed a flood of imprecation.

"Don't you worry, you old bloodsucker! Just wait and see whether I tell him what's up and blow this whole thing wide open or not! By the time I'm through your shop will be a shambles and you'll have no way to make a living!"

At this point the little monkey picked up his basket and ran off to search the streets for a certain person, but he couldn't find him. If Yün-ko should find this person, truly:

> Though Dame Wang's deeds were done in the past,
> Today the chickens would come home to roost.[21]

As a result of this event:

> The Spirit of the Perilous Paths[22] would strip
>   himself for action;
> The little monkey's revelations would lead
>   to disaster.[23]

> If you don't know who Yün-ko set out to look for, and
> If you want to know the outcome of these events,
> Pray consult the story related in the following chapter.

Chapter 5

YÜN-KO LENDS A HAND
BY CURSING DAME WANG;
THE HUSSY ADMINISTERS POISON
TO WU THE ELDER

If you ever apprehend the Ch'an enigma
posed by the word "romance";
You'll find that good affinities often
turn out to be bad affinities.[1]
In the heat of passion, everyone
becomes enamored of it;
Looked at dispassionately, everyone
comes to despise it.[2]
The flowers by the wayside ought not
to be plucked;
Natural beauty and sound substance
are safer by far.
A rustic wife, your own children,
and everyday fare;
Are unlikely to lead to either
lovesickness or penury.[3]

THE STORY GOES that Yün-ko, after his rough treatment at the hands of Dame Wang, had no place to vent his spleen. When he picked up his basket and ran off to search the streets it was Wu the Elder that he was looking for. He hadn't gone more than two blocks when whom should he see but Wu the Elder, shouldering his load of steamed wheat cakes, coming along the very street he was on.

As soon as he saw him Yün-ko stopped in his tracks and said to Wu the Elder, "I haven't seen you for ages. You're really putting on the fat aren't you?"

Wu the Elder put down his carrying pole and said, "I'm just the same as I've always been. Since when am I putting on any fat?"

"The other day," said Yün-ko, "I wanted to buy some bran, but couldn't find any, no matter where I looked. Everyone said you had some at home."

"I don't raise geese or ducks," said Wu the Elder. "What would I want with bran?"

"You say you've no use for bran," said Yün-ko. "In that case, how did you get so overstuffed yourself? Even if I picked you up by the feet and put you in a pot to boil, you wouldn't let off any steam?"

"You cocksucking monkey!" said Wu the Elder. "That's a fine suggestion to make! My wife isn't playing at ducks and drakes with anyone, so why should you call me a 'duck'?"[4]

"If your wife isn't playing at ducks and drakes with anyone," said Yün-ko, "she's playing at drakes and ducks."

Wu the Elder grabbed hold of Yün-ko and said, "Tell me who it is then."

"You're laughable," said Yün-ko. "You may be brave enough to grab hold of me, but I'll bet you aren't brave enough to bite off his left one for him."

"Good Little Brother," said Wu the Elder, "Just tell me who it is and I'll give you ten steamed wheat cakes."

"Steamed wheat cakes alone won't do the trick," said Yün-ko. "But if you treat me to three cups of wine I'll tell you."

"I didn't know you could drink," said Wu the Elder. "Follow me."

Wu the Elder shouldered his carrying pole and led Yün-ko to a small wineshop. When they got there he put down his load, took along a few steamed wheat cakes, and then ordered up some meat and a jug of wine.

When Yün-ko had finished these off he said, "Don't bother with any more wine, but I could use a few more slices of meat."

"Good Little Brother," said Wu the Elder, "please! Tell me who it is."

"Don't worry," said Yün-ko, "I'll tell you as soon as I've finished eating. And don't get too upset. I'll help you to nab him."

When Wu the Elder had watched the monkey finish off the meat and wine he said, "Now, tell me who it is."

"If you want to know," said Yün-ko, "take your hand and feel these lumps on my head."

"Where did you ever get such lumps from?" asked Wu the Elder.

"I'll tell you," said Yün-ko. "Today I took this basket of snow pears and set out to look for the Honorable Hsi-men, in the hope of getting a little something out of him. But I couldn't find him anywhere I looked. Someone on the street told me, 'He's probably in Dame Wang's teashop. He's carrying on an affair with Wu the Elder's wife and hangs around there all the time.'

"I had hoped that if I ran into him I could pick up thirty or fifty cash to spend, but that intolerable old pig and dog, Dame Wang, not only wouldn't let me into her room to look for him, but drove me out of her place with a couple of sharp raps on the head with her knuckles. So I set out especially to look for you. When I ran into you just now I needled you a few times, deliberately. If I hadn't needled you, you never would have asked anything about it."

"Really," said Wu the Elder.

"Can such things be?"[5]

"There you go again," said Yün-ko. "I was afraid you might be just such a fart of a fuck-off! The two of them are certainly having an easy time of it. All they have to do is wait until you're out of the way and then make out together in Dame Wang's room. And you ask me if it's true or if it's false! Do you think I'm just kidding you for the fun of it?"

When Wu the Elder heard this he said, "Brother, there's no reason for me to deceive you. That woman of mine has been going over to Dame Wang's place every day, allegedly to help her with some sewing of clothes, or shoes and stockings. When she comes home her face is red. My first wife left a daughter behind, and whenever that woman feels like it she:

Beats her in the morning and curses her at night,[6]

or doesn't give her any food to eat. Moreover, the last couple of days she's been acting rather peculiar, as if she wasn't any too happy to see me. In fact, I've been wondering what was wrong myself. What you've told me would explain it. Now then, I'd better leave my load in a safe place and go catch them in the act. What do you say?"

"For a man of your age," said Yün-ko, "you haven't any sense. That old bitch, Dame Wang, is not to be trifled with. If you have a run-in with her you're not likely to escape unscathed. Moreover, the three of them must have a prearranged signal, so if the old lady sees you come in to nab them, your wife will have time to hide. That Hsi-men Ch'ing is a pretty tough customer. He can handle twenty of the likes of you. If you fail to catch them in the act you may end up getting a good drubbing for your pains. On top of which, he's got both money and influence. If he were to lodge a complaint against you, and you were dragged into court without anyone to take your side, you could easily end up losing your life for nothing."

"Brother," said Wu the Elder, "everything you say is true; but how can I let off this head of steam?"

"I took a beating at Dame Wang's hands," said Yün-ko, "and I too have no place to vent my spleen. Let me suggest a move to you. Today, when you go home, don't kick up a fuss or say anything about it. Just act the same way you do every day. Tomorrow morning, make a smaller number of steamed wheat cakes than usual and come out to sell them. I'll be lying in wait at the mouth of the alley, and when I see Hsi-men Ch'ing go in I'll come and tell you. You can then shoulder your carrying pole and wait nearby while I go in and distract the old bitch, who's sure to pick a fight with me. At that point I'll throw my fruit basket out into the middle of the street as a signal for you to come charging in. I'll pin the old lady against the wall with my head while you dash into the room and raise the hue and cry. How's that for a plan?"

"If it goes as you say, Brother," said Wu the Elder, "I'll be greatly indebted to you. I've got several strings of cash here which I'll give you. Be sure to be there first thing in the morning to wait for me at the mouth of the alley on Amethyst Street."

Yün-ko collected his few strings of cash and some steamed wheat cakes and then went his way. Wu the Elder, for his part, paid the bill, shouldered his carrying pole, and made another round before heading for home.

It so happens that the woman, accustomed as she was to railing at Wu the Elder and abusing him in every way, had been sufficiently troubled in recent days by a bad conscience to go out of her way to be nice to him. That evening when Wu the Elder came home, shouldering his carrying pole, he acted just the way he always did and didn't bring anything up.

"Darling," said the woman, "how about a cup of wine?"

"I've just had three cups with another vendor," said Wu the Elder.

The woman then prepared supper and they ate it together. Of the events of that evening there is no more to tell.

The next day, after breakfast, Wu the Elder made only two or three trays of steamed wheat cakes and loaded them on his carrying pole. The woman was too preoccupied with Hsi-men Ch'ing to notice how many wheat cakes he made. Wu the Elder shouldered his carrying pole and went out to ply his trade. The woman could hardly wait until he was out the door before slipping over to Dame Wang's teashop to wait for Hsi-men Ch'ing.

To resume our story, Wu the Elder shouldered his carrying pole and headed straight for the mouth of the alley on Amethyst Street, where he found Yün-ko already on the lookout, with his fruit basket in hand.

"Has anything happened?" asked Wu the Elder.

"It's early yet," said Yün-ko. "You might as well make one of your regular rounds. By the time you're through that bastard will probably have shown up. You just wait nearby, don't go too far away."

Like a cloud scudding before the wind, Wu the Elder completed one of his regular rounds and came back again.

"You just watch for my fruit basket," said Yün-ko. "When it comes flying out, you go charging in."

Wu the Elder stowed his load in a safe place. But no more of this.

There is a poem that testifies to this:

Tigers deploy the revenants of their prey,[7]
  birds are snared with decoys;
Victims remain in the dark until the trap is sprung,
  while predators do as they please.
Yün-ko exposes Hsi-men Ch'ing's crime
  for all to see;[8]
But Dame Wang's handling of the affair
  is remarkable indeed.

To resume our story, Yün-ko picked up his basket and headed straight for the teashop, where he opened fire on Dame Wang with the words, "You old pig and dog! Just who did you think you were hitting yesterday?"

The old lady's character remained unaltered. Jumping to her feet, she shouted at him, "You little monkey! I've never had anything to do with you. What are you coming around here to abuse me again for?"

"If I curse you," replied Yün-ko, "for being a procuress and a pandering old bitch, it matters about as much as my prick!"

The old lady was enraged and, grabbing hold of Yün-ko, started to beat him with her fists.

With the shout, "You dare to strike me, do you!" Yün-ko threw the fruit basket in his hand out into the middle of the street.

The old lady tried to get a firmer grip on him, but the little monkey, with another cry of "You dare to strike me, do you!" put both arms around Dame Wang's waist, buried his head in the pit of her stomach, and pushed for all he was worth. He nearly knocked her over, but she backed into the wall, which prevented her from falling down. The monkey held her pinned against the wall with all his strength.

At this point Wu the Elder lifted up his clothes and came charging into the teashop in giant strides. When the old lady saw who it was and realized that he meant business, she tried to block his path, but the little monkey continued to hold her pinned against the wall with all his strength and wouldn't let her budge. All the old woman could do was to yell out, "Wu the Elder has come!"

Inside Dame Wang's room the woman, who was already entwined with Hsi-men Ch'ing, was barely able to extricate herself fast enough to rush to the door and hold it fast. Hsi-men Ch'ing, for his part, proceeded to dive under the bed.

Wu the Elder charged up to the door and gave it a shove, but he was unable to push it open and could only call out, "That's a fine thing you're up to!"

The woman was in a state of panic. Continuing to hold the door shut she said, "You're always shooting off your fucking mouth, boasting about how good you are at the martial arts, but when it comes to the crunch you're no use at all! Even a paper tiger can scare you to death!"

The woman's words were clearly intended to get Hsi-men Ch'ing to confront Wu the Elder and fight his way out of the predicament. Hsi-men Ch'ing was still under the bed, but when he heard these words they had the effect of stimulating him to action.

Crawling out from his hiding place he said, "Lady, it's not that I don't have what it takes. It's just that, for the moment, I couldn't think what to do." Then, unbarring the door, he called out, "Come in, if you dare!"

Yün-ko Lends a Hand by Cursing Dame Wang

Wu the Elder made a grab at him, but Hsi-men Ch'ing countered with a swift kick, and his assailant was so short that Hsi-men Ch'ing caught him squarely in the solar plexus with his foot and knocked him flat on his back.

When Hsi-men Ch'ing saw that Wu the Elder was down and out he took advantage of the confusion to beat a hasty retreat. Yün-ko also, seeing that the situation had taken a turn for the worse, abandoned Dame Wang and took to his heels. The neighbors in the area all knew that Hsi-men Ch'ing was a tough customer, and none of them wanted to interfere in the matter.

At this point Dame Wang attempted to get Wu the Elder back on his feet. When she saw that he was spitting blood and that his face had turned as sallow as wax, she called the woman out to fetch a bowl of water, with the help of which they succeeded in reviving him. Putting his arms over their shoulders, the two of them managed to help him through the back door and up to the second story room of his own house, where they put him to bed. Of the events of that night there is nothing more to tell.

The next day, when Hsi-men Ch'ing found out that nothing had come of the incident, he showed up at Dame Wang's place to keep his tryst with the woman as usual. Their only hope was that Wu the Elder would die.

The injuries he had sustained were serious enough to keep him from getting up or going out for five days. On top of which:

When he wanted soup, there was none to be had;
When he wanted water, there was none to be had.[9]

Every day he called on his wife for help, but she refused to respond. He had to lie there and watch as she dolled herself up before going out, and when she returned her face was red.

The woman even prohibited his daughter, Ying-erh, from coming to his aid, threatening her with the words, "You little wretch! If you give him so much as a cup of water to drink without telling me, you'd better look out."

Ying-erh was so intimidated by this that she didn't dare serve her father a mouthful of soup. On several occasions Wu the Elder fainted away from sheer indignation, but there was no one to pay any attention.

One day Wu the Elder told his wife he had something important to say to her and addressed her as follows: "As for what you've been up to, I caught you red-handed in the act of adultery, and you turned around and egged your lover into kicking me in the solar plexus, so that now:

Though I seek to live, I cannot live;
Though I seek to die, I cannot die,[10]

while all the time the two of you are off enjoying yourselves together. If I die it scarcely matters. I don't have the strength to contend with you any longer. But my younger brother, Wu the Second—you know what sort of a person he is—when he returns—as he will, sooner or later—he'll scarcely be willing to call it quits. If you consent to take pity on me, and help me to recover as soon as possible, when he comes back I won't say anything about it. But if you refuse to look after me, when he comes home he'll have something to say to you."

When the woman heard this speech she made no reply but slipped over to Dame Wang's place and repeated it, word for word, to the old woman and Hsi-men Ch'ing. When Hsi-men Ch'ing heard what she had to say it was:

> Just as though he had been dunked in a
> tub of ice water.[11]

"That's bad!" he said. "I understand that Captain Wu who killed the tiger on Ching-yang Ridge is the number one stout fellow in Ch'ing-ho district. But right now:

> Having been lovers for many a day;
> Our feelings and thoughts are one,
> We can never agree to be separated.[12]

If what you say is true, what are we to do? It's a bad situation all right!"

Dame Wang laughed sardonically and said, "I've never seen anything like it. You're the helmsman and I'm merely a sculler, but I'm not worried about it while you're in a state of panic."

"I may be a man," said Hsi-men Ch'ing, "but for all that, when it comes to situations like this, I don't know what to do. If you've got any ideas, please do whatever you can to protect us."

"If you want me to protect you," said Dame Wang, "I've got a plan that should do the trick. Do you want to be 'long-term man and wife' or 'short-term man and wife'?"

"Godmother," said Hsi-men Ch'ing, "what do you mean by 'long-term man and wife' and 'short-term man and wife'?"

"If you want to be 'short-term man and wife,' " said Dame Wang, "you should separate from each other this very day, wait until Wu the Elder has recovered, and offer him an apology. Then, when Wu the Second comes back, he won't say anything about it, and you can wait until he's sent away on another mission to get together again. That's what I mean by 'short term man and wife.' But if you want to be 'long-term man and wife,' to spend every day together without having to:

> Anticipate surprise and suffer fear,[13]

I've got a splendid plan for you. The only thing is it's not an easy subject to broach."

"Godmother," said Hsi-men Ch'ing, "please help us out. The only thing we want is to be 'long-term man and wife.' "

"This plan," said Dame Wang, "requires something that no one else has got, but which you, sir:

> As Heaven begets so Heaven disposes,[14]

happen to possess."

"Even if it were my eyes you wanted," said Hsi-men Ch'ing, "I'd gouge them out and give them to you. What is this thing anyway?"

"Right now," said Dame Wang, "this 'knockabout'[15] is in pretty bad shape. This presents you with the opportunity to take action against him while he's incapacitated. You, sir, should go home and pick up some arsenic from your pharmaceutical shop and then get the young lady to buy a dose of heart medicine, mix the arsenic in with it, and polish off this runt once and for all. If you cremate the body afterward you'll have gotten him completely out of the way, without leaving a trace behind. Then, even if Wu the Second comes back, what will he be able to do about it? It's always been the case that:

> In one's first marriage one must obey one's parents;
> In subsequent marriages one can suit oneself.[16]

Your brother-in-law will have nothing to say in the matter. You can continue to see each other clandestinely, and after half a year or a year the dust will have settled. Then, as soon as the mourning period for your husband expires, the gentleman can pop you into a sedan chair and take you into his household as a concubine. Then you can be 'long-term man and wife' and:

> Live happily ever after.

How's that for a plan?"

"Godmother," said Hsi-men Ch'ing, "this plan is splendid indeed. It's always been true that:

> If one wants to be able to enjoy life,
> One has to be prepared to risk death.[17]

Enough! Enough! Enough! One must either:

> Refuse to do something;
> Or not stop at anything."[18]

"That's the spirit," said Dame Wang. "This is a situation in which:

> One must cut the weeds and pull up the roots,
> So that new sprouts will not grow;
> If one cuts the weeds without pulling up the roots,
> When spring comes new sprouts will grow.[19]

The only problem remaining is how to proceed. You, sir, should go straight home and bring this ingredient as quickly as possible. I'll instruct the young lady on what she is to do. When the affair is accomplished I expect to be amply rewarded."

"Naturally," said Hsi-men Ch'ing, "that goes without saying."

There is a poem that testifies to this:

> Obsessed with thoughts of clouds and rain,
> the two of them are inseparable;
> Yearning for beauty, hankering after flowers,
> he will not call it quits.

In the final analysis, in this world
such things do happen;
Wu the Elder will lose his life
at the hands of a painted face.[20]

To resume our story, Hsi-men Ch'ing had not been gone for long when he returned with a packet of arsenic, which he handed over to Dame Wang, who put it away.

Turning her attention to the woman, she said, "Young lady, I'll tell you how to administer the medicine. Didn't Wu the Elder say to you, this very day, that he wanted you to help him recover? You must take advantage of this opening by playing up to him with every trick at your disposal. If he asks you for any medication, mix this arsenic in with some heart medicine before administering it to him. If he realizes that something is wrong and starts to struggle, just pour the rest of it down his throat before you jump off the bed. When the poison starts to take effect his stomach and intestines will burst and he may cry out. You must muffle his cries with a quilt so no one will hear, holding the quilt in place as tightly as you can. You must also heat a pan of hot water beforehand and put a rag to soak in it. When the poison takes effect there may be hemorrhaging from all his seven apertures as well as telltale marks where he has bitten his lips. After he stops breathing you must remove the quilt, take the rag that you have soaked in hot water, and wipe away any signs of blood. Then he can be popped into a coffin, carted out of town, and cremated. There's nothing to it."

"That's all very fine," said the woman, "but I'm afraid, when the time comes, I may lose my nerve and be unable to handle the corpse."

"That's no problem," said the old lady. "Just knock on the wall and I'll come over to help you."

"Do the best you can," said Hsi-men Ch'ing. "Tomorrow morning at the fifth watch I'll come by to see what's happened." Having said which, he made his way home.

Dame Wang took the arsenic and rolled it between her fingers into a fine powder, after which she gave it to the woman to take home and hide away in a safe place. The woman went upstairs to see how Wu the Elder was and found him:

With barely two breaths left in his body,[21]

manifestly on the brink of death. The woman sat down on the side of the bed and pretended to weep.

"What are you weeping about?" asked Wu the Elder.

The woman wiped away her tears and said, "In a moment of weakness I let that Hsi-men Ch'ing take advantage of me, but I never expected he would end up kicking you in the solar plexus. I've heard of a place that has good prescriptions for sale, and I'd like to go buy one for you, but I'm afraid you might be suspicious, so I haven't ventured to go and get it."

"If you help me to recover," said Wu the Elder, "so I'm all right again, I'll:

Wipe the slate clean with a single stroke,[22]

and won't even hold a grudge against you. When Wu the Second comes back I won't say anything about it. Please go buy the medicine as quickly as possible and help me to recover."

The woman picked up some copper cash and went directly to Dame Wang's place, where she sat down and got the old lady to buy the medicine for her.

Then she took it back upstairs and showed it to Wu the Elder, saying, "This is a dose of heart medicine. The doctor said if you take it late in the evening and then get a good night's sleep, with a couple of quilts over you to make you sweat, you can be up and about tomorrow."

"That's wonderful," said Wu the Elder. "I'm putting you to a lot of trouble. If you're willing to sacrifice a little sleep tonight, you can stay up and fix it for me when the time comes."

"Just relax and try to get some sleep," said the woman. "I'll take care of everything for you."

Gradually darkness began to fall. In the house the woman lit a lamp and heated a large pan of hot water, into which she put a rag to soak. She listened for the sound of the drum that signaled the night watches and eventually heard the third watch struck. First the woman poured the arsenic into a cup and then she scooped up a bowl of boiling water and took them upstairs.

"Darling, where did you put the medicine?" she called out.

"It's under the bed mat, beside my pillow," said Wu the Elder. "Hurry up and fix it for me."

The woman lifted up the mat, shook the medicine into the cup, and set the packet aside. Then she poured the hot water into the cup and, pulling a silver hairpin out of her hair, used it to stir the contents until it was all dissolved. With her left hand she helped Wu the Elder sit up in bed while with her right hand she held the medicine to his mouth.

Wu the Elder swallowed a mouthful and said, "Darling, this medicine really tastes awful."

"As long as it cures what ails you," the woman said, "what difference does it make whether it tastes awful or not?"

While Wu the Elder was swallowing his second mouthful the woman took advantage of the situation to pour the entire contents of the cup down his throat in one gulp. Then she laid him back down and hastily jumped off the bed.

Wu the Elder gave a groan and said, "Darling, no sooner did I swallow the medicine than my stomach began to hurt. It's bad! It's bad! It's more than I can take."

The woman then proceeded to take two quilts from the foot of the bed and put them hugger-mugger over his head and face.

"I'm suffocating," called out Wu the Elder as loudly as he could.

"The doctor told me," the woman responded, "that if I really made you sweat you'd get better that much faster."

Wu the Elder tried to say something more, but the woman was afraid he might put up a struggle so she jumped onto the bed, sat astride Wu the Elder's body,[23] and pressed down on the edge of the quilt with all her might, not letting up to the slightest degree. Truly:

Hot grease sears his chest and lungs;
Flames scorch his liver and intestines.
His heart cavity is encroached upon
by gleaming blades;
His entrails are rudely invaded
by steely knives.
His whole body feels as cold as ice;
His seven apertures all begin to hemorrhage.
His teeth are tightly clenched;
His three ethereal souls flee to the
City of the Unjustly Dead.
His throat is dry and parched;
His seven material souls head for the
Terrace of Homeward Gazing Spirits.[24]
The legions of Hell are further augmented
by one poison-eating ghost;
The world of the living is diminished
by one adulterer-seizing man.[25]

At this point Wu the Elder groaned twice and panted for a little while. Then his stomach and intestines burst and:

Alas and alack,

he was no longer able to move.

When the woman removed the quilt and saw that Wu the Elder had been:

Grinding and gnashing his teeth,[26]

and that he had hemorrhaged from all seven apertures, she was afraid. It was all she could do to jump off the bed and knock on the wall. When Dame Wang heard the knock she came over to the back door and gave a cough, at which the woman came downstairs to let her in.

"Is it all over or not?" asked Dame Wang.

"It's all over all right," said the woman, "but I've lost my nerve and can't handle it."

"What's so hard about it?" said Dame Wang. "I'll help you take care of everything."

The old lady rolled up her sleeves, scooped up a bucketful of hot water, threw the rag into it, and lugged it upstairs. Then she rolled up the quilts,

The Hussy Administers Poison to Wu the Elder

wiped away all traces of coagulated blood from around Wu the Elder's lips and seven apertures, and placed his clothes on top of the body. The two of them then carried him downstairs, one step at a time, and laid him out on the leaf of an old door. Once there, they combed his hair, placed a turban on his head, dressed him, and put on his shoes and stockings. Then they stretched a strip of white damask over his face and covered the corpse with a clean quilt. After they had gone back upstairs and cleaned everything up, Dame Wang went home and the woman commenced the charade of loudly bewailing the loss of her provider.

Gentle reader take note: It so happens that, generally speaking, the women of this world have three ways of weeping. If there are tears as well as sound, it is called weeping. If there are tears but no sound, it is called sobbing. If there are no tears but there is sound, it is called howling.[27]

The woman howled, without shedding a tear, for the remainder of the night.

The next morning at the fifth watch, before it was light, Hsi-men Ch'ing hurried over to find out what had happened. When Dame Wang had told him all the details he pulled out some silver and gave it to her to cover the cost of a coffin and the other funeral arrangements. Then they called the woman over for a conference.

When the woman arrived she said to Hsi-men Ch'ing, "Now that Wu the Elder is dead I'm completely dependent on you, sir. Don't put me in the position of:

> The rings that hold your hairnet in place: always
> at the back of your head."[28]

"What need is there for you to trouble yourself about that?" said Hsi-men Ch'ing.

"And if you should betray me," the woman asked, "what then?"

"If I ever betray you," said Hsi-men Ch'ing, "may I suffer the same fate as your Wu the Elder."

"Sir," said Dame Wang, "that's enough idle chatter for the time being. Right now there's only one thing that's important. Later this morning the local constable must supervise the encoffining ceremony, and if the coroner's assistant notices anything suspicious, what will we do then? The head coroner's assistant, Ho the Ninth, doesn't miss a trick. My only fear is that he may not permit the encoffining."

"That's no problem," said Hsi-men Ch'ing with a laugh. "I'll simply tell Ho the Ninth what to do. He wouldn't dare refuse a request from me."

"You'd better go speak to him immediately," said Dame Wang, "before it's too late."

Having turned the silver over to Dame Wang to buy the coffin, Hsi-men Ch'ing then went off to deal with Ho the Ninth. Truly:

The three luminaries cast shadows, but
who can catch them;
The ten thousand things have no roots, they
just arise of themselves.[29]
Concealed by the snow, the presence of the egrets
is not seen until they fly;
Hidden by the willows, the existence of the parrots
is not known until they speak.[30]

If you don't know what Hsi-men Ch'ing said to Ho
the Ninth, and
If you want to know the outcome of these events,
Pray consult the story related in the following chapter.

Chapter 6

HSI-MEN CH'ING SUBORNS HO THE NINTH;
DAME WANG FETCHES WINE
AND ENCOUNTERS A DOWNPOUR

How reprehensible is the wanton fellow, enamored
of the flowers by the wayside;
It is because of his insatiable lust that he
brings troubles on his head.
His body will perish and his life be lost
solely on this account;
His property will be destroyed and his family ruined
for this reason alone.
Romantic passion lasts but a moment; what value
does it have?
Its taste is quite ordinary; it is
nothing to boast about.
One day "catastrophe will arise within the
screen-wall of the house";[1]
And it will owe its inception to the
machinations of Dame Wang.[2]

THE STORY GOES that Hsi-men Ch'ing went off to deal with Ho the Ninth.

To resume our story, Dame Wang took the silver and set out to buy a coffin and appropriate objects to bury with the dead. She also bought incense, candles, paper money, and so forth. After she had returned she consulted with the woman, and they lighted a vigil lamp and placed it before Wu the Elder's spirit tablet.

The neighbors from the locality all came to see what was going on, and the woman pretended to hide her painted face as she shed crocodile tears.

"What illness did Wu the Elder die of?" the neighbors asked.

"My husband suffered from severe pains in the region of the heart," the woman replied. "Who could have anticipated that they would grow worse and worse as the days went by, until it became apparent that he was unlikely to recover? Unfortunately last night, during the third watch, he died. It's really terrible!" And she commenced once more the charade of loud weeping and wailing.

The neighbors were perfectly well aware that the deceased had died under suspicious circumstances, but they did not venture to inquire into them any too closely. They all attempted to comfort her with the words, "The dead are dead. The living must get on as best they can. Try to control your grief, young lady. The weather's too hot for it."

The woman had no choice but to pretend to thank them all, and they went their separate ways.

When Dame Wang had supervised the delivery of the coffin she went out again to request the attendance of the head coroner's assistant, Ho the Ninth, and to buy everything that was required for the encoffining ceremony and other household needs. Then she went to the Pao-en Temple, or Temple of Kindness Requited, and engaged two Ch'an monks to come that evening to keep vigil and perform a mass for the dead. It was not long before Ho the Ninth sent a couple of coroner's assistants ahead of him to take care of the preliminaries.

To resume our story, at about 10:00 A.M. Ho the Ninth himself set forth at a leisurely pace. When he arrived at the mouth of the alley on Amethyst Street he encountered Hsi-men Ch'ing, who called out to him, "Ho the Ninth, where are you headed?"

"I'm just going down the street here," replied Ho the Ninth, "to encoffin the corpse of Wu the Elder, who sold steamed wheat cakes."

"Walk a few steps with me," said Hsi-men Ch'ing. "I've got something to say to you."

Ho the Ninth followed Hsi-men Ch'ing into a small wineshop on the corner, where they occupied a private booth.

"Old Ninth, please take the seat of honor," said Hsi-men Ch'ing.

"Who am I," said Ho the Ninth, "to presume to sit down in your presence, sir?"

"Old Ninth," said Hsi-men Ch'ing, "why be so standoffish? Please, have a seat."

The two of them dickered politely for a while and then sat down. Hsi-men Ch'ing ordered the waiter to bring a bottle of their best wine. The waiter set out an array of appetizers, nuts, and so forth, suitable to accompany a drinking party, and then heated the wine for them.

Ho the Ninth was somewhat apprehensive. "Hsi-men Ch'ing has never bothered to have a drink with me before," he thought to himself. "This cup of wine today is sure to have something funny behind it."

The two of them had been drinking together for some time when, lo and behold, Hsi-men Ch'ing fumbled in his sleeve, pulled out an ingot of "snowflake" silver, and placed it in front of him, saying, "Old Ninth, please don't despise this, insignificant though it may be. I'll give you a further expression of my gratitude another day."

Ho the Ninth folded his hands in front of him and said, "Having never done the slightest thing to deserve it, sir, how could I possibly accept this

Hsi-men Ch'ing Suborns Ho the Ninth

silver from you? But if you have a command, sir, I could scarcely presume to refuse."

"Old Ninth," said Hsi-men Ch'ing, "don't be so standoffish. Please take it."

"Tell me what you have in mind, sir," said Ho the Ninth, "no matter what it is."

"It isn't anything much," said Hsi-men Ch'ing, "and in a little while the family will also give you something for your pains. The only thing is, right now, when you encoffin Wu the Elder's corpse, I'd be much obliged if you'd take care of everything, and:

> Draw an embroidered quilt over it,[3]

that's all. Need I say more?"

"I thought you were going to ask me to do something demanding," said Ho the Ninth. "What does a little thing like that matter? How could I possibly accept your silver for that, sir?"

"Old Ninth," said Hsi-men Ch'ing, "if you don't accept it, you'll be refusing me."

Ho the Ninth had always been rather afraid of Hsi-men Ch'ing for his unscrupulousness and his influence in official quarters, so he felt that he had no recourse but to accept the proffered silver.

After they had finished another few cups of wine, Hsi-men Ch'ing summoned the waiter and said, "Put it on the tab and come to my shop to collect the money tomorrow."

The two of them then went downstairs and out the door of the wineshop.

As they were on the point of parting Hsi-men Ch'ing said, "Old Ninth, be sure to remember. If you keep your mouth shut I'll reward you further on another day."

Having issued his instructions, he then went about his business.

Ho the Ninth was somewhat apprehensive. "It's my responsibility to encoffin Wu the Elder's corpse," he thought to himself. "Why should he give me these ten taels of silver? There's sure to be something funny about this business."

When he arrived at the door of Wu the Elder's house he found the pair of coroner's assistants that he had sent ahead waiting for him there. Dame Wang had also been waiting for a long time and had been questioning them about his whereabouts.

Ho the Ninth asked the coroner's assistants, "What illness did Wu the Elder die of?"

"His family says he died of heart trouble," said the coroner's assistants.

Ho the Ninth approached the door, pulled the hanging blind aside, and went inside.

Dame Wang greeted him with the words, "We've been waiting for you a long time. The Yin-yang Master's already been here half the day. Old Ninth, what's been keeping you so long?"

"Something came up that prevented me from getting here any sooner," said Ho the Ninth. "I'm afraid I'm a little late."

At this point he caught sight of the woman who came out from the interior of the house dressed in plain white clothes, with a white paper cap over her chignon, feigning tears.

"Try to control your grief, young lady," said Ho the Ninth. "Your husband is surely in Heaven by now."

The woman pretended to wipe away her tears, saying, "I can't tell you how terrible it is. My husband was stricken with heart trouble and in only a few days lost his life, just like that. It's really terrible to be so bereaved."

Ho the Ninth looked the woman over from top to toe and thought to himself, "Hitherto I've only heard tell of Wu the Elder's wife without ever having set eyes on her myself. So this is the sort of woman Wu the Elder managed to keep in his house. Hsi-men Ch'ing's ten taels of silver have not been spent for nothing."

Then he went over by the spirit tablet and prepared to examine Wu the Elder's corpse. As soon as the Yin-yang Master had finished reciting his text, Ho the Ninth lifted aside the funeral banderole and removed the strip of white damask that had been stretched over the face of the deceased. No sooner did he concentrate the gaze of those vigilant organs of his, with their:

> Five concentric rings,
> Eight precious attributes, and
> Two spots of magic liquid,[4]

than he perceived that Wu the Elder's:

> Fingernails were black,
> Lips were purple,
> Face was sallow,
> Eyes protruded,[5]

and knew he had been poisoned.

The two coroner's assistants who were standing to either side asked him, "Why is it that his face is purple, there are toothmarks on his lips, and signs of bleeding around his mouth?"

"Don't talk such nonsense!" said Ho the Ninth. "The weather's been extremely hot the last couple of days. A certain amount of deterioration is unavoidable under the circumstances."

He then proceeded, hugger-mugger,[6] to go through the motions of a formal examination of the corpse, presided over the encoffining, and directed his subordinates to drive the two "longevity nails" into either side of the lid of the casket.

Dame Wang did her best to expedite the proceedings and when they were finished produced a string of cash for Ho the Ninth and his men and sent them on their way.

"When will the interment take place?" he asked.

"The lady of the house," replied Dame Wang, "wants the funeral procession to take place on the third day, after which the body will be cremated outside the city wall."

The coroner's assistants then went their separate ways.

That evening the woman laid on a feast and invited guests. The second day four monks were engaged to recite sutras. Early on the morning of the third day, during the fifth watch, the coroner's assistants came to carry the coffin. There were also a few neighbors from the locality who put on mourning and joined in the funeral procession.

The woman donned her mourning attire, sat in a sedan chair, and all along the way continued the charade of loudly bewailing the loss of her provider. When they arrived at the crematorium outside the city walls a fire was ignited, the coffin, along with Wu the Elder's corpse, was completely incinerated, and his bones were scattered in the pond provided for that purpose.

It so happens that the refreshments provided for the guests at the funeral ceremony that day were all paid for by Hsi-men Ch'ing.

When the woman returned home she set up a spirit tablet in the upstairs room on which were inscribed the words "Spirit Tablet of My Deceased Husband, Wu the Elder." In front of the spirit tablet she lit a glass lamp, hung up some gilded funeral streamers, and made offerings of paper money, imitation gold and silver ingots, and the like.

That day when Hsi-men Ch'ing and the woman got together they sent Dame Wang back to her own home. The two of them then went upstairs and enjoyed themselves to their hearts' content. It was no longer the way it had been in Dame Wang's teashop when they had been confined to the furtive pleasures of:

Snitching chickens and filching dogs.[7]

Now that Wu the Elder was dead there was no one in the house to hinder them and they were able to:

Give free rein to their desires, and
Sleep together all night long.[8]

At the outset Hsi-men Ch'ing had been worried that the neighbors would realize what was going on, so he had always made a point of sitting around in Dame Wang's place for a while to keep up appearances. But now that Wu the Elder was dead he brought his body servant with him and went straight into the woman's house through the back door.

From this time on, he and the woman were inseparable.

Passion pervaded their breasts;
Their mutual love was like glue.[9]

He often stayed over with her for three or five nights in a row without going home. As a result, the members of his household, both high and low, were:

All at sevens and eights,

and became increasingly unhappy about the situation.

It so happens that the allure of feminine beauty ensnares men in such a way that:

Where there is initial success,
There will be ultimate disaster.[10]

There is a lyric to the tune "Partridge Sky" that testifies to this:

With lustful daring as big as the sky they can
no longer control themselves;
Their passions deep, their love fast, the two
are inseparable.[11]
In their greed for pleasure they no longer care
whether they live or die;
When infatuated who bothers to engage in
self-cultivation?

As affection grows deeper,
The passions cloy;
The greater the love, the more long-lasting
the resentment.
If one wished to dispel the enmity between
the states of Wu and Yüeh;[12]
Earth might age and Heaven waste away
before it could be accomplished.

Light and darkness alternate swiftly;
The sun and moon shoot back and forth like shuttles.

More than two months had now elapsed since Hsi-men Ch'ing and the woman first consummated their affair. One day the Dragon Boat Festival, on the fifth day of the fifth month, rolled around. Behold:

The swaying branches of the green willows
hang like emerald threads;
The spots of color formed by the pomegranate blossoms
are as red as rouge.
Ever so slightly, the breeze disturbs the curtains;
In whispering gusts, its coolness invades the doors.
Far and near, when the Dragon Boat Festival comes round;
In every house, goblets are raised in celebration.

Hsi-men Ch'ing was on his way back from a visit to the fair at the Temple of the God of the Eastern Peak[13] when he stopped in at Dame Wang's teashop and sat down.

The old woman hastily poured out a cup of tea and asked, "Where are you coming from, sir; and why don't you go over and look in on the young lady?"

"I've been at the temple fair today," said Hsi-men Ch'ing. "On a festive occasion like this she's very much on my mind, so I thought I'd come pay her a visit."

"Her mother, old Mrs. P'an, is here today," said Dame Wang. "I doubt if she's left yet. I'll run over there for a look and then report back to you, sir."

When the old lady went over to her neighbor's house by way of the back door she found her drinking wine with old Mrs. P'an, just as she had expected.

As soon as the woman saw who it was she hastened to offer her a seat and said, with a smile, "Godmother, you've arrived in the nick of time. Keep my mother company, and:

> If you drink a cup of wine on entering the door,
> You'll bear a bonny baby some day."[14]

"I haven't any old man," laughed the old lady, "so how could I produce a baby? But you're young and strong, perfectly fitted to produce one."

To which the woman replied, "As the saying goes:

> Young flowers bear no fruit;
> It's the old flowers that bear the fruit."

At this, Dame Wang turned to old Mrs. P'an and said, "Just look at the liberties your daughter takes with me. She's calling me an 'old beggar.'[15] But she'll find a use for this 'old beggar' yet."

"She's been sharp-tongued like that ever since she was a child," said old Mrs. P'an. "You've got to make allowances for her, Godmother."

It so happens that Dame Wang, having brought Hsi-men Ch'ing and the woman together, and enabled them to consummate their affair, devoted herself, early and late, to running errands for them, going out with the jug to buy wine, and so forth, and was dependent for her living on what she could make out of these transactions.

So she said to Chin-lien's mother, old Mrs. P'an, "This daughter of yours is just as clever as can be. She's a fine woman, make no mistake about it. I wonder what sort of man will have the luck to possess her in the future?"

"Godmother," said old Mrs. P'an, "since you're a matchmaker we must count entirely on you to bring that matter to a happy conclusion."

In the meantime the woman provided another place setting and poured out a cup of wine for her. Dame Wang drank a few cups with them until her face became bright red, but she was worried about keeping Hsi-men Ch'ing waiting too long, so she took the first opportunity to tip the woman a wink, said goodbye, and went home.

The woman realized that Hsi-men Ch'ing had come and did her best to expedite her mother's departure. Then she tidied up the room, lit some exotic incense, removed the remains of the repast she had been sharing with her mother, and prepared a brand new supply of wine and delicacies for the entertainment of Hsi-men Ch'ing. When that gentleman appeared on the terrace at the back of the house the woman came down the stairs to meet him, led him upstairs, greeted him with a bow, and offered him a seat.

It so happens that ever since Wu the Elder's death the woman had shown no inclination to wear mourning. She had put her husband's spirit tablet in a corner of the upstairs room and covered it with a sheet of white paper, and she neglected to set any offerings of soup or rice before it. Every day she dolled herself up, put on bright-colored clothing, made herself as attractive as possible, and enjoyed herself with Hsi-men Ch'ing.

Hsi-men Ch'ing had not visited her for the last two days, so the woman started out by giving him a hard time. "You unfaithful scoundrel! What do you mean by abandoning me like that? You must have found another sweetheart somewhere to think you can just leave me in the cold and neglect to pay any further attention to me."

"One of my concubines died the other day," said Hsi-men Ch'ing, "and I've been busy with the funeral arrangements for the last two days. Today I went to the temple fair and bought some hair ornaments, jewelry, clothes, and the like for you."

The woman was delighted by this. Hsi-men Ch'ing called in his page boy, Tai-an, and then took the gifts out of the felt bag he had been carrying and showed them to her one at a time. Not until he was finished did the woman bow in thanks and put them away.

The woman had beaten her stepdaughter, Ying-erh, into such a state of terrified submission that she no longer felt it necessary to conceal anything from her and actually ordered her to serve tea to Hsi-men Ch'ing. The woman herself set the table in order to keep him company while he drank his tea.

"There's no need for you to bother," said Hsi-men Ch'ing. "I've already given the money to Godmother to go out and buy wine, meat, appetizers, nuts, and so forth. On a festive occasion like this I wanted to spend a little time with you."

"This was originally prepared for my mother," said the woman, "but I saved enough of it to make a complete meal. If we wait until Godmother gets back it may be quite a while. Why don't we go ahead and start?"

The woman sat down next to Hsi-men Ch'ing:

> Cheek to cheek,
> Thigh to thigh, and
> Shoulder to shoulder,

and they began to drink wine together.

To resume our story, Dame Wang had picked up a basket, taken along an eighteen-ounce steelyard, and gone out into the street to buy wine and meat.

It happened, at that time, to be early in the fifth month, when heavy rains were a frequent occurrence. Though the red sun might appear to dominate the sky, a thunderhead might appear at any moment and release a downpour like an overturned basin. Behold:

Black clouds arise on all sides;
Dark fog immures the far heavens.
With a rushing sound,
It flies along, filling the heavens and
  blocking out the sun;
With pattering drops,
It beats a tattoo, as it strikes against
  the leaves of the plantain.
Assailed by a wild wind,
Skyscraping old cypresses
  are overturned;
Battered by thunderclaps,
The peaks of Mounts T'ai, Hua, Sung, and Ch'iao
  are shaken.
It quenches the flames and dispels the heat;
It moistens and nurtures the sprouts in the fields.
It quenches the flames and dispels the heat,
So that beauties are prone to appreciate it.
It moistens and nurtures the sprouts in the fields,
So that travelers are willing to forget the mud.

Truly:

The waters of the Yangtze, Huai, Yellow, and Chi rivers
  are newly augmented;
The emerald bamboo and the red pomegranate blossoms
  are rendered pristine.[16]

The old lady had picked up a bottle of wine, bought a basketful of fish, meat, chicken, goose, vegetables, fruit, nuts, and the like, and was returning along the street when she encountered this downpour. She ducked under the eaves of a house as quickly as she could and wrapped a kerchief around her head, but her clothes were completely soaked. She waited a while, until the rain let up a bit, and then raced for home like a cloud scudding before the wind.

Once inside the door, she put the provisions in the kitchen and then went upstairs, where she found the woman and Hsi-men Ch'ing drinking wine together.

"While you and the young lady have been living it up, sir," she said with an ingratiating smile, "just look at what's happened to my clothes. They're completely soaked. I'll have to ask you to replace them for me, sir."

"Just look at the old lady," said Hsi-men Ch'ing. "Did you ever see such an inveterate scrounger?"

Dame Wang Fetches Wine and Encounters a Downpour

"I'm no inveterate scrounger," said the old lady, "but at the very least, sir, you'll have to provide me with a bolt of aquamarine material."

"Godmother," said the woman, "what you need is some hot wine."

The old lady drank three cups with them and then said, "I'm going down to the kitchen to dry out my clothes."

After she had suited her actions to her words she cut up the chicken and goose, prepared the appetizers, put the fruit and nuts and so forth onto plates and saucers, and set them out in the upstairs room, together with some newly heated wine.

Hsi-men Ch'ing and the woman:

Poured out some more of the superior wine,
Shared with each other the rare repast, and
Fell to exchanging cups, thigh over thigh.

As he was drinking Hsi-men Ch'ing noticed that there was a *p'i-p'a*, or balloon guitar, hanging on the wall, and said, "I've heard for some time what a fine musician you are. Today, whatever happens, you'll have to entertain me with a song while I drink my wine."

"I only picked up a few lines when I started to study music as a child," laughed the woman. "I'm really not very good. You mustn't laugh at me, sir."

Hsi-men Ch'ing took the *p'i-p'a* down from the wall, lifted the woman onto his lap, and watched her as she placed the instrument on her knees:

Deftly extended her slender fingers,
Gently manipulated the icy strings,

and played a languid accompaniment as she sang a song to the tune "Liang-t'ou nan":

Without her headdress, too indolent
to perform her toilet,
Her clouds of black silk coiled in a chignon
and gleaming over her temples,
She fastens them in place with a slanting
gold hairpin.
She calls out, "Maidservant,
Open the clothes chest for me,
So I can put on an outfit of plain white silk."
So attired, she rivals Hsi-shih herself
in loveliness.
Emerging from her boudoir,
She calls out, "Maidservant,
Roll up the blind for me,
So I can burn a stick of evening incense."[17]

When Hsi-men Ch'ing heard this he was so delighted he scarcely knew what to do with himself.

Putting an arm around her powdered neck, he gave her a kiss as he praised her performance, saying, "Darling, whoever would have thought you were as smart as all that? Not one of the singing girls I've known in the streets and alleys of the licensed quarter can play or sing as well as you do."

"After all you've done for me," laughed the woman, "I'm content, for the present, to be:

Obedient to your every whim.

Just be sure you don't forget me in the future."

Hsi-men Ch'ing pinched her cheeks and said, "How could I ever forget you, darling?"

The two of them were:

Entranced by the clouds and intoxicated by the rain,[18]
Laughing and joking at each other's expense.

After a while Hsi-men Ch'ing took off one of her embroidered shoes, held it in his hand while he put a little cup of wine in it, and then drank a "shoe cup"[19] for the fun of it.

"My feet aren't as small as all that," said the woman. "Don't make fun of me, sir."

It wasn't long before the two of them began to feel the effects of the wine, whereupon they closed the door of the room, took off their clothes, got into bed, and began to play with each other.

Dame Wang put the crossbar on the front door and joined Ying-erh in the kitchen, where they made short work of the leftovers.

The two lovers in the upstairs room:

Tumbled and tossed like male and female phoenixes,[20]
As inseparable as fish from water,[21]

as they gave themselves over completely to pleasure. The woman's mastery of the arts of the bedchamber was equal to that of any prostitute, and she pulled out all the stops in her endeavors to please her partner. Hsi-men Ch'ing, too, was on his mettle and eager to:

Display his spearsmanship,[22]

to best advantage.

A woman of beauty and a man of talent,
Both of them were in the prime of life.

There is a poem that describes the picture they presented:

In the seclusion of the nuptial chamber
  the pillow and mat are cool;
The man of talent and woman of beauty
  approach the climax of their game.

No sooner have they embarked on "dipping the
red candle upside down";[23]
Than they suddenly switch to "punting
the boat by night."[24]
Rifling its fragrance, "the butterfly nibbles at
the calyx of the flower";[25]
Sporting with the water, "the dragonfly
darts, now high, now low."
When pleasure reaches its height passions are
intense, and feelings know no bounds;
As the mouth of the "divine turtle"
disgorges its "silvery stream."[26]

That day Hsi-men Ch'ing dallied in the woman's house until evening fell. As he was about to go home he left behind a few pieces of loose silver[27] to take care of her expenses. The woman did her best to keep him a while longer, but to no avail. Hsi-men Ch'ing put on his eye shades, walked out the door, and departed. After the woman had taken down the blind, closed the front door, and drunk a little more wine with Dame Wang, they went their separate ways. Truly:

Lingering at the door she saw young Master Liu
upon his way;
Amid the misty waters and the peach blossoms he was
soon lost to sight.[28]

If you want to know the outcome of these events,
Pray consult the story related in the following chapter.

Chapter 7

AUNTIE HSÜEH PROPOSES A MATCH WITH MENG YÜ-LOU; AUNT YANG ANGRILY CURSES CHANG THE FOURTH

I play the role of matchmaker and am really
 rather good at it;
Entirely owing to the assiduity with which
 I ply my two legs.[1]
My lethal lips are practiced at persuading
 widowers to remarry;
My trenchant tongue is capable of stirring
 the chaste widow's heart.
Lucky ribbons of festive red constantly
 adorn my head;
Party favors from wedding feasts are always
 present in my sleeves.
There is only one thing wrong
 with what I do;
Half my clients are helped but
 the other half are ruined.

THE STORY GOES that one day the same Auntie Hsüeh who was constantly to be seen around Hsi-men Ch'ing's household peddling costume jewelry set out with her box of trinkets and looked everywhere for Hsi-men Ch'ing but was unable to find him. Chancing to meet his page boy, Tai-an, she asked, "Where is your master?"

"Father's in the shop," replied Tai-an, "going over the accounts with Uncle Fu the Second."

It so happens that Hsi-men Ch'ing's family were the proprietors of a wholesale pharmaceutical business, the hired manager of which was named Fu Ming. His courtesy name was Tzu-hsin, and he was the second sibling in his generation of the family, which is why he was referred to as Uncle Fu the Second.

Auntie Hsüeh went straight to the door of the shop, pulled the hanging blind aside, and saw that Hsi-men Ch'ing was indeed inside, going over the accounts with his manager. She nodded to him and motioned for him to come outside. On seeing that it was Auntie Hsüeh, Hsi-men Ch'ing immediately abandoned his manager and came out to meet her, the two of them walking to a secluded spot where they could talk in private.

Auntie Hsüeh bowed to him with a word of greeting, and Hsi-men Ch'ing asked her what she had to say.

"I've come about a match that I'd like to propose to you, sir," said Auntie Hsüeh. "I guarantee she'll tickle your fancy, and she can take the place left by the death of your Third Lady. I've just been in the First Lady's quarters. She bought some of my trinkets and detained me for a cup of tea. I was there for an age, but I didn't dare bring up this subject. I thought it would be better if I found you first and broached it directly to you.

"The young lady in question is someone you probably already know about, sir. She's the legitimate widow of the owner of the Yang family's textile business outside the South Gate, and she's got a tidy sum of money at her disposal. She owns two Nanking beds, with retractable steps; four or five trunks full of clothing for all four seasons, figured gowns and so forth, packed so tightly you can't stick your hand into them; and pearl headbands and earrings, gold jewelry set with precious stones, and gold and silver bracelets and bangles, it goes without saying. In ready cash alone, she has more than a thousand taels of silver at her disposal. And she has two or three hundred bales of fine cotton drill[2] as well.

"Unfortunately, her husband died far away from home while he was out on the road selling textiles. She has been observing mourning for him for over a year now. She doesn't have any children of her own to worry about, only a young brother-in-law, who's just nine years old. There wouldn't be any point in maintaining her widowhood just for him. Her husband's paternal aunt is trying to persuade her to remarry.

"This year the young lady's no more than twenty-four or twenty-five. She's tall of stature and good-looking; in fact, when she's properly done up, she's as pretty as a figure on a decorative lantern. She's romantic and quick-witted, just as clever as can be, and as for the ability to take charge of a household, needlework and suchlike feminine accomplishments, backgammon and elephant chess, and so forth, that goes without saying. There's no reason for me to deceive you, sir. Her maiden name is Meng, she's the third sibling in her generation, and she lives on Stinkwater Lane. Also, she's an expert performer on the moon guitar. If you consent to see her, sir, I guarantee you'll:

> Hit the bull's-eye with the first arrow.[3]

How could anyone be as lucky as you, sir, to get all that dowry and a young lady to boot?"

When Hsi-men Ch'ing heard that the woman could play the moon guitar it struck a responsive note in his heart, so he asked Auntie Hsüeh, "How soon can I arrange to have a look at her?"

"I'll tell you what, sir," said Auntie Hsüeh, "having a look at her is not the first order of business. Right now the senior member of the Yang family is her husband's paternal aunt. There's also a maternal uncle of her husband, named Chang the Fourth, but since he's on the distaff side, he's:

Like the meat of the hickory nut: there's
always a husk in between.[4]

This old lady was originally married to Crooked-head Sun and lives in a house belonging to Eunuch Director Hsü on Halfside Street in the northern quarter of the city. Since Crooked-head died, the old lady has maintained her widowhood for thirty or forty years. She doesn't have any children of either sex and depends on her nieces and nephews for support.

"It's too late to do anything about it today, but tomorrow I'll come meet you, sir, and we'll go dump the whole proposition in her lap.

If you appeal for help, appeal to Chang Liang;
If you appoint a general, appoint Han Hsin.[5]

"The only thing this old lady cares about is money. She knows perfectly well that her nephew's widow is well provided for. She doesn't really care whom she marries as long as she can make a few taels of silver out of it. Promise her a little extra silver, sir, and throw in a bolt of that thin satin you have so much of at home. Then, if you go talk it over with her in person, and present her with a bearer's load of appropriate gifts, you'll:

Knock her over with one blow.[6]

If anyone else raises any objections, as long as you've got this old lady behind you, there isn't much they'll dare do about it."

This single conversation with Auntie Hsüeh had such an effect on Hsi-men Ch'ing that:

Joy manifested itself about his temples
and between his brows;
Delight spread itself across his cheeks
and smiling face.[7]

Gentle reader take note: The matchmakers of this world are not really interested in anything but making money for themselves. What do they care whether their clients end up dead or alive? They will describe a marriage prospect who holds no office as an officeholder, and a position as concubine as though it were a position as legitimate wife. They are such inveterate liars they would attempt to deceive Heaven itself, and there is no truth whatever to be found in their asseverations. Truly:

Though the matchmaker did her utmost
to promote the union;

Meng Yü-lou had already decided
to marry a rich man.
Those with affinities will meet though
separated by a thousand li;
Those without affinities will miss each other
though face to face.[8]

That day Hsi-men Ch'ing agreed with Auntie Hsüeh that the next day would be a good time to buy some presents and go to the northern quarter of the city to pay a visit to Aunt Yang. When Auntie Hsüeh finished her spiel she picked up her box of trinkets and departed. Hsi-men Ch'ing went back into the shop and continued to go over the accounts with Manager Fu. Of the events of that evening there is no more to tell.

The next day Hsi-men Ch'ing rose early and dressed himself to befit the occasion. Then he picked out a bolt of material, bought four trays of preserved fruit, and hired a bearer to carry them. Hsi-men Ch'ing rode on horseback, accompanied by his page boy, and Auntie Hsüeh led the way straight to the door of Aunt Yang's dwelling in the house belonging to Eunuch Director Hsü on Halfside Street in the northern quarter of the city.

Auntie Hsüeh went in first to alert Aunt Yang to the fact that she had a visitor.

"A man of property from hereabouts," she told her, "is respectfully waiting outside your door. He is interested in discussing a match with the young lady. I told him that you were the senior member of the Yang family and suggested that he should pay you a visit and discuss the matter before I would presume to take him outside the gate to see the lady herself. I brought him along with me today, and he has already dismounted and is waiting outside your door at this very moment."

"Ai-ya!" the old lady exclaimed when she heard this. "Matchmaker, why didn't you let me know ahead of time?"

On the one hand, she ordered her maidservant to sweep the parlor, tidy it up, and brew some good tea, while on the other hand, she said, "Please, invite him to come in."

Auntie Hsüeh lost no time in taking charge of the proceedings. First she had the load of gifts brought in and properly displayed, and it was only after the bearer had been dispatched with his empty containers that she invited Hsi-men Ch'ing to come in.

Hsi-men Ch'ing was wearing a large palmetto hat, a long gown fastened at the waist with a sash, and white-soled black boots. When he entered the door and met the old lady he bowed to her four times. Leaning on her staff, the old lady made haste to return his salutation.

Hsi-men Ch'ing would not let her proceed, protesting again and again, "Aunt, please accept my salutation."

The two of them dickered politely for a while until the old lady agreed to accept a half kowtow from him. They then sat down in the positions appropriate for guest and host while Auntie Hsüeh took her place to one side.

"What is the gentleman's name?" the old lady asked.

"I just told you," said Auntie Hsüeh, "but you've already forgotten. This is the Honorable Hsi-men Ch'ing, who is numbered among the most substantial men of property in Ch'ing-ho district. He owns the large wholesale pharmaceutical business on the street in front of the district yamen. He also engages in moneylending to both officials and functionaries. In his home:

> The piles of money reach higher than the dipper,
> The stores of rotting rice suggest a granary,

but he lacks a wife with the ability to take charge of the household. On hearing that the young lady from your family who lives outside the South Gate wishes to remarry, he has come especially in order to discuss this match with you."

"As long as the two of you relatives-to-be are both here," Auntie Hsüeh continued:

> "The holes in the water clock let it all spill out;[9]
> If you have anything to say, now's the time to say it.

There's no call for you to complain about the lies of us matchmakers. Since you're the senior member of the family on the bride's side, if anyone who had anything to say didn't come talk to you first, Aunt, who else should they talk to?"

"If you wanted to discuss a match with my nephew's widow," the old lady said, "all you needed to do was drop by for a chat. What need was there to go to the trouble of buying all these presents? You put me in a position in which it would be:

> Discourteous to refuse, and
> Embarrassing to accept."

"Worthy Aunt," said Hsi-men Ch'ing, "I'm afraid these presents are hardly worthy of the name."

The old lady bowed to him twice, expressed her gratitude, and had the presents put away, after which Auntie Hsüeh took the trays outside to where the bearer was waiting and then returned to keep them company.

Tea was served, and after they had finished drinking it, the old lady started the conversation by saying, "As far as I'm concerned:

> Not to speak up when you ought to is to be a coward.[10]

When my nephew was alive he succeeded in amassing a considerable sum for himself, and now that he has, unfortunately, died it has all fallen into the hands of his widow. At the very least she is worth more than a thousand taels of silver. Whether it is your wish, sir, to make her your concubine or your legitimate wife is no concern of mine. All I care about is that a proper sutra-reading should be performed on my nephew's behalf. As his paternal aunt

I am related to him by blood; it is not a distaff or marriage relationship. If you were to provide me with the cost of a coffin, it would not be as though I had made any exorbitant demands on you. In return, I'm prepared to hazard whatever face I've got left in this matter. I'll:

Cast myself in the role of a stinking rat,[11]

for the benefit of that old dog, Chang the Fourth, and stick up for the two of you, come what may. After she has been carried over your threshold, sir, if you were to permit her to pay me a visit now and then on birthdays and such occasions, and acknowledge me as a poor relation, I would endeavor not to inflict my poverty upon you."

"Madam," laughed Hsi-men Ch'ing, "you can relax on that score. I fully understand everything you've just said. Since you've broached the subject, madam, the cost of a single coffin is nothing to me. Even if it were ten coffins you wanted, I could afford it."

As he spoke, he reached inside the leg of his boot and drew out six ingots of five taels each, making a total of thirty taels of "snowflake" government silver.

Setting these down in front of her, he said, "This may not amount to much, madam, but I hope you will use it to buy a cup of tea. In the future, when the bride has been carried over my threshold, I will provide another seventy taels of silver and two bolts of satin toward your funeral expenses. You will always be a welcome guest in my home at any time of the year."

Gentle reader take note: In this world, money is like the brain and spinal cord of man in that it is the one indispensable thing that governs his every move.

When the black pupils of the old vixen's eyes saw the twenty or thirty taels of shiny government silver, she said with an ingratiating smile, "Worthy sir, I don't wish to be thought avaricious, but it has always been true that:

If the terms are settled at the outset,
Misunderstandings can be avoided later on."

"Madam," interjected Auntie Hsüeh from the side, "you're being more fastidious than you need to be. Such considerations are quite unnecessary in this case. The honorable gentleman is not that sort of person. After all he:

Sought to make your acquaintance with presents in hand.

You may not know it, madam, but even His Honor, the prefect, and His Honor, the district magistrate, consort with him. He is acquainted with people in many walks of life from all over the empire. You're not likely to make much of a dent in his resources."

This single conversation had such an effect on the old lady that she was ready to:

Fart ferociously and pee in her pants,[12]

in her excitement. After she had entertained her guests a while longer and they had drunk a second serving of tea, Hsi-men Ch'ing indicated that he was ready to be on his way. The old lady politely endeavored to detain him, but to no avail.

Auntie Hsüeh said, "Since we've been able to see you today, Aunt, and discuss this matter, tomorrow we can proceed to go outside the South Gate and take a look at the young lady."

"There's no need for the gentleman to take the trouble to pay a call in order to size up my nephew's widow," said the old lady. "Matchmaker, just tell her that I said, 'If you don't marry a man like this, what manner of man are you going to marry?' "

Hsi-men Ch'ing said his farewells and got up to go.

"Sir," said the old lady, "I didn't know you were coming, and I was unable to make proper preparations on the spur of the moment. Please forgive me for not offering you anything better."

Leaning on her staff, she accompanied him out the door and saw him several steps along his way before Hsi-men Ch'ing succeeded in persuading her to go back inside. Auntie Hsüeh remained outside to see Hsi-men Ch'ing into his saddle.

"Wasn't I right to propose this way of going about it?" she said. "It's much better to have started out by dumping the whole proposition in the old lady's lap than it would have been to rely on the good offices of anyone else. You go on home, sir," she continued. "I'm going to stay here and have another word with her. We've already agreed to meet and go outside the South Gate together first thing tomorrow."

Hsi-men Ch'ing pulled out a tael's worth of silver and handed it to Auntie Hsüeh to cover the hire of a donkey. After she had accepted the money he got on his horse and went home, while she remained behind at Aunt Yang's house, chatting and drinking wine until dark, before going home herself.

To make a long story short, the next day Hsi-men Ch'ing dressed himself to befit the occasion, slipped his betrothal gifts into his sleeve, and mounted a large white horse. Then, accompanied by his two page boys, Tai-an and P'ing-an, and by Auntie Hsüeh, riding a donkey, he proceeded outside the South Gate to the door of the Yang family compound on Stinkwater Lane off Hogmarket Street. This establishment consisted of a twenty-four-foot-wide frontage opening onto the street and five interior courtyards, receding along a vertical axis.

Hsi-men Ch'ing reined in his horse at the gate, and Auntie Hsüeh disappeared into the interior for some time before coming out to usher him in. After he had dismounted, the first thing he confronted was a two-story structure housing the main gate, which was situated on the south side of the street, facing north. Just inside the gate stood a gray screen-wall. Inside the ceremonial gate that led into the second courtyard the entrance was screened by a hedge of crape myrtle and a fence of woven bamboo splints.

The courtyard itself was decorated with pomegranate trees and potted miniature plants. Along a raised platform there stood a row of indigo vats for dyeing and two benches for fulling cloth.

Auntie Hsüeh pushed open the red latticework doors of the eighteen-foot-wide, south-facing reception hall, on the center of the back wall of which there hung in the place of honor a scroll depicting the Bodhisattva Kuan-yin of the Water Moon, accompanied by her attendant, Sudhana.[13] Landscape paintings by well-known artists hung on the other walls. There was also a marble standing screen, to either side of which stood tall, narrow-necked, bronze vases of the kind used in the game "pitch-pot."[14] All in all:

The chairs and tables were shiny, and
The screens and lattices were posh.

Auntie Hsüeh invited Hsi-men Ch'ing to take one of the seats reserved for distinguished guests and then disappeared into the interior once again.

After a while she came out and whispered in Hsi-men Ch'ing's ear, "The young lady hasn't finished her toilet yet. Please have a seat and wait a little longer, sir."

At this juncture a young servant brought out a cup of tea flavored with fruit kernels, and after Hsi-men Ch'ing had drunk it, she took the cup and its raised saucer away again.

Auntie Hsüeh, after all, was a matchmaker by profession, so she kept up an animated monologue:

Gesticulating with both hands and feet,[15]

for Hsi-men Ch'ing's benefit.

"Aside from Aunt Yang," she said, "the most important person in this family is the young lady. Of course there is her husband's younger brother, but he's still a minor and doesn't understand anything. Originally, when her late husband was still running the enterprise, in a single day, not even counting the silver, they sold enough blue cotton cloth of the kind used for making shoes to take in two large basketfuls of copper cash. He used to charge thirty cash a foot for the stuff. I've seen with my own eyes that on a given day they often had to feed as many as twenty or thirty dyers, and everything was managed by the young lady.

"She has two maidservants and a page boy at her beck and call. The older one, who's fourteen, and already dresses her hair in adult fashion, is called Lan-hsiang. The younger one's just eleven and is called Hsiao-luan. In the future, when she's carried across your threshold, they'll all come with her.

"If I succeed in bringing off this match for you, sir, I hope to be able to take out a mortgage on a couple of rooms in a better location than that out-of-the-way corner in the northern quarter where I'm living now. It's not convenient for me to get to your place from there. When you bought Ch'un-mei last year, sir, you promised me several bolts of muslin that you still haven't given me. I'll forget about that when this is all over if you'll compensate me for both occasions at once.

"On your way in just now, sir," she continued, "you must have noticed those two cabinets for displaying cloth. When Mr. Yang was still alive, I don't know how much money he put into the improvement of the retail shop that opens onto the street. This compound must also be worth seven or eight hundred taels of silver. It contains five interior courtyards and extends all the way back to the street that runs behind it. When she gets married, I'm afraid she'll have to leave it all to her young brother-in-law."

Auntie Hsüeh was still talking when a maidservant came out to summon her. Some time passed and then, lo and behold:

> To the tinkling of girdle pendants,
> Amid the fragrance of orchid and musk,

the woman herself appeared. She wore a kingfisher blue surcoat of figured silk, emblazoned with a mandarin square that featured an embroidered *ch'i-lin,*[16] over a wide-cut gown of figured scarlet silk. On her head:

> Pearls and trinkets rose in piles;
> A phoenix hairpin was half askew.

Hsi-men Ch'ing opened his eyes wide and took a good look at the woman. Behold:

> She is tall and slender in build;
> Modeled in plaster, carved of jade.
> Her figure is neither plump nor thin;
> Her stature is neither short nor tall.
> On her face, though barely visible,
> Are several inconspicuous pockmarks,
> That give her an air of natural beauty;
> Hidden beneath her skirt,
> Are a pair of tiny golden lotuses,
> That are well-formed and attractive.
> Two gold rings, set with pearls,
> Hang low beneath her ears;
> A pair of phoenix hairpins,
> Juts aslant at either temple.
> She has only to move,
> In order to make her openwork jade pendants tinkle;
> Wherever she sits,
> The reek of orchid and musk assails the nostrils.
> It is just as though Ch'ang-o has come down
> from her palace in the moon;
> She is exactly like the Goddess of Witches' Mountain
> descending her jasper steps.[17]

Hsi-men Ch'ing no sooner saw her than his heart was filled with delight. Auntie Hsüeh made haste to hold aside the portiere over the doorway in order to facilitate her entrance. The woman came in and:

Neither correctly nor precisely,

bowed and uttered a word of greeting, after which she sat down in a seat directly across from that occupied by her visitor. Hsi-men Ch'ing scrutinized her from head to toe with such intensity that the woman lowered her head.

Then he opened the conversation by saying, "My wife has been dead for some time and I would like to make you my legitimate wife and put you in charge of the household. What do you think of this proposal?"

"How old are you, sir," the woman asked, "and how long has your wife been dead?"

"I'm twenty-seven," said Hsi-men Ch'ing, "and I was born on the twenty-eighth day of the seventh month, at midnight. Unfortunately my former wife has been dead now for more than a year. I hardly dare ask how old you are, young lady?"

"I'm twenty-nine," the woman replied.

"So you're two years older than I am," said Hsi-men Ch'ing.

Auntie Hsüeh interjected from the side:

"When the wife is two years older,
Yellow gold never molders;
When the wife is three years older,
Yellow gold piles up like boulders."[18]

As she was speaking, a young maidservant came in carrying three servings of tea flavored with candied kumquats in carved lacquer cups inlaid with silver and provided with silver teaspoons in the shape of apricot leaves. The woman got up, brushed away a few drops of water from the rim of the first cup with her slender fingers, and handed it to Hsi-men Ch'ing. As he took the proffered cup in his hand, she bowed to him and expressed her good wishes.

Auntie Hsüeh seized the opportunity to step forward and lift the woman's skirt with her hand, revealing:

The upturned points of her tiny golden lotuses,
Barely three inches long,
But half a span in length,
Peeking out beneath her skirt.

She was wearing scarlet shoes that had tips decorated with cloud patterns of gold brocade and high white satin heels. As he beheld this sight, Hsi-men Ch'ing's heart was filled with delight.

The woman took the second cup of tea and handed it to Auntie Hsüeh, after which she took the remaining cup for herself and sat down again to keep them company while they drank.

Auntie Hsüeh Proposes a Match with Meng Yü-lou

Hsi-men Ch'ing then ordered Tai-an to present the square box containing his betrothal gifts, which consisted of two embroidered handkerchiefs, a pair of jeweled hairpins, and six gold rings. When these had been transferred to a tray and taken inside, Auntie Hsüeh prompted the woman to express her gratitude to Hsi-men Ch'ing with a bow.

"When are you planning to hold the ceremony, sir," the woman went on to ask, "so that I can make the necessary preparations?"

"Since you have deigned to accept my proposal," said Hsi-men Ch'ing, "I'll present you with some further insignificant gifts on the twenty-fourth day of this month, and hold the ceremony proper on the second day of the sixth month."

"If that's the way it's to be," the woman said, "I'll send someone tomorrow to inform my late husband's paternal aunt, who lives in the northern quarter of the city."

"Yesterday," said Auntie Hsüeh, "the gentleman paid her a call in order to discuss this matter."

"What did she say?" the woman asked.

"When she heard that the gentleman was interested in this match," Auntie Hsüeh replied, "she was as happy as could be, and suggested that I should bring him here so the two of you could meet. She said, 'If you don't marry a man like this, what manner of man are you going to marry? I'll support this match, come what may, and even undertake to act as guarantor.'"

"If that's really what Aunt said, everything will be fine," the woman said.

"My dear young lady," said Auntie Hsüeh, "surely you don't mean to suggest that a matchmaker such as myself would dare to fabricate a speech like that, do you?"

When she had finished speaking, Hsi-men Ch'ing said his farewells and got up to go.

Auntie Hsüeh accompanied him as far as the mouth of Stinkwater Lane and said, "Now that you've seen the young lady, sir, what do you think?"

"Auntie Hsüeh," said Hsi-men Ch'ing, "I am indeed deeply indebted to you."

"You go ahead, sir," said Auntie Hsüeh. "I want to have another word with the young lady before I leave."

Hsi-men Ch'ing mounted his horse and headed back into the city, but Auntie Hsüeh turned around and went inside again, where she said to the woman, "Young lady, with a husband like that you'll never have anything to worry about."

"Does Hsi-men Ch'ing have any women in his household or not?" the woman asked. "And what does he do for a living?"

"My dear lady," said Auntie Hsüeh, "even if he does have a few women about the place, none of them amount to anything. If what I say isn't true, when you get there you'll find out for yourself. His reputation is known to everyone. He is numbered among the most substantial men of property in Ch'ing-ho district, and he is renowned as the Honorable Hsi-men who owns a wholesale pharmaceutical business and lends money to both officials and functionaries. Even the district magistrate and the prefect consort with him. And recently he has become related to Commander Yang of the Eastern Capital, who recognizes him as a kinsman by marriage at four removes. No one dares to cross him."

The woman entertained Auntie Hsüeh with wine and a meal. Just as they were enjoying this repast together, who should turn up but Aunt Yang's page boy, An-t'ung, bearing a gift box containing sweetmeats that came from the country, including four slices of date cake made of glutinous millet flour, two pieces of candy, and several sugar dumplings made of glutinous rice flour.

"I've been sent to ask whether you've accepted that person's betrothal gifts or not," he reported. "My mistress says, 'If you don't marry a man like this, what manner of man are you going to marry?' "

"Please thank your mistress for her concern on my behalf," the woman said. "I have in fact already accepted his betrothal gifts."

"My Heavens!" said Auntie Hsüeh. "How lucky it is we matchmakers never tell anything but the truth. And now the good lady has sent her servant to confirm it."

The woman took the date cake and other sweetmeats out of the gift box and refilled it with a full complement of appetizers and cured meat. Then she gave it to An-t'ung along with fifty or sixty cash for himself and said, "When you get home, give my compliments to your mistress, and tell her that the other party has decided to make the formal presentation of his gifts on the twenty-fourth day of this month and to hold the wedding ceremony on the second day of the next month."

When the page boy had left Auntie Hsüeh said, "How about giving me a little something of whatever the lady sent you to wrap up and take home with me for the children?"

The woman gave her a piece of candy and ten sugar dumplings and she went out the door with:

> A thousand thanks and ten thousand
> expressions of gratitude.

But no more of this.

To resume our story, Chang the Fourth, the maternal uncle of Meng Yü-lou's deceased husband, had hopes of being able to exploit his relationship with his young nephew, Yang Tsung-pao, as a means of laying his hands on some of her property. He had a candidate of his own as a matrimonial prospect for her, for whom he was prepared to act both as advocate and guarantor. This was the widower Provincial Graduate Shang, the son of Prefectural Judge Shang who lived on Main Street. If someone else of no particular distinction had been proposed as a rival candidate he would have had a case to make; but when he heard, unexpectedly, that she was betrothed to Hsi-men Ch'ing, the owner of the wholesale pharmaceutical business in front of the district yamen, whom he knew to be possessed of clout in official circles, he felt himself to be stymied. After devoting much thought to the problem he decided that:

Of the thousand schemes and hundred plans,
The best plan is a frontal assault.

Chang the Fourth, therefore, paid the woman a visit and said to her, "Young lady, you really oughtn't to have accepted Hsi-men Ch'ing's betrothal gifts but should have gone along with my suggestion and married the son of Prefectural Judge Shang, the provincial graduate. He comes from a cultivated family that not only values poetry and propriety, but also possesses enough landed property for you to live on quite comfortably.

"He would certainly be preferable to Hsi-men Ch'ing. That bastard has been throwing his weight around in official circles for years. He's a tough customer. Moreover, he's already got a legitimate wife who's the daughter of Battalion Commander Wu. You're used to being a legitimate wife, and if you marry him you'll only be a concubine; won't that be quite a comedown for you? Moreover, he's already got three or four other bedmates about the place as well as maidservants who aren't old enough to put their hair up yet. If you enter his household, as the saying goes:

When people are many, mouths are many,

and you're likely to have a hard time of it."

"It's always been true," the woman said, "that:

A multitude of boats need not clog the channel.[19]

If there's already a First Lady in his household, I'm willing to acknowledge her seniority and be a younger sister to her. Even if he does have a few other bedmates about the place, if my husband takes a fancy to me, do you think I'll try to keep him to myself? And if he doesn't take a fancy to me, I can't very well physically restrain him, can I? I'm not afraid; even if there are a hundred people to contend with, I can scull my own boat. To say nothing of the wealthy and prominent, among whom there is hardly a household without four or five concubines, when you get right down to it, even the beggars in the streets:

With boys in hand and girls in arms,

often have three or four concubines tagging along at their heels. You're really making much ado about nothing. When I enter his household I'll know how to handle the situation so it won't be a problem for me."

"Young lady," said Chang the Fourth, "I've heard that this man is given to trading in human flesh and is an old hand at:

Beating his women and abusing his wives.

Whenever one of them fails to please him in any way, however slight, he calls in a go-between and disposes of her without more ado. Are you willing to expose yourself to this temper of his?"

"Old Fourth," the woman said, "you're mistaken. No matter how rough a man may be, he won't beat a wife who is diligent and knows what she's about. As a member of his household, if I manage to run a tight ship, so that:

> Words spoken inside do not get out, and
> Words spoken outside do not get in,[20]

what can he do to me? If a wife:

> Likes to eat but hates to work,
> Has a big mouth and a long tongue, and
> Devotes herself to stirring up trouble,

then:

> If her husband doesn't beat her,
> Should he beat the dog instead?"[21]

"But that's not all," said Chang the Fourth. "I've also heard he has a thirteen-year-old daughter at home who isn't married yet. I'm really afraid that if you enter his household you'll end up having to:

> Make three nests where there's only room for two.[22]

Just remember that:

> When people are many, mouths are many.

How will you ever be able to handle it?"

"Old Fourth," the woman said, "you don't know what you're talking about. As a member of his household I'll remember that:

> Seniors are senior, and
> Juniors are junior;

and that:

> The state of the river depends on what comes
> downstream from the source.[23]

If I treat his children well, there's no reason to fear that my husband will think ill of me, or that his children will be disrespectful. To say nothing of a single child, even if there were ten of them, it wouldn't be a problem for me."

"As I see it," said Chang the Fourth, "this is the sort of man whose:

> Conduct is lacking in rectitude.

He's always away from home:

> Sleeping among the flowers and lolling
> beneath the willows.[24]

Moreover, he's:

> Solid without, but hollow within,

and is up to his neck in debt. I'm only afraid he'll be the ruination of you."

"Old Fourth," the woman said, "you're mistaken again. Even if he does, sometimes, go out on the town and:

Careen about rather recklessly,[25]

as a woman:

I can only concern myself with what goes on
within the triple gates;
I can't concern myself with whatever may happen
without the triple gates.

You don't really expect me to follow him about all day long, do you? As the saying goes:

Money, in this world, is but a
sometime thing;[26]
Where is the family that is long rich
or forever poor?[27]

In fact, when you get right down to it, even His Majesty the Emperor himself, when he suffers from a temporary shortage of cash, has been known to appropriate the funds realized by the sale of brood mares from the Court of the Imperial Stud.[28] To say nothing of merchants, which of whom would ever be content to let his money sit idly at home, or scruple to:

Depend upon his wife's connections for his daily bread,[29]

if the need should arise? There's really no need for you to be so concerned about me."

Chang the Fourth saw that the only effect his arguments were having on the woman was to bring down her countercriticisms on his own head. Feeling that he had lost face, he finished his second cup of plain tea, got up, and departed. There is a poem that testifies to this:

Chang the Fourth, in uttering his hurtful words,
was only wasting his breath;
Marriage affinities, whatever one may think,
are predetermined.
The woman of beauty felt herself predisposed
in favor of Hsi-men Ch'ing;
Though he had talked himself hoarse
it would have been to no avail.

Chang the Fourth went home in a state of mortification and discussed the situation with his wife. They decided that the only thing to do was to wait until the day when the woman's trousseau was to be delivered to Hsi-men Ch'ing's household in advance of the wedding and then, making a pretext of protecting the interests of their nephew, Yang Tsung-pao, attempt to appropriate whatever they could of the woman's belongings.

To make a long story short, on the twenty-fourth day of the fifth month, Hsi-men Ch'ing arranged for the "presentation of the gifts." He invited his sister-in-law, who was married to his wife's eldest brother, to ride in the sedan chair and take charge of the gift-bearing procession. What with clothing and jewelry, formal gowns for all four seasons, preserved fruit, tea and pastries, bolts of cotton and silk, supplies of pongee and silk floss, the procession included more than twenty loads of gifts. On Meng Yü-lou's side, she invited Aunt Yang and her own elder sister to accept the gifts formally on her behalf and help to entertain the visitors, but there is no need to describe this in detail.

On the twenty-sixth, Meng Yü-lou engaged twelve Buddhist monks of high repute to recite a sutra and perform a "land and water" mass for the benefit of her deceased husband, after which his spirit tablet was burned. It was Aunt Yang who insisted on these observances.

As the day approached on which the trousseau was to be delivered to Hsi-men Ch'ing's household, Chang the Fourth recruited a number of neighbors from the locality to join him in coming to have a word with the woman. That day Auntie Hsüeh showed up with a few idlers who had been hired for the purpose by Hsi-men Ch'ing and ten or twenty soldiers that he had borrowed from the commandant's yamen.

As they started inside to move the woman's beds and curtains and the trunks in which her trousseau was packed, Chang the Fourth intercepted them and said, "Matchmaker, don't carry them away yet. I've got something to say about it."

After he had invited the neighbors to come inside and sit down, Chang the Fourth opened the parley by saying, "Distinguished neighbors, listen to me. The young lady is here, and I, Chang Lung, oughtn't to have to say it, but your husband, Yang Tsung-hsi, and your young brother-in-law, Yang Tsung-pao, are both my nephews, my elder sister's sons. Now, unfortunately, your husband is dead, but he succeeded in amassing a considerable sum for himself while he was alive. There are people who are trying to tell you what to do in this situation, and I, as a relative on the distaff side of the family, am not in a position to interfere in your affairs. Enough said. Nevertheless, my second nephew, Yang Tsung-pao, is a young karmic encumbrance, the weight of which will fall entirely on my shoulders. He and your husband were born of the same womb. Do you mean to maintain that he is not entitled to a portion of the family property?

"Now that all these distinguished neighbors are here today to act as witnesses—and, after all, whether you've got a tidy sum of money in your hands or not, there's no way I can prevent you from marrying someone if you want to—just open up your trunks and let everyone see for themselves what you've got in there, before letting them be carried off the premises. I'm not interested in taking anything away from you, but only in clarifying the situation. Young lady, what do you say?"

When the woman heard these words she started to cry and said, "Neighbors, listen to me. You are mistaken, sir. It's not as though I plotted with evil intent to murder my husband. Isn't it enough today that I have to bear the opprobrium for entering into another marriage? Whether or not my husband was successful in making money is public knowledge. But what few taels of silver he accumulated were all plowed back into this house. And the house I'm not taking with me. I'm leaving it all to my young brother-in-law. All the furnishings are being left absolutely intact. In fact, there are three or four hundred taels worth of outstanding debts, the papers for which have already been turned over to you to collect as they become due. Since when has there been any excess of silver over and above the expenditures required to maintain the establishment?"

"If you haven't any silver, then that's all there is to it," said Chang the Fourth. "All I'm asking you to do, now, is to open up your trunks in front of these witnesses so they can see for themselves whether you do indeed have any or not. Then you can carry it all off as you like. I'm not interested in taking anything away from you."

"No doubt you want to have a look at my shoes and footbindings too!" the woman said.

Just as they were beginning to wrangle, who should emerge from the rear of the house, leaning on her staff, but Aunt Yang.

"Aunt Yang is here," everyone said with one voice as they bowed to her in greeting.

After Aunt Yang had returned their salutation and sat down to keep them company, she addressed them as follows, "Distinguished neighbors: As the paternal aunt, I am related by blood; this is not a distaff or marriage relationship. Would anyone suggest that I have no say in this matter? The one who is dead was my nephew; the one who is alive is also my nephew.

Every one of the ten fingers,
Hurts equally if bitten.[30]

Quite aside from the fact that her husband really didn't have any money laid by; even if he had a hundred thousand taels of silver, you wouldn't be entitled to do anything more than take a look at it. She has no children and is still:

A young and delicate lass.

If you interfere and try to prevent her from remarrying, just what do you want to keep her around for, may I ask?"

In a chorus of loud voices the neighbors responded, "What Aunt Yang says makes sense."

"You don't mean to retain what she brought with her by way of a dowry from her own family, do you?" demanded the old lady. "She hasn't given me a thing behind anybody's back, yet you suggest that I'm being partial to her. Let's be fair about it. There's no reason for me to deceive any of you. This nephew of mine was so kind and just in everything he did that his loss is hard for me to bear. He was always so considerate to me. If that were not the case I wouldn't bother to concern myself about the matter."

Chang the Fourth eyed the old lady from one side and said, "Are you out of your mind?

The phoenix doesn't deign to alight where
there's no treasure to be had."

These words struck the old lady right on her sore spot. In an instant her face became purple with rage. Grabbing hold of Chang the Fourth, she started to curse him in earnest.

"Chang the Fourth," she said, "you'd better lay off that:

Wild and nonsensical talk.

I may be neither able nor talented, but at least I'm a certifiable member of the Yang family. You old oily mouth! What Yang family prick were you sired by?"

"I may have a different surname," said Chang the Fourth, "but my two nephews are the offspring of my own elder sister. You old bloodsucker! Don't you know that:

A girl faces outward from the moment she's born?[31]

You're engaged in:

Setting fires with one hand, and
Pouring water on them with the other."[32]

"You lousy, shameless, old dog-bone!" retorted Aunt Yang. "She's still:

A young and delicate lass.

Just what do you have in mind in wanting to keep her at home, may I ask? If you aren't hoping to slake your lust with her you must be plotting to fatten yourself at her expense."

"I'm not out for anybody's money," said Chang the Fourth. "But my nephew is my own sister's child, and if anything goes wrong, it's going to be me that's out of pocket, not you. You old gallows bird! You're out to:

Snatch the big, and
Snitch the little.
You may be a brown cat, but you've got a black tail."[33]

"Chang the Fourth!" Aunt Yang retorted. "You old beggar! You old slave! You old mealymouth! If you keep on talking such rot with your:

Deceitful mouth and duplicitous tongue,

you'll die so poor your family won't be able to afford the rope to hoist your coffin with!"

"You waggle-tongued old whore!" replied Chang the Fourth. "You've had to work so hard for your money you've burnt out your tail. No wonder you don't have any children."

This sally really got under Aunt Yang's skin. "Chang the Fourth, you louse!" she cursed at him. "You whoreson old dog! I may have no children, but I'm still better than your mother. She divides her time between Buddhist and Taoist temples, humping the bonzes and fucking the priests, while you're:

Still asleep in dreamland!"

At this point the two of them would have come to blows if the neighbors had not intervened, saying, "Old Fourth, let the lady have her say."

Meantime, Auntie Hsüeh, who had noticed that the two of them were preoccupied with their quarrel, took advantage of the confusion by placing herself at the head of Hsi-men Ch'ing's servants and hired hands, along with the soldiers who had been sent from the yamen. At her direction, they swooped down, hugger-mugger, on the woman's beds and curtains and the trunks containing her trousseau and carried them all off, any which way, like a gust of wind.

When Chang the Fourth realized what had happened his eyes swelled with rage, but:

Though he dared to be angry,
He dared not speak.[34]

The neighbors, for their part, seeing that there was nothing further to be done, attempted to smooth things over for a while and then went their separate ways.

On the second day of the sixth month Hsi-men Ch'ing dispatched a large sedan chair and four pairs of red silk lanterns to fetch the bride. Her elder sister, Mrs. Han, acted as her escort, and she was also accompanied by her young brother-in-law, Yang Tsung-pao, who had his hair done up in a topknot, wore a long green gown, and rode on horseback as he escorted his sister-in-law on her way to the wedding ceremony. Hsi-men Ch'ing rewarded him with a bolt of satin brocade and a jade belt buckle. The bride was accompanied by her two maidservants, Lan-hsiang and Hsiao-luan, whose job it was to:

Make the beds and fold the quilts.

She also brought along to wait on her the page boy, Ch'in-t'ung, who was just fourteen years old.

On the third day Aunt Yang and the woman's two sisters-in-law, the wives of her brothers, Meng the Elder and Meng the Second, came to participate in the "third-day celebrations." Hsi-men Ch'ing presented Aunt Yang with seventy taels of silver and two bolts of satin, and from that time on the families enjoyed uninterrupted relations.

Hsi-men Ch'ing prepared three rooms on the western side of the rear courtyard to serve as his new bride's living quarters. She was designated as the Third Lady in the hierarchy of his wife and concubines and bore the appellation Yü-lou, or Tower of Jade. Hsi-men Ch'ing gave orders that all the members of his household, from top to bottom, should address her as Third Lady.

Beginning with the evening of the wedding day he spent three successive nights in her room. Truly:

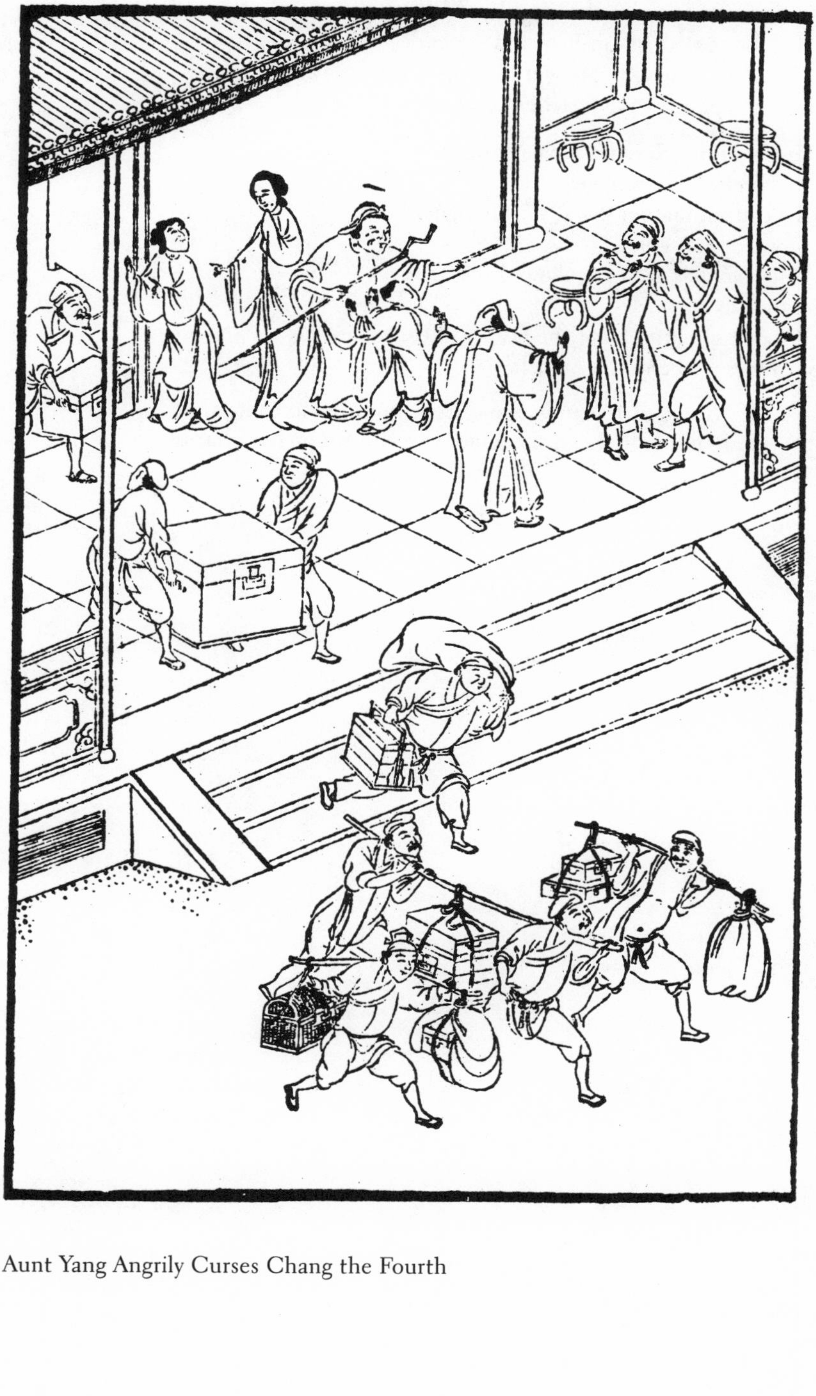

Aunt Yang Angrily Curses Chang the Fourth

Within the bed-curtains of gold lamé,
Two new partners performed their perennial roles;
Beneath the quilt of red brocade,
Two used objects were brought into play.[35]

There is a poem that testifies to this:

To encounter close up such a paragon
of feeling and romance;
Is a consummation that: "Without good fortune
one cannot enjoy."[36]
Wherever has Lieh-tzu allowed the wind
to carry him;[37]
When night after night the beauty of the moon
shines in the willow branches?[38]

If you want to know the outcome of these events,
Pray consult the story related in the following chapter.

Chapter 8

ALL NIGHT LONG P'AN CHIN-LIEN YEARNS FOR HSI-MEN CH'ING; DURING THE TABLET-BURNING MONKS OVERHEAR SOUNDS OF VENERY

In the silent bedchamber, all by herself,
she wonders;
The mandarin ducks are separated, no news
of him has come.
Before the fragrance of her powder has
vanished from his arm;
The *p'i-p'a* at the head of her bed is
covered with dust.
Her face has grown so thin it scarcely registers
in the phoenix mirror;
Her clouds of hair are so loose the jade hairpins
are falling out.
His mettlesome steed does not come; her gazing
eyes are tired;
All alone with her mandarin duck pillow, tears
flood her cheeks.

THE STORY GOES that from the time that Hsi-men Ch'ing took Meng Yü-lou into his household he:

Enjoyed himself with his new wife.[1]

They were:

Like glue and like lacquer.[2]

Moreover, the Ch'en family sent Auntie Wen to announce that they would like to have his daughter, Hsi-men Ta-chieh, carried across their threshold in marriage on the twelfth day of the sixth month. Hsi-men Ch'ing found himself so:

Pushed and pressured,

that he was unable to procure a bed for his daughter's trousseau in time for the occasion and had to supply her with one of the gilt lacquer Nanking beds with retractable steps that had formed part of Meng Yü-lou's dowry. What with the "third-day celebrations" and "ninth-day celebrations" attendant on this event, he was kept busy for more than a month and was unable to pay a visit to P'an Chin-lien.

As a consequence of this, every day found her:

Leaning against one doorjamb after another,
Wearing out her eyes with constant gazing.

She twice sent Dame Wang to inquire about Hsi-men Ch'ing, but the servants at his gate, who were familiar enough with the old lady and knew that she had been sent by P'an Chin-lien, paid scant attention, merely reporting that their master was busy.

The woman was frantic with longing. When the old lady reported the results of her mission, the woman vented her wrath on her stepdaughter, driving her out into the street, in her turn, to look for him. How could that little chit have dared to penetrate his:

Vast courtyards and secluded mansions?

All she did was to lurk in the vicinity of his gate a couple of times without catching sight of Hsi-men Ch'ing. When she returned home her stepmother spat in her face, slapped her, and abused her for being of no use. She even made her kneel on the floor until noon without giving her anything to eat.

At that time the summer solstice had already passed and the weather was extremely hot. The house was so uncomfortable the woman could hardly bear it and ordered Ying-erh to heat some water and prepare the tub so she could take a bath. She also put a tray of meat dumplings into the steamer so she would have something to offer him if Hsi-men Ch'ing happened to show up.

Wearing nothing but a short shift of thin floss silk, she sat on a low stool longing in vain for Hsi-men Ch'ing to come. Pouting with her lips, she cursed him a couple of times for a fickle scoundrel.

Bereft of thought or feeling,
Depressed and silent,

with her slender fingers she took off her two red embroidered shoes and used them to cast a "love hexagram"[3] in the hope of ascertaining whether Hsi-men Ch'ing would come or not. Truly:

In front of others she is reluctant to declare
herself too loudly;
Secretly she casts her lot with coins inquiring after
her distant lover.[4]

There are two songs to the tune "Sheep on the Mountain Slope" that testify to this:

Clad in "wave-tripping" silk stockings,
Looking almost natural,
Divested of their red-tipped shoes, which
now form a "love diagram,"

All Night Long P'an Chin-lien Yearns for Hsi-men Ch'ing

They are like lotus roots that have begun to sprout,
Like lotus pods that have shed their blossoms.
How were they ever bound tightly enough to make them
so very tiny?
Measured with a willow wand, they are
but half a span in length.
As for him,
He doesn't think of me;
As for me,
I think longingly of him.

Quietly taking down the bamboo blind,
Leaving the door to creak,
All I can do is lie underneath my quilt,
cursing his name.
How can you care so much for "misty willows,"
That you won't come to my place anymore?
"My eyebrows have lost their color; who will
repaint them for me?"[5]
Before whose house has he tethered his horse
to the green willows?
As for him,
He is unfaithful to me;
As for me,
I am yearning for him.[6]

At that time, after the woman had tried casting "love diagrams" for a while and realized that Hsi-men Ch'ing was not going to show up, she felt herself overcome by drowsiness, stretched out on her bed, and dozed off. When she woke up, about two hours later, she was not in the best of moods.

"I've heated the water, Mother," Ying-erh said. "Are you going to take a bath or not?"

"The dumplings must be done by now," the woman said. "Bring them in here so I can have a look."

Ying-erh hastened to obey and brought them into the bedroom. The woman counted them off, one by one, with her slender fingers. She had made a full tray of thirty dumplings, but now, though she counted them back and forth a number of times, she could only count twenty-nine. There was one dumpling missing.

"What could have happened to it?" she asked.

"I haven't any idea," said Ying-erh. "You must have counted wrong, Mother."

"I counted them myself, twice," the woman said. "I made thirty dumplings so I'd have something to offer your father if he comes by. Why did you have to go and snitch one? You're spoiled rotten, you wanton little slave! I suppose you were suffering from such:

Acute consumption or avid craving,

that you simply couldn't help eating this particular dumpling, while the rice I feed you:

Whether in large bowl or in small,

you can barely manage to choke down. What I'm going to do next is intended to teach you a lesson."

Thereupon:

Without permitting any further explanation,

she stripped the clothing off the little chit's body and picking up a riding crop proceeded to give her twenty or thirty strokes with it. She whipped the girl until she:

Howled like a stuck pig.

"If you don't confess," she threatened, "I'll certainly give you a hundred strokes."

When the girl could stand the beating no longer she cried out, "Don't whip me any more, Mother. I was desperately hungry and took one of them to eat."

"If you took it," the woman said, "why did you claim that I had counted wrong? You're nothing but a confirmed, mischief-making little whore! When that cuckold was still alive you may have gotten away with:

Telling tales and embroidering on the facts;

but where is he now? You think you can continue to be:

Up to your preternatural pranks,

right under my nose, do you? You mischief-making little whore! I'm going to beat your bottom right off for you!"

The woman whipped her a while longer and pulled her drawers back on before letting her up. Then she ordered her to stand beside her and cool her with a fan.

After she had fanned her for a while the woman said to her, "You lousy little whore! Stick your face over here, so I can give your cheeks a good scratching!"

Ying-erh really did stick her face out, and the woman gouged two bloody scratches in her cheeks with her sharp fingernails before letting her off.

After a while Chin-lien went over to her mirror stand to get dressed and put on some new makeup and then came out and stood inside the blind in the doorway. It just so happened that:

As providence would have it,

what should she see but Hsi-men Ch'ing's page boy, Tai-an, who was riding past her door on horseback with a package wrapped in felt tucked under his arm.

The woman called him to a halt and asked, "Where are you going?"

Now this page boy had always been glib with his tongue and had often accompanied Hsi-men Ch'ing when he visited the woman's house. She was in the habit of tipping him generously and always spoke up on his behalf when he was in hot water with Hsi-men Ch'ing. For this reason he was already on easy terms with the woman.

Dismounting from his horse, he said, "Father sent me to deliver a gift to the commandant's yamen."

The woman invited him inside and asked, "What's your father been up to at home? Why hasn't he come to see me or given me so much as a glimpse of his shadow for so long? It must be that he's found another sweetheart somewhere and put me in the position of:

> The rings that hold his hairnet in place: always
> at the back of his head."

"Father hasn't taken up with any sweetheart," said Tai-an. "It's just that the last few days he's had so much to do at home that he hasn't been able to get away and come to see you."

"Even if he has been busy at home," the woman said, "that's no reason to neglect me for half a month at a time without sending me so much as a word of news. It's obvious that I haven't been very much on his mind. Just what is it that's keeping him so busy, anyway?" she demanded of Tai-an. "Tell me all about it."

The page boy giggled but wouldn't tell her anything.

"There's been something to preoccupy him, that's all," he said. "Why do you insist on:

> Blowing aside the hairs only to look for trouble?"[7]

"My dear little oily mouth," the woman said, "if you don't tell me I'll never forgive you."

"If I tell you," the page boy said, "you mustn't tell Father that it was I who told you."

"I won't tell him, that's all," the woman said.

Tai-an then proceeded, thus and so, to give a full account, from beginning to end, of how Hsi-men Ch'ing had taken Meng Yü-lou into his household. Nothing might have happened if the woman had not heard about this, but having heard about it, she could not prevent the teardrops in her eyes from coursing down across her fragrant cheeks.

Tai-an was thrown into a panic by this response, and said, "It's precisely because you're so sensitive that I didn't want to tell you about it, and now that I have, look at the way you're carrying on."

The woman leaned against the doorjamb and gave a long sigh, saying, "Tai-an, you don't know how much love I've lavished on him, from the first day we met, and now, how can he just abandon me like this?"

As she spoke she was unable to prevent a copious fall of tears.

"Why should you torment yourself so?" said Tai-an. "At home, Mother doesn't even try to keep him in hand."

"Tai-an," the woman said, "listen to my plaint." There is another song to the previous tune that testifies to this:

My naughty lover is fickle;
He hasn't come for a month.
I've been alone beneath the mandarin duck quilt
for thirty nights.
His feckless affections are otherwise engaged,
While I remain an infatuated fool.
I never should have allowed myself
to become so involved.
"What is easily acquired is
easily relinquished."[8]
As for him,
His passion has cooled;
As for me,
It's just my luck.[9]

No sooner was she done than she started to cry all over again.

"Don't cry," said Tai-an. "I shouldn't wonder if Father turned up during the next couple of days, on his birthday. If you write a few words to him, I'll make sure that Father sees them, and he's certain to come."

"I'll really be beholden to you," the woman said. "If you can induce him to come, I'll make a pair of nice shoes for you to wear. I'll wait for him here in order to offer my birthday congratulations. If he doesn't come, I'll hold you accountable, you little oily mouth. And if he asks you what you were doing here, how will you answer him?"

"If Father asks me," said Tai-an, "I'll say that I was watering the horse in the street when you sent Granny Wang to ask me over and gave me this note, along with the injunction to tell him how much you wanted to see him."

"You little oily mouth," the woman laughed, "you're really:

A second Hung-niang: always able to
bring people together."[10]

When she had finished speaking she ordered Ying-erh to serve Tai-an a plateful of the steamed dumplings on the table, along with some tea. While this was being done she went inside, fetched a sheet of flowered notepaper, and:

Lightly grasping the jade tube, and
Gently toying with the sheep's hair brush,

dashed off a lyric to the tune "Mistletoe," which read as follows:

I'm taking my heartfelt words and
Sending them to you on this flowered notepaper.
I remember the time I first cut off
a lock of my black tresses for you.

I leaned against one doorjamb after another
and took down the bamboo blind,
Anticipating surprise and suffering fear for you,
trivial though they may have been.
And now you're actually betraying
my love.
If you're not going to come, return my
fragrant silk handkerchief.[11]

When she had finished composing her note she folded it into a lozenge-shaped lover's knot, sealed it, and gave it to Tai-an with the words, "Be sure to tell him, whatever he does, to come pay me a visit on his birthday. I'll be here waiting for him."

When Tai-an had finished eating his snack the woman also gave him several tens of cash.

As he was about to go outside and mount his horse she said to him, "When you get home and see your father, tell him, 'She really cursed you out.' And if he refuses to come, tell him, 'She's threatening to get into a sedan chair one of these days and come to pay you a visit herself.' "

Tai-an replied, "I feel just like:

A clapper-sounding southern salesman who runs into
a dung-cake peddler and exclaims:
'Don't bother to run through your inventory;
it only gives me the creeps!'
You'd crack melon seeds astride the wooden mule[12]
en route to your own execution:
How superfluous can you get?"

When he had finished speaking he mounted his horse and departed.

Every day the woman spent her time:

Waiting for long periods as well as short,

but it was just as though he were:

A stone sunk in the vast sea.[13]

She never caught so much as a glimpse of Hsi-men Ch'ing's shadow.

Seven days went by in this way until, finally, it was the day of his birthday. To the woman:

Each day was like three months of autumn;
Each night seemed like half a summer.[14]

She:

Waited all day,
Without any news of him;
Watched for a long time,
But caught not a glimpse of him.

Before she became aware of it she began to:

Silently gnash her silvery teeth, as
Tears overflowed her starry eyes.

When evening came she invited Dame Wang over, plied her with food and wine, and then pulled a silver hairpin with a gold head out of her hair and gave it to her, entreating her to go to Hsi-men Ch'ing's house on her behalf and press her invitation.

"If I show up this late in the day," said Dame Wang, "he'll already be:

Anticipating tea or recovering from wine,

and will certainly not consent to come. I'd do better to wait until first thing tomorrow morning to go to the gentleman's mansion and extend your invitation."

"Godmother," the woman said, "be sure you don't forget."

"Since when," the old lady asked, "have I ever undertaken anything for you without carrying it through?"

At this juncture the old lady, who was the sort who:

Wouldn't do anything except for money,[15]

having accepted the hairpin for her pains and drunk until her face was bright red, proceeded to make her way home.

It so happens that, in her bedroom, the woman:

Perfumed with incense the mandarin duck quilt, and
Deftly trimmed the silver lamp's wick,

but could not get to sleep. Giving vent to:

Long sighs as well as short,

she:

Tossed first this way and then that.

Truly, it is a case of:

She who is wont to diligently strum her *p'i-p'a*
late into the night;
When all alone in her deserted chamber can scarcely
bear to play it.[16]

At this juncture, accompanying herself on the *p'i-p'a*, she sang a suite of four songs to the tune "Making Silk Floss," which testifies to this:

In the beginning I loved you for
being so romantic;
We exchanged locks of our hair and
burned incense together.
When we sported with the clouds and rain
we were perfectly suited;
Behind my husband's back I carried on
an affair with you.
What did I care when people said, "Spilt water
can never be recovered?"[17]

If you are really betraying
  my true love,
You're: "Climbing a tree in search of fish,"[18]
  and deserve whatever you get.

Who would have thought you'd have
  found another sweetheart?
It makes me so mad I'm:
  "Half drunk and half crazy."
Leaning against the standing screen, I
  try to figure it out;
I don't understand it, how could you
  abandon me this way?
Though I: "Send letters and post notes,"
  you still refuse to come.
If you are really betraying,
  my affections,
If no one else gets to you first,
  Heaven will destroy you.

I certainly never loved you
  just for your money;
I loved you because I found you
  such an appealing lover.
You knew just how to handle me;
  you were always so clever.
I was a lovely flower that had
  just blossomed in the garden;
But once the butterfly had supped its fill
  it did not return.
Love of the kind that we once
  felt for each other,
Must have been predestined in a former life
  to be fulfilled in this.

I turn things over in my troubled heart
  until I'm depressed.
As the sayings go, "Women are
  easily infatuated,"
And, "Lovers alone are
  never satisfied."
The affair I had with you
  was my first;
It was a fresh flower I brought you;
  how could you give it up?

Now that you've found yourself
 another soul mate;
In the Temple of the God of the Sea[19]
 I'll bring an action against you.[20]

It so happens that all night long the woman:

Tossed first this way and then that,

but could not get to sleep.

The next morning she said to Ying-erh, "Go next door and see if Granny Wang has gone to invite your father or not."

Ying-erh did as she was told and, before long, came back and reported, "Granny Wang left a long time ago."

To resume our story, the old lady got up early in the morning and set out as soon as she had combed her hair and washed her face.

When she arrived at Hsi-men Ch'ing's gate she asked the servants on duty, "Is the gentleman at home?" but they all said, "We don't know," so she went over and waited by the wall across the street.

Before long, Manager Fu showed up to open the shop. The old lady went up to him, bowed and uttered a word of greeting, and then said, "May I trouble you with a question? Is the gentleman at home?"

"What do you want with him," said Manager Fu, "that you should be asking me so early in the morning? If you had asked anyone else, they wouldn't have known, but I'll tell you. Yesterday was the gentleman's birthday, and he spent the day entertaining guests in his home. They had been drinking all day long, and when evening came he took his friends off to the licensed quarter, where they must have made a night of it because he hasn't come home yet. That's where you ought to look if you want to find him."

After the old lady had bowed in gratitude and bade him farewell, she crossed the square in front of the district yamen and started along East Street in the direction of the lane that led into the licensed quarter. At this point, what should she see in the distance but Hsi-men Ch'ing coming toward her on horseback. He was accompanied by two page boys and was sufficiently the worse for wear so that:

His eyes were bleary with drink,

and he was:

Rocking backward and forward,

in the saddle.

"Sir!" the old lady hailed him in a loud voice. "Why don't you have a little less to drink?"

As she spoke, she stepped forward and brought him to a halt by taking hold of the horse's bit with her hand.

"You're Godmother Wang, aren't you?" Hsi-men Ch'ing inquired drunkenly. "What have you got to say for yourself?"

The old lady had whispered no more than a few words in his ear when Hsi-men Ch'ing said, "The page boy gave me the message when he got home. I know she must be angry with me. I'll go to her place right now."

Hsi-men Ch'ing followed the old lady, and the two of them carried on an animated dialogue all the way to their destination.

When they got to the woman's door, Dame Wang went in first and reported, "Young lady, I've got good news for you. Thanks to my efforts, in less than an hour I've succeeded in bringing the gentleman here with me."

When the woman heard that he had come, she hastily ordered Ying-erh to tidy up the room and then went out to welcome him. Hsi-men Ch'ing, who was still:

> More than a little addled with wine,

swaggered right in, fanning himself as he came, and bowed to the woman as he uttered a word of greeting.

The woman returned his salutation and said, "Sir:

> The more eminent you are, the harder you are to see.[21]

How could you simply drop me like this, without giving me so much as a glimpse of your shadow for so long? No doubt, with your new bride to keep you company at home, you're:

> Like glue and like lacquer,

and scarcely have any reason to think of me. How can you still claim, sir, that you haven't had a change of heart?"

"You shouldn't pay any attention to the nonsense people talk," said Hsi-men Ch'ing. "What would I want with a new bride anyway? It's only because my young daughter got married that I was kept busy for a few days and didn't have the time to pay you a visit. That's all there is to it."

"You think you can pull the wool over my eyes, do you?" the woman said. "If you haven't:

> Become enamored of the new and abandoned the old,

or found yourself a new sweetheart somewhere, you'll have to swear an oath on that all too vigorous body of yours before I'll believe you."

"If I ever betray you," said Hsi-men Ch'ing, "may I be afflicted with:

> Boils as big as bowls,
> Three to five years of jaundice,[22] and
> A bite on the balls by a centipede
> as big as a carrying pole."

"You lousy two-timer," the woman said, "what does:

> A bite on the balls by a centipede
> as big as a carrying pole,

have to do with you?"

As she spoke she reached out with her hand, snatched the hat off his head, and threw it on the floor. Dame Wang saw that it was a brand-new, tasseled, "tile-ridge" hat, shaped like the roof of a pavilion with flaring eaves,[23] and hastily picked it up and put it on the table for him.

"Young lady," she said, "you've been complaining about my failure to invite the gentleman here for you; and now look how you're treating him! If you don't put his hat back on for him he'll catch cold."

"Fat chance!" said the woman. "If that fickle ruffian died of a venereal chill, I wouldn't care."

As she spoke she pulled a pin out of his hair and held it in her hand while she examined it. It was a polished gold hairpin with two rows of characters engraved on it that said:

> The horse with the golden bridle neighs
> amidst the fragrant verdure;
> The visitor to the jade tower is drunk
> at apricot blossom time.[24]

It had been given to him by Meng Yü-lou, but the woman assumed that it was a gift from some singing girl, so she put it in her sleeve and refused to return it, saying, "And you claim not to have had a change of heart! Where did the hairpin I gave you get to, that you should be wearing this one from someone else?"

"As for that hairpin of yours," said Hsi-men Ch'ing, "the other day I got drunk and fell off my horse, so hard that my hat was knocked off and my hair came undone. When I looked for your pin I couldn't find it."

"You wouldn't fool a two-year-old child with that story," the woman said. "You mean to tell me you were so befuddled with drink that you couldn't even see a hairpin when it fell on the ground?"

"Young lady," interjected Dame Wang from one side, "you can't hold the gentleman to blame.

> He can detect a bee defecating forty li outside the city,
> But trips over a mangy elephant on his own doorstep:
> He can see things at a distance,
> But not close to home."

"It's bad enough to have her giving me a hard time," said Hsi-men Ch'ing, "without your joining in the fun."

The woman saw that he held in his hand a fine gold-flecked Szechwan fan, with red slats and a gold hinge-joint,[25] and proceeded to snatch it away from him and hold it up to the light.

It so happens that the woman was an old hand where anything about the relations between the sexes was concerned. When she saw that there were traces of tooth-marks all over the fan, confirming her suspicion that it had been given to him by some light-of-love:

> Without permitting any further explanation,

she broke it in two. By the time Hsi-men Ch'ing attempted to rescue it, it had already been torn to tatters.

"That fan was given to me by a friend named Pu Chih-tao,"[26] he protested. "I've only had it for three days, and you've torn it to tatters."

The woman had been harassing him for some time when Ying-erh came in with a cup of tea. Her stepmother told her to put it down and kowtow to Hsi-men Ch'ing.

"You've been nagging away for half the day already," said Dame Wang. "Enough is enough. Don't let yourselves miss the boat. I'll go downstairs and see to things in the kitchen."

The woman told Ying-erh to set up the table in the room where they were. In no time at all the wine and delicacies that had been prepared in advance for the celebration of Hsi-men Ch'ing's birthday, including, as might be expected, roast chicken, cooked goose, fresh fish, potted meat, fruits, and the like, were gotten ready, brought into the room, and set out on the table.

The woman opened a trunk and took out the things she had prepared for Hsi-men Ch'ing's birthday. She then arranged these on a tray and set it down in front of him, so he could see what she was giving him. There were: a pair of jet satin shoes; a pair of scent bags with the drawnwork inscription:

In secret tryst a lover's vow,
I'll follow you where'er you go;

a pair of russet satin kneepads, the borders of which were decorated with a motif of pines, bamboos, and plum blossoms, the "three cold-weather friends"; a sand-green waistband of Lu-chou pongee, decorated with the motifs of auspicious clouds and the symbolic representations of the "eight treasures," lined with watered-silk, fastened with purple cords, and enclosing a pocket filled with aromatic lysimachia and rose petals; and a hairpin in the shape of a double-headed lotus blossom, engraved with a pentasyllabic quatrain that read:

I have a lotus blossom with two heads;
To help keep your topknot in place.
As they grow from the same stem on your head,
So may we never abandon each other.

No sooner did Hsi-men Ch'ing see her gifts than his heart was filled with delight.

He pulled her into an embrace with one arm and gave her a kiss, saying, "Who would have thought you were as clever as this? Such skills are a rare thing."

The woman told Ying-erh to hold the winepot and pour a cup of wine for Hsi-men Ch'ing. Then:

Like a sprig of blossoms swaying in the breeze,
Just as though inserting a taper in its holder,

she kowtowed to him four times. Hsi-men Ch'ing hastened to pull her to her feet and the two of them:

Sat down shoulder to shoulder,
Exchanging cups as they drank.

Dame Wang took several cups of wine with them, until her face became bright red, and then said good-bye and went home, leaving the two of them to enjoy themselves as they pleased. After Ying-erh had seen Dame Wang on her way she locked the front door and went in to sit in the kitchen. The woman continued drinking wine with Hsi-men Ch'ing for some time.

Little by little evening began to fall. Behold:

Dense clouds obscure the evening peaks;
Dark mists streak the distant heavens.
Hosts of stars vie with the white moon
in their brilliance;
Green waters contend with the blue sky
in shades of aquamarine.
Monks make their way toward old temples;
Where, deep in the woods, they elicit
the cawing of crows.
Travelers head for desolate villages;
Where, among the lanes, they arouse
the barking of dogs.
Perched on his branch, the cuckoo cries
at the night moon;
Within the garden, the powdered butterfly
flirts with the flowers.[27]

At this point Hsi-men Ch'ing told his page boys to take the horse and go home since he had decided to spend the night at the woman's house. That evening the two of them were:

Just like cavorting sparrow hawks;
Exhausting themselves to please each other,
Indulging their lusts without restraint.

As the saying goes:

When joy reaches its zenith, it gives birth to sorrow;
When prosperity is at its height, adversity follows.[28]
Light and darkness alternate swiftly.

Let us now return to the story of Wu Sung. After taking charge of the district magistrate's letter and the consignment of presents, he set out from the district of Ch'ing-ho and escorted the shipment all the way to Defender-in-chief Chu Mien's establishment in the Eastern Capital. Once there, he duly turned over the consignment and engaged in several days of idle sightseeing; after which, having obtained a reply, he set out with his companions once again on the highway that led back to Shantung.

He had started out on his journey during the third or fourth month, but by now, on his return trip, the heat of summer had diminished and it was already early autumn. It rained continuously along the way, and the delays that this occasioned prevented him from returning in the expected time. What with one thing and another, the round trip was going to end up taking him more than three months. Held up as he was by the rains and flooding along the route, his spirit was troubled and he felt uneasy in mind and body.

Anxious to hurry back as fast as he could in order to see his elder brother, he dispatched one of the local recruits in his party to travel ahead and inform the district magistrate of their situation. He also privately entrusted him with a family letter for his brother, Wu the Elder, in which he said he would be home before long, no later than sometime in the eighth month.

The local recruit delivered his report to the district magistrate and then set out to look for Wu the Elder's house. It just so happened that:

As providence would have it,
Dame Wang was in the front of her shop at the time.

When the local recruit saw that the door of Wu the Elder's house was shut, he was about to call for someone to open up when the old lady asked him, "Who are you looking for?"

"I've been sent by Captain Wu," replied the local recruit, "to deliver a letter to his elder brother."

"Wu the Elder's not at home," the old lady said. "They've all gone out to pay a visit to the family graves. If you've got a letter for him, you might as well give it to me. As soon as he comes home I'll see that he gets it. It's all the same whether he gets it from you or from me."

Bowing to her with an expression of gratitude, the local recruit pulled out the family letter and handed it over to Dame Wang; after which he hurriedly leapt onto his horse and flew on his way.

Dame Wang took the letter and went over to the woman's house by way of the back door, which Ying-erh opened to let the old lady in. It so happened that the woman and Hsi-men Ch'ing had been at it for half the night and were sleeping late. It was almost lunchtime, but they weren't up yet.

"Sir! And young lady!" Dame Wang called out to them. "Get up! There's something urgent I need to tell you about." She then proceeded:

Thus and thus, and
So and so,

to relate what had happened. "Wu the Second has sent a local recruit to deliver a letter to his elder brother, saying that he'll arrive back before long. I accepted the letter on his behalf and managed to fob off the messenger with a few words. This matter will brook no delay. You must decide on the best thing to do as soon as possible."

If Hsi-men Ch'ing had not heard about this, nothing might have happened, but having heard these words, truly, it was just as though:

The eight-boned structure of his skull had been
split asunder;
Only to have poured into it half a bucketful
of icy snow.[29]

As soon as Hsi-men Ch'ing and the woman had gotten up and put on their clothes, they invited Dame Wang into the room and offered her a seat. She took out the letter and handed it to Hsi-men Ch'ing to read. Wu Sung said in the letter that he would arrive home no later than the Mid-autumn Festival, on the fifteenth day of the eighth month. This threw both of them into a panic.

"What are we going to do about this?" said Hsi-men Ch'ing. "Godmother, please do whatever you can to protect us.

Your kindness will be amply rewarded,
We will never dare to forget it.

Right now:

Our mutual passions are as deep as the sea;
We can't bear to be parted from each other.

But when that bastard, Wu the Second, comes back we'll have to separate. What can we do?"

"Sir," said the old lady, "what's so hard about that? As I pointed out to you once before:

In one's first marriage one must obey one's parents;
In subsequent marriages one can suit oneself.

It's always been the case that:

Brothers and sisters-in-law do not
ask after each other.[30]

Right now, Wu the Elder's 'hundredth day' is about to come up, and the young lady should engage a few Buddhist monks to preside over the burning of his spirit tablet. As soon as that ceremony is completed, and before Wu the Second gets back, you can pop her into a sedan chair, sir, and take her into your household as a concubine. Then, when that bastard, Wu the Second, arrives back, I'll explain the situation to him and he won't have anything to say in the matter. From then on the two of you can:

Live happily ever after,

and the whole damn business will come to nothing."

"Godmother," said Hsi-men Ch'ing, "you're absolutely right. Truly:

If you aren't tough enough,
You will never be secure."

That day, by the time Hsi-men Ch'ing and the woman had finished eating breakfast, they had decided that on the sixth day of the eighth month, which was Wu the Elder's "hundredth day," they would engage monks to perform the Buddhist rites and burn the spirit tablet of the deceased; and that on the evening of the eighth day Hsi-men Ch'ing would send a sedan chair to carry the woman across his threshold. Not long after the three of them had completed their deliberations, Tai-an came back with the horse to take Hsi-men Ch'ing home. But no more of this.

Days and nights speed by like arrows;
The sun and moon shoot back and forth like shuttles.

Before long it was the sixth day of the eighth month. Hsi-men Ch'ing had brought several taels of loose silver and two pecks of polished rice to the woman's house to defray the expenses of the religious observances. He sent Dame Wang to the Pao-en Temple to engage the services of six Buddhist monks, who were to come to the house and perform a "land and water" mass for the benefit of Wu the Elder, and then preside over the burning of his spirit tablet the same evening.

The foreman of the lay workers from the temple arrived early in the morning, at the fifth watch, bearing with him the sutras that would be used in the liturgy. He prepared the consecrated space in which the ceremony would be held and hung up Buddhist effigies. Dame Wang, in the kitchen, supervised the cook who had been engaged to prepare the vegetarian offerings that would be required for the occasion. Hsi-men Ch'ing spent the preceding night at the woman's house.

Before long the monks arrived and started to sound their hand-chimes and strike their drums and cymbals as they embarked upon their declamatory recitations. The liturgy included excerpts from the *Lotus Sutra*[31] and the *Litanies of Emperor Wu of the Liang Dynasty*.[32] That morning they dispatched petitions inviting the representatives of the Three Jewels, the Buddha, the Dharma, and the Sangha, to confer efficacy upon the ceremony by authenticating the covenant. These sacred beings were then invited to partake of the offerings presented to them. At noon the souls of the departed, on both land and water, were summoned to partake of the sustenance provided for their benefit, but there is no need to describe this in detail.

To resume our story, how could P'an Chin-lien bring herself to observe the appropriate abstentions? She remained in bed with Hsi-men Ch'ing and, though the sun was already high in the sky, they had not yet arisen. It was only when the monks requested the presence of the ordainer of the rites to burn incense, sign the petitions, authenticate the covenant, and worship Buddha that she got up, washed her face and combed her hair, made a specious show of putting on mourning, and came out to pay her respects before the Buddhist effigies.

When the company of monks caught sight of Wu the Elder's wife:

Each and every one of them became oblivious to
his Buddha nature and his meditative mind;
Each and every one of them lost control of
"the monkey of his mind and the horse of his will."[33]

All at sevens and eights,
They melted into a heap.

Behold:

The rector becomes flippant;
In reciting the Buddhas' names
he gets them backward.
The precentor becomes confused;
In chanting the words of the sutras
his intonation goes astray.
The incense-burning acolyte,
Knocks over the flower vase.
The candle-bearing ascetic,
Picks up the incense case instead.
The lector who declaims the covenant,
Reads the "Great Sung Empire"
as the "Great T'ang."
The teacher who enacts the rite of repentance,
Reads "Wu the Elder"
as "Grandfather Wu."
The abbot is so flustered;
He grabs the hand of an acolyte
instead of his drumstick.
The novice is so carried away;
He hammers on the pate of an old monk
instead of the bronze chime.
All the merit of their former austerities
comes to nothing in a moment;
Even a myriad guardian deities
could not reduce them to order.[34]

As soon as the woman had burned incense before the effigies, signed the petitions, and paid homage to Buddha, she returned to her room to keep Hsi-men Ch'ing company as before. A feast of wine and meat was laid on, and they gave themselves over to pleasure.

"If anything should come up," Hsi-men Ch'ing instructed Dame Wang, "just take care of it yourself. Don't let them come around and pester the lady of the house."

"You can relax, sir," the old lady said with a laugh. "Just leave those shaven-pated bastards to me. The two of you might as well enjoy yourselves."

Gentle reader take note: In this world Buddhist monks of such high virtue and attainments that they can remain:

Impervious to the temptations of the flesh,[35]

are few. A man of old has said:

In one word they are "bonzes,"
In two words they are "Buddhist monks,"
In three words they are "purveyers of demonic music,"
In four words they are "sex-starved hungry ghosts."[36]

Moreover, as Su Shih[37] has said:

The untonsured are not vicious,
The unvicious are not tonsured,
The vicious are most likely to be tonsured,
The tonsured are most likely to be vicious.[38]

The subject of this disquisition is how hard it is for monks to keep their vows. Living as they do in their high halls and spacious structures, occupying their sanctuaries and dormitories, supported by the alms of their benefactors so that they can count on three meals a day without having to plant or to plow, and without a worry in the world to occupy their minds, they are able to devote all their attention to lust. Laymen, on the other hand, no matter whether they be scholars, farmers, artisans, or merchants, and even though they be wealthy, distinguished, respected, and well-favored, are often so preoccupied with the pursuit of fame and profit or the demands of social intercourse that even though they have beautiful wives or young concubines at their disposal, the sudden recollection of some besetting problem, or the discovery that the rice-jar is empty and the woodshed short of fuel, is enough to make them lose all interest in such things. This is an arena in which they are no match for the monks.[39] There is a poem that testifies to this:

Sex-starved hungry ghosts, they are like
  long-haired monkeys among the beasts;
Disregarding their vows in the pursuit of lust,
  they sully the way of the patriarchs.
These creatures are only fit to be seen
  in their natural habitat;
They should never be invited into the decorated
  halls of one's home.[40]

That morning when the company of monks beheld the spectacle presented by Wu the Elder's wife, it made an indelible impression on them. When they came back from the temple, to which they had returned for their midday repast and a rest from their labors, the woman was in her room drinking wine and enjoying herself with Hsi-men Ch'ing.

It so happens that the woman's bedroom was right next to the consecrated space that had been set aside for the performance of the Buddhist ceremony. There was only the single thickness of a board wall between them. One of the monks, who had arrived before the rest, went up to the basin outside the woman's bedroom window to wash his hands. Suddenly he overheard the woman:

In a trembling voice and melting tones,
Sighing and moaning,
Panting and groaning,

just as though she were engaged in the act of sexual intercourse with someone in her room. At this the monk, pretending to wash his hands, stood there eavesdropping for quite a while.

He overheard the woman appealing in a soft voice to Hsi-men Ch'ing, "Daddy, how long are you going to keep on banging away like that? I'm afraid the monks may come back and hear something. Let me off for now and come as quickly as you can."

"There's no need to get so excited," said Hsi-men Ch'ing. I still haven't burnt the moxa on the top of your mons."[41]

Who would have thought that everything they said to each other was so clearly overheard by that shaven-pated rascal that he might well have ejaculated:

"Is it not delightful?"[42]

After a while, when the whole company of monks had reassembled and they resumed their performance of the liturgy, the word passed from mouth to mouth until they all knew that the woman was carrying on with a man in her room. Imperceptibly they began to reenact the imagined scene:

Miming it with their hands, and
Dancing it with their feet.[43]

By the time the Buddhist ceremony was nearing its completion that evening and the celebrants had moved outside to send the spirit of the departed on its way and burn the paper money that it would need in the other world, the woman had long since divested herself of her mourning and changed into a more colorful outfit. She and Hsi-men Ch'ing stood, shoulder to shoulder, just inside the hanging blind in the doorway, and watched the monks as they prepared to burn Wu the Elder's spirit tablet. Dame Wang brought out a bucket of water, a torch was lit, and in no time at all the spirit tablet and the Buddhist effigies were consumed by the flames.

The shaven-pated rascals with their cold eyes perceived the silhouettes of the man and the woman standing shoulder to shoulder inside the screen and were reminded of the goings-on they had overheard during the day. With one accord they fell to beating their drums and banging their cymbals as if their souls depended on it. A gust of wind blew the abbot's Vairocana hat onto the ground, exposing a bluish, finely polished, shiny pate. No one picked it up, but they all continued banging their cymbals, beating their drums, and:

Falling into a heap with laughter.

During the Tablet-burning Monks Overhear Sounds of Venery

"Reverend sir," called out Dame Wang, "the paper money has already been burnt. Why do you keep on banging away like that?"

"We still haven't burnt the incense on the top of the furnace,"[44] replied the monk.

When Hsi-men Ch'ing heard this he told Dame Wang to distribute the fee for their services as quickly as possible.

"Won't the lady who ordained the rites come out so we can thank her?" asked the abbot.

"Dame Wang," the woman said, "tell them I'd prefer to be excused."

"We'd better let her off for now," the monks replied, and went their way convulsed with laughter.

Truly:

> If one's real work had ever found favor in the eyes
>   of one's contemporaries;
> One would not have had to spend money on rouge
>   in order to paint peonies.[45]

There is a poem that testifies to this:

> Even while burning the spirit tablet
>   the wanton woman is dissatisfied;
> Listening by the wall-side eavesdropping monks
>   get an earful.
> If Buddhism or Taoism were really capable
>   of absolving her of her sins;
> Even the dead, on hearing of such things,
>   would be dispirited.

> If you want to know the outcome of these events,
> Pray consult the story related in the following chapter.

Chapter 9

HSI-MEN CH'ING CONSPIRES TO MARRY P'AN CHIN-LIEN; CAPTAIN WU MISTAKENLY ASSAULTS LI WAI-CH'UAN

THERE IS a lyric to the tune "Partridge Sky" that goes:

With lustful daring as big as the sky they can
  no longer control themselves;
Their passions deep, their love fast, the two
  are inseparable.
Preoccupied with the present and the pleasures
  that they share;
How can they anticipate what future dangers
  lurk within their screen-walls?

Greedy for delight,
They set their fancies free;
But the stouthearted hero, for his part,
  is bent on revenge.
The Lord of Heaven has his own way
  of disposing such affairs;
Victory and defeat, success and failure,
  never cease to alternate.[1]

The story goes that by the time Hsi-men Ch'ing and P'an Chin-lien were finished with the burning of Wu the Elder's spirit tablet they had already exchanged their mourning for more colorful garments. That evening they prepared a feast to which they invited Dame Wang in order to bid her farewell.

Chin-lien turned Ying-erh over to Dame Wang to look after and they then instructed her as follows: "When Wu the Second comes back, just say that the young lady had no way to support herself, and her mother urged her to take steps for the future, so she married a merchant from another town and went off with him."

The woman's trunks had already been dispatched to Hsi-men Ch'ing's house the day before. The broken-down furniture and old clothes that remained were all bequeathed to Dame Wang. Hsi-men Ch'ing also rewarded her for her exertions with a tael of silver.

The next day, in a single sedan chair, accompanied by four lanterns and escorted by Dame Wang and Tai-an, he had the woman carried off to his home. There was no one who lived on that street, whether far or near, who did not know about this affair, but they were all afraid of Hsi-men Ch'ing, who was not above resorting to strong-arm tactics and possessed both money and influence, so who would have dared to interfere?

Someone who lived in the locality composed a doggerel quatrain in commemoration of this event that sums it up very well:

Hsi-men Ch'ing's lack of shame
  is truly laughable;
"First seducing and then marrying,"[2]
  his ill fame is notorious.
Inside the sedan chair there sits
  a wanton whore;
While tagging at her heels there follows
  an old procuress.

When Hsi-men Ch'ing took the woman into his household he had the three ground-floor rooms of the two-storied belvedere in his garden made ready to serve as her living quarters. She had a little courtyard all to herself, to which the only entrance was a postern gate, and flowers and potted miniature plants had been provided for decoration. It was an extremely secluded place where people seldom came even during the daytime. One of the rooms served as her living room and another as her bedroom.

Hsi-men Ch'ing subsequently laid out sixteen taels of silver to buy her a black lacquer bedstead, elaborately adorned with gold tracery, bed curtains of scarlet silk with gold roundels, a dressing case ornamented with floral rosettes, and a complete complement of tables, chairs, and porcelain taborets embossed with patterns of ornamental brocade.

Wu Yüeh-niang, the First Lady of Hsi-men Ch'ing's household, employed two maidservants in her quarters, one of whom was named Ch'un-mei, or Spring Plum Blossom, and the other Yü-hsiao, or Jade Flute. Hsi-men Ch'ing reassigned Ch'un-mei to Chin-lien's quarters, directing her to serve her new mistress diligently and address her as Mother. He then laid out five taels of silver to buy another young maidservant, named Hsiao-yü, or Little Jade, to wait on Yüeh-niang, and a further six taels of silver to buy a scullery maid for Chin-lien, whose name was Ch'iu-chü, or Autumn Chrysanthemum.

P'an Chin-lien was designated as the Fifth Lady in the hierarchy of Hsi-men Ch'ing's wife and concubines. There was a former maidservant, named Sun Hsüeh-o, or Snow Moth, who had come into his household as part of the dowry of his deceased wife, née Ch'en. She was about nineteen years

Hsi-men Ch'ing Conspires to Marry P'an Chin-lien

old, petite in stature, and good-looking. Hsi-men Ch'ing had already granted her the right to wear the fret on her chignon that was a mark of nonservile status and had designated her as his Fourth Lady. That is why Chin-lien was designated as the Fifth Lady. Now that this matter has been explained we will say no more about it.

No sooner had this woman been brought across the threshold than the members of Hsi-men Ch'ing's household, both high and low, became unhappy about the situation.

Gentle reader take note: In this world, women with fire in their eyes are extremely numerous. No matter how worthy and intelligent a wife may be, or how much she may protest that she will not be annoyed if her husband should take a concubine, when she is actually confronted with the situation and sees her husband going off to someone else's room to enjoy the pleasure of:

> Sharing the same bed and a single pillow,

though she be ever so fine by nature, to a greater or lesser extent:

> Her countenance will sour and her heart be ill-disposed.

Truly:

> What a pity that, in its perfect fullness,
> the moon of this night;
> Should shed its pure radiance on other gardens,
> so near and yet so far.[3]

That evening Hsi-men Ch'ing slept in Chin-lien's chambers.

> Like fish sporting in the water;[4]
> Their pleasure could not be exceeded.

The next day the woman combed her hair and made herself up, put on her most attractive outfit, directed Ch'un-mei to accompany her with the ceremonial tea, and set out for the quarters of the First Lady, Wu Yüeh-niang, which were located in the rear of the residential compound. The purpose of this visit was to pay her respects to the ladies of the household and to present the First Lady with the customary pair of "presentation shoes," which had been made by her own hand.

From her seated position Yüeh-niang carefully scrutinized her visitor. She saw that the woman was no more than twenty-four or twenty-five years old and was very good-looking. Behold:

> Her eyebrows are shaped like willow leaves
> in early spring;
> Forever conveying a sense of longing
> for the clouds and rain.
> Her face is like peach blossoms
> in the third month;
> Covertly suggesting thoughts
> of breezes and moonlight.

Her slender waist is lissome;
So constricted as to render her
an idle swallow or languid oriole.
Her sandalwood mouth is dainty;
Attractive enough to drive bees to distraction
and butterflies to madness.
Her jade countenance is alluring,
a flower that can also speak;
Her fragrant visage is enticing,
a jade that exudes its own bouquet.[5]

As Wu Yüeh-niang:

Scanned her from head to foot,
Her glamour ran downward apace;
Surveyed her from foot to head,
Her glamour flowed up with her gaze.[6]
If one were to describe her glamour;
It is like a shining pearl
rolling on a crystal plate.
If one were to speak of her demeanor;
It is like a red apricot on a branch-tip
caught in the morning sun.[7]

When Yüeh-niang had looked her over for a while:

From her mouth no word was uttered, but
In her heart she thought to herself,

"When the servants came home they used to talk a lot about Wu the Elder's wife, but I had never set eyes on her. Now I can see that she really is as good-looking as they say. No wonder that ruffian of mine is so enamored of her!"

Chin-lien first kowtowed to Yüeh-niang and presented her with the customary pair of shoes. Yüeh-niang allowed her to kowtow to her four times. After this Chin-lien also paid her respects to Li Chiao-erh, Meng Yü-lou, and Sun Hsüeh-o, with whom she exchanged salutations on an equal footing as sisters. When these formalities were completed she stood to one side until Yüeh-niang ordered a maidservant to bring her a seat and had her sit down. Yüeh-niang directed the maidservants and other serving women in the household to address her as Fifth Lady.

The woman sat to one side and devoted her undivided attention to sizing up her new companions. She observed that Wu Yüeh-niang was about twenty-six years old and learned that she was called Yüeh-niang, or Moon Lady, because she had been born on the fifteenth day of the eighth month, the day of the Moon Festival. She had:

A face like a silver salver;
Eyes like apricots;
Was gentle in her movements;
Sedate, and of few words.

The Second Lady, Li Chiao-erh, had been a singing girl in the licensed quarter. She was pleasingly plump, rather heavy in build, and had the habit of merely giving a little cough when she was introduced to people. Although she was well versed in all the techniques that might be used to please a patron in bed, as might be expected of a well-known courtesan, she was no match for Chin-lien at the game of breeze and moonlight.

The Third Lady was Meng Yü-lou, who was the most recent addition to the household. She was about twenty-nine years old and had:

A pear-blossom complexion;
A willowy waist;
A tall stature;
And a melon-seed face,
With the addition of a few barely perceptible pockmarks.

She was possessed of a natural beauty, to be sure, but the golden lotuses that peeked out from underneath her skirt were neither all that big nor all that small.

The Fourth Lady, Sun Hsüeh-o, had entered the household as a personal maid. She was:

Petite in stature;
Dainty in demeanor;
Adept at making bouillabaisse;
And could do a pretty pirouette upon the emerald disk.[8]

Chin-lien was able to size them all up in her mind with one sweep of her eyes.

After the "third-day celebrations" were over she got up early every morning and came to Yüeh-niang's quarters, where she kept her company in doing needlework or making shoes. She always insisted on:

Fetching things, whether they were wanted or not; and
Doing things, whether they were called for or not.[9]

In giving orders to the maids and addressing Yüeh-niang, the words "First Lady" were seldom out of her mouth.

She didn't have to play up to her with every trick at her disposal very often before Yüeh-niang was so delighted she scarcely knew what to do with herself. Yüeh-niang started to address her as Sister Six because she was the sixth sibling in her generation of the family, presented her with some of her favorite articles of clothing and jewelry, and invited her to eat her meals and drink tea at the same table with her.

When Li Chiao-erh and the others saw the misguided favor that Yüeh-niang showered upon her they were not happy about it.

"We've been here a lot longer than she has," they grumbled, "but who pays any attention to us? How long has she been here, anyway, that she should be pampered so? Our elder sister doesn't know what she's doing."

Truly:

Though the preceding carriages have overturned
by the thousands;
The carriages that follow continue to overturn
in the same way.
No matter how clearly one may point out
the safest route;
One's honest words are misconstrued
as ill-meant advice.[10]

To resume our story, once Hsi-men Ch'ing had taken P'an Chin-lien into his household she found herself dwelling in:

Vast courtyards and secluded mansions,

and was provided with clothing and jewelry to match.

A woman of beauty and a man of talent,
Both of them were in the prime of life.

In everything they were:

Like glue and like lacquer;

She was:

Obedient to his every whim.

And as for their lewd desires, no day went by on which they were not gratified. But let us put this aside for a moment and say no more about it.

Let us now return to the story of Wu Sung. He arrived back in Ch'ing-ho district before the first ten days of the eighth month were over, reported immediately to the district yamen, and handed over the reply he had brought back from the capital. On reading it the district magistrate was very pleased to learn that his consignment of gold and other valuables had reached its destination safely. He rewarded Wu Sung with ten taels of silver and treated him to wine and food, but there is no need to describe all this.

Wu Sung then returned to his lodgings, changed his clothes and shoes, put on a new hat, locked the door of his room, and headed straight for Amethyst Street. When the neighbors who lived to either side saw that Wu Sung had come back, they felt so apprehensive they broke into a sweat.

"This is one of those times when:

Catastrophe will arise within the
screen-wall of the house,"

they said to themselves. "Once this wrathful god has returned he'll never be willing to call it quits. Something dire is bound to happen."

Wu Sung strode up to his elder brother's front door, pulled aside the bamboo blind, and poked his head inside. Catching sight of no one but the young girl, Ying-erh, who was twisting thread in the hallway under the stairs, he said to himself, "My eyes must be deceiving me?" He called out, "Sister-in-law," but there was no reply. He called out, "Elder Brother," but, again, there was no reply. "My ears must be playing tricks on me," he thought.

"Why is it that I don't hear any response from my elder brother or my sister-in-law?"

He went up to the young girl, Ying-erh, to ask what was going on, but when she saw that it was her uncle who had come back she was too frightened to say anything.

"Where have your father and mother gone?" Wu Sung demanded, but Ying-erh only started to cry and made no reply.

As he continued to press his inquiry Dame Wang, next door, overheard him and realized that it was Wu the Second who had returned. Fearful lest the cat be let out of the bag, she hurried over to help Ying-erh cover up the situation as best she could.

When Wu the Second saw that it was Dame Wang from next door he made her a bow and asked, "Where has my elder brother gone? And why is my sister-in-law nowhere to be seen?"

"Brother Two," the old lady said, "have a seat and I'll tell you all about it. After you left town, sometime in the fourth month, your elder brother came down with an awkward illness and died."

"When in the fourth month did my brother die?" Wu the Second demanded to know. "What kind of an illness was it? And whose medicine did he take?"

"It was on the twentieth day of the fourth month," said Dame Wang, "that your elder brother suddenly came down with an acute case of heart trouble. He was sick for eight or nine days.

> The gods were besought and diviners consulted.[11]

Every kind of medical prescription was tried, but nothing availed, and so he died."

"My elder brother never suffered from such an ailment before," said Wu the Second. "How could he get heart trouble and die, just like that?"

"Captain," said Dame Wang, "how can you talk that way?

> Weather is characterized by unexpected storms;
> Man is subject to unpredictable vicissitudes.[12]
> When you take off your shoes and socks today;
> Who knows whether you will put them on tomorrow?[13]
> Who can be sure that nothing will ever happen to him?"[14]

"Where is my elder brother buried at the present time?" Wu the Second demanded to know.

"By the time your elder brother breathed his last," said Dame Wang, "there wasn't a candareen left in the house. Your sister-in-law, after all, is like a legless crab. Where could she go to look for a grave site or anything like that? Fortunately a wealthy man in the neighborhood who was barely acquainted with Wu the Elder saw fit to help out by providing a coffin. There was nothing for it. After the body had lain in state for three days, it was carried outside the town and cremated."

"Where has my sister-in-law gone to now?" Wu the Second asked.

"She's still:

A young and delicate lass,"

said Dame Wang, "and had no means of support. She managed, somehow or other, to get through her hundred days of mourning, after which her mother urged her to take steps for the future. So, last month, she married a merchant from another town and went off with him. She left this karmic encumbrance of a step-daughter behind and asked me to look after her until you came back. Now that you're here, I can turn her over to you and thus fulfill my responsibilities in the matter."

When Wu the Second had heard her out, he thought to himself in silence for some time and then, abandoning Dame Wang unceremoniously, strode out the door and headed back to his lodgings in front of the district yamen. Opening the door, he went into his room, changed into a set of plain white garments, and sent his orderly out into the street to buy a hempen sash, a pair of cotton shoes, and a mourning cap to wear on his head. He also picked up some fruits and sweetmeats, incense sticks and candles, paper money and imitation gold and silver ingots, and so forth. Returning to his brother's home, he set up a new spirit tablet to Wu the Elder, prepared the soup and rice he had brought with him, lit lamps and candles on the table in front of the tablet, laid out the sacrificial wine and delicacies, and hung up funeral streamers with appropriate quotations from the sutras inscribed on them. It took him less than four hours, all told, to complete these arrangements.

A little after the first watch Wu the Second lit the incense, prostrated himself, and kowtowed, saying, "Elder Brother, hear me, if your departed soul be not too far away! When you were in this world you were of a meek disposition, and now that you are dead the circumstances remain unclear. Look you, if you have:

Suffered injustice and harbor resentment,

as the victim of a murder, appear to me in a dream. As your brother I will undertake to:

Requite your wrong and assuage your resentment."

Pouring the wine to make a libation, and burning the paper money, Wu the Second commenced to weep aloud, saying, "After all:

We came into this world by the same route."

He wept to such effect that among the neighbors to either side there were none who were not moved.

When Wu the Second had finished weeping he shared the soup and rice, wine and delicacies, with his orderly and Ying-erh. As soon as they had eaten he sought out two sleeping mats, instructed his orderly to bed down beside him in the room where they were, sent Ying-erh off to her own room, and then, taking the other mat for himself, lay down in front of the table on which Wu the Elder's spirit tablet was located.

It was around midnight and Wu the Second:

Tossed first this way and then that,

but could not get to sleep. All he could do was to give vent to long sighs. His orderly, meanwhile, lay there, snoring away, stretched out as if he were a dead man. Wu the Second got to his feet to look around and saw that the glass lamp on the table that held the spirit tablet seemed to be:

Half alight and half extinguished.

He sat down on the mat again and started to talk to himself, saying, "When my elder brother was alive he was of a meek disposition, and now that he is dead the circumstances remain unclear."

Before he had finished speaking he suddenly became aware of a gust of cold wind swirling up from underneath the table that held the spirit tablet. Behold:

Devoid of shape and form,
Neither fog nor mist;
Swirling like an eerie wind,
  its chill invades the bones;
Icy as a baleful breath,
  its cold penetrates the flesh.
Nebulous and dark,
It causes the lamplight before the tablet
  to grow dim;
Somber and spectral,
It makes the paper money on the wall
  fly every which way.
All too dimly, it conceals
  the poison-eater's ghost;
With a flutter, it ruffles
  his soul-inducting banner.[15]

This gust of cold wind made Wu the Second's hair stand on end. When he took a close look, he saw someone climbing out from underneath the table that held the spirit tablet, who called out to him, "Younger Brother, I died a grievous death!"

Wu the Second could not see him distinctly, but by the time he started forward to enquire further the cold wind had dissipated and the figure was no longer to be seen.

Wu the Second collapsed onto the mat and sat there thinking to himself, "How uncanny!

Was it a dream or not a dream?

Just now my elder brother wanted to tell me something, but my vital spirits caused his soul to disperse. It seems clear that this death of his must have been the result of foul play."

As he listened he heard the watchman strike the third quarter of the third watch. He looked over at his orderly, who was still fast asleep, and then, muttering unhappily to himself, "I'll have to wait till dawn before I can do anything about it," he fell into a fitful sleep.

Eventually, at the fifth watch, the cock crowed and it began to grow light in the east. The orderly got up to heat some water. After Wu the Second had washed and rinsed out his mouth, he woke up Ying-erh, so she could look after the house, and went out, taking the orderly with him.

As he went along the street he asked the neighbors who lived in the vicinity, "How did my elder brother come to die? And who has my sister-in-law married herself off to?"

The neighbors who lived on that street knew perfectly well what had happened, but they were all afraid of Hsi-men Ch'ing, so no one cared to interfere.

All they would say was, "Captain, there's no need to enquire any further. Dame Wang lives right next door. Just ask Dame Wang and you'll find out what you want to know."

A certain busybody also told him, "That Yün-ko who sells pears and Ho the Ninth, the coroner's assistant, are two people who know a good deal about it."

Wu the Second proceeded immediately to the commercial center of town to look for Yün-ko, but couldn't find him at first. Then he spotted the little monkey, carrying a basket woven out of willow osiers in his hand, on his way back from the rice store.

"Yün-ko," called out Wu the Second, "your brother salutes you."

When the young scamp saw that it was Wu the Second who accosted him, he said, "Captain Wu, you've shown up just a step too late. And another thing. My father's in his sixties and there's no one else to look after him. I can't very well let myself get involved in a lawsuit with you just for the fun of it!"

"Good Little Brother," said Wu the Second, "come with me." Leading him to the upper floor of a restaurant, he summoned the waiter and ordered him to have two meals prepared for them.

"You may be young, Little Brother," Wu the Second said to Yün-ko, "but you've got the filial desire to maintain your family. I'm afraid I don't have anything much to offer."

After groping around in his pocket, he produced five taels worth of loose silver and gave it to Yün-ko, saying, "You take this for the time being and use it to provide for your father's expenses. There's a matter in which you can be of use to me. Once it's taken care of I'll give you another ten taels or so of silver, which you can employ as capital in your trade. Now tell me in detail, whom did my elder brother quarrel with? Who plotted to do him in? And who carried my sister-in-law off in marriage? Tell me everything you know about it and don't conceal anything."

Yün-ko accepted the silver with alacrity, thinking to himself as he did so, "This five taels of silver is enough to provide for my father for three to five months. So even if I get involved in a lawsuit with him it won't matter."

"Brother Two," he said, "hear me out, and try not to get too upset at what I tell you."

Thereupon he told him the whole story, from beginning to end: how he had gone looking for Hsi-men Ch'ing to peddle some pears, how he had subsequently been beaten by Dame Wang, who wouldn't let him into her room, how he had helped Wu the Elder to catch them in the act of adultery, how Hsi-men Ch'ing had kicked Wu the Elder in the solar plexus, how he had suffered from pain in the region of the heart for several days, and then died under suspicious circumstances.

When Wu the Second had heard him out, he asked, "Is what you tell me really true?" Then he asked again, "And who did my sister-in-law marry herself off to?"

"Your sister-in-law," said Yün-ko, "was carried off to his own house by Hsi-men Ch'ing, so he could knock the bottom out of her at his leisure. And you ask me if it's true or if it's false!"

"You'd better not be lying," said Wu the Second.

"Even if I have to tell it in front of the magistrate," said Yün-ko, "I'll tell it the same way."

"Little Brother," said Wu the Second, "if that's the way things stand, let's have something to eat."

In no time at all they polished off a meal served in:

Large platters and large bowls.

When Wu the Second had paid the reckoning and the two of them had come downstairs, he said to Yün-ko, "You go home now and turn over the living expenses to your father. Early tomorrow morning meet me in front of the district yamen, and be prepared to testify on my behalf." Then he went on to ask, "Where does Ho the Ninth live?"

"It's a little late in the day to be looking for Ho the Ninth," said Yün-ko. "Before you came back, three days ago, he took himself off to who knows where."

Wu the Second let Yün-ko go his own way and then went home.

The next day Wu the Second got up early in the morning and went to Master Ch'en's house for assistance in drafting a formal complaint. Then he went to the front gate of the district yamen, where he found Yün-ko was already waiting. Taking him along with him, he went straight into the courtroom, knelt down, and began loudly to complain of a case of injustice.

When the district magistrate saw him, he recognized that it was Wu Sung and asked, "What is your plea? And what injustice do you have to complain of?"

Wu the Second pled as follows: "My brother, Wu the Elder, has been the victim of collusion between the influential malefactor, Hsi-men Ch'ing, and my sister-in-law, née P'an, with whom he has been carrying on an adulterous affair. The accused, having kicked my brother in the solar plexus, then contrived, at the instigation of Dame Wang, to conspire with his paramour in his murder. Ho the Ninth connived with them by fudging the coroner's inspection and cremating the body, thereby destroying the evidence of the crime. At the present time, Hsi-men Ch'ing has sequestrated my sister-in-law by taking her into his house as a concubine. The youngster, Yün-ko, who is now present, is prepared to testify to the truth of these allegations. I trust that Your Honor will see that justice is done."

When he had finished making his plea, Wu the Second presented the written text of his complaint. The district magistrate accepted it, and then asked, "Why is Ho the Ninth not here?"

"Ho the Ninth is aware of his culpability and has decamped," Wu the Second replied. "His whereabouts are unknown."

The district magistrate took Yün-ko's verbal deposition and then withdrew from the courtroom in order to consult with his subordinates.

It so happens that the district magistrate, the vice-magistrate, the assistant magistrate, and the docket officer had all of them, high and low, been engaged in hanky-panky with Hsi-men Ch'ing. For this reason they were unanimous in concluding that this case would be a difficult one to try.

When the district magistrate came back into the tribunal he summoned Wu Sung before him and said, "You are, yourself, a police captain on the staff of this court, and yet you seem to be ignorant of the law. It has always been true that:

> To prove adultery, you must nab both parties;
> To prove theft, you must produce the loot;
> To prove homicide, you must find the wound.[16]

The corpse of that elder brother of yours is no longer available as evidence, and you have not nabbed the accused in the act of adultery. For you to rely solely on the verbal allegations of this youngster in pressing a charge of murder against them is surely to make a travesty of justice. You ought not to act rashly but think it over to yourself.

> If you decide to proceed, then proceed;
> If you decide to desist, then desist."

"If Your Honor will permit me to speak," said Wu the Second, "all of these allegations are true. I have not invented a single one of them."

"You may rise, for the present," said the district magistrate. "Let me:

> Consider what course would be best.

If it turns out to be feasible to do so, I will have them arrested for you."

Only then did Wu the Second get to his feet and go outside. Yün-ko, however, was detained in the yamen and not permitted to return home.

It was not long before someone reported these events to Hsi-men Ch'ing, informing him that Wu the Second had returned and had taken Yün-ko with him to court to make a formal charge against him. Hsi-men Ch'ing was sufficiently alarmed by this development to send his trusted servants, Lai-pao and Lai-wang, with their sleeves full of silver, to take care of the officials involved, all of whom were bought off.

The next morning Wu the Second showed up in the courtroom bright and early and petitioned the district magistrate to proceed with the arrest of the accused. Who would have thought that this official coveted the bribe he had received?

As soon as the case was called, he said, "Wu the Second, you oughtn't to let yourself be misled by anyone else into becoming an antagonist of Hsi-men Ch'ing. The truth in this matter is not clear, and it would be a difficult case to try. As the sage has said:

> If even what one sees with one's eyes,
> May be feared suspect;
> How can words spoken behind one's back,
> Be completely trustworthy?[17]

You ought not to act rashly, on the spur of the moment."

The docket officer, who was standing to one side, also said, "Captain, since you work in the yamen, you must be acquainted with the law. In any case involving an accusation of homicide there are five prerequisites that must be possessed by the prosecutor before he can proceed to trial: the corpse of the victim, the wound, the medical cause of death, the weapon, and evidence that implicates the accused. The corpse of that elder brother of yours is no longer available as evidence. How can such a case be tried?"

"Since Your Honor denies my suit," said Wu the Second, "you must have your reasons."

He then recovered the written text of his complaint, left the courtroom, and returned to his lodgings with Yün-ko, whom he then released from his obligation and allowed to go home.

Scarcely aware of what he was doing, he gazed up to Heaven and gave a long sigh.

> Grinding and gnashing his teeth,

he kept muttering, "That damned whore!" to himself, over and over again. How was this man to find a vent for his anger?

Wu Sung headed straight for Hsi-men Ch'ing's wholesale pharmaceutical shop, with the intent of finding the culprit and taking matters into his own hands.

Manager Fu, who was in charge of the shop, was sitting inside the counter when Wu the Second strode up in an obviously belligerent mood, saluted him, and asked, "Is the Honorable Gentleman at home?"

Manager Fu recognized that it was Wu the Second and replied, "He's not at home, Captain. What have you got to say to him?"

"Walk a few steps with me, if you please," said Wu the Second. "I've got something to say to you."

Manager Fu did not dare to refuse and, coming outside, allowed Wu the Second to lead him to the mouth of an out-of-the-way alley for a chat. No sooner did they get there, however, than Wu the Second adopted a menacing manner, took hold of him by the lapel:

Opened wide his weird eyes,

and demanded, "Do you want to die, or do you want to live?"

"With all due respect, Captain," said Manager Fu, "I've never done anything to offend you. What are you so angry about, Captain?"

"If you want to die," said Wu the Second, "don't bother to reply. But if you want to live, tell me the truth. Where is that bastard, Hsi-men Ch'ing, at this moment? And how long is it since he took my sister-in-law into his household? If you tell me everything I ask, I'll let you go."

Manager Fu was not a courageous man. When he saw that Wu the Second meant business, he became panic-stricken and said, "Calm yourself, Captain! My position in his household is only that of an employee whom he hires for two taels of silver a month to manage his shop. I am not privy to his private affairs. The Honorable Gentleman really isn't at home. Just a little while ago he went out with an acquaintance to have a drink at the Great Tavern on Lion Street. I wouldn't dare tell you a lie."

It was only on hearing these words that Wu the Second released his grip and, with giant strides, flew off in the direction of Lion Street, like a cloud scudding before the wind. Manager Fu was so frightened it was some time before he could stir from the spot. Wu the Second made straight for the tavern just below the bridge on Lion Street.

To resume our story, Hsi-men Ch'ing was in the company of one of the black-robed lictors on the staff of the district yamen, who was known as Li Wai-ch'uan, or Leaky Li. This man played the role of influence peddler in both the district and the prefecture, intervening in public business on people's behalf, and keeping his ear to the ground as he ran back and forth, for a fee. If two parties were engaged in a lawsuit, he would peddle his services as a conduit of confidential information. Or if anyone wished to offer a bribe to the officials or functionaries, he would take a cut from both sides. For this reason he was known around the district yamen by the nickname Leaky Li.

That day, when he saw the district magistrate reject Wu Sung's suit, he had no sooner acquired the news than he came looking for Hsi-men Ch'ing to tell him that Wu the Second's suit had failed. Hsi-men Ch'ing had invited him to have a drink with him on the second floor of the tavern, where he presented him with five taels of silver.

Just as they were settling down to enjoy their drinks, Hsi-men Ch'ing happened to look out the window and caught sight of the formidable-looking Wu Sung, racing up toward the tavern from below the bridge. Realizing immediately that he could be up to no good, he excused himself on the pretext of going to the bathroom, leapt out a rear window, fled along the ridge of an adjacent roof, and jumped down into someone's rear courtyard.

Wu the Second dashed up to the front of the tavern and asked one of the waiters, "Is Hsi-men Ch'ing here?"

"The Honorable Hsi-men," the waiter replied, "is upstairs drinking wine with one of his acquaintances."

Quickening his pace and hiking up his clothes,

Wu the Second flew upstairs, where the only thing he saw was a man, occupying the place of honor, with a pair of painted singing girls sitting to either side of him. He recognized that it was Li Wai-ch'uan, the lictor from the district yamen, and knew that he must have come to tell Hsi-men Ch'ing the news.

Enraged, he went up to him and demanded, "Where has Hsi-men Ch'ing gone?"

When Li Wai-ch'uan saw that it was Wu the Second he was too dumbstruck to get a word out for some time. With a single movement of his leg, Wu the Second kicked over the table, smashing the cups and saucers to smithereens. The singing girls were frozen with fright. Wu the Second struck Li Wai-ch'uan right in the face with his fist.

Crying out, "Don't you . . . !" Li Wai-ch'uan jumped onto the bench he had been sitting on and tried to make his escape through the rear window, but Wu the Second picked him up with both hands and hurled him clear through the front window, so that he fell, headfirst, into the street below, and was knocked unconscious.

When the waiters on the ground floor saw that Wu the Second was running amok they were scared out of their wits. None of them dared to intervene. The pedestrians on either side of the street all stopped and stared. Wu the Second was still on the rampage. Racing downstairs, he saw that his victim was already half dead from the impact of his fall and lay there, at full length on the ground, unable to move anything but his eyes. Thereupon, square in the crotch, he gave him two additional kicks, with the result that:

Alas and alack;
He stopped breathing and died.

"Captain!" everyone exclaimed. "This man is not Hsi-men Ch'ing. You've attacked the wrong person."

"I asked him a question," said Wu the Second. "Why didn't he respond? That's why I assaulted him. Now, it appears that, without even suffering a beating, he has died."

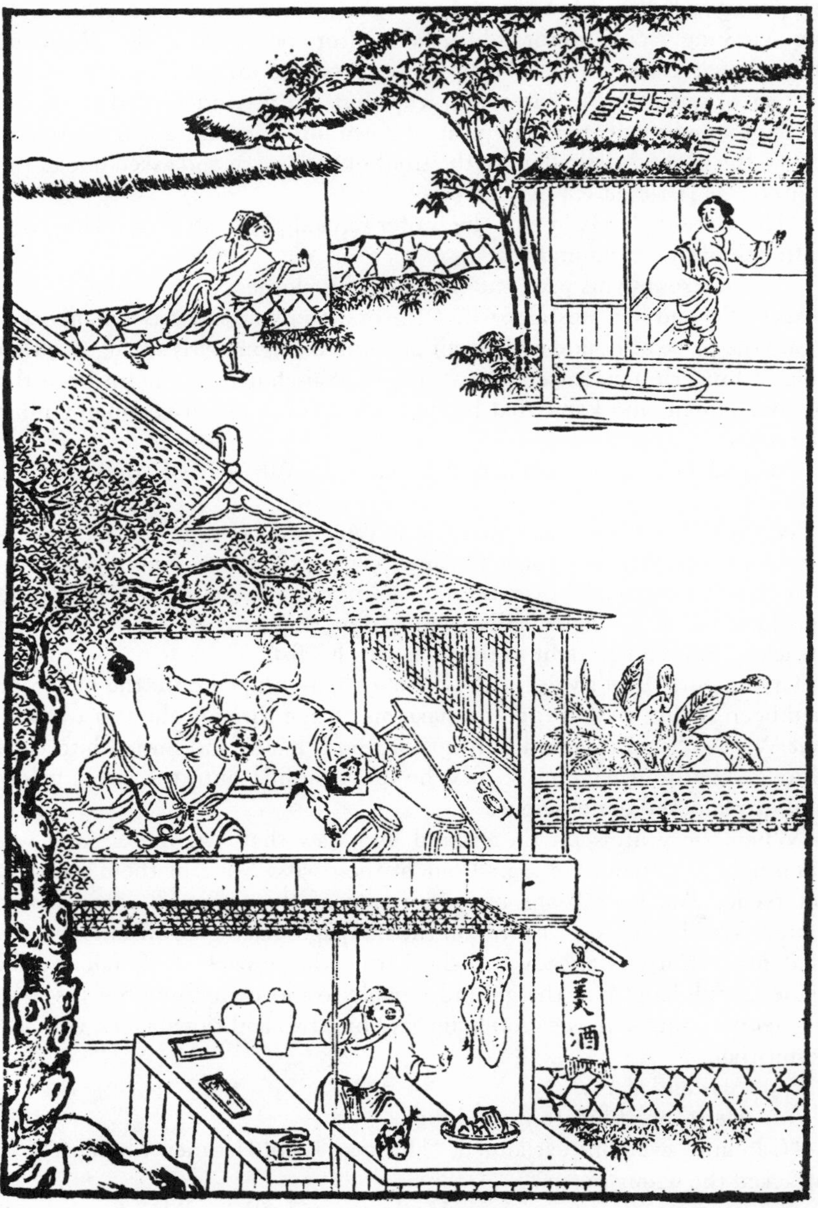

Captain Wu Mistakenly Assaults Li Wai-ch'uan

The local constable and the head of the relevant mutual security unit saw that a homicide had occurred but did not dare to accost Wu the Second directly in order to place him under arrest. All they could do was to gradually edge closer to him until they had him surrounded and then keep him under strict surveillance. The proprietor of the tavern, Wang Luan, and the two singing girls, whose surnames were Pao and Niu, were also taken into custody, after which they all proceeded to the yamen to appear before the district magistrate.

By this time:

> All Lion Street was dumbfounded;
> The district of Ch'ing-ho was disturbed.

The spectators who gathered in the streets could not be numbered.

They all said, "Hsi-men Ch'ing must not have been fated to die. When his assailant discovered that he had made good his escape, he took out his wrath on this man instead."

Truly:

> Mr. Chang drinks wine, but Mr. Li
>   gets drunk;
> The mulberry tree is cut with a knife,
>   but the willow bark is scarred.[18]
> While one person enjoys himself;
> Another is haled into court.
> Can such things be?

There is a poem that testifies to this:

> The hero, endeavoring to assuage his resentment,
>   suffers the rigors of the law;
> What can the Lord of Heaven be up to,
>   that such murk should be allowed to spread?
> In the Nine Springs the poison-eating sojourner
>   has died in vain;
> While, deep in her boudoir,
>   Chin-lien laughs her head off.

> If you want to know the outcome of these events,
> Pray consult the story related in the following chapter.

Chapter 10

WU THE SECOND IS CONDEMNED TO EXILE IN MENG-CHOU; HSI-MEN AND HIS HAREM REVEL IN THE HIBISCUS PAVILION

In the morning you may read the yogācāra sutras;
In the evening recite disaster-dispelling dhāranīs.
If you plant melons you will surely harvest melons;
If you plant beans you will surely harvest beans.
Sutras and dhāranīs have no minds of their own;
Once you have made your karma how can it be unmade?
Hell on the one hand and Heaven on the other;
Are only the consequences of our own actions.[1]

THE STORY GOES that once Wu Sung and the others had been taken into custody by the local constable and the head of the relevant mutual security unit, they all proceeded to the yamen to appear before the district magistrate.

Let us now return to the story of Hsi-men Ch'ing. Having leapt out a rear window on the second floor of the tavern and fled along the ridge of an adjacent roof, he had concealed himself in someone's rear courtyard.

It so happens that this was the residence of Old Man Hu, the doctor. While Hsi-men Ch'ing was still attempting to make himself inconspicuous, what should he see but a large, fat maidservant from Dr. Hu's household coming out to the privy to relieve herself. Just as she was in the process of jutting out her beefy behind, she suddenly caught sight of a man, on all fours, at the foot of the courtyard wall. Dashing back the way she had come, without even taking the time to put herself to rights, she screamed out, "Thief!" so lustily that Old Man Hu hurried into the courtyard to see what was the matter and recognized that it was Hsi-men Ch'ing.

"Congratulations, sir!" he said. "When Wu the Second failed to find you he killed the other person instead. The local constable has already taken him to the district yamen to appear before the magistrate. There is little reason to doubt that he will be convicted of a capital crime. You are free to go home, sir. Nothing will come of it."

Hsi-men Ch'ing then bade Old Man Hu a grateful farewell and swaggered off to his home, where he gave P'an Chin-lien a word-for-word account of everything that had happened. The two of them clapped their hands and laughed for joy, thinking that their only cause for worry had been eliminated.

"Spread a little extra money around, high and low," the woman advised Hsi-men Ch'ing. "See to it that they finish him off, so there'll be no danger of his ever getting free again."

Hsi-men Ch'ing sent his trusted servant, Lai-wang, to convey a set of gold and silver wine vessels and fifty taels of "snowflake" silver to the district magistrate. He also distributed a good deal of additional money, high and low, to the other functionaries, including the docket officer. The only purpose behind this largess was to see to it that Wu the Second was not treated leniently. The district magistrate accepted Hsi-men Ch'ing's bribe.

The next morning, at the early session of the court, the district magistrate took his place on the bench and the local constable and the head of the relevant mutual security unit escorted Wu the Second, along with the proprietor of the tavern and the singing girls who were to act as witnesses, into the courtroom and had them kneel down in front of the dais.

The district magistrate had altered his demeanor overnight. "Wu the Second, you rascal," he said. "Only yesterday you tried to bring a specious suit. I don't know how you could have shown such disrespect for the law. And now you have actually killed someone for no reason at all. What have you got to say in your defense?"

Wu the Second kowtowed and pled as follows: "I trust that Your Honor will see that justice is done on my behalf. My quarrel was really with Hsi-men Ch'ing, but when I unexpectedly ran into this man on the second floor of the tavern and asked him where Hsi-men Ch'ing had gone, he refused to give me an answer. In a momentary fit of rage, I wrongly killed him."

"This rascal is talking nonsense," proclaimed the district magistrate. "How could you have failed to recognize that he was a lictor on the staff of the yamen? You must have had an ulterior motive and are refusing to tell the truth."

Then he called out to his minions, "Put him to the question.

> Man is a miserable creature;
> Unless you beat him he'll never confess."[2]

From either side three or four lictors and jailers appeared, bearing a full panoply of instruments of torture. They turned Wu Sung over, and the blows of the light bamboo fell on him like rain. In no time at all they had administered twenty strokes, but, despite the beating, Wu the Second continued to protest, again and again, that he was being treated unjustly.

"In the past," he said, "there have been occasions when I exerted myself to the utmost on Your Honor's behalf. How can you show no pity for me now? Your Honor ought not to subject me to such cruel torture."

When the district magistrate heard these words he became even more incensed. "You scoundrel!" he replied. "You've killed someone with your own hands and you're still trying to tough it out. You can't stick anyone else with your own guilt." Then he called out, "Put the squeezers on him and give him a good squeezing."

Thereupon the finger-squeezers were applied to Wu Sung and, after being tightened in place, were struck fifty times with a heavy bamboo. He was then put into a long cangue and incarcerated in the district prison, while the witnesses in the case were temporarily detained in the gatehouse of the yamen.

Now among the vice-magistrate and other subsidiary officials there were some who had been on friendly terms with Wu the Second, who knew him to be a man of righteous and heroic cast, and who would have liked to help him out. But because they had all accepted Hsi-men Ch'ing's bribes, their mouths were sealed, and there was nothing they could do about it.

Wu Sung continued to protest that he was being treated unjustly, which delayed matters for a few days, but eventually he was driven into making a hugger-mugger confession. The docket officer on duty, the coroner's assistant, the head of the relevant mutual security unit, the witnesses, and so forth, were all escorted to Lion Street where a formal inquest was performed on Li Wai-ch'uan's corpse, and the inquest report form filled out. The said document read as follows:

> Wu Sung demanded reparation from the deceased for the unequal division of a sum of money, and, failing to receive satisfaction, in a drunken rage, assaulted him with both fists and feet and threw him to the ground with fatal results. The left rib cage, the face, the solar plexus, and the scrotum of the deceased all exhibit livid marks produced by injuries of varying degrees of severity.

After the inquest was completed they returned to the district yamen. One day, after a formal report of the particulars had been prepared, the prisoner was escorted under guard to Tung-p'ing prefecture to await the final disposition of his case.

Now the prefect of Tung-p'ing was named Ch'en Wen-chao.[3] He was a native of Honan and was an official of absolute integrity. As soon as he learned that the prisoner had arrived he took his position on the bench. What was this official like? Behold:

All his life he has been correct and upright;
By natural endowment he is worthy and perspicacious.
In his youth he studied his books
  by light reflected from the snow;[4]
Once grown up he responded to imperial inquiries
  in the Palace of Golden Bells.[5]
He constantly harbors
  a loyal and filial heart;

He is always motivated by
humane and kind considerations.
The population of his jurisdiction grows;
The taxes are honestly levied;
Common people who sing his praises
fill the streets.
The number of lawsuits is diminished;
Banditry and robbery are curtailed;
The clamor of elders extolling his virtues
is heard in the marketplace.
The people curb his carriage and tug at his stirrups;[6]
Enshrining his name in the history books
for a thousand years.
His merits are carved on stone and engraved on stelae;
So that his fame as a prefect will be acclaimed
for all time.
Correct and upright, of absolute integrity,
he is the father and mother of the people;
Worthy and good, square and proper,
he deserves the epithet "Azure Heaven."[7]

Now the prefect, Ch'en Wen-chao, already knew something about this case and gave immediate orders that both the accused and the witnesses should be brought before him. The first thing he did, right there in the courtroom, was to examine the report of the case that had been forwarded from Ch'ing-ho district as well as the various depositions and the recommended sentence. Truly, what did this report say? The text read as follows:

> Ch'ing-ho district reports a case of homicide to Tung-p'ing prefecture, as below: The accused, Wu Sung, twenty-seven years of age, is a native of Yang-ku district. Because of his unusual strength, the magistrate of Ch'ing-ho district appointed him to the post of police captain. On his return from an official mission, while preparing to make a ritual sacrifice in commemoration of his deceased elder brother, he learned that his sister-in-law, née P'an, had remarried before the expiration of her mourning period. The said Wu Sung, on making further inquiries in the streets, made his way, as he should not have done, to the second floor of Wang Luan's tavern in Lion Street, where he encountered the initially unknown but now identified Li Wai-ch'uan. Upon drunkenly demanding repayment of a prior loan of three hundred cash and meeting with a refusal from Li Wai-ch'uan, he engaged him, as he should not have done, in an affray, neither one being willing to submit to the other. In the course of being seized, beaten, kicked, and thrown to the ground, the victim suffered such severe injuries that he died on the spot. Two singing girls, surnamed Niu and Pao, were present at the time as witnesses of the affray. The accused was taken into custody by the local constable and the head of

the relevant mutual security unit. An official was deputized to proceed to the site of the crime, summon the coroner's assistant, the head of the relevant mutual security unit, the witnesses, and so forth, and conduct an inquest. Depositions were taken, bond was posted for the witnesses, and the inquest report form was duly filled out and submitted. If no conflicting evidence is adduced during retrial, the recommended sentence is as follows: According to the article of the penal code that reads "In cases of involuntary manslaughter resulting from an affray, no matter whether the fatal injury be inflicted by hand, foot, other object, or metal blade, the penalty shall be strangulation,"[8] Wu Sung should be sentenced to death by strangulation. The testimony of the proprietor of the tavern, Wang Luan, and the singing girls surnamed Niu and Pao indicates them to be innocent of any crime. The case is hereby duly forwarded to your tribunal for final disposition.

Date: The nth day of the eighth month of the third year of the Cheng-ho reign period.[9]

Signed: Li Ta-t'ien, District Magistrate
Yüeh Ho-an, Vice-Magistrate
Hua Ho-lu, Assistant Magistrate
Hsia Kung-chi, Docket Officer
Ch'ien Lao, Clerk, Office of Punishment

When the prefect had finished reading this document he called up Wu Sung, who knelt down in front of the dais, and asked him, "Why did you kill Li Wai-ch'uan?"

Wu Sung kowtowed and appealed to the prefect, saying, "Lord 'Azure Heaven,' to appear before you is to see the light of day. If you permit me to speak, I will presume to speak."

"Pray speak up, then," the prefect responded.

"I was actually bent on avenging the death of my elder brother," said Wu Sung. "In the course of seeking out Hsi-men Ch'ing, I wrongly assaulted and killed this person."

He then gave an account of the foregoing events, concluding as follows, "The truth is that I have:

Suffered injustice and harbor resentment.

The power of Hsi-men Ch'ing's money is too great for me to withstand. The only thing that rankles is that my brother, Wu the Elder, still bears a grudge in the nether world and has lost his life for nothing."

"You need not say another word," the prefect responded. "I already know all about it."

He then called up the clerk from the office of punishment, Ch'ien Lao, and ordered him to be given twenty strokes with the light bamboo, saying, "That district magistrate of yours doesn't deserve to continue in office. How can he have put justice up for sale so flagrantly?"

Thereupon, after taking the depositions of all the witnesses once again, he picked up his brush and rewrote Wu Sung's confession.

Turning to his subsidiary officials, he said, "This man was seeking to avenge the death of his elder brother when he wrongly killed this Li Wai-ch'uan. He is a man of honor, motivated by righteous indignation. This is not an instance of 'deliberate homicide of an innocent person.' "

On the one hand, he ordered that Wu Sung's long cangue be taken off and replaced with the lighter one prescribed for lesser offenses, and had him incarcerated in the prefectural prison, while he sent the witnesses back where they came from to await the final disposition of the case. On the other hand, he sent a dispatch to Ch'ing-ho district ordering the magistrate to apprehend the influential malefactor, Hsi-men Ch'ing; the sister-in-law of the accused, née P'an; Dame Wang; the youngster, Yün-ko; and the coroner's assistant, Ho the Ninth; to subject them to honest interrogation; and to report the results before taking any further action.

While Wu Sung was in prison in Tung-p'ing prefecture, since everyone knew that he was the victim of a miscarriage of justice, the jail warden and the guards actually provided him with food and wine without demanding a candareen for themselves.

It was not long before someone reported these events back to Ch'ing-ho district, and when Hsi-men Ch'ing got wind of them he was more alarmed than before. Ch'en Wen-chao was an official of absolute integrity, and he was afraid to try to bribe him. He had to go ask for help from the Ch'en family, to whom he was related by his daughter's marriage. That very night he dispatched one of their trusted servants, along with his own servants, Lai-pao and Lai-wang,[10] to travel to the Eastern Capital and deliver a letter to Yang Chien, the commander in chief of the Imperial Guard.

The commander, in his turn, sought the aid of the grand councilor and grand preceptor, Ts'ai Ching. The grand preceptor, fearing lest the reputation of District Magistrate Li be tarnished, immediately sent an urgent secret message to Ch'en Wen-chao in Tung-p'ing prefecture, directing him not to insist on haling Hsi-men Ch'ing and P'an Chin-lien into court.

Now this Ch'en Wen-chao had been the director of one of the two divisions of the Court of Judicial Review in the capital when he was promoted to the position of prefect of Tung-p'ing prefecture, and Grand Preceptor Ts'ai had been his examiner when he qualified for office by passing the civil service examinations. He was also aware that Yang Chien, as the commander in chief of the Imperial Guard, was an official who had the ear of the emperor himself. Thus:

> His obligations cancelled each other out.[11]

All he could do under the circumstances was to save Wu Sung from the death penalty. His judgment was therefore rendered as follows:

> Recommended sentence: that the accused shall be beaten forty strokes on the back with the heavy bamboo; that the name of his offense shall be tattooed on his face; and that he shall be condemned to military exile for life at a distance of 2,000 li.
>
> In addition: whereas Wu the Elder is already dead; and whereas his corpse is no longer available as evidence; and whereas nothing more than suspicions have been adduced as to the circumstances of his death; the matter shall not be pursued further. All other persons involved with this case may be released and permitted to return to their homes.

The records of the case were forwarded to the Ministry of Justice in the capital, and thence to the Censorate for ratification, and, one day, a directive came down ordering that the sentence be carried out without delay. Ch'en Wen-chao had Wu Sung brought out of prison, and the imperial decree was read out loud to him in the courtroom. His cangue was then removed, and there was no way to avoid the infliction of forty strokes on the back with the heavy bamboo. He was then fastened into a seven-and-a-half catty, ironclad, round-ended cangue, and two columns of gold-colored characters were tattooed on his face, preparatory to his removal to the prison camp at Meng-chou.

After the other persons involved in the case had been sent on their way, the prefect, right there in the courtroom, stamped the necessary documents with his seal and deputed two guards to escort Wu Sung to Meng-chou and turn him over to the authorities there.

That very day Wu Sung and the two guards left Tung-p'ing prefecture and returned to his brother's house in Ch'ing-ho district. He auctioned off whatever furnishings remained in order to provide the two guards with expense money along the way.

Then he approached a neighbor, Yao the Second, and asked him to look after Ying-erh for him, saying, "If, by imperial grace, an amnesty should ever be proclaimed that would allow me to return home:

> Your kindness will be amply rewarded,
> I will never dare to forget it."

The neighbors in the vicinity and the prominent householders who had been on good terms with Wu the Second, knowing that he was a man of honor who had had the misfortune to suffer this punishment, all helped him out with gifts of silver, or by providing food and wine, cash, or rice.

Wu the Second then went to his own lodgings and asked his former orderlies to bring out the bundle of his personal effects. That very day they set out on their journey, leaving Ch'ing-ho district, and wending their way along the highway toward Meng-chou. The weather was that of the middle month of autumn. With regard to this trip, truly:

Wu the Second Is Condemned to Exile in Meng-chou

If one is only able, somehow,
to preserve his foolish life;
He will be happy to go hungry
for the rest of his days.[12]

There is a poem that testifies to this:

The prefect, in investigating this case,
maintained the utmost impartiality;
He was successful in rescuing Wu Sung
from the brink of death.
Though he was condemned to military exile
in a distant prison camp;
The sickly verdure recovered its health
upon exposure to the genial breeze.[13]

Wu the Second set off on his way to military exile in Meng-chou. But no more of this.

To resume our story, when Hsi-men Ch'ing heard that his enemy had taken to the road, he felt as though:

The stone on his head had finally fallen to the ground;
The blockage in his heart had been miraculously removed.

He was as happy as could be.

Thereupon he ordered his servants, Lai-wang, Lai-pao, and Lai-hsing, to tidy up and sweep clean the Hibiscus Pavilion in the rear flower garden, set up standing screens, suspend gold-colored partitions, and make all the necessary preparations for a feast. Having engaged musicians to provide:

Wind and string instruments, song, and dance,

for their entertainment, he invited the First Lady, Wu Yüeh-niang, the Second Lady, Li Chiao-erh, the Third Lady, Meng Yü-lou, the Fourth Lady, Sun Hsüeh-o, and the Fifth Lady, P'an Chin-lien, to join him in a party for the:

Jollification of the entire family.

The wives of his household retainers, along with maidservants and waiting women, stood in attendance on either side. What were the revels like that day? Behold:

Incense smolders in precious tripods;
Blossoms are displayed in golden vases.
The table service is an array of
exotic antiques from Hsiang-chou;[14]
The hanging blinds are adorned with
shining pearls from Ho-p'u.[15]
Crystal platters,
Are piled high with the magic jujubes and pears
that confer immortality;

Chrysoprase goblets,
Are filled to the brim with the jade and carnelian hued
nectars of the gods.
There are deep-fried dragon livers,
And roast phoenix entrails;
Truly, one has but to use one's chopsticks
to exhaust ten thousand cash.
There are black bears' paws,
And purple dromedaries' pads;
When these are presented after the wine
their fragrance suffuses the table.

And there are also:

Tenderly steamed fragrant rice garnished with
red lotus blossoms;
And neatly sliced gray mullet large enough to
swallow an official seal;[16]
Bream and carp from the I and Lo rivers,
Truly, more costly than beef or lamb;[17]
As well as longans and litchis,
Verily, the finest fruits of the Southeast.
As the phoenix tablets are crushed,[18]
Foaming whitecaps of brick tea
break in white jade cups;
As the carnelian liquid is poured,
The pure bouquet of vintage wine
bursts from the golden flagon.
In fine, the sumptuousness of this repast
could put Lord Meng-ch'ang to shame;[19]
This feast, alone, required such wealth
as might have beggared Shih Ch'ung.[20]

On this occasion, as soon as Hsi-men Ch'ing and Wu Yüeh-niang had occupied the positions of honor, the rest of the ladies, Li Chiao-erh, Meng Yü-lou, Sun Hsüeh-o, and P'an Chin-lien, arrayed themselves on either side and the drinking began:

With the raising of glasses and passing of cups;[21]
Amid clustering blossoms and clinging brocade.

Who should appear at this juncture but the page boy, Tai-an, who led into their presence a young boy and a young girl, with their hair cut straight across their foreheads, prepossessing in appearance, and carrying a pair of gift boxes.

"They're from Eunuch Director Hua's house, next door," he said. "They've brought over some flowers for the ladies to put in their hair."

The two messengers went up and kowtowed to Hsi-men Ch'ing, Yüeh-

Hsi-men and His Harem Revel in the Hibiscus Pavilion

niang, and the others, and then stood to one side, saying, "Our mistress has sent us over to deliver this box of pastries and some flowers for Madam Hsi-men to wear in her hair."

Yüeh-niang pulled aside the hanging blind to take a look at the gifts. One box contained stuffed, spiced, gold-colored pastries, of a kind reserved for use in the imperial palace. The other box contained newly picked fresh plantain lilies.

"I've been the occasion of putting your mistress to too much trouble once again, I fear," said Yüeh-niang, utterly delighted.

She saw to it that the two of them were offered something to eat and then gave the young girl a handkerchief and the young boy a hundred cash.

"Tell your mistress many thanks," she said, and then asked the young girl, "What's your name?"

"I'm called Hsiu-ch'un," she replied, "and the boy's called T'ien-fu."

After they were gone, Yüeh-niang turned to Hsi-men Ch'ing and said, "This lady from the Hua household next door is really nice. She's always sending her page boy and maidservant over here with gifts for me, and I'm afraid I haven't yet done anything to reciprocate."

"It hasn't even been two years," responded Hsi-men Ch'ing, "since Brother Hua the Second took this woman to wife. He tells me himself that she has a most accommodating disposition, otherwise she'd never consent to keep two such attractive young girls as personal maids."

"Not long ago," said Yüeh-niang, "in the sixth month, when the old gentleman of their household passed away, I met her by the graveside while attending the funeral. She is petite in stature and has a round face, delicately curved eyebrows, and a fair complexion. She seems very considerate by nature and must still be quite young, not more than twenty-three or twenty-four."

"You don't know the story," said Hsi-men Ch'ing. "She was originally the concubine of Privy Councilor Liang Shih-chieh when he was regent of the Northern Capital at Ta-ming prefecture, so her union with Hua Tzu-hsü is a case of remarriage, though she brought him a considerable fortune."

"The fact that she has sent over these gift boxes indicates a desire to get better acquainted," said Yüeh-niang. "We are next-door neighbors, after all. We mustn't be remiss in our social obligations. One of these days we'd better send something over there in return."

Gentle reader take note: It so happens that the maiden name of Hua Tzu-hsü's wife was Li. Because she was born on the fifteenth day of the first month, and someone had made her family a gift of a pair of fish-shaped vases on that day, her informal name was P'ing-erh, or Vase. She had formerly been a concubine in the household of Privy Councilor Liang Shih-chieh in Ta-ming prefecture. Privy Councilor Liang was the son-in-law of Grand Preceptor Ts'ai Ching in the Eastern Capital.[22] His wife was extremely jealous by nature and had beaten numbers of maidservants and concubines to death and buried them in the rear flower garden. Li P'ing-erh, consequently, resided outside the women's quarters in her husband's studio, where she had a waiting woman to look after her.

It happened that on the fifteenth day of the first month of the first year of the Cheng-ho reign period,[23] during the Lantern Festival, Privy Councilor Liang and his wife were enjoying themselves on the upper floor of the Blue Cloud Tavern, when Li K'uei slaughtered their entire household, old and young alike, during a bandit raid on Ta-ming prefecture.[24] Privy Councilor Liang and his wife were forced to flee for their lives. On this occasion Li P'ing-erh managed to escape the carnage, along with her waiting woman, but not before she had appropriated a necklace of one hundred large, Western Ocean[25] pearls and a pair of onyx gemstones weighing a good two ounces, with which she made her way to the Eastern Capital to seek refuge with relatives.

At that time Eunuch Director Hua had just been promoted from his post in the imperial palace to the position of grand defender of Kuang-nan. Because his nephew, Hua Tzu-hsü, was still without a mate, he sent a matchmaker to propose a marriage, and Li P'ing-erh thus entered the household as a legitimate wife. When the old eunuch departed to take up his post in Kuang-nan, he took them with him, but after they had lived there for something over half a year, he unfortunately fell ill and petitioned the throne for permission to retire to his native place. Because he was originally from Ch'ing-ho district, it was there that he had come to live in retirement.

Now that Eunuch Director Hua had died, his entire estate fell into the hands of Hua Tzu-hsü, who made it a daily practice to frequent the licensed quarter with his friends, one of whom was Hsi-men Ch'ing. They had formed a club, of which Hsi-men Ch'ing was the senior member.

The second member was named Ying Po-chüeh, or Sponger Ying. He had started life as the son of Master Ying, the merchant, who owned a fine-silk-goods store, but once the business had come into his hands, he had lost his capital and fallen on hard times. He now made his living by squiring young rakes about the licensed quarters and picking up whatever he could along the way. He was an expert performer at kickball and knew all there was to know about such games as backgammon and elephant chess.

The third member was named Hsieh Hsi-ta, or Tagalong Hsieh, whose courtesy name was Tzu-ch'un. He, too, was a profligate hanger-on as well as being an expert performer on the *p'i-p'a*. He had nothing to do every day but to haunt the licensed quarter and live off:

> The tea and rice afforded by romance.

There were also other members with names such as Chu Jih-nien, or Sticky Chu; Sun Kua-tsui, or Blabbermouth Sun; Wu Tien-en, or Heartless

Wu; Yün Li-shou, or Welsher Yün; Ch'ang Shih-chieh, or Cadger Ch'ang; Pu Chih-tao, or No-account Pu; and Pai Lai-ch'iang, or Scrounger Pai. There were ten of them in all.[26] Pu Chih-tao had died recently, and Hua Tzu-hsü, or Nobody Hua, had been allowed to take his place.

Every month the ten of them met together somewhere and engaged the services of two singing girls so they could enjoy themselves:

Amid clustering blossoms and clinging brocade.

The other members of the club, observing that Hua Tzu-hsü was the profligate scion of a eunuch household and that he had:

Money to spend and silver to squander,[27]

were anything but backward in encouraging him to patronize singing girls in the licensed quarter, with the result that he often stayed out for three or five nights in a row without going home. Truly:

On the purple roads spring is at its height;
In the red bowers the music is intoxicating.
How long a span of life are we allotted?
Not to enjoy it is to live in vain.[28]

Now that this matter has been explained, we will say no more about it.

To resume our story, that day Hsi-men Ch'ing and his wife and concubines enjoyed a feast in the Hibiscus Pavilion for the:

Jollification of the entire family.

The party did not break up until evening. By the time Hsi-men Ch'ing retired to P'an Chin-lien's quarters he was already half drunk and, exhilarated by the wine, wanted to play at clouds and rain with her. The woman hastily lit some incense and laid out the bedding, after which they:

Took off their clothes and went to bed.

Hsi-men Ch'ing, however, did not proceed directly to the clouds and rain. Knowing that the woman was partial to "toying with the flute,"[29] he sat down inside the green gauze mosquito netting and ordered her to get down on all fours beside him. After:

Lightly adjusting her golden bracelets,

she took hold of his organ with both hands and popped it into her mouth. Hsi-men Ch'ing:

Bent his head in order the better to savor,
The marvelous sight as it went in and out.
She sucked it audibly for some time, until
Their lewd excitement was redoubled.

At this point Hsi-men Ch'ing called out to Ch'un-mei to come in and bring them some tea. The woman was afraid the maidservant would see what they were up to and hastily let down the bed curtains.

"What are you afraid of?" asked Hsi-men Ch'ing. "Brother Hua the Second next door," he went on, "actually has two attractive young girls as maid-

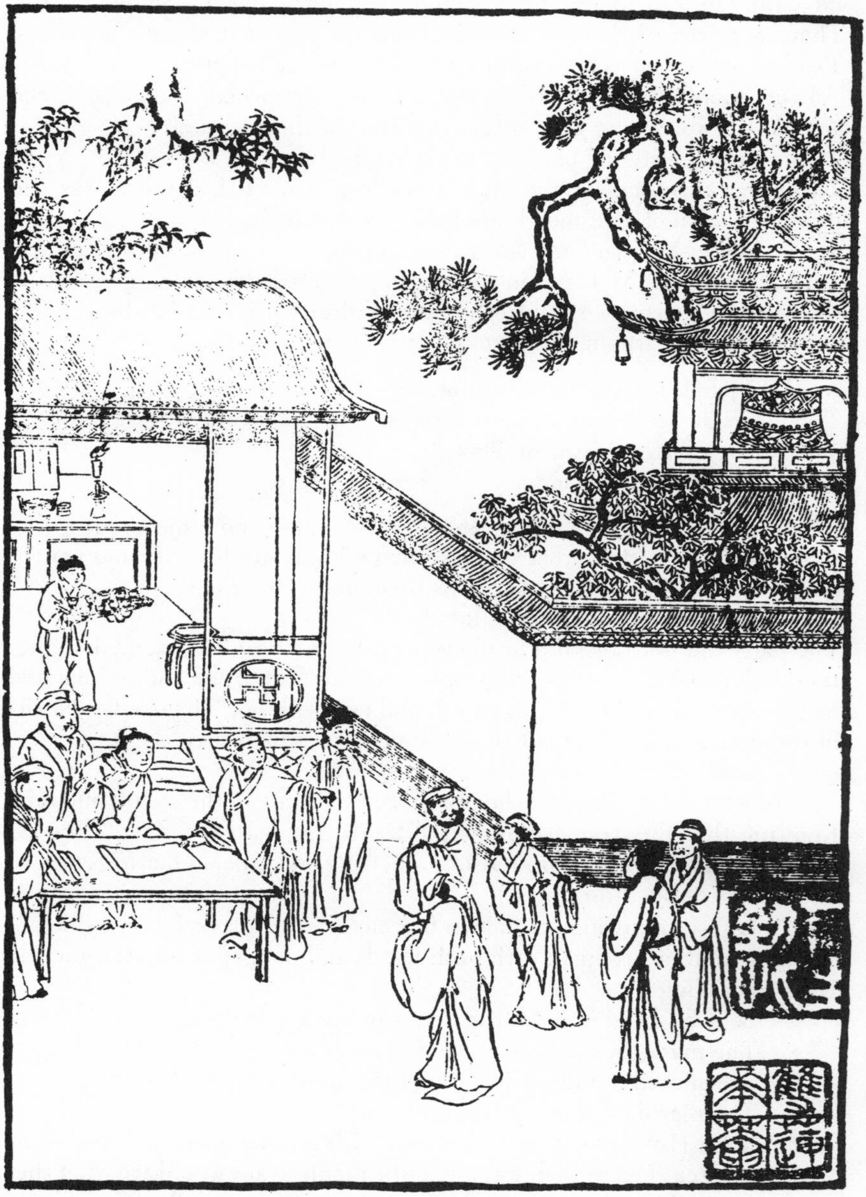

Hsi-men Ch'ing and His Cronies Form the Brotherhood of Ten

servants in his rooms. The one who delivered the flowers today was the youngest. There is another one, as old as Ch'un-mei, whom Brother Hua the Second has already had his way with. I caught sight of her once, when she had followed her mistress to the front door, and could see that she has a good figure. Who would have thought that Brother Hua the Second, young as he is, would carry on that way in his own house?"

When the woman heard this, she gave him a look, saying, "You crazy good-for-nothing! I'd just be wasting my breath on you! If you want to have your way with this maidservant, go ahead and take her. What need is there to:

Beat around the bush; or
Point out a mountain and promise a millstone.[30]

Why drag anyone else into it? In the first place, I'm not that sort of person; and, in the second place, she's not really my maidservant to begin with. If that's the way things stand, tomorrow I'll pay a visit to the rear compound and leave the way open for you. Just call her into the room and have your way with her. That's all there is to it."

When she had finished speaking, she went back to "toying with the flute" until Hsi-men Ch'ing ejaculated. Only then did they go to sleep:

Arm around head and thigh over thigh.

Truly:

Past mistress of the intimate arts,
  she caters to her lover's whim;
How quick she is, and diligent,
  to "play the purple flute."[31]

There is a lyric to the tune "Moon on the West River" that testifies to this:

The scent of orchid and musk pervades
  the gauze netting;
The delicate beauty is an old hand at
  "playing the flute."
Her snow-white jade body is visible
  through the bed curtains;
It's enough to make one's "ethereal and
  material souls take flight."

On jade wrists she gently adjusts
  golden bracelets;
Both of them are passionate,
  "half drunk, half crazed."
The talented gentleman is moved
  to enjoin his partner,
"Take it easy, so you can go on sucking
  a little longer."[32]

The next day, sure enough, the woman went to pay a visit to Meng Yü-lou's quarters in the rear compound. Hsi-men Ch'ing called Ch'un-mei into the room and had his way with the young girl.

When spring touches the apricot and peach trees,
their new buds burst into red flower;
When the breeze plays among the willow fronds,
they are made to bend their green waists.[33]

From this day on, her mistress treated her with special favor, no longer sending her to the kitchen to:

Do the cooking or clean the stove,

but only asking her to serve inside her own rooms, to:

Make the beds and fold the quilts,

or to fetch tea. She presented her with some of her favorite articles of clothing and jewelry, and encouraged her to bind her feet in order to keep them delectably tiny.

It so happens that Ch'un-mei was quite unlike Ch'iu-chü. She was naturally intelligent, enjoyed repartee, was quick on the uptake, and rather good-looking. Hsi-men Ch'ing was very partial to her. Ch'iu-chü, on the other hand, was stupid and dull, and could not be relied upon to perform her tasks. She was the one who got beaten by her mistress. Truly:

The swallows and sparrows round the pond
make quite a clamor with their chatter;
All appeal to humanity and righteousness
and judge each other stupid or worthy.
Though they may belong to different species,
they are alike in being birds of the air;
And yet, noble and base, high and low,
even they are not all the same.

If you want to know the outcome of these events,
Pray consult the story related in the following chapter.

Chapter 11

P'AN CHIN-LIEN INSTIGATES THE BEATING OF SUN HSÜEH-O; HSI-MEN CH'ING DECIDES TO DEFLOWER LI KUEI-CHIEH

When the woman, for her part,
  is "as jealous as can be";
The wastrel, on his part,
  "does just as he pleases."
Susceptible to "clever words
  and deceptive phrases";
He cares nothing for "new loves
  and old affections."
Once out the door, he
  "feels the tug of red sleeves";
And finds another place to
  "peddle his romantic feelings."
Each day becomes "a Cold Food
  or a Lantern Festival";[1]
Who will not "cater to his whims
  or connive in his ruin"?[2]

THE STORY GOES that once P'an Chin-lien was established in Hsi-men Ch'ing's household she:

Relied on his favor to become arrogant;
Transmuting the "cold" into the "hot,"

to such effect that, day or night, there was no longer any peace and quiet to be had. She was extremely suspicious by nature and was forever:

Listening at the fence or eavesdropping by the wall,

on the lookout for an excuse to make trouble. Nor was her maidservant, Ch'un-mei, any model of forbearance.

One day, as ill luck would have it, Chin-lien was upset over some insignificant matter and spoke a few intemperate words to Ch'un-mei. Ch'un-mei, having no place else to vent her spleen, went back to the kitchen in the rear compound and started:

Pounding the table and banging the pans,
in no mood to be trifled with.

Sun Hsüeh-o, who found this behavior annoying, twitted her sarcastically with the words, "You crazy good-for-nothing! If you're hard up for a man, go be hard up someplace else. I can do without your high-handedness around here."

When Ch'un-mei, who was still at the height of her ill-humor, heard these words, she flared up immediately.

"Just who is insinuating that I'm on the lookout for a man?" she demanded to know.

Hsüeh-o saw that she was really out of sorts and managed to keep her mouth shut. Ch'un-mei, however, took off in a huff for the front compound, where she gave Chin-lien a provocative word-for-word account of this exchange:

Thus and thus, and
So and so,
with a few additional details thrown in for good measure, such as, "She claimed that you connive with me to share our favors with him as a means of keeping him all to ourselves."

Chin-lien had had a bellyful. She was already feeling rather tired from having to get up earlier than usual in order to see off Wu Yüeh-niang on her way to a funeral. She took a nap and then went out to sit in the pavilion in the garden.

While she was there, who should come strolling along but Meng Yü-lou, who addressed her with an ingratiating smile, saying, "Sister, how come you're so silent and glum?"

"I don't even want to talk about it," said Chin-lien. "I'm feeling all tired out this morning. Where've you come from, Sister Three?"

"I've just paid a visit to the kitchen in the rear compound," said Meng Yü-lou.

"And what did that woman have to say to you?" asked Chin-lien.

"Sister didn't have anything to say," replied Yü-lou.

Although Chin-lien said no more about it at the time, she stored up the resentment in her heart and, henceforth, regarded Sun Hsüeh-o as her enemy. But no more of this.

The two of them did some needlework together for a while when Ch'un-mei appeared with a pot of hot water and Ch'iu-chü with two cups of tea. After finishing their tea, the two of them set out the pieces of a board game and started to play with each other.

Just as they were at a critical point in their game, the page boy, Ch'in-t'ung, whose job it was to watch the garden gate, suddenly appeared and announced, "Father has come home."

The two women made haste to put the game away, but Hsi-men Ch'ing, who had already crossed the threshold of the garden, caught sight of them.

They were wearing their everyday chignons enclosed in frets of silver filigree, from which two tufts of hair were allowed to escape at either temple, pendant onyx earrings, blouses of white silk, pink vests, drawnwork skirts, and two pairs of tiny shoes, the up-turned points of which were adorned with red mandarin ducks. Each of them appeared to him to be:

Modeled in plaster, carved of jade.

Without his even being aware of it, Hsi-men Ch'ing's face became wreathed in smiles, and he blurted out, "They look just like a pair of painted faces, and they'd cost a pretty penny too."

"We're no painted faces," declared Chin-lien. "But if that's what you're looking for, you can find the genuine article in the rear compound."

At this sally, Meng Yü-lou excused herself and started back toward her own quarters, but Hsi-men Ch'ing caught her with one hand and said, "Where are you off to? Do you have to leave as soon as I show up? Tell me the truth, now; when I'm not at home, what do the two of you do around here?"

"We're bored to distraction," said Chin-lien, "and were only playing a couple of rounds of a board game here. We really haven't stolen anything. How were we to know that you would turn up?"

As she spoke, she helped him off with his outer clothes and then said, "You've come back from the funeral early today."

"Most of the guests at the reception," said Hsi-men Ch'ing, "were either eunuchs or official colleagues of the deceased. Moreover, the weather was hot. I couldn't stick it out, so I came home before it was over."

"Why isn't our elder sister home yet?" asked Meng Yü-lou.

"Her sedan chair has probably reached the city walls by now," said Hsi-men Ch'ing. "I've already sent two servant boys back to meet her."

When he had finished taking off his outer clothes, he sat down and asked, "What do the two of you wager when you play games together?"

"We were only playing for the fun of it," said Chin-lien. "Why should we have to wager anything?"

"Let me play a game with you," proposed Hsi-men Ch'ing. "Whoever loses will have to forfeit a tael of silver and treat the rest of us."

"But we don't have any money," said Chin-lien.

"If you don't have any money," said Hsi-men Ch'ing, "you can pull out one of your fancy hairpins and pawn it with me. It all comes to the same thing."

Thereupon, they set up the board and the three of them played a game together. P'an Chin-lien lost. While Hsi-men Ch'ing was still counting the pieces, the woman upset the board and then ran over beside a clump of sweet-smelling daphne, leaned against an ornamental rock, and pretended to busy herself picking flowers.

When Hsi-men Ch'ing located her, he said, "All right, little oily mouth! It was you who lost the game, and now you're trying to hide over here, are you?"

When the woman saw Hsi-men Ch'ing coming, she broke into giggles, saying, "You crazy good-for-nothing! It was Meng the Third who lost, but you didn't dare enforce the rules on her, but have come to bother me instead."

As she spoke, she tore the petals off the flowers in her hand and scattered them all over Hsi-men Ch'ing.

Stepping forward, Hsi-men Ch'ing embraced her with both arms, pushed her up against the ornamental rock:

Stuck out his clove-shaped tongue;
Mingled his sweet spittle with hers,

and began to toy with her in earnest.

At this juncture, Yü-lou appeared on the scene and called out, "Sister Six, the First Lady has arrived home. I'm going back to the rear compound."

Only then did the woman abandon Hsi-men Ch'ing.

"Brother, I'll have something more to say to you later," Chin-lien said to him as she went off to accompany Yü-lou on her way back to the rear compound.

When they had paid their respects to Yüeh-niang, she asked them, "What are the two of you laughing about?"

"Today Sister Six played a board game with Father," replied Yü-lou, "and lost a tael of silver. Tomorrow she'll have to play host and invite you to join the fun."

Yüeh-niang smiled. Chin-lien, on this occasion, did no more than put in a pro forma appearance before Yüeh-niang and then head back to the front compound in order to keep Hsi-men Ch'ing company. She ordered Ch'un-mei to light some incense in her room and to prepare the bathing tub and heat some bath water so that that evening she and Hsi-men Ch'ing could:

Emulate the pleasures of fish in the water.[3]

Gentle reader take note: Although Wu Yüeh-niang was the First Lady of the house and occupied the master suite, she was sick so much of the time that she hadn't been able to take effective charge of household affairs. All she really did was to go out and pay the social calls that propriety demanded. The household expenditures and receipts were all in the hands of the ex-courtesan, Li Chiao-erh. Sun Hsüeh-o was in charge of the wives of the household retainers who worked in the kitchen, and it was her responsibility to supply the needed food and drink to the separate quarters of the various residents. For example, if Hsi-men Ch'ing spent the night in one of his concubine's quarters and needed anything to eat or drink, or a particular kind of soup, it was Hsüeh-o's responsibility to see that it was duly prepared, and the maidservants from the rooms in question would come to fetch it. But no more of this.

That evening Hsi-men Ch'ing remained in Chin-lien's quarters where they drank wine for a while, and then, when they had finished bathing, went to bed.

The next day was one of those occasions on which:

Something was destined to happen.

Hsi-men Ch'ing had promised Chin-lien that he would visit the fair at the Temple of the God of the Eastern Peak and buy some pearls for her to make into a headband. For this reason he rose early and expressed a desire for some lotus-blossom cakes and pickled fish and vermicelli soup for breakfast. As soon as he got up he asked Ch'un-mei to go to the kitchen and order these things for him, but she refused to budge.

"Don't send her back there," said Chin-lien. "There's someone there who goes around saying that I encourage her to connive with me in sharing your favors as a means of keeping you all to ourselves. She's forever:

Pointing at the pig but cursing the dog,[4]

and abusing the two of us every way she knows how. What would you want to send her back there for?"

"Who is it that says that sort of thing or abuses her?" Hsi-men Ch'ing demanded to know. "Tell me who it is."

"What's the point of talking about it?" said Chin-lien.

"Even basins and jugs have ears.[5]

Just don't send her back there, but send Ch'iu-chü instead, that's all."

Hsi-men Ch'ing, therefore, called in Ch'iu-chü and told her to go back to the kitchen and give Hsüeh-o his instructions. Enough time went by in which to eat two meals; the woman had already set the table, but still no food was forthcoming. By this time Hsi-men Ch'ing was getting very hot and bothered.

When the woman saw that Ch'iu-chü had not returned she turned to Ch'un-mei and said, "You go back there and see what's going on. That slave still hasn't come back. She must have:

Taken root and sent up sprouts,

by now."

Ch'un-mei was rather out of sorts to begin with and marched off to the kitchen in a huff.

When she saw that Ch'iu-chü was still waiting for the food, she started to curse at her, saying, "You lousy, sleepy-eyed slave! Mother's going to beat the legs right off you! 'Why haven't you come back?' she'd like to know. Father's being kept waiting. As soon as he's eaten he wants to go to the temple fair. There he is up front, anxious to be on his way, and getting increasingly hot and bothered. I've been sent to see if I can drag you back with me."

If Sun Hsüeh-o had not heard these words nothing might have happened, but having heard them, she became enraged and started to curse, saying, "You crazy little whore! You may think I'm like:

The Mohammedan bowing to Mecca;[6]
So whoever shows up gets a bow.

But:

The saucepan is beaten out of iron;
Things take a little time to make.

The congee I had already prepared, he doesn't want to eat. Instead, all of a sudden, he comes up with a brand new idea, and expects me to start grilling cakes and making soup. How was I supposed to know what he wanted? After all, I'm not a:

Tapeworm in his belly."[7]

Ch'un-mei was incensed at her cursing and responded, "Stop talking through your cunt! If the master hadn't ordered us to come for it, who would have dared to demand anything of you? Whether you come up with it or not, we're going back up front and report. Why make such a fuss about it?"

Taking hold of Ch'iu-chü by the ear, she set off toward the front compound.

"Like mistress, like slave," muttered Hsüeh-o. "Do you think you can carry on so high-handedly, and remain in favor, forever?"

"If you've got the favor,
You might as well flaunt it,"

said Ch'un-mei. "I wouldn't sell the two of us short if I were you."

Thereupon, she marched off in a fit of high dudgeon.

When Chin-lien saw her come in the door, her face waxen with rage, dragging Ch'iu-chü behind her, she asked, "What's the matter?"

"Why don't you ask her?" said Ch'un-mei. "When I went, she was still mooning around in the kitchen, waiting, while the other one:

Just as slow and easy as you please,

had only started to knead the dough. Although I probably shouldn't have, I said, 'Father's up front waiting, and Mother wants to know why you haven't come back yet. She's sent me here to get you.' Whereupon that insignificant harlot started to curse me, calling me 'slave' a thousand times, if not ten thousand times. She said, 'Father seems to think I'm like:

The Mohammedan bowing to Mecca;
So whoever shows up gets a bow.

Someone must have been putting ideas in his head. The congee I had already prepared, he doesn't want to eat. Instead, out of the blue, he comes up with a brand new idea, and calls for cakes and soup.' She was so busy with her cursing in the kitchen that she couldn't get around to the cooking."

"Just as I said," interjected the woman, "you shouldn't have sent her back there. As long as someone's so ill-disposed toward her, and claims that she and I are keeping you all to ourselves here in our quarters, she's bound to get nothing but abuse for her pains."

When Hsi-men Ch'ing heard this he became enraged. Marching back to the kitchen:

Without permitting any further explanation,
he kicked Hsüeh-o several times and cursed her, saying, "You lousy, splay-legged whore! When I sent her here to ask after the cakes, what did you curse her for? You called her a slave, did you? Why don't you:

Piddle a bladderful of piss, and
Take a good look at yourself?"[8]

Hsüeh-o had to suffer Hsi-men Ch'ing's kicking and abuse, but:

Though she dared to be angry,
She dared not speak.

Hsi-men Ch'ing had hardly gone out the kitchen door when Hsüeh-o turned to the wife of the head servant, Lai-chao, whose nickname was "The Beanpole," and said, "This must be my unlucky day! It's a good thing you were here to see it. I didn't say anything to her. She came marching in here like an avenging spirit:

Making all kinds of threatening noises,

and dragging the other maidservant away. Then she went:

Talebearing and embroidering on the facts,[9]

in front of the master, so that he came storming in here and abused me this way for no reason at all. I'm going to keep my eyes peeled from now on. The two of them are like mistress, like slave. Do they think they can carry on so high-handedly forever? They'll come a cropper if they don't watch out."

Unbeknownst to her, Hsi-men Ch'ing had overheard everything she said. He came back in and struck her several additional blows with his fist, cursing as he did so, "You lousy slave of a whore! And you still claim you weren't abusive to her, when I've heard you cursing her with my own ears?"

Hsi-men Ch'ing beat her until:

The pain was difficult to bear,

and then went back to the front compound. Hsüeh-o was left in the kitchen with the tears running down her face. Convulsed with sobs, she began to cry out loud.

Wu Yüeh-niang had just gotten up and was in the master bedroom combing her hair.

"What's the ruckus in the kitchen all about?" she asked Hsiao-yü.

Hsiao-yü came back and reported, "Father wanted some cakes to eat before going to the temple fair. They say the lady in the kitchen was cursing at Ch'un-mei, from the Fifth Lady's quarters, when Father overheard her and gave her a few kicks. That's why she's started to cry."

"I don't remember his ever asking for cakes before," said Yüeh-niang. "But all she needed to do was to make them up as fast as she could and send him on his way. What need was there for her to curse the maidservant from the other quarters?"

Thereupon, she sent Hsiao-yü to the kitchen to urge Hsüeh-o and the servants' wives to hurry up with the preparation of the soup. Hsi-men

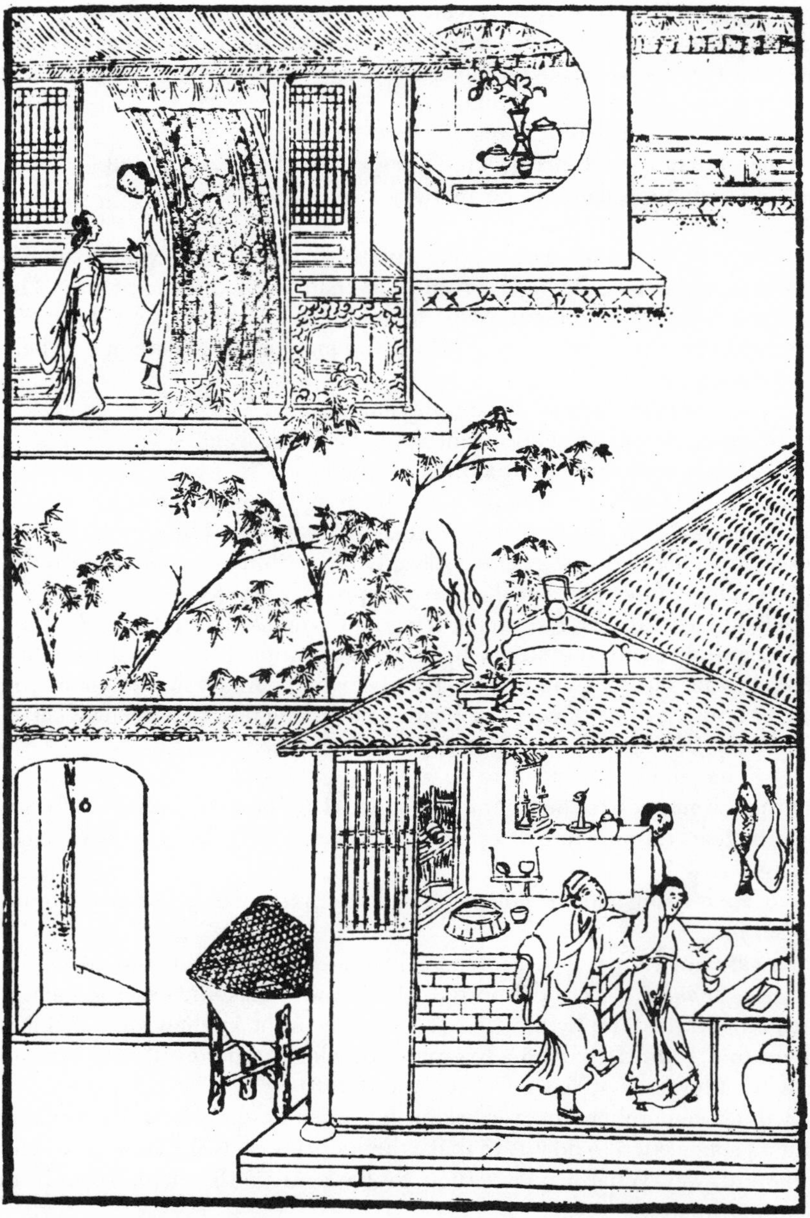

P'an Chin-lien Instigates the Beating of Sun Hsüeh-o

Ch'ing finally ate his breakfast, mounted his horse, and set off for the temple, accompanied by one of his page boys. But no more of this.

Sun Hsüeh-o couldn't get over her resentment at what had happened, so she went into Yüeh-niang's room and started telling her about it. But she didn't realize that Chin-lien had stolen up outside and was standing by the window, eavesdropping.

Chin-lien saw that Hsüeh-o was inside the room and overheard her saying to Yüeh-niang and Li Chiao-erh, "She's got him completely monopolized. Behind your back:

> There's nothing she won't do.[10]

Mother, you don't know that whore. When you get right down to it, she's more insatiable than any mere adulteress. She can't stand to go even a single night without a man. She's always up to something behind your back.

> Things no one else would do;
> She can bring herself to do.[11]

Originally, when she was living in her own home, she poisoned her husband to death. And now that she's here, she's trying her best to bury the rest of us alive. She's turned our husband into an angry fighting cock who glares at us as though he doesn't even see us."

"I don't remember your ever acting this way before," said Yüeh-niang. "If he sent a maidservant from the front compound to ask for cakes, all you needed to do was to make them up as best you could and send him on his way. What need was there for you to start cursing her for no good reason?"

"I'll call her bald or blind if I like!" retorted Hsüeh-o. "Just a little while ago, when that maidservant worked for you, if she refused to do as she was told when I was on duty in the kitchen, I would give her a smack with the back of a knife. And you didn't say anything about it. But now that she's fallen into the hands of that other one, she's started to carry on as though she owns the place."

While they were still talking, Hsiao-yü came in and said, "The Fifth Lady is outside."

A minute later, Chin-lien came into the room and said to Hsüeh-o, "If I really did do in my former husband, you had no business allowing your husband to bring me into the household in the first place. That way I could never have monopolized him or taken your place away from you. As for Ch'un-mei, she wasn't even my own maid to begin with. If you're so angry about it, all you have to do is make her go back to serving the First Lady. That way if you want to quarrel with her, I won't get dragged into it. No one feels good about losing a husband and having to marry another, but, right now, there's really nothing difficult about it. Just wait till he gets home and have him give me a writ of divorce. I'll go, and that will be the end of it."

"I don't know what's at the bottom of all this," said Yüeh-niang, "but it would help if the two of you would be a little more sparing of words."

"Just look at her, Mother," protested Hsüeh-o:

"Her mouth is like the Huai River in spate.[12]

Nobody can get the better of her. And she's always wagging her tongue in front of our husband, turning him against us, so he scarcely recognizes us any more."

"If you had your way," she continued, turning to Chin-lien, "except for Mother, the rest of us would all be driven away, so you'd be the only one left."

Wu Yüeh-niang just sat there and let the two of them continue to trade insults, without saying a word. It didn't take long for it to heat up even further.

"You may call me a slave," said Hsüeh-o, "but it's you who are the real slave."

They were on the verge of coming to blows when Yüeh-niang decided she had had enough of it and told Hsiao-yü to drag Hsüeh-o back to the kitchen.

P'an Chin-lien, for her part, went straight back to her quarters, where she:

Took off her fancy attire,
Washed away her makeup,
Let loose her raven locks, and
Left her flowery countenance in disarray.

She wept until:

Her two eyes were the color of peaches,

and threw herself down on her bed.

When the sun began to set in the west, Hsi-men Ch'ing came back from the temple fair, carrying four ounces of pearls in his sleeve. No sooner did he enter her room and see the state she was in than he asked, "What's the matter?"

The woman started to cry out loud, demanding a writ of divorce from Hsi-men Ch'ing and pouring out, thus and so, the entire story.

"I certainly never loved you just for your money, and now that I've joined my fate to yours, how can you let anyone abuse me so? She said I had done in my husband, a thousand times, if not ten thousand times. What's it to me if I:

Pick up something that I already have, or
Lose something that never belonged to me?

If I have to do without a maidservant, so be it. What do I want with a maid from someone else's quarters to wait on me, if I have to take all this abuse for it? I've got one shadow too many as it is."

If Hsi-men Ch'ing had not heard these words nothing might have happened, but having heard them:

The spirits of his Three Corpses[13] became agitated;
The breaths of his Five Viscera[14] ascended to Heaven.[15]

Like a whirlwind he descended upon the kitchen, seized Hsüeh-o by the hair, and proceeded to beat her with a short stick as hard as he could.

Luckily for her, Wu Yüeh-niang intervened, grabbing him by the hand and saying, "Why doesn't everyone take things a little easier? You're just upsetting the master of the house."

"You lousy, splay-legged whore!" exploded Hsi-men Ch'ing. "I heard you cursing in the kitchen with my own ears, and you're still trying to drag other people into it. If I don't beat your bottom right off for you, I might as well forget it."

Gentle reader take note: As a direct result of the beating of Sun Hsüeh-o this day, P'an Chin-lien would find that:

Though her deeds were done in the past,
The chickens would come home to roost.

There is a poem that testifies to this:

Chin-lien, by relying on her husband's favor,
could count on his support;
But, in so doing, she aroused the deepest enmity
in Sun Hsüeh-o.
It has always been true that gratitude for kindness
and festering resentment;
Even in a thousand or ten thousand years
will never be allowed to gather dust.[16]

On this occasion, after Hsi-men Ch'ing had beaten Hsüeh-o, he returned to the front compound and endeavored to mollify Chin-lien. He brought out from his sleeve the four ounces of pearls that he had bought at the temple fair that day and gave them to her to make into a headband. When the woman saw that her husband had taken action on her behalf and thereby enabled her to vent her spleen, there was no reason for her to be anything but delighted. From this time on:

Whatever she asked for, she received tenfold,[17]

and the favor shown her was even greater than it had been before.

One day thereafter, she fulfilled her obligation by giving a little party in the garden to which she invited only Wu Yüeh-niang, Meng Yü-lou, and Hsi-men Ch'ing, so the four of them could have a drink together.

To make a long story short, Hsi-men Ch'ing had formed a club, the membership of which consisted of ten friends, who met together once a month for a drinking party.[18]

The first of them was named Ying Po-chüeh, or Sponger Ying. He was the decadent scion of what had once been a substantial family, but had managed to completely squander his patrimony, and now made his living by squiring wealthy young rakes about the licensed quarters and picking up whatever he could along the way. His nickname was Beggar Ying.

The second was named Hsieh Hsi-ta, or Tagalong Hsieh. He had inherited the right to a position as a battalion commander in the Ch'ing-ho Guard, but, having lost his parents while still a child, had become:

A dedicated idler, devoted to his leisure.[19]

He was an expert performer at kickball and also liked to gamble. Having abandoned his prospects of a career, he was now a confirmed hanger-on.

The third was named Wu Tien-en, or Heartless Wu. He had been a yin-yang master on the staff of the district yamen, but had been removed from his post for cause. He now made his living by hanging around in front of the yamen and acting as a guarantor for loans to the local officials and functionaries. This was how he had become acquainted with Hsi-men Ch'ing.

The fourth was named Sun T'ien-hua, whose nickname was Sun Kua-tsui, or Blabbermouth Sun. He was more than fifty years old and specialized in talking his way into the brothels in the licensed quarter without purchasing their wares.[20] He made himself useful to the singing girls by:

Delivering letters and passing notes,

or helping them to attract customers, thus depending for his living on the emoluments of romance.

The fifth, who was the younger brother of Assistant Regional Commander Yün, was named Yün Li-shou, or Welsher Yün.

The sixth, who was the nephew of Eunuch Director Hua, was named Hua Tzu-hsü, or Nobody Hua.

The seventh was named Chu Jih-nien, or Sticky Chu.

The eighth was named Ch'ang Shih-chieh, or Cadger Ch'ang.

The ninth was named Pai Lai-ch'iang, or Scrounger Pai.

Together with Hsi-men Ch'ing, they made ten in all. The other members of the club, out of consideration for Hsi-men Ch'ing's supply of ready cash, insisted on his taking the position of senior member. Every month they met together somewhere for a drinking party, at which they took turns playing host.

One day it was the turn of Hua Tzu-hsü to convene the club at his home, which was right next door to that of Hsi-men Ch'ing. As befitted the household of a eunuch, everything was done on a lavish scale, with:

Large platters and large bowls.

The others had already arrived, but Hsi-men Ch'ing was busy that day, and by midafternoon had still failed to show up, though they were careful to keep a place for him.

When Hsi-men Ch'ing finally arrived, he was immaculately dressed and accompanied by four page boys. The whole company got up from their seats to welcome him. When they had finished with the social amenities, the host sat down in the appropriate place and Hsi-men Ch'ing took the seat of honor. A performer with a painted face and two other singing girls were there to entertain them, playing a *p'i-p'a*, a psaltery, and a mandola, and singing in front of the gathering. Truly, words are inadequate to describe:

The graceful beauty of the denizens of the Pear Garden;[21]

Whose beauty and talent both approached perfection.

Behold:

Their silk garments are like drifts of snow;
Their jeweled chignons are like storeyed clouds.
They have cherry mouths, apricotlike faces,
and peach-colored cheeks;
They possess willow waists, orchidaceous hearts,
and epidendronlike natures.
The sound of their singing is melodious;
Their voices are like the warbling of orioles
as they sport upon the branch.
The style of their dancing is fastidious;
Their postures resemble the pacing of phoenixes
as they move among the flowers.
Their tunes adhere to classic standards;
Their music has the air of spontaneity.
Their dancing waylays the bright moon
into shining on the pleasure-houses of Ch'in;
Their singing diverts the moving clouds
into hovering atop the bordellos of Ch'u.
High or low, allegro or andante,
they adhere to the appropriate modes;
Spitting out jade and expectorating pearls.
Light or heavy, scherzando or legato,
they follow the prescribed melodies;
Like plangent metal or tinkling jade.
The bridges on the psaltery are ranged like wild geese;
making each note distinct.
The wood of the clappers is inlaid with red ivory;
so every beat sounds new.[22]

After a little while, when:

Three rounds of wine had been consumed; and
Two suites of songs had been performed,

the three singing girls laid aside their instruments, came forward, and:

Like sprigs of blossoms swaying in the breeze;
Sent the pendants of their embroidered sashes flying,

as they kowtowed to the company. Hsi-men Ch'ing called for his page boy, Tai-an, and instructed him to take three sealed gift packets out of his letter case. There were two mace for each of them. After they had kowtowed once again to express their gratitude, they withdrew.

Hsi-men Ch'ing then asked his host, Hua Tzu-hsü, "What's the name of this girl? She can really sing!"

Before his host could reply, Ying Po-chüeh interjected, "You're certainly becoming rather forgetful not to recognize her, sir. The one who was playing the psaltery is Brother Hua the Second's sweetheart, Wu Yin-erh, or Silver, from the back alley in the licensed quarter. The one who was playing the mandola is Greenhorn Chu's daughter, Chu Ai-ai, or Love. And this one who was playing the *p'i-p'a* is the daughter of Auntie Li the Third, from Second Street. She's the younger sister of Li Kuei-ch'ing and her informal name is Kuei-chieh, or Cassia. Since her paternal aunt is a member of your household, how can you pretend not to know her?"

Hsi-men Ch'ing laughed, saying, "It's been six years since I saw her last, and she's grown up to be a woman already."

A little later, when they had run out of wine, the girls came out to replenish their drinks, and Kuei-chieh performed her task most ingratiatingly, engaging them in flirtatious conversation as she did so.

Hsi-men Ch'ing asked her, "What are Auntie Three and your sister, Kuei-ch'ing, doing at home these days? Why haven't they paid me a visit recently, or come to see your aunt?"

"My mother's been in bad shape since last year," said Kuei-chieh. One of her legs is partially paralyzed to this day, so she can't even walk without someone to lean on. My elder sister, Kuei-ch'ing, has been engaged by a merchant from the Huai region for the last six months. He's always taking her off to stay with him in his inn, and he won't let her come home for two or three days at a time. There's hardly anyone to be relied on at home these days. My mother is completely dependent on me to come out and sing every day, helping to entertain the few gentlemen that we're acquainted with. It's a hard life. We simply haven't had the time to pay a visit at your house, or look in on my aunt. How is it, Father, that you haven't been inside the quarter for such a long time? And why haven't you let my aunt come home to visit with my mother?"

When Hsi-men Ch'ing saw that her manner was congenial and her conversation clever and sprightly, he felt himself rather attracted to her.

"If I arranged with two of my friends to escort you back to your place today," he asked, "how would that be with you?"

"Don't joke with me, Father," said Kuei-chieh. "How could:

> Such distinguished feet tread on such humble ground?"[23]

"I'm not joking," said Hsi-men Ch'ing; and he actually reached into his sleeve, pulled out his handkerchief, along with a toothpick and a box of breath-sweetening lozenges, and gave them to Kuei-chieh as a pledge.

"When do you plan to leave?" asked Kuei-chieh. "I ought to send the servant back home right away, to let them know, so they'll be able to make some preparations."

"As soon as the party breaks up," said Hsi-men Ch'ing, "we can set out together."

Not long thereafter, when they had finished passing around the wine, it was lamplighting time and the party broke up. Hsi-men Ch'ing invited Ying

Po-chüeh and Hsieh Hsi-ta to join him, and, without even bothering to go home, they set out, on horse and mule back, to accompany Kuei-chieh into the licensed quarter, to the Li family establishment. Truly:

Into the brocaded nest,
It is not nearly as good to venture
as it is to stay away;
Into the red floss noose,
It is easy enough to stick your head
but hard to extricate it.[24]

There is a song to the tune "The Water Nymphs" that testifies to this:

A human pitfall, secretly constructed,
like an underground dugout;
A circean cave, as artfully designed
as a penitentiary;
A charnel house, openly laid out
like a butcher shop;
Its sole purpose is to love you to death
while devouring you alive.
On its signboard you will find written
in large characters:
"For the cost of his entertainment
the patron will receive no discount;
For the expenses incurred
the madam alone will accept payment;
For the price of their favors
the girls will not extend credit."[25]

When Hsi-men Ch'ing and the others had escorted Li Kuei-chieh's sedan chair to the door of her establishment, Li Kuei-ch'ing came out to meet them and ushered them into the main room. After they had finished with the appropriate amenities, they invited her old mother to come out so they could pay their respects. Before long, the old procuress made her appearance, hobbling along with the aid of a stick, for she suffered from partial paralysis on one side of her body.

When she saw Hsi-men Ch'ing she saluted him with the words, "My Heavens! It's my distinguished kinsman. What wind has blown you this way?"

Hsi-men Ch'ing laughed, saying, "I've been so busy recently I haven't been able to stop by. I hope you won't take it amiss."

"And who may these two gentlemen be?" asked the procuress.

"They're two good friends of mine," said Hsi-men Ch'ing, "Brother Ying the Second and Hsieh Hsi-ta. We had a meeting of our club at the Hua residence today and ran into Kuei-chieh there, so we decided to see her home together. Bring on the wine. We'd be happy to have three cups with you."

The procuress asked her three guests to be seated at the upper end of the room while she busied herself with seeing that tea was served, a dining table wiped off, and wine and delicacies prepared. In a little while a servant came in with the table, the lamps and candles were lit, and an array of wine and foodstuffs appeared.

Kuei-chieh returned to her room and changed her clothes before coming back out to help entertain them. It was truly:

A nest of breezes and moonlight;
A lair of orioles and flowers.

There was nothing for it for the two sisters but to:

Fill their golden goblets to the brim; and
Tune their jade mandolas to one melody,

as they sang and served the wine. There is a poem that testifies to this:

Inside glass goblets,
The amber fluid is rich.
From the small press the wine drips
in pearls of red.
Frying dragons and roasting phoenixes
weep jade fat.
Silk screens and embroidered curtains
contain the perfumed air.
Blow dragon flutes!
Beat alligator drums!
Let white teeth sing!
Slender waists dance!
All the more, since verdant spring
must not be spent in vain,
And silver lamps reflect the voices
of alluring damsels.
No wine now wets the earth
of Liu Ling's[26] tomb.[27]

On this occasion, Li Kuei-ch'ing and Li Kuei-chieh sang a suite of songs together, while at the table the guests were having such a good time that:

Drinking vessels and game tallies lay helter-skelter.[28]

Turning to Kuei-ch'ing, Hsi-men Ch'ing said, "Since the two of you are both here today, and I've heard for a long time what an accomplished performer of southern melodies Kuei-chieh has become, why not ask her to sing us a song, as a means of encouraging our two guests to have another cup of wine? What do you think?"

"We really oughtn't to put her to the trouble," said Ying Po-chüeh, "but are prepared to wash our ears in hopes of hearing a superb performance."

Hsi-men Ch'ing Decides to Deflower Li Kuei-chieh

Kuei-chieh simply sat there with a smile on her face for some time, without making a move.

It so happens that Hsi-men Ch'ing had gotten the idea into his head that he might like to deflower Kuei-chieh, and that was why he had first expressed a desire to hear her sing a solo. This fact did not escape the practiced eyes of the denizens of the quarter, who:

Knew a ghost when they saw one,

and had already guessed 80 or 90 percent of what was afoot.

Li Kuei-ch'ing, who was sitting by her side, was the first to speak, saying, "I'm afraid our Kuei-chieh has been spoiled ever since she was a child. She's always been rather shy, by nature, and doesn't like to sing for people on a merely casual basis."

At this, Hsi-men Ch'ing called for his page boy, Tai-an, drew a five-tael ingot of silver out of his letter case, and placed it on the table, saying, "This doesn't amount to anything, but may help to defray the cost of Kuei-chieh's makeup for the time being. On another day I'll send over a few sets of brocade clothing for her."

Kuei-chieh hastily rose to her feet and expressed her thanks, after which a maidservant was directed to put the money away, on the one hand, while on the other, a small table was placed out for her, and Kuei-chieh was invited to leave her place at the main table and sing for them.

Thereupon, Kuei-chieh:

Neither hurriedly nor hastily;
Lightly raising her silken sleeves,
Setting her beige skirt in motion,

and with a pink, tasseled handkerchief, decorated with a motif of:

Fallen blossoms on flowing water,

dangling from the mouth of her sleeve, sang a song to the tune "Stopping the Clouds in Flight:"

Though her demeanor is nonchalant,
She has outdone every rival in the quarter
to take top billing.
Her every move is escorted by a fragrant breeze,
And never fails to elicit respect.
Ch'a!
She is a piece of jade sullied in the muck;
Hardly run of the mill.
With a single, unaccompanied song,
She takes her audience by storm.
Just like the epiphany
in King Hsiang's dream.[29]
Just like the epiphany,
in King Hsiang's dream.[30]

By the time she had finished her song, Hsi-men Ch'ing was so delighted he scarcely knew what to do with himself. He ordered Tai-an to take the horse home with him, and that evening he spent the night in Li Kuei-ch'ing's room. Merely because Hsi-men Ch'ing felt an inclination to deflower this girl, and Ying Po-chüeh and Hsieh Hsi-ta were on the spot to aid and abet him in this enterprise, he took the bait.

The next day he sent a page boy to his house to fetch fifty taels of silver and also to a silk goods store to buy four sets of clothing, explaining that he planned to deflower Li Kuei-chieh. When Li Chiao-erh heard that it was her own niece, from her old establishment, that he was planning to deflower, how could she have been anything but delighted? She promptly produced a silver ingot of fifty taels weight and gave it to Tai-an to deliver to the licensed quarter.

A set of jewelry was made up, clothing was tailored, tables of food were ordered, and with:

Wind and string instruments, song and dance;
Amid clustering blossoms and clinging brocade,

there were three days of nuptial festivities. Ying Po-chüeh and Hsieh Hsi-ta also persuaded Blabbermouth Sun, Sticky Chu, and Cadger Ch'ang to come up with five candareens each, in the way of a gift, when they came to offer their congratulations. Every last thing, including the bedding, was paid for by Hsi-men Ch'ing. Day after day they regaled themselves in the licensed quarter with:

Unlimited quantities of meat and wine.

But no more of this.

Amid dancers' skirts and singers' clappers
he is forever seeking novelty;
But when all the yellow gold is spent
nothing but his body remains.
A word of advice to wealthy young men:
"Don't spend it all too fast;
The practice of economy is like good medicine,
for it can cure poverty."[31]

If you want to know the outcome of these events,
Pray consult the story related in the following chapter.

Chapter 12

P'AN CHIN-LIEN SUFFERS IGNOMINY FOR ADULTERY WITH A SERVANT; STARGAZER LIU PURVEYS BLACK MAGIC IN PURSUIT OF GAIN

How laughable is the parvenu Hsi-men Ch'ing;
Whoever possesses money is welcomed as a patron.
His whole household is in a state of disorder;
Who cares about standards of decency or propriety?
His days are spent consorting with boon companions;
His nights devoted to sleeping with a painted woman.
Though this may not be a long-lived relationship;
It still counts as "a fling in the spring breeze."[1]

THE STORY GOES that Hsi-men Ch'ing was so infatuated by Li Kuei-chieh's beauty that he lingered in the licensed quarter for nearly half a month, without going home. Wu Yüeh-niang sent a servant with his horse to bring him home on numerous occasions, but the proprietors of the Li family establishment even hid his clothes and hat, so reluctant were they to let him leave the premises. As a result, the women in his household were all left at loose ends.

This might have been tolerated by the rest of them, but as for P'an Chin-lien:

She was still in the springtime of her youth,
  not thirty years old;
The flames of her desire could not be banked,[2]
  but flared up ten feet high.

Every day, without fail, she and Meng Yü-lou would make their way to the front gate, looking as though they were:

Modeled in plaster, carved of jade;
Displaying white teeth and red lips,

and lean against the doorjamb as they gazed out into the street, often remaining there until dusk.

In the evening when Chin-lien returned to her room she found that:

On her glossy pillow, amid deserted bed curtains,
There was no companion on the Phoenix Terrace.[3]

Unable to sleep, she would wander into the garden where she:

Gently paced the flower-strewn moss, and
Watched the moon bobbing beneath the water;

fearful lest Hsi-men Ch'ing's:

Heart should prove as difficult to capture.
She objected to the lovemaking of the tortoiseshell cats,
For the tumult it engendered in her fragrant heart.

At the time when Meng Yü-lou had entered the household she had brought with her a page boy named Ch'in-t'ung, who was about fifteen years old and had just begun to wear his hair in adult style. He was:

Bright-eyed and clean-cut,

as well as being:

Artful and accomplished.

Hsi-men Ch'ing had entrusted the keys of the garden to him and made him responsible for keeping it properly swept. At night he slept in a small side chamber just outside the garden gate.

During the day, P'an Chin-lien and Meng Yü-lou often met in the pavilion in the garden and did needlework together, or played board games with each other. This page boy was adept at performing little favors and, when he saw that Hsi-men Ch'ing had arrived home, was in the habit of coming to let the women know before telling anybody else. For this reason Chin-lien was fond of him and often invited him into her room and treated him to a drink of wine. As a result, the two of them:

Morning after morning and evening after evening;
Exchanged looks with eyes and eyebrows,[4]

until they both began to get ideas.

It happened that Hsi-men Ch'ing's birthday on the twenty-eighth day of the seventh month was approaching. When Wu Yüeh-niang realized that he was still in the licensed quarter, so enamored of the mist and flowers that he had no thought of return, she sent the page boy, Tai-an, to take his horse to the Li establishment and try to bring him back home.

P'an Chin-lien secretly addressed a note to him and gave it to Tai-an, with the injunction, "Slip this to your father inconspicuously, and tell him, 'The Fifth Lady hopes you'll come home as soon as possible.' "

Tai-an did not dare to be remiss, but mounted the horse and proceeded straight to the Li family establishment in the licensed quarter. What should he see when he got there but Sponger Ying, Tagalong Hsieh, Sticky Chu, Blabbermouth Sun, and Cadger Ch'ang, the whole bunch of them in fact, keeping Hsi-men Ch'ing company as he embraced his painted lady:

Amid clustering blossoms and clinging brocade;
Enjoying themselves as they drank up the wine.

When Hsi-men Ch'ing saw that Tai-an had arrived, he asked, "What have you come for? Is everything all right at home?"

"Everything's all right at home," replied Tai-an.

"Tell Uncle Fu the Second to try to collect those unpaid bills that are still outstanding in the shop up front," said Hsi-men Ch'ing. "I'll look over the accounts when I get home."

"The last few days Uncle Fu the Second has collected quite a few of them," said Tai-an. "He'll present the accounts when you get home."

"Did you bring that outfit for your Aunt Kuei-chieh?" asked Hsi-men Ch'ing.

"I've got it right here," replied Tai-an.

He then reached into his felt bag, drew out a red blouse with a blue skirt to match, and handed them to Kuei-chieh. Kuei-chieh and Kuei-ch'ing both bowed to express their thanks, and the present was put away. After which, they made haste to give orders that Tai-an should be properly entertained with food and wine in the servants' quarters.

As soon as the page boy had finished his food and wine he came back into the main room to await his instructions, and he took advantage of the occasion to approach Hsi-men Ch'ing and:

Whisper into his ear in a low voice,[5]

"The Fifth Lady at home asked me to deliver this note. She hopes you'll come home as soon as possible."

Just as Hsi-men Ch'ing was reaching out his hand to take it, Li Kuei-chieh caught sight of the transaction and, assuming it to be a love letter from some prostitute in the front sector of the quarter, snatched it out of his hands and tore it open to see for herself. It turned out to be a sheet of fancy note paper with a diapered border, on which there were a few lines of handwriting. Kuei-chieh handed it to Sticky Chu and asked him to read it out loud to her.

Sticky Chu saw that the missive was in the form of a pair of songs to the tune "The Wind Scatters the Plum Blossoms" and proceeded to declaim them to the company, as follows:

Yearning for him at twilight,
Longing for him by day;
I've tired myself out waiting,
  but my lover doesn't come.
Solely on his account, only for his sake,
  I've worn myself to a frazzle.
Alas, beneath my brocade coverlet,
  I sleep alone.[6]

The lamp is guttering out,
Everyone else is asleep;
All that remains, peeping through my window,
  is the bright moon.

Sleeping alone, even if my heart
were hard as iron;
How could it endure the desolation
of this night?[7]

The note was signed:

Respectfully,
Your favorite, P'an the Sixth

When Kuei-chieh heard the contents of this missive, she left the table, went back to her room, threw herself down on the bed, and lay there with her face to the wall.

To resume our story, as soon as Hsi-men Ch'ing realized that Kuei-chieh was upset, he took the note and tore it to shreds and then, in front of everybody, kicked Tai-an twice with his booted foot. He also sent someone twice to ask Kuei-chieh to return, but she did not come back. Hsi-men Ch'ing was so flummoxed by this that he made his way back to her room himself and carried her out to rejoin the party.

Upon his return he said to Tai-an, "I order you to take the horse and go home. If any whore at my place sends you here again, no matter who it is, when I get back I'll beat her to a stinking pulp!"

Tai-an returned home in tears, but we will say no more of that.

"Kuei-chieh," said Hsi-men Ch'ing, "there's no need to be so upset. This note is not from anyone else, it's only from the fifth concubine back at my place, asking me to go home because there's something she needs to take up with me. That's all there is to it."

Sticky Chu continued the joke, saying, "Kuei-chieh, don't you believe him. He's only trying to fool you. This P'an the Sixth is really a prostitute from another part of the quarter that he's recently taken up with. She's a real looker. You shouldn't let him off the hook."

Hsi-men Ch'ing laughed and pretended to hit him, saying, "You goddamned louse! All you ever do is plague people to death. She's giving me enough trouble as it is without you and your nonsense on top of everything else."

"It's you who are in the wrong, brother-in-law," said Li Kuei-ch'ing. "As long as you have people at home to keep you in line, what need is there for you to deflower a painted woman in the first place? You might as well stick to the ones you've already got, period. How long have the two of you been together, after all, that you should already be prepared to abandon her?"

"You've got a point there," interjected Sponger Ying. "Sir," he continued, turning to Hsi-men Ch'ing, "if you'll only take my advice, you won't have to go home, on the one hand, and Kuei-chieh won't have to be upset, on the other. From this day on, let's agree that if anyone gets into such a spat again, each of the culprits will have to forfeit two taels of silver and buy meat and wine to treat the rest of us."

And sure enough, the four or five boon companions at the table:

> The talkers talking,
> The jokers joking;
> Playing at guess-fingers or gaming at forfeits,
> Enjoying themselves as they drank up the wine,

finally succeeded in mollifying Kuei-chieh. Hsi-men Ch'ing embraced her and sat her on his lap with an ingratiating smile, while the two of them passed the same cup of wine back and forth between them as they drank.

Before long, seven cups of tea were brought in on a vermilion tray of bright red lacquer. The teacups were the color of snowy linen, the teaspoons were in the shape of apricot leaves, and the tea itself, which was flavored with marinated bamboo shoots, sesame seeds, and osmanthus, was of a bewitching fragrance.

When a cup had been placed in front of each of them, Ying Po-chüeh said, "I know a song to the tune "Imperial Audience" that describes the virtues of tea:

> The tender leaves,
> Of this high-grade tea,
> Are nourished by the spring breeze.
> Though, if neglected, they will wither away;
> The slightest infusion brings out their true colors.
> Incomparable, extraordinary;
> Hard to depict or to describe;
> Often savored in the mouth;
> When drunk, you long for them;
> When sober, you adore them;
> But a single armful will cost you a bundle.[8]

Tagalong Hsieh laughed, saying, "If the Honorable Gentleman is:

> Spending his money and wasting his goods,

without hoping to get such an armful, what else could he be hoping for? Now, everyone ought to pitch in, by singing a song if he knows one, or, if he can't sing, by telling a joke, to help Kuei-chieh down her wine."

Tagalong Hsieh, himself, was the first to tell a joke. "Once upon a time there was a mason who was engaged to repave a courtyard in the licensed quarter. Because the madam had been less than generous with him, he surreptitiously stuck a brick in her covered drain.[9] As a result, when it rained, her whole courtyard filled up with water. The madam, in a state of consternation, sought him out, gave him all he could eat or drink, weighed out a mace of silver, and begged him to get rid of the water for her. The mason consumed the food and wine and then stealthily removed the brick from her drain, whereupon all the water immediately drained away. 'Foreman,' asked the madam, 'what was the problem?' To which the mason replied, 'The problem with your drain was the same as it is with you:

It's only dough that makes things flow;
Without the dough, there'd be no flow.'"

It so happens that this joke reflected badly on Kuei-chieh's profession, which induced her to speak up, as follows, "I've got a joke of my own with which to regale you gentlemen. Once upon a time, the Taoist adept Sun Ssu-miao[10] had prepared a feast and wished to summon his guests, so he sent the tiger who was customarily in attendance beneath his dais to invite them. The tiger proceeded to eat each and every one of the guests while they were en route to the feast. The Taoist waited until evening, but not a single guest had arrived. Everyone told him, 'That tiger of yours must have eaten the guests on their way here.' Before long the tiger arrived and the Taoist asked him, 'What has become of the guests I sent you to invite?' To which the tiger, who could speak the language of men, replied, 'You should know, master, that I've never been known to invite people to partake of anything. The only thing I'm any good at is devouring people.'"[11]

This joke reflected badly on the whole bunch of them.

"It would seem," said Sponger Ying, "that all we know how to do is free-load off your patron, without being able to stand him a treat in return."

Thereupon, he extracted a silver-plated earpick from his hair that weighed one mace. Tagalong Hsieh contributed the pair of gilded rings he used to hold his hairnet in place, which were found to weigh nine and a half candareens. Sticky Chu pulled an old handkerchief out of his sleeve, which was assessed at a value of two hundred discounted cash. Blabbermouth Sun divested himself of the white cotton breechcloth he wore around his loins, which was pawned for enough to buy two and a half jars of wine. Cadger Ch'ang had nothing he could contribute, so he asked Hsi-men Ch'ing for the loan of a full mace of good-quality silver.

The entire proceeds of the collection were handed over to Li Kuei-ch'ing, to defray the expenses of standing Hsi-men Ch'ing and Kuei-chieh a treat. Kuei-ch'ing turned the money over to the servant, who managed to buy a mace worth of crabs, a mace worth of pork, and a chicken. The Li establishment threw in a few side dishes of its own, and everything was duly prepared in the kitchen and served up in:

Large platters and large bowls.

Once the company was seated they scarcely needed an invitation before setting to.

The telling is slow;
What happened was quick.

Behold:

Everyone's mouth goes into motion,
Each of them lowers his head to the task.
Obscuring the sky and bedimming the sun,[12]
They are like a swarm of locusts
all descending at once;
Squinting their eyes and hunching their shoulders,
They are like starving prisoners
just let out of jail.
This one sets to with flailing arms,
As though it has been years
since he saw food or wine;
That one holds his chopsticks together,
As if it has been ages
since he attended a feast.
One of them has sweat pouring from his face,
As he engages in a grudge match
with a chicken bone;
Another wipes the oil from his lips,
As he wolfs down bristle and rind
with his hog's flesh.
When they have eaten but a while,
The cups and plates are in a state of disarray;[13]
By the time they are through,
The chopsticks lie about helter-skelter.
The cups and plates are in a state of disarray;
As spic-and-span as though washed.
The chopsticks lie about helter-skelter;
As neat and clean as though scoured.
This one rates the designation
Commander in Chief of the Gourmands;
That one has earned the sobriquet
General of the Trenchermen.[14]
The wine pots are drained dry,
but they continue to upend them;
The platters are quite empty,
yet they scan them in vain.

Truly:

Delicacies of every variety
have perished in but a moment;
Sacrificed upon the altar
in the Temple of the Five Viscera.[15]

On this occasion, the bunch of them cleaned the place out as thoroughly as any Buddha King of Purifying Light[16] could have done. Hsi-men Ch'ing and Kuei-chieh barely had two cups of wine apiece, and a few meager gleanings from the dishes on the table, before everything was gobbled up by the ravenous horde.

That day two of the chairs at their table were broken. The page boy who waited out front with the horse was not invited in for a snack, so he knocked the image of the tutelary god off its pedestal in the shrine by the door and deposited a bulging pile of hot shit in its place. On his way out the door, Blabbermouth Sun stuffed the gilded brass Buddha from the Li family's parlor into his waistband. Sponger Ying, pretending to kiss Kuei-chieh, snitched a gold-filled pin from her hairdo. Tagalong Hsieh pocketed Hsi-men Ch'ing's Szechwan fan. Sticky Chu went into Kuei-ch'ing's room to have a look at himself and made off with her mercury-backed mirror. Even the discount on the mace of silver that Cadger Ch'ang had borrowed from Hsi-men Ch'ing was put onto the reckoning.

It so happened that this bunch of men had nothing better to do than keep Hsi-men Ch'ing company in his revels. What a time they had together! There is a poem that testifies to this:

The prostitutes of the licensed quarter
  are as coquettish as monkeys;
They are only fit to be visited
  on the impulse of the moment.
If one allows himself to become infatuated,
  with no sense of satiety;
To whom can he safely entrust
  the keys to his coffers?

His boon companions continued to cluster around Hsi-men Ch'ing:

Enjoying themselves as they drank up the wine.

But let us put this aside for a moment and return to the story of Tai-an.

When the page boy returned home with the horse, Wu Yüeh-niang was sitting in her room with Meng Yü-lou and P'an Chin-lien.

As soon as she saw Tai-an, she asked, "Have you brought your father back with you or not?"

Tai-an had been crying so hard that both his eyes were as red as could be. He gave an account, thus and so, that concluded, "I only got kicked and cursed by Father for my pains. And he also said, 'Whoever sends after me again will hear from me when I get home.'"

"Just look at him," said Yüeh-niang. "How unreasonable can you get? If he won't come home, so much for that; what business does he have abusing the page boy? How can he allow himself to be so bewitched by that vixen?"

"It's bad enough to kick a page boy," said Meng Yü-lou, "but how can he threaten to abuse us into the bargain?"

"Nine out of ten of those whores in the licensed quarter," said P'an Chin-lien, "don't have any real feelings for their customers. As the saying goes:

Not even shiploads of gold and silver,
Can fill up the camps of mist and flowers."

Chin-lien simply blurted out what she had to say, without remembering that:

Even if you only talk along the road,
There may be someone lurking in the grass.[17]

Ever since Tai-an had returned from the licensed quarter, Li Chiao-erh had stolen up outside and had been standing by the window, eavesdropping. When she overheard P'an Chin-lien abusing the members of her own household to Yüeh-niang and referring to them as whores a thousand times, if not ten thousand times, she secretly stored up the resentment in her heart and, henceforth, regarded Chin-lien as her enemy. But no more of this. Truly:

Honeyed words and plausible speeches
can make the twelfth month warm;
Cruel words that are hurtful to others
can turn the sixth month cold.[18]
Chin-lien's only consideration was
the need to make herself heard;
How could she anticipate that a bystander
could be the cause of calamity?

We will say no more for the moment about the enmity that Chin-lien incurred in Li Chiao-erh, but return to the story of that woman herself.

When Chin-lien returned to her room:

Each half hour was like three months of autumn;
Each two-hour period seemed like half a summer.

Knowing that Hsi-men Ch'ing was not coming home that night, she sent her two maidservants off to sleep, made a pretense of going out for a stroll in the garden, invited Ch'in-t'ung into her room, drank wine with him until he was drunk, closed the door:

Took off her clothes and unfastened her girdle,

and proceeded to couple with him. Truly:

With lustful daring as big as the sky,
what is there to fear?
Amid mandarin duck curtains the clouds and rain:
a lifetime of passion.[19]

Behold:

One of them shows total disregard
for ethical norms or distinctions of status;
The other does not discriminate between
above and below or high and low.

One of them, inspired by perverse lustful daring,
Cares nothing for the severity of her husband;
The other, carried away by lecherous desires,
Ignores a clear-cut violation of the law.
One of them, breathing heavily with staring eyes,
Sounds like an ox snoring in the willow's shade;
The other, with coy words and inarticulate cries,
Reminds one of an oriole warbling among the flowers.
One of them, murmurs in her partner's ear
of passions evoked by clouds and rain;
The other, swears by the pillow side
to be as faithful as the hills and seas.
The garden with its hundred flowers,
Has been transformed into a pleasure ground;
The bedroom of his lawful mistress,
Has turned into a Kingdom of Cockaigne.
Almost before they know it, a glob
of donkey's spunk,
Has been deposited in Chin-lien's
jadelike body.[20]

From this time on, every night the woman invited the page boy into her room for a repeat performance and sent him on his way again before dawn. She secretly let him have two or three of her gold-headed pins to wear in his hair, and she also gave him the brocade scent bag she wore suspended at her waist, together with the gourd toggle that held it in place, so he could wear them under his clothes.

How could she have known that this page boy:

Was not the sort to abide by his lot,[21]

but constantly went out into the street to drink and gamble with his fellow servants, where he was so indiscreet as to allow these gifts to be seen? As the saying goes:

The best way to avoid being found out,
Is not to do it in the first place.[22]

One day wind of this came to the ears of Sun Hsüeh-o and Li Chiao-erh, who said to each other, "That lousy whore is forever hypocritically protesting her own virtue. How is it, then, that today she's been caught red-handed committing adultery with a page boy?"

The two of them went off together to tell Yüeh-niang about it, but Yüeh-niang expressed herself repeatedly to be incredulous.

"It's all because the two of you are on the outs with her," she said. "But how can you help offending Sister Meng the Third by such an accusation? She'll say you're just trying to get rid of her page boy."

This response reduced the two to silence.

Sometime after this, the woman was carrying on with the page boy in her room one night when she forgot to close the back door. Her maidservant, Ch'iu-chü, happened to come out to relieve herself and saw what was going on. The next day she reported what she had seen to Hsiao-yü in the rear compound, and Hsiao-yü mentioned it to Hsüeh-o. Hsüeh-o and Li Chiao-erh again sought out Yüeh-niang and told her about it.

It happened to be the twenty-seventh day of the seventh month, the eve of Hsi-men Ch'ing's birthday, and he had just come back from the licensed quarter to celebrate it. The two of them recounted everything, thus and so.

"The maidservant from her own quarters has reported it with her own mouth. It's not just a case of our trying to do her in. If you won't say anything about it, we'll go tell Father ourselves. You'd do as well to forgive a whore like that as you would to forgive a scorpion!"

"He's only just come home," said Yüeh-niang, "and it's a special day for him to boot. If you two disregard me and insist on telling him about it, in a little while, when the trouble starts, you'll have to look out for yourselves."

The two of them did not take Yüeh-niang's advice, but waited until Hsi-men Ch'ing came into his room and then told him all about how Chin-lien had been committing adultery with the page boy.

If Hsi-men Ch'ing had not heard these words nothing might have happened, but having heard them:

> Anger flared up in his heart, and
> Malice accrued in his gall.[23]

Marching out to the front compound, he sat down and called out in a loud voice for Ch'in-t'ung.

It was not long before someone reported these events to P'an Chin-lien.

In a state of panic she sent Ch'un-mei to call the page boy into her room, where she enjoined him, "Whatever happens, don't admit to anything!"

She demanded back the pins he was wearing in his hair, but she was so flustered she forgot to recover the scent bag with the gourd toggle.

Summoned into the front reception room, the page boy was made to kneel in front of Hsi-men Ch'ing, who ordered three or four servants to stand by with heavy bamboo canes.

"You lousy slave!" Hsi-men Ch'ing addressed him, "Do you acknowledge your crime?"

Ch'in-t'ung was too frightened to answer for some time.

Hsi-men Ch'ing ordered his minions, "Take off his hat and pull out the pins in his hair. I want to take a look at them. He's been seen sporting two gold-headed silver pins." Then, addressing him directly, he demanded, "What's become of the gold-headed silver pins you've been wearing?"

"I've never had any silver pins," said Ch'in-t'ung.

"The slave is still up to his tricks," said Hsi-men Ch'ing. "Strip off all his clothes and beat him with the bamboo."

The two or three servants in attendance set about their task. One of them, while engaged in stripping off his clothes, took down his trousers, disclosing the fact that underneath them he was wearing a jade-colored damask tunic, from the waist-string of which there hung a brocade scent bag with a gourd toggle.

Hsi-men Ch'ing noticed it immediately and called out, "Bring it here so I can have a look at it."

Recognizing it as the very object that P'an Chin-lien customarily wore suspended at her waist, he became enraged.

"Where did you get this?" he demanded. "Tell me the truth. Who gave it to you?"

The page boy was so frightened that it was some time before he could open his mouth to reply.

"It's something I picked up one day while I was sweeping in the garden," he said. "Nobody gave it to me."

Hsi-men Ch'ing gnashed his teeth in rage and shouted out the order, "Tie him up and give him a real thrashing."

Then and there Ch'in-t'ung was bound, hand and foot, and the blows of the cane fell on him like rain. In no time at all they had administered thirty strokes of the heavy bamboo, so severely that:

> The skin was broken, the flesh was split, and
> Fresh blood flowed down his legs.[24]

Hsi-men Ch'ing also gave orders to his chief household retainer, Lai-pao: "Pluck out the hair on the slave's temples and throw him out of here. See that he never sets foot on the threshold again."

When Ch'in-t'ung had kowtowed to his master, still weeping and wailing, he was given the gate. This page boy, only because:

> Last night he flirted with the nymph who keeps the books
> in the Palace of the Jade Emperor;
> Today, guilty of a clear-cut violation of Heaven's law,[25]
> is banished to the realms below.

There is a poem that testifies to this:

> Tigers deploy the revenants of their prey,
> birds are snared with decoys;
> Chin-lien was not the sort to remain chaste
> within her empty boudoir.
> Today she's in an untenable position
> for adultery with a servant;
> From now on, if she encounters criticism
> she has no one to blame but herself.

On this occasion, Hsi-men Ch'ing had Ch'in-t'ung beaten and then ejected him from the household.

When P'an Chin-lien, in her room, heard what had happened, it was:

Just as though she had been dunked in a tub of ice water.

Before long, Hsi-men Ch'ing came into her quarters. The woman trembled with fright as if the pulse had stopped beating in her body. When she went up to him, obsequiously, to take his outer garments, Hsi-men Ch'ing slapped her in the face so hard he knocked her down. He ordered Ch'un-mei to lock the front and back gates and not let anyone in. Then he got himself a small chair, sat down in the courtyard underneath the flower arbor, pulled out a riding crop, and, brandishing it in his hand, commanded, "Whore! Take off your clothes and get down on your knees."

The woman, troubled as she was by a bad conscience, did not dare to disobey. She actually took off all her clothes, above and below, and knelt down before him:

Hanging her powdered face in shame,

not daring to utter a sound.

"You lousy whore!" said Hsi-men Ch'ing. "There's no use pretending you're:

Still asleep in dreamland.

I've just gotten the truth out of that slave. He's confessed to everything. Tell me the truth. While I've been away from home, how many times have you made out with him?"

"My Heavens!" the woman wept. "You really do me a mortal injustice, that's all there is to it. During the whole time you've been away from home the last half month or so, I've spent my days in the company of Sister Meng the Third, doing needlework together, and in the evenings I've locked the gate early and gone to bed. Without some reason I haven't presumed to step outside the postern gate. If you don't believe me, just ask Ch'un-mei, that's all. If I'd been indulging in any:

Illicit salt or illicit vinegar,[26]

she could hardly fail to know about it." Then, calling to Ch'un-mei, she said, "Sister, come over here and tell your father all about it."

"You lousy whore!" Hsi-men Ch'ing cursed. "They say you gave two or three of your gold-headed hairpins to that page boy on the sly. How can you deny it?"

"They do me a mortal injustice, that's all there is to it," the woman said. "It's all the doing of some backbiting whore, who will come to a bad end, eating her heart out when she sees how often you come to my room to spend the night, and angry enough to try to nail me with such a preposterous[27] story. As for the hairpins you've given me, there are only so many of them, and every last one is accounted for. Take a look for yourself. What could I be thinking of to give them to that slave for no reason at all? Someone like that, who hardly even makes the grade as a slave! He's such a babe in the woods it would be no exaggeration to say he hasn't even learned to piss yet. It's all a story someone has made up out of whole cloth to get back at me."

"Forget about the hairpins," said Hsi-men Ch'ing, reaching into his sleeve and pulling out Ch'in-t'ung's scent bag. "This is something that belongs to you. How did it come to be discovered hanging underneath the clothes of that page boy? Brazen that out if you can."

As he spoke, the gorge rose within him and he brought down the riding crop, with a whistling slash, across her pale and fragrant flesh. He struck the woman so hard that:

> The pain was difficult to bear, and
> Tears streaked her powdered face.

"Please, Father!" she blubbered. "If you let me speak, I'll speak. If you don't let me speak, you can beat me to death if you like, and make a stinking mess of the place. As for this scent bag and its gourd toggle; while you were away from home one day, I was going past the banksia rose trellis, on my way into the garden to do some needlework with Sister Meng the Third, when my girdle came undone. It must have fallen off at that time. I've looked for it everywhere. Who could have known that this slave would pick it up? I certainly never gave it to him."

This explanation happened to accord perfectly with what Ch'in-t'ung had just stated in the front reception room when he said he had picked it up in the garden. Moreover, when Hsi-men Ch'ing saw the woman's flowerlike body, which had been stripped stark naked, kneeling before him as she uttered her:

> Winsome sobs and melting words,[28]
> His anger flew to Java,

and he became 80 or 90 percent disposed to clemency.

Calling over Ch'un-mei, he sat her in his lap, and asked her, "Has the whore really been engaged in hanky-panky with the page boy or not? If you tell me to forgive the whore, I'll forgive her."

Affecting the:

> Coquetry and petulance of a spoiled child,[29]

Ch'un-mei sat down in his lap and said, "As for that, Father, needless to say, all day long Mother and I have been:

> As inseparable as the lip and the cheek.[30]

How could she have had anything to do with that slave? This is all something fabricated by someone who is jealous of Mother and me. Father, you ought to think what you're doing, or you'll only make an ugly reputation for yourself, which won't sound any too good when it gets abroad."

With these few words she succeeded in reducing Hsi-men Ch'ing to silence. Throwing aside the riding crop, he told Chin-lien to get up and put on her clothes, on the one hand, while he also gave orders to Ch'iu-chü to fetch something to eat and set the table so they could have a drink.

P'an Chin-lien Suffers Ignominy for Adultery with a Servant

The woman thereupon filled a cup of wine to the brim and, holding it in front of her with both hands, knelt down on the ground:

Like a sprig of blossoms swaying in the breeze;
Sending the pendants of her embroidered sash flying,

as she offered it up to him.

Hsi-men Ch'ing admonished her as follows: "I'll forgive you this once. But whenever I'm away from home, I want you to:

Cleanse your heart and reform your ways.[31]

Lock the doors early and don't allow yourself to:

Give way to foolish fancies.[32]

If I find out anything, I certainly won't forgive you again."

"I hear and I obey," the woman said, and then:

Just as though inserting a taper in its holder,

she kowtowed to Hsi-men Ch'ing four times. Only then did she take her place at the table and keep him company as they drank wine together. Truly:

If you're going to be a human being,
don't be a woman;
Or your every joy and sorrow will be
dependent on another.[33]

This woman, P'an Chin-lien, had been so favored by Hsi-men Ch'ing in the past as to lose all sense of decorum, but today she had brought this shameful ignominy on herself. There is a poem that testifies to this:

No matter how congenial and compliant
Chin-lien might appear;
She flaunted her favor to compete for affection
and thereby aroused enmity.
Had it not been for Ch'un-mei's intervention
on the day in question;
How could her parents' legacy of skin and flesh
have borne up under the lash?

While Hsi-men Ch'ing was still drinking wine in Chin-lien's room, they were interrupted by the sound of a page boy knocking at the gate, who announced that Hsi-men Ch'ing's brothers-in-law, Wu Yüeh-niang's eldest brother Wu K'ai[34] and second brother Wu the Second, along with his shop manager, Fu Ming, his daughter and son-in-law, and other relatives, had arrived in the front reception room to offer presents and wish him a happy birthday. Only then did Hsi-men Ch'ing relinquish Chin-lien, readjust his clothing, and go out front to entertain his guests.

On this occasion, there were gifts from Ying Po-chüeh, Hsieh Hsi-ta, and the other members of the club, and Li Kuei-chieh's establishment in the licensed quarter also sent a servant with a gift. Hsi-men Ch'ing was kept busy in the front compound, acknowledging the presents people had sent and issuing invitations. But no more of this.

To resume our story, when Meng Yü-lou heard that Chin-lien had been thus humiliated, she waited until Hsi-men Ch'ing was out of the house, took pains to evade the notice of Li Chiao-erh and Sun Hsüeh-o, and came to pay Chin-lien a visit.

Finding her lying on her bed, she asked, "Sister Six, what's the real story behind this? Tell me all about it."

Her eyes brimming over with tears, Chin-lien sobbed out, "Sister Three, just look at what that insignificant whore has done. Today, behind my back, she's provoked our husband into giving me such a beating. From now on, the enmity between those two whores and me will be as deep as the sea."

"Even if you had a bone to pick with them," said Yü-lou, "you didn't have to do it in such a way that my page boy got thrown out of the household, did you? Sister Six, don't let yourself get too depressed about it. After all, it's not as though our husband will no longer listen to anything we have to say. If he doesn't come into my quarters someday soon, there won't be anything I can do about it, but if he does come into my quarters, I'll see if I can't put in a good word for you."

"Many thanks for your help, Sister," said Chin-lien. She then called in Ch'un-mei to bring them some tea, and they sat down and chatted together for a while, until Yü-lou said good-bye and returned to her own quarters.

That evening, because Wu Yüeh-niang's sister-in-law, Wu K'ai's wife, was visiting in the master suite, Hsi-men Ch'ing went to Yü-lou's quarters to spend the night.

Yü-lou took the opportunity to say to him, "You really oughtn't to flout Sister Six's feelings for you. She never did anything like that. It's all because, in the past, she's had words with Li Chiao-erh and Sun Hsüeh-o, and now, for no reason at all, these charges have been trumped up against my page boy. Without so much as enquiring into the:

Blue or red, black or white,[35]

of the situation, you've done him an injustice. You mustn't blame Sister Six. You've really been too hard on her. I'm prepared to swear an oath on her behalf. If anything like that had really happened, do you think Elder Sister wouldn't have told you?"

"I asked Ch'un-mei about it," said Hsi-men Ch'ing, "and she said the same thing."

"She's in her room right now," said Yü-lou, "feeling miserable. Why don't you go look in on her?"

"I know," said Hsi-men Ch'ing. "I'll go to her quarters tomorrow."

Of the events of that evening there is no more to tell.

The next day was Hsi-men Ch'ing's birthday, and a lot of distinguished guests had been invited to attend a party, including the commandant, Chou Hsiu,[36] the judicial commissioner, Hsia Yen-ling, the militia commander, Chang Kuan, and Hsi-men Ch'ing's brother-in-law, Wu K'ai. A sedan chair was dispatched to bring Li Kuei-chieh, and the services of two other singing girls were also engaged, to sing at the daylong celebration.

When Li Chiao-erh saw that her niece had come, she led her in to meet Yüeh-niang and the others, and she was invited to sit down in the master suite and have a cup of tea. She asked to meet P'an Chin-lien, and maidservants were sent after her twice, but Chin-lien refused to put in an appearance, claiming that she felt out of sorts.

In the evening, when Kuei-chieh was about to go home, she came to say goodbye to Yüeh-niang, who gave her a vest of cloud-patterned damask, a handkerchief, and some other trinkets, and, together with Li Chiao-erh, accompanied her to the main gate.

On their way, Kuei-chieh herself went up to Chin-lien's postern gate in the garden, saying, "Come what may, I'd really like to meet the Fifth Lady."

When Chin-lien heard she had come, she sent Ch'un-mei to shut the postern gate and:

Lock it tight as an iron bucket, so that
Not even Fan K'uai himself could get through,[37]

while repeating, quite audibly, the words, "I won't let her in."

As a result of this rebuff, the prostitute returned home:

Her face crimson with mortification.

Truly:

Distribute your favors widely;
In this life you never know where
  you will meet again.
If you make a lot of enemies;
You'll encounter them in a tight spot
  where there's no escape.[38]

We will say no more for the moment about how Li Kuei-chieh went home, but return to the story of Hsi-men Ch'ing. That evening he appeared in Chin-lien's quarters and she met him at the door with her:

Cloudy locks in disarray, and her
Flowery countenance dispirited,

as she helped him off with his clothes. She waited on him with tea and hot water to wash his feet, playing up to him with every trick at her disposal in the endeavor to please him. That night as they shared pillow and mat:

Like fish sporting in the water;
She humbled herself to the most shameful acts.
There was no length to which she would not go.[39]

"Darling," she said, "who is there in the whole household who really loves you? Out of all these cases of:

Cohabitation amid the dewdrops,[40]

among all these 'remarried goods,' you and I are the only ones who really understand each other. When the others see how much you care for me, and how much time you spend with me, it makes them angry, and they fabricate things behind my back and try to make trouble between us. My foolish lover, what have you been thinking of, to allow yourself to be made the instrument of someone else's revenge? How could you have treated the person you love with such heartless cruelty? As the saying goes:

If you beat domestic fowl,
they'll hop around in circles;
If you beat wildfowl,
they'll fly high into the sky.[41]

Even if you were to beat me to death, I'd still be right here in this room. Where else would I dare go? Just the other day, for example, when you were in the licensed quarter and kicked and cursed your page boy—fortunately Elder Sister from the master suite and Sister Meng the Third were there to corroborate this—didn't I say something—and it was well-intentioned—about my fears that the painted woman in that establishment would exhaust your vitality—that the singing girls in the licensed quarter are only in it for the money and don't have any real feelings for their customers—what do they really care for you? How was I to know that this would be overheard by an interested party and that the two of them would connive against me behind my back? It's always been the case that:

When other people are out to get you it's seldom fatal;
It's only when Heaven is out to get you that it's fatal.

Later on:

With the passage of time the truth will become clear.[42]

The only thing is you've got to stand up for me, that's all."

On this occasion, with no more than these few words she succeeded in mollifying Hsi-men Ch'ing. That night the two of them:

Indulged their lusts without restraint.

The next day Hsi-men Ch'ing had his horse prepared and set off for the licensed quarter with the two page boys, Tai-an and P'ing-an, in attendance.

To resume our story, Li Kuei-chieh was all dressed up and engaged in entertaining a customer. When she heard that Hsi-men Ch'ing had arrived, she hastily returned to her room, where she:

Washed away her makeup,
Took off her pins and earrings,
Threw herself down on the bed, and
Pulled the coverlet over her head.

Upon his arrival, Hsi-men Ch'ing had to wait a long time before anyone came out to keep him company. At long last, the old lady appeared, bowed to him in greeting, and offered him a seat.

"How now, Kinsman?" the madam said. "It's been days since you've paid us a visit."

"It's only on account of all the busywork in connection with my birthday," said Hsi-men Ch'ing. "There isn't anyone to be relied on at home."

"My daughter imposed on your hospitality the other day," said the madam.

"Why didn't her elder sister, Kuei-ch'ing, come with her that day?" asked Hsi-men Ch'ing.

"Kuei-ch'ing is not at home," the madam replied. "Her patron has taken her to stay with him in his inn and hasn't let her come home the last few days."

They talked for a long time. After a while, someone brought tea and she kept him company while he drank it.

"What's become of Kuei-chieh?" Hsi-men Ch'ing finally asked.

"You mean you don't know about it, Kinsman?" the madam asked. "It's childish of her, and I don't know what it was that happened, but she was upset about something when she came home that day. She's been out of sorts ever since and has taken to her bed. In fact, she hasn't set foot outside her room from that time to this. It's really too cruel of you, Kinsman, not to have come to see her."

"Is that so?" said Hsi-men Ch'ing. "I didn't know anything about it." And he went on to ask, "Which room is she in? I'll go pay her a visit."

"She's sleeping in her bedroom at the back of the house," the madam replied, and immediately ordered a maidservant to show him the way.

Hsi-men Ch'ing went back to her room, where he found the painted woman with:

> Raven locks in disarray, and
> Pale countenance unadorned,

sitting on the bed, with the coverlet wrapped around her, and her face to the wall. When she saw it was Hsi-men Ch'ing, she made no response of any kind.

"What went wrong when you were at my place the other day?" he asked.

Receiving no reply, he asked again, "Who was it who upset you? Tell me all about it."

He kept on asking for a long time before Kuei-chieh replied, saying, "Well, anyway, it was the Fifth Lady of your household. Since you've already got someone who's so good at:

> Playing up to people and trading on her looks,

what need is there for you to bother yourself with whores like me? We may have been born to the trade, but when we put our legs in the air we do a better job of it than any of those amateurs on the outside, no matter what their social standing. I wasn't there in my professional capacity the other day, to provide entertainment, but came to bring you a gift, like the other guests. The First Lady treated me very cordially, as did the other two ladies, and presented me with clothes and trinkets. Under the circumstances, if I hadn't asked to be introduced to her, she would have said that we denizens of the licensed quarter were ignorant of the rules of proper behavior. Having heard people say there was a Fifth Lady in your household, I assumed I might ask to be introduced to her. But she refused to make an appearance. When I was about to come home, together with my aunt, I went to say goodbye to her, but she sent her maidservant to shut the gate in my face. Really:

She wouldn't know a favor if she saw one."

"Don't hold it against her," said Hsi-men Ch'ing. "She was really feeling out of sorts that day. If she had been feeling all right, she could hardly have refused to come out and meet you. What a whore she is! Why, several times, on account of her backbiting and troublemaking, I've been on the verge of giving her a beating."

Kuei-chieh brushed Hsi-men Ch'ing across the face facetiously with the back of her hand and said, "What a shameless fellow! You'd actually beat her, would you?"

"You don't know what I'm capable of," said Hsi-men Ch'ing. "Except for my regular wife, it's nothing for me to give any one of the other concubines or maidservants a beating. When you get right down to it, if twenty or thirty strokes with a riding crop are not enough to subdue them, I'll even go so far as to cut off their hair, whether they like it or not."

"Decapitation's too good for you," said Kuei-chieh. "This calls for 'delinguification,' if there's any such thing. You probably:

Bow down to them thrice, and
Say yes to them twice,[43]

for all I know. If you're really up to it, when you get home, just cut off a single hank of hair, and bring it here to show me. Only then will I acknowledge your claim to fame as a real devotee of the licensed quarters."

"Are you willing to shake on it?" asked Hsi-men Ch'ing.

"I'd shake on it a hundred times," said Kuei-chieh.

That day Hsi-men Ch'ing spent the night in the licensed quarter. The next day, around dusk, he said goodbye to Kuei-chieh and mounted his horse to return home.

Kuei-chieh said:

"My eyes are on the lookout for the flag of victory,
My ears are always on the alert for good tidings.

Darling, if the quest for this object proves unsuccessful, you needn't expect to see me again."

Hsi-men Ch'ing's dander was up as a result of her needling, and he was already inebriated by the time he returned home. He didn't go anywhere else, but headed straight for P'an Chin-lien's quarters in the front compound. When the woman saw that he was in his cups, she waited on him with more than usual care. In reply to her questions, he said he didn't want any food or wine, but ordered Ch'un-mei to wipe off the cool bamboo bed mat and then close the door and leave them alone.

Sitting down on the bed, he ordered the woman to take off his boots. The woman did not dare to refuse. In no time at all she had taken off his boots and helped him into bed. But Hsi-men Ch'ing did not go to sleep. Sitting up on a pillow, he ordered the woman to take off her clothes and kneel down on the surface of the bed before him.

The woman was so apprehensive she broke into a sweat. Without any idea what it was all about, she knelt down on the bed and began to weep out loud in a quavery voice, saying, "Father, if you'd only give me a clear-cut idea of what's going on:

I'd be prepared to die if I must.[44]

Even when you:

Keep me on tenterhooks,[45]

all evening and I do my level best to watch my step, I don't seem to be able to suit your fancy. How can I bear it when all you do is saw away at me with a blunt knife?"

"You lousy whore!" cursed Hsi-men Ch'ing. "If you don't take off your clothes I'm going to lose my patience."

"The riding crop's hanging on the other side of the door," he called out to Ch'un-mei. "Bring it here for me, will you?"

Ch'un-mei deliberately refused to come into the room. Only after he had called for some time did she push open the door and come in:

Just as slow and easy as you please.

She saw the woman kneeling on the surface of the bed in the lamplight, with her hair tumbled before her like oil pouring from an overturned table. Hsi-men Ch'ing repeated his order, but she didn't budge.

"Ch'un-mei, my sister," the woman pled with her. "Help me! He's going to beat me."

"Little oily mouth," said Hsi-men Ch'ing. "Don't pay any attention to her. Just fetch me the riding crop so I can give this whore a beating."

"Father, how can you carry on so shamelessly?" demanded Ch'un-mei. "What business of yours has Mother ever ruined, that you should take the word of some whore, whose only interest is to:

Stir up a storm in untroubled waters,[46]

and persist in making such capricious demands on her? How can you expect anyone to be:

Of one heart and one mind,

with you under the circumstances? You'll be lucky if they give you a second glance."

Ch'un-mei refused to obey him, latched the door behind her, and went off to the front of the compound.

Hsi-men Ch'ing, finding himself:

At a loss for what to do next,

laughed loudly and said to Chin-lien, "I won't beat you then. You can get up. If I ask you for something, will you give it to me, or won't you?"

"Darling," the woman said, "my whole body, bones and flesh alike, is completely at your disposal. Whatever it is you may want, I could not refuse to comply. But I don't know what it is you've set your heart on."

"What I want," said Hsi-men Ch'ing, "is a lock of the best hair from the crown of your head."

"Dear heart," the woman said, "any part of my body is yours for the asking. You can burn it with moxa wherever you like and I'll go along with you. But to cut off my hair is out of the question. The very thought of it scares me to death. From the time I left my mother's womb twenty-five years ago, I've never done anything like that. On top of which, recently the hair has already begun to thin out on the crown of my head. You really ought to take pity on me, that's all."

"You were upset at my annoyance with you just now," said Hsi-men Ch'ing, "but when I ask you for something, you refuse to comply."

"If I didn't comply with your desires," said the woman, "with whose should I comply?" She then went on to ask, "Tell me the truth. What do you want this hair of mine for, anyway?"

"I want to make a hairnet," said Hsi-men Ch'ing.

"If you want to make a hairnet," said the woman, "I'll make it for you. Just don't give it to that whore so she can use it to cast a spell on me."

"I won't give it to anybody, that's all," said Hsi-men Ch'ing. "I only want your hair to make the main cord of a hairnet to bind my topknot with."

"If all you want it for is to make a cord for your topknot," said the woman, "I'll cut it off for you."

Thereupon, the woman undid her hair and let Hsi-men Ch'ing himself take a pair of scissors and neatly cut off a large lock from the crown of her head. He wrapped it in paper and put it in his wallet.

The woman then fell into Hsi-men Ch'ing's arms and, weeping coquettishly, said, "I'll do anything you want. I only hope you don't forget your feelings for me. No matter how stuck you become on anyone in the quarter, just don't abandon me."

That night they:

Enjoyed each other even more than usual.

The next day Hsi-men Ch'ing got up and, as soon as the woman had fed him his breakfast, went outside, mounted his horse, and headed straight for the licensed quarter.

"Where's the hair you've cut off her head," Kuei-chieh demanded.

"I've got it right here," replied Hsi-men Ch'ing. He then reached into his wallet, pulled it out, and handed it to Kuei-chieh. She opened it and took a look, and when she saw that it was really a lock of beautiful hair, as glossy and black as oil, she promptly tucked it into her sleeve.

"Now that you've seen it, give it back to me," said Hsi-men Ch'ing. "Last night she made all kinds of difficulties about cutting this hair. It was only when I changed countenance and got angry that she let me cut off this single lock of it. I fooled her by saying I only wanted it to make the main cord of a hairnet to bind my topknot with, and then brought it straight here to show you. You can see, I'm as good as my word."

"What sort of a rarity is this," said Kuei-chieh, "to have put you into such a state? When you're ready to go home I'll give it back to you. If you're as afraid of her as all that, you shouldn't have cut it off in the first place."

"Who's afraid of her?" laughed Hsi-men Ch'ing. "It's just that I don't want to go back on my word."

Kuei-chieh induced Kuei-ch'ing to keep him company for a drink of wine, and then, as soon as she was out of sight, inserted the woman's hair into the linings of her shoes, so she could trample her underfoot every day. But no more of this.

Now that she had Hsi-men Ch'ing in her clutches, she kept him there for several consecutive days, without letting him go home.

From the time that Chin-lien allowed the cutting off of this lock of her hair, she became dispirited. Every day she:

Confined herself to her room,
Too languid to consume tea or food.

Wu Yüeh-niang, consequently, sent a page boy after a certain Dame Liu, whose services were frequently called upon in the household, to come and take a look at her.

"Madam has contracted a black humor," the old lady said, "which continues to rankle in the heart and can't be eliminated. Your head aches, you feel nauseous, and you have no appetite."

On the one hand, she opened her medicine bag and left behind two doses of medicine, in the form of black pills, which were to be taken in the evening along with a decoction of ginger, while, on the other hand, she said, "I'll get my old man to come by tomorrow and ascertain whether or not you're fated to suffer any calamities during the current year of your horoscope."

"So your old man can also tell fortunes, can he?" said Chin-lien.

"Even though he's blind," said Dame Liu, "there are two or three things he can do. First of all, he's an expert at the Yin-yang School of fortune-telling and can either avert peoples' calamities or offer them protection against them. Secondly, he's well versed in acupuncture, moxabustion, and the treatment of pyogenic infections of the skin. His third skill is one that I really shouldn't talk about, but he's always helping people to perform 'turnabouts.' "

"What does the word 'turnabout' mean?" asked the woman.

"Well, for example," said Dame Liu, "if a father and son are at odds, or two brothers are not getting along harmoniously, or a legitimate wife and a concubine are quarreling with each other; if one of the parties calls on the services of my old man, he can employ a counteractive agent on his or her behalf in order to keep the other party in check, or provide him or her with a philter containing a counteractive spell that, if given to the other party to drink, will cause, within three days, the father and son to become intimate, the brothers to become harmonious, or the wife and concubine to cease to quarrel. Or if someone's business is not doing well, or his real estate is not prospering, he can 'open the door to wealth' for him, or enable him to 'turn a profit.' And as for such things as the treatment of disease, the performance of ritual purification, the exorcism of the spirits of baleful stars,[47] or the invocation of the Great Dipper, he's good at all of them. For this reason people all call him Stargazer Liu.

"There was one case, I remember, of a newly married daughter-in-law, of humble social origin, who was somewhat light-fingered and was constantly stealing things from her mother-in-law's household and taking them back to her own family. Whenever her husband found out about it she was regularly beaten. My old man was able to perform a 'turnabout' for her, by writing two spells, which were burnt, and the ashes buried under the water jar. The whole family drank water from the jar, after which the daughter-in-law could steal things right in front of their eyes without their noticing it. He also provided her with a counteractive agent, which was placed under her pillow, with the result that whenever her husband slept on that pillow it was just as though his hands had been restrained and he no longer beat her."

When P'an Chin-lien heard this, she took it to heart and ordered her maidservant to provide Dame Liu with tea and something to eat. When the latter was about to leave, Chin-lien wrapped up three mace of silver for her medical services. She also weighed out an additional five mace to enable her to buy paper money and other ritual objects, and asked her to bring her blind husband back with her at breakfast time the next day to burn the spirit money for her. Dame Liu then took her leave and went home.

The next day, sure enough, bright and early in the morning, Dame Liu showed up with the blind rascal in tow and proceeded to come straight in through the front gate. That day Hsi-men Ch'ing was still in the licensed quarter, from which he had not yet returned home.

The page boy in charge of the gate asked the blind man where he thought he was going, to which Dame Liu replied, "Today we've come to burn paper for the Fifth Lady."

"Dame Liu," said the page boy, "if you've come to burn paper for the Fifth Lady, you can lead him right in, but look out for the dog."

The old lady took her husband by the hand and led him straight to P'an Chin-lien's parlor, where they had to wait a long time before the woman finally appeared. The blind man saluted her and then sat down.

The woman told him the eight characters that determined her horoscope,[48] and after the blind rascal had performed some calculations on the fingers of his hand, he said, "Madam was born in a *keng-ch'en* year, in a *keng-yin* month, on an *i-hai* day, during the hour *chi-ch'ou*. Since the solar term 'Spring Begins' fell on the eighth day of the first month that year, one day before the day of your birth, your horoscope begins in the first month of the year. According to the orthodox interpretation of the Tzu-p'ing School,[49] although this horoscope of yours is certainly splendid and remarkable, you will not, in this life, receive any support from your 'husband star,' which corresponds to the stem *keng*. There will also be some difficulty as far as your 'children star' is concerned. The element wood, associated with the stem *i* in the combination *i-hai* that designates the day of your birth, is the governing element in your horoscope, but your horoscopic 'body' cannot be said to 'flourish' when this element occurs in the first month. If the effect of this unpropitious factor is not counteracted, the element is likely to burn itself up. Moreover, the reduplication of the element metal, associated with the stem *keng* in the combinations *keng-ch'en* and *keng-yin* that designate the year and month of your birth, indicates that the influence of the baleful star Yang-jen, or Ram's Blade, is too great. This will create difficulties for your 'husband star.' Only after you have gained the ascendancy over two husbands will you be all right."

"I already have," the woman said.

The blind rascal then continued, "As for this horoscope of yours, madam, excuse me for saying so, but the Tzu-p'ing School attaches great importance to the horoscopic categories called the 'killer' and the 'seal,' which would correspond, in your case, to the elements metal and water. These two elements would normally be quite compatible, but the presence of the element water, associated with the stem *kuei*, in the 'one-sided seal' pertaining to the combination *i-hai* that designates the day of your birth, and the recurrence of the same element in the horoscopic category called 'injurer of the official' pertaining to the combination *keng-ch'en* that designates the year of your birth, indicates an excess of water that produces a 'collision' with your governing element of wood. This is inadequately compensated for by the presence of the element earth, associated with the stem *chi* in the combination *chi-ch'ou* that designates the hour of your birth. Since the stem *keng*, which is your 'official,' and the stem *hsin*, which is your 'killer,' are both associated with the element metal, they conflict with each other. As the authorities say:

> If the 'killer' is in the ascendant for a man,
> he will exercise authority and power;
> If the 'killer' is in the ascendant for a woman,
> she is sure to 'punish' her husband.

"All of this indicates that you must be intelligent, adept at adapting yourself to changing circumstances, and sure to attract the favorable or unfavorable attention of others. But there is one problem. This year of your horo-

Stargazer Liu Purveys Black Magic in Pursuit of Gain

scope is a *chia-wu*[50] year, and the indications are that during this 'annual fatal period' calamities are likely to occur. You are fated to suffer difficulties resulting from encounters with the influence of the two baleful stars Hsiao-hao, or Little Waster, and Kou-chiao, or Strangler. Although you may escape unharmed, the indications are that there will be disharmony resulting from the 'matched shoulders' between your governing element and that associated with the stem *chia* in the designation of this year in your horoscope, both of which are wood. The wagging tongues of petty persons may often cost you some groaning and discomfort."

When the woman had heard him out, she said, "I'd be much obliged to you, sir, if you could do whatever you can to effect a 'turnabout' on my behalf. I've got a tael of silver here for you, sir, as a token of my gratitude. I hope it will suffice to buy you a cup of tea. I don't ask for anything else; all I want is to keep petty persons at a distance, and to be assured of the love and respect of my husband."

Retiring into her bedroom, she pulled out two of her hair ornaments and handed them to the blind rascal, who accepted them and tucked them into his sleeve.

"If you want me to effect a 'turnabout,' " he said, "I'll take a piece of willow wood and carve a pair of male and female effigies out of it. They must be inscribed, respectively, with the sets of eight characters that determine your and your husband's horoscopes, and then bound together with seven times seven, or forty-nine, strands of red thread. A strip of red gauze must be fastened over the eyes of the male effigy, love grass must be stuffed into its heart cavity, its hands must be secured with needles, and, below, its feet must be stuck together with glue. The effigy must then be concealed inside the pillow on which he sleeps. In addition to this, I will write a spell for you, using vermilion ink, which you must burn to ashes, and surreptitiously stir into a cup of strong tea. If your husband drinks the tea and sleeps, the same night, on the pillow, in no more than three days, the magic will naturally take effect."

"Please, sir," the woman asked, "tell me, what's the significance of these four things?"

"I'll explain them to you, madam," the blind rascal said. "The fastening of the gauze around the eyes is to make you appear in your husband's sight as captivating and voluptuous as Hsi-shih. The stuffing of the heart cavity with love grass is to make him love you in his heart. The securing of the hands with needles is to prevent him from daring to strike you, no matter what you do, so that, in fact, he'll even get down on his knees to you. The sticking together of the feet with glue is to make it impossible for him to go out and sow any more wild oats."

When the woman heard tell that:

Such things could be,

she was utterly delighted. Thereupon, the incense, candles, and paper money were all prepared and the ceremony of burning spirit money on the woman's behalf was duly carried out.

The next day Stargazer Liu sent his wife to deliver the spell for the making of the philter and the other counteractive agents that he had promised. The woman took care of everything just as she had been told. Having burnt the spell to ashes, she stirred it into some good tea and, when Hsi-men Ch'ing came home, had Ch'un-mei serve it to him. That night the two of them:

> Shared a single pillow on the same bed.

As time passed:

> One day became two,
> Two days became three,

and they became:

> As inseparable as fish from water, and
> Enjoyed each other as usual.

Gentle reader take note: No matter whether your household be great or small, it is best to avoid the services of priests and nuns, Buddhists and Taoists, wet nurses and go-betweens. There is no telling what they will do behind your back. A poet of yore has left us some words of admonition, in the form of a quatrain, that express this very well:

> To the formal reception room of your house
> never admit female professionals;
> Always keep your back door securely locked
> in order to deny them admission.
> If you have a well in your courtyard,
> repair even the slightest fissure;
> Then your catastrophes will be few
> and your stars of good fortune many.

> If you want to know the outcome of these events,
> Pray consult the story related in the following chapter.

Chapter 13

LI P'ING-ERH MAKES A SECRET TRYST OVER THE GARDEN WALL; THE MAID YING-CH'UN PEEKS THROUGH A CRACK AND GETS AN EYEFUL

Since there's no such thing in this life
  as complete satisfaction;
In one's way of coping with the world
  do not be too demanding.[1]
It's a good thing always to pay heed
  only to the words of superior men;
When disputes arise never listen
  to the words of petty persons.[2]
Only regard the customs of the age
  as a source of amusement;
While respecting the intentions of others
  by keeping them at a distance.
If one were to address perceptive women with
  a word to the wise;
It would be, "Don't ever confide your troubles
  to your sweetheart."[3]

THE STORY GOES that one day earlier that summer,[4] on the fourteenth day of the sixth month, when Hsi-men Ch'ing came in from the front compound and went into Yüeh-niang's room, she said to him, "While you were out today, the Hua household sent a page boy over with a note inviting you for a drink. 'Ask him to come over whenever he gets home,' he said."

Hsi-men Ch'ing looked at the invitation, which read, "Can you join me for a chat at Wu Yin-erh's place in the licensed quarter at noon today? Come over to my place so we can go together. I do hope you can make it."

Hsi-men Ch'ing thereupon dressed himself to befit the occasion, ordered two of his attendants to prepare his best horse, and proceeded directly to the Hua household next door. How could he have known that Hua Tzu-hsü would not be at home? His wife, Li P'ing-erh, was standing on the raised stone platform just inside the second gate, the unfinished vamp of a sand-green Lu-chou pongee shoe in her hand. She was wearing a summer outfit that consisted of:

A chignon enclosed in a fret of silver filigree,
Pendant amethyst earrings in gold settings,
A blouse of pale lavender silk, opening down the middle,
And a white silk skirt with drawnwork borders,
Beneath which there peeked out a pair of tiny shoes,
The points of which bore the beaks of red phoenixes.

Hsi-men Ch'ing, quite unaware of what was in store for him, proceeded through the gate, and the two of them ran smack into each other.

Hsi-men Ch'ing had already had her on his mind for some time. Although he had caught a glimpse of her by the graveside at the old Eunuch Director's funeral the previous summer, he had not yet had a chance to savor the details. Now that he was able to meet her face to face and saw that she had a naturally fair complexion, was petite in stature, and had a face shaped like a melon seed and delicately curved eyebrows, before he knew it:

His ethereal souls flew beyond the sky, and
His material souls dispersed among the nine heavens.[5]

Stepping forward with alacrity, he gave her a deep bow, and the woman returned his salute, after which she turned around and disappeared into the interior of the house. But she sent out the maidservant with her hair cut straight across her forehead, named Hsiu-ch'un, to ask Hsi-men Ch'ing to take a seat in the parlor, while she herself stood just inside the postern gate:

Half revealing her captivating countenance,

and addressed him, saying, "Please sit down for a little while, sir. He's gone out on an errand just now, but he'll be back any minute."

Before long she sent out a maidservant with a cup of tea, and while Hsi-men Ch'ing was drinking it, she conversed with him from the other side of the gate, saying, "At this drinking party over there that he's invited you to today, sir, whatever happens, for my sake, couldn't you urge him to come home a little earlier than usual? Our two menservants will both accompany him, leaving only these two maidservants and myself, so there won't be anyone to be relied on at home."

"Sister-in-law," said Hsi-men Ch'ing, "you're certainly in the right. My brother really ought to:

Pay more attention to his family affairs.

Since you have so instructed me, Sister-in-law, I'll be sure to stick by his side.

Together we'll go and together return.

How could I do anything detrimental to my brother's interests?"

While they were still speaking, who should appear but Hua Tzu-hsü himself, and the woman returned to her own quarters.

Hua Tzu-hsü saluted Hsi-men Ch'ing and then said, "How good of you to accept my invitation. Something came up just now that I simply had to run out and take care of. Forgive me for not being here to greet you myself."

Thereupon, they took their places as guest and host, and a page boy was ordered to bring tea.

It was not long until they had done with the tea, and Hua Tzu-hsü instructed the page boy, "Tell Mother to prepare the refreshments. I'm going to share three cups of wine with Mr. Hsi-men here before we set off."

Then, turning to his guest, he continued, "Today is the birthday of Wu Yin-erh from the licensed quarter, and so I've invited you to join me in paying her a visit in order to celebrate the occasion."

"My Good Brother," said Hsi-men Ch'ing, "why didn't you say so before?"

Turning to Tai-an, he ordered, "Go home at once, get five mace of silver put into a sealed packet, and bring it back to me here."

"What need is there for you to put yourself to such trouble, Brother?" protested Hua Tzu-hsü. "I'm afraid I'm to blame."

When Hsi-men Ch'ing saw that the servants were setting up a table, he said, "Brother, there's no need to entertain me here. Let's go into the quarter and do our drinking there."

"I wouldn't presume to detain you," said Hua Tzu-hsü. "Just stay a little longer."

Whereupon, in:

> Large platters and large bowls,

such delicacies as chicken feet and fresh pork were set before them. A high-stemmed silver goblet in the shape of a sunflower was provided for each of them. There were also four "spring rolls" left over when they had finished eating, which they saved as a treat for the boys who tended their horses.

Before long, after Tai-an had returned with the requested gratuity, the two of them mounted their horses and set off together. Hsi-men Ch'ing was accompanied by Tai-an and P'ing-an, and Hua Tzu-hsü by T'ien-fu and T'ien-hsi, so they had four page boys in their retinue as they made their way directly to Madam Wu the Fourth's establishment in the back alley of the licensed quarter in order to celebrate Wu Yin-erh's birthday.

After they got there:

> Amid clustering blossoms and clinging brocade,
> Song and dance and wind and string instruments,

they continued drinking until the first watch before the party broke up. Hsi-men Ch'ing saw to it that Hua Tzu-hsü got stinking drunk, while at the same time, in response to Li P'ing-erh's request, he actually accompanied him on his way home. When the calls of the page boys had succeeded in getting someone to open the front gate, they helped their master into the parlor and set him down. Li P'ing-erh and her maidservants, carrying lamps and candles, came out and supported Hua Tzu-hsü on his way into the interior of the house.

His mission accomplished, Hsi-men Ch'ing was about to take his leave when the woman came back out to thank him.

"My poor husband is a sorry lot and something of a sot," she said. "It's very kind of you to have put up with him for my sake and to have brought him home with you. Please don't laugh at my solicitude, sir."

"How would I dare?" replied Hsi-men Ch'ing, hastening to make a low bow in response to her salutation. "Since you gave me my marching orders this morning, Sister-in-law, I have shown myself capable of:

> Leading the army forth, and
> Leading it back again.

How could your wish that I should accompany your husband home be anything but:

> Imprinted in my heart and engraved on my bones?[6]

Had I failed to do so, it would not only have added to your worries, but would have shown me to be:

> Undependable in the performance of my task.

The people at that establishment would have had Brother in their clutches if I hadn't insisted on urging him to leave. But as we passed by the gate of the Star of Joy establishment—the one that features the painted face, Cheng Ai-hsiang, whose nickname is Cheng Kuan-yin, or Goddess of Mercy Cheng, and who's quite a looker—Brother would have ventured in there, if I hadn't done everything in my power to stop him. 'Brother,' I said to him, 'let's go home. There's time enough to come another day. Sister-in-law's at home worried to death about you.' It was only then that he consented to come straight home with me. Otherwise, if he'd gone into the Cheng place, he wouldn't have been home all night.

"With all due respect, Sister-in-law—I really shouldn't say this sort of thing—but Brother's a fool. With such a young wife and such a large house to look after, how can he simply abandon you and stay away from home for whole nights at a time? It doesn't make any sense."

"It's just as you say," the woman responded. "Simply because of this philandering of his, and his refusal to take anyone's advice, I get so upset here at home that my body aches all over. From now on, sir, whenever you run into him in the licensed quarter, whatever happens, for my sake, urge him to come home as soon as possible.

> Your kindness will be amply rewarded,
> I will never dare to forget it."

Now this Hsi-men Ch'ing was the sort of man of whom it is said:

If you hit him on the top of his head,
The soles of his feet will ring.

He had been a habitué of the world of breeze and moonlight for so many years that there wasn't much he didn't know about anything. Therefore, on this particular day, the fact that the woman was opening up a wide avenue of approach to herself was not lost on him.

His face wreathed in smiles, he laughed, saying, "How can you talk that way, Sister-in-law? Really! What are friends for, anyway? I'll certainly do my best to admonish my brother. You can rest assured, Sister-in-law."

The woman bowed to him again to express her thanks and also directed a young maidservant to bring out a cup of tea, flavored with fruit kernels, in a carved lacquer cup with a silver spoon.

When Hsi-men Ch'ing had finished the tea, he said, "I'd better be on my way. Be careful not to let anyone into the house."

Whereupon, he took his leave and went home.

From this time on, Hsi-men Ch'ing made up his mind that he would contrive to make a conquest of this woman. Time and again he saw to it that Sponger Ying, Tagalong Hsieh, and the rest of that crowd detained Hua Tzu-hsü in the licensed quarter, carousing all night long, while he slipped out and made his way back to his own home. Once there, he would stand around in front of the gate until the woman and her two maidservants appeared at the front gate next door. She noticed that it was Hsi-men Ch'ing, who gave a discreet cough as he passed in front of her door. First he would head east, then turn around and go west, or come to a halt in front of the gateway across the street and stare fixedly in the direction of her door. The woman would show herself in the doorway and then, when she saw him coming, duck inside, only to stick her head out again as soon as he had passed by. As for:

The messages in their eyes and the expectations
in their hearts;
There was no longer any need to express them in words.

One day, as Hsi-men Ch'ing was standing in front of his gate, the woman sent her young maidservant, Hsiu-ch'un, to invite him over.

"What are you inviting me for, Sister?" Hsi-men Ch'ing pointedly asked. "Is your father at home or not?"

"Father's not at home," Hsiu-ch'un replied. "It's Mother that's inviting you, sir. There's something she wants to ask you."

This was just the signal Hsi-men Ch'ing had been waiting for. He complied with alacrity, was shown into the parlor, and took a seat.

After some time, the woman came out and saluted him, saying as she did so, "I'm extremely grateful for your consideration the other day.

It is imprinted in my heart,
My gratitude knows no bounds.

Since my poor husband went out last, it's been two days in a row now that he hasn't come home. I wonder if you happen to have come across him or not, sir?"

"Yesterday, along with three or four others, he was drinking in the Cheng family establishment," said Hsi-men Ch'ing. "Something happened to come up that brought me home, and today I haven't had a chance to go into the quarter, so I don't know whether he's still there or not. If I'd been there I could hardly have failed to urge him to come home as early as possible. I'm well aware how upsetting it is for you, Sister-in-law."

"It's just as you say," the woman responded. "I suffer constantly from his refusal to take anyone's advice, his frequent resort to the quarter:

Sleeping among the flowers and lolling
beneath the willows,

and his refusal to pay any attention to family affairs."

"If one had to assess Brother's character," said Hsi-men Ch'ing, "he's certainly humane and righteous enough, but he does have this one flaw."

As they were talking, the young maidservant brought tea, and they drank it together. Hsi-men Ch'ing was afraid Hua Tzu-hsü might come home and thought it imprudent to linger, so he prepared to take his leave.

The woman, for her part, begged Hsi-men Ch'ing, in no uncertain terms, "If you happen to go there tomorrow, whatever happens, urge him to come home as soon as possible. Your kindness will be rewarded. You can be sure I'll make it worth your while, sir."

"Say no more, Sister-in-law," said Hsi-men Ch'ing. "After all, Brother and I are just like that together."

After saying which, Hsi-men Ch'ing went home.

The next day, when Hua Tzu-hsü came back from the licensed quarter, the woman complained to him, saying, "While you've been out:

Indulging your taste for wine and sex,

we've become more than a little obligated to our next-door neighbor, the Honorable Hsi-men, who has, more than once, helped to see you safely home. You really ought to buy him a present of some kind to express your gratitude if you don't want to fall behind in your social obligations."

Hua Tzu-hsü immediately bought four boxes of presents and a jar of wine and sent the page boy, T'ien-hsi, to deliver them to Hsi-men Ch'ing's household. Hsi-men Ch'ing accepted them and gave the messenger a generous tip, but we will say no more of this.

Wu Yüeh-niang, who was present on this occasion, asked, "What is the Hua household sending you this batch of presents for?"

Hsi-men Ch'ing replied, "This must be because, the other day, when

Brother Hua the Second invited me to join him in the licensed quarter to help celebrate Wu Yin-erh's birthday, he got drunk, and I had to help him to get home. And also because his wife is aware that I constantly urge him not to spend the night in the quarter but to go home as early as possible, and she can't get over her feelings of gratitude at my consideration. I imagine she must have suggested to Brother Hua the Second that he buy these presents in order to thank me."

Wu Yüeh-niang folded her hands in front of her chest and made him a bow in the manner of a Buddhist priest, saying, "Brother, you really ought to take a good look at yourself. You're just like:

> The earthenware idol preaching to the idol of clay.

You, too, stay away from home for days at a time:

> Seducing people's daughters and carrying on
> with their wives,

and you have the face to preach to someone else's husband."

"I don't suppose," she continued, "that you're planning to simply accept these presents from them without doing anything in return. Whose name was written on the card that came with the gifts, anyway? If it was his wife's name, then we can write an invitation in my name today and invite her over for a visit. She's been anxious to make our acquaintance for some time. If it was her husband's name, invite him or not, as you please. It's no business of mine."

"It was in Brother Hua the Second's name," said Hsi-men Ch'ing. "I'll invite him over tomorrow, that's all."

The next day, sure enough, Hsi-men Ch'ing made the necessary preparations and invited Hua Tzu-hsü over for a visit. They spent the better part of the day drinking together.

When he got home, Li P'ing-erh said to him, "We mustn't be remiss in our social obligations. We sent him a set of presents and he has reciprocated by inviting you over for a drink. Some day soon you ought to make the necessary preparations and invite him back over here for a drink. Turnabout is fair play."

> Light and darkness alternate swiftly.

Before long the Double Yang festival,[7] on the ninth day of the ninth month, rolled around. Hua Tzu-hsü took advantage of the occasion to engage the services of two singing girls, and sent an invitation to Hsi-men Ch'ing to come over and enjoy the chrysanthemums with him. He also invited Sponger Ying, Tagalong Hsieh, Sticky Chu, and Blabbermouth Sun to keep them company. Playing the game:

> "Passing the Flower to the Beat of the Drum,"[8]

they:

> Enjoyed themselves as they drank up the wine.

There is a poem that testifies to this:

The raven and the hare[9] move in their orbits
as swiftly as arrows;
Among the festivals in the human world
it is again the Double Yang.
The red leaves on a thousand branches
supply autumn color;
The yellow blossoms on the garden paths
emit unusual fragrance.
But the black-hatted young official is not seen
ascending the heights;
He is still dreaming of a silk-clad young lady
offering him wine.
Amid embroidered hangings, behind latticed doors,
they gaze at each other;
From this time on, their mutual love
will never be forgotten.

That day the bunch of them continued to drink until after the lamps had been lighted. At this juncture Hsi-men Ch'ing happened to get up from his place and go outside to relieve himself. He did not anticipate that Li P'ing-erh would be standing there, eavesdropping, just on the other side of the latticework partition, and the two of them ran smack into each other. Before Hsi-men Ch'ing could get out of the way, the woman, who had hastily withdrawn behind the postern gate on the west side of the courtyard, surreptitiously sent her maidservant, Hsiu-ch'un, to waylay him in the shadows.

"Mother has sent me to ask you, sir," she whispered, "if you won't take it easy on the wine and go home as early as you can. Right now she's contriving a way to hustle Father off to the quarter to spend the night. This evening, thus and so, Mother would like to have a word with you."

When Hsi-men Ch'ing heard this:

His delight knew no bounds.

He returned to the party, after relieving himself, and from that point on surreptitiously disposed of his drinks, concealing what he was doing behind his sleeve. As the singing girls continued to play their instruments, sing, and ply the guests with wine, he pretended to be too drunk to have any more.

Before long it was already the first watch, and Li P'ing-erh kept coming back impatiently to eavesdrop outside the screen. She saw that Hsi-men Ch'ing was sitting in the place of honor, pretending to have fallen asleep, while Sponger Ying and Tagalong Hsieh were sitting there, as if their bodies were nailed to their chairs. They were so drunk they bobbed about like the float valve in an oil jar, but they wouldn't get up to go. It got so bad that

Sticky Chu and Blabbermouth Sun finally left, but the two of them still wouldn't budge. Li P'ing-erh was beside herself.

Hsi-men Ch'ing eventually got up to go, but Hua Tzu-hsü wouldn't let him get away.

"I must not have done my duty as a host today," he said. "Brother, how can you refuse to stay a little longer?"

"I'm really drunk," said Hsi-men Ch'ing, "I can't swallow another drop." Whereupon, making a deliberate display of:

Swaying to the east and tumbling to the west,

he prevailed upon his two page boys to help him back home.

"I don't know what's the matter with him today," said Sponger Ying, "that he kept refusing to have anything more. He got drunk when he'd hardly had anything to drink. But since our host has gone to so much trouble on our behalf, let's ask our two sisters here to bring out some larger cups, and we'll have another forty or fifty rounds before breaking up."

When Li P'ing-erh heard this, from her vantage point on the other side of the screen, she cursed them unremittingly for a pair of slobber-pussed jailbirds, and inconspicuously sent the page boy, T'ien-hsi, to call Hua Tzu-hsü out for a word with her.

"If you want to go on drinking with that bunch," she told him, in no uncertain terms, "you can take yourselves into the licensed quarter, this minute, and do your drinking there. Don't stick around the house and bother me anymore. Before I know it, it'll be:

The third watch in the middle of the night,

and you'll still be:

Burning oil and wasting fuel.

I've had enough of it."

"If I go into the licensed quarter with them at this hour," said Hua Tzu-hsü, "I'll never make it back home tonight. You'd better not give me a hard time about it."

"You go ahead," the woman said. "I'll not give you a hard time about it, that's all."

This was just the signal Hua Tzu-hsü had been waiting for. He came back and told the others about it, thus and so, saying, "Let's go into the licensed quarter."

"Really?" said Sponger Ying. "Sister-in-law said that? It's no use trying to fool us. You'd better go back and ask Sister-in-law again before we get going."

"My wife just spoke to me about it a minute ago," said Hua Tzu-hsü. "She told me not to come home till tomorrow."

"I've got it," said Tagalong Hsieh. "She just couldn't take any more of Beggar Ying's palaver. Now that our brother's succeeded in getting her permission, we can go without anything to worry about."

Thereupon, along with the two singing girls, the whole party set off for the licensed quarter. T'ien-fu and T'ien-hsi accompanied their master, Hua Tzu-hsü, and his two guests. When they arrived at Wu Yin-erh's place in the back alley of the quarter it was already the second watch. They called until someone opened the gate. Wu Yin-erh had already gone to bed, but she got up, lit some candles in the reception room, and invited them to come in and have a seat.

"The patron of your establishment," explained Sponger Ying, "invited us to his place to enjoy the chrysanthemums and have a drink today. Having already drunk to the point where we can't stop, he's also invited us to look in on you here in the quarter. Whatever you've got in the house to drink, serve it up, so we can continue drinking."

We will say no more, for the moment, about Hua Tzu-hsü's drinking bout in the licensed quarter, but return to the story of Hsi-men Ch'ing.

When he arrived home, still feigning drunkenness, he went into P'an Chin-lien's quarters. No sooner had he taken off his outer clothes, however, than he went out into the front garden and sat down to await a signal from Li P'ing-erh's side of the wall. After some time had passed, he heard them chasing the dog and locking the gate on the other side. Not long after this, what should appear in the dark shadows over the wall but the maidservant, Ying-ch'un. She pretended to be calling a cat, but when she saw Hsi-men Ch'ing sitting in the pavilion, she gave him a message. Hsi-men Ch'ing then moved over a table and a bench and, by mounting on top of them, was able to get over the wall. A ladder had already been put in place on the other side.

Now that Hua Tzu-hsü was out of the way, Li P'ing-erh had already:

Removed her headdress,
Carelessly coiled her raven locks, and
Adorned herself with demure elegance,

before coming out to stand in the veranda. When she saw Hsi-men Ch'ing come over the wall:

Her delight knew no bounds.

She welcomed him into her room, which was brightly illuminated by lamps and candles, and where she had already laid out a magnificent spread of wine and delicacies, condiments and appetizers.

There was a small pot:

Filled to the brim with fragrant wine.

The woman:

Lifting high a jade goblet,

with both hands, allowed Ying-ch'un to fill it from the wine pot, and then offered it to Hsi-men Ch'ing with a deep bow, saying, "We've been obligated to you in the past, sir, and you have even gone to the trouble of entertaining us. It's enough to make me:

Uneasy in my heart.

Li P'ing-erh Makes a Secret Tryst over the Garden Wall

Today I took it upon myself to prepare this cup of watery wine and invite you over, sir, as a means of expressing some small part of my inadequate feelings. And then I've had to contend with the refusal of those two goddamned slobber-pusses to leave. I was really beside myself. But now I've succeeded in packing them all off to the licensed quarter."

"My only fear is that Brother Two might come home," said Hsi-men Ch'ing.

"I've already told him to spend the night there and not come back," said the woman. "The two menservants have both gone with him. There's no one else left at home but these two maidservants and Old Mother Feng, who looks after the gate. She's been a servant in my family since I was a child and is completely trustworthy. The front and back gates are already locked."

When Hsi-men Ch'ing heard this, he was completely delighted. The two of them then sat down together:

> Shoulder to shoulder and thigh over thigh,
> Exchanging cups as they drank,

while Ying-ch'un stood at their side to pour the wine and Hsiu-ch'un went back and forth to serve the food. When they began to feel the effects of the wine; within the brocade bed curtains, the maids:

> Perfumed with incense the mandarin duck quilt, and
> Put in its place the coral pillow.

The servants then removed the table at which they had been drinking and put the latch on the door, after which the two of them:

> Got into bed and engaged each other in amorous sport.

It so happens that well-to-do households are equipped with double windows, the outer layers of which are called shutters, and the inner layers, casements. When the woman sent her maidservants out of the room, she closed the two casements on the inside, so that even though the room was illuminated by lamps and candles, no one could see in from the outside.

Now the maidservant, Ying-ch'un, was already sixteen years old and knew something of the world. When she saw that the two of them were going to engage in an illicit liaison that night, she stealthily pulled a hairpin out of her headdress, poked a hole in the paper of the lower part of the casement, and peeped inside. Truly, what were the two of them doing with each other? Behold:

> By the gleam of lamplight,
> Amid mermaid silk curtains;
> One comes, the other goes,
> One butts, the other lunges.
> One of them stirs his jade arms into motion,
> The other raises her golden lotuses on high.
> This one gives vent to the warbling of an oriole,

The Maid Ying-ch'un Peeks through a Crack and Gets an Eyeful

That one gives voice to the twittering of a swallow.
It is just like Chang Chün-jui's rendezvous
with Ts'ui Ying-ying;[10]
It much resembles Sung Yü's secret tryst
with the Goddess of Witches' Mountain.[11]
Promises to be as faithful as the hills and seas,
Still resonate within their ears;
The butterfly is enamored, the bee distraught,
They are not yet willing to call a halt.
The engagement is protracted,
The coverlet disturbed by crimson waves,[12]
Until the transfusing touch of the "magic rhinoceros
horn"[13] penetrates her creamy breast;
The battle is prolonged,
The bed curtains clipped by silver hooks,
Until the twin arcs of her painted eyebrows
wilt on her jade face.

Truly:

The third time that lip meets lip
passion is stronger than ever;
A single melting sensation suffuses the body
when lovers meet in secret.

While the two of them were in the room playing at clouds and rain, who would have thought that everything they did was so clearly seen and heard by Ying-ch'un from her vantage point outside the window that she might well have exclaimed:

"Is it not delightful?"[14]

She could hear everything that they said.

"How old are you?" Hsi-men Ch'ing asked the woman.

"I was born in the year of the ram," said Li P'ing-erh, "so, this year, I'm twenty-two."

She then went on to ask, "How old is your first lady?"

"My wife was born in the year of the dragon," said Hsi-men Ch'ing, "which would make her twenty-five."

"So she's three years older than I am," said the woman. "One of these days I ought to buy a set of presents and go pay a call on your First Lady. My only fear is that she may not be any too friendly."

"My wife has always had a most accommodating disposition," said Hsi-men Ch'ing. "If that were not the case, how could I ever manage to keep so many bedmates around the place?"

"When you came over here, just now," the woman went on to ask, "did the First Lady know about it or not? If she should ask you about it, what would you say?"

"My wives all live in the rear compound," said Hsi-men Ch'ing, "four courtyards back from the front of the house. The only exception is my fifth concubine, née P'an, who lives all by herself in a two-storied belvedere in the front garden, but she doesn't dare interfere with me."

"And how old is the Fifth Lady?" the woman asked.

"She was born in the same year as my wife," replied Hsi-men Ch'ing.

"That's good," the woman said. "If she doesn't think it presumptuous of me, I'd like to acknowledge her as an elder sister. Someday soon, if you can get hold of the outlines of the First Lady's and the Fifth Lady's feet for me, I'll make two pairs of shoes for them, myself, and take them over with me, as a token of my feelings."

The woman then pulled out two gold pins from among those that held her headdress in place and gave them to Hsi-men Ch'ing, enjoining him, "If you should go into the licensed quarter, don't let Hua Tzu-hsü see them."

"I understand," Hsi-men Ch'ing promised.

Thereupon, the two of them:

> Like glue and like lacquer,

dallied with each other until the fifth watch, when:

> The cock crowed outside the window, and
> The eastern horizon began to grow light.

Hsi-men Ch'ing, fearing that Hua Tzu-hsü might come home, got up and put his clothes in order.

"You can climb over the wall the same way you came," the woman said.

The two of them agreed on a set of signals between themselves. Whenever Hua Tzu-hsü was safely out of the way, a maidservant on this side would look over the wall and give a surreptitious cough as a signal, or first throw a piece of tile over the wall to see if the coast was clear before climbing up to communicate with him. Hsi-men Ch'ing could then use a ladder to climb over the wall, where he would find another already in place to receive him. The two of them could thus:

> Communicate across the intervening wall,[15]

as they engaged in:

> Pilfering jade and purloining perfume.[16]

As long as they did not go in and out the main gates, there would be no way for the neighbors in the vicinity to find out about their clandestine affair.

There is a poem that testifies to this:

> In your eating, go easy on the salt and vinegar;
> Don't bother to go places where you don't belong.
> If you want to be respected, study diligently;
> If you don't want a deed discovered, don't do it.[17]

To resume our story, as the day dawned, Hsi-men Ch'ing climbed back over the wall the way he had come and went to P'an Chin-lien's room.

Chin-lien, who was still in bed, asked him, "Where did you go off to yesterday without anyone's knowing it? You didn't come home all night, and you didn't tell me where you were going."

"Once again," explained Hsi-men Ch'ing, "it was Brother Hua the Second who sent a page boy over to invite me to join him on an excursion into the licensed quarter. We've been drinking half the night, and I came home as soon as I could tear myself away."

Although Chin-lien believed him, the shadow of a doubt still lingered in her mind.

One day, after dinner, she and Meng Yü-lou were sitting in the pavilion in the garden doing some needlework together when a piece of tile came flying over the wall and landed right in front of them. Meng Yü-lou was so preoccupied with stitching the sole of the shoe she was working on that she didn't notice anything. But P'an Chin-lien swiftly surveyed the scene and caught an indistinct glimpse of a white face that poked over the top of the wall and then immediately withdrew.

Chin-lien nudged Yü-lou, pointing to the place where the head had appeared, and said, "Look, Sister Three, that was the older of the two maidservants in the Hua household next door. She must have climbed up to look at our flowers over the wall and then, on seeing us here, gotten down again."

Although this is all that she said at the time, she didn't let it go at that.

Later the same evening, Hsi-men Ch'ing arrived home after a social engagement and came into Chin-lien's quarters. When she helped him off with his outer garments and asked if he wanted anything, he expressed no interest in food or tea of any kind, but made a beeline for the front garden. P'an Chin-lien, on the principle that:

> One thief knoweth another,

decided to spy on him and observed that, after he had sat there for some time, the same maidservant as before peeked over the wall, whereupon Hsi-men Ch'ing clambered up a ladder and disappeared over the wall himself.

Once there, he was met by Li P'ing-erh, who conducted him into her room for a rendezvous, but there is no need to describe this in detail.

P'an Chin-lien returned to her room where, all night long, she:

> Tossed first this way and then that,

but could not get to sleep.

At dawn the next day, who should appear but Hsi-men Ch'ing, who pushed open the door to her room and came inside. The woman pretended to be asleep and did not pay him any attention. Hsi-men Ch'ing, who was already feeling somewhat uneasy about the situation, came up and sat down beside her on the edge of the bed.

When the woman saw what he was doing, she jumped up into a sitting position herself, took hold of him by the ear with one hand, and berated him, saying, "You unfaithful scoundrel! Where did you really go off to last night, anyway; leaving your old mother to fret the whole night through?"

"No sooner do I let you out of my sight," she continued, "than you're up to your old tricks. But I already know all about them, and you're beginning to try my patience. Tell me the truth at once, all this while, how many times have you made out with that whore in the Hua household next door? If you confess to everything, I may let you off the hook; but if you try to deceive me by so much as a single word, the next time you set one foot over there, I'll raise such a hue and cry before you can get your other foot over the threshold, you fickle jailbird, that:

You'll die without a plot to be buried in.[18]

"You've been arranging to have your cronies latch onto her husband and keep him overnight in the licensed quarter while you're here making out with his wife. If it's trouble you want, I'll give you enough so that:

When you've had your fill, there'll be enough left over
for you to wrap up and take home with you.

No wonder, yesterday, when Sister Meng the Third and I were in the garden doing our needlework, what should appear but that elder maidservant from her place:

Sticking out her head and craning her neck,

over the wall? It turns out she was nothing but a ghost-snatching demon sent by that whore to snatch you away. You think you can fool your old mother, do you? The other night when that cuckold of hers supposedly invited you to join him for an excursion into the licensed quarter, it was his own home that was the licensed quarter, wasn't it?"

If Hsi-men Ch'ing had not heard these words nothing might have happened, but having heard them, he was flustered enough to adopt the posture of a dwarf.

Stamping his feet in exasperation, he knelt down on the ground with an ingratiating laugh and pleaded with her, saying, "You crazy little oily mouth! Not so loud! The truth of the matter is that, thus and so, she asked how old the two of you were and said that, someday soon, if she can get hold of the outlines of your feet, she'll make a pair of shoes for each of you. She'd also like to acknowledge you both as elder sisters. She's quite content to be a younger sister to you."

"I don't need that whore to acknowledge me as any older brother or older sister," exclaimed Chin-lien. "She steals other people's husbands and then comes around offering to do them little favors as a means of cementing the relationship. Your old mother is:

Not the sort of person to let dust
be thrown in her eyes.[19]

She thinks she can get away with that kind of mischief right under my nose, does she?"

As she spoke, she pulled open his trousers with one hand, exposing to view his limp and flaccid organ, which still had a silver clasp fastened around it.

"Tell me the truth," she demanded. "How many times did you make out with that whore last night?"

"Only once that would really count," replied Hsi-men Ch'ing.

"You'll have to swear an oath on that all too vigorous body of yours before you can get me to believe that," said the woman. "One time only and it's:

> As soft as driveling snot and thick as gravy.[20]

It might as well have been stricken with paralysis. The slightest sign of vitality would be cause for hope."

As she spoke, she removed the clasp with a single motion of her hand, and continued to berate him, saying, "You shameless ruffian!

> You may be a brown cat, but you've got a black tail.

No wonder I turned the place upside down looking for it, and all the time it was you who had spirited the thing away in order to screw around with that whore."

Affecting an ingratiating smile, Hsi-men Ch'ing said, "You crazy little whore! You'll be the death of me yet. She has repeatedly asked me to convey the message that someday soon she'll come over and kowtow to you. And she's going to make a pair of shoes for you too. Yesterday she sent her maidservant over for an outline of the feet of the one from the Wu family. And today she asked me to deliver this pair of hairpins in the shape of the character for long life to you as a present."

Thereupon he took off his cap, pulled them out of his headdress, and presented them to Chin-lien. Taking them into her hand and looking them over, Chin-lien saw that they were a pair of gold, openwork pins, in the shape of the character for long life, which had been deeply chased in intaglio and inset with azurite. It was obvious from the extraordinary intricacy of the craftsmanship that they had been manufactured for imperial use and came from the palace.

Chin-lien was utterly delighted and said, "Well, if that's the way things stand, I won't say any more about it, that's all. When you go over there in the future, I'll act as a lookout, so the two of you can screw away to your hearts' content. How would that be?"

Hsi-men Ch'ing was so delighted he put both arms around her and said, "My precious child, if you really do that, it will prove the truth of the adage:

> You don't raise a child in the hope it will
>   shit gold and piss silver;
> All you can hope for is that it will
>   respond empathetically to you.[21]

Tomorrow I'll go myself and buy you a set of patterned clothing to express my gratitude."

"I don't trust that:

Honeyed mouth and sugared tongue,

of yours," the woman responded. "If you want your old mother to fix things up for the two of you, you'll have to agree to three conditions."

"No matter how many conditions you impose, I'll agree to them all," said Hsi-men Ch'ing.

"The first condition," the woman said, "is that you will have to give up frequenting the licensed quarter. The second condition is that you must do as I say. The third condition is that when you go over to sleep with her, when you come home, you must tell me all about it, without deceiving me by so much as a single word."

"Those conditions are no obstacle," said Hsi-men Ch'ing. "I'll agree to all of them, and make an end to it."

From this time on, whenever Hsi-men Ch'ing came back after spending the night next door, he would regale the woman with an account of his adventures.

"Li P'ing-erh has a naturally fair complexion," he would say. "Her face is shaped like a melon seed. She's very amorous and she drinks like a fish. We often bring a box of delicacies inside the bed curtains and play cards there and drink for half the night before going to sleep."

One day, he reached into his sleeve and pulled out an object, which he handed to Chin-lien to look at, saying, "This is an album of paintings from the Palace Treasury that the old eunuch director obtained during his service in the Imperial Household Department. The two of us consult it by lamplight and then attempt to emulate the proceedings."

Chin-lien took the album in her hand and opened it up to take a look. There is a lyric that testifies to this:

Mounted on patterned damask in the imperial palace,
Fastened with ivory pins on brocade ribbons;
Vividly traced in outlines of gold,
  enhanced by blue and green colors;
The square painting on each folio leaf
  is neatly framed.
The women vie with the Goddess of Witches' Mountain,
The men resemble that handsome paragon, Sung Yü.[22]
Pair by pair, within the bed curtains, they show
  themselves to be practiced combatants.
The names of the positions are
  twenty-four in number;[23]
Each one designed to arouse the
  lust of the beholder.

Chin-lien, having perused it from beginning to end, was reluctant to let it out of her hands and, turning it over to Ch'un-mei, said, "Put it away safely in my trunk so we can amuse ourselves with it whenever we want to."

"You can look it over for a few days," said Hsi-men Ch'ing, "but then you'll have to return it to me. This is a prized possession, belonging to someone else, which I borrowed to bring home and look at, on condition that I return it to her afterward."

"If it belongs to her, what's it doing in my house?" demanded Chin-lien. "I didn't take it out of her hands. And even if I had, she couldn't get it out of me now."

"It wasn't you who asked her for it," said Hsi-men Ch'ing. "It was I who borrowed it. You crazy little slave. Stop fooling around."

As he spoke, he went after her and tried to wrest the album out of her hand.

"If you try to grab it," said Chin-lien, "I'll go you one better. I'll tear it to shreds and then nobody will be able to enjoy it."

"I guess I'm outmaneuvered," said Hsi-men Ch'ing with a laugh. "Do as you like with it, but return it when you're through, that's all. If you give this back to her, she's got another remarkable object I can borrow for you in the future."

"My child, whoever taught you to be so disingenuous?" said Chin-lien. "Bring it here first, and then I'll let you have this album back."

The two of them continued their badinage for some time.

That evening, in her room, Chin-lien:

> Perfumed with incense the mandarin duck quilt,
> Deftly trimmed the silver lamp's wick,
> Made herself up alluringly, washed her private parts,

and, together with Hsi-men Ch'ing, opened up the album inside the bed curtains, preparatory to:

> Enjoying the pleasures of connubial bliss.

Gentle reader take note: Black magic and sorcery have existed since ancient times. If you look at the way in which Chin-lien, from the time she prevailed upon the blind Stargazer Liu to effect a "turnabout" on her behalf, in no time at all contrived to so complicate the situation that Hsi-men Ch'ing's:

> Annoyance and anger were transformed into favor,

while her:

> Seclusion and disgrace were transmuted to joy,

with the result that he no longer dared to control her; can the existence of such arts be doubted? Truly:

> Though you may be as devious as any demon,
> You'll drink the water she's washed her feet in.[24]

There is a lyric to the tune "Partridge Sky" that testifies to this:

She remembers that time in the studio
  when they had just met;
The clouds and rain they enjoyed together
  were known to only a few.
When evening came, the phoenix and his mate
  alighted on adjacent pillows;
Left untrimmed, the silver lamp
  shed only a half-light.

Thinking of the past,
Her dreaming soul deluded;
Tonight she is all too happy to enjoy
  the pleasures of connubial bliss.
Tumbled and tossed like male and female phoenixes,
  their pleasure knows no bounds.
From this time on, surely, the pair of them
  will never be separated.[25]

If you want to know the outcome of these events,
Pray consult the story related in the following chapter.

Chapter 14

HUA TZU-HSÜ SUCCUMBS TO CHAGRIN AND LOSES HIS LIFE; LI P'ING-ERH INVITES SEDUCTION AND ATTENDS A PARTY

The message in her eyes and expectation in her heart
will brook no further delay;
She is not content merely to fiddle with
her hairpin of jade.[1]
When spring blooms on her smiling countenance
the flowers look seductive;
At the slightest perturbation of her delicate brows
the willows droop in sorrow.
While blushes suffuse her peachlike cheeks
she dreams of matrimony;
As the chill invades her orchid-scented chamber
she longs for togetherness.
If only she could contrive to comply
with Ssu-ma Hsiang-ju's wishes;
Without suffering the fate of Cho Wen-chün
when she sang the "Song of White Hair."[2]

THE STORY GOES that one day when Wu Yüeh-niang was feeling out of sorts, her sister-in-law, the wife of Wu K'ai, came to pay her a visit and she invited her to stay overnight.

While she was entertaining her visitor in her room, the page boy, Tai-an, happened to come in, carrying his master's felt bag, and reported, "Father's come home."

Wu K'ai's wife promptly moved over to Li Chiao-erh's quarters in order to get out of the way.

Before long, Hsi-men Ch'ing came in, took off his outer garments, and sat down. Hsiao-yü brought him a cup of tea, but he didn't drink it.

Yüeh-niang noticed that he looked rather worried and asked, "Why is it that you've come home so early from your club meeting today?"

"It was Ch'ang Shih-chieh's turn to entertain us today," said Hsi-men Ch'ing, "but he doesn't have room in his own house, so he invited us to make an excursion to the Temple of Eternal Felicity, at Wu-li Yüan, outside the South Gate. Then Brother Hua the Second invited Brother Ying the Second and several of the rest of us, four or five in all, to join him for a drink at Cheng Ai-hsiang's place in the licensed quarter. Just as we were beginning to enjoy ourselves, all of a sudden, a group of official lictors appeared, and:

Without permitting any further explanation,

arrested Brother Hua the Second and took him into custody. This development caught all of us completely off guard, and in my alarm I fled to Li Kuei-chieh's place and hid out for a while. Still uneasy about it, I sent someone to make inquiries.

"It turns out that Hua the Elder, Hua the Third, and Hua the Fourth, from Brother Hua the Second's branch of the old eunuch's family, are suing him for a share of the family property. They have filed a suit in the prefectural yamen at K'ai-feng, the Eastern Capital, and, since the suit has been accepted, the authorities in this district have been ordered to arrest the defendant. It was only after ascertaining the facts that we felt secure enough to break up and come home."

When Yüeh-niang had heard him out, she said, "It serves you right! You've been spending altogether too much of your time hanging around and playing the god with that bunch, without so much as thinking of coming home. All you want to do is fool around outside. It's only appropriate that something like this today should happen before you're ready to call it quits. If you don't give it over now, sooner or later you're going to get involved in a brawl in which they'll drag you off somewhere and:

Pound you into a bloody sheep's head,[3]

before you abandon this kind of behavior once and for all.

"When your legitimate wife, at home, gives you her well-meant advice, you seldom pay any attention. But whenever a whore in the licensed quarter says a few words to you, you prick up your donkey's ears and do as she says. Truly:

The words of your family
  are wind in your ears;
The words of outsiders
  are sutras in letters of gold."

"Who would have the:

Seven heads and eight galls,

to assault me?" scoffed Hsi-men Ch'ing.

"You good-for-nothing," Yüeh-niang responded. "You're given to shooting off your mouth at home all right, but if it came to the crunch, you'd be so terrified your tongue would hang out."

As they were talking, who should come in but Tai-an, who reported, "Hua the Second's wife, next door, has sent T'ien-fu to ask Father if he would step over there to have a word with her."

This was just the signal Hsi-men Ch'ing had been waiting for, and he lost no time in starting on his way.

"One of these days," said Yüeh-niang, "if you don't watch out, it's going to be you that gets nabbed."

"It's right next door," said Hsi-men Ch'ing. "What harm can it do? I'll just go over and see what she has to say."

Thereupon, he went over to Hua Tzu-hsü's place. Li P'ing-erh sent a page boy to invite him into the rear of the house for a talk. What should he see when he got there but the woman, with her:

> Silk tunic in disarray, and
> Pale countenance unadorned,

coming out of her room, so frightened her face had turned as sallow as wax?

Kneeling down before Hsi-men Ch'ing and making repeated supplications, she said, "Sir, there's no help for it!

> If you won't do it for the priest's sake,
>   do it for the Buddha's.[4]

As the saying goes:

> When calamities strike the home,
> Neighbors help each other out.

It's all because of my poor husband's refusal to take anyone's advice, coupled with his unwillingness to pay any attention to serious family affairs. He reposes his trust in the people he fools around with outside and stays away from home for days at a time. It's only appropriate that today he should have allowed himself to be taken advantage of and gotten himself into this kind of a fix.

"And now that it's come to the crunch, at this late date, he sends his page boy to me and wants me to pull strings and get him off the hook. I'm only a woman, after all, about as much good as a legless crab; where does he think I'm going to go to find the strings to pull on his behalf? I get so angry when I think of his refusal to take anyone's advice, I'm tempted to let him be dragged off to the Eastern Capital and beaten to a pulp. It would serve him right. The only thing that deters me is that it would reflect unfavorably on the late old eunuch director's reputation.

"I hadn't any alternative, sir, but to ask you to come over and appeal to your generosity. Forget about him! But if you could only find it in you, for my poor sake; if you know of any strings to pull, whatever happens, be good enough to pull one. I just don't want to see him abused, that's all."

When Hsi-men Ch'ing saw the woman kneeling before him, he quickly said, "Sister-in-law, please get up. It's no problem. At first, today, I didn't know what was going on. We were all at the Cheng establishment drinking wine together when a group of official lictors suddenly appeared and carried brother off to the Eastern Capital."

"It's a long story,"

the woman said. "The trouble is being caused by the nephews of my father-in-law, the late eunuch director, who belong to the same collateral branch of the family as the one from which my husband was adopted. The eldest nephew, Hua the Elder, Hua the Third, Hua the Fourth, and my husband are all natural brothers. The eldest is called Hua Tzu-yu, the third is called Hua Tzu-kuang, the fourth is called Hua Tzu-hua, and my husband is called Hua Tzu-hsü. They are all the consanguineous nephews of the old eunuch director.

"Although the old gentleman had succeeded in amassing a tidy fortune for himself, he saw clearly enough that this husband of mine would not amount to anything; so, when he came back from Kwangtung, he put his property into my hands for safekeeping. He even went so far, at times, as to give my husband a regular caning. The other nephews, too, had tasted enough of the stick at his hands not to dare to interfere.

"Last year, when the old gentleman died, Hua the Elder, Hua the Third, and Hua the Fourth were given something in the way of furniture and household effects to take home with them, but they didn't receive so much as a candareen's worth of silver. I said at the time, 'We'd better take care of them by giving them a little something.' But this husband of mine spent all his time fooling around on the outside and was unwilling to pay any attention at all to serious matters. Now, today, they've been able to:

Act so quietly not a breath of air escaped,

and he's allowed himself to be undone."

When she had finished speaking, she let herself go and began to weep out loud.

"Don't worry, Sister-in-law," said Hsi-men Ch'ing. "I was afraid it would be something big. But, as it turns out, it's only a case of members of the same branch of the family suing each other over the division of property. It shouldn't be too difficult to handle. As long as you want me to, I'll:

Treat my brother's affairs as my own, and
Treat my own affairs as my brother's.

No matter what you ask of me, I'll be only too happy to comply."

"If you'll only deign to help out, sir," the woman said, "everything will be fine. I'll need to know, though, how much money will be required in order to pull the necessary strings, so I can get it ready."

"It won't require all that much," said Hsi-men Ch'ing. "I understand that Prefect Yang, who presides over the prefectural yamen in K'ai-feng, the Eastern Capital, is a protégé of the grand preceptor, Ts'ai Ching. Grand Preceptor Ts'ai, along with my kinsman by marriage at four removes, the commander in chief of the Imperial Guard, Yang Chien, are both people who have the ear of the reigning emperor himself. If these two men can be induced to interest themselves on your behalf, and they both speak to Prefect Yang, he could hardly refuse to comply. No matter how important a matter it might be, that ought to take care of it. Now we will certainly need to make a present to Grand Preceptor Ts'ai, but since Commander in Chief Yang is related to me by marriage, he will probably refuse to accept anything."

The woman then went into her room, opened a trunk, and brought out sixty large ingots of silver, weighing fifty taels each, making a total of three thousand taels, which she handed over to Hsi-men Ch'ing to expend, both high and low, as he saw fit, in the endeavor to pull the necessary strings.

"Half of that would do," said Hsi-men Ch'ing. "What need is there to use so much?"

"If there's anything left over, you can keep it for me, sir," the woman said. "Concealed behind my bed there are four lacquer chests decorated with gold tracery that contain python robes, jade-ornamented girdles, jeweled cap buttons, chatelaines, pendants, and bracelets, as well as valuable jewels and objets d'art. If you could take these off my hands at the same time, sir, and keep them over at your place, I could ask for them whenever I need anything. If I don't take precautions ahead of time, but leave everything to him, we're going to end up having trouble making ends meet. It's obvious that:

> Three fists are no match for four hands.[5]

If we let ourselves be outnumbered, sooner or later they'll get the better of us and make off with the property, and I'll be left in the lurch with nowhere to turn."

"But what will happen when Brother Hua the Second comes home and starts looking for this stuff?" asked Hsi-men Ch'ing.

"These are all things," the woman replied, "that the old gentleman, while he was still alive, personally handed over to me for safekeeping. My husband doesn't know a thing about them. You can feel free to take charge of them, sir."

"If that's what you want me to do," said Hsi-men Ch'ing, "I'll send someone over to move them as soon as I get home."

Thereupon, he went straight home and consulted with Yüeh-niang about it.

"As for the silver," said Yüeh-niang, "we can send page boys over to carry it back in food boxes. But if we bring the stuff in the chests in at the front door, we can hardly avoid attracting the attention of the neighbors. The best thing to do is, thus and so; if we hoist it over the wall at night, it will be less conspicuous."

Hsi-men Ch'ing was greatly delighted by this suggestion and immediately dispatched the four servants, Lai-wang, Tai-an, Lai-hsing, and P'ing-an, with two sets of food boxes, to carry the three thousand taels of silver over to his house on their carrying poles. Later that evening, when the moon rose, Li P'ing-erh, on her side, together with her two maidservants, Ying-ch'un and Hsiu-ch'un, by putting a bench on top of a table, managed to hoist the chests up to the top of the wall. Hsi-men Ch'ing, on his side, accompanied only by Yüeh-niang, Chin-lien, and Ch'un-mei, set up a ladder to receive them. They spread a strip of felt over the top of the wall and then hoisted the chests over the top, one at a time, and deposited them in Yüeh-niang's room.

You may well ask:

"Can such things be?"
If you want to get rich,
You've got to take risks.

There is a poem that testifies to this:

Wealth and success are often attained
by strokes of good luck;
Profit and fame, on the other hand,
bring troubles of their own.
If you are destined to attain them,
you will do so in the end;
If you are not destined to attain them,
no amount of effort will avail.[6]

Hsi-men Ch'ing had succeeded in taking into his own possession a considerable quantity of his neighbor's disposable wealth, in the form of gold and silver and other valuables, without the other residents of the neighborhood being any the wiser. The same day he had the requisite monies packed up, requested a letter of introduction from his son-in-law's family, the Ch'en household, and sent a servant off to deliver them to the Eastern Capital.

Along the way this messenger:

Each morning took to the purple road;
Each evening tramped the red dust,[7]

until, one day, he arrived in the Eastern Capital and turned over the letter and presents to the commander in chief of the Imperial Guard, Yang Chien. The latter, in his turn, requested the grand councilor and grand preceptor, Ts'ai Ching, to send a note to Prefect Yang in the prefectural yamen at K'ai-feng.

Now this prefect was named Yang Shih,[8] his courtesy name was Kuei-shan, and he was a native of Hung-nung district in the province of Shensi. He had passed the *chin-shih* examination in the year 1103 and had risen to the position of chief minister of the Court of Judicial Review before receiving his current appointment as prefect of K'ai-feng. He was an official of absolute integrity. But the grand preceptor, Ts'ai Ching, had been his examiner in the *chin-shih* examination and Yang Chien was a favored and highly placed official, so he could hardly refuse to do the requested favor.

At the same time Hsi-men Ch'ing had also dispatched a letter to Hua Tzu-hsü, informing him of the steps that were being taken on his behalf, and saying, "The officials involved have all been taken care of. When you appear in court and are interrogated about the whereabouts of the inherited property, simply say that all of the money has been spent and that nothing remains but the houses and real estate."

To resume our story, one day Prefect Yang Shih ascended the tribunal, and the functionaries of the six local offices stood in attendance. Behold:

His official conduct is honest and correct;
His actions reveal integrity and intelligence.
He always harbors a compassionate disposition;
He constantly possesses benevolent intentions.
In cases of disputes over the ownership of land,
He distinguishes between the crooked and the straight
  before taking action.
In instances of mutual contention or affrays,
He weighs the lightness or heaviness of the offense
  before passing sentence.
In moments of leisure he fingers the zither
  or entertains guests;
He also devotes himself to the investigation
  of the condition of the people.
Despite the fact that he is a presiding official
  in the capital,
He really is a father and a mother to the people
  in his jurisdiction.[9]

That day, Prefect Yang Shih ascended the tribunal and ordered that Hua Tzu-hsü be taken out of the lockup and brought before him. When the parties to the suit had been assembled in the courtroom and knelt down before the dais, the prefect began his interrogation as to the whereabouts of the inherited property.

All Hua Tzu-hsü would say was, "After the death of the old eunuch director, the money was all expended on the funeral and services for the dead. All that remains are two houses and a country estate. As for the furniture and household effects, they have all been divided up among the other members of the family."

"It is difficult to ascertain anything about the property of eunuchs," pronounced Prefect Yang. "It is a case of:

Easy come, easy go.[10]

Since the money has apparently all been spent, I hereby rule that the presiding magistrate of Ch'ing-ho district be ordered to depute functionaries to assess Eunuch Director Hua's two houses and country estate, to sell them off for their market value, to divide up the proceeds among Hua Tzu-yu and the other two plaintiffs, and to report back to me in writing."

Hua Tzu-yu and the others wanted to kneel down before the tribunal and petition the prefect to continue to hold Hua Tzu-hsü in custody until the whereabouts of the missing money could be determined, but Prefect Yang angrily rejected their petition, saying, "You rascals are lucky to have escaped a beating. When this eunuch director of yours died, why didn't you bring a suit at that time, instead of waiting until now when:

The affair is over and the circumstances have changed,

to kick up such a fuss and waste the paper and brushes required to file a suit?"

Thereupon, without beating Hua Tzu-hsü a single stroke, he signed an order authorizing the return of the defendant to Ch'ing-ho district, and the assessment of the real estate. But no more of this.

No sooner did Hsi-men Ch'ing's retainer, Lai-pao, ascertain the facts about the disposition of the case than he traveled back, post haste, to report to his master. When Hsi-men Ch'ing heard that the prefect, Yang Shih, had proven responsive to pressure and had released Hua Tzu-hsü and allowed him to return home, he was extremely pleased.

Li P'ing-erh invited Hsi-men Ch'ing over to her place to discuss the matter and said to him, "Why don't you get together a few taels of silver and buy the house we're living in? After all, it won't be long now before I'm completely yours."

Hsi-men Ch'ing went home and broached the issue with Wu Yüeh-niang.

"No matter what it's officially assessed at," Yüeh-niang said, "you ought not to enter into an agreement to buy that house. What will you do if her husband should start to suspect something?"

Hsi-men Ch'ing made a mental note of what she had said.

Not many days thereafter, Hua Tzu-hsü arrived home. The district magistrate of Ch'ing-ho deputed Vice Magistrate Yüeh to carry out the assessment, with the following results. The eunuch director's mansion, located on Main Street in An-ch'ing ward, was evaluated at 700 taels of silver. It was sold to a distaff relative of the imperial family named Wang. The country estate outside the South Gate was evaluated at 655 taels of silver. It was sold to the commandant, Chou Hsiu. All that remained was the modest house in which Hua Tzu-hsü was currently residing. It was evaluated at 540 taels of silver, but because it was right next door to Hsi-men Ch'ing's property, no one dared to buy it.

Hua Tzu-hsü repeatedly sent people over to make representations, but Hsi-men Ch'ing stalled, maintaining that he couldn't afford it, and refused to rise to the bait. The district magistrate was anxious to settle the matter so that he could file the required written report. Li P'ing-erh, in desperation, secretly sent Old Mother Feng over to Hsi-men Ch'ing's place to suggest that he use 540 taels of the silver she had deposited with him to make the purchase. Only then did Hsi-men Ch'ing agree, and the silver was duly weighed out in the presence of the officials. Hua the Elder even signed the paper that formalized the transaction.

That very day the necessary documents were completed and a report was sent up to the higher authorities. The sale of the old eunuch's real estate holdings had produced, in all, a total of 1,895 taels of silver, which was evenly divided among the three plaintiffs.

Hua Tzu-hsü had come out of this lawsuit without anything for himself. His money, his houses, and his landed property were all gone. Not a trace remained of the 3,000 taels of silver, in large ingots, that had been stored in his coffers.

In a state of severe perturbation he demanded an accounting of Li P'ing-erh. "How was the silver that you provided to Hsi-men Ch'ing actually spent? And how much of it is left over? After all, we have to come up with the money to buy another house."

The only result of these queries was that he had to endure four or five days of abuse at the hands of his wife.

"Phooey! You muddleheaded troll!" she railed at him. "Day after day you neglected your proper concerns, going out and:

> Sleeping among the flowers and lolling
> beneath the willows,

without bothering to come home. It only serves you right that someone should have been lying in wait for you and succeeded in luring you into this trap.

"Once you landed in jail, you sent someone to speak to me, urging me to pull strings on your behalf. I'm only a woman, after all. I've scarcely ventured out so far as the front gate.

> I may be able to run, but I can't fly.[11]

What do I know about such things? Who do I know, anyway, that might be able to pull strings for you?

> Even if I were made of iron, how many nails
> could you get out of me?

I had to run all over the place, saying 'Please sir' and 'I beg you, madam,' before I could find anyone that could be of any use. If you haven't planted any seeds in the past, when the going gets rough, who's going to pay any attention to you?

"Thank goodness, our next-door neighbor, Hsi-men Ch'ing, out of consideration for our former relationship, was willing, despite the coldness of the weather and the ugly winds that were blowing, to send his servant all the way to the Eastern Capital, where he succeeded in bringing this affair of yours to a satisfactory conclusion.

"But now that you've escaped the clutches of the law and find yourself with:

Both feet on level ground again,[12]

what do you do but:

Once your life's been saved, think of money;
Once your wound's been healed, forget the pain,

and come home to demand an accounting of your wife?

"Even if there were anything left over, it wouldn't be yours to fritter away on your own gratification. After all, I've still got the note you sent me. If I didn't have your written authorization, it's not very likely that I'd have laid out your money in order to pull strings for you entirely on my own hook, or have simply handed it over to somebody, is it?"

"Of course I sent you that note," said Hua Tzu-hsü. "But the truth of the matter is I was hoping there would be something left over. We've got to come up with enough money to buy another house and have something to live on before we can worry about anything else."

"Phooey!" his wife exclaimed. "What a nincompoop! I'm just wasting my breath on you. If you'd only paid some attention a little bit earlier, instead of:

Ignoring things when you're flush, and
Starting to worry when you're in the hole!

You may accuse me of spending too much a thousand times, or ten thousand times if you like, but where do you suppose those three thousand taels of yours went, anyway? I wouldn't underestimate the appetites of people like the grand preceptor, Ts'ai Ching, or the commander in chief of the Imperial Guard, Yang Chien, if I were you. If they had been offered any less, do you suppose you could have escaped with impunity from your bout with the law, without suffering so much as a lash with a wisp of straw on your cuckold's body, only so you could come home and shoot off your mouth?

"Hsi-men Ch'ing is no connection of yours. You've got no claim on him. And which of your beloved relatives or friends would have been willing to:

Travel north and journey south,

or go to such lengths or spend so much money, in order to come to your rescue? When you got home you should have laid on a feast and invited him over to express your appreciation, instead of:

Trying to sweep it all under the rug with a
single stroke of the broom,[13]

or demanding that everything be accounted for after the fact."

It did not take very many such pointed and derisive speeches to reduce Hua Tzu-hsü to silence.

The next day Hsi-men Ch'ing sent Tai-an over with a gift to Hua Tzu-hsü to help calm his flustered spirits. Hua Tzu-hsü reciprocated by preparing a feast, hiring two singing girls, and extending an invitation to Hsi-men Ch'ing to express his gratitude. He intended to take advantage of the occasion to ask what had become of his money, and he hoped to be able to rely on Hsi-men Ch'ing for the return of several hundred taels of silver, which would enable him to buy another house.

Li P'ing-erh did not want this to happen, so she secretly sent Old Mother Feng over to say to Hsi-men Ch'ing, "Don't accept this invitation. Provide him with a false account of how the money was spent, claiming that it was all used up in taking care of the officials involved in the case, both high and low."

Hua Tzu-hsü did not catch on, but sent his servant over two or three times to press the invitation. Hsi-men Ch'ing actually went so far as to hide out in the licensed quarter, while ordering his servants to report that he was not at home. Hua Tzu-hsü was giddy with rage at this treatment, but all he could do was stamp his feet in frustration.

Gentle reader take note: As a rule, when a wife has had a change of heart and no longer sees eye to eye with her husband, even a man with the strength and resolution to chew up nails will find it difficult to defend himself against her secret wiles. It has always been true that:

> Man is responsible for what lies outside the household;
> Woman is responsible for what lies within it.[14]

Yet, on many occasions a man's reputation is ruined by a woman. Why is this so? It is always because he doesn't know how to handle her. To sum it up in a nutshell, the secret lies in the saying:

> The husband sings and the wife follows.[15]

Where:

> Beauty and virtue attract each other,
> Affinities are mutually compatible,
> The man admires the woman, and
> The woman admires the man,

one can, perhaps, be confident that there will be no problem. But, if the slightest distrust develops between them, it will soon turn into revulsion and hatred. As for the likes of Hua Tzu-hsü, who spent his days in:

> Insensate dissipation, and
> Unrestrained license;

for such a man to hope that his wife would not get other ideas into her head, was futile indeed. Truly:

> If one's own resolution is supported,
> There is no tempest that can shake it.[16]

There is a poem that testifies to this:

If success and accomplishment could be won
by intelligence and effort;
In ancient times Tao Chih[17] would have
been made a marquis.
If one's actions are righteous, one is truly
deserving of respect;
If one is lustful and uncaring, how can one fail
to be ashamed?[18]
The scion of the Hsi-men family was given over to
lust and dissipation;
His adulterous and fickle paramour was nothing but
a captivating wench.
Hua Tzu-hsü became so engorged with rage
his tender guts gave way;
But another day, in the court of the underworld,
he would be revenged.

To make a long story short, Hua Tzu-hsü could only scrape together 250 taels of silver, with which he bought a house on Lion Street for them to live in. He was already suffering from the ill effects of his rage, and no sooner had they completed their move than he was unfortunate enough to come down with an acute intestinal fever.

He took to his bed early in the eleventh month and was unable to get up again thereafter. Li P'ing-erh responded to his entreaties by calling in Dr. Hu from Main Street, but later had to dispense with him in order to save money. From then on it was merely a matter of time.

One day became two,
Two days became three,

until finally, on the last day of the month:

Alas and alack;
He stopped breathing and died.

At the time of his death he was twenty-three years of age. No sooner had he taken to his bed than his eldest servant, T'ien-hsi, absconded with five taels of silver and vanished without leaving a trace.

Once Hua Tzu-hsü was dead, Li P'ing-erh lost no time in sending Old Mother Feng to ask Hsi-men Ch'ing over for a consultation. A casket was purchased, the encoffining ceremony completed, sutras were duly recited, and Hua Tzu-hsü's body was escorted out to the graveyard and buried. Hua the Elder, Hua the Third, and Hua the Fourth, together with their wives, all came to offer their condolences, and after they had returned from accompanying the coffin to its final resting place they went their separate ways.

Hua Tzu-hsü Succumbs to Chagrin and Loses His Life

On the day of the funeral Hsi-men Ch'ing also had Wu Yüeh-niang arrange for a table of food and wine in their name so that they could offer a sacrifice at the graveside of the deceased.

That day, when Li P'ing-erh had returned home in her sedan chair, she procured a spirit tablet for her dead husband and set it up in her room. But, although she went through the motions of keeping vigil for him, all she could think of was Hsi-men Ch'ing. Even while Hua Tzu-hsü was still alive she had encouraged Hsi-men Ch'ing to make free with her two maidservants, and now that he was dead the two families became closer than ever.

Before long it was the ninth day of the first month and Li P'ing-erh had ascertained that it was P'an Chin-lien's birthday. Even though the fifth of the seven weekly commemorations of Hua Tzu-hsü's death had not yet been observed, she bought presents, got into her sedan chair, all dressed up in a white satin jacket over a skirt of blue brocade, with a white hempen snood over her chignon, held in place with a pearl headband, and came to pay a call in honor of Chin-lien's birthday. Old Mother Feng carried her felt bag, and T'ien-fu escorted her sedan chair.

The first thing she did after crossing the threshold was to kowtow to Wu Yüeh-niang four times:

> Just as though inserting a taper in its holder,

saying as she did so, "The other day at the graveside I'm afraid I provided you with but meager fare. And thank you very much for your lavish present."

After she had paid her respects to Yüeh-niang, she asked to be presented in turn to Li Chiao-erh and Meng Yü-lou. It was only then that P'an Chin-lien came in.

"So this is the Fifth Lady," the visitor exclaimed, as she kowtowed once again, repeating as she did so, "Elder Sister, please accept my salutation."

Chin-lien demurred at first and the two of them dickered politely for a while until they settled the matter by kowtowing to each other. Chin-lien thanked her for her birthday presents. The visitor was also introduced to Wu Yüeh-niang's sister-in-law, the wife of her elder brother, Wu K'ai, and to Chin-lien's mother, Old Mrs. P'an.

Li P'ing-erh then asked to be allowed to pay her respects to Hsi-men Ch'ing, but Yüeh-niang told her, "Today he's gone to the Temple of the Jade Emperor outside the Eastern Gate to attend the *chiao* rites of cosmic renewal[19] in honor of the Jade Emperor's birthday."

She urged her visitor to sit down, and another serving of tea was called for and consumed. After some time had passed, who should come wandering in but Sun Hsüeh-o.

Li P'ing-erh, observing that she was slightly less well dressed than the others, got up and asked, "Who might this lady be? Since I did not know of her, I'm afraid I didn't ask to be presented to her."

"She's just one of my husband's young ladies," said Yüeh-niang.

Li P'ing-erh Invites Seduction and Attends a Party

Li P'ing-erh hastily prepared to kowtow to her, but Yüeh-niang intervened, saying, "There's no need for you to go to all that trouble. A bow to each other will be quite sufficient."

When the two of them had finished saluting each other as directed, Yüeh-niang invited Li P'ing-erh into her own room to change her clothes and instructed a maidservant to set up a table in the parlor and serve tea.

Before long wine was brought in, and they:

Drew round the newly replenished brazier, and
Decanted the finest Yang-kao[20] vintage.

Thereupon, Wu K'ai's wife, Old Mrs. P'an, and Li P'ing-erh, took the seats of honor, Yüeh-niang and Li Chiao-erh assumed the role of hosts, Meng Yü-lou and P'an Chin-lien sat to one side, and Sun Hsüeh-o, not daring to presume on their company for too long, went back to look after things in the kitchen.

Yüeh-niang, observing that Li P'ing-erh never refused a drink, served a round of wine herself and then directed Li Chiao-erh and the others each to serve a round in turn.

They joshed with their guest freely, saying, "Mrs. Hua, you've moved so far away that we sisters must:

Spend more time apart than together.[21]

You no longer give us a thought. It would really be too cruel of you if you don't promise to visit us again."

"If it hadn't been for P'an the Sixth's birthday," said Meng Yü-lou, "you wouldn't even have come to see us today."

"My dear First Lady, and Third Lady," said Li P'ing-erh, "thanks to the kindness all of you have shown me, I've wanted to come and pay you a visit for a long time. But, on the one hand, I'm still in mourning, and on the other hand, after my poor husband's death, there's been no one to look after the place. In fact, I've hardly observed my husband's fifth weekly commemoration yet. If I hadn't been afraid of offending the Fifth Lady, I wouldn't have ventured to come today."

She then went on to ask, "First Lady, when does your birthday come?"

"It's a bit early yet for my birthday," said Yüeh-niang.

"The First Lady's birthday," said P'an Chin-lien, taking over the conversational lead, "is on the fifteenth day of the eighth month. I hope, whatever happens, you'll be able to come visit us then."

"Needless to say," said Li P'ing-erh, "I'll be sure to come."

"Now that you're here," said Meng Yü-lou, "why don't you give us the pleasure of your company by making a night of it, and not bothering to go home?"

"I really would welcome the chance to have a good talk with all of you," said Li P'ing-erh. "To tell you the truth, I find myself living in reduced circumstances, a newcomer to the neighborhood, and ever since my poor husband died, there's been no one to look after the place. The back wall of my house abuts on the garden of that distaff relative of the imperial family named Ch'iao. It's as desolate as can be, and at night there are often fox spirits about:

Pitching bricks and tossing tiles,[22]

and I'm afraid. We used to have two page boys, but the eldest of them has run away. T'ien-fu, here, looks after the front gate, but the back of the house is completely deserted. I'm entirely dependent on Old Feng. She's been with me a long time, and she often comes over to do the laundry and help the maidservants make shoes. I'm really beholden to her."

"How old is Mother Feng?" asked Yüeh-niang. "She certainly looks like a good, dependable body. I've never even heard her raise her voice."

"She's fifty-five years old this year," said Li P'ing-erh. "She was born in the year of the dog. She has no children of her own, either male or female, and depends on matchmaking for her living. I supply her with clothes from time to time. Ever since the recent death of my poor husband I've asked her to come over and keep me company. At night she sleeps on the same k'ang with the maidservants."

"There you are," said P'an Chin-lien, who was always quick on the uptake, "as long as you've got Old Feng to look after the house for you, you might just as well spend the night here. After all, since Mr. Hua is dead, there's no longer anyone to tell you what to do."

"If you'll do as I say," said Meng Yü-lou, "you'll send Old Feng home with the sedan chair and forget about going yourself."

Li P'ing-erh only smiled, without uttering a sound.

As they were talking:

Several rounds of wine had been consumed.

Old Mrs. P'an was the first to get up and make her way toward the front of the compound. P'an Chin-lien then followed in her mother's wake and went off to her own quarters.

"I've already had enough wine," Li P'ing-erh kept insisting, as she refused to accept any more, but Li Chiao-erh said, "How is it that you've been willing enough to drink at the hands of the First Lady and the Third Lady, but when I offer you wine, you refuse to drink any? It's really too discriminatory."

Thereupon, she picked up a larger cup and proceeded to fill it.

"My dear Second Lady," protested Li P'ing-erh, "I really can't manage any more. I'm not just pretending."

"After you've finished this cup," said Yüeh-niang, "you can rest awhile."

Only then did Li P'ing-erh accept the proffered cup and put it down in front of her while she continued to engage them in animated conversation.

Meng Yü-lou, noticing that Ch'un-mei was standing to one side, asked her, "What's your mother doing up front, anyway? You go up there and invite both your mother and Old Mrs. P'an to come back here. Tell them that the First Lady invites them back to help her keep Mrs. Hua company while she drinks wine."

Ch'un-mei had not been gone for long when she returned and said, "Old Mrs. P'an is not feeling well and has gone to bed. Mother is in her room putting on her makeup. She'll be here any minute."

"I've never seen anything like it," said Yüeh-niang. "After all, you're one of the hostesses, and yet, before anyone even knows what you're up to, you abandon your guest and run off to your own room. I don't know how many times a day this sister of mine has to redo her face. Whenever she feels like it she runs off to do it again. She's fine enough in other respects, but about this one thing she's still rather childish."

While she was still speaking, who should appear but P'an Chin-lien. She was wearing a saffron-colored jacket of Lu-chou silk that opened down the middle and was decorated with a motif of wild geese holding bulrushes in their mouths. It had a stiff-standing white satin collar with purfled edging and gilt buttons that depicted honeybees rifling chrysanthemum blossoms. Beneath this she wore a drawnwork skirt with a foot-wide, gold-spangled border representing sea horses sporting in the waves, shoes of scarlet silk with high white satin heels, and figured ankle leggings. She also sported pendant onyx earrings and a pearl headband. In fact, she was dressed identically with Meng Yü-lou. Yüeh-niang, on the other hand, had on a scarlet silk jacket, a plain blue satin cloak, and a skirt of sand-green pongee, while on her head she wore a fret over her chignon, enclosed in a sable toque.

Meng Yü-lou was the first of the party to catch sight of Chin-lien as she made a conspicuous entrance:

> Heavily made up and richly attired,

with a gold pin in the shape of the character for long life carelessly stuck in the hair over her temple.

She proceeded to josh her, saying, "A fine wench you are, Slavey Five. You're the one who was you know what 'under a lucky star'[23] this very day, yet you've abandoned your guest and run off to hide in your room. And you call yourself a human being!"

Chin-lien laughed loudly and gave her a playful slap.

"You're a pretty nervy wench, Slavey Five," exclaimed Yü-lou. "It's your turn to offer our guest a drink."

"I've already had more than a little at the hands of the Third Lady," said Li P'ing-erh. "I've reached my limit."

"What you had to suffer at her hands is her business," said Chin-lien. "I, too, make bold to offer you a cup."

Thereupon, she tucked up her sleeves, filled a large cup to the brim, and presented it to Li P'ing-erh, who merely allowed it to sit in front of her, without venturing to take a drink.

Yüeh-niang, who had withdrawn into the master suite with her sister-in-law, Wu K'ai's wife, came out and saw that Chin-lien had sat down to help entertain Li P'ing-erh.

"Why doesn't Old Mrs. P'an come out and provide some company for our guest?" she asked.

"My mother isn't feeling well," replied Chin-lien. "She's stretched out in my room, and even if you send for her, she won't come."

Yüeh-niang caught sight of one of the pins in the shape of the character for long life that was visible in the hair over Chin-lien's temple and asked Li P'ing-erh, "Where was this pair of pins that you gave Sister Six made? They're really very fine. In the future I'd like to get them reproduced so we could each have a pair to wear."

"If you'd like some, First Lady, I still have a few more of them at home," said Li P'ing-erh. "One day soon I'll send over an additional pair for each of you. They are made to imperial specifications and were smuggled out of the palace by the old eunuch, my late father-in-law. Workmanship of this kind is not to be found on the outside."

"I was only having a little joke at your expense," said Yüeh-niang. "There are such a lot of us, you could scarcely be expected to have that many to give away."

As the group of womenfolk continued to drink and amuse themselves, the sun was gradually sinking in the west. Old Mother Feng, who had been plied with wine in Sun Hsüeh-o's quarters at the rear of the compound, came out with a very red face and urged Li P'ing-erh to make up her mind either to leave or, if not, to send the sedan chair back home.

"Don't go," said Yüeh-niang to her guest. "Just tell Old Feng to go home with the sedan chair."

Li P'ing-erh merely said, "There's no one to look after the place. I'll come again sometime soon to pay my respects to all of you. There'll be time enough for me to stay the night another day."

"Why be so insistent on having your own way?" said Meng Yü-lou. "It looks as though none of us carries much weight with you, but if you won't send the sedan chair off, just wait until Father comes home in a little while; you can be sure he'll try to persuade you to stay, too."

This argument had the effect of overcoming Li P'ing-erh's objections. Taking out the keys to the house, she handed them to Old Mother Feng, saying, "Since all these ladies are so insistent on my staying, if I were to refuse, it would only show that:

> I didn't know a favor when I saw one.

You can dismiss the sedan chair for today, but tell the bearers to come back for me tomorrow. When you and the page boy get home, be careful not to let anyone into the house."

She also called Old Mother Feng over to her and:

> Whispered into her ear in a low voice,

"Tell my head maid, Ying-ch'un, to get the keys to the trunk in my bedroom and take four pairs of pins in the shape of the character for long life out of the small jewelry box with the gold tracery on it. Bring these to me first thing tomorrow morning. I want to give them to the four ladies here."

When Old Mother Feng had received her instructions she took formal leave of Yüeh-niang.

"Have something to drink before you go," Yüeh-niang said.

"I've had both food and wine just now in the quarters of the young lady at the rear of the compound," said Old Mother Feng. "I'll be back first thing tomorrow morning."

Whereupon, with:

A thousand thanks and ten thousand
  expressions of gratitude,

she made her exit. But no more of this.

Shortly thereafter, when Li P'ing-erh refused to have anything more to drink, Yüeh-niang invited her into the master suite to have some tea with her sister-in-law.

All of a sudden, who should come in but the page boy, Tai-an, carrying his master's felt bag. Hsi-men Ch'ing had come home, and his first words upon lifting aside the portiere and entering the room were, "So Mrs. Hua is here."

Li P'ing-erh jumped hastily to her feet and the two of them exchanged salutations, after which she sat back down again. Yüeh-niang called Yü-hsiao to help Hsi-men Ch'ing off with his things.

Turning to Wu K'ai's wife and Li P'ing-erh, Hsi-men Ch'ing said, "Today I've been attending the *chiao* rites of cosmic renewal in celebration of the birthday of the Jade Emperor at his temple outside the Eastern Gate. It was my turn to preside this year. Otherwise, I would have come home after the vegetarian feast at noon. As a consequence I had to join the others in going over the accounts in Abbot Wu's room and, what with one thing and another, have been tied up all this time."

He then went on to ask, "I take it that Mrs. Hua is not going to go home today?"

"She kept refusing our invitations and proposing to leave," said Meng Yü-lou, "until, by combining our efforts, we carried the day by main force."

"There's no one to look after the place," said Li P'ing-erh. "I can't help worrying about it."

"Don't talk such rot!" said Hsi-men Ch'ing. "The night patrols have been very strict recently. What is there to be afraid of anyway?

If the wind so much as stirs a blade of grass,

all I'd have to do is send a note to Commandant Chou Hsiu and he'd:

Act upon it even in defiance of the law."[24]

"Why have you been neglecting Mrs. Hua so?" he added. "Has she been given anything to drink, or hasn't she?"

"All of us have been trying our hands at persuading her," said Meng Yü-lou, "but she affects an inability to drink."

"You're not up to the task," said Hsi-men Ch'ing. "Let me give it a try. She's got no mean capacity."

Although Li P'ing-erh said the words, "I can't handle any more," she made no effort to withdraw.

Thereupon, the maidservants were instructed to reset the table and an elaborate spread of meat and vegetable dishes, along with other dainties of every kind, which had been prepared in anticipation of Hsi-men Ch'ing's return, was laid before them. Sister-in-law Wu, sensing that the time had come to take flight, asserted that she did not wish to have any more wine and withdrew to Li Chiao-erh's quarters to get out of the way.

Thereupon, Li P'ing-erh was seated in the place of honor, Hsi-men Ch'ing drew up a chair across from her and assumed the role of host, Wu Yüeh-niang sat on the k'ang with her feet on the frame of the brazier, and Meng Yü-lou and P'an Chin-lien sat down at the other two sides of the table. As soon as the five of them had taken their places they started to decant the wine. They didn't use small cups either, but called for large goblets of chased silver.

It was a case of:

> First a cup for you,
> Then a cup for me.

As the saying goes:

> Romantic affairs are consummated over tea, and
> Wine is the go-between of lust.

As the cups passed back and forth, the woman continued to drink until:

> Her painted eyebrows drooped low, and
> Amorous glances escaped the corners of her eyes.

Truly:

> A pair of peach blossoms bloomed upon her cheeks,[25]
> Her brows and eyes proclaiming her a wanton wench.

When Yüeh-niang saw that the two of them were:

> As stuck on one another as sugar candy,[26]

and that:

> The conversation was becoming rather risqué,[27]

she found it so offensive that she withdrew to her own room and sent for her sister-in-law to keep her company, leaving the other three to entertain their guest.

They continued drinking until the third watch. By that time Li P'ing-erh's:

> Starry eyes were all a blur.

Hardly able to stand on her own legs, she asked Chin-lien to accompany her to the bathroom in the rear of the compound.

Hsi-men Ch'ing, too, was:

Swaying to the east and tumbling to the west,

as he went into Yüeh-niang's room to ask her where they should put their guest for the night.

"Let her sleep in the room of the one whose birthday she came to celebrate," said Yüeh-niang.

"Where shall I spend the night, then?" asked Hsi-men Ch'ing.

"Spend the night wherever you like," said Yüeh-niang. "Or, better yet, go spend it with her if you want."

"Whoever heard of such a thing?" laughed Hsi-men Ch'ing, and he called for Hsiao-yü to help him off with his clothes. "I'll sleep in here tonight, then."

"Don't be so delirious," said Yüeh-niang. "Or do you want to provoke me into a real tirade? If you stay here, where do you suppose my sister-in-law is going to sleep?"

"Enough! Enough!" said Hsi-men Ch'ing. "I'll go and sleep with Meng the Third." Whereupon, he went off to Yü-lou's quarters to spend the night.

After she had accompanied Li P'ing-erh to the bathroom, P'an Chin-lien took her up to her own quarters in the front part of the compound, and that night she shared a bed with Old Mrs. P'an.

The next morning Li P'ing-erh got up and was combing her hair in front of the mirror when Ch'un-mei brought her some hot water to wash her face and helped her with her toilet. She noticed how clever Ch'un-mei was and, knowing that she was a maidservant who had enjoyed Hsi-men Ch'ing's sexual favors, she made her a present of a gold chatelaine with three pendant charms in the shape of three miniature toilet articles.

Ch'un-mei immediately reported this gift to her mistress and Chin-lien was profuse in her thanks, saying, "I've put you to the additional expense of being so generous to her."

"You really are lucky, Fifth Lady, to have such a fine maid," said Li P'ing-erh.

That morning Chin-lien had Ch'un-mei open the gate to the garden and took Li P'ing-erh and Old Mrs. P'an on an extended tour of the entire premises.

Li P'ing-erh noticed that a gate had been opened in the wall that had formerly separated Hsi-men Ch'ing's residence from hers, and asked, "When is Father Hsi-men going to start construction on the new building?"

"Recently he had the yin-yang master come over to give him an appraisal," said Chin-lien. "He's planning to:

Break ground and start construction,
Put it up and top it off,

in the second month. He's going to tear down your old house and combine the two pieces of property into one, erect an artificial hill and a summerhouse in the front, and make a large garden out of it. Then he's planning to build another three-room belvedere, to be called the Flower-viewing Tower, which will be lined up with my own to form one boundary of the grounds."

Li P'ing-erh made a mental note of everything she was told.

While the two of them were still talking together, Yüeh-niang sent Hsiao-yü to invite them back to the rear of the compound for some tea. The three of them then made their way to the master suite where they found Wu Yüeh-niang, Li Chiao-erh, and Meng Yü-lou keeping Sister-in-law Wu company as they waited for them, with the tea things already laid out.

Just as everyone was enjoying the tea and the snacks that accompanied it, who should suddenly appear but Old Mother Feng. When they had offered her a seat and served her some tea, Old Mother Feng pulled an old kerchief out of her sleeve, in which the four pairs of pins in the shape of the character for long life were wrapped, and handed it to Li P'ing-erh. No sooner had she accepted them than she presented one pair to Yüeh-niang, and afterward, a pair each to Li Chiao-erh, Meng Yü-lou, and Sun Hsüeh-o.

"These must have cost you a pretty penny," said Yüeh-niang. "This will never do."

"My dear First Lady," laughed Li P'ing-erh, "It's not as though they were genuine rarities. I'm only offering them to you to give away to someone if you like."

Yüeh-niang and the others bowed in gratitude before venturing to stick the pins in their hair.

"I hear that your front door opens right on the Lantern Market," said Yüeh-niang. "It must be quite exciting. If we go for a look at the lanterns someday soon, we'll come pay you a visit. Pray don't pretend you're not at home."

"Let me extend an invitation to all of you ladies for that day," said Li P'ing-erh.

"You may not know it, elder sister," said Chin-lien, "but I've heard that the fifteenth is actually our guest's birthday."

"That settles it," said Yüeh-niang. "If it's really your birthday, every last one of us will come to wish you many happy returns."

"My humble abode is scarcely fit to accommodate a snail,"

laughed Li P'ing-erh, "but if you ladies deign to visit me, consider yourselves invited."

It was not long before they finished their morning repast, after which wine was served and they fell to drinking again. The time passed swiftly as they enjoyed each other's company until the sun began to sink in the west and the sedan chair came back to pick her up. Li P'ing-erh said her farewells, and her sorority of hostesses could not persuade her to stay any longer. Before leaving, she asked if she might be permitted to say good-bye to Hsimen Ch'ing.

"He had to get up early this morning," said Yüeh-niang, "and go outside the city gate to see off the district vice-magistrate."

Only then, with:

A thousand thanks and ten thousand
expressions of gratitude,

did Li P'ing-erh get into her sedan chair and go home. Truly:

The coupled halves of the peach stone
serve to evoke a chuckle;
Because inside, it will be found, lie
yet another couple.[28]

If you want to know the outcome of these events,
Pray consult the story related in the following chapter.

Chapter 15

BEAUTIES ENJOY THE SIGHTS
IN THE LANTERN-VIEWING BELVEDERE;
HANGERS-ON ABET DEBAUCHERY
IN THE VERDANT SPRING BORDELLO[1]

As the sun sinks amid the western hills,
  the moon rises in the east;
Even the span of a hundred years
  is like wind-blown tumbleweed.
Before one knows it, the red-cheeked lad
  one so admires,
In the twinkling of an eye turns into
  a white-haired gentleman.
Do not waste the fullness of your youth,
  so quickly does it pass;[2]
Even Heaven-scaling wealth and success
  are as evanescent as clouds.
One might as well seek to divert oneself
  among scarlet skirts;
Hugging the turquoise and cuddling the red
  in houses of pleasure.

THE STORY goes that:

Light and darkness alternate swiftly,

and before anyone knew it, the fifteenth day of the first month was at hand. The day before, Hsi-men Ch'ing sent his page boy, Tai-an, to deliver four trays of preserved fruit, two trays of sweetmeats in the shape of birthday peaches, a jug of wine, a tray of birthday noodles, and a set of heavy silk brocade clothing to Li P'ing-erh in honor of her birthday. The gifts were sent in Wu Yüeh-niang's name, accompanied by a card that read, "Respectfully presented with straightened skirts by the lady, née Wu, of the Hsi-men household."

Li P'ing-erh had just gotten up and was still engaged in doing her toilet. Calling Tai-an into her bedroom, she said, "I'm afraid I imposed upon your First Lady's hospitality the other day, and now she has gone to the further trouble of sending me these gifts."

"Mother sends her greetings," said Tai-an, "and Father sends his greetings too. They told me to say, 'It's only a little something for you to give away to someone if you like.' "

Li P'ing-erh told Ying-ch'un to set up a small table outside in the parlor. There Tai-an was entertained with tea and four little boxes of delicacies. As he was about to leave, she gave him two mace of silver and a handkerchief of shot silk decorated with the symbolic representations of the "eight treasures."

"When you get home," she said, "please convey my greetings to all the ladies of the house. I'll send Old Mother Feng around with written invitations. Whatever happens, I hope they will all condescend to pay me a visit tomorrow."

When Tai-an kowtowed and went outside she also gave him a hundred cash for the two carriers who had brought the boxes containing her presents.

Li P'ing-erh lost no time in dispatching Old Mother Feng with a letter box containing five written invitations, inviting Wu Yüeh-niang, Li Chiao-erh, Meng Yü-lou, P'an Chin-lien, and Sun Hsüeh-o to visit her on the fifteenth. At the same time she also sent Hsi-men Ch'ing a private note asking him to drop in on her later that evening to help celebrate her birthday.

The next day Wu Yüeh-niang, having told Sun Hsüeh-o to stay behind and look after the house, set out with Li Chiao-erh, Meng Yü-lou, and P'an Chin-lien in four sedan chairs. All of them were dressed in clothing of figured brocade. Accompanied by the page boys Lai-hsing, P'ing-an,[3] Tai-an, and Hua-t'ung, they arrived in front of Li P'ing-erh's newly purchased house, which was located in the Lantern Market on Lion Street.

The house consisted of a twenty-four-foot-wide frontage and three interior courtyards, receding along a vertical axis. The first part of the building was a two-story structure with windows on the upper floor that opened directly over the street. Inside the ceremonial gate that led into the second courtyard there was a row of three rooms on either side and a formal reception hall. A passageway through an antechamber led into the third courtyard, which contained three bedrooms and a kitchen. The open space behind the third courtyard, abutted directly on the garden of a distaff relative of the imperial family named Ch'iao.

Li P'ing-erh, knowing that Wu Yüeh-niang and the others were coming to see the lanterns, had furnished the second-story room that overlooked the street with standing screens, chairs and tables, and an array of decorated lanterns. She first ushered her guests into the formal reception hall and then, after they had performed the customary exchange of greetings, invited them back to the parlor in the rear courtyard for some tea. When they had finished changing their clothes in her room, tea was served, but there is no need to describe this in detail.

At noontime Li P'ing-erh invited her guests to return to the reception hall where four place settings had been provided and two singing girls, named

Tung Chiao-erh and Han Chin-ch'uan, had been engaged to entertain them as they enjoyed the feast. After:

Five rounds of wine had been consumed; and
Three main courses had been served,

Wu Yüeh-niang and the others were invited to go up to the second-story room that overlooked the street to enjoy the display of lanterns as they continued their feast.

Hanging blinds of speckled bamboo had been let down under the eaves, from which an array of brightly colored lanterns were suspended. Wu Yüeh-niang was wearing a full-sleeved jacket of figured scarlet material, a stylish green silk skirt, and a sable cloak. Li Chiao-erh, Meng Yü-lou, and P'an Chin-lien all wore white satin jackets and blue silk skirts, over which Li Chiao-erh also wore a brocaded aloeswood-colored vest, Meng Yü-lou a brocaded green vest, and P'an Chin-lien a brocaded scarlet vest. On their heads:

Pearls and trinkets rose in piles;
Phoenix hairpins were half askew,

while, from just behind the hair over their temples, there dangled innumerable pendant earrings in the shape of miniature lanterns of every description.

Leaning out of the windows of the second-story room, they looked down on the Lantern Market below where:

Crowds of people had congregated; and
The merrymaking was at its height.

Several tens of elaborate lantern-stands had been erected in the street, and peddlers were busy hawking their wares on all sides.

The men and women come to see the lanterns;
Were red as flowers and green as willows.
Carriages and horses rumbled like thunder;
Hills of lanterns soared into the Milky Way.[4]

What did this wonderful Lantern Market look like? Behold:

Insinuating themselves among the mountain rocks, a pair
  of dragons sports in the water;
Concealed amid the sunset clouds, a solitary crane
  ascends to the heavens.
Golden Lotus lanterns,
Tower of Jade lanterns,
Scintillate like a cluster of pearls;
Lotus blossom lanterns,
Hibiscus lanterns,
Scatter a thousand embroidered rosettes.[5]
Hydrangea lanterns,
Are chaste and immaculate;
Snowflake lanterns,

Are tumbled and tossed.
Scholar lanterns,
Bow and scrape, advance and retreat,
Preserving the manners of Confucius and Mencius;
Housewife lanterns,
Display virtuous demeanors and gentle dispositions,
Emulating the fidelity and resolve of Meng Chiang.[6]
There is a Buddhist monk lantern,
Depicting Yüeh-ming and the courtesan Liu Ts'ui;[7]
And an underworld assessor lantern,
Showing Chung K'uei seated with his little sister.[8]
There is a shamaness lantern,
Fluttering her feathered fan,
Pretending to subdue evil spirits;
And a Liu Hai lantern,
Bearing the golden three-footed toad on his back,
As it gobbles its string of cash.[9]
There are camel lanterns,
And green lion lanterns,
Bearing priceless rarities,
Snorting and roaring;
As well as gibbon lanterns,
And white elephant lanterns,
Proffering treasures fit to ransom cities,
Gamboling and playing.
All arms and legs,
Crab lanterns,
Cavort in the clear waves;
With gaping mouths and long beards,
Catfish lanterns,
Gulp down green algae.
Silver moths vie with one another in brilliance,
Snowy willows compete with each other in beauty;
Pair by pair, they follow in the wake of brocade sashes
    and dangling pomanders,
Branch by branch, they brush against decorated pennants
    and turquoise carriage curtains.[10]
Fish and dragons sport on the sand,
As the Seven Perfected Ones and the Five Ancients[11]
    present their vermilion texts;
Tasseled portieres are suspended,
While the Nine Barbarians and the Eight Tribes
    come to offer their tribute.

Parading village mummers,
Troupe after troupe, drum up a dreadful din;
Peddlers of toys and knickknacks,
Item by item, tout the uniqueness of their wares.
Among the revolving lanterns,
One comes, the other goes;
Amid the suspended lanterns,
One bobs up, another down.
There are vitreous vases,
Depicting only a beautiful woman or rare flower;
As well as mica screens,
Portraying paradises on both mountains and seas.
To the east,
There are bedsteads of carved lacquer,
And bedsteads of inlaid mother-of-pearl,
The golds and greens of which blend their hues;
To the west,
There are lanterns spangled with gold,
And lanterns striped with colors,
Producing brocade effects that dazzle the eye.
To the north,
There are exhibited antiques and curios;
To the south,
Calligraphy, painting, vases, and incense burners.
Patrician youths are out in force,
From beneath low balustrades their kickballs
rise into the clouds;
Wellborn young ladies escort each other,
As within lofty belvederes they show off
their good looks.
The booths of the fortune-tellers are massed like clouds,
The stalls of the physiognomists are arrayed like stars;
They are prepared to expatiate on one's fortune
in the impending spring,
Or determine the success or failure of a lifetime
with sure precision.
Then there are those,
Professional storytellers,
Who, standing on a slope,
Relate in doggerel and song the exploits of Yang Yeh;[12]
And see those others,
Itinerant Buddhist monks,
Who, clapping their sounding cymbals,

Elaborate upon the adventures of Tripitaka.[13]
The sellers of Lantern Festival dumplings,
Make imposing piles of their ingredients;
The makers of artificial plum blossoms,
Attach them ubiquitously to dead branches.
Paper cutouts of spring moths,
Stuck rakishly in the hair over the temples,
  quiver in the east wind;
Gold-flecked gimcrack hairpins,
Twinkle atop chignons with a glitter
  that rivals the sun's.
Standing screens depict the extravagant Shih Ch'ung
  and his brocaded windbreak;[14]
Beaded portieres display the twin perfections
  of plum blossom and moonlight.
Though the attractions of the hills of lanterns
  cannot be exhaustively ennumerated;
They surely must portend a bumper harvest
  and a happy year to come.

Wu Yüeh-niang contemplated the spectacle for a while, after which, observing that the crowd below was getting rowdy, she and Li Chiao-erh withdrew to the table and sat down to enjoy their wine. P'an Chin-lien and Meng Yü-lou, however, along with the two singing girls, continued to lean out over the windowsills and gaze at the scene below. P'an Chin-lien went so far as to tuck up the sleeves of her white satin jacket, revealing the brocaded lining and exposing her ten slender fingers, which sported six gold stirrup-shaped rings. Leaning halfway out the window, she cracked melon seeds with her teeth and spit the empty shells onto the heads of the people below. All the while she and Meng Yü-lou maintained a steady stream of laughter and banter.

One minute she called out, "Elder Sister, come and see. Look at the two hydrangea lanterns hanging from the eaves of the house over there:

One comes, the other goes;
Bobbing up, bobbing down.

They're really something to see."

The next minute she said, "Second Sister, come and see. On the stand just across the street there's a big fish lantern with all kinds of small fry, turtles, shrimp, crabs, and so forth, tagging at its heels. They're really fun to watch."

A minute later she called to Meng Yü-lou, saying, "Third Sister, just look at the old lady lantern and the old man lantern over here."

As she spoke, a sudden gust of wind blew up and tore a gaping hole in the abdomen of the old lady lantern. When Chin-lien saw what had happened she laughed uproariously.

This had the effect of attracting the attention of the sightseers below.

Rubbing shoulders and nudging backs,
Lifting their heads and gazing upward;
Jammed together into an indivisible mass,
Treading on one another's heels,

in no time at all a considerable crowd of onlookers had gathered. Among them were to be found some dissolute young scamps who were not averse to offering their own assessments of the situation.

One said, "They must be dependents of some princely or noble household on an outing."

Another hazarded, "They must be the seductive concubines of some relative of the imperial family, come to see the lanterns. Otherwise, what are they doing dressed in palace style?"

Another ventured, "They must be whores from the licensed quarter that some big spender has engaged to entertain him while he enjoys the lanterns."

Still another strolled over and said, "I'm the only one who can identify them. None of you will ever guess right. If you take them for whores, how do you account for the other four at the back? I'll tell you who they are: those two women don't belong to just anybody. They might as well be mates of King Yama himself or concubines of the General of the Five Ways. They're the womenfolk of the Honorable Hsi-men Ch'ing who owns the wholesale pharmaceutical business on the street in front of the district yamen and engages in moneylending to both officials and functionaries. You'd be well-advised to leave them alone. They must have come here along with his wife to see the lanterns.

"The one wearing the brocaded green vest I don't recognize, but the one wearing the brocaded scarlet vest with the turquoise beauty patch on her face looks like the wife of Wu the Elder who used to peddle steamed wheat cakes on the street. When Wu the Elder tried to catch her in the act of adultery in Dame Wang's teashop, the Honorable Gentleman just mentioned gave him such a kick that he died of the effects, after which he took her into his household as a concubine. Later on, her brother-in-law, Wu Sung, came back from the Eastern Capital and lodged a complaint against him, but ended up killing the lictor, Li Wai-ch'uan, by mistake, so that Hsi-men Ch'ing was able to get his assailant condemned to military exile, while he himself got out of the affair completely unscathed. She hasn't shown herself in public for the last year or two, but she's looking better than ever."

At this point another busybody chimed in, saying, "What's the point of wasting our time talking about the likes of them? Let's move along."

When Wu Yüeh-niang, from her vantage point in the upstairs room, became aware that a large crowd had assembled below, she told Chin-lien and

Beauties Enjoy the Sights in the Lantern-viewing Belvedere

Yü-lou to come back and join her at the table, where they listened to the two singing girls perform songs in celebration of the lantern festival while they drank their wine.

After a while, Yüeh-niang indicated that she was ready to make her departure by saying to her hostess, "I've had enough to drink. The Second Lady and I will go ahead home, but we'll leave our two sisters behind to keep you company a little longer and show our appreciation for your hospitality. Our husband isn't at home today, so there's no one to look after the place. When only the maidservants are there, I can't help worrying about it."

Li P'ing-erh could hardly let them go without a protest.

"My dear First Lady," she said, "I've scarcely had a chance to show my respects to you. Since your arrival today I haven't even had the opportunity to help you to a proper serving of anything. It's a festival occasion, after all, and yet you want to go home before the lanterns are lit or dinner is served. Even if Father Hsi-men is out today, as long as the young ladies are there, what is there to worry about? Wait until the moon rises, at least, and I'll see you all home myself."

"It's not that," said Yüeh-niang. "It's just that I'm not accustomed to drinking so much. If I leave my two sisters behind it will be just as though I were here myself."

"Even if you don't want any more yourself," said Li P'ing-erh, "that's no reason why the Second Lady shouldn't have another cup. The other day, at your house, I accepted cup after cup without demur, and you ladies refused to let me off. Now that you've been good enough to visit these cramped quarters of mine, though I have nothing to offer, you must let me do the best I can."

Thereupon, she took a large silver goblet and handed it to Li Chiao-erh, saying, "Second Lady, you must have a cup, no matter what. I know the First Lady has had enough, so I don't dare offer her a big one, but only a little one."

So saying, she filled a cup to the brim and offered it to Yüeh-niang, and then did the same for Li Chiao-erh, encouraging her as she did so with the words, "Second Lady, do drain this cup."

Yüeh-niang gave two mace of silver to each of the singing girls, and then, after waiting for Li Chiao-erh to finish her wine, got up to go.

Turning to Yü-lou and Chin-lien, she said, "The two of us will go on ahead. When we get home, I'll send a page boy back with a lantern to fetch you. Do come home then; there's no one to look after the place."

Yü-lou assented to this suggestion. Li P'ing-erh then saw Yüeh-niang and Li Chiao-erh out the door and into their sedan chairs before returning upstairs to keep Yü-lou and Chin-lien company as they continued to drink wine. Gradually, as it grew late:

The jade hare rose in the east,[15]
and the lanterns on the second floor were lit. The singing girls entertained them with songs as they drank their wine. But no more of this.

To resume our story, that day Hsi-men Ch'ing had invited Ying Po-chüeh and Hsieh Hsi-ta to dine with him at home, after which they set out together to enjoy the sights in the Lantern Market. When they arrived at the eastern end of Lion Street Hsi-men Ch'ing, because he knew that Yüeh-niang and the others were being entertained in the front second floor room of Li P'ing-erh's house and he didn't want his companions to see them, did not proceed to the western end of the street where the big lanterns were displayed, but came to a halt when he had gotten no further than the shop that sold gauze lanterns.

No sooner had he turned around than he ran into Blabbermouth Sun and Sticky Chu, who saluted him with the words, "We haven't seen you for ages, Brother, but you've been very much in our thoughts."

Seeing that he was accompanied by Ying Po-chüeh and Hsieh Hsi-ta, they upbraided them, saying, "A goddamned fine couple of fellows you are; going out on the town with our elder brother without giving us the word!"

"Brother Chu," said Hsi-men Ch'ing, "you're doing them an injustice. We've only just run into each other on the street."

"Well now, where are you headed, then, after you've seen the lanterns?" asked Sticky Chu.

"We might as well go to the Great Tavern right here on Lion Street and have a few drinks together," said Hsi-men Ch'ing. "I'd invite you all home with me if it weren't for the fact that my womenfolk are all out at a party today."

"Rather than letting you treat us to a round at the tavern," said Sticky Chu, "why don't we all go into the licensed quarter together and pay a visit to Li Kuei-chieh? It's only appropriate on a festival occasion like this that we should go wish her a happy new year and have some fun together. The other day when we were over at her place she appealed to us, and actually broke down and cried, saying that ever since she became indisposed last month not even your shadow has been into the quarter to see her. All we could do was to say that you must be busy in order to cover up for you. Since you're free today, we'll be happy to accompany you inside to pay her a visit."

Hsi-men Ch'ing, who was preoccupied by his assignation with Li P'ing-erh later that evening, tried to excuse himself, saying, "I'm afraid I can't make it today; I've got something to do. How about tomorrow?"

But he was quite unable to withstand the urgings of his cronies who:

Dragged him off, dead or alive.

Thereupon, he consented to go into the licensed quarter with them. Truly:

The shadows of the flowers under the willows
hold down the dust on the road;
Each time one sets out to enjoy them
one's pleasure is renewed.
If one could only assess the sums spent for a smile
in the metropolis;
Who knows how many commoners' households
they would serve to support?[16]

When Hsi-men Ch'ing and his companions arrived at the Li family establishment they found Li Kuei-ch'ing, all made up, standing in the doorway. She ushered them into the main room and greeted each of them in turn.

Sticky Chu then called out in a loud voice, "Invite Auntie Li the Third to come out at once! It's only thanks to our combined efforts that we've induced the Honorable Gentleman to pay you a visit."

Before long, the old procuress made her appearance, hobbling along with the aid of a stick.

After they had finished with the appropriate amenities, she said to Hsi-men Ch'ing, "I hope we haven't been remiss in the entertainment we've provided you, Kinsman. How is it that you haven't dropped in to see my daughter for such a long time? You must have taken up with a new sweetheart somewhere else."

"You've hit the nail on the head, madam," interjected Sticky Chu. "The Honorable Gentleman has recently had his eye on another tart of incomparable beauty and has been spending all his free time at her place. He doesn't give a thought to your Kuei-chieh any longer. In fact, if the two of us hadn't run into him in the Lantern Market just now and dragged him along with us, he wouldn't be here now. If you don't believe me, just ask Blabbermouth Sun here." Then, pointing at Ying Po-chüeh and Hsieh Hsi-ta, he continued, "And this goddamned pair, for their part, are:

Deities of the same persuasion."[17]

When the old procuress heard these words she cackled out loud, saying, "Well, Brother Ying, we've never done anything to get on the wrong side of you. Why don't you use your good offices to put in a word for us with our kinsman here? However complicated his affairs in the quarter may be, as the saying goes:

A practiced profligate doesn't confine his attentions
to a single whore;
A practiced whore doesn't reserve her blandishments
for a single patron.
The hole in the cash has much the same shape
wherever you find it.

There's no need for me to boast about our Kuei-chieh's looks. The gentleman has eyes of his own and doesn't require anyone to point out the obvious to him."

"To tell the truth," interposed Blabbermouth Sun, "this new tart that Brother's taken up with isn't even an inhabitant of the quarter. She's an outsider who doesn't give a fuck for the insiders."

When Hsi-men Ch'ing heard this he chased Blabbermouth Sun around the room, pretending to hit him, exclaiming as he did so, "Madam, don't pay any attention to this:

God-damned and man-condemned,[18]

old oily mouth! All he ever does is plague people to death."

This exhibition only caused Blabbermouth Sun and the rest to collapse in a heap with laughter.

Hsi-men Ch'ing then proceeded to pull three taels of silver out of his sleeve and hand them to Li Kuei-ch'ing, saying, "On this festival occasion I'd like to stand my friends a treat."

"I really couldn't agree to such a thing," Kuei-ch'ing affected to reply. "Give it to my mother."

"How now?" Auntie Li responded. "My kinsman must think so little of us that he doesn't think we can afford to furnish a feast, even on a festival occasion, for the entertainment of his distinguished friends. If you have to reach into your own pocket to defray the expenses, it will look as though we denizens of the licensed quarter are only interested in money after all."

At this juncture Ying Po-chüeh interrupted her, saying, "Auntie, if I were you I'd take what you're offered. As the saying goes:

Don't risk your luck by refusing the first gleanings
of the New Year: stash them away.

Just bring on the wine, now, as quickly as you can."

"That will never do," said the procuress, but even as she persisted in her protestations she accepted the silver and slipped it into her sleeve.

Making a deep bow, she said, "Thank you for your generosity, Kinsman."

"Wait a minute, Auntie," said Ying Po-chüeh. "I've got a story for you. A certain young man was having an affair with a prostitute in the licensed quarter. One day, just for the fun of it, he disguised himself as a pauper and paid a visit to his regular establishment. When the madam saw how shabby his clothing was, she paid him no attention and let him sit there for some time without even offering him a cup of tea. The young man said, 'Auntie, I'm hungry. If you've got any rice, please bring me something to eat.' To which the old procuress replied, 'The bin is completely dry. Where would I get you any rice from?' 'Since you're out of rice,' the young man said, 'If you have any water, please bring me a little to wash my face with.' To which the old procuress replied, 'We haven't been able to pay the water carrier, so he hasn't delivered any water the last few days.' At this, the young man reached into his sleeve, pulled out a silver ingot weighing ten taels, put it on the table in front of him, and told her to buy rice and order water with it. This flustered the old procuress so much that she blurted out, 'Kinsman, would you rather eat your face before washing your rice, or wash your rice before eating your face?' "

Everyone laughed uproariously at this.

"I see you're still as quick to make fun of people as ever," said Auntie Li. "It so happens that, as the saying goes:

> Such a thing may be said, but
> It ain't necessarily so."

"Lend an ear," said Ying Po-chüeh, "I've got something else to tell you. The Honorable Gentleman has recently engaged the services of Brother Hua the Second's former sweetheart, Wu Yin-erh, from the back alley of the quarter. He isn't interested in your Kuei-chieh any longer. If we hadn't dragged him along with us today, do you think he'd be here now?"

"I don't believe you," laughed the procuress. "Our Kuei-chieh can be said, without exaggeration, to be superior to Wu Yin-erh in every way. Our establishment and our kinsman's family are bound together by ties that:

> The sharpest knife could never sever.

What do you take our kinsman for, anyway? He's seen enough of the world, if you get right down to it, to know the value of true gold when he sees it."

When they had finished with their palaver, four folding armchairs were set up in the parlor, on which Ying Po-chüeh, Hsieh Hsi-ta, Sticky Chu, and Blabbermouth Sun sat down, in the positions of honor, while Hsi-men Ch'ing assumed the place of host, across from them. The old lady then excused herself in order to supervise the preparation of the wine and accompanying delicacies for the party.

Sometime after her departure, Li Kuei-chieh herself finally appeared. Her hair was done up in a casual "bag of silk" chignon in the Hang-chou style, fastened in place with a gold filigree pin. Her coiffure was further augmented by plum-blossom-shaped ornaments with kingfisher feather inlays, a pearl headband, and gold lantern earrings. She was wearing a white satin jacket that opened down the middle, with purfled edging and green brocade sleeve linings, over a red silk skirt. Indeed, she was so made up as to look as though she were:

> Modeled in plaster, carved of jade.

After having:

> Neither correctly nor precisely,

made a bow to the company and uttered a word of greeting, Kuei-chieh sat down with Kuei-ch'ing at the two unoccupied ends of the table. Before long, one of the girls of the establishment brought in seven cups of tea on a square tray of painted lacquer. The teacups were the color of snowy linen, the silver teaspoons were in the shape of apricot leaves, and the tea itself, which was flavored with attar of roses and the kernels of melon seeds, was of a bewitching fragrance. Kuei-ch'ing and Kuei-chieh served a cup to each of their guests and kept them company until the tea was finished and the raised saucers were cleared away.

A servant then came in to wipe off the table and began to lay out the delicacies to go with the wine. Just at this juncture, from behind the hanging blind over the door, a number of shabbily dressed young men, known to the trade as "cribbers," were observed:

Sticking out their heads and craning their necks,

awaiting the right moment to make their way inside and kneel down in front of the company.

They held three or four pints of melon seeds in their hands, which they presented to the host with the words, "A humble offering to Your Honor on this festival occasion."

Hsi-men Ch'ing recognized their leader as a fellow called Yü Ch'un, or Stupid Yü, and asked him, "Which of you are here today?"

"Tuan Mien, or Half-baked Tuan, Sha San, or Yokel Sha, and Nieh Yüeh, or Tiptoe Nieh, are just outside," replied Stupid.

Half-baked Tuan and the others then came inside and, noticing that Ying Po-chüeh was one of the company, kowtowed to him, saying, "Master Ying, you're here too."

Hsi-men Ch'ing stood up, announced that he would take the melon seeds, and then, rummaging in his purse for a tael's worth of silver, tossed it on the floor.

When Stupid Yü had picked it up, he and his companions kowtowed on their hands and knees, saying, "Thank you for your generosity, sir," and beat a hasty retreat.

There is a song to the tune "Imperial Audience" that describes the conduct of these "cribbers."

Assembling at one place,
Congregating at another,
Their status may be low, but their pretensions
  are great.
If you rub them the wrong way, they'll
  give you a hard time.
No part of the licensed quarter
  is off their beat.
At parties they'll join the fun,
Ever ready with idle conversation;
Only after doing their turn
  will they disperse.

The money they make isn't much,
So why do they make such a fuss?
They live off the spittle licked from
the tiger's mouth.[19]

As soon as Hsi-men Ch'ing had gotten rid of the "cribbers," wine was served and the party settled down to drink. Kuei-chieh:

Filled the golden cups to the brim,
Dangling her pair of red sleeves.
Dainties were prepared of the rarest kind,
Fruits were provided just in season.
Hugging the turqoise and cuddling the red,
The flowers were gorgeous and the wine heady.

After:

Two rounds of wine had been consumed,

Kuei-ch'ing and Kuei-chieh, one playing the psaltery and the other the *p'i-p'a*, accompanied themselves as they sang the song suite on the beauties of spring, the first number of which, to the tune "Flowers in Brocade," begins with the words:

The fair weather is balmy.[20]

Just as they were in full voice, three young men appeared, wearing black clothing and brown leather boots, who were known to the trade as "ball clubbers."

They held a gift box containing a roast goose and two bottles of vintage wine in their hands, which they presented to the company, after making a half obeisance, with the words, "A humble offering to Your Honor and his distinguished friends on this festival occasion."

Hsi-men Ch'ing was already acquainted with them. The first was called Pai T'u-tzu, or Baldy Pai, also known as Mohammedan Pai, the second, Hsiao Chang Hsien, or Trifler Chang, and the third, Lo Hui-tzu, or Mohammedan Lo.

"Wait outside a little while," he said to them, "until we've finished our wine. Then we'll come out and kick three rounds with you."

So saying, he sent them on their way with four plates of delicacies from the table, a large jug of wine, and a saucerful of savories for their refreshment.

When the "ball clubbers" had eaten their fill and inflated their ball, Hsi-men Ch'ing came outside and played a round of kick-about with them in the courtyard. After him it was Kuei-chieh's turn, and she joined a pair of them to form a triangular threesome in which the other two faced off as receivers to field her endeavors. As she did her best to "hook" and "chip" with her kicks, they were lavish with meretricious praise, and whenever she made a mistake they were quick to retrieve the ball for her.

Hangers-on Abet Debauchery in the Verdant Spring Bordello

When they were through, they made up to Hsi-men Ch'ing in the hope of reward, saying, "Kuei-chieh's 'ball-handling' is more professional than ever. When she 'volleys' with a 'flick pass' or a 'chip kick' we hardly know what to do with ourselves. In another year or two she and her sister will rank among the best 'ball-handlers' on this side of the quarter. There won't be another 'hooker' or 'chippy' in the same league. Already they're ten times better than the girls from the Tung establishment on Second Street."

By the time Kuei-chieh had kicked two rounds:

Dust had settled about her eyebrows,
Sweat had moistened her cheeks;
She was panting and puffing, and
Her limbs ached with exhaustion.

Extracting a folding fan from her sleeve, she endeavored to cool herself with it while she stood hand-in-hand with Hsi-men Ch'ing and watched Kuei-ch'ing engage Hsieh Hsi-ta and Trifler Chang in the same three-cornered game of kick-about. Baldy Pai and Mohammedan Lo stood on the sidelines, emptily gesturing with their feet and running back and forth to retrieve the ball when any of the players made an error.

There is another song to the tune "Imperial Audience" that describes the conduct of these "ball clubbers."

Idle when at home,
Forever on the make,
No honest trade for them,
Yet their kickballs are never
far from their sides.
Every day they haunt the street corners,
Paying no heed to the poor,
But toadying to the rich.
From early morning till late at night,
They seldom eat a full meal.
Though they never make much money,
They make ends meet by hiring out
the favors of their wives.

Hsi-men Ch'ing was still in the licensed quarter, looking on at his companions as they challenged each other to backgammon, played at kickball, and drank wine, when Tai-an arrived on horseback to fetch him.

Approaching his master as inconspicuously as possible he:

Whispered into his ear in a low voice,

"The First Lady and the Second Lady have already gone home. Mrs. Hua told me to ask you to come over as soon as you can."

On hearing this message, Hsi-men Ch'ing gave Tai-an whispered instructions to take the horse around to the back door and wait for him there.

Then, without even taking another drink, he accompanied Kuei-chieh back to her room and sat down with her for only a few minutes, after which, feigning the need to answer a call of nature, he came out to the back door, jumped on his horse, and disappeared in a cloud of dust.

Before he had made good his departure, Ying Po-chüeh sent the servant of the house out to intercept him, but Hsi-men Ch'ing merely said, "I've got something to attend to at home," and refused to return.

He did remember, however, to leave Tai-an a tael and five mace of silver with which to take care of the three "ball clubbers." The proprietors of the Li family establishment were so worried lest Hsi-men Ch'ing be on his way to visit Wu Yin-erh's place in the back alley that they sent a maidservant after him who tailed him all the way to the gate of the quarter before coming home. Ying Po-chüeh and the rest continued drinking, and it was not until the second watch that the party finally broke up. Truly:

If any curse me, curse away;
I'll have my pleasures anyway.

If you want to know the outcome of these events,
Pray consult the story related in the following chapter.

Chapter 16

HSI-MEN CH'ING IS INSPIRED BY GREED
TO CONTEMPLATE MATRIMONY;
YING PO-CHÜEH STEALS A MARCH
IN ANTICIPATION OF THE CEREMONY

Doubt not the existence of beauties who can
 topple kingdoms and cities;
Yet dreams of clouds and rain on Witches' Mountain
 are ever deluded.
Too great an infatuation with rouge and powder
 can melt the sturdiest bones;
And lead one to neglect the claims of friendship
 in favor of moth eyebrows.
In Warm Soft Country one's prowess
 is still undiminished;
Affected by the Alluring Breeze one's
 carriage remains dashing.
The heedless fellow is not awake to
 the evanescence of spring;
Having spent a thousand for a night of pleasure
 he is reluctant to quit.

THE STORY GOES that as soon as Hsi-men Ch'ing had made his way out the gate of the licensed quarter that day, with Tai-an in attendance, he whipped up his horse and headed straight for Li P'ing-erh's house on Lion Street. Arriving at her front door and dismounting, he saw that the gate was tightly shut and surmised that her guests must already have returned home in their sedan chairs. He told Tai-an to rouse Old Mother Feng, who opened the door for them.

When Hsi-men Ch'ing came in, Li P'ing-erh was standing in the candle-lit reception room:

Her flowery headdress in perfect order,
Her white mourning-clothes very becoming,

as she leaned against the latticework of the door, cracking melon seeds with her teeth.

As soon as she saw that Hsi-men Ch'ing had arrived, she:

Lightly moved her lotus feet,[1]
Gently lifted her beige skirt,

and descended the steps to welcome him, saying as she did so, "If you'd come a little earlier your Third Lady and Fifth Lady would still have been here. They only got into their sedan chairs and departed for home a few minutes ago. Your First Lady left early today. She said you weren't at home. Where have you been?"

"This morning," said Hsi-men Ch'ing, "I set out with Brother Ying the Second and Hsieh Hsi-ta to see the lanterns. We had hardly passed by your front door when we happened to run into a couple of friends who dragged us off to visit one of the establishments in the licensed quarter. We've been carrying on there ever since. I was afraid you might be waiting for me, so when the page boy showed up I pretended to have to go to the bathroom and made my escape through the back door. If I hadn't taken matters into my own hands that crew would have hung onto me so tenaciously I could never have gotten away."

"Thank you very much, sir, for your generous presents," said Li P'ing-erh. "Your ladies refused to stay any longer. They kept saying there was no one at home to look after the place, but I can't help feeling rather left in the lurch."

Thereupon:

More vintage wine was poured, and
Another rare repast was spread.

In the reception room:

Decorated lanterns were lit up,
Heat-holding drapes were let down.
Animal-shaped briquettes replenished golden braziers,
The scent of ambergris wafted from jeweled censers.

On the festive board:

Rare delicacies rose in piles,

From the goblet's rim:

Fragrant wine overflowed.

The woman handed Hsi-men Ch'ing a cup of wine and then kowtowed to him, saying, "Now that my poor husband is dead I'm completely alone in the world. I offer you this cup of wine today in the hope that you will accept responsibility for me in the future. Sir, if you only saw fit not to reject me for my inadequacies, I'd be more than willing to:

Make the beds and fold the quilts,

for you. If you could just permit me to play the role of a younger sister among the ladies of your household:

I'd be prepared to die if I must.

But I don't know what you think about this."

Hsi-men Ch'ing Is Inspired by Greed to Contemplate Matrimony

As she spoke her eyes brimmed over with tears.

Hsi-men Ch'ing accepted the wine and said with a smile, "Please get up. Since you have deigned to express so much love for me, rest assured that where any request from you is concerned:

It is imprinted in my heart.

As soon as your mourning period is over you can leave the rest to me. There's no need for you to worry any more about it. Today is your birthday. Let's drink to it."

Hsi-men Ch'ing, thereupon, drank off the wine and then, after refilling the cup, offered it in return to the woman. She bade him take the seat of honor, and Old Mother Feng went off to busy herself with the preparations in the kitchen. Before long she brought in a serving of birthday noodles.

As they ate, Hsi-men Ch'ing asked who had provided the entertainment during the day, and Li P'ing-erh replied, "Tung Chiao-erh and Han Chin-ch'uan were here today. When the party broke up they accompanied your Third Lady and Fifth Lady home to pick up some artificial flowers they had been promised."

Hsi-men Ch'ing sat on the left side of the table and the two of them fell to drinking together:

Exchanging cups as they drank.

Li P'ing-erh's maidservants, Ying-ch'un and Hsiu-ch'un, stood in attendance, pouring wine and fetching food for them as occasion demanded. Who should come forward at this juncture but Tai-an, who prostrated himself on the floor and kowtowed to Li P'ing-erh, wishing her a happy birthday.

Li P'ing-erh promptly rose to her feet and returned his salute, telling Ying-ch'un as she did so, "Get Old Mother Feng to set aside some noodles and savories in the kitchen, along with a jug of wine, for Tai-an."

"As soon as you've finished eating," Hsi-men Ch'ing told him, "you can go home with the horse."

"When you get there," said Li P'ing-erh, "if your mistress should ask, don't tell her that your master is here."

"Leave it to me," said Tai-an. "I'll just say that Father is spending the night in the licensed quarter and wants me to come and fetch him in the morning."

Hsi-men Ch'ing nodded approvingly, and Li P'ing-erh was as pleased as could be. "What a clever lad," she said.

"He doesn't miss a wink."[2]

She ordered Ying-ch'un to fetch two mace of silver for him, saying, "Here's a little something to help you celebrate the festival. Buy yourself some melon seeds to crack. If you bring me the outlines of your feet sometime soon, I'll make a nice pair of shoes for you."

Tai-an hastily kowtowed, saying, "How could I dream of such a thing?" and then withdrew to the kitchen.

When he had finished eating he led the horse outside, and Old Mother Feng put the crossbar on the front door to secure it for the night.

Li P'ing-erh and Hsi-men Ch'ing played at guess-fingers as they drank. After a while, a set of thirty-two ivory dominoes[3] was brought out. A madder red strip of felt was placed over the table and the two of them played dominoes and drank by the light of the suspended lanterns.

They enjoyed themselves in this way for some time, after which Li P'ing-erh ordered Ying-ch'un to light the candles in her bedroom.

It so happened that after the death of Hua Tzu-hsü, Hsi-men Ch'ing had already enjoyed the favors of both Ying-ch'un and Hsiu-ch'un, so there was no need to hide anything from them. They were instructed to prepare the bed and to bring along the food boxes and wine service from the reception room.

Thereupon, inside the bedstead, within the purple brocade curtains, the woman exposed her powder-white body and was joined by Hsi-men Ch'ing. With their:

> Fragrant shoulders huddled together, and
> Jade bodies snuggled up against each other,

the two of them continued to play dominoes and drink wine out of large goblets.

As they were so engaged, Li P'ing-erh asked Hsi-men Ch'ing, "When are you going to be finished with the reconstruction work you plan to do over there?"

"I'm only waiting until sometime next month to:

> Break ground and start construction,"

replied Hsi-men Ch'ing. "I'm going to tear down your old house and combine the two pieces of property into one. Then I'll erect an artificial hill and a summerhouse in the front, and make a garden and pleasure ground out of it. I'm also planning to build another three-room belvedere, like the one I already have, and call it the Flower-viewing Tower."

"In the tea chest over there behind the bed," the woman said, pointing as she spoke, "I've got forty catties of aloeswood, two hundred catties of white wax, two jars of quicksilver, and eighty catties of imported pepper stored away. If you will have it taken away sometime soon and sold off for its cash value, I'll contribute the proceeds of the sale to your building expenses. If you don't see fit to reject me for my inadequacies, please, whatever happens, tell your First Lady when you get home that I'd be more than willing to play the role of a younger sister among the ladies of your household. It wouldn't matter where I was ranked in the hierarchy. Darling, I just can't go on without you."

As she spoke a cascade of tears began to fall from her eyes.

Hsi-men Ch'ing solicitously endeavored to wipe them away with his handkerchief, saying, "Your feelings are fully understood by me. But we'd better wait until your period of mourning is over, on the one hand, and until I've finished the new construction work, on the other. Otherwise, if I took you into my household, you'd have no place to stay."

"If you really intend to take me into your family," the woman responded, "be sure, whatever you do, to locate the quarters you build for me next to those of your Fifth Lady. I don't know what I'd do without her, she's such a nice person. She and the Third Lady, née Meng, who lives in the rear compound, were just as friendly as could be to me on our very first meeting. The two of them are so alike they seem less like fellow-wives than sisters born of the same mother. Only your First Lady seems somewhat ill-disposed, as though:

Nobody amounts to much in her eyes."

"Actually," said Hsi-men Ch'ing, "this humble wife of mine, née Wu, has a most accommodating disposition. If that were not the case, how could I ever manage to have so many bedmates at my disposal? What I plan to do is to build a three-room belvedere on your former property for you to live in, just like the one on mine, and provide access through two postern gates. What do you think of that?"

"Sweetheart," the woman replied, "that would please me no end."

Thereupon, the two of them:

Tumbled and tossed like male and female phoenixes,
Indulging their lusts without restraint.

It was the fourth watch before they finally:

Fell asleep on the same pillow,
Shoulder to shoulder and thigh over thigh.

The next day it was past lunchtime before they stirred. The woman had not yet combed her hair when Ying-ch'un brought in some congee. She and Hsi-men Ch'ing had hardly finished half a bowl of the congee when wine was brought in and the two of them fell to drinking again.

It so happened that Li P'ing-erh was fond of doing it doggie fashion. Getting down on all fours, she made Hsi-men Ch'ing sit on the pillow and insert himself into her inverted flower while she:

Moved back and forth as she wished.

Just as the two of them were approaching their climax, what should they hear but Tai-an knocking at the gate, having arrived on horseback to fetch his master. Hsi-men Ch'ing called him over to the window and asked him what was up.

"There are three merchants from Szechwan and Hu-kuang waiting for you at home," replied Tai-an. "They have some excellent stock to dispose of and would like to weigh it out with Uncle Fu the Second and settle accounts. They are asking only a hundred taels down to conclude a contract, with the balance due in the middle decade of the eighth month. The First Lady sent me to ask you to come home and take care of the matter."

"You didn't say I was here, did you?" asked Hsi-men Ch'ing.

"I told her you were at Li Kuei-chieh's place in the licensed quarter," said Tai-an. "I didn't tell anyone you were here."

"She doesn't know how to handle things," said Hsi-men Ch'ing. "All she had to do was tell Uncle Fu the Second to take care of it. What need was there to send for me?"

"Uncle Fu the Second proposed to do just that," replied Tai-an, "but the merchants wouldn't agree to it. They refused to sign the contract until they had seen you in person."

"As long as they've sent the boy after you," said Li P'ing-erh:

"Business comes first.

If you don't go home you'll only upset the lady of the house."

"You don't know these lousy southern bastards," said Hsi-men Ch'ing. "They never come knocking at your door, trying to unload their goods, unless the market is slow and they've got nowhere else to dispose of them. You've got to buy on time, for three months or half a year. If you pay them off any sooner than that they'll start getting ideas. I've got the largest store in the whole Ch'ing-ho district and do the largest volume of business. It wouldn't matter how long I kept them waiting, they'd still have to come looking for me in the end."

"To refuse a business deal,
Is to risk making an enemy,"

said Li P'ing-erh. "Why don't you do as I say; go on home, take care of them, and come back later? After all:

There are as many days ahead of us as there are
leaves on the willow tree."[4]

Hsi-men Ch'ing acknowledged the force of Li P'ing-erh's rhetoric by slowly getting up, combing his hair and washing his face, donning his hairnet, and putting on his clothes. After Li P'ing-erh had provided him with something further to eat, without more ado, he put on his eye-mask and rode home on horseback.

There were four or five merchants waiting for him in the shop who went about their business as soon as he had supervised the weighing out of the merchandise, settled the account, and signed the contract.

Hsi-men Ch'ing then paid a visit to P'an Chin-lien's quarters.

"Where did you go yesterday?" she demanded to know. "If you tell the truth, I'll forget it; but if you don't, I'll kick up a real rumpus."

"Since you were all out being entertained at the Hua house," said Hsi-men Ch'ing, "I went for a tour of the Lantern Market with a few of my friends, after which we went into the licensed quarter and made a night of it. I didn't get home until the page boy came to fetch me this morning."

"The page boy went to fetch you all right," said Chin-lien, "but I doubt if any part of the licensed quarter saw so much as your ghost. So much for that! You lousy two-timer, you still think you can fool me do you? That whore yesterday was so anxious to get us out of the way it was obvious she was:

Up to her preternatural pranks.

She must have invited you over so you could screw the night away. She didn't let you go till you were screwed out, I dare say. And as for that lousy jailbird, Tai-an:

He's such a practiced old hand,

he had one story for the First Lady and another story for me.

"Initially, when he came back with the horse and the First Lady asked him, 'Why hasn't your father come home? Who's place is he drinking at?' he replied, 'He went for a tour of the Lantern Market with Uncle Ying the Second and that crowd. They're all in the licensed quarter now, having a party at Li Kuei-chieh's place. He told me to come back and fetch him in the morning.'

"Later on, however, when I called him into my room and interrogated him myself, he just giggled and wouldn't say anything. Only after I began to give him a hard time did he say, 'Father's really at Mistress Hua the Second's place on Lion Street.' The lousy jailbird! How did he know that you and I are:

Of one heart and one mind?

You must have told him it was all right to tell me."

"I did nothing of the sort," said Hsi-men Ch'ing evasively.

Seeing that concealment was no longer possible, however, he went on to tell her all about Li P'ing-erh's invitation of the previous night.

"When I arrived she offered me a cup of wine and apologized for the scant entertainment she had been able to provide you. Then she started to weep and wail, telling me that her household was understaffed, that the rear part of the property was deserted, and that she was afraid to be alone there at night. Her one desire is that I will marry her. She asked when I was going to finish building the new house. She also showed me several hundred taels worth of aromatics, wax, and other valuable goods, and suggested that I broker them for her and keep the proceeds to help defray the building expenses. She wants me to start on the construction work as soon as possible so she can move in next to you and be a sister of yours. But I fear you may not agree to that."

"It's not as though I have:

A shadow too many,

here as it is," said the woman. "I only hope she does move in. That would be fine by me. This place of mine is completely deserted, and I'd love to have somebody to keep me company. It's always been true that:

A multitude of boats need not clog the channel,
A multitude of carts need not block the road.[5]

I could hardly refuse her the same sort of welcome I once received myself. It's not as though she were trying to take my place away from me or anything like that. My only fear is that:

Other people may not be as well disposed as I am.

You'll have to find out what the First Lady thinks about it."

"It's only something to talk about at the moment," said Hsi-men Ch'ing. "Her mourning period isn't even over yet."

Their colloquy at an end, the woman was helping Hsi-men Ch'ing off with his white satin jacket when an object fell out of his sleeve with a tinkling sound. Taking it in her hand, she found it had a heavy feel to it and was about the size of a fowling pellet. She scrutinized it for some time but couldn't tell what it was. Behold:

To the tune "Immortal at the River"

First introduced as a product
  of the barbarian armies;
It has found its way by recommendation
  to the capital itself.
Its body is miniature,
  its interior hollow.
Once set in motion
  by the merest touch;
It will roll around spontaneously,
  stridulant as a cicada.

Adept at arousing consternation
  in the beauty's heart;
A veteran contributor
  to the vigor of the loins;
Its sobriquet is "Brazenfaced
  Valiant Vanguard."
On the victory honors list
  forever number one;
It has won renown as
  "The Titillating Bell."[6]

The woman examined it for some time before asking, "What on earth is it? And why does it give me a numb feeling halfway up my arm?"

"This is something you wouldn't be familiar with," Hsi-men Ch'ing laughed. "It's called a 'titillating bell' and comes from the southern country of Burma. Good ones cost four or five taels of silver."

"What do you do with it?" the woman asked.

"If you put it in your 'crucible' before doing the deed," said Hsi-men Ch'ing:

"It's too wonderful for words."

"You've been experimenting with Li P'ing-erh, haven't you?" the woman said.

Thereupon, Hsi-men Ch'ing gave a full account of the events of the preceding night, with the result that Chin-lien's:

Lecherous desires were suddenly aroused.

Though it was broad daylight, the two of them:

Took off their clothes and went to bed.

Truly:

Who knows what reason there might be
that Wang-tzu Ch'iao,[7]
No sooner learned to "play the flute"
than he became transported.[8]

To make a long story short, one day Hsi-men Ch'ing met with the appropriate brokers and weighed out the aromatics, wax, and other goods that had been stored in the tea chest behind Li P'ing-erh's bed. In all he was able to realize 380 taels of silver by the sale. Li P'ing-erh kept only 180 taels out of this sum for her own expenses and turned over the balance to Hsi-men Ch'ing to help defray the cost of the new building.

The yin-yang master was consulted and the eighth day of the second month chosen to:

Break ground and start construction.

Hsi-men Ch'ing turned over five hundred taels of silver to his head servant, Lai-chao, and his manager, Pen the Fourth, and put them in charge of procuring the necessary bricks, tiles, lumber, and stone, supervising the work, and handling the accounts.

This Pen the Fourth, whose name was Pen Ti-ch'uan, or Scurry-about Pen, was a young man who was by nature:

Dashing and affected,
Versatile and clever.

He had begun his career as a flunky in the household of one of the imperial eunuchs. But because he:

Was not the sort to abide by his lot,
Took his cut of both outgo and income,[9]

and got caught cooking the books, he had been dismissed. He supported himself for a while as a catamite, after which he took a job as a servant in a well-to-do household. From this position he had subsequently absconded with a wet nurse, whom he took as his wife, and set himself up as a dealer in the secondhand clothes trade. On top of all this he was also a proficient performer on the *p'i-p'a*, the flute, and other wind instruments.

Hsi-men Ch'ing was so impressed by the variety of his talents that he often patronized him, allowing him to weigh out the goods in his wholesale pharmaceutical business and earn commissions as a middleman. As a result, he had come to feel, in matters both great and small, that he could hardly do without him.

On the appointed day, Pen Ti-ch'uan and Lai-chao supervised the artisans of the various trades as they began the construction work. First they demolished the old house on what had been the Hua property and took down the intervening wall, then they laid the foundations and erected a summerhouse, an artificial hill, pavilions, terraces, and other recreational facilities. This was not the work of a day, but there is no need to describe it exhaustively.

Light and darkness alternate swiftly,
The sun and moon shoot back and forth like shuttles.

Hsi-men Ch'ing had remained at home overseeing the construction of his new garden for more than a month when the hundredth-day anniversary of Hua Tzu-hsü's death, which fell in the first decade of the third month, became imminent. Li P'ing-erh invited Hsi-men Ch'ing over beforehand to discuss the arrangements.

"I intend to burn Hua Tzu-hsü's spirit tablet," she said. "I don't know whether you plan to sell this house or not, but I wish you would send someone over to look after it and take me into your own household as soon as possible. I don't want to stay here any longer than necessary. At night it's completely deserted and I'm afraid. There are often fox spirits about doing their best to drive me to distraction. When you get home, please tell the First Lady that if she would only take pity on me it would save my life. It wouldn't make any difference where you chose to rank me in the hierarchy, I'd be more than willing to:

Make the beds and fold the quilts,

for you without repining." As she spoke:

Her tears fell like rain.

"There's no need to get so upset," said Hsi-men Ch'ing. "I already mentioned what you told me to my wife and Fifth Lady after I got home the other day. Just wait until the house I'm building for you is finished. By that time your mourning period will be nearly over. It won't be any too late to have you carried over the threshold then."

"Fine enough," said Li P'ing-erh. "But if it's really true that you intend to marry me, I wish you'd expedite the building of the house and take me over there as soon as possible. If I were able to live for even a day as a member of your household:

I'd be prepared to die if I must.

As long as I stay here:

Each day is like a year."[10]

"I understand what you're saying," responded Hsi-men Ch'ing.

"Even if the house isn't finished on time," said Li P'ing-erh, "once I've burnt the spirit tablet I could occupy the upper floor of the Fifth Lady's belvedere for a few days and then move into the new building after it's completed. Whatever else you do, when you get home speak to the Fifth Lady about it. I'll be waiting for your answer. The tenth of the third month is the hundredth-day anniversary of his death. I'll have to have a sutra reading and burn his spirit tablet then."

Hsi-men Ch'ing gave his assent and stayed overnight with the woman.

The next day he repeated everything she had said, word for word, to P'an Chin-lien.

"Of course, that would be fine," said Chin-lien. "I'd be perfectly happy to set aside a room or two for her to live in. It's the others I'd be worried about. You'll have to find out what the First Lady thinks about it. As far as I'm concerned:

> There's water enough in the channel
> for all the boats.[11]

It all depends on what our elder sister has to say."

Hsi-men Ch'ing went straight to Wu Yüeh-niang's room. He found her combing her hair and proceeded to give her a complete account of Li P'ing-erh's desire to marry into the family, from beginning to end.

"You really can't very well marry her," said Yüeh-niang. "In the first place: her mourning period isn't over yet. In the second place: you were formerly on intimate terms with her husband. And in the third place: you've already been engaged in hanky-panky with her, first buying their house and then stashing away all the valuables she entrusted to you for safekeeping. As the saying goes:

> The loom may stay put, but the shuttle gets around.[12]

I've heard people say that Hua the Elder from her husband's branch of the family is a tough customer. If any word of this should get about you'd only be:

> Inviting lice onto your own head to scratch.[13]

What I say is in your own best interests, but:

> Be you Chao, Ch'ien, Sun, or Li;[14]
> I've had my say, you may do as you please."

With these few words she succeeded in reducing Hsi-men Ch'ing to silence. He went out to the front reception hall and sat down in a chair all by himself to ponder the situation. He didn't see how he could either convey this reply to Li P'ing-erh or refuse to go back and see her. After thinking it over for some time he returned to Chin-lien's room.

"When you went to see our elder sister, what did she say?" asked Chin-lien.

Hsi-men Ch'ing told her everything Yüeh-niang had said.

"Her objections are certainly reasonable enough," said Chin-lien. "First you bought his house and now you want to marry his wife into the bargain, a woman with whom you only became acquainted through your long-standing relationship with her husband. And there's another thing to consider too. Since even between friends:

Though there may be no secrets, there
are some constraints,

if it ever came to the attention of the authorities, they would take a dim view of it."

"I think I could handle that," said Hsi-men Ch'ing. "What worries me is that bastard, Hua the Elder. No doubt he resents the fact that he:

No longer has an arena for his tricks.

If he finds out about this and tries to make trouble on the grounds that her mourning period isn't over yet, what am I to do? Right now I'm at a loss how to reply to her."

"Phooey! What's so hard about that?" said Chin-lien. "Tell me, are you planning to give her your answer today or tomorrow?"

"She wants me to give her an answer of some kind today," replied Hsi-men Ch'ing.

"When you go there today then," said Chin-lien, "this is what you do. Say to her, 'I talked it over with the Fifth Lady when I got home, but there are such quantities of raw pharmaceuticals in storage on the second floor of her belvedere that there'd be no place to put your furniture if you moved in. You might as well wait a little longer. Your house is 70 or 80 percent completed already. I'll urge the artisans to speed up their work on the decorating, painting and varnishing, and other finishing touches, and by the time they're through your mourning period will be nearly over. If I take you in then, everything will be in proper order. That would be a lot better than having you move in on top of the Fifth Lady right now, while you're still in a ritual status that makes you:

Neither fish nor fowl.

You'd only get in each other's way and find it difficult to keep up appearances.' If you do as I suggest, I guarantee she'll give up the idea."

Hsi-men Ch'ing was so delighted by what he heard that he set out for Li P'ing-erh's house without delay.

"How did it go with that request of mine when you got home?" the woman asked.

"The Fifth Lady said," reported Hsi-men Ch'ing, "that you'd do better to wait until they've finished painting and varnishing your new house before moving in. Right now there's so much stuff:

Strewn about higgledy-piggledy,

on the second floor of her place that if you went over there there'd be no place to store your things. And there's another problem as well. If your husband's eldest brother should complain that your mourning period isn't over yet, what would we do then?"

"He wouldn't dare interfere in my affairs," said the woman. "Quite aside from the fact that:

Each of us has his own life to live,

and that a formal settlement of the matter of the disputed property has already been reached; as far as I'm concerned:

In one's first marriage one must obey one's parents;
In subsequent marriages one can suit oneself.

It's always been the case that:

Brothers and sisters-in-law do not
  ask after each other.

My husband's eldest brother has no business interfering in my private affairs. As it is, he can see I'm having a hard time making a go of it, but what does he care? If he so much as lets off a fart, by the time I'm finished with him, he'll:

Die in his chair,
Not daring to die in his bed.

You can relax on that score, sir. He won't dare give me any trouble."

"As for this house of yours," she then went on to ask, "how soon is it going to be finished anyway?"

"I've already instructed the artisans," said Hsi-men Ch'ing, "to give priority to the three-room belvedere I'm building for you. By the time they're done with the painting and varnishing it will be the beginning of the fifth month."

"My darling," the woman said, "push ahead with it as fast as you can. I'm willing to wait until then if I must."

When they had finished talking, a maidservant brought in wine and the two of them fell to enjoying themselves and drinking together for the rest of the night.

From this time on, Hsi-men Ch'ing came to see her every three to five days, without fail, but there is no need to describe this in detail.

Light and darkness alternate swiftly.

The construction work in Hsi-men Ch'ing's residential compound had already been under way for more than two months, and the three-room belvedere, called the Flower-viewing Tower, was nearing completion. All that remained was the summerhouse, for which the foundation had not yet been laid.

One day the Dragon Boat Festival, on the fifth day of the fifth month, rolled around.

In each household artemisia leaves adorn the gate,
In every dwelling efficacious charms deck the door.[15]

Li P'ing-erh prepared a feast in honor of the occasion and invited Hsi-men Ch'ing over to share the festival *tsung-tzu* with her, on the one hand,

and to discuss the date she would be carried over his threshold, on the other. They decided that on the fifteenth day of the fifth month she would engage Buddhist priests to hold a sutra-reading and burn the spirit tablet of her deceased husband, after which Hsi-men Ch'ing would arrange to have her carried over his threshold.

Hsi-men Ch'ing then asked Li P'ing-erh, "On the day you burn the spirit tablet, are you planning to invite Hua the Elder, Hua the Third, and Hua the Fourth, or not?"

"I'll send them each an invitation," the woman replied. "They can come or not as they please."

Now that their plans had been made, all that remained was to wait for the fifteenth day of the fifth month. The woman engaged the services of twelve monks from the Pao-en Temple, who came to her home on the appointed day to perform the sutra-reading and preside over the burning of the spirit tablet.

The same day, Hsi-men Ch'ing wrapped up three mace of silver as a birthday present for Ying Po-chüeh. In the morning he also gave five taels of silver to Tai-an and instructed him to buy chicken, goose, duck, and whatever else was needed for a feast that evening to celebrate the end of Li P'ing-erh's mourning period. Then, taking P'ing-an and Hua-t'ung with him to look after the horse, he set out in the early afternoon for Ying Po-chüeh's house.

Among those attending the party that day were Tagalong Hsieh, Sticky Chu, Blabbermouth Sun, Heartless Wu, Welsher Yün, Cadger Ch'ang, Scrounger Pai, and the new recruit to the company, Scurry-about Pen. All ten members of the club were present, not one of them having failed to put in an appearance. Two boy actors had also been engaged to play and sing for them.

After everyone had been served with wine and they had taken their places at the table, Hsi-men Ch'ing called the two boy actors over to him. He recognized the first of them to be Wu Yin-erh's younger brother, Wu Hui.

The other, whom he did not recognize, knelt down and said, "I am Cheng Ai-hsiang's elder brother, Cheng Feng."

Hsi-men Ch'ing, who occupied the seat of honor, rewarded each of them with two mace of silver.

The party continued until the sun began to sink in the west. At this juncture Tai-an arrived with a horse to fetch his master.

Coming right up to the table, he whispered into Hsi-men Ch'ing's ear, "The lady would like you to come over as soon as you can."

Hsi-men Ch'ing responded with a wink, and Tai-an had started on his way out of the room when he was called to a halt by Ying Po-chüeh, who demanded, "You lousy dog-bone! Come over here and tell me the truth. If you don't tell the truth, I'll give your little ear a permanent twist. How many birthdays do you think your Daddy Ying has in a year, that you should come with the horse to fetch your father while the sun is still high in the sky? Where are you off to anyway? And who really sent you here? It may have been one of your mistresses at home, but it may just as well have been that 'Eighteenth Youngster'[16] from the licensed quarter. If you don't tell me, a hundred years will go by before I ever put in a good word with your father to find this little dog-bone of his a wife."

Tai-an's only response was to say, "The truth is: nobody sent me. I feared it was getting late and thought Father might want to be on his way, so I brought the horse along early to await his convenience."

Ying Po-chüeh harassed him a while longer, without effect, and then said, "If you don't tell me what's afoot, and I find out about it later on, see if I don't settle accounts with you, you little oily mouth."

So saying, he poured out a cup of wine and selected half a saucerful of savories for Tai-an to eat when he had retired from their presence.

After some time, Hsi-men Ch'ing withdrew to the bathroom in order to adjust his toilet.

Summoning Tai-an, he drew him aside and asked him, "Who all showed up at the Hua house today?"

"Hua the Third is off in the country somewhere," reported Tai-an. "And Hua the Fourth is at home suffering from an eye ailment. No one came from either of their families. Only Hua the Elder and his wife showed up. After they had eaten their fill of the vegetarian fare, the husband went home first, leaving his wife behind. When she was ready to leave, Mistress Hua called her into her room and presented her with ten taels of silver and two sets of clothes, for which she actually kowtowed in gratitude."

"Did she have anything to say?" asked Hsi-men Ch'ing.

"She didn't venture so much as a word about it," replied Tai-an. "All she said was that when Mistress Hua is carried over your threshold she'd like to pay you a call on the 'third-day celebrations.' "

"Did she really say that?" asked Hsi-men Ch'ing.

"How would I dare lie about it," responded Tai-an.

When Hsi-men Ch'ing heard this his heart was filled with delight. "Are the oblations completed as yet?" he went on to ask.

"The monks left some time ago," replied Tai-an. "The spirit tablet has already been burned. Mistress Hua said she'd like you to come over as soon as you can."

"I understand," said Hsi-men Ch'ing. "Go outside and take care of the horse."

Tai-an was on his way out when, unexpectedly, Ying Po-chüeh, who had been eavesdropping in the corridor, suddenly accosted him with a shout, which gave him quite a start.

"You lousy little dog-bone!" he cursed. "You wouldn't tell me anything, but I've already contrived to hear all about it. A fine thing your father and you are up to!"

"You crazy dog!" said Hsi-men Ch'ing. "Don't make such a fuss or everyone in the place will find out about it."

"If you'd taken me into your confidence in the first place," said Ying Po-chüeh, "I might not have said anything about it."

Thereupon he went right back to the table and, thus and so, told everyone the whole story.

Taking hold of Hsi-men Ch'ing, he said, "Brother, what sort of a person are you anyway?

Can such things be,

that you should keep them to yourself without even letting your brothers in on them? Even if Hua the Elder had had anything to say about it, all you would have had to do was give us the word. Once we had spoken to him, he would have gone along with anything, never fear. If he had dared to utter so much as a single 'no,' we would have given him his lumps, make no mistake about it.

"Honestly, though, is this marriage set, or isn't it? Tell us all about it. Really! What are friends for, anyway? If there's anything we can do for you, we'd be willing to:

Go through fire for you, or
Go through water for you.[17]

In fact:

We seek not to have been born the same day;
We seek only to die, every man for himself.[18]

As long as we're prepared to treat you this way, unless you have some reason you haven't disclosed, why should you want to keep us in the dark?"

Tagalong Hsieh picked up where he left off.

"Brother," he said, "if you refuse to tell us any more, we'll make such a fuss in the licensed quarter that Li Kuei-chieh and Wu Yin-erh will hear about it and everyone will be embarrassed."

Hsi-men Ch'ing laughed, saying, "All right, then, I'll make a clean breast of it. The wedding has all been arranged."

"The day for the ceremony, when you have her carried over the threshold, hasn't been set yet, has it?" asked Ying Po-chüeh.

"The day you carry our sister-in-law over the threshold," said Tagalong Hsieh, "we'll come to congratulate you. Whatever else you do, Brother, you'll have to engage four singing girls and invite us to a wedding feast."

"That goes without saying," said Hsi-men Ch'ing. "Of course, all of you will be invited."

"Rather than waiting to congratulate our brother on a future occasion," said Sticky Chu, "why don't we offer him a toast in advance?"

Thereupon, Sponger Ying presented the toast, Tagalong Hsieh held the flagon, Sticky Chu proffered some viands, and the rest of them all knelt down too, to keep them company. The two boy actors were also dragged into the act, being made to kneel down and sing the song suite entitled "Thirty Melodies," which begins with the words:

How happy this auspicious day.[19]

Hsi-men Ch'ing was made to swallow three or four cups of wine in a row.

"Brother," said Sticky Chu, "on the day you invite us to the feast, you must be sure to include Cheng Feng and Wu Hui as well. That's settled then. Whatever happens, the two of you must go."

Cheng Feng, deferentially covering his mouth with his hand, replied, "We promise to report to your home for duty at an early hour."

Before long, after everyone had been served with wine, they returned to their places, sat down, and embarked upon another bout of drinking.

The day gradually waned and Hsi-men Ch'ing grew restless. As soon as he thought no one was looking, he got up and tried to slip away, but Ying Po-chüeh attempted to block the door and prevent his escape.

"Brother Ying," intervened Tagalong Hsieh, "let him go. We wouldn't want to spoil his plans and arouse the resentment of our sister-in-law."

Hsi-men Ch'ing seized the opportunity to leap on his horse and disappeared in a puff of smoke.

When he arrived at Lion Street, Li P'ing-erh had already divested herself of her mourning and changed into a more colorful outfit. In the reception room:

Ablaze with lamps and candles,[20]

the table was laid with a full complement of wine and delicacies, with a single folding armchair standing at its head.

Not until Hsi-men Ch'ing had assumed the place of honor was a jug of wine broached and decanted. A maidservant held the flagon, from which Li P'ing-erh proceeded to fill a cup to the brim and offer it to her guest.

She then kowtowed to him four times:

Just as though inserting a taper in its holder,

and said, "Today the spirit tablet of my poor husband has been burnt. If you, sir, deign not to reject me, I will enjoy the pleasure of:

Waiting upon you with towel and comb,

thereby:

Fulfilling my desire for connubial bliss."

When she rose to her feet after completing her obeisances, Hsi-men Ch'ing also got up from his seat and proffered the woman a cup of wine in return. Only then did they sit down to enjoy themselves together.

"Did Hua the Elder or his wife have anything to say today?" Hsi-men Ch'ing asked.

Ying Po-chüeh Steals a March in Anticipation of the Ceremony

"After the noon vegetarian meal," replied Li P'ing-erh, "I invited them into my room and told them about your intentions. He expressed nothing but pleasure at the news and didn't have a word to say against it. All he said was that he'd have his wife pay you a call on the 'third-day celebrations.' I gave them ten taels of silver and two sets of clothes. The two of them were as happy as could be and thanked me again and again on their way out the door."

"If that was their only response," said Hsi-men Ch'ing, "I might as well let them come calling; what does it matter? But if they utter a single word of criticism, I'll never forgive them."

"If either of them so much as lets a hot fart on the subject," asserted Li P'ing-erh, "I won't let them get away with it."

Thereupon, Old Mother Feng brought out some soup and an assortment of appetizers from the kitchen. Li P'ing-erh had taken the trouble to:

Wash her hands and trim her nails,

before personally preparing some miniature steamed dumplings with a stuffing of minced scallions and mutton. From a chased silver goblet filled with southern wine, Hsiu-ch'un poured out two cups for her mistress and her visitor. Hsi-men Ch'ing drank only the first half-cupful of his wine and presented the remainder to Li P'ing-erh.

One goes, the other comes;

and thus they proceeded to drink several cups in a row. Truly:

The sway of passion takes one's years away;
The force of setting makes the wine flow free.[21]

Because the day of her marriage was impending, Li P'ing-erh was even happier than usual. Her face was wreathed in smiles.

"While you were drinking just now at the Ying place," she said, "you kept me waiting a long time. I was afraid you might get drunk, so I sent for Tai-an to ask you to come over as soon as possible. Did anyone there catch on?"

"Beggar Ying, as usual, guessed that something was afoot," replied Hsi-men Ch'ing. "He pressured the page boy into letting out a few words about it, and then clowned around for a while. The members of the club demanded a chance to offer their congratulations, so I guess I'll have to engage singing girls and throw a party for them. They also ganged up on me and made me swallow a few cups of wine. As soon as I thought no one was looking, I tried to slip away, but they blocked the door, and:

Argued the pros and cons,

among themselves before letting me go."

"The fact they let you go shows they understand a thing or two," said Li P'ing-erh.

Hsi-men Ch'ing, having noticed that:

Her drunken demeanor invited license; and
Her passionate eyes expressed desire,

lost no time in abandoning all restraint. He:

Stuck out his clove-shaped tongue; and
Nuzzled her apricot cheeks.

Li P'ing-erh embraced Hsi-men Ch'ing, saying, "My darling, if you really do plan to marry me, make it as soon as possible. It's inconvenient for you to have to come and go this way. Don't leave me here to long for you day and night."

When she had finished speaking, they:

Tossed first this way and then that;
Till they were intertwined into one.

Truly:

A beauty who could topple kingdoms and cities
belonged to Emperor Wu of Han;[22]
A goddess who could make clouds and make rain
appeared to King Hsiang of Ch'u.[23]

There is a poem that testifies to this:

In passion's thrall breast presses close to breast;
In tender aftermath arms are gently enlaced.
Let the silver lamp burn brightly as it will;
They're still afraid it's nothing but a dream.[24]

If you want to know the outcome of these events,
Pray consult the story related in the following chapter.

Chapter 17

CENSOR YÜ-WEN IMPEACHES COMMANDER YANG; LI P'ING-ERH TAKES CHIANG CHU-SHAN AS MATE

To the tune "Partridge Sky"

She remembers that time in the studio
when they had just met;
The clouds and rain they enjoyed together
were known to only a few.
When evening came, the phoenix and his mate
alighted on adjacent pillows;
Left untrimmed, the silver lamp
shed only a half light.

Thinking of the past,
Her dreaming soul deluded;
Tonight she is all too happy to enjoy
the pleasures of connubial bliss.
Tumbled and tossed like male and female phoenixes,
their pleasure knows no bounds.
From this time on, surely, the pair of them
will never be separated.[1]

THE STORY GOES that the twentieth day of the fifth month was the birthday of Commandant Chou Hsiu of the Regional Military Command. When the day came, Hsi-men Ch'ing sealed up five mace of silver and two handkerchiefs in a packet, as his contribution toward the cost of the celebration. Then, having dressed himself to befit the occasion, he mounted a large white horse and, accompanied by four page boys, set off for the commandant's home to offer his birthday greetings. Among the others attending the party were the judicial commissioner, Hsia Yen-ling, the militia commander, Chang Kuan, the battalion commanders Ching Chung[2] and Ho Chin, and other military officials. The guests were met with drinks at the door and received to the strains of martial music. A southern-style play, of the genre known as hsi-wen,[3] was performed for their entertainment, and four singing girls had been engaged to ply the guests with wine.

Tai-an took Hsi-men Ch'ing's outdoor clothes and went home with the horse. When the sun began to sink in the west, Tai-an set out on horseback to fetch his master.

As he was passing by the western end of Lion Street he ran into Old Mother Feng and asked her, "Mother Feng, where are you going?"

"Mistress Hua sent me to ask your master over," replied Old Mother Feng. "Silversmith Ku has finished the jewelry she ordered for the betrothal ceremony and delivered it today in a box. She wants your master to come and see it. She also has something she wants to talk to him about."

"My master's at Commandant Chou's place attending a party today," said Tai-an. "I'm on my way to fetch him. You can save yourself a trip. When I get there I'll give him the message."

"I'm imposing on you," said Old Mother Feng, "but, whatever you do, be sure to mention it. Mistress Hua is waiting for him."

Tai-an whipped up his horse and headed straight for the commandant's headquarters. The officials at the party were devoting themselves to their cups and having a high time of it.

Tai-an went up to Hsi-men Ch'ing's place at the table and said to him, "On my way back from home with the horse just now, I ran into Old Mother Feng in the street. Mistress Hua had sent her to invite you over. She said that Silversmith Ku had delivered the jewelry and she wanted you to come and see it. She also has something she wants to talk to you about."

When Hsi-men Ch'ing heard this, he gave Tai-an some savories, soup, and rice to eat and prepared to make his departure. Commandant Chou was reluctant to let him go, blocking the door and foisting a large cup of wine upon him.

"Since you do me the honor, sir," said Hsi-men Ch'ing, "I will drink this cup at your behest. But there is something I must attend to that prevents me from enjoying your hospitality to the full. Forgive me. Forgive me."

Thereupon, he:

Drained it in one gulp,

bade farewell to Commandant Chou, got on his horse, and headed straight for Li P'ing-erh's house. When he had finished the tea with which the woman welcomed him, Hsi-men Ch'ing told Tai-an to take the horse home and come to fetch him in the morning.

After Tai-an had left, Li P'ing-erh told Ying-ch'un to get the jewelry out of its box for Hsi-men Ch'ing to look over. All ablaze like golden fire, it was a fine set of jewelry indeed.

When it had been put away, Hsi-men Ch'ing said, "You won't have to wait any longer than the twenty-fourth for the presentation of the betrothal gifts, and we'll hold the ceremony proper next month, on the fourth."

The woman's heart was filled with delight. She promptly brought out the wine, and she and Hsi-men Ch'ing drank deeply and unburdened themselves to each other. After they had been drinking for a while, she ordered a maidservant to wipe off the cool bamboo bed mat in her room, and the two of them took their places inside the gauze netting.

The incense was redolent of orchid and musk;
The bedspread was fashioned of mermaid silk.

Taking off their clothes, they sat:

Shoulder to shoulder and thigh over thigh;
Drinking wine and making merry with each other.

After some time:

The glint of spring pervading their eyes;[4]
They were carried away by lecherous desires.

Hsi-men Ch'ing started out by engaging the woman in the sport of clouds and rain for a while. After that, responding to a drunken whim, he ordered her to lie down across the mat and indulge him by "toying with the flute." Behold:

To the tune "Moon on the West River"

The scent of orchid and musk pervades
the gauze netting;
The delicate beauty lightly proceeds
to "play the flute."
Her snow-white jade body is visible
through the bed curtains;
It's enough to make one's "ethereal and
material souls take flight."

A single cherry might describe
her tiny mouth;
Tender stalks are not as gentle
as her fingers.
The talented gentleman is moved
to remark to his partner,
"I never knew the magic rhinoceros horn
could feel so good."[5]

At this juncture, Hsi-men Ch'ing, who was in his cups, playfully asked the woman, "In the old days, when your Hua Tzu-hsü was still alive, did you ever do anything like this with him?"

"When he wasn't asleep he was in dreamland,"

the woman replied. "How could I ever have had the patience to do this sort of thing with him? All he ever wanted to do was fool around outside. And even when he came home, I wouldn't ordinarily let him touch me. Moreover, as long as the old eunuch director was alive, we slept in separate rooms. As for my husband, I used to curse him till he looked as though:

His head had been sprayed with dog's blood.[6]

If he gave me any trouble, all I had to do was tell the old eunuch about it and he'd give him a regular caning. He scarcely counted as a human being. What sort of stuff do you think he was made of, anyway? If I had played around this way with him it would only have given me the creeps. Who is there besides you who could suit me so perfectly? You're just what the doctor ordered. By day and by night, all I do is long for you."

The two of them fooled around for a while and then got back to business. Ying-ch'un waited on them, bringing in a small square box filled with assorted dainties, including nuts, rissoles, chicken and goose giblets and feet, and rose- and chrysanthemum-flavored cakes. A small gold flagon was:

Filled to the brim with carnelian-hued nectar.

From dusk, when the lamps and candles were lighted, they intermittently played with one another and drank until the time of the first watch.

All of a sudden they were interrupted by the sound of loud knocking at the outer gate. When they sent Old Mother Feng to open the door and see who it was, it turned out to be Tai-an.

"I told him to come and fetch me tomorrow," said Hsi-men Ch'ing. "What's he doing coming back at a time like this?"

When he called him into the room to question him, the page boy made his way as far as the door in a state of obvious agitation. Hsi-men Ch'ing and the woman were still in bed, so he did not dare go inside, but he spoke to them from the other side of the portiere.

"Your daughter and son-in-law have arrived," he said, "along with a large number of boxes. The First Lady sent me to ask you to come home as quickly as possible to discuss the situation with her."

When Hsi-men Ch'ing heard this, he didn't know what to make of it.

"At such an hour, what could have happened?" he wondered. "I'd better go home and see what's going on."

He got up hastily. The woman helped him on with his clothes and heated a cup of warm wine for him to drink.

Whipping up his horse, he went straight home, where he found the rear reception room brightly lit with lamps and candles. His daughter and son-in-law were both there, along with a large pile of boxes, beds and curtains, and other family belongings.

Hsi-men Ch'ing could hardly believe his eyes.

"What are you doing arriving home at such an hour?" he demanded.

His son-in-law, Ch'en Ching-chi, kowtowed and said, with tears in his eyes, "Recently our kinsman, the venerable Yang Chien, was impeached by a supervising secretary in the Office of Scrutiny, with the result that an imperial edict has come down ordering his arrest and incarceration in the South Prison to await the final disposition of his case. His protégés, relatives, and employees have all been tentatively sentenced to public exposure in the cangue and military exile. Yesterday his factotum, Yang Sheng, by traveling day and night, managed to get word of this to my father. My father was thrown into such a state of consternation by the news that he directed me to take your daughter, along with some boxes of family belongings, and seek temporary lodging with you until things blow over. He himself immediately set off for my paternal aunt's place in the Eastern Capital, to find out whatever more he could. When things return to normal:

> Your kindness will be amply rewarded,
> He will never dare to forget it."

"Did your father give you a letter, or anything?" asked Hsi-men Ch'ing.

"I've got his letter right here," said Ch'en Ching-chi, pulling it out of his sleeve and handing it to him.

Hsi-men Ch'ing broke open the seal and found that it read as follows:

> Respectfully indited by his devoted servant, Ch'en Hung,[7] for the perusal of my most virtuous kinsman, Hsi-men Ch'ing:
>
> I will dispense with the customary formalities. The northern barbarians are currently encroaching upon our frontiers, and their incursions have extended beyond the borders of Hsiung-chou. The failure of the minister of war, Wang Fu,[8] to dispatch adequate defense forces has resulted in a military debacle in which our kinsman, the venerable Yang Chien, is also implicated. They have both been impeached on charges of the utmost gravity by a supervising secretary of the Office of Scrutiny.
>
> His Majesty is incensed and has ordered their arrest and incarceration in the South Prison, pending a formal inquiry by the Three Judicial Offices. Their protégés, relatives, and employees have all, in accordance with precedent, been tentatively sentenced to military exile in frontier guard units.
>
> On hearing this news, my entire family has been thrown into consternation, having no place to turn. I have taken the initiative of sending my son and your daughter, along with what they are able to carry with them in the way of boxes of family belongings, to seek temporary refuge in your household. I am leaving immediately for the capital, where I plan to stay with my elder sister's husband, Chang Shih-lien,[9] and await word of the final disposition of the case.
>
> Once my affairs are in sufficient order to permit my return home:
>
> Your kindness will be amply rewarded,
> I will never dare to forget it.
>
> Fearing that there may be some repercussions in the district, I have also ordered my son to provide you with five hundred taels of silver, in the hope that, as my kinsman, you will do what you can to cope with the situation.

Censor Yü-wen Impeaches Commander Yang

I shall endeavor to requite you
in the future;
Not forgetting your kindness
as long as I live.[10]

Written in haste, by lamplight, I am unable to express myself more fully.

Date: The twentieth day of the middle month of summer.

Signed: Hung, again, respectfully salutes you.

By the time Hsi-men Ch'ing finished reading the letter he was extremely perturbed. He instructed Wu Yüeh-niang to prepare food and wine for his daughter and son-in-law, and ordered the servants to sweep out the three rooms on the eastern side of the courtyard in front of the main reception hall for the couple to stay in. The boxes of valuables were all stored away in Yüeh-niang's room in the master suite. Ch'en Ching-chi brought out the five hundred taels of silver and turned them over to Hsi-men Ch'ing to cover whatever expenses might be incurred in attempting to cope with the situation.

Hsi-men Ch'ing summoned his manager, Wu Tien-en, and gave him five taels of silver, along with instructions to go that very night to the office of the chief clerk in the district yamen and make a copy of whatever relevant documents had come down from the Eastern Capital. What did the texts in the government gazette actually say?

Memorial Submitted by Yü-wen Hsü-chung,[11] Supervising Secretary of the Office of Scrutiny for War, and Others

In Re: An Urgent Request for an Imperial Decision in Favor of Summary Execution for the Traitorous Ministers Who Abuse Their Power and Betray the National Interest, with a View toward Reinvigoration of Our Armed Forces and Elimination of the Barbarian Threat

Your servant has heard that the danger posed by the barbarians has existed since ancient times. In the Chou dynasty, the Hsien-yün; in the Han, the Hsiung-nu; in the T'ang, the T'u-chüeh; and in the Five Dynasties, the Ch'i-tan, all gradually became strong. And since our own Imperial Sung dynasty was established, the Great Liao has made incursions into the Central Plain for no little while. But I have never heard of a state being threatened by barbarians from without when it did not already harbor barbarians within.[12] As the proverb says:

When frost descends, the bell
of Feng-shan sounds;
When rain falls, the plinth under
the pillar sweats.[13]

That like breeds like is a necessary principle. The situation is analogous to that of a sick individual whose vital organs have long been ravaged by disease. When his natural vitality is sapped from within, he becomes susceptible to the penetration of malign influences from without. Once the entire body has become infected, not even Pien Ch'üeh of Lu[14] would be able to save him. How could he then long endure?

The present situation of the empire is just like that of an invalid in the final stages of debilitation. The ruler resembles his head; the chief ministers resemble his vital organs; and the lesser officials resemble his four limbs. If Your Majesty sits in state upon the throne above, and your officials fulfill their responsibilities below, the natural vitality of the body politic will be replenished within; its defenses will be strong without; and the menace of barbarian invasion will be eliminated.

At the present time, among those whose conduct has led to the menace of barbarian invasion, no one is more culpable than the grand academician of the Hall for the Veneration of Governance, Ts'ai Ching. His artful, specious, cunning, and dangerous nature, further abetted by the lack of integrity or shame, permits him to engage, indifferently, in slander and flattery. Above, he is incapable of supporting his sovereign in the exercise of his prerogatives, assisting in the primary tasks of ordering and transforming the realm. Below, he is incapable of promoting virtue or implementing policy, protecting and cherishing the common people. Solely devoted to fattening himself at public expense, he curries imperial favor in order to consolidate his position; engenders factions in order to conceal his traitorous designs; deceives his sovereign by keeping him in the dark; and underhandedly stigmatizes men of worth. The corps of loyal servants of the state has been dispersed;[15] the hearts of the citizens of the realm have turned cold; yet an unbroken stream of high officials, clad in crimson and purple, continues to congregate at his door.

Recently, as a result of the failure of his policy in the Ho-Huang region, the initiation of hostilities with the Liao, the cession of the three commandaries, the revolt of Kuo Yao-shih,[16] and the sudden proliferation of our losses, the Chin barbarians have broken their covenant and encroached upon the heartland of the empire. These egregious examples of betrayal of the national interest are all due to Ts'ai Ching's malfeasance.

Wang Fu is rapacious, mediocre, and unreliable; his conduct more befitting that of a buffoon. Having been dredged up by Ts'ai Ching, to whose recommendation he owes his post in the government, he was, before long, mistakenly entrusted with military power. He is ready to engage in appeasement in order to maintain his position, but is quite without any policy to advance. Recently, on the occasion of Chang Ta's annihilation at T'ai-yüan,[17] he was too panic-stricken to know what to do. And now that the barbarians are threatening the interior, he has fled south with his wife and children, concerned only for his personal safety.[18] The enormity of this betrayal of the national interest is such that execution is too good for him.

Yang Chien was originally nothing but a gilded and pampered youth who, by availing himself of inherited privilege, and thereby exploiting the favor shown to the dead, has succeeded in obtaining access to military power and unwarranted responsibility for external defense. He is but an arrant traitor, feigning loyalty,[19] whose pusillanimity knows no parallel.

These three officials have conspired to form a cabal that fosters corruption in both the capital and provinces and is like a noxious venom gnawing at Your Majesty's vitals. For years now, their conduct has invited catastrophes and induced anomalies, destroying the health and vitality of the body politic. The burdens of corvée and taxation are heavy and vexatious; the common people are dislocated and scattered; banditry is rife; the barbarians have ceased to be loyal; the resources of the empire are exhausted; and the moral bonds that hold society together have broken down. Though we were to pluck out the hairs of our heads, they would not suffice to enumerate the crimes of Ts'ai Ching and his coadjutors.[20]

If your servants, who but await punishment in the aforesaid office in the discharge of their responsibilities as censors, were to see these traitorous ministers betray the national interest without calling the fact to Your August Majesty's attention, they would fail in their obligations to ruler and father, above, and violate the principles to which they have devoted a lifetime of study, below. We, therefore, humbly request an imperial decision, whether it be to relinquish Ts'ai Ching and the other malefactors of his faction to the hands of the penal authorities, in order to display your clemency; to subject them to the extreme penalty, in order to demonstrate their conspicuous disgrace; or to sentence them to public exposure in the cangue, in accordance with precedent, and condemn them to military exile on the distant frontier,[21] where they may contend against monsters and demons.[22]

Should such measures be adopted, there would be reason to hope that the favor of Heaven might be restored[23] and the hearts of the people made glad. Should the law of the land be thus reaffirmed, the barbarian threat would dissolve of itself. The empire would then be fortunate indeed! Your subjects would then be fortunate indeed!

This memorial had elicited an imperial rescript that read as follows:

Let Ts'ai Ching remain in office, for the time being, in order to assist Us in Our government. Let Wang Fu and Yang Chien be remanded to the Three Judicial Offices, which will conduct a joint inquiry and report the result to Us.

Respectfully received and respectfully acted upon.

There followed a quotation from the report of the joint inquiry by the Three Judicial Offices, which read as follows:

Wang Fu, Yang Chien, and the other malefactors of their faction are found guilty of malfeasance in regard to their military commands. In permitting the barbarians to penetrate deeply beyond our frontiers and wreak havoc with our populace, they have sustained heavy losses of officers and men and abandoned control of our

> territories. For such crimes the penalty prescribed by law is execution. Among the henchmen, clerical subofficials, functionaries, relatives, and adherents who have abetted them in their iniquities are Tung Sheng, Lu Hu, Yang Sheng, P'ang Hsüan, Han Tsung-jen, Ch'en Hung, Huang Yü,[24] Hsi-men Ch'ing,[25] Liu Sheng, Chao Hung-tao, and others. For all of the above whose names have been ascertained, the recommended sentence is: public exposure in the cangue for one month, followed by military exile in frontier guard units.

If Hsi-men Ch'ing had not read these documents nothing might have happened, but having read them:

In his ears all he heard was a
sighing rush of air,
As his ethereal and material souls fled
he knew not where.

Truly:

The shock affected all six of his vital organs,
including liver and lungs;
The fright damaged the three bristles and seven
apertures of his heart.[26]

Hsi-men Ch'ing immediately turned his attention to the task of getting together a quantity of gold, silver, and valuable antiques, and seeing that they were properly packed.

He then summoned his servants, Lai-pao and Lai-wang, into his bedroom and gave them secret orders:

Thus and thus, and
So and so:

"Hire horses for yourselves and leave for the Eastern Capital this very night to find out what's happening. Make no effort to seek out the place where my relative by marriage, Ch'en Hung, is staying. If you get wind of any adverse repercussions, do your best to fix things up by any means you can think of, and hurry back to report to me."

Hsi-men Ch'ing had already provided the two men with twenty taels for their traveling expenses. Early in the fifth watch they hired drivers and set out on their way to the Eastern Capital. But no more of this.

Hsi-men Ch'ing was unable to get to sleep all night long. Early the next morning he directed Lai-chao and Pen the Fourth to put a stop to the construction work in the garden and send all the artisans of the various trades home for the time being. He gave orders that the main gate of his compound was to be kept tightly closed every day, that his servants were not to venture outside the premises except on specific business, and that if anyone were to knock they should not be admitted.

Hsi-men Ch'ing confined his activities to his own quarters, restlessly walking outside and then back in again from time to time.

Worry piled upon worry;
Depression augmented by depression;[27]

he was just like:

A millipede on a hot surface,[28]

and forgot his undertaking with Li P'ing-erh as effectively as though it had been:

Relegated to outer space, beyond the nine heavens.[29]

When Wu Yüeh-niang saw the way he kept to his room every day:

His brows contracted by melancholy;
His face exhibiting a worried hue;[30]

she said to him, "It's a matter that primarily concerns the family of our kinsman by marriage, Ch'en Hung. After all:

For every injustice there is a perpetrator;
For every debt there is a creditor;[31]

why should you be so upset over something that hardly concerns you?"

"You're only a woman; what would you know about such things?" said Hsi-men Ch'ing. "Ch'en Hung is our relative by marriage, and those two karmic encumbrances, my daughter and son-in-law, have moved into our house to live. This is an inescapable fact. The neighbors in the locality who have had reason to be annoyed with us in the past are extremely numerous. As the saying goes:

The loom may stay put, but the shuttle gets around.
When the sheep is beaten, the colt and donkey tremble.[32]

If there should be any troublemakers about to point the finger at us or:

Pull up the trees to investigate the roots,[33]

you and I would be hard put to protect ourselves."

Truly:

Though you sit in your house behind closed doors,
Catastrophe may yet strike you out of the blue.[34]

Hsi-men Ch'ing remained at home in a state of deep depression, but we will say no more about it.

To resume our story, Li P'ing-erh waited first one day and then another, but nothing happened. She sent Old Mother Feng to Hsi-men Ch'ing's place twice in succession, but the main gate was:

Locked tight as an iron bucket, so that
Not even Fan K'uai himself could get through.

She waited around half the day, but nobody came out, so there was no way for her to discover what was going on.

When the twenty-fourth finally arrived, Li P'ing-erh again sent Old Mother Feng to Hsi-men Ch'ing's place to deliver the jewelry she had had made for their betrothal and to ask him to come and have a word with her. Unable to get anyone to open the gate, she was waiting under the eaves of the house across the street when who should appear but Tai-an, who came out to water the horse.

On catching sight of her, Tai-an said, "Old Mother Feng, what are you doing here?"

"Mistress Hua sent me to deliver the jewelry," said Old Mother Feng. "Why is there so little sign of activity around here? She wants your master to come over and have a word with her."

"My master has been occupied with inconsequential affairs for some days," said Tai-an, "and hasn't had any free time. You'd better take the jewelry back with you for the time being. When I get done watering the horse I'll be sure to tell my master what you've said."

"My good fellow," said Old Mother Feng, "I'll wait right here if you'll just take the jewelry inside and speak to your master about it. Mistress Hua is annoyed enough with me as it is."

Tai-an was prevailed upon to tether the horse and go back inside. After some time he came out again and reported, "I've told my master what you said and he's agreed to accept the jewelry. He wants you to tell Mistress Hua to wait a few days longer until he's able to pay her a visit and speak to her in person."

Old Mother Feng went straight home and reported this message to her mistress, who had no alternative but to wait a few days longer.

Before she knew it, the fifth month came to an end and she found herself in the first decade of the sixth month.

> Pining by day and longing by night;
> Of news from her lover she has none.
> Beset by dreams, harried in spirit;
> Her day of consummation is delayed.

Truly:

> Too indolent to paint her moth eyebrows,
> Too abashed to retouch her powdered face;
> Her bosom swells with unexpressed resentment,
> Her jadelike spirit is utterly distraught.

The woman waited expectantly for Hsi-men Ch'ing, but he did not come. Every day:

> Her intake of tea and food diminished,
> Her spirits became ever more deranged.

At night:

> Sleeping alone upon her pillow,
> She tossed and turned obsessively.

Suddenly she heard a knocking at the gate and seemed to see Hsi-men Ch'ing coming in. The woman:

> Welcomed him at the door with a smile, and
> Led him into the room by the hand.

She asked him why he had failed to keep their tryst, and
Each of them expressed their innermost thoughts.
Inseparable and impassioned,
They devoted the night to pleasure.
Only when the cock crowed and the day dawned,
Did he extricate himself and return home.

The woman awoke with a start and gave a great cry, but:

Her soul had already escaped.

Old Mother Feng hurried into the room to see what was amiss.

"Hsi-men Ch'ing just left," the woman said. "Have you locked the gate after him yet?"

"Your longing has addled your wits," said Old Mother Feng. "How could the Honorable Gentleman have been here? I haven't seen so much as his shadow."

From this time on, the woman's:

Dreamscapes were haunted.

Night after night she was disturbed by fox spirits with:

Assumed names and appropriated identities,

who came to sap her vitality. Gradually her countenance grew wan and emaciated; she lost her appetite and took to her bed.

One day Old Mother Feng said to the woman, "I've asked that doctor, Chiang Chu-shan, who lives at the end of Main Street, to come and see you."

This man was still young, no more than thirty.

Petite in stature,
Precious in bearing;

he was as frivolous and untrustworthy a person as you could find.

Invited into the woman's bedroom, he found her with:

Misty locks and cloudy tresses,
Lying huddled in her bedclothes;

looking, for all the world, as though she were suffering from insurmountable grief.

After he had consumed the obligatory tea, a maidservant placed a cushion in the appropriate spot and Chiang Chu-shan approached the bed and proceeded to palpate the patient's pulse. The fact that the woman was good-looking was not lost upon him as he embarked upon his diagnosis.

"In attempting to ascertain the cause of your indisposition just now, I find that your hepatic pulse is thready, becoming full after passing the *ostium pollicare*[35] on the wrist; whereas your yin pulses are sluggish in their ascent from the *ostium pollicare* to the *linea piscis*[36] at the foot of the thenar eminence. This indicates a condition, engendered by the six desires and seven passions, in which:

Yin and yang contend with one another,
Producing alternate fevers and chills;

and is characterized by a feeling of internal melancholic congestion that cannot be dissipated.

It appears to be malaria but is not malaria,
It seems to be the ague but is not the ague.

By day you feel:

Enervated and sleepy,
Lacking all vitality;

and by night:

Your spirit will not keep to its abode,
But dallies with demons in your dreams.

If not treated in time, it may develop into a consumptive inflammation of the bones, which is nearly always fatal.[37] What a pity! What a pity!"

"If you will be good enough to prescribe an efficacious remedy," the woman said, "should I recover I will see that you are amply rewarded."

"I will, of course, do my best," said Chiang Chu-shan. "If you take my medicine I am sure you will be restored to perfect health."

When the consultation was over he got up to go. Li P'ing-erh gave Old Mother Feng five mace of silver and sent her after him to fetch the prescription.

That evening the woman took the medicine he had prescribed and was able to sleep undisturbed. Gradually her appetite improved and she began to comb her hair again and get up and about. In the space of a few days her spirits were back to normal.

One day, having prepared a feast and set aside three taels of silver, she sent Old Mother Feng to invite Chiang Chu-shan to come over so she could thank him for his pains.

Now, ever since Chiang Chu-shan had diagnosed Li P'ing-erh's illness he had been coveting her[38] for no little while. Thereupon he no sooner heard the invitation than he changed his clothes and presented himself. He was ushered into the reception room where the woman, resplendantly attired, came out to greet him. After the tea had been twice replenished, she invited him into her boudoir where:

Wine and viands were already laid out,
Amid the frangrance of orchid and musk.

The young maidservant, Hsiu-ch'un, stood in attendance, ready to present him with the three taels of silver on a platter decorated with gold tracery.

The woman:

Lifting high a jade goblet,

came forward and saluted him, saying, "The other day, when I was feeling so out of sorts, you were good enough to prescribe an efficacious remedy that provided immediate relief. Today I have prepared a meager cup of watery wine and invited you here to express my gratitude."

"That was only my professional responsibility," said Chiang Chu-shan, "something that principle required. What need is there to make so much of it?"

Then, seeing the three taels that were being offered in return for his services, he said, "How could I presume to accept such generous remuneration?"

"It is but a paltry expression of my gratitude, far less than propriety would demand," the woman said. "I sincerely hope that you will be good enough to accept it."

Only after repeated demurrals did Chiang Chu-shan consent to take it.

The woman presented him with the wine and they took their seats. After:

> Three rounds of drinks had been consumed,

Chiang Chu-shan stole a glace at the woman and saw that she was:

> Modeled in plaster, carved of jade;
> Astonishingly seductive and voluptuous.

Without further ado he determined to see if he could get a rise out of her.

"I hardly dare ask," he said, "how old you are, young lady?"

"I'm twenty-three," the woman responded.

"There's another thing I'm curious about." he said. "Why on earth should someone like you, still in the flower of youth, born and bred in respectable circumstances, with ample means to supply all your needs, have been suffering the other day from a melancholic congestion and feeling of insufficiency?"

When the woman heard this, she smiled, and said, "I will not deceive you, sir. Since my poor husband passed away my domestic circumstances have been desolate. I am all alone in the world and beset by worry and longing. How could I avoid falling ill?"

"How long has it been, in fact, since your husband died?" asked Chiang Chu-shan.

"My poor husband," the woman replied, "during the eleventh month of last year, came down with an acute intestinal fever and died. It must be nearly eight months ago by now."

"Who prescribed for him?" asked Chiang Chu-shan.

"Dr. Hu from Main Street," the woman replied.

"You don't mean that Hu the Quack who lives in Eunuch Director Liu's house on East Street, do you?" said Chiang Chu-shan. "He never attended the Imperial Academy of Medicine as I did. What does he know about the pulse? Why did you call upon someone like that?"

"It was only because my neighbors recommended him," the woman said, "that I engaged his services. But my poor husband was simply not fated to live. It had nothing to do with him."

"Do you have any boys or girls?" Chiang Chu-shan went on to ask.

"No," the woman replied.

"What a pity," said Chiang Chu-shan, "that in the youthful prime of life you should be living the lonely life of a widow, without any children to keep you company. Why don't you seek some means of improving your lot? If you resign yourself to such melancholy seclusion how can you help becoming ill?"

"Recently I have entered into an engagement to be married," the woman said. "I'll be crossing my husband's threshold sometime soon."

"May I ask who it is you plan to marry?" inquired Chiang Chu-shan.

"It's the Honorable Hsi-men Ch'ing, who owns the wholesale pharmaceutical business on the street in front of the district yamen," the woman replied.

When Chiang Chu-shan heard this, he said, "That's bad! That's bad! Why would you want to marry him? I've often been called on to perform medical services in his household and know all about it. He's nothing but an influence peddler in the district yamen, and a loan shark as well. His home is a veritable flesh market. Not counting the maidservants, he's already got five or six bedmates, of higher and lower status, about the place, whom he subjects to a regular caning if they get out of hand. Whenever one of them fails to please him in any way, however slight, he calls in a go-between and disposes of her without more ado. He's:

> The foreman of the wife-beaters,
> The leader of the lotharios.

"It's a good thing you told me about it. Otherwise, if you had entered his household, it would have been like:

> A moth darting into the flame.[39]

You would have been trapped, unable to escape in any direction, and it would have been too late to think better of it. Moreover, he has recently been implicated in an affair involving his kinsman by marriage and is holed up in his home, unable to come out. The construction work he has undertaken is only half-finished and has all been abandoned. Documents have been dispatched from the Eastern Capital ordering the prefectural and district authorities to arrest the implicated parties. It looks as though the buildings he was working on are likely to end up being confiscated by the government. Why on earth, for no good reason, would you want to marry someone like that?"

With this single speech he reduced the woman to tight-lipped silence. On top of everything else, there were all the valuables that she had stashed in Hsi-men Ch'ing's household.

She pondered this for some time and kicked herself, thinking, "No wonder when I invited him again and again he never showed up. It really was because he was embroiled in something at home."

She also noticed that Chiang Chu-shan's conversation was animated and his demeanor unassuming and respectful.

"If I could only manage to marry someone like that in the future," she thought to herself. "I wonder if he already has a wife or not."

"I am much indebted to you for your advice," she went on to say. "If any family of your acquaintance should have a suitable match to propose, I would have no reason to refuse it."

Chiang Chu-shan rose to the bait. "May I ask what sort of person you have in mind, so I can come tell you about it if I should hear of anyone that fits the bill?"

"It really wouldn't matter to me whether his social status were high or low," the woman said. "Someone just like you would be fine."

If Chiang Chu-shan had not heard these words nothing might have happened, but having heard them:

His joy was so great,
He lost his bearings.[40]

Thereupon, he got up from his seat, knelt down before her, and said, "I will not deceive you. I have lost my helpmate and no longer have anyone to look after me.[41] I have been living the life of a widower for some time and have no children. If you should be so considerate as to bestow your affections upon me and consent to a marriage alliance, it would fulfill the wish of a lifetime. Though I should have to:

Carry rings and knot grass,[42]
I will never dare to forget it."

The woman smiled and took him by the hand, saying, "Please get up. I don't even know how long you've been a widower, or how old you are. If you would like to marry me, you must engage a go-between to propose the match in order to fulfill the demands of propriety."

Chiang Chu-shan went down on his knees again and importuned her as follows: "I am twenty-eight years old and was born on the twenty-seventh day of the first month at six o'clock in the morning. Unfortunately, my poor wife died last year. I possess but meager resources and my origins are humble. Since you have been good enough to grant your gracious consent, what need is there for the intercession of a matchmaker?"[43]

When the woman heard these words she smiled, saying, "If you don't have any money, I have an old waiting woman here, named Feng, who can serve as go-between and witness. There's no need for you to present any betrothal gifts. All we need to do is pick an auspicious day and I will take you into my household as my husband. What do you think?"

Chiang Chu-shan hastily threw himself at her feet, with the words, "Young lady, you are like:

Another set of parents to me,
A reborn father and mother.[44]
This must have been fated in a prior existence,[45]
Such good fortune would suffice for three lives."[46]

Li P'ing-erh Takes Chiang Chu-shan as Mate

Then and there, in the room they were in, the two of them exchanged loving cups, and the marriage contract was concluded. Chiang Chu-shan continued to drink with her until evening before going home.

The woman discussed the situation with Old Mother Feng, saying, "Since Hsi-men Ch'ing's household is implicated in such an affair:

> The outcome is unpredictable.

Moreover, I'm so alone here that when I fell ill I was lucky to escape with my life. Under the present circumstances, I might just as well take this doctor as my husband and try to make a go of it with him; why not?"

The next day she sent Old Mother Feng to communicate with him. She had selected the eighteenth day of the sixth month as the most auspicious date for the occasion, and when the time came she brought Chiang Chu-shan across the threshold and they became man and wife.

After the "third-day celebrations" were over, the woman got together three hundred taels worth of capital and had a twelve-foot-wide segment of the frontage of her residence opened up to serve as a dispensary for Chiang Chu-shan. As a result:

> Everything was put on an entirely new footing.[47]

Originally, when he made calls on his patients, he had had to go on foot. But now he was able to buy a donkey to ride. He cut quite a figure as he came and went in the streets. But no more of this. Truly:

> Even a puddle of stagnant water,
> completely undisturbed,
> May yet find its surface ruffled
> by the spring breeze.[48]

> If you want to know the outcome of these events,
> Pray consult the story related in the following chapter.

Chapter 18

LAI-PAO TAKES CARE OF THINGS IN THE EASTERN CAPITAL; CH'EN CHING-CHI SUPERVISES THE WORK IN THE FLOWER GARDEN

It is deplorable, but man's heart is
  more venomous than a snake;[1]
Who is aware that the eye of Heaven rolls as
  relentlessly as a wheel?
The property once purloined from one's
  neighbor to the east;
Will someday revert to the
  family on the north.
Unrighteous riches are like snow
  sprinkled with scalding water;
Unearned property is like sand
  propelled by the tide.
If one takes craft and cunning to be
  the secret of success;
It will prove as evanescent as the
  morning and the evening clouds.[2]

AT THIS POINT the story divides into two. We will say no more, for the moment, about Chiang Chu-shan's marriage into Li P'ing-erh's household, but return to the story of Lai-pao and Lai-wang's trip to the Eastern Capital to fix things up on Hsi-men Ch'ing's behalf.

Every morning they took to the purple road;
Each evening they tramped the red dust.
When hungry they ate, when thirsty they drank;[3]
Proceeding by moonlight, enveloped in stars.[4]

One day, they arrived at the Eastern Capital, entered through the Myriad Years Gate, and sought out an inn at which to take lodgings for the night.

The next day, they set out to see what they could learn in the streets. By listening to the "wind-borne words"[5] of passersby, who:

Put their heads together to whisper,[6]
Gossiping in the streets and discoursing in the alleys,[7]

they ascertained that on the previous day the report of the joint inquiry with regard to the minister of war, Wang Fu, had elicited an imperial rescript confirming the sentence of execution after the Autumn Assizes. But because not all of the relatives and adherents of Commander Yang Chien had yet been apprehended, a final determination of his case was still pending, though further developments were expected to occur that very day.

Lai-pao and his companion, carrying their presents with them, lost no time in making their way to the gate of Ts'ai Ching's residence. Since they had come to the capital to take care of things twice before, they already knew their way around. Taking their stand beneath the commemorative arch on Dragon's Virtue Street, they waited to see what they could find out about the situation inside the mansion.

Before long, they saw a figure, clad in black, hurriedly coming out of the grand preceptor's residence and heading toward the east. Lai-pao recognized him to be the factotum, Yang Sheng, on the domestic staff of Commander Yang Chien.

He was on the verge of stopping him to ask how matters stood when he thought to himself, "The master didn't tell me to call on him." So he held his peace and let him go his way.

After waiting for some time, the two of them went up to the door of the mansion and saluted the gatekeeper with a deep bow, saying, "Might we ask, is His Honor, the grand preceptor, at home or not?"

"His Honor is not at home," the gatekeeper replied. "He has not yet returned from the deliberations at court. Why do you ask?"

"If you would be so kind," Lai-pao continued, "as to invite out the majordomo, Chai Ch'ien; I have something to report to him."

"The majordomo, Uncle Chai, is also not in," the functionary replied. "He went out together with His Honor."

"Wait a minute," Lai-pao thought to himself. "He's not being very forthcoming. He must be expecting to receive a little something for his pains."

Thereupon, he pulled a tael's worth of silver out of his sleeve and handed it to him.

The functionary took it and then asked, "Is it His Honor you want to see, or His Excellency, the academician? If it's His Honor you want, the person to go through is the principal majordomo, Chai Ch'ien. If it's His Excellency you want, the person to go through is the secondary majordomo, Kao An. Each of them has his own responsibilities. Moreover, His Honor has not yet returned from court; only His Excellency, the academician, is at home. If you have something to take up with him, I can invite out Majordomo Kao for you. Whatever your business may be, he can arrange an interview with His Excellency for you. It's all the same."

Lai-pao took advantage of the occasion by equivocating, "We are here on business from the household of Commander Yang."

When the functionary heard this, he dared not be remiss, but went straight into the mansion. After some time, Kao An appeared.

Lai-pao hastily made his obeisance and offered him ten taels of silver, saying, "I am a servitor of Commander Yang's who came to get the news from His Honor along with the factotum, Yang Sheng. Because I stopped on the way to get something to eat, I'm a bit late. It never occurred to me that he would come right ahead, so I was unable to catch up."

Kao An accepted the gratuity, saying, "Your factotum, Yang Sheng, left just a minute ago. His Honor is still detained at court. If you will wait a little bit, I'll see if I can arrange an interview for you with His Excellency."

So saying, he conducted Lai-pao past the great reception hall in the second courtyard, through an interior gate on one side, and up to a spacious eighteen-foot-wide structure that was situated with its back to the north and its front facing south. This building was adorned with a green-painted balustrade and displayed a vermilion plaque over the lintel that had been presented by the emperor himself. It was inscribed with four large gold characters in the imperial hand, set off against an intaglio ultramarine ground, that read "The Academician's Music Chamber."

It so happened that Ts'ai Ching's son, Ts'ai Yu,[8] was also a favorite of the emperor's. At the time in question he held concurrently the posts of academician of the Hall of Auspicious Harmony, minister of rites, and superintendent of the Temple of the Supreme Unity.

Lai-pao waited outside the door while Kao An went in to confer with his master. When he came out, he summoned Lai-pao to follow him inside and kneel in the middle of the hall. A beaded blind was suspended at the upper end of the room, behind which Ts'ai Yu was seated, wearing an informal gown and a soft cap.

"Where do you come from?" he asked.

"I am a servant of Commander Yang's kinsman, Ch'en Hung," Lai-pao replied. "I came in the company of the commander's factotum, Yang Sheng, in order to ask His Honor for news. Unexpectedly, he got a head start on me, and I have been unable to catch up with him."

Thereupon, he pulled a document out of his breast pocket and handed it up.

When Ts'ai Yu saw that the words "Five hundred piculs of white rice"[9] were written on it, he called Lai-pao to come up closer, and said to him, "His Honor, because of the allegations against him on the part of the censors, has for some days now avoided participation in the work of the Secretariat. Responsibility for such matters, including yesterday's report of the joint inquiry of the Three Judicial Offices, is in the hands of the minister of the right, Li Pang-yen.[10] It is said that, with regard to the accusations against Commander Yang, news leaked out of the palace yesterday that His Majesty is disposed to be magnanimous and will reserve the matter for special treatment. Those of his subordinates and employees whose names have been ascertained will be tried as soon as the investigation is completed. You would be well advised to go to Li Pang-yen's place to make your plea."

Lai-pao kowtowed repeatedly, saying, "I have no entrée to Minister Li's mansion. I hope that Your Excellency will deign to show me some consideration, for Commander Yang's sake."

"Go to the area just north of the Heavenly River Bridge," Ts'ai Yu responded, "and look for a great gateway standing at the top of a rise. Ask for the residence of the minister of the right, grand academician of the Hall for Aid in Governance, and concurrently minister of rites, Li Pang-yen. Everyone will know where it is. However, I might as well send someone from my staff to take you there."

There and then, he ordered an usher to fetch a sheet of stationery, affixed his seal to it, and sent the majordomo, Kao An, to escort him to Minister Li's place and argue, thus and so, on his behalf. Kao An took the document and accompanied Lai-pao out the gate of the mansion, where they picked up Lai-wang to carry the presents. After traversing Dragon's Virtue Street they headed straight for the gate of Li Pang-yen's mansion above the Heavenly River Bridge.

It so happened that Li Pang-yen had just returned home after the morning audience. He was at the door, dressed in a scarlet crepe robe, with a jade-ornamented girdle about his waist, in the act of seeing off a senior official, who got into his sedan chair and went his way. When he returned to the reception hall, the gatekeeper announced that His Excellency, the academician Ts'ai Yu, had sent his majordomo to see him. He first summoned Kao An into his presence and talked to him for a while before calling on Lai-pao and Lai-wang to come inside, where they knelt down below the dais at the upper end of the hall. Kao An stood to one side and passed up Ts'ai Yu's sealed letter and the list of presents. Lai-pao then proceeded to make a formal presentation of the gifts from below.

When Li Pang-yen saw them, he said, "In view of the fact that you are asking a favor on behalf of His Excellency, Ts'ai Yu, and that you also represent a kinsman of Commander Yang's, how could I ever accept these presents? Moreover, as far as Commander Yang is concerned, yesterday His Majesty's heart was moved to clemency, so his problems are already over. The only thing is that a number of his subordinates, because of the gravity of the charges brought by the censors, are sure to be tried and sentenced."

There and then, he ordered an attendant clerk to fetch the list of names that had been forwarded by the Office of Scrutiny the day before and show it to Lai-pao. It read as follows:

> Under the name of Wang Fu: clerical subofficial Tung Sheng; henchman Wang Lien; and foreman Huang Yü.
>
> Under the name of Yang Chien: miscreant clerical subofficial Lu Hu; factotum Yang Sheng; domestic clerks Han Tsung-jen and Chao Hung-tao; foreman Liu Sheng; relatives and adherents Ch'en Hung, Hsi-men Ch'ing, Hu the Fourth, etc.

All of the above-named persons:
Fall into the category of
mere falcons and hounds;[11]
Are of the same ilk as the
"fox who flaunted the tiger's might."[12]

By manipulating their superiors they have been able to take advantage of their power to do harm to others. In rapaciousness and cruelty they are without parallel, and the catalogue of their abuses has reached mountainous proportions. On their account the common people have been made to knit their brows and the marketplaces are in an uproar.

We humbly request that Your Majesty relinquish the members of this entire faction to the hands of the judicial authorities and either condemn them to military exile on the distant frontier, where they may contend against monsters and demons, or subject them to condign punishment, in order to reaffirm the law of the land. They ought not to be permitted to remain at large for even a single day.

When Lai-pao read this document, he was thrown into consternation and kowtowed repeatedly, pleading, "I am a retainer of Hsi-men Ch'ing's. I hope Your Honor will see fit to open wide your all-embracing heart and save my master's life."

Kao An also got down on his knees and made a plea on his behalf.

When Li Pang-yen saw that he was being offered five hundred taels of silver to deal with but a single name, he could hardly refuse to do the requested favor. There and then, he ordered his attendants to bring in his writing desk, took up his brush, and so altered the name on the document that, instead of reading Hsi-men Ch'ing, it read Chia Lien.[13] At the same time he indicated his acceptance of the presents and had them put away.

When Li Pang-yen had finished taking care of the matter, he wrote a note in reply to the academician Ts'ai Yu, and also rewarded Kao An, Lai-pao, and Lai-wang with a sealed packet containing fifty taels of silver. Once they were out in the street, Lai-pao and Lai-wang took their leave of the majordomo, Kao An, and went back to their inn, where they got their luggage together, paid the bill, and set out posthaste to return to Ch'ing-ho district.

As soon as they arrived home, they went to see Hsi-men Ch'ing and told him, from beginning to end, everything they had done in the Eastern Capital. When Hsi-men Ch'ing heard what they had to say it was:

Just as though he had been dunked in a
tub of ice water.

"It's a good thing I sent someone to take care of things," he said to Wu Yüeh-niang. "Otherwise, who knows what might have happened?"

Truly, on this occasion, Hsi-men Ch'ing's life was like:

Lai-pao Takes Care of Things in the Eastern Capital

The setting sun that has already sunk
behind the western hills;
When it is summoned forth once more
to scale the Fu-sang tree.[14]

Only then did he feel as though:

The stone on his head had finally fallen to the ground.

By the time two days had gone by, his gate was no longer closed, the construction work in his garden was resumed, and he began, gradually, to appear in public again.

One day, Tai-an was riding on horseback along Lion Street when he noticed that a large pharmaceutical shop had been opened in the front part of Li P'ing-erh's residence, with sizable stocks of raw and prepared pharmaceuticals visible within. There was a small red counter, a lacquered plaque over the door, and a shop sign hanging outside. Business appeared to be brisk.

When he got home, he told Hsi-men Ch'ing about it.

Not yet knowing that Chiang Chu-shan had married into Li P'ing-erh's household, Tai-an merely said, "Mistress Hua has acquired a manager somewhere and opened a pharmaceutical shop."

On hearing this, Hsi-men Ch'ing only half believed it.

One day, in the middle decade of the seventh month, when:

The autumn wind begins to sough, and
The jade dew grows more chilly,[15]

Hsi-men Ch'ing was riding his horse along the street when he ran into Ying Po-chüeh and Hsieh Hsi-ta.

The two of them called him to a halt and when he dismounted saluted him, saying, "Brother, where've you been keeping yourself all this while? We went by your place several times but saw that the gate was shut and didn't venture to intrude. We've been utterly at a loss for lo, these many days. Really, Brother, what have you been up to at home, anyway? Have you taken our new sister-in-law to wife? You haven't invited us yet to help celebrate the occasion."

"It was something I didn't feel like mentioning," said Hsi-men Ch'ing. "Because the Ch'en family, to whom I'm related by marriage, got into a sticky predicament, I had to busy myself with their affairs for a few days. The wedding has had to be postponed."

"We didn't know you had anything to worry about," said Ying Po-chüeh. "But now that we've run into you today, we're not about to let you get away scot-free. Come share three cups with us at Wu Yin-erh's place in the licensed quarter. It will help dispel your gloom."

So saying:

Without permitting any further explanation,

they dragged Hsi-men Ch'ing off into the licensed quarter, leaving Tai-an and P'ing-an to follow after them with the horse. Truly:

On the return trip one only grieves
  that the days are short;
When homesick one is prone to regret
  that the horse is slow.
Worldly wealth, painted faces, and wine
  in the sing-song houses;
Who is there who is not deluded
  by these three things?[16]

That day, Hsi-men Ch'ing allowed himself to be dragged off to Wu Yin-erh's place by the two of them, where they proceeded to drink the day away. Not until evening began to fall and he was half inebriated did they let him go.

Whipping up his horse, he was passing by the end of East Street on his way home when he ran into Old Mother Feng, who was coming from the south in a great hurry.

Hsi-men Ch'ing reined in his horse and asked, "Where are you going?"

"Mistress Hua sent me to attend the Ullambana[17] services at the temple outside the South Gate," replied Old Mother Feng. "She asked me to have a coffer of paper money burned on behalf of the deceased Hua Tzu-hsü. I have had to hurry in order to get back before the gates are closed."

"Is Mistress Hua at home and well?" asked Hsi-men Ch'ing, drunkenly. "I'll come have a word with her tomorrow."

"Why should you ask after her anymore, sir?" demanded Old Mother Feng. "You had a ready-made, fully cooked meal there for the asking, but you let someone snitch the pot away from under your very nose."

When Hsi-men Ch'ing heard these words, he was astonished.

"You don't mean to say she's married someone else?" he asked.

"Mistress Hua sent me over to your place to deliver the jewelry again and again," Old Mother Feng replied. "But I was never able to see you. Your gate was closed. I persuaded your servant to go inside and urge you to action, but you didn't pay any attention. Now someone else has taken her. What have you got to say about it?"

"Who is it?" demanded Hsi-men Ch'ing.

Old Mother Feng told him the whole story, from beginning to end. How, during the third watch in the middle of the night, the woman had been troubled by fox spirits and had fallen ill. How she gradually approached the brink of death. How she had engaged Dr. Chiang Chu-shan who lived on Main Street to come and see her. How she had taken his medicine and subsequently recovered. How, on such and such a day, she had brought him across the threshold and they had become man and wife. And how she had now produced three hundred taels worth of capital and set him up with a pharmaceutical shop of his own.

If Hsi-men Ch'ing had not heard about this nothing might have happened, but having heard about it, he was so angry he tried to stamp his feet though he was still on horseback.

"That's bad!" he called out. "If you'd married anyone else, it wouldn't bother me. But how could you bring yourself to marry a stunted little cuckold like that? What can he do for you?"

Thereupon he whipped up his horse and headed straight home. He had just dismounted and was going through the inner gate when he came upon Wu Yüeh-niang, Meng Yü-lou, P'an Chin-lien, and his daughter, Hsi-men Ta-chieh, in the courtyard outside the front reception hall, where they were amusing themselves by skipping rope[18] in the moonlight. As soon as they saw that Hsi-men Ch'ing had come home, Wu Yüeh-niang, Meng Yü-lou, and Hsi-men Ta-chieh withdrew to the rear of the compound. P'an Chin-lien, alone, remained behind, leaning against one of the pillars of the reception hall while she fiddled with her shoe.

"So you whores are bored enough to scream, are you!" Hsi-men Ch'ing shouted at her, drunkenly. "Don't you have anything better to do than jump rope?"

As he spoke, he went up to Chin-lien and kicked her twice. When he arrived in the rear of the compound, instead of going into Wu Yüeh-niang's room to change his clothes, he went back to an anteroom on the western side of the front courtyard that he was accustomed to use as a study, where he demanded his bedding and proposed to spend the night. All the while, he proceeded to:

Beat the maidservants, and
Abuse the page boys,

giving every indication of being in a foul mood.

His womenfolk huddled together in consternation, not knowing how to account for it. Wu Yüeh-niang was very critical of Chin-lien.

"You could tell he was drunk when he came in," she said. "All you had to do was take a few steps to get out of his way. Instead of which, you did everything you could to attract his attention, doubling up with laughter and fiddling with your shoe. As a result:

The locust and the grasshopper,
Are cursed in the same breath."[19]

"It's bad enough to abuse us," said Meng Yü-lou, "but how can he call our elder sister a whore? The unprincipled good-for-nothing!"

"It seems I'm the only one in the house fit to be taken advantage of," said Chin-lien, picking up where Yü-lou had left off. "The three of you were all there, just as I was, but I'm the only one who got kicked. It would appear that some people are more privileged than others."

This incensed Yüeh-niang, who said, "Then why didn't you get him to give me a kick too, just for starters? If you're not privileged around here, I'd like to know who is? You don't know your place, you lousy baggage, but at least I keep quiet about it; while you're always spouting off, yakkety-yak, with that mouth of yours!"

When Chin-lien saw that Yüeh-niang was angry, she tried to deflect the conversation in an effort to cover her tracks.

"Sister," she said, "that's not it at all. The fact is, whenever he gets upset anywhere, for whatever reason, he vents his spleen on me. He's always opening his eyes wide and threatening a thousand, if not ten thousand, times to beat me to a stinking pulp."

"Whoever told you to provoke him in the first place?" Yüeh-niang demanded.

> If he doesn't beat you,
> Should he beat the dog instead?"

"Elder Sister," said Yü-lou, "why don't you call in the page boy and ask him where he's been drinking today? Why should he have gone out in a perfectly good mood in the morning and come home in such a state?"

In no time at all, Tai-an was summoned into their presence and subjected to interrogation.

"You lousy jailbird!" Yüeh-niang railed at him. "If you don't tell the truth, I'll send for one of the older servants to hang you up and give you a real flogging. You and P'ing-an will both get ten strokes with the heavy bamboo."

"Don't beat me, mistress," said Tai-an. "I'll tell you the truth. Today the master, along with Uncle Ying the Second and company, had a drinking party in the Wu family establishment in the licensed quarter. They broke up early and, as he was passing the end of East Street on the way home, he ran into Old Mother Feng. She told him that Mistress Hua, having waited for him in vain, had married that Dr. Chiang Chu-shan who lives on Main Street. The master was as upset as could be all the way home."

"I can well believe it," said Yüeh-niang. "So that shameless perverted whore had such hot pants she couldn't wait to get married, did she? And now he comes home and vents his spleen on us."

"Mistress Hua didn't marry herself off to Dr. Chiang Chu-shan," said Tai-an. "She brought him across the threshold into her own household. And now she has put up the capital he needs to open a really prosperous big pharmaceutical shop. When I came home and told the master about it, he didn't, at first, believe it."

"If you stop to consider it," said Meng Yü-lou, "how long has her husband been dead, anyway? To marry someone like that, before her mourning period is even over, simply won't do at all."

"Nowadays," said Yüeh-niang, "who pays any attention to what will, or won't, do? It's not as though she were the only one with such hot pants she couldn't wait to get married until the mourning period for her husband was over. From whores like that, who spend all their time with their lovers:

Lolling in their cups, or
Snoozing in a stupor,[20]

what kind of marital fidelity can you expect?"

Gentle reader take note: This speech of Yüeh-niang's;

Hit two people with one swipe of the stick.[21]

Both Meng Yü-lou and P'an Chin-lien had remarried before their mourning periods were over. When they heard these words, all they could do was return to their quarters, feeling somewhat discomfited. But enough of this. Truly:

One may find things less than satisfactory
eight or nine times out of ten;
But it is seldom wise to tell anyone about
even two or three of them.[22]

To resume our story, that evening Hsi-men Ch'ing spent the night in the anteroom on the west side of the front courtyard.

The next day, he arranged to have his son-in-law, Ch'en Ching-chi, cooperate with Pen the Fourth in the task of supervising the construction work in the garden and handling the accounts, and he reassigned Lai-chao to responsibility for the main gate. His daughter, Hsi-men Ta-chieh, spent the daylight hours in the rear of the compound, joining in the amusements of Wu Yüeh-niang and the other womenfolk, and only in the evening returned to the rooms on the eastern side of the front courtyard to sleep. Ch'en Ching-chi, on the other hand, spent his days in the garden supervising the construction work and did not venture as far as the rear reception hall unless asked. His meals were brought out to him from the back of the compound by page boys. As a result, the female members of Hsi-men Ch'ing's household had not even had a chance to meet him.

One day, Hsi-men Ch'ing was away from home, attending a farewell party for Battalion Commander Ho Chin of the Provincial Surveillance Commission. Wu Yüeh-niang had been feeling concerned for some time that ever since Ch'en Ching-chi had moved in with them he had been working hard supervising the construction in the garden, and they had never even invited him for a meal to express their appreciation for his labors.

On this occasion, she said to Meng Yü-lou and Li Chiao-erh, "I've wanted to do something about it, but have been afraid my husband would criticize me for interfering; if I don't do anything, though, it just doesn't seem right to me. When someone else's child is visiting you and gets up early and goes to bed late every day, working as hard as he can, to accomplish some task on your behalf, is it right that no one should think of some way of thanking him for his efforts?"

"Sister," said Meng Yü-lou, "you're the mistress of the household. If you don't concern yourself about it, who else is going to do so?"

Wu Yüeh-niang thereupon sent orders to the kitchen to prepare a table of wine, delicacies, and savories, and at noon she invited Ch'en Ching-chi to come in and share a meal with them.

Ch'en Ching-chi dropped his work, told Pen the Fourth to take over, and went straight into the rear compound. When he had finished bowing and paying his respects to Yüeh-niang, he sat down to one side. Hsiao-yü provided him with tea and, after he had done drinking it, brought in a table for him and served up a selection of vegetable dishes and hors d'oeuvres.

"Son-in-law," said Yüeh-niang, "you've been working hard every day supervising the construction in the garden. I've wanted to invite you in for a visit, but haven't had the opportunity. Today your father-in-law is not at home and I'm not otherwise engaged, so I've prepared a cup of watery wine as a means of expressing our appreciation for your labors."

"Your son is much indebted to both of you for your kindness," said Ching-chi. "What labors have I performed that you should put yourself to so much trouble?"

Yüeh-niang offered him a drink and Ching-chi sat down again to one side. Before long, the full complement of delicacies arrived, and Yüeh-niang kept him company for a while as he drank.

"Go and invite our daughter to join us," she said to Hsiao-yü.

"Mistress Ch'en is busy right now," said Hsiao-yü. "She'll be here in a minute."

Before long, they heard the sound of dominoes[23] being played in the inner room.

"Who is it playing dominoes?" Ching-chi asked.

"Your wife is playing dominoes with my maidservant, Yü-hsiao," replied Yüeh-niang.

"You can see she has no sense of propriety," said Ching-chi. "When you call for her, she doesn't come, but stays in the room and goes on with her game."

Sometime later, Hsi-men Ta-chieh lifted aside the portiere and came into the parlor, where she sat down across from her husband to have a drink with him.

"Is our son-in-law any good at dominoes?" Yüeh-niang asked.

"He knows something of the rudiments," said Mistress Ch'en.

At that time, Wu Yüeh-niang thought of Ch'en Ching-chi only as a worthy son-in-law and did not realize that, in fact, he was a young scamp. When it came to poetry, lyrics, songs, or rhapsodies; backgammon and elephant chess; or the various word games played by breaking characters down into their component parts, there was:

Nothing he had not mastered,
Little he did not know.

There is a lyric to the tune "Moon on the West River" that testifies to this:

Artful and accomplished from his youth,
Romantic and dashing as can be;

He loves to wear duck green, spend
newly minted silver,
Or take a hand at backgammon
or elephant chess.

Master of the *p'i-p'a*, pipes, and woodwinds;
Adept at fowling, horse racing, and kick-ball;
There is only one chink in his armor:
When he sees a pretty face he's a goner.

"Since your husband knows his dominoes," said Yüeh-niang, "why don't we all go inside and play a few hands together?"

"You and my wife play, Mother," said Ching-chi. "Your son really oughtn't to presume."

"It's all in the family, Son-in-law," said Yüeh-niang. "What is there to worry about?"

So saying, she led the way into the inner room. There they found Meng Yü-lou sitting on the bed, over which a madder-red strip of felt had been placed, playing with the dominoes.

On seeing Ch'en Ching-chi come in, she got up to go, but Yüeh-niang said, "It's only our son-in-law, not an outsider. Just give him a bow in greeting."

Then, turning to Ch'en Ching-chi, she said, "This is your Third Lady."

Ching-chi promptly made her a bow and Yü-lou returned his salute.

Thereupon Yü-lou, Mistress Ch'en, and Yüeh-niang played a threesome together, while Ching-chi kibitzed on the sidelines. After they had played for a while, Mistress Ch'en lost and stepped down, allowing Ching-chi to take her place.

When play was resumed, Meng Yü-lou melded a double six, a one-six, and a double one to produce the combination known as "Heaven and Earth Separated."[24] Ch'en Ching-chi added a five-six and another double six to Yü-lou's double six to produce the combination known as "One Spot Short."[25] Wu Yüeh-niang put down a pair of double fours and a double three, attempting to make the combination known as "Eight that Don't Add Up,"[26] but could not play her double three on the double one.

Trying first this and then that,

she was unable to combine her dominoes with those on the board in order to make a scoring combination.

Just at that moment, P'an Chin-lien lifted aside the portiere and walked in. She was wearing a chignon enclosed in a fret of silver filigree into which she had inserted a fresh cactus flower.

Looking as captivating as ever, she laughed, saying, "I was wondering who it could be in here, and it turns out to be Master Ch'en."

When Ch'en Ching-chi swiveled his neck to see who had come in, she burst upon his sight to such effect that:

On Seeing P'an Chin-lien Ch'en Ching-chi Loses His Wits

His heart quivered, his eyes wavered, but
His soul had already escaped.

Truly:

Five hundred years ago these lovers were
fated to meet this day;
Thirty years of bliss may be the result of
just such an encounter.[27]

"This is your Fifth Lady," said Yüeh-niang. "Just give her a bow in greeting, Son-in-law."

Ching-chi promptly stepped forward to make her a deep bow, and Chin-lien returned his salute.

"Take a look at this, Sister Five," said Yüeh-niang. "The young fledgeling has got the old corbie beat."

Chin-lien stepped closer, leaning against the bedrail with one hand and flirting a white gauze circular fan with the other, as she advised Yüeh-niang, saying, "That's not the best way to play your dominoes, Elder Sister. If you put the double three over there instead, you'll have the combination "Heaven All Different,"[28] which will beat Master Ch'en and Sister Three."

Just as the group of them were in the midst of enjoying their domino game, who should come in, carrying his master's felt bag, but Tai-an, who said, "Father's come home."

Yüeh-niang hurriedly told Hsiao-yü to escort Master Ch'en out by the postern gate.

When Hsi-men Ch'ing had dismounted and come inside he went first to the front part of the compound to take a look at the construction work and then slipped into P'an Chin-lien's quarters.

Chin-lien made haste to receive him and helped him off with his outdoor things, saying, "You're home early from your farewell party today."

"Battalion Commander Ho Chin of the Provincial Surveillance Commission has just been promoted to the post of commander of Hsin-p'ing Stockade," said Hsi-men Ch'ing. "All his acquaintances from the entire guard battalion went out to the suburbs to see him off. Since he sent me an invitation, I could hardly decline to show up."

"You could use something to drink," said Chin-lien. "I'll tell the maidservant to bring you some wine."

Before long, a table was prepared for a drinking party and appropriate dishes were set before them. As they were drinking, Hsi-men Ch'ing brought up the fact that the ridgepole of the summerhouse in the garden would be put in place within a few days. A lot of friends and relatives would be invited, who would bring boxes of candied fruit, wine, and congratulatory red banners to commemorate the occasion; and they would have to hire caterers to supply a feast for their entertainment.

When they had talked for a while, it began to grow late. Ch'un-mei took a lamp and returned to her room, leaving the two of them to go to bed by themselves.

Because he had gotten up early to go to the farewell party, Hsi-men Ch'ing was tired. After only a few cups of wine he became drunk. No sooner did his head hit the pillow than he was:

> Snoring thunderously;
> Stertorously unwakable.

The weather was that of the third decade of the seventh month, so the nights were still rather hot. Under the circumstances, how could P'an Chin-lien be expected to get to sleep?

Suddenly, she became aware of the thunderous drone of mosquitoes inside the green gauze netting. Standing up, stark naked, she took a lighted candle in her hand and searched the interior of the net for mosquitoes, burning them one at a time as she found them.

Looking down, she saw Hsi-men Ch'ing, lying faceup on the pillow, fast asleep. She shook him but could not wake him up. The organ that lay between his loins was constricted by a clasp so that:

> It was tumid and long.[29]

Before she knew it, her:

> Lecherous desires were suddenly aroused.

Putting down the candlestick, she began to manipulate his organ with her slender fingers. After she had toyed with it for a while, she squatted down and began to suck it, moving it first this way and then that.

Hsi-men Ch'ing woke up and cursed at her, "You crazy little whore! Your daddy's asleep and you still want to plague him to death."

So saying, he got up and sat on the pillow, telling her to stay where she was and suck away. Meanwhile, he:

> Bent his head to observe the action,[30]
> In order to augment his pleasure.[31]

Truly:

> No wonder the beauty has become
> so extremely libidinous;
> Late at night she practices in secret
> on the purple phoenix flute.

There is a lyric composed of double meanings on the subject of the mosquito that testifies to this:

To the tune "Treading the Grass"

> I love its diminutive body,
> And its attenuated waist.
> With its throbbing sussuration
> it's forever buzzing about.
> At dusk, when people forget to close
> their red doors,

It surreptitiously sneaks inside
  the gauze netting.

Gently nuzzling the fragrant flesh,
Casually enamored of the jade body,
Whatever its mouth touches
  it stains with rouge.
In one's ears it produces
  a constant hubbub;
Late at night, refusing
  to let one sleep.

The woman continued to toy with him for about the time it would take to eat a meal when Hsi-men Ch'ing suddenly had an idea. He summoned Ch'un-mei to decant some wine and stand beside the bed with flagon in hand. Then he moved the candle onto the backboard of the bed and ordered the woman to turn around and get down on all fours in front of him. Inserting his organ into hers in order to:

Poke up the fire on the other side of the mountains,[32]

he told her to move back and forth as she liked while he proceeded to drink and enjoy himself from his superior vantage point.

"You insinuating ruffian!" the woman cursed at him. "Since when did you come up with this brand new way of doing things? How weird can you get? With the maidservant looking on to boot! What do you think you're up to?"

"I've told you before," said Hsi-men Ch'ing, "your sister P'ing-erh and I often used to do it like this. We'd get her maidservant, Ying-ch'un, to hold the flagon and pour the wine for us. It's amusing to do it this way."

"I'd only be wasting my breath on you!" said the woman. "My sister P'ing-erh! Sister my prick! What are you dragging that whore into it for? As far as I'm concerned:

Even the best intentions go quite unrequited.[33]

That whore had such hot pants she couldn't wait for you, but went off and married somebody else, didn't she?

"The other day, when you came home after you'd been drinking and found the three of us skipping rope in the courtyard together, you singled me out to vent your spleen on. I was the only one you chose to kick; and for that I was even given a hard time in certain quarters. It would seem that I'm the only one fit to be taken advantage of around here."

"Who gave you a hard time?" Hsi-men Ch'ing asked.

"After you came in the other day," the woman said, "the lady in the master suite got into quite an altercation with me. She accused me of talking back to her and called me a baggage who didn't know my place. The more I think about it, the more it seems that:

All you get for raising toads is dropsy.[34]

So now everyone's down on me."

"That's not it," said Hsi-men Ch'ing. "I'm not down on you. What happened the other day was that brother Ying the Second and that bunch dragged me off to Wu Yin-erh's place for a drink. On my way home I ran into Old Mother Feng in the street and she told me, thus and so, all about it. I was so angry I was stupefied. If she'd married anyone else, I could have taken it; but Dr. Chiang Chu-shan, that lousy stunted little cuckold! It's a wonder Hua the Elder hasn't bitten his balls off! What can he do for her that she should take him into her household and set him up with the capital to open a rival store and start doing business, as cool as you please, right under my nose?"

"It's a wonder you have the face to mention it," the woman said. "Didn't I tell you at the time that:

> The first one to cook the rice is the first to eat?[35]

But you didn't pay any attention to me and insisted on getting Elder Sister's permission. As the saying goes:

> To defer when you differ,
> Is to give up the dipper.[36]

It was your mistake. You've got no one to blame but yourself."

Hsi-men Ch'ing was so exasperated by these few words of the woman that:

> The fire that ignited in the core of his crater,
> Turned half the cloud-capped volcano into magma.

"Let her do as she likes," he said. "If that undutiful whore says another word about it, she'll find out soon enough how much attention she can expect to get from me."

Gentle reader take note: It has always been true that malicious words and deceitful conduct are not unknown even between rulers and ministers, fathers and sons, husbands and wives, and elder and younger brothers; to say nothing of friends. If even so worthy and chaste a wife as Wu Yüeh-niang, who enjoyed the status of principal consort, could become abruptly alienated from her husband merely because Hsi-men Ch'ing chose to listen to the mischievous pillow talk of P'an Chin-lien, how much the more should one be on one's guard in matters of more moment.

From this time on, relations between Hsi-men Ch'ing and Wu Yüeh-niang were so embittered that they refused to speak to each other when they met. Yüeh-niang let him spend the night with whomever he liked and made no attempt to interfere. No matter whether he arrived late or departed early, she paid no attention. Even when he came into their rooms to get something she would tell the maidservant to deal with it and pay him no heed. Thus the two of them let their feelings for each other grow cold. Truly:

> Though the preceding carriages have overturned
> by the thousands;
> The carriages that follow continue to overturn
> in the same way.

No matter how clearly one may point out
  the safest route;
One's honest words are misconstrued
  as ill-meant advice.

To resume our story, from the time that relations between Hsi-men Ch'ing and Wu Yüeh-niang became embittered, P'an Chin-lien saw that her husband had succumbed to her wiles and believed that she had gained her objective. Every day she plucked up her spirits and:

Tricked herself out conspicuously,
To curry favor and court affection.

As a result of her meeting with Ch'en Ching-chi in the rear compound that day, she had noticed that the young scamp was:

Artful and accomplished,

and got it into her head to see if she could seduce him; but she was too afraid of Hsi-men Ch'ing to dare try anything. Whenever her husband was out of the house, however, she would send her maidservant to invite him into her room for a cup of tea, and they often spent their time playing board games together.

One day, the ridgepole of Hsi-men Ch'ing's newly constructed summer-house was ready to be put in place, and relatives and friends came to commemorate the occasion by hanging up congratulatory red banners. Many of them also brought boxes of candied fruit. The artisans of the various trades were all presented with gifts in reward for their services. The male guests were entertained in the main reception room, and it was sometime in the afternoon before the party broke up. Hsi-men Ch'ing waited to see that everything was properly put away and then went back to the rear compound to get some sleep.

Ch'en Ching-chi came into Chin-lien's room and asked for some tea.

Chin-lien, who was sitting on the bed fiddling with her *p'i-p'a*, said, "You mean to tell me they've been celebrating up front for half the day, ever since the ridgepole was put in place, and you haven't had anything to drink, but have to come into my room looking for tea?"

"Your son would not deceive you, ma'am," said Ching-chi, "but since I got up in the middle of the night I've been busy these ten hours or more and haven't had anything to eat or drink."

"Where's your father-in-law?" the woman asked.

"He's gone to the rear compound to get some sleep," Ching-chi replied.

"Well, if you really haven't had anything," the woman said, turning to Ch'un-mei, "Get some of those stuffed steamed-shortcake pastries out of my cabinet and give them to Master Ch'en to eat."

Thereupon, four saucers of savory appetizers were dished up on Chin-lien's bed table for the delectation of the young scamp.

As he ate, he noticed that the woman was strumming her *p'i-p'a* and asked her, playfully, "Fifth Lady, what tune is that you're playing? Why don't you sing me a song?"

"My good Master Ch'en," the woman laughed, "I'm not the one you're after. Why should I sing you a song? Just wait till your father-in-law gets up and see if I don't tell him what you've been doing."

Ching-chi promptly fell to his knees with an ingratiating giggle and pled with her, "I beseech you, Fifth Lady, take pity on me. Your son will not dare do it again."

At this, the woman couldn't help laughing.

From that time on, the young scamp and the woman:

Became more intimate by the day.[37]
Drinking tea and eating meals;
Traversing rooms and entering chambers;[38]
Engaging in badinage and repartee;
Rubbing shoulders and nudging elbows;[39]
They carried on without restraint.

Wu Yüeh-niang, taking him to be no more than a boy, allowed her disingenuous son-in-law the run of the house. By so doing she showed herself to be blind to her own shortcomings. Truly:

Knowing only how to rifle flowers
in order to elaborate honey;
The bee knows not for whom it labors
to provide something sweet.[40]

It is deplorable, but Hsi-men Ch'ing's vigilance
leaves much to be desired;
This fact encourages his peach and plum blossoms
to smile in the spring breeze.
Under his layers of embroidered quilts
there sleeps a rogue;
With three meals of delicacies a day
he nurtures a tiger.
Enamored of her person, his son-in-law
covets his concubine;
Attracted by his wealth, he is prepared
to do his father-in-law in.
And there is yet another privilege
of which he can boast;
Traversing rooms and entering chambers
he can dally as he likes.[41]

If you want to know the outcome of these events,
Pray consult the story related in the following chapter.

Chapter 19

SNAKE-IN-THE-GRASS SHAKES DOWN CHIANG CHU-SHAN; LI P'ING-ERH'S FEELINGS TOUCH HSI-MEN CH'ING

When flowers bloom they do not disdain
  the plots of the poor;
The moon shines on mountains and rivers
  so that all are bright.
In this world the heart of man alone
  remains vile;
In all things demanding that Heaven
  show him favor.
The foolish, the deaf, and the dumb
  everywhere prosper;
While the clever and the intelligent
  suffer in poverty.
The year, month, day, and hour of birth
  determine it all;
However calculated, events are controlled
  by fate rather than man.[1]

THE STORY GOES that Hsi-men Ch'ing had been constructing a formal garden and summerhouse in his residential compound for nearly half a year before the final decorating, painting, and varnishing were completed. From front to back:

Everything was put on an entirely new footing.

The housewarming celebrations lasted for several days. But no more of this.

One day, during the first decade of the eighth month, Hsi-men Ch'ing was invited to help celebrate the birthday of Judicial Commissioner Hsia Yen-ling at his newly purchased country estate. He had engaged the services of four singing girls, a band of musicians, and a troupe of tumblers and acrobats to entertain his guests. At ten o'clock in the morning, Hsi-men

Ch'ing, having dressed himself to befit the occasion, set off on horseback, accompanied by four page boys.

Wu Yüeh-niang, during her husband's absence, prepared a feast of wine and delicacies and invited Li Chiao-erh, Meng Yü-lou, Sun Hsüeh-o, Mistress Ch'en, and P'an Chin-lien to join her. They opened the gate of the new garden and proceeded to enjoy it at their leisure. When they surveyed the scene within:

Flowers and trees, pavilions and terraces,
Stretched before them as far as the eye could see.[2]

Truly, it was a fine garden. Behold:

At the main entrance, fifteen feet high,
There stands a red-lacquered memorial arch;
All the way round, in twenty segments,
There stretches a crenellated wall of crushed limestone.
At the portal there is a gate tower;
Terraces and kiosks spread in all directions.
There are artificial hills and genuine waters;[3]
Blue-green bamboos and glaucous pine trees.
The structures that are high but not pointed
are called terraces;
Whereas those that are lofty but not forbidding
are called kiosks.

If one wishes to enjoy the four seasons, there are places for each of them:

In spring there is Swallow-flight Hall,
Where cypress and cedar vie in verdancy.
In summer there is Brookside Lodge,
Where lotus and water lily display their colors.
In autumn there is Halcyon House,
Where the golden chrysanthemum braves the frost.
In winter there is Hidden Spring Grotto,
Where the white plum blossom gathers snow.

Just see how:

Capricious blossoms immure the narrow paths;
Lissome willows brush the carved balustrades.
Tossed in the breeze, willow fronds
raise their mothlike eyebrows;
Laden with raindrops, flowering crab apples
display their delicate features.
Before Swallow-flight Hall,
The daffodils seem about to open but haven't opened;
Behind Hidden Spring Grotto,
The holly is in half bloom but not yet full bloom.

The pale plum blossoms east of the Lowland Bridge
  bloom and fade;
The redbuds above the Cloud Repose Pavilion
  are not yet in flower.
By the ornamental rocks,
The elecampane has just blossomed;
Beside the painted railings,
The dianthus has just appeared.
With a flutter of wings the purple swallows
  penetrate the curtains;
In a burst of song the yellow orioles
  traverse the shadows.

And there are also:

Moon windows and snowy grottoes;

Not to mention:

Waterside retreats and breezy pavilions.
The banksia rose arbor,
Runs into the rose-leaved raspberry trellis;
The peach tree with its thousand leaves,
Confronts the willow of the three springs.

And there are also:

Lilacs,
Mimosa,
Caragana,
Yellow roses,
Jasmine,
And narcissus.

In front and behind the summerhouse there are:

Juniper hedges and bamboo-lined walks,
Serpentine streams and square pools.
Plantains and palm trees shade the steps;
Helianthus and pomegranate catch the sun.
Amid the waterweeds frolicking fish
  startle the beholder;
Among the flowers powdered butterflies
  dance in pairs.

Truly:

The peonies have hardly begun to reveal
  their bodhisattvas' faces;
Before the litchis are ready to put forth
  their mārarājas' heads.[4]

Thereupon, Wu Yüeh-niang led the other womenfolk into the garden.

Some hold hands as they wander
  along the flowery paths;
Others, seated on the fragrant grass,
  compare botanical specimens.
One, approaching the balustrade to survey the scene,
Playfully picks red lovers' beans
  to toss at the goldfish;
Another, leaning on the railing to enjoy the flowers,
Gigglingly flirts her silken fan
  to startle the butterflies.

Wu Yüeh-niang made her way to the highest point in the garden, the Cloud Repose Pavilion, where she proceeded to play a board game with Meng Yü-lou and Li Chiao-erh. P'an Chin-lien, along with Mistress Ch'en, and Sun Hsüeh-o, ascended the Flower-viewing Tower, from which they could see extending before them:

The tree peony grove,
The garden peony bed,
The crab apple bower,
The seven sisters trellis,
And the banksia rose arbor;

Not to mention:

That "cold-enduring gentleman," the bamboo,[5]
And that "snow-despising grandee," the pine.[6]

Truly:

All four seasons produce their
  never-fading flowers;
All eight festivals appear one
  everlasting spring.[7]
Such a vision is not exhaustible;
Such a view exceeds comprehension.[8]

Before long, the wine was served. Wu Yüeh-niang took the seat of honor, with Li Chiao-erh sitting across from her. To either side of them, Meng Yü-lou, Sun Hsüeh-o, P'an Chin-lien, and Mistress Ch'en sat down in order of precedence.

"I forgot to invite Master Ch'en," said Yüeh-niang. Turning to Hsiao-yü, she said, "Quickly! Run up front and ask our son-in-law to join us."

It was not long before Ch'en Ching-chi presented himself:

His head adorned with an ultramarine silk cap,
His body clad in an informal gown of purple satin,
His feet shod in white-soled black boots.

After making his bow of greeting, he sat down next to his wife, Mistress Ch'en.

After they had been drinking for a while:

With the raising of glasses and passing of cups,

Wu Yüeh-niang went back to playing board games with Li Chiao-erh and Mistress Ch'en, while Sun Hsüeh-o and Meng Yü-lou climbed the Flower-viewing Tower to enjoy the view.

Chin-lien wandered off by herself, beside the flower beds in front of the artificial hill, where she amused herself by batting at the butterflies[9] with her round white-silk fan. Unexpectedly, Ch'en Ching-chi, who had crept up behind her to see what she was up to, addressed her, saying, "Fifth Lady, you don't know how to go about batting a butterfly. Let me show you how it's done. These butterflies dart up one second and down the next, as if they can't make up their minds. They certainly are elusive creatures."

Chin-lien swiveled her powdered neck and gave him a sidelong glance. "You lousy short-life!" she berated him. "If anyone should overhear you, you'd be done for; though I suppose you're too far gone to care."

With a giggle, Ch'en Ching-chi pounced up to her, embraced her, and gave her a kiss. The woman responded by giving him a shove with her free hand that knocked the young scamp head over heels.

Though neither of them realized it, this scene had been observed from a distance by Meng Yü-lou, atop the Flower-viewing Tower, who now called out, "Sister Five, come over here. I've got something to tell you." Only then did Chin-lien abandon Ching-chi and go off to climb the tower.

Thus it happened that neither of the two butterflies were caught that day.

Though they may have made a swallows' tryst
or orioles' assignation;[10]
The bee's antennae had no more than grazed
the corolla of the flower.[11]

Truly:

Though distracted bees and wanton butterflies[12]
are sometimes to be seen;
Once they fly into the pear blossoms
they disappear from view.[13]

On seeing that the woman was gone, Ch'en Ching-chi returned to his room without a word. Finding himself beset by melancholy, he improvised a song to the tune "Plucking the Cassia" in order to dispel his depression.

I saw her rakishly sporting a spray of blossoms;
Smiling as she toyed with her spray of blossoms.
On her ruby lips she wore no rouge;
But looked as though she did wear rouge.
When we met the other day,
And then met again today;
She seemed to have feelings for me,

But displayed no feelings for me.
Though she wished to consent;
She never gave her consent.
It looked as though she refused me;
But she really never did refuse me.
When can we make another assignation;
When will we ever see each other again?
If we don't meet,
She may long for me;
When we do meet,
I still long for her.[14]

We will say no more, for the moment, about Wu Yüeh-niang and the others as they feasted in the garden, but return to the story of Hsi-men Ch'ing's visit to Judicial Commissioner Hsia Yen-ling's country estate outside the South Gate.

On his way home, after the party was over, he happened to pass through the Southern Entertainment Quarter.[15]

Now in days gone by, Hsi-men Ch'ing had been a habitué of the:

Three quarters and two alleys,

of the pleasure precincts, so all the "knockabouts" there were known to him. The people called "knockabouts" at that time, during the Sung dynasty, corresponded to what are vulgarly referred to today as "bare sticks." Among these were two men, named Snake-in-the-grass, Lu Hua, and Street-skulking Rat, Chang Sheng, who had often been patronized by Hsi-men Ch'ing, and belonged to the:

Chicken-pinching and dognapping ilk.

Hsi-men Ch'ing caught sight of the two of them that day as they were engaged in a gambling game and pulled up his horse in order to have a word with them. The two men immediately came up and greeted him by falling to one knee, asking, "Sir, where are you headed at such an hour?"

"Today is the birthday of His Honor, Hsia Yen-ling, of the Judicial Commissioner's Office," said Hsi-men Ch'ing. "He invited some of us to his country estate outside the South Gate to help celebrate the occasion. There is a favor I'd like to ask of you. Will you agree to do it or not?"

"Needless to say, sir," the two replied, "we are mindful of everything you've done for us in the past. If you now have a task for us to perform:

Though we should have to go through fire and water,
We would not decline to suffer ten thousand deaths."[16]

"If that's the way you feel about it," said Hsi-men Ch'ing, "come to my house tomorrow and I'll give you your instructions."

"Why wait till tomorrow?" the two demanded. "Tell us about it now. Really, what's up?"

Hsi-men Ch'ing then:

> Whispered into their ears in a low voice,

and related the whole story of how Chiang Chu-shan had deprived him of Li P'ing-erh. "All I want you two fellows to do is to help me vent my spleen," he concluded.

Still on horseback, Hsi-men Ch'ing hitched up his clothes and groped for his wallet, which turned out to contain four or five taels worth of loose silver. Pouring it all out and handing it to the two men, he said, "Take this and buy yourselves some wine to drink. If you manage to pull this affair off successfully for me, I'll reward the two of you further."

Lu Hua refused to accept the money, saying, "It's not as though you haven't already done us any favors in the past, sir. I thought you might want to send us:

> Down to the floor of that great sea, the Eastern Ocean,
> To wrest the horn from the Green Dragon's head;
> Or up to the very summit of Mount Hua, the Western Peak,
> To wrench the tusk from the White Tiger's jaws;

in which case, we might not be able to comply. But if it's only such a piddling task as this, where's the difficulty? This silver I absolutely refuse to accept."

"If you won't take it," said Hsi-men Ch'ing, "I won't trouble you any further." Whereupon, he told Tai-an to repossess the silver, whipped up his horse, and started on his way.

Chang Sheng, however, stopped him, saying, "Lu Hua, you don't understand His Honor's disposition. If you don't take what you're offered, it will seem as though we're trying to get out of it."

Lu Hua then accepted the silver and kowtowed on his hands and knees, saying, "Just go home and relax, sir. In two days or less, you can absolutely rely on us to give you something to laugh about."

"As for me," said Chang Sheng, "if you could only manage, in the future, to wangle some sort of position for me with His Honor Hsia on the staff of the Judicial Commissioner's Office, that would be quite sufficient."

"Is that all?" said Hsi-men Ch'ing. "That goes without saying."

Gentle reader take note: Afterward, Hsi-men Ch'ing did recommend Chang Sheng to Hsia Yen-ling, who got him a job on the domestic staff of Chou Hsiu, the commandant of the Regional Military Command. But this is a subsequent event; having mentioned it, we will say no more about it.

These two "knockabouts" took their newly acquired silver and went back to gambling as before. By the time Hsi-men Ch'ing had ridden into the city through the South Gate and arrived home, the sun was already setting in the west.

When Wu Yüeh-niang and the others heard that he had come home they all went back to the rear compound. Only P'an Chin-lien remained in the summerhouse to see that everything was properly put away. Hsi-men Ch'ing did not go back to the rear compound but came straight into the garden. When he saw the woman supervising the clearing up in the pavilion, he asked, "What have you all been up to here during my absence?"

"Today," Chin-lien said with a smile, "Elder Sister and the rest of us decided to open up the gate and have a look at the garden for ourselves. How could we have known you would get home so early?"

"Hsia Yen-ling really put himself out today," said Hsi-men Ch'ing. "It was at his country estate. He had engaged four singing girls and four acrobats to entertain us, and there were only five guests there. Because I was worried about the distance, I left early."

The woman helped him off with his outdoor things and then said, "You could use something to drink. I'll tell the maidservant to bring you some wine."

"You can take the rest of the dishes away," Hsi-men Ch'ing instructed Ch'un-mei. "Just leave a few saucers of delicacies and decant a flagon of grape wine for me."

Sitting down in the place of honor, he noticed that the woman was wearing a blouse of aloeswood-colored moiré with variegated crepe edging, which opened down the middle, over a drawnwork skirt of white glazed damask. Shoes of scarlet iridescent silk, with white soles, satin high heels, and gold-spangled toes were visible beneath her skirt. On her head she wore a chignon, enclosed in a fret of silver filigree, in front of which there was a tiara of jade, enchased with gold, representing the scene "plucking the cassia in the moon palace." Her hair was further adorned with plum-blossom shaped ornaments with kingfisher feather inlays, and a host of trinkets were stuck about the temples, which had the effect of further enhancing:

The fragrant redness of her ruby lips, and
The glossy whiteness of her powdered face.

Before he knew it, Hsi-men Ch'ing's:

Lecherous desires were suddenly aroused.

Taking her two hands in his, he embraced her and gave her a kiss. Shortly thereafter, Ch'un-mei brought in the wine and the two of them passed the same cup back and forth between them. As they drank they sucked each other's tongues so assiduously that the sound of the sucking was quite audible. The woman then hitched up her skirt and sat in his lap. Once there, she took a sip of wine and then proceeded to transfer it into the mouth of her companion like a bird feeding its young, after which she picked up a fresh lotus pod from the table with her slender fingers and fed it to him.

"That's not very appetizing," protested Hsi-men Ch'ing. "Why feed me that?"

"My son," the woman said, "don't push your luck. You'd do better not to refuse anything from your mother's hand."

Thereupon, she put a fresh walnut kernel in her mouth and passed it to him before desisting.

Hsi-men Ch'ing wanted to play with the woman's breasts, so she unfastened the gold chatelaine with its three pendant charms that she wore at her collar and held it between her teeth while she pulled open her silk blouse, revealing:

> The beautiful unblemished jade, of
> Her fragrant and creamy bosom;
> Her tight and squeezy breasts.

Hsi-men Ch'ing fondled and caressed them for some time, sucking at the teats like a young calf. The two of them laughed and joked together as they:

> Enjoyed to the full the pleasures of connubial bliss.

In the midst of his euphoria, Hsi-men Ch'ing said to the woman, "I've got something to tell you that will give you something to laugh about in a day or two. You may have heard that Dr. Chiang Chu-shan has opened a pharmaceutical shop right under my nose. Well, one of these days, you can rely upon it, he's going to look as though he's opened a fruiterer's shop on his own face."

"Why's that?" the woman asked.

Hsi-men Ch'ing told her the whole story of how he had run into Lu Hua and Chang Sheng outside the South Gate that day.

"What a depraved creature you are," the woman laughed. "There's no telling how much evil karma you will have accumulated before you're through."

She then went on to ask, "Isn't that Dr. Chiang the same Dr. Chiang whom we often call in to perform medical services here? He always looks circumspect and polite enough to me. He lowers his gaze whenever he sees anyone. The poor fellow! You really oughtn't to give him such a hard time."

"He's got you fooled," said Hsi-men Ch'ing. "You say he lowers his gaze when he sees you. That's only the better to ogle your feet."

"You delirious oily mouth!" the woman exclaimed. "He actually ogles the feet of other people's wives!"

"You don't know the half of it," said Hsi-men Ch'ing. "Someone nearby called on him once while he was on his way home carrying a fish from the market. When he was intercepted, he said, 'Let me take the fish home first, and come after that.' His interlocutor said, 'I've got someone seriously ill at home. Please, doctor! Come right away.' This Chiang Chu-shan then followed him home. The sick person was on the second floor so he was invited upstairs. It turned out to be a woman who was ill, and a good-looking one at that. When he came into the room, she stuck her hand out so he could palpate her pulse. The rascal had her wrist in his hand when he suddenly thought of his fish, which had been left hanging on a curtain hook downstairs, and forgot himself, asking, 'You don't have a pussy down there do you?' When her husband, who was standing there in the same room, heard this, he strode over, grabbed him by the hair, and beat him to a stinking pulp. He not only lost his fee, but had his clothes torn to tatters by the time he made his escape."

"A likely story!" the woman said. "I don't believe a cultivated man like that would do any such thing."

"If you go by appearances," said Hsi-men Ch'ing, "you'll miss the boat. As far as he's concerned:

Outside he may be the picture of propriety;
But inside he harbors cunning and villainy."

When the two of them had talked and laughed with each other for a while, they stopped drinking wine, finished putting the things away, and went back to Chin-lien's room to spend the night. But no more of this. Let us put this strand of our narrative aside for a moment.

To resume our story, two months or so had now passed since Li P'ing-erh brought Chiang Chu-shan across her threshold in wedlock. Initially, out of his desire to please her, Chiang Chu-shan had concocted various aphrodisiacs. He had even bought some "Yunnanese ticklers,"[17] "ladies' delights,"[18] and the like in front of the city gate, in the hope of arousing her passion. What he failed to realize, however, was that the woman had already experienced every kind of:

Violent storm and sudden downpour,[19]

at the hands of Hsi-men Ch'ing, so that his inexperienced efforts often left her unsatisfied. Little by little she began to despise him, until the day finally came when she smashed the sexual implements to smithereens with a stone and threw them all away.

"You're just like a shrimp or an eel," she railed at him, "with no real strength in your loins. What's the point of your buying all this junk to titillate your old lady with? I thought I was getting a real hunk of meat, but it turns out you're:

Good enough to look at, but not fit to eat.[20]

You're about as much use as a 'pewter spearhead'[21] or a 'dead turtle'!"

Li P'ing-erh cursed her husband till he looked as though:

His head had been sprayed with dog's blood,

and drove him out to sleep in the shop up front, though it was the third watch in the middle of the night.

From then on, she could think of no one but Hsi-men Ch'ing, and she refused to let her husband into her bedroom. Every day she nagged him about the accounts and tried to monitor the expenditure of her capital.

One day, feeling that he had had a bellyful, Chiang Chu-shan had gone into the shop and was sitting there behind the narrow counter when who should appear but two men, staggering and stupefied with drink, who made their way in and sat down on a bench.

"Have you got any 'dog-yellow' in this shop of yours?" one of them demanded.

"You're pulling my leg," laughed Chiang Chu-shan. "I've only got 'ox-yellow.'[22] Who ever heard of 'dog-yellow'?"

"Well, if you haven't any 'dog-yellow,' " his interlocutor continued, "I suppose 'ice-ashes' will do. Let me see some. I'll buy a few ounces from you."

"Pharmaceutical houses only carry 'ice-crystals,' "[23] said Chiang Chu-shan, "the best quality of which comes from Borneo in the South Seas. Who ever heard of 'ice-ashes'?"

"It's no use asking him," the other one said. "He's only been open a few days and could hardly be expected to carry pharmaceuticals like these. We'd do better to go to the Honorable Hsi-men Ch'ing's shop."

"Come over here," the first one said. "We'd better get down to serious business. Brother Chiang, there's no use pretending you're:

Still asleep in dreamland.

The principal and interest on those thirty taels of silver you borrowed from Brother Lu here three years ago when your wife died are mounting up. We've come to collect from you today. If we'd simply demanded payment as soon as we entered the door, seeing as how you've managed to marry money and open a brand new shop, we were afraid it might reflect on your reputation.[24] So we thought we'd do you a good deed by starting out with a few words of nonsense, so you could see the need to take your medicine. If you refuse to take your medicine, you'll have to repay him the silver just the same."

When Chiang Chu-shan heard these words he was stupefied with amazement. "But I never borrowed any silver from him," he stated.

"If you didn't borrow the money," said his interlocutor, "why should we be dunning you for it? It has always been true that:

Flies don't cluster on eggs
  unless they're cracked.[25]

You'd better not stick to that line."

"I don't even have the honor to know the names of you gentlemen," said Chiang Chu-shan.

"I've never met you before.[26]

On what grounds can you simply appear and demand money of me?"

"Brother Chiang," his interlocutor stated, "you are mistaken. It has always been true that:

Those who achieve office are seldom poor, and
Those who repudiate debts are seldom rich.

Remember those days before you made a place for yourself when you had to peddle your nostrums with bell in hand like any mountebank. It was Brother Lu here who came to your aid then and made it possible for you to arrive at your present state."

"My surname is Lu and my given name is Hua," the other one asserted. "In such and such a year you borrowed thirty taels of silver from me to pay for your wife's funeral expenses. Including principal and interest, you owe me forty-eight taels by now. You'll have to repay me whether you like it or not."

"Since when did I ever borrow any money from you?" Chiang Chu-shan demanded in consternation. "And even if I did, there would have been a contract and a guarantor."

"I was the guarantor," stated Chang Sheng. Whereupon, reaching into his sleeve, he pulled out a contract and waved it in his face.

Chiang Chu-shan was so angry his face had turned as sallow as wax. "You gallows bird!" he cursed. "You servile cur! You think you can play the 'knockabout,' coming in here from out of nowhere and intimidating me, do you?"

When Lu Hua heard these words he reacted with outrage. From the other side of the narrow counter he sent a clenched fist whistling across that flew right into Chiang Chu-shan's face, knocking his nose to one side. At the same time he started pulling the pharmaceuticals off the shelves and hurling them into the street.

"You lousy 'knockabout'!" cursed Chiang Chu-shan. "How dare you despoil my merchandise?"

All he could do was call for T'ien-fu to come to his aid, but Lu Hua kicked him into a corner with one swing of his foot and he was too frightened to make a further move.

Chang Sheng pulled Chiang Chu-shan out from behind the narrow counter and made a show of staying Lu Hua's hand, saying, "Brother Lu, you've already waited long enough as it is. Give him another couple of days to come up with the cash, and make an end of it. What do you say, Brother Chiang?"

"I never borrowed his money in the first place," said Chiang Chu-shan. "But even if I had, you could have raised the issue more politely. What's the idea of all this rough stuff?"

"Brother Chiang," said Chang Sheng, I can see that:

> You've swallowed the flesh of a bitter olive,
>   but the pleasing aftertaste is coming out;[27]
> You've only endured a slap with a flour sack,
>   but you've done a complete about-face.[28]

If you had only changed your tune a little earlier, I might have asked Brother Lu to forgive you some of the interest. As it is, even if you have to do it in two or three installments, the only thing to do is pay it off. It won't get you anywhere to talk tough and refuse to acknowledge it. After all, you can hardly expect him to simply forget it."

When Chiang Chu-shan heard these words, he said, "I can't take any more of this! I'll go to court with him. Who ever saw the color of his money?"

"Have you been hitting the bottle again this morning?" Chang Sheng responded.

Without any warning, Lu Hua struck Chiang Chu-shan another blow with his fist, knocking him flat on his back and nearly precipitating him headfirst into an open drain. His hairdo came undone, and his cap and headband were covered with filth.

"In broad daylight too!"[29] Chiang Chu-shan started screaming at the top of his voice. This attracted the attention of the head of the local mutual security unit, who proceeded, without more ado, to truss him up with a length of rope.

When Li P'ing-erh, inside the house, heard the sound of this altercation and came to peek out through the front door blind, she was just in time to see the local constable leading her husband away in bonds and was so angry she was stupefied. She sent Old Mother Feng out to take down the plaque over the door and the shop sign. The better part of the pharmaceuticals that had been thrown into the street had been appropriated by passersby. There was nothing to do but close up shop and return inside to sit it out.

It was not long before someone reported these events to Hsi-men Ch'ing, who immediately dispatched a message to the local constable telling him to hale the suspect before the Judicial Commissioner's Court first thing the following morning. At the same time he sent a personal note about the case to Commissioner Hsia Yen-ling.

Next morning, the prisoner was brought into the courtroom. When Judicial Commissioner Hsia had taken his position on the bench, he read the deposition of the arresting officer and summoned Chiang Chu-shan before him.

"I see that your formal name is Chiang Wen-hui," he said. "Why did you borrow money from Lu Hua and then not only refuse to repay it, but abuse him into the bargain. Such conduct is reprehensible."

"I don't even know this person," said Chiang Chu-shan, "nor have I ever borrowed money from him. I was in the process of trying to reason with him, but he wouldn't pay any attention, and started kicking and beating me. He even despoiled me of my merchandise."

Commissioner Hsia then called Lu Hua before him and asked for his side of the story.

"He originally borrowed the money from me to pay for his wife's funeral expenses," said Lu Hua. "Since then, it's been three years by now that he's postponed paying me back. The other day I heard that he had married into someone's family and had gone into business for himself in a big way. But when I asked him to settle up, he started to hurl every kind of abuse at me, even claiming that I was despoiling his merchandise. I've got the contract for the original loan right here. This Chang Sheng was the guarantor. I hope Your Honor will look into the matter."

Snake-in-the-grass Shakes Down Chiang Chu-shan

As he spoke, Lu Hua reached into his breast pocket and pulled out a contract, which he handed up to the bench. When Commissioner Hsia opened it, he found that it read as follows:

> The contracting party, Chiang Wen-hui, a physician of this district, finding himself without sufficient funds to defray the funeral expenses of his deceased wife, has arranged, through the good offices of the guarantor, Chang Sheng, to borrow the sum of thirty taels of silver from one Lu Hua at a rate of 3 percent interest, compounded monthly, for his personal use, and undertakes to repay the principal and interest by a year from this date. If he should default, his personal effects to the equivalent value are offered as collateral. Lest questions should arise in the future, this written contract is set down as evidence of the above transaction.[30]

When Commissioner Hsia finished perusing this document, he struck the table in high dudgeon, saying, "It's outrageous! In the face of the guarantor and the contract, how can he continue to deny his liability? I can see this rascal is given to:

Hairsplitting and logic-chopping.[31]

He has the look of a reneger about him." So saying, he called out to his minions, "Take him down and give him a good flogging with the heavy bamboo!"

Thereupon:

Without permitting any further explanation,

three or four lictors turned Chiang Chu-shan over on the ground and gave him thirty hard strokes with the heavy bamboo. They beat him so severely that:

The skin was broken, the flesh was split, and
Fresh blood flowed down his legs.

Two runners were then dispatched to escort Chiang Chu-shan to his place of residence, and a bench warrant was issued authorizing the requisition of thirty taels of silver with which to make restitution to Lu Hua; failing which, the prisoner was to be remanded to the yamen for further detention.

Chiang Chu-shan's legs had been beaten so severely that he was barely able to waddle. When he made his way home, weeping and wailing, and pled with Li P'ing-erh to give him the money to pay off Lu Hua, she spat in his face and cursed him, saying, "You shameless cuckold! Whose money do you think you're giving away? You've got a nerve demanding money of me. If I'd known that:

Even if you lost your head, you'd leave
a stump of debts behind,[32]

I'd never have been blind enough to marry you. You turtle! You're:

Good enough to look at, but not fit to eat."

When the two runners and the plaintiffs, who were waiting outside, heard the woman berating her husband, they kept up their unremitting pressure, calling out, "Chiang Wen-hui, if you can't raise the money, there's no point in delaying any further. Let's go back and report to the yamen."

Chiang Chu-shan had to come out to placate the runners and then go back inside to continue pleading with his wife. Getting down on his knees, so his torso looked as though it were sticking straight out of the ground like a post,[33] and weeping and wailing as he spoke, he said, "Just look upon it as a good deed, like a pilgrimage to:

> The mountains of the four directions or
> the five sacred peaks;[34]
> Almsgiving, or providing vegetarian
> meals for monks.

If you don't give me these thirty taels of silver, and I have to go back to court, how will my lacerated buttocks ever take another flogging? It will be the death of me, that's all."

The woman had no alternative but to dole out thirty taels of "snowflake" silver to her husband. Chiang Chu-shan, in due course, turned this over to Lu Hua in the presence of the magistrate, who tore up the contract and thus brought the matter to a conclusion.

Lu Hua and Chang Sheng took the thirty taels of silver they had thus obtained and paid a visit to Hsi-men Ch'ing to report on the success of their venture. Hsi-men Ch'ing invited them into the summerhouse and entertained them with wine and food while they regaled him with their exploits. He was absolutely delighted and said, "You two have enabled me to vent my spleen, which was all I wanted."

Lu Hua offered to turn over the thirty taels of silver to Hsi-men Ch'ing, but he refused to accept it, saying, "You two take it and buy yourselves a jug of wine. You can regard it as an expression of my thanks. I may have further favors to ask of you in the future."

The two of them thanked him again and again as they got up to go and then set off with the silver in hand to resume their gambling. Truly:

> He was ever prepared to enjoy the pleasure of,
> "abusing the innocent and good";
> As a makeshift substitute for the delight of,
> "addiction to clouds and rain."[35]

To resume our story, when Chiang Chu-shan went home after handing over the silver in the judicial commissioner's courtroom, his wife refused to let him stay there.

"Just who do you think you are?" she demanded. "You might as well regard the whole episode as a fit of delirium on my part, and those thirty taels of silver as the fee for your treatment. The sooner you move out of here the better. If I let you stay any longer, I'm likely to discover that even the value of this house of mine will not suffice to pay off your debts."

Chiang Chu-shan realized that they had come to a parting of the ways and hobbled off on his painfully wounded legs, weeping and wailing, to look for a place to stay. He had to leave behind all the stock that had been purchased with his wife's money. She pressed him to remove the medical supplies, mortar and pestle, pharmacological sieve, and other impedimenta that he had brought with him, and the two of them severed their relationship forthwith. At their final parting, as he was on his way out the door, the woman even sent Old Mother Feng to dip up a pewter basin full of water and throw it after him, saying:

"At last my enemy has been removed from my sight."

From the day that she got rid of Chiang Chu-shan, the woman could think of no one but Hsi-men Ch'ing. She heard, moreover, that the difficulties he had been in had come to nothing, and she much regretted what she had done. Every day found her:

Too languid to consume tea or food,
Too lazy to paint her moth eyebrows;
Leaning against one doorjamb after another,
Wearing out her eyes with constant gazing;

longing in vain for someone to come. Truly:

His pillow words remain,
But now his love is dead;
In her room he is not seen,
In silence her soul melts.[36]

We will say no more for the moment about how Li P'ing-erh longed for Hsi-men Ch'ing, but relate instead how, one day, Tai-an happened to pass by her house on horseback and noticed that the front door was shut tight, the pharmaceutical shop was no longer open for business, and everything looked as quiet as could be. When he arrived home he reported this to Hsi-men Ch'ing, who said, "I imagine the beating he got was more than that stunted little cuckold could take. He's probably confined to his room while he recuperates. It'll be half a month, at best, before he can come out and resume business." He saw no need to take any further action in the matter.

One day, it was Wu Yüeh-niang's birthday, on the fifteenth day of the eighth month, and a lot of female guests were being entertained in the main reception hall. Because Hsi-men Ch'ing and Yüeh-niang were no longer on speaking terms, he took himself off to the licensed quarter to pay a visit to Li Kuei-chieh's establishment. Once there, he said to Tai-an, "Take the horse home right away, and come back to fetch me this evening."

Later on, he sent someone to invite Ying Po-chüeh and Hsieh Hsi-ta to join him for a game of backgammon. Li Kuei-ch'ing was also at home that day, and the two sisters kept their guests company and plied them with wine. After a while, they all went into the courtyard together and amused themselves by playing at "pitch-pot."[37]

As the sun was setting in the west, Tai-an came back with the horse to fetch his master. Hsi-men Ch'ing was in the toilet at the rear of the establishment, engaged in the act of defecation. When he caught sight of Tai-an, he asked, "Is everything all right at home?"

"Everything's all right at home," replied Tai-an. "The guests in the main reception hall have already left and the things have all been put away. The First Lady has asked her eldest brother's wife and Aunt Yang to come back to her own room and visit for a while.

"Mistress Hua from Lion Street sent Old Mother Feng over today to deliver some birthday presents to the First Lady, including four trays of preserved fruit, two trays of sweetmeats in the shape of birthday peaches, birthday noodles, a bolt of material, and even a pair of shoes she had made for her with her own hands. The First Lady gave Old Mother Feng a mace of silver and explained that you weren't at home, but didn't bother to invite her over."

Hsi-men Ch'ing noticed that Tai-an's face was red and asked him, "Where've you been drinking?"

"Just now," said Tai-an, "Mistress Hua sent Old Mother Feng to invite me over and offered me some wine. I told her I didn't drink, but she put so much pressure on me I ended up taking two cups after all. That's why my face is red.

"Mistress Hua has now come to regret what she did. She cried like anything when she saw me. When I told you what had happened the other day, you hardly believed me. It seems that the very day Chiang Chu-shan was released from the Judicial Commissioner's Court, she sent him packing. She's really very sorry for what she did, and still has her heart set on marrying you.

"She's a lot thinner than she used to be. She begged me to ask you to go see her, no matter what, and get you to decide what you're going to do. If you indicate your assent, she wants me to go right back and let her know about it."

"That lousy worthless whore!" said Hsi-men Ch'ing. "If she's already found a husband for herself, that ought to be that. What does she want to continue bothering me for?

"Well, if that's the way things stand, I haven't the time to go see her. Tell her to forget about the ritual presentations of tea and betrothal gifts. Let her pick a good day and I'll have the whore carried across my threshold, and be done with it."

"I understand," said Tai-an. "She's waiting at her place for me to go back and give her the word. I'll get P'ing-an and Hua-t'ung to come wait on you here."

"Go ahead," said Hsi-men Ch'ing. "I understand."

Tai-an went out through the gate of the licensed quarter and straight to Li P'ing-erh's house, where he told her what had happened. The woman's heart was filled with delight.

"Good Little Brother," she said, "I'm very much indebted to you today for settling this matter with your master for me."

Thereupon, Li P'ing-erh took the trouble to:

> Wash her hands and trim her nails,

before going into the kitchen and personally preparing some dishes, so she could regale Tai-an with food and wine.

"I'm shorthanded here," she said. "I hope you can come over tomorrow, no matter what, to help T'ien-fu supervise the movers in carrying my stuff over to your place."

She hired five or six porters, with their carrying poles, and it took them four or five days to get everything moved. Hsi-men Ch'ing didn't even bother to tell Wu Yüeh-niang what was happening, but simply had her effects piled on the upper floor of the newly erected Flower-viewing Tower.

On the afternoon of the twentieth day of the eighth month, Hsi-men Ch'ing dispatched a large sedan chair, a length of red satin, and four lanterns, together with an escort consisting of Tai-an, P'ing-an, Hua-t'ung, and Lai-hsing, to have the woman carried across his threshold. Li P'ing-erh sent Old Mother Feng to take her two maidservants to their new home ahead of time and waited for her return before getting into the sedan chair and setting off herself. She turned her own house over to Old Mother Feng and T'ien-fu to look after.

Hsi-men Ch'ing did not go out anywhere that day, but sat in the new summerhouse, wearing an informal gown and everyday hat, awaiting the woman's arrival. When her sedan chair was set down in front of his gate, a long time elapsed before anyone came out to receive her.

Meng Yü-lou went to the master suite and said to Yüeh-niang, "Sister, you are the mistress of the household. Right now she's already at the gate. If you don't go out to receive her, how can you help annoying our husband? He's just sitting in the summerhouse, and the sedan chair has already been at the gate for an age, without anyone going out to meet it. Under the circumstances, how can she be expected to come in?"

Wu Yüeh-niang was in a quandary. On the one hand, she could go out to receive her, but she was still angry about it and didn't want to give in. On the other hand, if she refused to go out, she was afraid of Hsi-men Ch'ing's violent temper. Finally, after pondering the matter for a while, she:

> Lightly moved her lotus feet,
> Gently lifted her beige skirt,

and went out to receive her.

Li P'ing-erh, holding the ritual "precious vase"[38] in her arms, was conducted directly to the new dwelling that had been constructed for her. Her two maidservants, Ying-ch'un and Hsiu-ch'un, had already had time to put everything in proper order, so she had nothing to do but await the arrival of Hsi-men Ch'ing that evening.

How could she have anticipated that Hsi-men Ch'ing was still so angry with her that he refused to enter her chamber?

The next day she had to come out and make a formal visit to Wu Yüeh-niang's quarters in the rear compound, where she paid her respects to the other female members of the household and was designated, in order of precedence, as the Sixth Lady. As was customary, a large feast was held on the third day, to which many female guests and relatives were invited. But her husband had yet to appear in her chamber.

The evening of her arrival he had gone to P'an Chin-lien's quarters to spend the night.

"She's your bride, after all," said Chin-lien, "and this is her first day in your home. How can you leave her in the lurch at such a time?"

"You don't know her," said Hsi-men Ch'ing. "That whore has a little too much fire in her eyes for my taste. I'll give her the cold shoulder for a couple of days and then go in to her in my own good time."

On the third day, after the guests had departed, Hsi-men Ch'ing still refused to set foot in her chamber, but went, instead, to Meng Yü-lou's quarters in the rear compound to sleep. In the middle of the night, when Li P'ing-erh saw that her husband had avoided coming into her room for the third night in a row, she sent her two maidservants off to sleep, abandoned herself to her tears, and then, alas, stood up on her bed, threw her foot bindings over the rafter, and hanged herself. Truly:

The enamored branches having failed to intertwine
  beneath the mandarin duck curtain;
Her resentful soul is the first to find its way
  to the realm of the Nine Springs.[39]

The two maidservants, who had dozed off, awoke to find the lamp guttering out and were getting up to trim the wick when they suddenly saw their mistress suspended over the bed. Frightened into a state of panic, they ran next door to call Ch'un-mei, saying, "Our mistress has hanged herself."

P'an Chin-lien hurriedly got up and came over to see for herself. She found the woman, dressed completely in scarlet, hanging down, stiff and straight, over the bed. She and Ch'un-mei promptly cut the foot bindings by which she was suspended and laid her down. Only after they had administered artificial respiration for some time did she spit up a mouthful of colorless saliva and regain consciousness.

"Run back to the rear compound and ask your master to come here," Chin-lien said to Ch'un-mei.

Hsi-men Ch'ing was in Meng Yü-lou's room, drinking wine, not having gone to bed yet. Before this happened, Meng Yü-lou had been remonstrating with him, saying, "How can you bring her into your household and then not darken her doorstep for three days in a row without arousing ill feelings? It makes it look as though we give this one thing priority over everything else, and insist upon our rights of seniority, begrudging her even one night of your company."

"Let her wait a full three days, then I'll go," said Hsi-men Ch'ing. "You don't know her. That whore's got a tendency to:

> Wolf down the rice in her bowl,
> While keeping one eye on the pot.[40]

If you think about it, she has nothing to reproach me for. From the time her husband died, right up to the present, we've been on the closest of terms. What promises didn't she make to me? And then, at the last minute, she up and married that Dr. Chiang Chu-shan. As though I were no match for that scoundrel! So now, what's she running after me for?"

"You have every right to be upset," said Yü-lou. "But she also was imposed upon."

As they were talking, they heard the sound of knocking at the inner gate. Yü-lou sent Lan-hsiang to see who it was, and she reported that Ch'un-mei had come to fetch her master because the Sixth Lady had hanged herself in her room.

Meng Yü-lou lost no time in urging Hsi-men Ch'ing on his way, saying, "I told you you ought to go look in on her, but you paid no attention. It's not surprising something like this has happened."

Thereupon, with lighted lanterns, they set out for the front compound to see for themselves. When Wu Yüeh-niang and Li Chiao-erh heard what had happened, they also got up and went to her room. They found Chin-lien holding Li P'ing-erh up in a sitting position and asked, "Sister Five, have you given her any ginger extract yet?"

"When I first got her down, I gave her some," Chin-lien replied.

Li P'ing-erh choked for some time before she was able to cry audibly. Only then did Yüeh-niang and the others feel as though:

> The stone on their heads had finally
> fallen to the ground,

so they could tuck her back in bed and return to their own rooms to get some rest.

It was not until noon or thereabouts the next day that Li P'ing-erh was able to get down some congee and broth. Truly:

> Her body was like the moon at the fifth watch
> as it is swallowed by the hills;
> Her life was like a lamp at the third watch
> as it begins to run out of oil.[41]

"Don't you believe that whore," said Hsi-men Ch'ing to Li Chiao-erh and the others, "she's only putting on that suicide act to scare us. I'm not going to let her get away with it. Wait and see. This evening I'm going to go into her room and get her to stage another hanging for my benefit before I believe her. And if she balks at the idea, I'll give her a good taste of the riding crop. That lousy whore! Who does she take me for, anyway?"

When his womenfolk heard these words, they all broke into a sweat on Li P'ing-erh's behalf.

That evening, sure enough, they saw Hsi-men Ch'ing conceal a riding crop in his sleeve and head for her room. Meng Yü-lou and P'an Chin-lien ordered Ch'un-mei to lock the door and not let anyone in, while they took up positions by the postern gate that led into Li P'ing-erh's courtyard and eavesdropped to see what was happening inside.

To resume our story, when Hsi-men Ch'ing saw that the woman was lying facedown on her bed, crying, and that she made no move to get up when she saw him come in, he was more than a little annoyed. The first thing he did was to chase her two maidservants into an empty room and tell them to stay there. Then he sat down on a chair, pointed his finger at the woman, and reviled her, saying, "Whore! If you were really sorry for what you did, what need was there to come to my house to hang yourself. You should have stuck it out with that stunted little cuckold of yours. Who asked you to come here? I haven't done you any harm, so what are you pissing those tears out of your cunt for? I've never seen anyone hang themselves before. Today you can put on a command performance for my benefit."

Thereupon, he pulled out a length of cord and threw it in her face, ordering the woman to hang herself. Li P'ing-erh remembered what Chiang Chu-shan had told her, that Hsi-men Ch'ing was:

> The foreman of the wife-beaters,
> The leader of the lotharios.

"What did I ever do in a previous incarnation to deserve such a fate?" she thought to herself. "Today, with my eyes wide open, I've plunged right into the fiery pit all over again."

The more upset she became the harder she cried.

This made Hsi-men Ch'ing even angrier. "Get down off that bed," he ordered. "Take off your clothes and get down on your knees."

The woman was dilatory about taking off her clothes, until Hsi-men Ch'ing turned her over on the surface of the bed, pulled the riding crop out of his sleeve, and gave her a few strokes with the whip. Only then did she take off all her clothes, above and below, and, trembling with fright, kneel down before him on the surface of the bed.

Hsi-men Ch'ing sat down again and proceeded to subject the woman to a thorough interrogation, from beginning to end, saying, "I told you, clearly enough, to wait a little while, because I was tied up by something at home. So why did you ignore my request and rush into a marriage with that scoundrel, Dr. Chiang Chu-shan? If you'd married anyone else, it wouldn't have bothered me. But that stunted little cuckold! What could he do for you? You brought him across your threshold and then supplied the capital to set him up in business, opening a shop right under my nose, in order to take away my livelihood."

"I've already told you," the woman said, "how much I regret what I did, but it's too late to do anything about that now. It was only because you left me and didn't come back that I began to go crazy with longing. The garden of that distaff relative of the imperial family named Ch'iao, which abuts on the rear of my compound, is haunted by fox spirits. At the third watch in the middle of the night they constantly:

> Assumed names and appropriated identities,

appearing to me in your guise in order to sap my vitality, and departing only when the day dawned and the cock crowed. If you don't believe me, just ask Old Feng or the two maidservants. They'll corroborate my story.

"As time passed, my vitality was so sapped that I gradually approached the brink of death and would certainly have perished before long. It was only then that Dr. Chiang Chu-shan was engaged to see me and, like a fool, I:

> Fell right into the paste pot,[42]

and allowed the scoundrel to take advantage of me. He said that you were implicated in some affair and had gone off to the Eastern Capital. It was only for lack of an alternative that I went down the road I did.

"How could I have known he was the sort of scoundrel who:

> Even if he lost his head, would leave
> a stump of debts behind?

Before I knew it, his creditors were banging on the gate and he was:

> Haled before the judge and exposed in the courtroom.[43]

There was nothing I could do but:

> Swallow my anger and keep my own counsel.

It cost me several taels of silver to do it, but I sent him packing without delay."

"I hear you tried to get him to make out a complaint against me," said Hsi-men Ch'ing, "over all those things of yours I have in storage. If so, what are you doing in my house today?"

"Why you! It ought to go without saying," the woman said. "If I ever did any such thing, may my body rot completely away!"

"Even if you had," said Hsi-men Ch'ing, "it wouldn't scare me. They say that:

> If you have the means, you can change husbands at will.

But I'm not about to let you get away with that sort of thing. I might as well tell you the truth. Those two guys who beat up the doctor:

Thus and thus, and
So and so,

were acting on my instructions. I had only to:

Put in motion one of my schemes,

in order to fix that scoundrel so he had:

No place to run.

All I would have to do is:

Resort to one of my devices,

in order to put you, too, in a position to be:

Haled before the judge."

"I know it was all a trick of yours," the woman said, "but take pity on me. If I'm left all by myself in some deserted place, it will be the death of me, that's all."

As she spoke, Hsi-men Ch'ing's wrath was gradually assuaged.

"Whore!" he demanded. "Come over here. Let me ask you. How do I stack up compared to that scoundrel, Dr. Chiang Chu-shan?"

"How can he be compared to you?" the woman said.

"You're the sky;
He's a shard of brick.
You're higher than the Thirty-third Heaven;
He's lower than the Ninety-ninth Hell.

Quite aside from the fact that you are:

Chivalrous by nature and open-handed with your wealth,
Have a voice like plangent bronze and tinkling jade,[44]
Command a clever and articulate tongue,[45]
Dress in silks and wear brocades,[46] and
Are ever attended by three or five servants;[47]

thereby showing yourself to be:

A man above other men;

even the delicacies that constitute your daily fare are such things as he would never see, were he to live for hundreds of years. How can he be compared to you? You're just what the doctor ordered. Ever since I experienced love at your hands, by day and by night all I do is long for you."

This last statement had such an effect on Hsi-men Ch'ing that:

His delight knew no bounds.

Throwing aside the riding crop, he helped the woman to her feet and allowed her to get dressed, after which he took her onto his lap and said, "My child, what you say is true. What does that scoundrel know about anything? To him:

A saucer may look as big as the sky."

With that, he called for Ch'un-mei and told her, "Set the table at once and then go back to the rear compound and fetch us some food and wine as quick as you can."

Truly:

To the east the sun is shining, to the west
  there are clouds;
Just as you think it will never clear, it
  is already clear.[48]

If you want to know the outcome of these events,
Pray consult the story related in the following chapter.

Chapter 20

MENG YÜ-LOU HIGH-MINDEDLY INTERCEDES WITH WU YÜEH-NIANG; HSI-MEN CH'ING WREAKS HAVOC IN THE VERDANT SPRING BORDELLO

In this world one has a role to play
  for three score years and ten;
What need is there both day and night
  to overtax one's spirits?
The affairs of this world in the end
  bring naught but regret;
The fleeting luxury that beguiles the eye
  is wont to prove unreal.
Poverty and want, wealth and distinction,
  are allocated by Heaven;
Success and failure, glory and luxury,
  are but dust in a crack.
So why not let yourself go, enjoying
  pleasures as they come;
Rather than waiting for the gray hairs
  to invade your temples?[1]

THE STORY GOES that Hsi-men Ch'ing was so affected by the few:

Soft-spoken sentiments and tender words,

addressed to him by Li P'ing-erh in her bedroom that:

His anger turned to joy.[2]

After he had helped her to her feet and allowed her to get dressed, the two of them fell to:

Hugging and embracing each other,
As inseparable as they could be.

Meanwhile, he called Ch'un-mei into the room and told her to set the table and then go to the rear compound to fetch some wine.

To resume our story, ever since Hsi-men Ch'ing went into Li P'ing-erh's quarters, P'an Chin-lien and Meng Yü-lou had been standing outside the postern gate eavesdropping upon the events within. The door of Li P'ing-erh's room was closed, but Ch'un-mei was waiting in attendance, all by herself, in the intervening courtyard. Chin-lien had taken Yü-lou by the hand, and the two of them were gazing through the cracks in the gate to see what they could observe. They saw that her room was lit by lamp and candle light, and could tell that the two were talking inside, but were unable to overhear what was being said.

"We're not as well off as that lousy little piece Ch'un-mei," said Chin-lien. "She can hear everything perfectly."

Ch'un-mei listened surreptitiously outside the window for a while and then strolled over toward the gate.

"What's going on inside the room," Chin-lien demanded in a whisper.

When Ch'un-mei heard the question, she came over and relayed the story to the two auditors on the other side of the gate, saying, "Father told her to take off her clothes and get down on her knees, but she wouldn't take her clothes off, so Father got angry and gave her a few strokes with the riding crop."

"Did she take them off when he whipped her?" asked Chin-lien.

"Only when she realized how angry he was," said Ch'un-mei, "was she frightened enough to take her clothes off and kneel down before him on the bed. Father's interrogating her right now."

Meng Yü-lou, who was afraid Hsi-men Ch'ing might overhear them, said, "Sister Five, let's go over to the other side," and proceeded to pull Chin-lien around to the postern gate on the west side of the courtyard. It was early in the third decade of the eighth month and the moon had just come up. Chin-lien cracked melon seeds with her teeth as the two of them stood there in the dark shadows and chatted together, while they waited for Ch'un-mei to come out with a further report.

"Our sister must have thought she was in for a tasty treat," Chin-lien said to Yü-lou. "The only thing she wanted was a chance to move in here, and now:

> Before being able to so much as shake her head,[3]

she's had to face this initiatory ordeal, and brought down these strokes of the whip on herself. As for that totally inconsiderate good-for-nothing of ours, as long as you go along with him he may be all right, but:

> He's just like hot taffy;
> Whether you try to twist it or whether you don't,
> you get stuck either way.[4]

Remember what happened to me when that slavey of a concubine tried to nail me with her talebearing? And then there was that prostitute from the quarter. No matter how circumspect I tried to be, she got him to give me a hard time. How I cried over it! As for you, Sister, how long have you been here, anyway? You still don't know what you're up against."

Not long after the two of them had begun their conversation, the postern gate was heard to open and Ch'un-mei came out on her way to the rear compound.

Unexpectedly, her mistress, who was standing in the dark shadows, demanded, "You little piece, where are you off to?"

Ch'un-mei laughed, but continued on her way.

"You crazy little piece," said Chin-lien. "Come over here. I want to ask you something. What are you in such a hurry for, anyway?"

Only then did Ch'un-mei stop and give an account, thus and so, of what had happened.

"First she cried, and then did a lot of talking," she said, "until Father so far relented that he lifted her up and embraced her. Then he had her put her clothes back on and told me to set the table. Right now, I'm on my way to the rear compound to fetch some wine for them."

When Chin-lien heard this, she turned to Yü-lou and said, "That lousy shameless good-for-nothing!

The thunder may have been loud, but
The raindrops didn't amount to anything.[5]

To hear him tell it, he was going to give her a real thrashing, raise royal hell with her; but when it came to the crunch, nothing happened at all. I can see it now. I'll bet you anything, when she brings the wine, he'll have Ch'un-mei serve it. The lousy little piece! You'd think she didn't have any maidservants of her own. If you go fetch his wine for him, when you get to the rear compound that slavey of a concubine, Hsüeh-o, is likely to start shooting off her cunt about it the way she did before. I've had enough of that, thank you."

"As long as Father sent me, what's it all to me?" said Ch'un-mei, as she went off with a giggle.

"That little piece of mine is the limit," said Chin-lien. "When I give her a regular job to do, she's so slow to get a move on, you'd think she was dead. I don't know why it is, but whenever there's some;

Pussyfooting errand,[6]

to be run for anyone else, she's ready to:

Stick her head into any cranny,[7]

to get a crack at it, and takes off like a flash. You know perfectly well she's got two maidservants of her own, but you'll run your legs off in their stead. What's it to you? That little piece of mine is like:

The radish peddler who tags along after the salt vendor:
forever horning in where she doesn't belong."[8]

"Why do you suppose it is?" said Yü-lou. "If I tell my own senior maidservant, Lan-hsiang, to get to work on something, she may look like she's going to, but she doesn't. While if her master puts her up to any piece of mischief, she not only obeys, but goes off like a flash too."

As they were talking, who should suddenly turn up from the rear compound but Yü-hsiao, who said, "I see the Third Lady is still here. I've come to fetch you."

"You crazy little bitch! You gave me quite a start," exclaimed Yü-lou, who then went on to ask, "Does your mistress know you're here?"

"I put my mistress to bed some time ago," said Yü-hsiao. "I was coming out to the front compound to see what was up, just now, when I ran into Ch'un-mei, on her way back to fetch some wine and appetizers."

"What happened after the master went into her room?" she then went on to ask.

"When he went into her room," Chin-lien interjected, "it was the same old story:

> Like the ugly lady with the pointed head who tried to
> improve matters by banging it against the privy wall:
> She's got everything shipshape."

Yü-hsiao had to ask Yü-lou again for an explanation, and she told her all that had happened.

"You don't mean to say, Third Lady," exclaimed Yü-hsiao, "that he really made her take off her clothes and get down on her knees, and then gave her five strokes with the riding crop?"

"He only started whipping her when she refused to get down on her knees," said Yü-lou.

"So he whipped her over her clothes," said Yü-hsiao. "If he'd whipped her without them, how could her fair white skin ever have endured it?"

"You crazy little bitch," laughed Yü-lou. "You're really sensitive enough to:

> Empathize with the sorrows of the ancients."[9]

As they were talking, who should appear but Ch'un-mei and Hsiao-yü, with the wine and appetizers. Ch'un-mei had the wine and Hsiao-yü was carrying a square box with the food. They headed straight for Li P'ing-erh's room.

"You lousy little piece!" said Chin-lien. "I don't know why it is, but whenever you get wind of a job like this, you seem to think it's:

> Like a rat stationed in the clouds:
> The 'furry pest' Heaven has to offer."[10]

"Well, make your delivery and get it over with," she ordered. "And let her own maidservants look after her from now on. Don't you pay any further attention to them. I've got something for you to do."

Ch'un-mei merely giggled and went inside with Hsiao-yü. Once there, they laid the wine and food out on the table and then came outside again, leaving Ying-ch'un and Hsiu-ch'un in the room to wait on them.

When Yü-lou and Chin-lien had finished questioning them, Yü-hsiao said, "Third Lady, let's go back to the rear compound," and the two of them went off together.

Chin-lien told Ch'un-mei to lock the postern gate and then went back to her room to spend a solitary night. But no more of this. Truly:

> What a pity that, in its perfect fullness,
> the moon of this night;
> Should shed its pure radiance on other gardens,
> so near and yet so far.[11]

Eavesdroppers Discuss Li P'ing-erh's Feat of Reconciliation

We will say no more, for the moment, about P'an Chin-lien's solitary night, but turn instead to Hsi-men Ch'ing and Li P'ing-erh. The two of them:

Indulged their mutual affection,
Drinking wine and talking together,

until the middle of the night before they:

Spread the kingfisher-colored quilt,
Laid out the mandarin duck pillows,
Got into bed and prepared to sleep.

Indeed:

Under the flickering lamplight,
They remind one of phoenixes singing a duet
within a mirror;
Enveloped in fragrant incense,
They resemble butterflies doing a pas de deux
among the flowers.

Truly:

This evening let the silver lamp burn
brightly as it will;
They're still afraid this tryst of theirs is
nothing but a dream.[12]

There is a lyric to the tune "Partridge Sky" that testifies to this:

Her eyebrows lightly penciled,
her comb stuck askew;
She has no heart to continue
doing her embroidery.
Deep within cloudy windows,
in misty chambers;
Her orchidaceous heart
studies to please.

Beautiful as can be,
Ever more lovely;
She is a goddess incarnate,
unknown to this world.
From now on she can abandon
that lovesick refrain;
Brocade itself is no fit simile
for such a consummation.[13]

The two of them slept until lunchtime the next day. Li P'ing-erh was just getting up to look in the mirror and comb her hair when who should appear but Ying-ch'un, who had been to the kitchen in the rear compound. She was carrying four saucers of fancy appetizers: one of squash and eggplant julienne in a sweet sauce, one of Chinese cabbage vinaigrette, one of smoked pork, and one of minced shad preserved in fermented red mash. In addition there was a bowl of boiled squab and another of junket flavored with yellow leeks. These were accompanied by two silver-mounted bowls of fresh white fragrant nonglutinous rice and two pairs of ivory chopsticks.

The woman had rinsed out her mouth and joined Hsi-men Ch'ing in drinking half a cup of wine when she turned to Ying-ch'un and said, "Decant some of that Chin-hua wine[14] in the silver flagon that was left over from yesterday."

Goblets were set out and she kept Hsi-men Ch'ing company as they drank two bumpers apiece before she washed her face and completed her toilet. She then proceeded to open up her trunks and display her valuables, jewelry, and clothing for Hsi-men Ch'ing's benefit. She brought out the necklace of one hundred large, Western Ocean pearls that she had originally appropriated from the household of Privy Councilor Liang Shih-chieh and showed it to him. She also produced an onyx cap button in a gold setting, which she said had belonged to the late eunuch director. Detached from its cap and put on the scales, it turned out to weigh four mace and eight candareens. Li P'ing-erh suggested to Hsi-men Ch'ing that he take it to a silversmith and have it made into a pair of pendant earrings for her.

She also brought out a fret of gold filigree that weighed nine ounces and asked Hsi-men Ch'ing, "Do the First Lady and the others have frets like this one or not?"

"Some of them do have frets of silver filigree," said Hsi-men Ch'ing, "but none of them has anything as elaborate as this."

"I'd better not wear it, then," the woman said. "Take it to the silversmith for me, to be melted down, and then have him make me a pin for holding my chignon in place, in the shape of nine golden phoenixes holding strands of pearls in their beaks. With whatever's left over, have him make me a tiara of jade, enchased with gold, representing 'the goddess Kuan-yin in her full glory' like the one the First Lady wears in front of her coiffure."

Hsi-men Ch'ing accepted these commissions, combed his hair and washed his face, put on his clothes, and prepared to go out.

"There's no one to look after the other house," said Li P'ing-erh. "Whatever you do, you ought to go by there to check things out and assign someone to take care of it in T'ien-fu's place so he can come and serve here at home. Mother Feng, the old good-for-nothing, is getting so doddery I don't feel right leaving her there all by herself."

"I'll do just as you say," said Hsi-men Ch'ing, as he put the fret and the cap button into his sleeve and headed for the door.

He was on his way out of the compound when he was unexpectedly accosted by P'an Chin-lien, who was standing by the postern gate on the east side of the courtyard with her hair in disarray and an unwashed face.

"Brother, where are you off to?" she demanded. "At this hour of the morning you look:

Day-blind enough to catch a sparrow in the eye."

"I've got an errand to run," said Hsi-men Ch'ing.

"You crazy good-for-nothing," said Chin-lien. "Come back here. What are you in such a hurry for, anyway? I've got something to say to you."

When Hsi-men Ch'ing saw how importunate she was, he had no alternative but to come back and allow himself to be led into her room.

The woman sat down on a chair and, taking his two hands in hers, said, "I'll only be wasting my breath on you. Are your legs on fire, you crazy three-inch good-for-nothing? No one's going to:

Stew you in a pot and eat you.[15]

What are you so anxious to get away with, anyway? Come over here. I want to ask you something."

"That's enough, you little whore!" said Hsi-men Ch'ing. "Why be so importunate? I've got an errand to run. I'll tell you when I get back."

As he spoke he started outside, but the woman felt his sleeve and, detecting something heavy in it, said, "What's this? Take it out and show it to me."

"It's the wallet I carry my silver in," said Hsi-men Ch'ing.

The woman didn't believe him and, sticking her hand into his sleeve to see for herself, pulled out the fret of gold filigree.

"This is her fret, isn't it?" she said. "Where are you taking it?"

"She asked me whether any of you had frets like this one," said Hsi-men Ch'ing, "and I told her you didn't. So she wants me to take it to the silversmith to be melted down and made into another two pieces of jewelry for her to wear."

"What does this fret weigh," asked Chin-lien, "and what does she want it made into?"

"It weighs nine ounces," said Hsi-men Ch'ing. "She wants it made into a nine-phoenix pin and a tiara of jade, enchased with gold, representing 'the goddess Kuan-yin in her full glory,' like the one the First Lady wears in front of her coiffure."

"A nine-phoenix pin," said Chin-lien, "would only take three ounces and five or six mace of gold, at the most. And as for that tiara of the First Lady's, I've weighed it myself, and it only comes to one ounce and six mace. Whatever you do, have him use what's left over to make another nine-phoenix pin, just like hers, for me."

"She wants the setting of that 'Kuan-yin in her full glory' to be solid and sturdy," said Hsi-men Ch'ing.

"Even if it were made solid and sturdy," said Chin-lien, "it wouldn't take more than three ounces. At the very least, barring any monkey business, he ought to be able to squeeze two or three extra ounces of gold out of it, which would be enough to make a pin for me."

"You little whore!" laughed Hsi-men Ch'ing. "All you care about is gaining petty advantages for yourself. You've got to have your finger in every pie."

"My son," said Chin-lien, "you would do well to heed your mother's words. If you don't get that pin made up for me, I'll have something further to say to you."

Hsi-men Ch'ing put the fret back in his sleeve, laughed, and started out the door.

"Brother," joked Chin-lien, "you've met your match at last."

"What do you mean I've met my match?" demanded Hsi-men Ch'ing.

"If you haven't met your match," said Chin-lien, "how come, last night:

> The thunder may have been loud, but
> The raindrops didn't amount to anything?

You were threatening to give her a real thrashing and make her hang herself. But this morning all she had to do was pull out a fret in order to:

> Make a ghost at the millstone out of you.[16]

You dog of an oily mouth! There's nothing you won't do for her."

"You little whore!" laughed Hsi-men Ch'ing, as he finally made his exit. "All you ever do is talk nonsense."

To resume our story, Wu Yüeh-niang was sitting in her room with Meng Yü-lou and Li Chiao-erh when they suddenly heard a servant outside calling for Lai-wang, but unable to find him. Who should it turn out to be but P'ing-an, who lifted aside the portiere on the threshold.

"What do you want him for?" asked Yüeh-niang.

"Father is waiting impatiently for him," said P'ing-an.

Yüeh-niang took her time in responding, before finally saying, "I've sent him on an errand."

It so happens that earlier that morning Yüeh-niang had sent him to Nun Wang's monastery to deliver a votive gift of incense, oil, and white rice.

"I'll simply tell Father you've sent him on an errand," said P'ing-an.

"You crazy slave!" Yüeh-niang retorted angrily. "Tell him whatever you like."

P'ing-an was so taken aback by her response that he went out without daring to utter another word.

Yüeh-niang turned to Yü-lou and the others and said, "If I say anything about it, he claims it's none of my business. If I don't say anything, I get so frustrated I could burst. He's brought that person into our household, bag and baggage, so why doesn't he just sell off that house of hers and be done with it? What's the point of all this rot about:

> Ringing bells and beating drums,[17]

in order to protect the place? In any case, she's already got that Old Mother Feng of hers there, so the most we need to do is send an unmarried page boy over to spend the nights. Does he think the house is going to walk away on him? After all:

If you're going to be a wet nurse,
You've got to handle the shit that goes with the job.

But no one else but Lai-wang and his wife will do, despite the fact that she's suffering from:

Seven ailments and eight pains.[18]

If she should happen to come down with something and take to her bed over there, who would look after her?"

"Elder Sister," said Yü-lou, "you are my senior, and I may be speaking out of turn, but you are the mistress of the household. The fact that you and our husband are not on speaking terms makes it difficult for any of the rest of us to know what to do and leaves the servants with nowhere to turn. The way our husband has been carrying on the last few days:

Alienated from this one and abusive of that,

indicates that he, too, is completely at loose ends. Wouldn't you be willing to consider, for our sake, saying a few words to him and making it up somehow?"

"Third Sister Meng," said Yüeh-niang, "you'd better get those ideas out of your head. I haven't picked any quarrel with him. He's simply making a show of his temper for no reason at all. I don't care how long a face he pulls, that's not going to get me to give him another look. He's been calling me an undutiful whore behind my back. How have I been undutiful, I'd like to know? It's only now, after I've allowed him to bring six or seven bedmates into the place, that he's discovered how undutiful I am. It's always been true that:

If you wish to get along, say what people want to hear;
If you try to be honest, you'll only arouse antagonism.[19]

"As for my husband, originally, when I did what I could to talk you out of marrying her, I was thinking only of your own best interests. Since you had already stashed away all those valuables of hers, and bought her husband's house into the bargain, if you were then revealed to have designs upon his wife, and it had come to the attention of the authorities, they would have taken a dim view of it. On top of which, her mourning period wasn't even over yet, so you really couldn't very well marry her, I said.

"How was I to know that behind my back the trap had already been sprung? Every day:

Betrothal gifts were exchanged between them,[20]

while I was the only one kept in the dark. They might as well have:

Put a water crock over my head.[21]

One day he claimed he was 'spending the night in the quarter,' and the next day he claimed he was 'spending the night in the quarter.' How was I to know that all he wanted was to get her into his own house so he could 'spend the night in the quarter' the more conveniently?

"He's so susceptible to other people's:

Showy glamor and gaudy airs,[22]

they can:

Conjure dragons and depict tigers,

as a cover for their:

Two faces and three knives,[23]

and he thinks they're:

As wonderful as can be.[24]

Meanwhile, people like myself, who try to be honest, but whose:

Good advice proves bitter to the taste,[25]

can't even get his attention, and end up being treated like enemies. Truly:

Though the preceding carriages have overturned
by the thousands;
The carriages that follow continue to overturn
in the same way.
No matter how clearly one may point out
the safest route;
One's honest words are misconstrued
as ill-meant advice.

"If you won't pay any attention to me, I won't demand anything of you. So long as you don't begrudge me three meals a day, I'll make do as though I no longer had a husband at all, and live the life of a widow here in my room. The rest of you had better let me do as I like. It's none of your business."

This speech of Yüeh-niang's left Yü-lou and the others at a loss for words for some time.

At this juncture, who should appear but Li P'ing-erh, who had combed her hair and made herself up in order to come to the master suite and offer Yüeh-niang and the others the customary ceremonial tea. She was wearing a silk blouse of scarlet brocade that opened down the middle, over a long trailing skirt of kingfisher-blue figured silk, and was accompanied by Ying-ch'un, bearing a silver pitcher of hot water, and Hsiu-ch'un, with a box of tea. Yüeh-niang ordered Hsiao-yü to bring her a seat and had her sit down. A little later Sun Hsüeh-o also came in, and after Li P'ing-erh had served tea to each of them in turn they all sat down together.

P'an Chin-lien, who had a sharp tongue, broke the ice by saying, "Sister Li, come over here and kowtow to your elder sister. To be frank with you, our elder sister and Father have not been on speaking terms with each other for quite a while now, all on your account. We've just spent half the day interceding with her for your sake. Some day soon you really ought to prepare a feast for them and see if you can't get the old couple to make it up somehow."

"I'll do just as you say, Sister," said Li P'ing-erh.

Thereupon, she knelt down on the floor in front of Yüeh-niang and:

> Like a sprig of blossoms swaying in the breeze;
> Sending the pendants of her embroidered sash flying;
> Just as though inserting a taper in its holder;

kowtowed to her four times.

"She's only pulling your leg, Sister Li," said Yüeh-niang.

Turning, then, to Chin-lien, she continued, "Fifth Sister, you can all give up your efforts to persuade me. I've already sworn an oath. If I live to be a hundred, I'll never be reconciled to him."

As a result of this, none of them dared bring it up again.

Chin-lien had picked up a small brush and was standing beside Li P'ing-erh, smoothing her coiffure with it, when she noticed that she was wearing in her hair a gold openwork pin in the shape of a cricket and an ornamental comb decorated with the motif of pines, bamboos, and plum blossoms, the "three cold-weather friends," in gold filigree.

"Sister Li," she said, "you really oughtn't to wear anything as intricate as this cricket pin. It's likely to get tangled in your hair. Something like that gold-enchased 'Kuan-yin in her full glory' that our elder sister wears in her coiffure would be better. It's more solid and sturdy."

Li P'ing-erh replied quite innocently, "I plan to get the silversmith to make one just like it for me."

A little later, Hsiao-yü and Yü-hsiao came up to replenish her tea and took advantage of the occasion to tease her.

Yü-hsiao began by asking, "Sixth Lady, what office in the Imperial City was that old eunuch director of yours originally attached to?"

"He started out as director of the Firewood Office in the Imperial Palace," said Li P'ing-erh, "and served in the Imperial Bodyguard. Later on he was promoted to the position of grand defender of Kuang-nan."

"It comes as no surprise, then," laughed Yü-hsiao, "that yesterday you seemed to be so intimately acquainted with the stick."

"Last year the community heads and elders from all the villages outside the city walls were looking for you everywhere," chimed in Hsiao-yü. "They wanted you to go to the Eastern Capital on their behalf."

Li P'ing-erh, who was still a bit slow on the uptake, asked, "Why were they looking for me in particular?"

"They said you really knew how to abase yourself effectively in pleading for flood relief," laughed Hsiao-yü.

"Yesterday:

> You were like the old biddy from the countryside on a
> pilgrimage to the Temple of the Thousand Buddhas,"

resumed Yü-hsiao.

> "You kept on kowtowing as if there were no end in sight."

"The other day, it is reported," Hsiao-yü continued, "the emperor sent four border patrol agents[26] to ask if you would consent to go abroad in order to make a marriage alliance with the Huns. Is that really so?"

"I didn't know anything about it," said Li P'ing-erh.

"They said you had an irresistible way of saying 'Huney,' " laughed Hsiao-yü.

These sallies reduced Yü-lou and Chin-lien to helpless laughter.

"You crazy little stinkers!" Yüeh-niang finally intervened. "Go on about your business. Haven't you anything better to do than tease her?"

By this time Li P'ing-erh was so embarrassed her face had become a patchwork of red and white blotches. She was so ill at ease she didn't know whether to get up or stay put, but finally escaped to her own quarters.

Some time later, Hsi-men Ch'ing came into her room to tell her that Silversmith Ku had agreed to make the jewelry to her specifications.

In the course of consulting with her, he said, "Tomorrow we'll send out invitations asking the male friends of the family to come to a wedding reception on the 25th. We can scarcely avoid sending an invitation to Hua the Elder."

"His wife came to the third-day feast," said Li P'ing-erh, "and was anxious that he be invited. It doesn't matter. You might as well go ahead and invite him."

"As for the other house," she continued, "I guess Old Mother Feng can handle it, after all. If you would just send someone to take turns with T'ien-fu spending the night over there, that ought to take care of it. There's no need to make Lai-wang move in. My elder sister in the master suite says his wife is in such poor health she won't be able to go with him."

"I didn't know anything about it," said Hsi-men Ch'ing.

He proceeded forthwith to summon P'ing-an and instructed him, "You and T'ien-fu take turns, on alternate days, spending the night at the house on Lion Street." But no more of this.

To make a long story short, in no time at all it was the 25th, the day of the wedding feast for male friends and relatives in Li P'ing-erh's honor. The main reception hall was decorated with flowers, and four singing girls as well as a troupe of tumblers and acrobats were engaged for the occasion. The brothers-in-law, Hua the Elder and Wu K'ai, were seated at the head table. Wu Yüeh-niang's younger brother, Wu the Second, and her eldest sister's husband, Mr. Shen, were seated at the second table. Ying Po-chüeh and Hsieh Hsi-ta were seated at the third table. Sticky Chu and Blabbermouth Sun were seated at the fourth table. Cadger Ch'ang and Heartless Wu were seated at the fifth table. Welsher Yün and Scrounger Pai were seated at the sixth table. Hsi-men Ch'ing took his place as host with his managers, Fu Ming and Scurry-about Pen, and his son-in-law, Ch'en Ching-chi, arrayed to either side.

Before the feast, shortly after noon, Li Kuei-chieh, Wu Yin-erh, Tung Yü-hsien, and Han Chin-ch'uan arrived in their sedan chairs and were entertained by Yüeh-niang in the master suite. The male guests, upon their arrival, were seated in the newly erected summerhouse and served tea. After everyone had arrived, they moved into the main reception hall where the tables were already set up, with place cards indicating who was to sit in the positions of greater and lesser honor at each table.

The appetizers consisted of wildfowl wrapped in pastry and a soup of eight ingredients. The first main course was roast goose. As the food was being served, the musicians struck up a tune and the tumblers put on a performance, which turned out to be a comic farce of the genre known as hsiao-lo yüan-pen.[27] After they went off, the two boy actors, Li Ming and Wu Hui, came on to play and sing for the company. They were followed by an instrumental interlude, after which the four singing girls came in to ply the guests with wine.

At this juncture, from his place at the table, Ying Po-chüeh spoke up, saying, "Today is our elder brother's wedding feast. Though it may not be my place to do so, I have screwed up the courage to request that our new sister-in-law be invited out so we may pay her our respects. That would put the seal on our intimacy. What *I* think may not matter too much, but your esteemed kinsman Hua the Elder, your two brothers-in-law, and Mr. Shen are all here today. What else did they come for?"

"My insignificant concubine is far too unworthy to receive such an honor," said Hsi-men Ch'ing. "Pray excuse her."

"That's no way to talk," said Hsieh Hsi-ta. "You promised us beforehand. Were it not for our sister-in-law, why should we have come? Moreover, our sister-in-law's esteemed kinsman, Hua the Elder, is here.

At first only a friend,
Now he is our kinsman.

It's not as though she were being invited out to meet a stranger. What is there to worry about?"

Hsi-men Ch'ing laughed but did not make a move.

"Brother," said Ying Po-chüeh, "don't laugh. We've all brought our reception fees with us. We're not asking her to come out and meet us for nothing."

"You dog!" said Hsi-men Ch'ing. "All you ever do is talk nonsense."

Unable to resist these repeated importunities any longer, he called over Tai-an and told him to convey the request to the rear compound.

After some time, Tai-an reappeared and reported, "The Sixth Lady begs to be excused."

"That's enough of your monkey business, you little dog-bone," said Ying Po-chüeh. "You think you can fool me by pretending to go inside and then coming up with such a tale? You may swear as much as you like, but if you stick to your story, I'll have to go back there myself."

"You don't mean to suggest I'd try to fool the likes of you, do you?" protested Tai-an. "Go ahead back, then, and see for yourself."

"You think I wouldn't dare?" said Ying Po-chüeh. "After all, the garden is familiar territory. Suppose I go inside and drag out the whole lot of your mistresses, how would that be?"

"That big pug of ours is something fierce," said Tai-an. "I'd hate to see you lose your balls."

Ying Po-chüeh made a great show of jumping up from his place, chasing after Tai-an, and giving him a couple of kicks.

"A fine little dog-bone you are!" he laughed. "You know how to get at me all right. Now go back there again, as quick as you can, and invite her out. If you fail, it'll cost you twenty of the best with the cane."

This performance caused everyone, including the four singing girls, to burst into laughter.

Tai-an returned to the host's position at the foot of the hall and stood there watching his master, without making a move.

Hsi-men Ch'ing, finding himself:

At a loss for what to do next,

had no alternative but to call Tai-an over and instruct him, "Tell the Sixth Lady to get herself ready and come out to meet the guests."

After Tai-an had been gone for some time he came out again and asked Hsi-men Ch'ing to go inside. The servants of the guests were then herded outside and the inner gate was closed. The four singing girls went back to the interior to supply a musical accompaniment for Li P'ing-erh's entrance. Meng Yü-lou and P'an Chin-lien did their best to encourage her, helping to smooth her coiffure and put on her jewelry, before pronouncing her ready to go out.

Brocaded rugs and embroidered carpets were laid down in the reception hall, whereupon:

Amid the fragrance of orchid and musk,
To the strains of strings and woodwinds,

conducted on her way by the four singing girls, the woman made her appearance at last.

She was wearing a full-sleeved robe of scarlet variegated silk over a skirt of sand-green material, sprigged with gold-stemmed and green-leaved flowers. Behold:

Her waist is encircled by,
A lady's girdle inset with plaques of green jade;
Her wrists are enclosed in,
Gold bangles that double as sleeve-weights.
On her breast there lies,
An amulet suspended from a necklace;
By her skirt is heard,
The tinkling of girdle pendants.

Hsi-men Ch'ing's Cronies Make a Fuss over His New Bride

On her head,
Pearls and trinkets rise in piles;
Beside her temple,
A jeweled hairpin is half askew.
Gold rings with amethyst pendants,
Hang low beneath her ears;
Phoenix pins with dangling pearls,
Jut from either side of her chignon.
Her powdered face makes a perfect ground
 on which to display beauty marks;
Her beige skirt only enhances the sight
 of her tiny red mandarin duck shoes.
It is just as though Ch'ang-o has come down
 from her palace in the moon;
She is exactly like the Goddess of Witches' Mountain
 deigning to grace the feast.

The four singing girls, playing the *p'i-p'a*, psaltery, and three-stringed banjo, clustered around her as she saluted the company with a formal kowtow:

Like a sprig of blossoms swaying in the breeze;
Sending the pendants of her embroidered sash flying.

There was not a man present who did not make haste to rise from his place and return her salute.

To resume our story, Meng Yü-lou, P'an Chin-lien, and Li Chiao-erh clustered around Wu Yüeh-niang behind a hanging screen in the reception hall to see what they could hear and see of the proceedings. They heard the singing girls perform the song to the tune "Clever Improvisation" that begins with the words:

How pleased we are by your success,

and then continues:

Heaven has made this perfect match;
Like male and female phoenix
 are husband and wife.

They then proceeded to the next song in the suite, to the tune "Flirtatious Laughter," which begins with the words:

Gayly laughing we celebrate this happy occasion,
By raising our phoenix goblets on high.
To the sound of ivory clappers, silver psaltery,
 and jade flute,
Let them bring on in cups and platters,
The fruits of sea and land to grace
 the auspicious feast.

The song concluded with the words:

May they live happily together as husband and wife
forever and ever.[28]

At this point Chin-lien turned to Yüeh-niang and said, "Elder Sister, listen to what they're singing. She's only a concubine, after all. That really isn't an appropriate song suite to sing on a day like this. If they're to be like fish in the water, and 'live happily together as husband and wife for ever and ever,' where does that leave you?"

Now although Yüeh-niang was a good person by nature, when she heard these words she couldn't help being somewhat dismayed and feeling resentful in her heart. She also observed the way in which Ying Po-chüeh, Hsieh Hsi-ta, and the rest of the company carried on when Li P'ing-erh came out to greet them. It seemed as though they:

Wished they had more mouths than nature had provided,[29]

the better to praise her with.

"This sister-in-law of ours," rhapsodized Ying Po-chüeh, is truly something:

Seldom seen in the universe,[30]
Without peer in this world.[31]

Quite aside from the fact that she is:

Compliant and virtuous by nature, and
Dignified and stately in demeanor;[32]

she cuts such a striking figure that in all the world you could hardly hope to find the like. Who else but our elder brother deserves to enjoy such good fortune? We who have been privileged to see her today will have been the gainers though we should die tomorrow."

At the conclusion of this peroration he called out to Tai-an, "Make haste to escort your mistress back to her quarters. I fear we may be overtaxing her. It isn't worth the risk."

When Wu Yüeh-niang and the others overheard this speech they cursed him unremittingly for a rot-talking, glib-tongued jailbird.

After an appropriate time Li P'ing-erh prepared to withdraw. The four singing girls, observing that she had money at her disposal, all made up to her, saying:

Ma'am this and ma'am that,

as they adjusted her trinkets and straightened her clothes for her. In fact:

There was no length to which they would not go.[33]

When Wu Yüeh-niang returned to the master suite she felt very much out of sorts. Who should appear in her room at this juncture but Tai-an and P'ing-an, bearing a lot of complimentary gifts of cash, bolts of material, articles of clothing, and other expressions of regard on a pair of trays.

Yüeh-niang wouldn't even look at them, but said angrily, "You lousy jailbirds! Take them up to the front compound, why don't you. What do you want to bring them in here for?"

"Father told us to bring them into your room," said Tai-an.

Yüeh-niang told Yü-hsiao to take care of them, and she tossed them onto the bed.

Before long, her eldest brother, Wu K'ai, after finishing the second course of the banquet, came into the rear compound to pay his sister a visit. When Yüeh-niang saw her brother come into the room, she hastily proceeded to greet him with a kowtow:

Like a sprig of blossoms swaying in the breeze,

and then sat down with him.

"My wife imposed on your hospitality the other day," said Wu K'ai. "And I'm much obliged to your husband for sending along a sampling from the feast. When she got home she told me that my brother-in-law and you were not on speaking terms, and I had made up my mind to come say something to you about it, even before receiving your husband's invitation today.

"Sister, if you persist in this course, all the good feeling you have built up in the past will be lost. It has always been true that:

Foolish men fear their wives, but
Virtuous women fear their husbands.[34]
The 'three obediences' and 'four virtues,'
Are the norms that govern female conduct.[35]

From now on, Sister, don't try to interfere with anything he wants to do. I dare say my brother-in-law would never do anything really wrong. Only by playing the role of a 'Mr. Yea-sayer'[36] can you show what a dutiful wife you are."

"No doubt if I'd been a more dutiful wife I wouldn't have aroused such antagonism in the first place!" said Yüeh-niang sarcastically. "Now that he's got this rich baby of his, a poor officer's daughter like myself might just as well be dead for all he cares. It's none of your business. Leave it to me. Let him do as he pleases. You lousy ruffian! Since when have you been so concerned about me, anyway?"

As she spoke, Yüeh-niang broke into tears.

"Sister," said Wu K'ai. "It's not right of you to carry on this way. You and I are not that sort of people. You really ought to put a stop to it immediately. If the two of you are on good terms with each other, it makes it much more propitious for relatives like myself to come visiting."

He remonstrated with her for a while, after which Hsiao-yü came in to serve tea. When they were done with the tea, Yüeh-niang told Hsiao-yü to set the table and invited her brother to stay and have some wine with her.

"Needless to say, Sister," said Wu K'ai, "I'm already stuffed with wine and food from the feast. I just came in to pay you a visit."

Wu K'ai sat a little longer until a page boy was dispatched from the front compound to invite him to rejoin the party, whereupon he said his farewells and followed him back outside. Thereafter, the company continued to drink until after the lamps were lighted before finally breaking up. The four singing girls each received a gold lamé handkerchief and five mace of silver from Li P'ing-erh that day and went home in a happy state.

From this time on, Hsi-men Ch'ing spent several nights in a row in Li P'ing-erh's room. This might have been tolerated by the rest of his womenfolk, but P'an Chin-lien was in high dudgeon about it. She did her best to provoke ill feeling between Wu Yüeh-niang and Li P'ing-erh by criticizing the former behind her back and alleging that she was intolerant of others. Li P'ing-erh innocently fell into Chin-lien's toils, addressing her as Elder Sister and becoming more intimate with her than ever. Truly:

> On first meeting one should express no more than
> three-tenths of one's thoughts;
> Never under any circumstances should one disclose
> the whole content of one's heart.[37]

From the time that Hsi-men Ch'ing brought Li P'ing-erh over his threshold, in the course of doing which he had picked up two or three dubious increments to his property, his affairs became more prosperous than ever. On his country estate outside the walls and in his residential compound:

> Everything was put on an entirely new footing.
> The rice and millet overflowed his granaries,
> His mules and horses became teeming herds,
> His slaves and servants were arrayed in ranks.[38]

Hsi-men Ch'ing changed the name of Li P'ing-erh's page boy, T'ien-fu, or Heavenly Blessing, to the more elegant Ch'in-t'ung, or Lute Boy, which had formerly been the designation of that servant of Meng Yü-lou's who had been driven out of the house for his suspected adultery with P'an Chin-lien. He also bought two new page boys, whom he named Lai-an and Ch'i-t'ung. The four maidservants, Ch'un-mei from P'an Chin-lien's quarters, Yü-hsiao from the master suite, Ying-ch'un from Li P'ing-erh's quarters, and Lan-hsiang from Meng Yü-lou's quarters, were dressed in identical outfits of clothing and jewelry and sent out to an anteroom on the western side of the front courtyard to be instructed in the arts of singing and performing on musical instruments by Li Chiao-erh's younger brother, the musician Li Ming. Ch'un-mei learned to play the *p'i-p'a*, Yü-hsiao the psaltery, Ying-ch'un the three-stringed banjo, and Lan-hsiang the two-stringed barbarian fiddle. Every day Li Ming was regaled with:

> Three teas and six repasts,[39]

and he received five taels a month as wages.

Hsi-men Ch'ing also had a twelve-foot-wide segment of the frontage of his residence opened up, and he weighed out two thousand taels of silver to his manager, Scurry-about Pen, with which to start a pawnshop on the premises. His son-in-law, Ch'en Ching-chi, was given charge of the keys of both shops and made responsible for collecting unpaid debts, but he did not handle the stock. Scurry-about Pen kept the accounts and weighed out the merchandise, while the manager, Fu Ming, was in overall charge of both the pharmaceutical business and the pawnshop, with responsibility for assessing the silver and buying the stock. The second floor of P'an Chin-lien's belvedere was used as a warehouse for the pharmaceuticals, and the second floor of Li P'ing-erh's dwelling was lined with shelves for the accommodation of the articles of clothing and jewelry, antiques, books, paintings, and curios pledged by customers of the pawnshop.

The outlay of silver in the pawnshop on any given day was considerable. Every day Ch'en Ching-chi got up early and went to bed late. He carried the keys and went over the receipts and expenditures with the manager. He wrote a good hand and was quick at arithmetic. When Hsi-men Ch'ing saw all this, he was as pleased as could be.

One day, while they were sharing a meal in the front reception hall, he said to him, "Son-in-law, the fact that you show such aptitude for business here in my household would be a source of great comfort to your father in the Eastern Captital if he only knew about it. I, too, have found someone I can trust. As the saying goes:

> If you have a son, rely on your son;
> If you lack a son, rely on your son-in-law.[40]

In consideration of what you and my daughter are to me, if I should happen to die without a son of my own, all this property of mine might someday be yours."

"Your son has suffered the misfortune," said Ch'en Ching-chi, "of seeing his family implicated in legal trouble. Distantly separated from his father and mother, he has sought refuge here with his parents-in-law and has been fortunate enough to find favor in their sight.

> My obligations to you are so great,
> I can hardly repay them dead or alive.

But I am still young and ignorant. My only hope is that you will both be patient with me. How could I presume to expect anything more?"

When Hsi-men Ch'ing saw that he had a way with words and was intelligent and quick-witted, he was more pleased with him than ever. From that time on, he relied on him to handle all the correspondence that came in or out of the household, in matters great or small, in the form of letters, invitations, lists of presents, and so forth. When guests came, he was always invited to help entertain them, and whenever Hsi-men Ch'ing drank tea or ate a meal his company was felt to be indispensable.

How could he have known that this young scamp was really:
A needle in a wad of cotton;
A thorn in the flesh?[41]
Or that he was given to:
Constantly peeping through embroidered curtains
to steal a peek at Chia Wu;
Frequently invading the innermost chambers
to purloin the perfume of Han Shou?[42]
There is a poem that testifies to this:

A winsome son-in-law on the "eastern couch"[43]
is much to be desired;
How much the more so if he is in his prime,
a prepossessing youth.
When guests are entertained he always finds
a place at the table;
As a matter of course he is given free run
of the postern gates.
In both front compound and rear courtyard[44]
he flirts egregiously;
Under the guise of foolish frolicking
he hides his treachery.
However much you may sing his praises
for being "half a son";
In the final analysis his bones and flesh
form no link with your own.

Days and nights speed by like arrows;
The sun and moon shoot back and forth like shuttles.
Before one has finished enjoying the mid-autumn moon,
The chrysanthemums are blooming on the eastern hedge.
High in the sky the desolate wild geese
wing their way south;
Before you know it, snowflakes cover the ground.

One day, during the third decade of the eleventh month, Hsi-men Ch'ing's club convened for a drink in the home of his friend Cadger Ch'ang, but the party began to break up early. Before even waiting for the lamps to be lit, Hsi-men Ch'ing got up to go, along with Sponger Ying, Tagalong Hsieh, and Sticky Chu, and the four of them set off on horseback together. No sooner had they emerged from Cadger Ch'ang's gate than, lo and behold:
Dense masses of dark clouds,
appeared in the heavens and, all of a sudden:
Fluttering and swirling,
A skyful of snowflakes came drifting down.

"Brother," said Sponger Ying, "if we were to go home at such an hour as this our families would hardly be prepared to receive us. I know it's been some time since you've been into the licensed quarter to see Li Kuei-chieh. Today, just as 'Meng Hao-jan Braved the Snow to Look for Plum Blossoms,'[45] we ought to take advantage of the fact that it's snowing to go pay her a visit."

"Brother Ying the Second is right," said Sticky Chu. "Every month, whether you're kept away by wind and rain or not, you shell out twenty taels of silver to maintain her as your mistress. If you don't even bother to visit her, she's certainly having an easy time of it."

Allowing himself to be persuaded by this barrage of:

First a word from you,
Then a sentence from me,

on the part of his three companions, Hsi-men Ch'ing, there and then, redirected his horse into East Street and headed in the direction of the licensed quarter. By the time they arrived at Li Kuei-chieh's establishment it was already getting dark. They found the lamps and candles in the reception room already lit and a maidservant busy sweeping the floor. After the old lady and Li Kuei-ch'ing had come out to greet them, four folding chairs were set out and they sat down.

"I'm afraid Kuei-chieh arrived late at your house the other day," said the old procuress, "and imposed on your hospitality. Thank you also for the handkerchief and trinkets your Sixth Lady was kind enough to give her."

"She fared none too well, I fear," said Hsi-men Ch'ing. "I didn't want to keep them too late, so as soon as the guests left, I sent them home."

As he spoke, the madam ordered tea to be served, and when they were done with the tea, a maidservant set the table and furnished it with appropriate appetizers.

"What's become of Kuei-chieh?" Hsi-men Ch'ing finally asked.

"Kuei-chieh has been at home waiting for you for days on end, Kinsman," the madam said, "but you have not seen fit to pay her a visit. Today just happens to be her fifth maternal aunt's birthday, and she sent a sedan chair for her, so she's gone out to help celebrate her aunt's birthday."

Gentle reader take note: It so happens that in this world Buddhist monks, Taoist priests, and singing girls are three professions of which it may be said:

If they do not see the color of your money,
They will not open their eyes.
Despising the poor and toadying to the rich;[46]
Prevarication and trickery,
Are two things they cannot do without.

The fact is that Li Kuei-chieh had not really gone out to help celebrate her fifth maternal aunt's birthday. In recent days, seeing that Hsi-men Ch'ing was remiss in coming to see her, she had taken up with a certain Ting the Second, whose sobriquet was Ting Shuang-ch'iao, the son of Mr. Ting, the silk merchant, from Hang-chou. Having disposed of a thousand taels worth of silk, he was staying at an inn in the vicinity and was in the habit of coming into the licensed quarter to patronize the prostitutes without his father's knowledge. His first move had been to offer ten taels of silver and two sets of heavy Hang-chou silk clothing for Li Kuei-chieh's favors, as a consequence of which he had spent the last two nights with her. Only a moment ago, he had been drinking with Li Kuei-chieh in her room when Hsi-men Ch'ing had unexpectedly arrived. The old procuress had hurriedly bundled Kuei-chieh and her customer off to a little-used room in the third courtyard at the back of the house to get them out of the way.

At this juncture, Hsi-men Ch'ing, who took the madam's story at face value, said, "Well, old lady, even if Kuei-chieh isn't here, bring on the wine and we'll await her return at our leisure."

The old procuress retired to the kitchen and did her best to expedite the proceedings, so that wine and delicacies, along with additional appetizers, were quickly forthcoming and soon covered the surface of the table. As for Li Kuei-ch'ing:

> The bridges on her psaltery were ranged like wild geese;
> The songs that she performed were set to new melodies;

as she endeavored to entertain them. The company was soon busy:

> Playing at guess-fingers or gaming at forfeits.

Just as they were settling down to enjoy their drinks, Hsi-men Ch'ing happened to go to the back of the house to relieve himself. This was one of those occasions on which:

> Something was destined to happen.

Suddenly he became aware of the sound of people laughing in an anteroom on the eastern side of the courtyard. As soon as he had finished relieving himself he went up to the window of the room in question and stole a peek. What should he see inside but Li Kuei-chieh drinking wine in the company of a southerner who was wearing a square-cut scholar's cap. Before he knew it:

> A fire blazed up in his heart.[47]

He strode back to the front of the house and, with a single movement of his hand, turned over the table at which his companions were drinking, smashing the saucers and cups to smithereens. He then called out the four page boys who had accompanied him to look after the horse, P'ing-an, Tai-an, Hua-t'ung, and Ch'in-t'ung, and:

> Without permitting any further explanation,

ordered them to smash up the doors, windows, walls, beds, and curtains of the Li family establishment.

Sponger Ying, Tagalong Hsieh, and Sticky Chu did their best to restrain him, but to no avail. Hsi-men Ch'ing continued to protest, again and again, that he was going to drag out that jailbird of a southerner and that painted

Hsi-men Ch'ing Wreaks Havoc in the Verdant Spring Bordello

face, truss them up together with a single length of rope, and lock them up in his gatehouse.

Now Ting the Second was not a brave man, and when he heard the rumpus that was being kicked up outside he was so frightened he hid under the bed in the inner room and called out to Kuei-chieh to save him.

"Phooey!" said Kuei-chieh. "You can depend on my mother, whatever happens. It doesn't amount to anything. Let him blow off steam if he wants to, but no matter how he blusters, you stay where you are."

To resume our story, when the old procuress saw that Hsi-men Ch'ing had made a wreck of the place:

Neither hurriedly nor hastily,

she made her appearance, hobbling along with the aid of a stick, and said a few inconsequential words to smooth things over. This had the effect of making Hsi-men Ch'ing even angrier and, pointing his finger at her, he began to curse. There is a song to the tune "Courtyard Full of Fragrance" that testifies to this:

Madam, you are not a good sort of person.
Welcoming the new and seeing off the old,[48]
You live off beauty by prostituting it.
With specious words you would deceive me,
Faultfinding here and eulogizing there.[49]
In your house alone I must have spent,
At least a thousand taels of yellow gold.
You sell dog meat advertised as mutton.[50]
I'll tell you what you really are:
One of those vixens who bewitch people,
Whose every wile is absolutely false.

The madam responded in kind:

Good sir, let me tell you something.
If you stop patronizing my daughter,
I'll find a replacement for you.
My whole house looks only to her,
For its means of livelihood.
If we are to feed and clothe ourselves,
We are dependent on her for firewood and rice.
There is no excuse for your raving like thunder.[51]
You may object that we are lacking in good faith,
But you forget your own deficiencies;
She's not your wedded wife by aid of go-between.

When Hsi-men Ch'ing heard her reply, he became even angrier, and almost came to blows with the old lady. This was only prevented thanks to the strenuous efforts of Sponger Ying, Tagalong Hsieh, and Sticky Chu, who had to intervene physically in order to restrain him.

After creating this great disturbance, Hsi-men Ch'ing swore an oath never to cross the threshold of the Li family establishment again and then mounted his horse and rode home through the snow. Truly:

To sleep with every casual flower, when they
  number in the millions;
Is not as good a plan as going home to share
  a bed with your wife.
Even though, beside your pillow, she may leave
  something to be desired;
She will sleep with you until the morrow dawns
  without demanding money.[52]

Or again:

Such women do no weaving and their
  menfolk do not plow;
The flaunting of their beauty is their
  only stock in trade.
Though your wealth be measured by the peck
  or by the cartload;
It will not suffice to fill the madam's
  bottomless pit.

Or again:

Their false feelings and specious sentiments
  resemble the real thing;
With deceptive phrases and clever words[53]
  they put on a good show.
How many otherwise intelligent gentlemen
  have been done in by them?
Only after death will their tongues
  be plucked out in Hell.[54]

If you want to know the outcome of these events,
Pray consult the story related in the following chapter.

Appendix I

TRANSLATOR'S COMMENTARY ON THE PROLOGUE

The first half of the first chapter, including the prologue, of the *Chin P'ing Mei tz'u-hua* has been completely rewritten in the B and C recensions of the text on which the existing English translations are based.[1] This is the first attempt, therefore, to present this material to the English-speaking world in the form in which it was originally written. The prologue presents a rather enigmatic introduction to the novel and is not self-explanatory, although it exemplifies many of the rhetorical techniques that inform the rest of the text. I have chosen, therefore, to append a brief commentary to help prepare the reader for what is to follow.

Although the prologue is not an easy document to interpret, I believe that a close reading will show that it succeeds admirably, albeit subtly, in prefiguring every one of the major issues with which the novel is concerned. As such it must be considered an integral part of the work, and any interpretation of the novel as a whole must take it into account.

It begins with a lyric by the thirteenth-century poet Cho T'ien, which appears to restate the conventional view that women are to be blamed for the failures of even some of the greatest men of the past. But in the explication of the words *passion* and *beauty* that immediately follows, it is not alleged that temptation, in the form of beauty, is the cause of passion, but that the two are interdependent, in that the presence of either one can give rise to the other. It follows from this that the moral responsibility for the excesses to which passion so often leads must be borne by the individual who allows this response to go unchecked within himself rather than by the one who evokes it. One of the major themes of the novel is the unfortunate consequences, for both society and the individual, of failure to take moral responsibility for one's acts. A line of poetry that is repeated three times in the course of the novel makes this point with unmistakable clarity: "Beauty does not delude people, they delude themselves."[2] Thus the apparent point of the opening lyric is subtly undercut by the passage of explication that immediately follows it, leaving readers to decide for themselves. This is one of the most consistently employed rhetorical strategies of the author, who delights in juxtaposing seemingly incompatible points of view in order to stimulate reflection on the part of the reader.

This brief excursus on the relationship between passion and beauty introduces the statement by Wang Yen (256–311) that "It is people just like ourselves who are most affected by passion." As pointed out in chapter 1, note 7, this is the punch line of a famous anecdote that reads as follows:

"When Wang Yen's infant son died, Shan Chien came to offer his condolences. Wang Yen was beside himself with grief. Shan Chien said, 'It was only a babe in arms, so why carry on to such an extent?' To which Wang Yen replied, 'Sages may be able to forget their feelings, and the lower order of men may lack feeling altogether. It is people just like ourselves who are most affected by passion.'"

The occurrence of this quotation on the first page of the novel is significant for two reasons. First, it indicates that the author intends to focus his attention on that middle range of human beings into which most of his readers, who are neither sages nor insensate brutes, must fall, rather than creating a gallery of plaster saints and cardboard villains with whom his readers could not be expected to feel much affinity. Second, it adumbrates one of the author's major thematic concerns—the consequences of irresponsibility in high places.

Wang Yen was one of the most prominent men in the political and cultural life of his time, and he ended his career as chief minister, yet he has been held to be largely responsible for the fall of the Western Chin dynasty (265–317), which took place a few years after his death. He had already attracted favorable attention while still in his teens, but there was something ominous in his character that disturbed his uncle, Yang Hu (221–278), a famous paragon of moral rectitude. A near contemporary of his, Sun Sheng (c. 303–373), reported the following anecdote, as translated by Richard B. Mather: "Wang Yen's father, Wang I, had a notification of censure and was about to be dismissed from his post. Yen was in his seventeenth year at the time, and went to see his uncle, Yang Hu, to plead his father's cause. His words were unusually impressive, but Hu did not grant his request. Yen thereupon shook out his clothes and rose to depart. Hu, looking back, said to the other guests, 'This man will certainly have a flourishing reputation and occupy a great position in his own age, but at the same time, the one who will destroy the morals and harm the good influences of his age will also certainly be this man.' "[3]

Another near contemporary, Lu Lin (fl. fourth century), commented after Wang Yen's death, as translated by Mather: "Although Wang Yen occupied an exalted office, he did not restrict himself with his duties. The contemporary age was so influenced by him that people felt ashamed to talk about the Moral Teaching . . . [i.e., Confucianism], and from clerks in the Imperial Secretariat on down, everybody admired the principle of folding the hands in silence, and took the neglect of duty for their ideal. Although all was still at peace within the Four Seas, those who understood the true state of affairs realized that they were on the verge of ruin."[4] There can be little doubt that the author of the *Chin P'ing Mei* felt that the society of his day was on the verge of ruin for the same reasons.

The next paragraph of the prologue continues the explication of the opening lyric by defining "Hook of Wu" as the name of a sword and providing a seemingly gratuitous list of the names of some famous swords of antiquity. As pointed out in chapter 1, note 9, this passage is reminiscent of the penultimate paragraph of Hsün-tzu's most famous essay, entitled "Man's Nature Is Evil," where he also lists the names of some famous swords of antiquity and ends by saying, as translated by Burton Watson, "but if they had not been subjected to the grindstone, they would never have become sharp, and if men of strength had not wielded them, they would never have been able to cut anything."[5]

As pointed out in chapter 1, note 9, it is clear that the sword serves Hsün-tzu as a metaphor for realized human potential, the raw material of which must undergo the tempering and grinding of proper socialization before it can be put to effective use. And even then, to continue the metaphor, if it is not to grow blunt or rusty it must be properly maintained, which, in human terms, requires one to subject oneself to a continuous regimen of self-cultivation. It was not the fact that the swords of Hsiang Yü and Liu Pang had not been sharp, but the fact that their self-indulgence had allowed them to become blunted, that resulted in their moral and political failures. It is just such a lack of self-cultivation that enables the protagonists of the *Chin P'ing Mei* to be so acute in detecting the misdeeds of others and so obtuse in applying these lessons to themselves. As Dame Wang says of Hsi-men Ch'ing, "He can detect a bee defecating forty li outside the city, but trips over a mangy elephant on his own doorstep."[6]

The prologue then goes on to recount selectively the events leading up to the death of Hsiang Yü, the most powerful man in China during the interregnum between the Ch'in and Han dynasties. The description is based on that in the *Shih-chi* (Records of the historian), by Ssu-ma Ch'ien (145–c. 90 B.C.), which is justifiably regarded as one of the most famous passages in Chinese literature.[7] In the original source it is made clear that Hsiang Yü's downfall is due more to his own hubris than to any external cause. Three times he declares that it is Heaven that is destroying him, and twice that this outcome is due to no fault of his own. His attitude is a perfect exemplification of the truth of Hsün-tzu's dictum that "He who understands himself does not blame others; he who understands destiny does not blame Heaven. He who blames others will come to grief; he who blames Heaven lacks resolution. To fail in oneself and place the blame on others, is this not to be deluded?"[8]

Every educated Chinese reader is familiar with the biography of Hsiang Yü in the *Shih-chi* and could be expected to recognize it as the source of the account of his death given in the prologue to the *Chin P'ing Mei*. Knowledge of the source would thus have the effect of undercutting, or even contradicting, the validity of the point apparently being made on the surface of the text through the use of selective quotation. This is another of the rhetorical strategies most frequently resorted to by the author of the *Chin P'ing Mei*. Again and again, when the source of an allusion is located, its true significance for the interpretation of the text turns out to lie in some part of the work that is not quoted directly. This device is, of course, a commonplace to students of classical Chinese poetry, who often find that the correct interpretation of an allusion is dependent on the identification of its source and familiarity with its contents, but its occurrence in the major works of vernacular literature has not been adequately recognized. The text of the *Chin P'ing Mei* is a veritable pastiche of unidentified quotations and allusions, almost as dense as those to be found in the work of such Western authors as Joyce or Nabokov. Until the sources of these quotations and allusions are located and interpreted, the meaning of the text will remain enigmatic.

As the prologue continues, it describes at some length the events leading up to the horrible fate of Lady Ch'i, the favorite consort of the founding emperor of the Han dynasty. As the poem by Fan Ch'eng-ta (1126–93) that is quoted at the conclusion of this passage points out, both Hsiang Yü and Liu Pang, for all their vaunted might, "proved powerless to protect their beauties." This theme clearly foreshadows the inability of Hsi-men Ch'ing to prevent the death of his favorite concubine, Li P'ing-erh,[9] which is in fact the outcome of his own tyrannical insistence on having sexual intercourse with her, against her will, during her menstrual period.[10] After her death Hsi-men Ch'ing is inconsolable and cries out, "Heaven must be blind to leave me so destitute. . . . What have I ever done to anyone that Heaven should now see fit to rob me so egregiously of my beloved!"[11] Once again, this is a perfect illustration of the truth of Hsün-tzu's dictum that "It is only an enlightened ruler who is able to show love to those whom he loves; a benighted ruler is sure to endanger those whom he loves."[12]

This point implies that Hsi-men Ch'ing's role in the novel is meant to be analogous to that of a benighted ruler. There is no doubt in my mind that this is precisely what the author intends to suggest by beginning his novel, which ostensibly focuses on the household of a middle-class man-about-town, with a prologue that deals with the exploits of two famous contenders for the throne. If this were not the case, the prologue would be both superfluous and irrelevant.

But this implication is not confined to the prologue. Innumerable clues, planted inconspicuously in the narrative, indicate that Hsi-men Ch'ing is intended to function as a surrogate, not only for the feckless Emperor Hui-tsung (r. 1100–25) of the world ostensibly depicted in the novel, but also for the Chia-ching emperor (r. 1521–66) and/or the Wan-li emperor (r. 1572–1620) of the author's own time. Hsi-men Ch'ing's six wives are surrogates for the "six traitors," or six evil ministers, who are traditionally blamed for the fall of the Northern Sung dynasty. In a less specific sense, they may also be seen as analogues of the ministers of the Six Ministries that comprised the administrative core of the central government. Hsi-men Ch'ing's sycophants, servants, and employees, in their turn, act as surrogates for the eunuchs and lesser functionaries in the imperial administration. By deliberately restricting his focus to the events in a single middle-class household, but subtly suggesting to the reader that this microcosm stands in an analogical relationship to the society as a whole, the author is able to attack the abuses of the day with far greater candor and analytical rigor than would have been possible, or safe, if he had attacked the reigning monarch and the existing political and social structure directly.

The analogy between the household and the state, as well as that between the roles of husband and wife and ruler and minister, are ancient and hallowed components of the Chinese cultural tradition. It is the latter analogy that lends poignancy to the remark in the prologue that "The way of a wife or concubine who wishes to serve her husband faithfully and yet keep her head and neck intact within her own windows is hard." There can be no doubt that this statement is intended to apply not only to the unfortunate plight of the women in the prologue, and in the novel proper, but also to that of the actual or prospective officials from whose ranks the bulk of the novel's readers could be expected to come.

The story of the favoritism displayed toward Lady Ch'i by Emperor Kao-tsu, his willingness to consider replacing the heir apparent with her son, and the fatal consquences that this had for both of them clearly foreshadows the story of the relationship between Hsi-men Ch'ing and Li P'ing-erh and her son in the novel. But both of these stories also have a special relevance to crucial events of the Wan-li reign period (1573–1620), during which the novel was probably written. The most divisive and protracted controversy of this long and controversy-ridden reign, beginning as early as 1584, was over the issue of whether or not the emperor intended to prefer the son of his favorite consort, Cheng Kuei-fei (c. 1568–1630), by designating him heir apparent instead of the emperor's eldest son by another wife.[13] The author's contemporaries could scarcely have failed to see that this story, which looms so large in the prologue, and the corresponding elements of the plot that loom so large in the novel, might be interpreted as having some relevance to the events of their own day.

By saying this, however, I do not mean to imply that the *Chin P'ing Mei* is a roman à clef in any meaningful sense of the term. There is no one-to-one correspondence between the characters and incidents of the novel and those of sixteenth-century China, or any other period of Chinese history. The author undoubtedly believed that the moral laws he intended his work to exemplify were universally valid and that the lessons that might be derived from it were, consequently, as true for any one period of history as for another. By the same token, they were as true for the household of a bourgeois social climber as they were for the imperial court. In fact he makes an explicit statement to this effect in the couplet, "This has always been so, in ancient as in modern times; it is as true for the exalted as for the humble."

The author's method is to write about the sexual and emotional relations between ordinary men and women and the analogous relations between the ruler and his ministers at one and the same time, rather than merely using one set of terms as substitutes for the other. Thus, when the focus shifts from household to court, or from sexual promiscuity to political irresponsibility, each sphere of conduct is intended to suggest and illuminate relevant aspects of the other, rather than merely to stand for it. Thus the *Chin P'ing Mei* is allegorical only in the sense that its characters and incidents are intended to be suggestive of analogous characters and incidents wherever and whenever they may occur, but not in the sense that they stand, in any consistent way, for a corresponding set of relationships in some other sphere. One of the functions of the prologue is to prepare the reader to look for such meaningful links between seemingly disparate elements and to consider the relationship betwen the parts and the whole.

In the paragraph immediately following the lengthy exposition of the opening lyric we encounter the quotation: "Gentlemen who presume on their talents are lacking in virtue and women who flaunt their beauty are dissolute. If only they were able to maintain the fullness of their gifts while taking care to avoid the overflow of excess, they could be upright men and virtuous women." As pointed out in chapter 1, note 28, this passage comes from the author's comment at the end of a famous tenth-century tale about the tragic consequences of an adulterous liaison accomplished by climbing over an intervening wall. The plot of this tale prefigures in many of its details the affair between Hsi-men Ch'ing and his neighbor's wife, Li P'ing-erh, which is consummated for the first time when he climbs over the garden wall for an assignation.[14] But this quotation also foreshadows one of the major themes of the novel, which is the consequences of excess in the sexual, economic, and political spheres. If this fault is allowed to go unchecked it results in debauchery, avarice, and tyranny, any one of which may lead, as they do in the novel, to death.

In the ensuing paragraph we are told that "this book is an instance of a beautiful woman who is embodied in a tiger and engenders a tale of the passions." This, obviously, is a reference to P'an Chin-lien, the female protagonist of the novel, who first encounters her nemesis, Wu Sung, as a result of his exploit in slaying a tiger with his bare fists,[15] and who is herself disemboweled by him near the end of the book[16] in revenge for her murder of his brother.[17] The first syllable of her given name associates her with the lethal element, metal, and in turn, according to the traditional Chinese system of correlative correspondences, with the carnivorous animal, the tiger, and with autumn, the season of death. It comes as no surprise, therefore, that she accomplishes the murder of her rival Li P'ing-erh's baby son with the help of a cat, which is, of course, a tiger in miniature.[18]

Toward the end of the prologue we are told that the setting of the story to follow is the district of Ch'ing-ho in the prefecture of Tung-p'ing. I have already explained in the introduction why I think that the choice of Ch'ing-ho as a setting for the novel may have been intended as an ironic commentary on the action, deriving its force from the doctrine of the rectification of names, of which Hsün-tzu is the most famous proponent. Since, historically speaking, the district of Ch'ing-ho was never part of the prefecture of Tung-p'ing, the author of the *Chin P'ing Mei* must have made a conscious choice in asserting such a relationship. I suggest that he may have done so because of its literary associations. The prefecture of Tung-p'ing was located in a low-lying swampy area of western Shantung Province, along a major transportation artery between North and South China. Around the middle of the third century A.D. the famous poet Juan Chi (210–63) served for a time as governor of Tung-p'ing and wrote a *fu*, or rhapsody, about it in which he describes it as a sink of unparalleled iniquity. I will quote at some length from the relevant portions of Donald Holzman's translation of this work:

There is a vile place, reached through side roads,
  Where there are heaps of deer and pigs;
It is not made beautiful by the fair and clean,
  But is the resort of the filthy and impure. . . .
[Here] the Three Chin concocted their alliances
  And Cheng and Wei[19] spread their disorder. . . .
That is why violence ran loose within families
  And poisoned hate sprang up between husband and wife.
These people still had boundless desires to do bad:
  How could it be long before they gave vent to them? . . .
With its back to the mountains, facing the waters,
  The region was filthy, full of egotism,
So that in the small quarters and border towns
  No one would deny the bad things said of it. . . .
Arrogant menials from small towns
  Lived here.
The waterways lead, by the quickest route,
  To Lake Tung-t'ing and to the state of Ch'u,
And they carry [southern] influences [to Tung-p'ing],
  Directly to it, and to its entire domain.
Thus they inherited [southern] customs
  And were without rules, without models:
Not barbarians, they still followed no laws,
  And came to do harm.
. . . in their cooperative ventures, each vaunts his own power;
  They turn away from reason and towards debauchery.
Extolling the passions and chasing after profit,
  The only thing they respect is excess.[20]

Thus, as early as the third century of our era, the literary reputation of Tung-p'ing was established as a region characterized by filth and impurity, political intrigue, licentious popular culture, familial violence, marital discord, runaway egotism, disruption of the social hierarchy, disdain for southern culture on the part of its northern inhabitants (despite or because of its pervasive influence), illegality, contempt for reason and restraint, debauchery, passion, and excess. It would be hard to imagine a more appropriate geographic setting for the sordid story that is unfolded in the *Chin P'ing Mei*.

I hope that the above remarks will prove sufficient to demonstrate that the prologue to the *Chin P'ing Mei tz'u-hua*, although it may appear somewhat confusing at first reading, in fact succeeds in adumbrating all of the major issues raised in the body of the novel and must be regarded not only as an integral part of the work, but as essential to any interpretation of the author's intended meaning.

Appendix II

TRANSLATIONS OF SUPPLEMENTARY MATERIAL

1. Song suite beginning with the tune "Flowers in Brocade," the first line of which is "The fair weather is balmy." See chapter 15, note 20. This song suite is performed twice in the *Chin P'ing Mei tz'u-hua*, vol. 1, ch. 15, p. 9a, ll. 1–2; and vol. 4, ch. 78, p. 20a, l. 3. It is preserved in *Tz'u-lin chai-yen*, 2:618–23; and *Yung-hsi yüeh-fu, ts'e* 12, pp. 57a–59a. The following translation is based on the text as given in *Tz'u-lin chai-yen*.

TO THE TUNE "FLOWERS IN BROCADE" (NORTHERN STYLE):

The fair weather is balmy,
Spring is at its most beautiful.
Now lightly warm, now lightly cool,
It reveals itself in flowering branches.
Deep in secluded courtyards,
The swallows suddenly return.
On purple roads and fragrant streets,
Fine steeds with golden bridles neigh.
Parks and woods are bright with silks,
Peach and apricot blossoms vie in fragrance.
The sounds of imperial music,
Drift across the Dragon Pool.
Fragrant verdure gradually blends
  into the green mist.
Truly, on such a fine day,
One revels joyously in the beautiful scene.

TO THE TUNE "GOLD LAMÉ CURTAINS" (SOUTHERN STYLE):

The lingering cold is chilly;
Layers of emerald curtains are drawn.
Throughout the imperial capital, spring has returned.
The east wind grows more importunate.
The scene is at its most beautiful;
Bright with silks and jewels.
Having moistened the flowers, the rain has cleared.
The rain has cleared,
And the flowering branches reach to the ground.

The smell of flowers permeates the fragrant streets;
Subtly invading the sleeves of the passersby.
On Bronze Camel Street, they have roamed everywhere.
They have roamed everywhere,
In love with the long days and genial sun.

TO THE TUNE "PLUCKING THE CASSIA" (NORTHERN STYLE):

On the roads of the pleasure quarter
  lissome willows are trailing;
On the banks of the Wei River
  the genial sun lingers.
Reds and purples exude fragrance;
Plum branches lose their powdery blooms;
Peach trees venture into flower;
Crab apples and pears vie with their snowy blossoms.
Blowing the willow catkins
  the fragrant breeze is gentle;
Embracing the roving wheels
  the emerald grass is luxuriant.
Let carnelian goblets overflow;
Exchange songs and lyrics.
Meeting with times of peace
  and glorious days;
In every place they celebrate
  the season of the flowers.

TO THE TUNE "RIVER WATER" (SOUTHERN STYLE):

Spring colors live up to the revelers' desires;
The fragrant breeze penetrates their silks.
See how they compete to display flowery lanterns;
How the light of the moon shines refulgently;
And how, clustering on the branches of fiery trees,
Tens of thousands of candles envelop them.
The silver river and pearly dipper grow dim.
This festive day, the fifteenth of the first month,
Surpasses the revels at the Jasper Pool.
Bright lotus lamps illuminate the hills of lanterns,
Truly, they are magnificent.
Crowds surge about vermilion wheels, traffic on
  the celestial streets is slow.
Reining in their jeweled horses are the
  imperial guards by their ten thousands,
Watching until the shadows of the trees fall east
  and the moon sinks west.

TO THE BINARY TUNES "WILD GEESE ALIGHT" AND "VICTORY SONG" (NORTHERN STYLE):

Arabesques of incense float from jeweled censers;
The oriole's song shatters the silence of dawn.
Spring breezes waft the fragrance of flowery plants;
Lingering sunlight enhances rivers and mountains.

Frowning-eyebrow willow leaves expand their greens;
Rain-drenched crab apple blossoms drip in threads.
Village mummers and country folk enjoy themselves;
At the Lustration Festival wine cups are set afloat.
Everyone must know,
The myriad nations are now all at peace;
Upon prescribed topics,
One must compose poetry on phoenix notepaper.

TO THE BINARY TUNES "REITERATIVE BROCADE" AND "INTOXICATED IN THE EAST WIND" (SOUTHERN STYLE):

Our only fear is that greens darken the alleyways,
And spring will soon depart.
Our only fear is that greens darken the alleyways,
And spring will soon depart.
The cuckoo cries,
Only causing the flowers to fall and
  the willow catkins to fly.
The effects of the east wind permeate everything;
On these fine days when spring is in its glory,
Half the flowers have already fallen,
Leaving only a few branches of peony behind.
Outside the painted pavilions,
One is surrounded by misty peaks and emerald waves.
Behold: swings kick into view behind the walls,
Revealing pearls and kingfisher feather ornaments,
Which set off to perfection golden bridle trappings.
Our only fear is that greens darken the alleyways,
And spring will soon depart.

Climbing high towers, leaning on
  all the balustrades,
On the eve of the spring festival, fires are
  prohibited, one eats cold food.
Windblown red petals stick to the picnic mats.
In the I-ch'un Park there is banqueting.

Begrudging what remains of spring,
One lies intoxicated in the slanting sunlight.
In the shadow of the weeping willow trees,
The calls of auspicious birds awaken the slumberer.
As one traverses the twenty-four divisions
  of the flowering cycle,
One can calculate how much of the glorious season
  has already gone by.

TO THE BINARY TUNES "RIVER-BOBBED OARS" AND "SEVEN BROTHERS" (NORTHERN STYLE):

Traversing willow paths,
Crossing peach tree streams,
Skimming the clear waves,
Pairs of swallows fly.
Fragrant verdure grows wild and luxuriant;
Fallen willow catkins lie soiled in mud.
Cuckoos cry incessantly,
But cannot call a halt to spring's
  wending way.
Only the myriad willow fronds
  impede its progress.

The beautiful scene basks in genial sunlight.
Truly: as greens darken reds dwindle.
The most touching element is a pair of orioles,
Warbling to the humans,
Harmonizing with the notes of pipe and song.
As the sun moves, flower shadows traverse
  hanging painted screens.
Truly: Chinese and barbarians alike share in
  the enjoyment of these years of peace.

TO THE TUNE "WAVE-BOBBING OARS" (SOUTHERN STYLE):

The realm of luxury,
Is apparent in the picturelike towers and terraces.
Beside the dance floors, swallows kick
  blossoms into flight.
Performing new music, the mandola and psaltery
  are tuned to a low pitch.
As though calling to the revelers, orioles
  compete in song.

TO THE BINARY TUNES "PLUM BLOSSOM WINE" AND "ENJOYING THE SOUTH" (NORTHERN STYLE):

See how in spring pools,
Brocadelike carp leap.
Hear how in green trees,
Yellow orioles warble.
Everything conveys the idea of spring.
Each is content;
Each is happy.
The east wind blows the willow catkins,
Skidding over the green verdure,
As far as the horizon.
They cannot be restrained,
Seeing spring on its way,
Alighting on the fallen blossoms,
Entangled in floating gossamer.
Outside the ornate mansion,
West of the little bridge,
The new plums are like beans,
The willow leaves like eyebrows.

Remember mid-spring in the Southern Park,
  homeward bound, treading the green;
After doing a stint on the swing,
  showing off one's silken garments.
Slowly singing "Golden Threads" and
  toasting with golden goblets;
Idly apostrophizing the peonies and
  appreciating the yellow roses.
Truly: an auspicious festival in a glorious season,
Thanks to the unification of the Great Ming,
  favoring Chinese and barbarian alike.

CODA:

Of all the beauteous seasons of the year,
  one must remember,
Throughout the human world, the glory of spring
  is most enjoyable.
May the good fortune and long life of our
  Sage Sovereign equal Heaven.

2. Song suite to the tune "Thirty Melodies," the first line of which is "How happy this auspicious day." See chapter 16, note 19. This song suite is per-

formed twice in the *Chin P'ing Mei tz'u-hua*, vol. 1, ch. 16, p. 11a, l. 9; and vol. 2, ch. 31. p. 15a, l. 5. It is preserved in *Sheng-shih hsin-sheng*, pp. 513–14; *Tz'u-lin chai-yen*, 1:235–37; and *Yung-hsi yüeh-fu, ts'e* 16, pp. 8a–9a. The following translation is based on the text as given in *Sheng-shih hsin-sheng*.

To the tune "Thirty Melodies":

How happy this auspicious day;
The planet Venus has appeared, dimly discernible
  amid variegated clouds.
See how the jade tree before the reception hall,
Has once again put forth a magic sprout.
Having been invited to attend the feast,
We offer a curved kingfisher feather
  with a sharp quill,
And a round gold embroidery frame
  of paltry diameter,
As tokens of esteem for this lovely new face;
And in the hope that you will remain a happy pair,
And continue to live harmoniously together
  for a hundred years.
Five hundred years ago your destiny
  was sealed,
Only to be fulfilled today.
Here in your magistrate's tribunal,
  on the occasion of this birthday,
We offer a toast to your long life.
As pure as jade,
As captivating as a flower,
This is the flawless jewel of the age.
At this feast to celebrate the bathing of the child,
On this auspicious day,
The whole household is happy as can be.
Necklaces and bracelets hold in place
  the mermaid silk.
Our only wish is that,
Your longevity be that of a mountain,
Your good fortune as deep as the sea,
And that you share glorious success.
The happy hubbub at this elegant feast
  is not inconsiderable.
Truly: the Queen Mother of the Western Pool
  has temporarily abandoned paradise;
Immortal lads amid the clouds proffer
  the peaches of immortality.

With her patent of nobility she is entitled
   to a coach and four,
The phoenix headdress and cloud-patterned cape.
Surrounded by attendant beauties,
Entitled to golden insignia and purple seal-ribbons,
He has returned to his old home,
Where, dressed in motley, he can join his family
   in enjoying the season.
If the proper rites are not observed it may
   give rise to resentment;
Human nature is such that one must be chary
   of too intimate relationships.
We are happy to live in an era of good government
   when the people are not disturbed,
And wish the nation to be at peace and
   the wind and rain harmonious.
A jade *ch'i-lin* has fulfilled the bear's
   portent of a noble birth.
So now that famous beauty, the elder Ch'iao,
   is as lucky as her little sister,
And with a baby to boot,
To bring glory to its ancestors,
And continue the family tradition of
   wearing gold and sable.
Tortoise and crane portend good fortune,
   sporting in pool and pavilion;
Pine and cypress intertwine their branches,
   intimating endurance.
Grain grows in double ears; phoenixes
   alight in respect.
They are like birds that fly only in pairs,
   like mating phoenixes.
Shadows of flowers tumble and toss on the screen;
The sound of singing resounds in the air.
The dancers with willowy waists like Hsiao-man's
   are danced out;
The tune "Rainbow Skirts and Feathered Garments"
   is finally over;
As they turn their heads, cloud-shaped palace
   head ornaments fall out.
The ornate halls are deep,
The gardens and courtyards secluded.
The incense floating from jeweled censers
   is curling upwards.

Roll up the embroidered curtains
and beaded portieres;
Let the swallows come and nest
if they will.
We are confronted with crimson peaches,
seemingly afire,
Just as they should be.
We see butterflies, one pair after another,
flying around us.
At this auspicious feast, this
festival of flowers,
The small zither and great zither
are in harmony.
Let us enjoy the music of
pipes and woodwinds;
Unbutton our collars,
Open our mouths in laughter;
Give way to drunkenness, empty
the golden flagons;
And leave the red apricot blossoms to revel
on their branch tips.
May your wealth and distinction flourish
like the three months of spring,
And may the voice of the cuckoo never be heard
to portend their end.

CODA:

May the incense of your sacrifices never cease,
your flowers never grow old;
May your good fortune be deep as the Eastern Sea,
your longevity ever increase;
May you fulfill your days with mutual respect
and enjoy your life together.

3. Song suite beginning with the tune "Clever Improvisation," the first line of which is "How pleased we are by your success." See chapter 20, note 28. This song suite is performed and partially quoted in the *Chin P'ing Mei tz'u-hua*, vol. 1, ch. 20, p. 10b, ll. 2–4. It is preserved in *Ts'ai-lou chi*, scene 20, p. 69, ll. 3–11; *Sheng-shih hsin-sheng*, pp. 418–20; *Tz'u-lin chai-yen*, 2:1272–75; *Yung-hsi yüeh-fu, ts'e* 16, pp. 32b–33b; and *Ch'ün-yin lei-hsüan*, 3:1971–73. The following translation is based on the text as given in *Sheng-shih hsin-sheng*.

TO THE TUNE "CLEVER IMPROVISATION":

How pleased we are by your success,
You have been doubly favored.
Heaven has made this perfect match;
Like male and female phoenix
  are husband and wife.
Wearing golden seal and purple ribbon,
  marks of glory and distinction,
Today we thank our parents,
Profoundly grateful for their loving care.
Chorus:
How happy we are to meet again,
How happy we are to meet again.
In the decorated hall ranks of pearls
  and head ornaments are arrayed.
The happy hubbub of feasting and music
  is graced with a spring breeze.
This day we will renew our marriage vows,
Enjoying the pleasures of connubial bliss,
Like fish sporting in the water.

TO THE TUNE "FLIRTATIOUS LAUGHTER":

Gayly laughing we celebrate this happy occasion,
By raising our phoenix goblets on high.
To the sound of ivory clappers, silver psaltery,
  and jade flute,
Let them bring on in cups and platters,
The fruits of sea and land to grace
  the auspicious feast.
The name of the winner of top honors is
  emblazoned on the tiger placard.
Behold: in perfumed hall and painted chamber
  we feast from brazen vessels.
May they live happily together as husband and wife
  for ever and ever.

TO THE TUNE "CONGRUENT WAYS":

Formerly we feared the shame of
  public exposure;
Our temporary anger was only
  a pretense.

We did not anticipate that you
would reject us;
At that time we had no way of
keeping you.
But now that we have arrived at the present day,
Let us enjoy ourselves and endeavor
to get drunk.
Endeavor to get drunk,
But never forget the role played in the past
by the gaily colored ball.

To the tune "The Doll":

How joyous our delight as tortoiseshell mats
are spread for the feast.
In the fine haze, incense curls from golden
lion-shaped censers.
We are surrounded by red, encircled by emerald,
like piles of embroidered brocade.
Hear how the musicians play in perfect unison;
Truly: it is a model occasion.

To the tune "Imposter's Song":

In spring we enjoy this famous park;
the flowers are like silks;
The scene is most remarkable.
Amid ten li of lotus blossoms
oars move lightly;
Everything is perfect.
In the decorated hall, day after day,
fine feasts are spread.
Do not fail to take advantage of
such auspicious occasions,
Such auspicious occasions;
But give others cause to celebrate the story of
The Gaily Colored Tower.

To the tune "Sacred Bhaiṣajya-Rāja":

The notes are harmonious,
The melodies entrancing;
Happily we celebrate the occasion
by providing this feast.
Never parted for a moment,

Following in each other's steps;
In such a good marriage, truly,
   we will never separate,
But enjoy forever the pleasures
   of connubial bliss.

TO THE TUNE "PLUM BLOSSOM WINE":

At every festival, in every season,
May our wishes be granted, our moods happy.
Let fragrant breezes sweep courtyards
   gay with the sound of song.
Pour frothing bumpers,
Float golden wine cups.
Chorus:
In decorated halls let happy laughter reign.
Who is as lucky as you and I,
Sharing the delights of the nuptial chamber,
Able to spend the rest of our lives
   with branches entwined?
Crimson curtains and embroidered hangings,
Hide fairy caverns, the realms of the blessed.
It is just like stumbling on the
   Peach Blossom Spring.
Such glory and distinction,
Are unmatched in this world.
Chorus:
In decorated halls let happy laughter reign.
Who is as lucky as you and I,
Sharing the delights of the nuptial chamber,
Able to spend the rest of our lives
   with branches entwined?

CODA:

It seems we must have been united
   in a former life;
How happy we are to have met again
   in this incarnation.
Father and mother, husband and wife,
Are reunited and all wish them well.

NOTES

INTRODUCTION

1. Some of this introduction has already appeared in a slightly different form in my article entitled "A Confucian Interpretation of the *Chin P'ing Mei*," in *Proceedings of the International Conference on Sinology, Section on Literature, August, 1980* (Taipei: Academia Sinica, 1981), pp. 39–61.

2. On the possible implications of this construction of the title, see Katherine Carlitz, "Puns and Puzzles in the *Chin P'ing Mei*: A Look at Chapter 27," *T'oung Pao* 67, 3–5 (1981): 237.

3. The term "beauties of spring" is ambiguous since it also implies "beauties of sex," or "sex appeal."

4. See Chang Chu-p'o's essay entitled "*Chin P'ing Mei* tu-fa" (How to read the *Chin P'ing Mei*), which is part of the prolegomena in *Chang Chu-p'o p'i-p'ing Ti-i ch'i-shu Chin P'ing Mei* (Chang Chu-p'o's commentary on the number one marvelous book *Chin P'ing Mei*), ed. Wang Ju-mei et al., 2 vols. (Chi-nan: Ch'i-Lu shu-she, 1988), 1:49–50, item 106; and "How to Read the *Chin P'ing Mei*," trans. David T. Roy, in *How to Read the Chinese Novel*, ed. David L. Rolston (Princeton: Princeton University Press, 1990), p. 242, item 106.

5. See *Hou-ts'un Ch'ien-chia shih chiao-chu* (Liu K'o-chuang's poems by a thousand authors edited and annotated), comp. Liu K'o-chuang (1187–1269), ed., and annot. Hu Wen-nung and Wang Hao-sou (Kuei-yang: Kuei-chou jen-min ch'u-pan she, 1986), *chüan* 7, p. 206, l. 6.

6. See C. T. Hsia, "*Chin P'ing Mei*," in his *The Classic Chinese Novel* (New York: Columbia University Press, 1968), pp. 165–202. The quotations are on pp. 168 and 180, respectively.

7. For a book-length demonstration of this proposition, see Mary Elizabeth Scott, "Azure from Indigo: *Hong lou meng*'s Debt to *Jin Ping Mei*," Ph.D. dissertation, Princeton University, 1989, passim.

8. See *Chin P'ing Mei tz'u-hua* (Story of the plum in the golden vase), 5 vols., fac. repr. (Tokyo: Daian, 1963).

9. See P. D. Hanan, "The Text of the *Chin P'ing Mei*," *Asia Major*, n.s. vol. 9, part 1 (1962): 14–33.

10. See P. D. Hanan, "A Landmark of the Chinese Novel," in *The Far East: China and Japan*, ed. Douglas Grant and Millar Maclure (Toronto: University of Toronto Press, 1961), p. 325.

11. See P. D. Hanan, "Sources of the *Chin P'ing Mei*," *Asia Major*, n.s. vol. 10, part 1 (1963): 23–67.

12. See Andrew H. Plaks, "*Shui-hu chuan* and the Sixteenth Century Novel Form: An Interpretive Reappraisal," *Chinese Literature: Essays, Articles, Reviews* 2, 1 (1980), pp. 3–6; and *The Four Masterworks of the Ming Novel* (Princeton: Princeton University Press, 1987), passim.

13. The term "dialogically" is borrowed from the usage of the Russian critic M. M. Bakhtin and is discussed at length on pp. xliii–xlv.

14. James Joyce used the term "work in progress" as a provisional name for *Finnegans Wake* from 1924 until it was published in 1939. See Richard Ellmann, *James Joyce* (New York: Oxford University Press, 1982), p. 563.

15. The term "the figure in the carpet" refers to a famous short story of that title by Henry James (1896) that deals with a seemingly irrecoverable pattern of significance inconspicuously woven into the fabric of a work of art. See Henry James, *The Figure in the Carpet and Other Stories* (New York: Penguin Books, 1986), pp. 357–400; and what James himself had to say about it in the preface to the New York edition of his works, in ibid., pp. 44–46.

16. Shen Te-fu (1578–1642) claims that Yüan Hung-tao himself told him at a meeting that took place in Peking in 1606 that a complete manuscript of the *Chin P'ing Mei* was then in the possession of a bibliophile named Liu Ch'eng-hsi (d. 1621). See *Wan-li yeh-huo pien* (Private gleanings of the Wan-li reign period [1573–1620]), by Shen Te-fu, 3 vols. (Peking: Chung-hua shu-chü, 1980), vol. 2, *chüan* 25, p. 652, ll. 2–3. The passage in which the above statement occurs is the most detailed account that we have of the prepublication history of the *Chin P'ing Mei*. It has been translated in Hanan, "The Text of the *Chin P'ing Mei*," pp. 46–48. For further information on Liu Ch'eng-hsi, see Ma Tai-loi, "Ma-ch'eng Liu-chia ho *Chin P'ing Mei*" (The Liu family of Ma-ch'eng and the *Chin P'ing Mei*), *Chung-hua wen-shih lun-ts'ung* (Collections of essays on Chinese literature and history), no. 1 (1982): 111–20.

17. The second preface to this edition is dated to a month that corresponds to the period from December 28, 1617, to January 25, 1618, in the Western calendar. For a description of this edition, which is the one on which this translation is based, see Hanan, "The Text of the *Chin P'ing Mei*," pp. 2–39. I accept the arguments of Wei Tzu-yün and André Lévy that this was probably the first printed edition. See Wei Tzu-yün, *Chin P'ing Mei t'an-yüan* (The origins of the *Chin P'ing Mei*) (Taipei: Chü-liu t'u-shu kung-ssu, 1979), pp. 87–89 and passim; and André Lévy, "About the Date of the First Printed Edition of the *Chin P'ing Mei*," *Chinese Literature: Essays, Articles, Reviews* 1, 1 (January 1979): 43–47.

18. See Hanan, "The Text of the *Chin P'ing Mei*," pp. 1–10.

19. An excellent, unexpurgated, modern reprint of the B edition, which includes the rudimentary upper margin and interlineal commentary by an unknown critic, is available under the title *[Hsin-k'o hsiu-hsiang p'i-p'ing] Chin P'ing Mei* ([Newly cut illustrated commentarial edition] of the *Chin P'ing Mei*), 2 vols. (Chi-nan: Ch'i-Lu shu-she, 1989). On this commentary, see Andrew H. Plaks, "The Chongzhen Commentary on the *Jin Ping Mei*: Gems amidst the Dross," *Chinese Literature: Essays, Articles, Reviews* 8, 1 and 2 (July 1986), pp. 19–30.

20. An excellent modern reprint of this edition, which is expurgated, but in which every deletion is scrupulously indicated, is available in *Chang Chu-p'o p'i-p'ing Ti-i ch'i-shu Chin P'ing Mei*. This edition reprints Chang Chu-p'o's prechapter, upper margin, and interlineal commentary in full. On the importance of this commentary in the history of Chinese literary criticism, see David T. Roy, "Chang Chu-p'o's Commentary on the *Chin P'ing Mei*," in *Chinese Narrative: Critical and Theoretical Essays*, ed. Andrew H. Plaks (Princeton: Princeton University Press, 1977), pp. 115–23.

21. For a study of one significant aspect of this problem, see Indira Suh Satyendra, "Toward a Poetics of the Chinese Novel: A Study of the Prefatory Poems in the *Chin*

P'ing Mei tz'u-hua," Ph.D. dissertation, University of Chicago, 1989, pp. 22–86 and passim.

22. *Kin Pei Bai* (Chin P'ing Mei), trans. Ono Shinobu and Chida Kuichi, 3 vols. (Tokyo: Heibonsha, 1962).

23. *The Golden Lotus: A Translation, from the Chinese Original, of the Novel Chin P'ing Mei*, trans. Clement Egerton, 4 vols. (London: Routledge & Kegan Paul, 1972).

24. *Djin Ping Meh: Schlehenblüten in goldener Vase*, trans. Otto and Artur Kibat, 6 vols. (Hamburg: Verlag Die Waage, 1967–83).

25. *Fleur en Fiole d'Or (Jin Ping Mei cihua)*, trans. André Lévy, 2 vols. (Paris: Gallimard, 1985).

26. I use the term "implied author," in contradistinction to the "real author," who has not been identified, in the sense defined by Wayne Booth in *The Rhetoric of Fiction* (Chicago: University of Chicago Press, 1961), pp. 67–86 and passim.

27. See Patrick Hanan, "The Early Chinese Short Story: A Critical Theory in Outline," *Harvard Journal of Asiatic Studies*, vol. 27 (1967): 192–97; also in Cyril Birch, ed. *Studies in Chinese Literary Genres* (Berkeley: University of California Press, 1974), pp. 323–28; and Hanan, *The Chinese Vernacular Story* (Cambridge: Harvard University Press, 1981), pp. 59–68.

28. I use the term "formal realism" as defined by Ian Watt in *The Rise of the Novel* (Berkeley: University of California Press, 1957), pp. 9–34; and discussed by Patrick Hanan in "The Early Chinese Short Story," pp. 175–78.

29. See the preface signed Hsin-hsin Tzu (Master of Delight) in *Chin P'ing Mei tz'u-hua*, vol. 1, pp. 1–11. This preface, together with a second preface, a colophon, and eight lyrics that appear before the beginning of the text in this edition, are all translated and annotated below.

30. This point was impressed upon me by Patrick Hanan in conversations that took place in the mid-1960s and has also been forcefully stated by Wei Tzu-yün in his *Chin P'ing Mei t'an-yüan*, pp. 19–25.

31. For an argument to this effect, see ibid., pp. 26–32.

32. See *Shih-chi* (Records of the historian), by Ssu-ma Ch'ien, 10 vols. (Peking: Chung-hua shu-chü, 1972), vol. 7, *chüan* 74, p. 2348. Translation adapted from *Records of the Historian*, trans. Yang Hsien-yi and Gladys Yang (Hong Kong: Commercial Press, 1974), p. 74. For an excellent summary of the life and thought of Hsün-tzu, see the general introduction to *Xunzi: A Translation and Study of the Complete Works*, trans. John Knoblock, vols. 1 and 2 (Stanford: Stanford University Press, 1988–90), vol. 1, pp. 3–128.

33. See *Hsün-tzu yin-te* (A concordance to *Hsün-tzu*) (Taipei: Chinese Materials and Research Aids Service Center, 1966), p. 111, ll. 16–17.

34. See Paul Varo Martinson, "*Pao* Order and Redemption: Perspectives on Chinese Religion and Society Based on a Study of the *Chin P'ing Mei*," Ph.D. dissertation, University of Chicago, 1973, passim. See also Martinson, "The *Chin P'ing Mei* as Wisdom Literature: A Methodological Essay," *Ming Studies*, no. 5 (Fall 1977): 44–56.

35. See Andrew H. Plaks, "Neo-Confucian Issues in Ming-Ch'ing Fiction," ms., Princeton University, 1977, esp. pp. 9–11. See also his *The Four Masterworks of the Ming Novel*, pp. 156–77 and 497–512.

36. See Peter Halliday Rushton, "The Narrative Form of *Chin P'ing Mei*," Ph.D. dissertation, Stanford University, 1978, esp. pp. 187–264. See also Peter Rushton,

"The Daoist's Mirror: Reflections on the Neo-Confucian Reader and the Rhetoric of *Jin Ping Mei*," *Chinese Literature: Essays, Articles, Reviews* 8, 1 and 2 (July 1986): 63–81.

37. See Katherine Carlitz, "The Role of Drama in the *Chin P'ing Mei*: The Relationship between Fiction and Drama as a Guide to the Viewpoint of a Sixteenth-Century Chinese Novel," Ph.D. dissertation, University of Chicago, 1978, esp. pp. 36–57. See also her "The Conclusion of the *Jin Ping Mei*," *Ming Studies*, no. 10 (Spring 1980): 23–29; and *The Rhetoric of Chin p'ing mei* (Bloomington: Indiana University Press, 1986), pp. 28–52 and passim.

38. See *Chin P'ing Mei tz'u-hua*, vol. 1, ch. 1, p. 9a, l. 9; ch. 19, p. 1a, l. 4; vol. 5, ch. 84, p. 10a, l. 10; and ch. 94, p. 1a, l. 4.

39. See *Meng-tzu yin-te* (A concordance to Meng-tzu) (Taipei: Chinese Materials and Research Aids Service Center, 1966), p. 41, 4B.12. Translation from *Mencius*, trans. D. C. Lau, (Baltimore: Penguin Books, 1970), p. 130.

40. See *Hsün-tzu yin-te*, ch. 23, p. 88, ll. 16–18. Translation from *Hsün Tzu: Basic Writings*, trans. Burton Watson (New York: Columbia University Press, 1963) p. 163.

41. See Wm. Theodore de Bary, "Individualism and Humanitarianism in Late Ming Thought," in *Self and Society in Ming Thought*, ed. Wm. Theodore de Bary (New York: Columbia University Press, 1970), p. 195.

42. See *Hsün-tzu yin-te*, ch. 23, p. 88, ll. 13–15. Translation from Watson, *Hsün Tzu*, p. 163.

43. On the distinction between "showing" and "telling" as critical concepts, see Booth, *The Rhetoric of Fiction*, pp. 3–64 and passim.

44. The allusion is to Friedrich Nietzsche, *Human, All Too Human* (1878).

45. There is abundant classical sanction for the use of microcosm and macrocosm as tools of analysis. For example, a line in the *Huai-nan tzu* (Book of the Prince of Huai-nan), an eclectic work compiled under the auspices of the Prince of Huai-nan, Liu An (d. 122 B.C.), reads, "By way of the small one can perceive the great; by way of the near one can suggest the far." See *Huai-nan hung-lieh chi-chieh* (Collected commentaries on the *Huai-nan tzu*), ed. Liu Wen-tien, 2 vols. (Taipei: T'ai-wan Shang-wu yin-shu kuan, 1969), vol. 2, *chüan* 17, p. 7b, l. 10. Po Chü-i (772–846), a famous T'ang poet who is frequently quoted in the *Chin P'ing Mei*, wrote a poem one couplet of which reads, "By means of the small one may illuminate the great; / One can employ the household as a metaphor for the state." See *Ch'üan T'ang shih* (Complete poetry of the T'ang), 12 vols. (Peking: Chung-hua shu-chü, 1960), vol. 7, *chüan* 424, p. 4655, l. 6.

46. J. Hillis Miller, "Introduction," in Charles Dickens, *Bleak House* (Baltimore: Penguin Books, 1975), pp. 11–29.

47. See L. Carrington Goodrich and Chaoying Fang, eds., *Dictionary of Ming Biography*, 2 vols. (New York: Columbia University Press, 1976), 1:315.

48. Ibid., 1:325.

49. *Hsün-tzu yin-te*, ch. 1, p. 1, ll. 15–16. Translation from Watson, *Hsün Tzu*, p. 17.

50. *Hsün-tzu yin-te*, ch. 9, p. 30, ll. 3–4. Translation from Watson, *Hsün Tzu*, p. 50.

51. *Hsün-tzu yin-te*, ch. 9, p. 31, ll. 8–11. Translation from Watson, *Hsün Tzu*, pp. 54–55.

52. See Carlitz, "The Role of Drama in the *Chin P'ing Mei*," pp. 57–67; Arthur F. Wright, "Sui Yang-ti: Personality and Stereotype," in *The Confucian Persuasion*, ed. Arthur F. Wright (Stanford: Stanford University Press, 1960), pp. 61–65.

53. For the text of Ch'en Tung's (1086–1127) contemporary indictment of the "six traitors"—Ts'ai Ching (1046–1126), T'ung Kuan (1054–1126), Wang Fu (1079–1126), Liang Shih-ch'eng (d. 1126), Li Yen (d. 1126), and Chu Mien (1075–1126)—all of whom figure in the *Chin P'ing Mei*, see *Huang-ch'ao pien-nien kang-mu pei-yao* (Chronological outline of the significant events of the imperial [Sung] dynasty), comp. Ch'en Chün (c. 1165–c. 1236), pref. dated 1229, 2 vols., fac. repr. (Taipei: Ch'eng-wen ch'u-pan she, 1966), vol. 2, *chüan* 29, pp. 27b–30a; *Hsüan-ho i-shih* (Forgotten events of the Hsüan-ho reign period [1119–25]) (Shanghai: Shang-hai ku-tien wen-hsüeh ch'u-pan she, 1955), pp. 83–85; and *Proclaiming Harmony*, trans. William O. Hennessey (Ann Arbor: Center for Chinese Studies, University of Michigan, 1981), pp. 106–9.

54. See *Hsi-yu chi* (The journey to the west), 2 vols. (Peking: Tso-chia ch'u-pan she, 1954), vol. 1, ch. 14; and *The Journey to the West*, trans. Anthony C. Yu, 4 vols. (Chicago: University of Chicago Press, 1977–1983), vol. 1, ch. 14.

55. See Tu Kuo-hsiang, "Lun Hsün-tzu te 'Ch'eng-hsiang p'ien'" (On Hsün-tzu's "Ch'eng-hsiang" chapter), in his *Tu Kuo-hsiang wen-chi* (Collected essays of Tu Kuo-hsiang) (Peking: Jen-min ch'u-pan she, 1962), pp. 158–83. This chapter of the *Hsün-tzu* has been translated into English by Göran Malmqvist in his monograph entitled "The *Cherng Shiang* Ballad of the *Shyun Tzyy*," *Bulletin of the Museum of Far Eastern Antiquities*, vol. 45 (1973): 63–89.

56. Watson, *Hsün Tzu*, p. 4.

57. See the essay by Chang Chu-p'o, "*Chin P'ing Mei* tu-fa," pp. 25–50, items 26 and 76; and my translation, "How to Read the *Chin P'ing Mei*," pp. 202–43, items 26 and 76. See also Hsia, *The Classic Chinese Novel*, p. 181; and John C. Y. Wang, "The Cyclical View of Life and Meaning in the Traditional Chinese Novel," in *Études d'Histoire et de Littérature Chinoises Offertes au Professeur Jaroslav Průšek*, ed. Yves Hervouet (Paris: Presses Universitaires de France, 1976), pp. 296–98.

58. Harold L. Kahn, *Monarchy in the Emperor's Eyes: Image and Reality in the Ch'ien-lung Reign* (Cambridge: Harvard University Press, 1971), p. 227.

59. See *Hsün-tzu yin-te*, ch. 18, pp. 67–68. This passage has been translated into English in *The Works of Hsüntze*, trans. Homer H. Dubs (London: Arthur Probsthain, 1928), pp. 198–202.

60. The best analysis of the ending of the novel known to me is in Carlitz, *The Rhetoric of Chin p'ing mei*, pp. 128–45.

61. See item 8 in Chang Chu-p'o, "*Chin P'ing Mei* tu-fa"; and Roy, "How to Read the *Chin P'ing Mei*."

62. *Hsün-tzu yin-te*, ch. 19, p. 71, ll. 18–19. Translation from Watson, *Hsün Tzu*, p. 94.

63. See *Shui-hu ch'üan-chuan* (Variorum edition of the *Outlaws of the Marsh*), ed. Cheng Chen-to et al., 4 vols. (Hong Kong: Chung-hua shu-chü, 1958), chs. 23–27.

64. See Wu Hsiao-ling, "*Chin P'ing Mei tz'u-hua* li te Ch'ing-ho chi i Chia-ching shih-ch'i te Pei-ching wei mo-hsing ch'u-t'an" (A preliminary study of the fact that Ch'ing-ho in the *Chin P'ing Mei tz'u-hua* is modeled on the Peking of the Chia-ching

reign period), *Chung-wai wen-hsüeh* (Chung-wai literary monthly) 18, 2 (July 1989): 107–22.

65. See *Hsün-tzu yin-te*, ch. 12, p. 44, l. 15. For another translation, see Knoblock, *Xunzi: A Translation and Study of the Complete Works*, 2:177, ll. 24–29.

66. See his famous essay entitled "The Rectification of Names," in *Hsün-tzu yin-te*, ch. 22, pp. 82–86; and Watson, *Hsün Tzu*, pp. 139–56.

67. See "*Chin P'ing Mei* pa" (Colophon to the *Chin P'ing Mei*), by Hsieh Chao-che, a hitherto unnoticed document that was discovered in 1976 by Ma Tai-loi of the University of Chicago in a rare edition of Hsieh Chao-che's *Hsiao-ts'ao chai wen-chi* (Collected prose from the Small Grass Script Studio), pref. dated 1626 (original edition in Sonkeikaku Library, Tokyo), *chüan* 24, pp. 30b–31b. For a reproduction and study of this important text, see Ma Tai-loi, "Hsieh Chao-che te '*Chin P'ing Mei* pa"' (Hsieh Chao-che's "Colophon to the *Chin P'ing Mei*"), *Chung-hua wen-shih lun-ts'ung*, no. 4 (1980): 299–305.

68. See *Pei-ho chi-yü* (Supplementary account of the northern section of the Grand Canal), by Hsieh Chao-che (1567–1624), in *Ssu-k'u ch'üan-shu chen-pen, erh-chi* (Rare volumes from the *Complete library of the four treasuries*, second series), 400 vols. (Taipei: T'ai-wan Shang-wu yin-shu kuan, 1971), vol. 138, *chüan* 3, p. 16b.

69. See *Hsün-tzu yin-te*, ch. 26, pp. 94–95. Two of these pieces are translated in *Chinese Rhyme-Prose: Poems in the Fu Form from the Han and Six Dynasties Periods*, trans. Burton Watson (New York: Columbia University Press, 1971), pp. 123–25. For a succinct discussion of this enigmatic text, see David R. Knechtges, *The Han Rhapsody: A Study of the Fu of Yang Hsiung* (Cambridge: Cambridge University Press, 1976), pp. 18–21.

70. See *Han-shu* (History of the Former Han dynasty), comp. Pan Ku (32–92), 8 vols. (Peking: Chung-hua shu-chü, 1962), vol. 4, *chüan* 30, p. 1756, ll. 2–3. Translation adapted from that in Hellmut Wilhelm, "The Scholar's Frustration: Notes on a Type of *Fu*," in *Chinese Thought and Institutions*, ed. John K. Fairbank (Chicago: University of Chicago Press, 1957), pp. 312–13.

71. See Hsia, *The Classic Chinese Novel*, p. 176.

72. See *Chin P'ing Mei tz'u-hua*, vol. 4, ch. 80, pp. 2a–2b.

73. Robert Scholes, *Elements of Fiction* (New York: Oxford University Press, 1967), p. 37.

74. See Vladimir Nabokov, *The Annotated Lolita*, ed. and annot. Alfred Appel, Jr., (New York: Vintage Books, 1991), pp. lvi–lvii.

75. *Hsün-tzu yin-te*, ch. 9, p. 27, ll. 4–6. Translation from Watson, *Hsün Tzu*, p. 38.

76. *Hsün-tzu yin-te*, ch. 9, p. 28, ll. 9–11. Translation from Watson, *Hsün Tzu*, p. 43.

77. *Chin P'ing Mei tz'u-hua*, vol. 3, ch. 49, p. 1b, ll. 2–5. The wording of this memorial is drawn from the biography of Tseng Hsiao-hsü in the *Sung shih* (History of the Sung dynasty), comp. T'o-t'o (1313–55) et al., 40 vols. (Peking: Chung-hua shu-chü, 1977), vol. 38, *chüan* 453, p. 13319, ll. 7–9.

78. *Chin P'ing Mei tz'u-hua*, vol. 1, ch. 6, p. 7b, l. 10. In my translation of this poem in chapter 6 I have rendered the words of the text, which literally mean "clear stream," as "silvery stream" in order to suggest this equation.

79. *Chin P'ing Mei tz'u-hua*, vol. 1, ch. 6, p. 7b, l. 11.

80. Carlitz, "The Role of Drama in the *Chin P'ing Mei*," pp. 68–69.

81. For an annotated translation of this climactic scene, see David T. Roy, trans., "Selections from *Jin Ping Mei*," *Renditions*, no. 24 (Autumn 1985), pp. 58–62. For a further exploration of this topic, see Indira Satyendra, "Metaphors of the Body: The Sexual Economy of the *Chin P'ing Mei tz'u-hua*," paper presented at the annual meeting of the Association for Asian Studies, New Orleans, April, 1991.

82. Hsia, *The Classic Chinese Novel*, p. 186.

83. See Sigmund Freud, *Civilization and Its Discontents*, trans. Joan Riviere (New York: Doubleday Anchor Books, n.d.), passim.

84. *Hsün-tzu yin-te*, ch. 32, p. 109, ll. 18–21. The quotation from the *Book of Songs* is from the fourth stanza of song no. 260. See *Mao-shih yin-te* (Concordance to the Mao version of the *Book of songs*) (Tokyo: Japan Council for East Asian Studies, 1962), p. 71, no. 260, l. 6. Translation from Arthur Waley, trans., *The Book of Songs* (London: Allen and Unwin, 1954), p. 142, ll. 5–6.

85. For well-informed surveys of the current state of *Chin P'ing Mei* studies, see the translator's introduction to Lévy, *Fleur en Fiole d'Or*, 1: xxxvii–lxxi; and Plaks, *The Four Masterworks of the Ming Novel*, pp. 55–72.

86. See David T. Roy, "The Case for T'ang Hsien-tsu's Authorship of the *Jin Ping Mei*," *Chinese Literature: Essays, Articles, Reviews* 8, 1 and 2 (July 1986), pp. 31–62.

87. M. M. Bakhtin, *The Dialogic Imagination: Four Essays*, ed. and trans. Caryl Emerson and Michael Holquist (Austin: University of Texas Press, 1981), pp. 47–49.

88. Ibid., pp. 262–63.

89. Ibid., p. 301.

90. Ibid., p. 417.

91. John C. Duggan called this contemporary example to my attention. For a study of such rhetorical devices in the *Chin P'ing Mei* and their influence on later fiction, see David L. Rolston, "Nonrealistic Uses of Oral Performing Literature in Traditional Chinese Fiction: The Model of the *Jin Ping Mei cihua* and Its Influence," forthcoming in *Chinoperl*. See also Satyendra, "Toward a Poetics of the Chinese Novel," pp. 87–190.

92. For an important study of this subject, see "Intertextuality in Chinese Full-length Fiction," in David L. Rolston, "Theory and Practice: Fiction Criticism, and the Writing of the *Ju-lin wai-shih*," 4 vols., Ph.D. dissertation, University of Chicago, 1988, 2:270–424.

93. Brian Boyd, *Vladimir Nabokov: The Russian Years* (Princeton: Princeton University Press, 1990), p. 300.

94. *The Story of the Stone*, by Cao Xueqin, trans. David Hawkes and John Minford, 5 vols. (Baltimore: Penguin Books, 1973–86), 1:46.

PREFACE TO THE *CHIN P'ING MEI TZ'U-HUA*

1. It may be thought that I have annotated the text of this preface too heavily, but I have done so advisedly. I wish to demonstrate that the writer of the preface, if he was not also the author of the novel, must have been extremely familiar not only with the contents of the *Chin P'ing Mei*, but also with the rhetorical techniques of the author. He shows himself to be conversant with an enormous range of both classical and popular literature, and he interweaves quotations from both types of sources in

a manner indistinguishable from that of the author. The degree of intertextuality between the preface and the novel as well as its sources is striking. This is not characteristic of the second preface or the colophon that follow. These observations are intended to reinforce the contention that if this preface to the *Chin P'ing Mei* is not by the author himself, it remains the earliest and by far the most important statement about the author's intentions and deserves to be taken seriously by all students of the novel.

2. The identity of the Scoffing Scholar of Lan-ling has not been established. I believe that the author may have adopted this pseudonym in order to suggest an affinity with Hsün-tzu, the great Confucian philosopher of the third century B.C., who served as the magistrate of Lan-ling in what is now Shantung Province, and whose name has, therefore, come to be associated with that place. For an elaboration of this hypothesis, see the introduction to this volume.

3. The seven feelings natural to mankind are defined in the *Li-chi* (The book of rites) as joy, anger, sadness, fear, love, disliking, and liking. See *Li-chi*, in *Shih-san ching ching-wen* (The texts of the thirteen classics) (Taipei: K'ai-ming shu-tien, 1955), ch. 7, p. 45, l. 6; and *Li Chi: Book of Rites*, trans. James Legge, 2 vols. (New Hyde Park, N.Y.: University Books, 1967), 1:379. In the Buddhist version of this concept, melancholy is sometimes substituted for sadness.

4. The phrase that I have rendered "appeals to every taste" means literally "minced and roasted for every mouth." For its first occurrence, see *T'ang chih-yen* (A gleaning of T'ang anecdotes), by Wang Ting-pao (870–c. 954) (Shanghai: Ku-tien wen-hsüeh ch'u-pan she, 1957), *chüan* 10, p. 112, l. 10.

5. The phrase that I have rendered "as intricately articulated as the conduits of the circulatory system" is from Chu Hsi's (1130–1200) preface to his commentary on the *Chung-yung* (Doctrine of the mean), written in 1189. Since the *Chung-yung* is one of the *Ssu-shu* (Four books), which formed the basis of Confucian education during the Ming and Ch'ing dynasties, and Chu Hsi's commentaries on these works were the standard interpretations, the wording of his prefaces would have been familiar to every educated Chinese during the sixteenth century. See *Ssu-shu chang-chü chi-chu* (Collected commentary on the paragraphed and punctuated text of the *Four books*), by Chu Hsi (Peking: Chung-hua shu-chü, 1983), p. 16, l. 1. A variant of the same phrase is employed by Li K'ai-hsien (1502–68) to describe the plot of the *Shui-hu chuan* (Outlaws of the marsh). See Li K'ai-hsien, *Tz'u-nüeh* (Pleasantries on lyrical verse), in *Chung-kuo ku-tien hsi-ch'ü lun-chu chi-ch'eng* (A corpus of critical works on classical Chinese drama), comp. Chung-kuo hsi-ch'ü yen-chiu yüan (The Chinese Academy of Dramatic Arts), 10 vols. (Peking: Chung-kuo hsi-chü ch'u-pan she, 1959), 3:286, l. 12.

6. The phrase that I have rendered "the atmosphere is redolent of rouge and powder" occurs in a comment by Kao Ju (fl. 16th century) on a category of books in his private library that includes the names of five of the nine works referred to later in this preface to the *Chin P'ing Mei*. In fact his library contained all but the last two of these nine works. The preface to the catalogue of his library is dated 1540. For the comment in question, see *Pai-ch'uan shu-chih* (A catalogue of the hundred streams), by Kao Ju (Shanghai: Ku-tien wen-hsüeh ch'u-pan she, 1957), *chüan* 6, p. 90, l. 12.

7. The *Shih-ching*, the oldest anthology of Chinese poetry (12th–7th centuries B.C.), is one of the Confucian classics. For a translation of the song in question, see Waley, *The Book of Songs*, pp. 81–82.

8. This is a quotation from Book 3 of the *Lun-yü* (The analects of Confucius). See *The Analects of Confucius*, trans. Arthur Waley (London: Allen and Unwin, 1949), p. 99. The same quotation also occurs in Yüan dynasty drama. See *Yüan-ch'ü hsüan* (An anthology of Yüan tsa-chü drama), comp. Tsang Mao-hsün (1550–1620), 4 vols. (Peking: Chung-hua shu-chü, 1979), 3:1168, l. 19.

9. This is a quotation, with an insignificant textual variant, from Book 4 of the *Lun-yü*. See Waley, *The Analects of Confucius*, p. 102. The same quotation also occurs in *Yüan-ch'ü hsüan*, 3:1206, l. 4; and the *Shui-hu chuan*. See *Shui-hu ch'üan-chuan*, vol. 4, ch. 110, p. 1655, l. 2.

10. Of Lu Ching-hui nothing is known. The authorship of this collection of tales in the literary language is elsewhere attributed to Ch'ü Yu (1341–1427), author's preface dated 1378. See *Chien-teng hsin-hua*, by Ch'ü Yu, in *Chien-teng hsin-hua [wai erh-chung]* (New wick-trimming tales [plus two other works]), ed. and annot. Chou I (Shanghai: Ku-tien wen-hsüeh ch'u-pan she, 1957). Six of these tales have been translated into English in *The Golden Casket: Chinese Novellas of Two Millennia*, trans. Wolfgang Bauer and Herbert Franke, trans. from the German by Christopher Levenson (New York: Harcourt Brace and World, 1964), pp. 219–63; and a seventh has been translated by Paul W. Kroll, under the title "The Golden Phoenix Hairpin," in *Traditional Chinese Stories: Themes and Variations*, ed. Y. W. Ma and Joseph S. M. Lau (New York: Columbia University Press, 1978), pp. 400–403.

11. This short tale by Yüan Chen (775–831), which is believed to be autobiographical, is probably the best-known and most influential love story in the literary language. For the text of this tale, see *Ying-ying chuan* (Story of Ying-ying), in *T'ang Sung ch'uan-ch'i chi* (An anthology of literary tales from the T'ang and Sung dynasties), ed. Lu Hsün (Peking: Wen-hsüeh ku-chi k'an-hsing she, 1958), pp. 127–36. For a study and translation, see James R. Hightower, "Yüan Chen and 'The Story of Ying-ying,'" *Harvard Journal of Asiatic Studies*, vol. 33 (1973): 90–123.

12. The author's postface to this collection of literary language tales is dated 1428. See *Hsiao-p'in chi* (Emulative frowns collection), by Chao Pi. (Shanghai: Ku-tien wen-hsüeh ch'u-pan she, 1957).

13. Lo Kuan-chung (fl. 14th century) is one of the names to which the authorship of this long vernacular novel is traditionally attributed, although there is no extant edition of the text that antedates the sixteenth century. The nucleus of the plot of the *Chin P'ing Mei* is derived from this novel, and it is the single work that exerted the greatest influence on the author. For a critical modern edition of the text, with variorum notes, see *Shui-hu ch'üan-chuan*.

14. The authorship of this long love tale in the literary language, to which there is a preface dated 1486, has traditionally been attributed to Ch'iu Chün (1421–95), although that attribution has recently been convincingly challenged. See Hung-lam Chu, "The Authorship of the Story *Chung-ch'ing li-chi*," *Asia Major*, third series, vol. 1, part 1 (January 1988): 71–82. For a text of this novelette, see *Yen-chü pi-chi* (A miscellany for leisured hours), ed. Lin Chin-yang (fl. early 17th century), 3 vols., fac. repr. of Ming ed., in *Ming-Ch'ing shan-pen hsiao-shuo ts'ung-k'an, ch'u-pien* (Collectanea of rare editions of Ming-Ch'ing fiction, first series) (Taipei: T'ien-i ch'u-pan she, 1985), vol. 2, *chüan* 6, pp. 1a–40b, and vol. 3, *chüan* 7, pp. 1a–30a, upper register.

15. Of Lu Mei-hu nothing is known. A work of this title is listed in Kao Ju's catalogue, the *Pai-ch'uan shu-chih*, *chüan* 6, p. 90, ll. 9–10, where the authorship is

attributed to one Lu Min-piao. This is also a long love tale in the literary language. For a text of this novelette, see *Yen-chü pi-chi*, vol. 3, *chüan* 9, pp. 16b–32a, and *chüan* 10, pp. 1a–39b, upper register.

16. Chou Li was a prolific author and compiler who flourished in the second half of the fifteenth century. A work of this title is listed in Kao Ju's catalogue, the *Pai-ch'uan shu-chih*, *chüan* 6, p. 89, ll. 10–11, where it is described as being in five *chüan* and containing twenty-seven items. It is probably a collection of literary language tales, but I have not been able to locate a copy of it.

17. This anonymous mid-sixteenth-century work, the full title of which is the *Ju-i chün chuan*, is a scurrilous novelette in the literary language that purports to describe the sexual exploits of the T'ang empress Wu Tse-t'ien (r. 684–705). I have used the Japanese movable-type edition, the colophon of which is dated 1880.

18. This is an early Ming vernacular story of unknown authorship that purports to relate an episode from the life of the well-known poet Chang Hsiao-hsiang (1132–69). For a version of the text, entitled *Chang Yü-hu su nü-chen kuan chi* (Chang Yü-hu spends the night in a Taoist nunnery), see *Yen-chü pi-chi*, vol. 2, *chüan* 6, pp. 6b–24b, lower register. The most significant thing about this list of nine works is that quotations from most, if not all, of them can be demonstrated to have been worked into the text of the *Chin P'ing Mei*. This indicates that the author of the preface, if he was not also the author of the novel, was thoroughly familiar with the text of the novel as well as the nature and contents of the sort of works upon which the author drew.

19. These poetic conceits are derived from a couplet in a poem by Han Yü (768–824). See *Ch'üan T'ang shih*, vol. 5, *chüan* 340, p. 3815, l. 2.

20. This phrase occurs in the sixteenth-century novel *Hsi-yu chi* (The journey to the west), the earliest extant edition of which was published in 1592. See *Hsi-yu chi*, attributed to Wu Ch'eng-en (c. 1500–82), vol. 2, ch. 53, p. 608, l. 13; and Yu, *The Journey to the West*, vol. 3, ch. 53, p. 36, l. 13; or *Journey to the West*, trans. W. J. F. Jenner, 3 vols. (Beijing: Foreign Languages Press, 1982–86), vol. 2, ch. 53, p. 380, ll. 17–18. A variant of this phrase occurs as early as the T'ang dynasty in the text of an inscription for a Buddhist monastery by Li Ch'iao (644–713). See *Ch'üan T'ang wen* (Complete prose of the T'ang), 20 vols. (Kyoto: Chūbun shuppan-sha, 1976), vol. 6, *chüan* 248, p. 11a, l. 3.

21. This phrase echoes the final clause of Chu Hsi's preface to his commentary on the *Ta-hsüeh* (The great learning), which, like his preface to the *Chung-yung* referred to above in note 5, was written in 1189. This preface, like that to the *Chung-yung*, would have been familiar to every educated reader in sixteenth-century China. See Chu Hsi, *Ssu-shu chang-chü chi-chu*, p. 2, l. 13.

22. Yao and Shun are legendary emperors from Chinese prehistory who are traditionally believed to have reigned during the third millennium B.C. In the Confucian tradition they have been extolled as archetypes of sage rulership.

23. This phrase occurs in *Yüan-ch'ü hsüan*, 4:1331, l. 13; *Yüan-ch'ü hsüan wai-pien* (A supplementary anthology of Yüan tsa-chü drama), comp. Sui Shu-sen, 3 vols. (Peking: Chung-hua shu-chü, 1961), 2:574, l. 9; and the early Ming tsa-chü drama entitled *Yü-ch'iao hsien-hua* (A casual dialogue between a fisherman and a woodcutter), in *Ku-pen Yüan Ming tsa-chü* (Unique editions of Yüan and Ming tsa-chü drama), ed. Wang Chi-lieh, 4 vols. (Peking: Chung-kuo hsi-chü ch'u-pan she, 1958),

vol. 4, scene 4, p. 12a, l. 2. The same phrase also occurs in the text of the *Chin P'ing Mei*. See *Chin P'ing Mei tz'u-hua*, vol. 1, ch. 8, p. 11b, l. 4.

24. This phrase occurs in a poem by Han Yü. See *Ch'üan T'ang shih*, vol. 5, *chüan* 341, p. 3824, l. 3. It also occurs in a lyric from an early vernacular story entitled *Chien-t'ieh ho-shang* (The monk's billet-doux). See *Ch'ing-p'ing shan-t'ang hua-pen* (Stories printed by the Ch'ing-p'ing Shan-t'ang), ed. T'an Cheng-pi (Shanghai: Ku-tien wen-hsüeh ch'u-pan she, 1957), p. 8, l. 16. The same lyric is quoted twice, with some textual variations, in the *Chin P'ing Mei*. See *Chin P'ing Mei tz'u-hua*, vol. 1, ch. 20, p. 3b, ll. 7–9; and vol. 5, ch. 83, p. 8a, ll. 5–8.

25. This phrase occurs in the first line of verse 55 of a suite of one hundred songs to the tune "Hsiao-t'ao hung" that retells the story of the *Ying-ying chuan* (see note 11 above). See the sixteenth-century anthology *Yung-hsi yüeh-fu* (Songs of a harmonious era), pref. dated 1566, 20 *ts'e*, fac. repr. (Shanghai: Shang-wu yin-shu kuan, 1934), *ts'e* 19, p. 42b, l. 10. According to Yeh Te-chün, this suite of songs is by a Ming dynasty figure named Wang Yen-chen. See *[Chi-p'ing chiao-chu] Hsi-hsiang chi* (The romance of the western chamber [with collected commentary and critical annotation]), ed. and annot. Wang Chi-ssu (Shanghai: Shang-hai ku-chi ch'u-pan she, 1987), p. 297.

26. This phrase first occurs in a work by Ch'ang Ching (d. 550) that is quoted in his biography in the history of the Northern Wei dynasty (338–534). See *Wei shu* (History of the Northern Wei dynasty), comp. Wei Shou (505–72), 8 vols. (Peking: Chung-hua shu-chü, 1974), vol. 5, *chüan* 82, p. 1807, l. 9. It also occurs in the *Ming-feng chi* (The singing phoenix), a famous ch'uan-ch'i drama, probably written between 1567 and 1572, that deals with the history of the Chia-ching reign period (1522–66) and attacks the corrupt chief minister Yen Sung (1480–1565) and his coterie. This was a pioneering work in the history of Chinese drama in that it dealt realistically with nearly contemporaneous events. As such it may have served as an inspiration to the author of the *Chin P'ing Mei*. See *Ming-feng chi, Liu-shih chung ch'ü* edition (Taipei: K'ai-ming shu-tien, 1970), scene 27, p. 112, l. 10. For a description and analysis of the *Ming-feng chi*, see Cyril Birch, "Some Concerns and Methods of the Ming *Ch'uan-ch'i* Drama," in Birch, *Studies in Chinese Literary Genres*, pp. 229–37.

27. This phrase first occurs in a lyric by the eleventh-century poet Liu Yung (cs 1034). See *Ch'üan Sung tz'u* (Complete *tz'u* lyrics of the Sung), comp. T'ang Kuei-chang, 5 vols. (Hong Kong: Chung-hua shu-chü, 1977), 1:13, lower register, ll. 3–4. It also occurs in *Yüan-ch'ü hsüan*, 3:1264, l. 3; and the *Chin P'ing Mei tz'u-hua*, vol. 1, ch. 1, p. 12a, l. 4.

28. This phrase first occurs in a work entitled *Chien-wen lu* (A record of things seen and heard) by Hu No (fl. late 10th century), the father of the famous Confucian teacher Hu Yüan (993–1059). It is no longer extant in its complete form, but twenty-three items from it are included in the collectanea entitled *Lei-shuo* (Categorized records) compiled by Tseng Ts'ao in 1136. The item in which this phrase occurs concerns Li Yü (937–78), the famous lyric poet who was the last emperor of the Southern T'ang dynasty (937–75). He spent the final three years of his life in captivity in the Northern Sung capital of K'ai-feng, during which time the Sung emperor, T'ai-tsung (r. 976–97), visited the Han-lin Academy one day and found him sitting in a position of lesser honor than that of some of his former officials. On seeing this

one of the emperor's courtiers was led to remark, "He didn't know how to cultivate the way of the ruler. All he could do was descant upon the breeze and apostrophize the moon. It is only appropriate that he should have come to this." See *Lei-shuo*, comp. Tseng Ts'ao, 5 vols. (Peking: Wen-hsüeh ku-chi k'an-hsing she, 1955), vol. 2, *chüan* 19, p. 13a, ll. 4–6. The implications of this anecdote are most appropriate to the *Chin P'ing Mei*, one of the dominant themes of which is the moral and social consequences of irresponsible rulership. The same phrase also occurs in the twelfth-century chantefable on the theme of the *Ying-ying chuan* by Tung Chieh-yüan. See *Tung Chieh-yüan Hsi-hsiang chi* (Master Tung's Western chamber romance), ed. and annot. Ling Ching-yen (Peking: Jen-min wen-hsüeh ch'u-pan she, 1962), *chüan* 1, p. 3, l. 11; and *Master Tung's Western Chamber Romance*, trans. Li-li Ch'en. (Cambridge: Cambridge University Press, 1976), p. 7, l. 5. It is also found in an anonymous Ming tsa-chü drama entitled *Chang Yü-hu wu-su nü-chen kuan* (Chang Yü-hu mistakenly spends the night in a Taoist nunnery), which deals with the same stuff-material as the *Yü-hu chi* (see note 18 above). See *Ming-jen tsa-chü hsüan* (An anthology of Ming tsa-chü drama), comp. Chou I-pai (Peking: Jen-min wen-hsüeh ch'u-pan she, 1958), scene 4, p. 624, l. 6.

29. These two lines are derived, with some textual variation, from a couplet in a poem by Hsieh Chin (1369–1415). See his *Hsieh hsüeh-shih wen-chi* (Collected works of Academician Hsieh), 10 *chüan*, preface dated 1562 (microfilm copy in the East Asian Library, University of Chicago), *chüan* 4, p. 15a, ll. 5–6. This poem is also attributed to T'ang Yin (1470–1524). See *T'ang Po-hu ch'üan-chi* (Complete works of T'ang Yin) (Taipei: Tung-fang shu-tien, 1956), *wai-chi, chüan* 2, p. 2b, ll. 1–2. Four lines of the same poem, including the two quoted here, also occur in the *Chin P'ing Mei tz'u-hua*, vol. 2, ch. 25, p. 1b, ll. 4–6.

30. A variant of this proverbial phrase occurs as early as the *Huai-nan tzu* (Book of the Prince of Huai-nan), a collection of Taoist lore compiled under the auspices of Liu An (179–122 B.C.), the Prince of Huai-nan. See *Huai-nan hung-lieh chi-chieh*, vol. 1, *chüan* 12, p. 28b, ll. 1–2. It also occurs in the *Chin P'ing Mei tz'u-hua*, vol. 1, ch. 8, p. 9a, l. 3; and vol. 4, ch. 78, p. 29a, l. 9.

31. This line is from a famous poem by Lu K'ai addressed to his friend Fan Yeh (398–445), the compiler of the *Hou-Han shu* (History of the Later Han dynasty). See *Hsien-Ch'in Han Wei Chin Nan-pei ch'ao shih* (Complete poetry of the Pre-Ch'in, Han, Wei, Chin, and Northern and Southern dynasties), comp. Lu Ch'in-li, 3 vols. (Peking: Chung-hua shu-chü, 1983), 2:1204, l. 7.

32. This line is based on two couplets from an early ballad traditionally attributed to Ts'ai Yung (132–192). See ibid, 1:192, l. 9. The relevant lines read: "A stranger came from far away / And gave me a pair of carp. / I summoned my son to cook the carp / In which there was a letter on a square of silk."

33. This phrase occurs in the *Chien-teng yü-hua* (More wick-trimming tales), by Li Ch'ang-ch'i (1376–1452), author's preface dated 1420, in *Chien-teng hsin-hua [wai erh-chung]*, *chüan* 1, p. 153, l. 12; and *Yü-ching t'ai* (The jade mirror stand), a sixteenth-century ch'uan-ch'i drama by Chu Ting. See *Yü-ching t'ai, Liu-shih chung ch'ü* edition (Taipei: K'ai-ming shu-tien, 1970), scene 33, p. 89, l. 7.

34. A variant of this couplet is quoted in the fourteenth-century anthology of moral aphorisms entitled *Ming-hsin pao-chien* (A precious mirror to illuminate the mind), preface dated 1393, as being from a work of moral exhortation attributed to

Wei Hua-ts'un, a woman of the fourth century who was one of the founders of Taoist liturgiology. See *Ming-hsin pao-chien* (Microfilm copy of a Ming edition in the East Asian Library, University of Chicago), *chüan* 1, p. 9a, l. 10. The same passage is quoted in the *Shui-hu ch'üan-chuan*, vol. 2, ch. 36, p. 563, l. 3; and in the *Chin P'ing Mei tz'u-hua*, vol. 5, ch. 88, p. 1a, l. 4.

35. This expression, which employs a rare character for the word "evaded," is derived from a passage in the *Shu-ching* (Book of documents) that reads, "Calamities produced by Heaven may be avoided, but calamities of one's own making cannot be evaded." See *The Shoo King or The Book of Historical Documents*, trans. James Legge (Hong Kong: University of Hong Kong Press, 1960), p. 207. The implications of this passage are highly relevant to the *Chin P'ing Mei*, which is very much concerned with the consequences of failure to take responsibility for one's own actions. The same expression also occurs in the epilogue to a literary tale by Huang-fu Mei (fl. early 10th century) entitled *Fei-yen chuan* (The story of Pu Fei-yen), in *T'ang Sung ch'uan-ch'i chi*, p. 165, l. 9. The author of the *Chin P'ing Mei* was demonstrably familiar with this passage because he quotes from the same epilogue in the prologue to the first chapter of his novel. See note 28 to chapter 1 below. This expression also occurs in the *Hsi-yu chi*, vol. 2, ch. 95, p. 1075, l. 10.

36. I have not been able to locate the original source of this proverbial couplet. The first half of the couplet occurs in the same form in the *Chin P'ing Mei tz'u-hua*, vol. 4, ch. 79, p. 1a, l. 8, at the opening of the chapter in which Hsi-men Ch'ing dies as a consequence of sexual excess. A variant occurs in the roughly contemporaneous ch'uan-ch'i drama by Chou Lü-ching entitled *Chin-chien chi* (The brocade note), *Liu-shih chung ch'ü* edition (Taipei: K'ai-ming shu-tien, 1970), scene 15, p. 48, l. 7.

37. This couplet is from the *Ch'ien-tzu wen* (Thousand-character text), a famous children's primer composed of a thousand different characters and traditionally attributed to Chou Hsing-ssu (d. 521). See the text as printed in *Dai Kan-Wa jiten* (Great Chinese-Japanese dictionary), comp. Morohashi Tetsuji, 13 vols. (Tokyo: Taishūkan shoten, 1960), 2:523, upper register, l. 4. The same couplet occurs in the roughly contemporaneous ch'uan-ch'i drama *Mu-tan t'ing* (The peony pavilion) by T'ang Hsien-tsu (1550–1616), the author's preface of which is dated 1598. See *Mu-tan t'ing*, ed. and annot. Hsü Shuo-fang and Yang Hsiao-mei (Peking: Chung-hua shu-chü, 1959), scene 17, p. 81, ll. 6–7; and *The Peony Pavilion*, by Tang Xianzu, trans. Cyril Birch (Bloomington: Indiana University Press, 1980), scene 17, p. 80, ll. 16 and 18.

38. This line occurs in the *Chu-tzu yü-lei* (Classified sayings of Master Chu), a collection of the sayings of Chu Hsi as recorded by his disciples that was published in 1270. See *Chu-tzu yü-lei*, comp. Li Ching-te, 8 vols. (Taipei: Cheng-chung shu-chü, 1982), vol. 1, *chüan* 1, p. 8b, l. 8. It also occurs in a collection of aphorisms compiled by Ch'ien Ch'i (1469–1549) entitled *Ch'ien Kung-liang Ts'e-yü* (Penetrating aphorisms of Ch'ien Ch'i). See the edition of this work included in the *Ts'ung-shu chi-ch'eng* (A corpus of works from collectanea), 1st series (Shanghai: Shang-wu yin-shu kuan, 1936), vol. 374, p. 11, l. 6.

39. This line is from a lyric by Su Shih (1037–1101). See *Ch'üan Sung tz'u*, 1:280, upper register, l. 6. A variant occurs in the *Chin P'ing Mei tz'u-hua*, vol. 4, ch. 63, p. 12b, l. 1.

40. This phrase is from a memorial to the throne by Ch'en Fan (d. 168) in which he descibes the inevitable results of specious speech and behavior. See *Hou-Han shu*, comp. Fan Yeh, 12 vols. (Peking: Chung-hua shu-chü, 1965), vol. 8, *chüan* 66, p. 2169, l. 14.

41. This phrase occurs in the first line of a preface (dated 1588) by Yü Hsiang-tou (c. 1550–1637) to the *Hsi-Han chih-chuan* (Chronicle of the Western Han dynasty), a historical novel attributed to Hsiung Ta-mu (fl. mid 16th century). See *Ch'üan-Han chih-chuan* (Chronicle of the entire Han dynasty), 12 *chüan* (Chien-yang: K'o-ch'in chai, 1588), in *Ku-pen hsiao-shuo ts'ung-k'an, ti-wu chi* (Collectanea of rare editions of traditional fiction, fifth series) (Peking: Chung-hua shu-chü, 1990), 2:487, l. 2.

42. Hsin-hsin tzu, the Master of Delight, has not been identified, but there is a sixteenth-century ch'uan-ch'i drama entitled *Huan-hun chi* (The return of the soul), the authorship of which is attributed to Hsin-hsin k'o, a very similar pseudonym. There is a facsimile reproduction of this play available in the *Ku-pen hsi-ch'ü ts'ung-k'an, erh-chi* (Collectanea of rare editions of traditional drama, second series) (Shanghai: Shang-wu yin-shu kuan, 1955), item 5. For the attribution of authorship, see *Yüan-shan T'ang ch'ü-p'in* (The Yüan-shan T'ang critical classification of ch'uan-ch'i dramas), by Ch'i Piao-chia (1602–45), in *Chung-kuo ku-tien hsi-ch'ü lun-chu chi-ch'eng*, 6:118, l. 2.

PREFACE TO THE *CHIN P'ING MEI*

1. Yüan Hung-tao (1568–1610) praised the *Chin P'ing Mei*, of which he had only seen the first part, in a letter to Tung Ch'i-ch'ang (1555–1636) in the tenth month of 1596, and again in a well-known brief composition entitled "The Rules of Drinking," which was written in 1605–6. See Hanan, "The Text of the *Chin P'ing Mei*," pp. 39–46. It is also reasonable to assume that he praised it verbally to his contemporaries.

2. *T'ao-wu* was the name given to the annals of the state of Ch'u in ancient times. It is no longer extant but is mentioned in the book of *Mencius*. See *The Works of Mencius*, trans. James Legge (Hong Kong: Hong Kong University Press, 1960), p. 327. According to the traditional interpretation, the word *t'ao-wu* was the name of a ferocious mythological beast and was chosen as the title of a historical work because it was expected to serve as an admonitory negative example.

3. The words that I have rendered as "villain" and "clown" are the technical terms *ching* and *ch'ou* that are used to designate the corresponding role types in traditional Chinese drama.

4. Ch'u Hsiao-hsiu has not been identified. However, if this preface is by Feng Meng-lung, as a number of scholars have suggested, it may be significant that there was a prominent clan of this name in Su-chou, which was also his native place. See note 6 below.

5. The story of Hsiang Yü (232–202 B.C.), the Hegemon-King, who was the most powerful figure in China during the interregnum between the Ch'in (221–207 B.C.) and Han (202 B.C.–A.D. 220) dynasties, is memorably told by Ssu-ma Ch'ien (145–c. 90 B.C.) in the *Shih-chi* (Records of the historian), the first comprehensive history of China. See *Records of the Grand Historian of China*, trans. Burton Watson, 2 vols.

(New York: Columbia University Press, 1961), 1:37–74. It also figures prominently in the prologue to the *Chin P'ing Mei*. It has been dramatized many times, but the play referred to here is most likely to be the ch'uan-ch'i drama *Ch'ien-chin chi* (The thousand pieces of gold) by Shen Ts'ai (fl. 15th century), two of whose other works are referred to by name in the *Chin P'ing Mei*. Scene 14 of this play is entitled "Night Feast," and Hsiang Yü's suicide at Wu-chiang occurs in scene 41. See *Ch'ien-chin chi*, by Shen Ts'ai, *Liu-shih chung ch'ü* edition (Taipei: K'ai-ming shu-tien, 1970), pp. 44–47 and 130–34.

6. Chinese dragons are often depicted with a large pearl dangling before their open jaws, so the pseudonym Pearl-juggler inevitably suggests the word "dragon." Eastern Wu is an archaic designation of the Su-chou region in modern Kiangsu Province. For these reasons it has been suggested that this pseudonym may refer to Feng Meng-lung (1574–1646), the famous connoisseur and purveyor of vernacular literature, who was a native of Su-chou and whose given name contains the word "dragon." Since Feng Meng-lung is known to have been one of the early admirers of the *Chin P'ing Mei* and to have urged its publication while it was still circulating in manuscript only, I am inclined to think that he may well have been the author of this preface. See Hanan, "The Text of the *Chin P'ing Mei*," p. 47.

7. This date corresponds to the period from December 28, 1617, to January 25, 1618, in the Western calendar.

COLOPHON

1. The Chia-ching reign period extended from 1522 to 1566. The question of whether the *Chin P'ing Mei* was written during the Chia-ching or the Wan-li (1573–1620) reign periods is still a matter of controversy. For the reasons given on p. xlii of my introduction to this translation, I hold to the latter view.

2. Cheng and Wei were the names of two petty states in ancient China the popular music of which was regarded as licentious. Confucius is traditionally believed to have edited the *Book of Songs* in which airs from Cheng and Wei are included.

3. The identity of Nien-kung has not been established.

PREFATORY LYRICS

1. These four lyrics may all be by the prominent Yüan dynasty (1279–1368) Buddhist cleric Ming-pen (1263–1323). The first, second, and fourth occur together, without attribution, in an anthology of Buddho-Taoist poetry and liturgical material compiled c. 1347, so they are at least as old as the fourteenth century. See *Ming-ho yü-yin* (Lingering notes of the calling crane), comp. P'eng Chih-chung, *ts'e* 744–45 in *Cheng-t'ung Tao-tsang* (The Cheng-t'ung [1436–49] Taoist canon) (Shanghai: Shang-wu yin-shu kuan, 1926), *chüan* 6, pp. 5b–6a. In a work completed in 1688 Shen Hsiung claims to have personally seen copies of the first two lyrics in Ming-pen's own hand. See *Ku-chin tz'u-hua* (Comments on lyrics ancient and modern), comp. Shen Hsiung, in *Tz'u-hua ts'ung-pien* (A collectanea of talks on lyrics), comp. T'ang Kuei-chang, 5 vols. (Peking: Chung-hua shu-chü, 1986), 1:796, ll. 9–13. In another work compiled in 1707 under imperial auspices, the first three lyrics are quoted in full and attributed to Ming-pen. See *Li-tai tz'u-hua* (Talks on lyrics chro-

nologically arranged), comp. Wang I-ch'ing et al., in *Tz'u-hua ts'ung-pien*, 2:1293, ll. 6–12. We also know that Ming-pen liked to compose lyrics to this tune because there are eight other examples of his extant. See *Ch'üan Chin Yüan tz'u* (Complete lyrics of the Chin and Yüan dynasties), comp. T'ang Kuei-chang, 2 vols. (Peking: Chung-hua shu-chü, 1979), 2:1161–62. I feel that these four lyrics are all of a piece and were probably composed by a single author, possibly as part of a series. Despite the fact that T'ang Kuei-chang accepts the attribution of only the third lyric to Ming-pen, consigning the other three to the category of anonymous authorship, I am inclined to accept them all as being by the same author. For a monograph on Ming-pen's role in intellectual history, see Chün-fang Yü, "Chung-feng Ming-pen and Ch'an Buddhism in the Yüan," in *Yüan Thought: Chinese Thought and Religion under the Mongols*, ed. Hok-lam Chan and Wm. Theodore de Bary (New York: Columbia University Press, 1982), pp. 419–77.

2. Golden Valley was the name of the country villa of Shih Ch'ung (249–300), a man whose wealth and fondness for ostentation has made his name proverbial for those qualities. See *Shih-shuo Hsin-yü: A New Account of Tales of the World*, by Liu I-Ch'ing; trans. Richard B. Mather (Minneapolis: University of Minnesota Press, 1976), ch. 9, p. 264, item 57, n. 1.

3. This line is a quotation from a poem by T'ao Ch'ien (365–427), a poet famous for qualities diametrically opposite to those represented by Shih Ch'ung. See *Hsien-Ch'in Han Wei Chin Nan-pei ch'ao shih*, 2:1010, l. 2. For a translation of the poem in question, see *T'ao Yüan-ming: His Works and Their Meaning*, trans. A. R. Davis, 2 vols. (Cambridge: Cambridge University Press, 1983), 1:154.

4. The "four vices" is a traditional topos that is elaborated upon ubiquitously in Chinese popular literature. It acquired additional significance, however, during the Wan-li reign period because of an incident that occurred in January 1590, when the left case reviewer in the Court of Judicial Review, a man named Lo Yü-jen (cs 1583), submitted a scathing memorial to the throne in which he accused the emperor himself of being addicted to drunkenness, lust, avarice, and anger. This created a furor that was probably not forgotten until near the end of the reign in 1620. The fact that the author of the *Chin P'ing Mei* placed these lyrics on the four vices in such a prominent position at the head of his text may go a long way toward explaining why the novel was not published until the final years of the Wan-li reign period even though it had been circulating in manuscript and attracting a good deal of attention among the literary elite from at least as early as 1596. So long as the memory of this incident remained fresh, any work that highlighted the four vices in such a way ran the risk of being interpreted as a veiled attack on the reigning emperor. The complete text of Lo Yü-jen's memorial may be found in *Wan-li ti-ch'ao* (Transcriptions from gazettes of the Wan-li period), 3 vols., fac. repr. (Taipei: Cheng-chung shu-chü, 1969), 1:468–74.

5. The term "cinnabar fields" is the conventional rendering of an important concept in Taoist physiological alchemy that might be translated more functionally as "regions of vital heat." There were three of them in the human body: an upper one in the head, a middle one in the thorax, and a lower one in the abdomen. For more on this esoteric subject, see Joseph Needham and Lu Gwei-djen, *Science and Civilisation in China*, vol. 5, part V, *Spagyrical Discovery and Invention: Physiological Alchemy* (Cambridge: Cambridge University Press, 1983), pp. 38–39 and passim.

6. A variant form of this couplet occurs in the anonymous early Ming ch'uan-ch'i drama *P'o-yao chi* (The dilapidated kiln). See *P'o-yao chi*, item 19 in *Ku-pen hsi-ch'ü ts'ung-k'an, ch'u-chi* (Collectanea of rare editions of traditional drama, first series) (Shanghai: Shang-wu yin-shu kuan, 1954), *chüan* 1, scene 4, p. 11b, l. 3.

7. A variant form of this couplet is traditionally attributed to Hsü Shou-hsin (fl. 11th century), a semilegendary figure who was, at one time, sometimes numbered among the Eight Immortals of popular Taoism. See *Sung-shih chi-shih* (Recorded occasions in Sung poetry), comp. Li O (1692–1752) and Ma Yüeh-kuan (1688–1755), 14 vols. (Shanghai: Shang-wu yin-shu kuan, 1937), vol. 13, *chüan* 90, p. 2174, l. 5. It occurs in the form given here in Yüan drama. See *Yüan-ch'ü hsüan*, 2:632, ll. 3–4; and 4:1368, ll. 3–4. It also occurs in the form given here, without attribution, in the *Ming-hsin pao-chien, chüan* 1, p. 11a, ll. 9–10.

8. A variant form of this couplet occurs in Yüan drama. See *Yüan-ch'ü hsüan*, 4:1504, l. 16. The same variant form also occurs in a fifteenth-century ch'uan-ch'i drama. See Shen Ts'ai, *Huan-tai chi* (The return of the belts), item 32 in *Ku-pen hsi-ch'ü ts'ung-k'an, ch'u-chi, chüan* 1, scene 6, p. 13b, l. 4. This drama is represented in the novel as being performed on two separate occasions in Hsi-men Ch'ing's household. See *Chin P'ing Mei tz'u-hua*, vol. 4, ch. 65, p. 13b, l. 9; and vol. 4, ch. 76, p. 7a, l. 11.

CHAPTER 1

1. There is no prologue designated as such in the text. I have chosen to set it apart from the remainder of the chapter in order to emphasize its importance. For an attempt to explicate its significance, see appendix I.

2. I have chosen to translate the names of the poetic genres *tz'u* and *ch'ü*, both of which were originally written to preexisting tunes, as "lyric" and "song," respectively. In most cases, when examples of these genres are copied into the text of the novel, the name of the tune is supplied; but in some instances, such as this, it is omitted. In all such cases, when I have been able to ascertain the name of the tune, I supply it.

3. Liu Pang (256–195 B.C.) is the name of the founder of the Han dynasty (206 B.C.–A.D. 220), who reigned from 206 to 195 B.C. For the classic account of his career, see *Shih-chi*, vol. 2, *chüan* 8, pp. 341–94; and Watson, *Records of the Grand Historian of China*, 1:77–119.

4. Yü-chi is the name of a favorite of Liu Pang's rival, Hsiang Yü, who accompanied him at the crucial battle of Kai-hsia in 202 B.C. See *Shih-chi*, vol. 1, *chüan* 7, p. 333; and Watson, *Records of the Grand Historian of China*, 1:70–71.

5. Lady Ch'i was the name of a favorite concubine of Liu Pang, whose tragic story is memorably related by Ssu-ma Ch'ien. See *Shih-chi*, vol. 2, *chüan* 9, pp. 395–97; and Watson, *Records of the Grand Historian of China*, 1:321–23.

6. As Patrick Hanan has pointed out in his "Sources of the *Chin P'ing Mei*," p. 33, n. 23, this lyric is by Cho T'ien (fl. early 13th century). See *Ch'üan Sung tz'u*, 4:2481. The proximate source is the middle-period (c. 1400–c. 1575) vernacular story entitled *Wen-ching yüan-yang hui* (The fatal rendezvous), published by Hung P'ien ca. 1550. See *Ch'ing-p'ing shan-t'ang hua-pen*, p. 154. For an annotated French translation of this story, under the title "Le rendez-vous d'amour où les cous sont coupés,"

see André Lévy, *Études sur le Conte et le Roman Chinois* (Paris: École Française d'Extrême-Orient, 1971), pp. 195–210.

7. The proximate source of this quotation is the prologue of the story *Wen-ching yüan-yang hui*, p. 155, l. 1. The ultimate source is Wang Yen (256–311). In the *Shih-shuo hsin-yü* (A new account of tales of the world), by Liu I-ch'ing (403–444), the anecdote in which this quotation occurs is assigned to Wang Jung (234–305), Wang Yen's first cousin. See *Shih-shuo hsin-yü chiao-chien* (A critical edition of the *Shih-shuo hsin-yü*), ed. Yang Yung (Hong Kong: Ta-chung shu-chü, 1969), ch. 17, item 4, pp. 488–89; and Mather, *Shih-shuo Hsin-yü*, p. 324. In the *Chin shu* (History of the Chin dynasty [265–420]), however, this anecdote is assigned to Wang Yen. See *Chin shu*, comp. Fang Hsüan-ling (578–648) et al., 10 vols. (Peking: Chung-hua shu-chü, 1974), vol. 4, *chüan* 43, pp. 1236–37. Commentators have determined the latter attribution to be the correct one. The anecdote reads as follows: "When Wang Yen's infant son died, Shan Chien came to offer his condolences. Wang Yen was beside himself with grief. Shan Chien said, 'It was only a babe in arms, so why carry on to such an extent?' To which Wang Yen replied, 'Sages may be able to forget their feelings, and the lower order of men may lack feeling altogether. It is people just like ourselves who are most affected by passion.'"

8. As W. L. Idema has pointed out in his "Zhu Youdun's Dramatic Prefaces and Traditional Fiction," *Ming Studies*, vol. 10 (Spring 1980): 17–18, this quotation occurs in conjunction with the preceding one in at least three earlier sources, in all of which it is attributed to the famous Buddhist figure Hui-yüan (334–416). See *Ch'ui-chien lu ch'üan-pien* (Record of breathing into a sword-guard, complete edition), by Yü Wen-pao (fl. c. 1250) (Peking: Chung-hua shu-chü, 1959), part 4, p. 107; Chu Yu-tun's (1379–1439) preface to his play *Chen Yüeh-o ch'un-feng Ch'ing-shuo t'ang* (Chen Yüeh-o: Spring breeze at Ch'ing-shuo Pavilion); microfilm copy of the original edition, preface dated 1406, in the Peking Library, pp. 1a–1b; and the prologue of the story *Wen-ching yüan-yang hui*, in *Ch'ing-p'ing shan-t'ang hua-pen*, p. 155. I have not been able to locate this quotation in the extant works of Hui-yüan.

9. These are all the names of famous swords of antiquity. This passage is reminiscent of the penultimate paragraph of Hsün-tzu's most famous essay, entitled "Man's Nature is Evil." See *Hsün-tzu yin-te*, p. 90, ll. 87–89, which is translated by Burton Watson as follows: "Ts'ung of Duke Huan of Ch'i, Ch'üeh of T'ai-kung of Ch'i, Lu of King Wen of the Chou, Hu of Lord Chuang of Ch'u, and Kan-chiang, Mu-yeh, Chü-ch'üeh, and Pi-lü of King Ho-lü of Wu were all famous swords of antiquity, but if they had not been subjected to the grindstone, they would never have become sharp, and if men of strength had not wielded them, they would never have been able to cut anything." See Watson, *Hsün Tzu*, p. 170. The sword here serves Hsün-tzu as a metaphor for realized human potential, the raw material of which must undergo the tempering and grinding of proper socialization before it can be put to effective use. And even then, to continue the metaphor, if it is not to grow blunt or rusty it must be properly maintained, which, in human terms, requires one to subject oneself to a continuous regimen of self-cultivation. The relevance of this passage to the argument of the *Chin P'ing Mei* is that it was not that the swords of Hsiang Yü and Liu Pang had not been sharp but the fact that their self-indulgence allowed them to become blunted that resulted in their moral and political failures.

10. The First Emperor of the Ch'in dynasty (221–207 B.C.) was the title assumed by Ying Cheng (259–210 B.C.), the king of the state of Ch'in, when he succeeded in unifying China in 221 B.C.

11. The O-pang Palace was an ostentatious edifice of enormous proportions across the river from the Ch'in capital of Hsien-yang, work on which began in 212 B.C. It is said that a labor force of more than 700,000 men was drafted to work on its constuction. See *Shih-chi*, vol. 1, *chüan* 6, p. 256; and Yang and Yang, *Records of the Historian* (Hong Kong: Commercial Press, 1974), p. 179.

12. The first four lines of this passage of parallel prose, with their formulaic boxing of the compass, occur in very similar form in at least three earlier works of vernacular literature. See *Ch'in ping Liu-kuo p'ing-hua* (The p'ing-hua on the annexation of the Six States by Ch'in), originally published in 1321–23 (Shanghai: Ku-tien wen-hsüeh ch'u-pan she, 1955), p. 3; *San-kuo chih p'ing-hua* (The p'ing-hua on the history of the Three Kingdoms), also published in 1321–23 (Shanghai: Ku-tien wen-hsüeh ch'u-pan she, 1955), p. 2; and *Hua Kuan So ch'u-shen chuan* (The story of how Hua Kuan So got his start in life), originally published in 1478, in *Ming Ch'eng-hua shuo-ch'ang tz'u-hua ts'ung-k'an* (Corpus of prosimetric tz'u-hua narratives published in the Ch'eng-hua reign period [1465–87] of the Ming dynasty), 12 *ts'e* (Shanghai: Shanghai Museum, 1973), *ts'e* 1, p. 1a. For an English translation of the last passage, see *The Story of Hua Guan Suo*, trans. Gail Oman King (Tempe, Ariz.: Center for Asian Studies, Arizona State University, 1989), p. 30.

13. The Hung Canal was located in what is now Honan Province. This event took place in 203 B.C. See *Shih-chi*, vol. 1 *chüan* 7, p. 331; and Watson, *Records of the Grand Historian of China*, 1:68.

14. Fan Tseng (275–204 B.C.) was one of Hsiang Yü's principal advisers. For his biography, see *Shih-chi*, vol. 1, *chüan* 7, pp. 300–25 passim; and Watson, *Records of the Grand Historian of China*, 1:41–64 passim.

15. Han Hsin (d. 196 B.C.) was one of Liu Pang's principal generals and the architect of his decisive victory over Hsiang Yü at Kai-hsia in 202 B.C. For his biography, see *Shih-chi*, vol. 8, *chüan* 92, pp. 2609–30; and Watson, *Records of the Grand Historian of China*, 1:208–32.

16. See *Shih-chi*, vol. 1, *chüan* 7, p. 333; and Watson, *Records of the Grand Historian of China*, 1:70.

17. This poem is by Hu Tseng (fl. late 9th century), whose verses on famous historical themes appear ubiquitously in Chinese vernacular fiction. See *Ch'üan T'ang shih*, vol. 10, *chüan* 647, p. 7423, l. 4.

18. On the day in 209 B.C. when Liu Pang, who was only a minor functionary at the time, decided to become an outlaw, he cut in two a white snake that lay across his path. This symbolic act has been taken to mark the inception of his revolt against the Ch'in dynasty. See *Shih-chi*, vol. 1, *chüan* 8, p. 347; and Watson, *Records of the Grand Historian of China*, 1:80–81.

19. The information in the above paragraph occurs in almost the same words in the earliest extant edition of the famous historical novel *San-kuo chih t'ung-su yen-i* (The romance of the Three Kingdoms), preface dated 1522, attributed to Lo Kuan-chung, 2 vols. (Shanghai: Shang-hai ku-chi ch'u-pan she, 1980), vol. 1, *chüan* 4, p. 201, ll. 13–15. The text reads "two years later," but I have emended it to "three years later" to bring it into conformity with historical fact. For evidence that this was part

of an established formula, see ibid., l. 14; and *Yüan-ch'ü hsüan wai-pien*, 1:146, ll. 9–10.

20. Prince Ju-i of Chao (d. 194 B.C.), the third son of Liu Pang, was poisoned by Empress Lü after her husband's death. See *Shih-chi*, vol. 2, *chüan* 9, p. 397; and Watson, *Records of the Grand Historian of China*, 1:322–23.

21. Empress Lü (242–180 B.C.), the first wife of Liu Pang, was a ruthless and strong-minded woman who took over the reins of power after the death of her son, Emperor Hui (r. 195–188 B.C.), and reigned in her own right from that time until her death in 180 B.C. For her biograpy, see *Shih-chi*, vol. 2, *chüan* 9, pp. 395–412; and Watson, *Records of the Grand Historian of China*, 1:321–40.

22. Kao-tsu, "supreme ancestor," is the posthumous title conferred upon Liu Pang, the first emperor of the Han dynasty (r. 206–195 B.C.). He is usually referred to by this title.

23. Chang Liang (d. 189 B.C.) was one of Liu Pang's principal advisers. For his biography, see *Shih-chi*, vol. 6, *chüan* 55, pp. 2033–49; and Watson, *Records of the Grand Historian of China*, 1:134–51.

24. For this episode, see *Shih-chi*, vol. 6, *chüan* 55, pp. 2044–47; and Watson, *Records of the Grand Historian of China*, 1:145–49. The second line of this song has been inadvertently omitted. I have supplied it from the original text in the *Shih-chi*, loc. cit., p. 2047, l. 8.

25. See *Shih-chi*, vol. 2, *chüan* 9, p. 397; and Watson, *Records of the Grand Historian of China*, 1:323. Watson translates the relevant passage as follows: "Empress Lü later cut off Lady Ch'i's hands and feet, plucked out her eyes, burned her ears, gave her a potion to drink which made her dumb, and had her thrown into the privy, calling her the 'human pig.'" He also adds a note: "Early Chinese privies consisted of two parts, an upper room for the user and a pit below in which swine were kept. Apparently Lady Ch'i was thrown into the lower part, hence the epithet."

26. This poem was written in 1170 by Fan Ch'eng-ta (1126–93) on the occasion of a visit to the site of Yü-chi's tomb near Ssu district in what is now Anhui Province. See *Fan Shih-hu chi* (Collected works of Fan Ch'eng-ta), 2 vols. (Peking: Chung-hua shu-chü, 1962), vol. 1, *chüan* 12, p. 145. The same poem, with some textual variants, is quoted without attribution in the 1588 edition of the *Ch'üan-Han chih-chuan*, *chüan* 2, p. 35b, ll. 4–5.

27. The proximate source of this sentence is the vernacular story *Wen-ching yüan-yang hui*, p. 155, l. 3.

28. The proximate source of these lines is ibid., p. 166, ll. 13–14. The ultimate source is the literary tale by Huang-fu Mei entitled *Fei-yen chuan*, p. 165, ll. 8–9; see also Jeanne Kelly, trans., "The Tragedy of Pu Fei-yen," in Ma and Lau, *Traditional Chinese Stories*, p. 176.

29. The Yellow Springs is a traditional Chinese metonym for the land of the dead.

30. The proximate source of most of the preceding eight lines of text is the vernacular story *Wen-ching yüan-yang hui*, p. 157, ll. 1–2.

31. The probable source of these two lines is the middle period vernacular story entitled *Hsin-ch'iao shih Han Wu mai ch'un-ch'ing* (Han Wu-niang sells her charms at New Bridge Market). See *Ku-chin hsiao-shuo* (Stories old and new), ed, Feng Meng-lung (1574–1646), 2 vols. (Peking: Jen-min wen-hsüeh ch'u-pan she, 1958), *chüan* 3, p. 63, l. 10; and Robert C. Miller and the editors, trans., "Han Wu-niang

Sells Her Charms at the New Bridge Market," in Ma and Lau, *Traditional Chinese Stories*, p. 313.

32. The probable source of this couplet is the early Ming novel *San Sui p'ing-yao chuan* (The three Sui quash the demons' revolt), fac. repr. (Tokyo: Tenri daigaku shuppan-bu, 1981), *chüan* 2, ch. 6, p. 11a, l. 7. For an explication of the prologue, see appendix I.

33. The Cheng-ho reign period corresponds to the years 1111–18.

34. Emperor Hui-tsung (1082–1135) occupied the throne during the years 1100–25.

35. The Sung dynasty lasted from 960 to 1279.

36. Kao Ch'iu (d. 1126) is a historical figure. For his biography, see *Hui-chu lu* (Records for chowrie waving conversation), by Wang Ming-ch'ing (1127–c. 1214) (Peking: Chung-hua shu-chü, 1961), *hou-lu, chüan* 7, p. 176. He is one of the principal villains in the novel *Shui-hu chuan*. See *Shui-hu ch'üan-chuan*, vol. 1, ch. 2, pp. 16–21 and passim; and Shapiro, *Outlaws of the Marsh*, vol. 1, ch. 2, pp. 15–24 and passim. He is also the principal villain in the sixteenth-century ch'uan-ch'i drama *Pao-chien chi* (The story of the precious sword) by Li K'ai-hsien (1502–68), completed in 1547, which is one of the most important sources drawn upon by the author of the *Chin P'ing Mei*. See *Pao-chien chi*, by Li K'ai-hsien, in Fu Hsi-hua, ed., *Shui-hu hsi-ch'ü chi, ti-erh chi* (Corpus of drama dealing with the *Shui-hu* cycle, second series) (Shanghai: Ku-tien wen-hsüeh ch'u-pan she, 1958), pp. 1–98 passim.

37. Yang Chien (d. 1121) is a historical figure. For his biography, see *Sung shih*, vol. 39, *chüan* 468, p. 13664.

38. T'ung Kuan (1054–1126) is a historical figure. For his biography, see *Sung shih*, vol. 39, *chüan* 468, pp. 13658–59; Herbert Franke, ed., *Sung Biographies*, 4 vols. (Wiesbaden: Franz Steiner Verlag, 1976), 3:1090–97; and A *Compilation of Anecdotes of Sung Personalities*, comp. Ting Ch'uan-ching; trans. Chu Djang and Jane C. Djang (N.p.: St. John's University Press, 1989), pp. 543–48.

39. Ts'ai Ching (1046–1126) is a historical figure. For his biography, see *Sung shih*, vol. 39, *chüan* 472, pp. 13721–28; Franke, *Sung Biographies*, 3:1029–35; and Djang and Djang, A *Compilation of Anecdotes of Sung Personalities*, pp. 517–26.

40. For the story of how the baleful stars descended to earth to be incarnated in human form, see *Shui-hu ch'üan-chuan*, chs. 1–2, 42, and 71; and Shapiro, *Outlaws of the Marsh*, chs. 1, 42, and 71.

41. Sung Chiang (fl. 1117–21) is a historical figure, although very little is known about him. He is the principal hero of the *Shui-hu chuan*. For a succinct survey of the available information about the historical figure, see Richard Gregg Irwin, *The Evolution of a Chinese Novel: Shui-hu-chuan* (Cambridge: Harvard University Press, 1966), pp. 9–18.

42. Wang Ch'ing and T'ien Hu are fictional bandit leaders whose uprisings are suppressed by Sung Chiang and his followers on behalf of the imperial government in certain editions of the *Shui-hu chuan*, the earliest extant datable exemplar of which was published in 1594.

43. Fang La (d. 1121) is a historical figure. For his biography, see *Sung shih*, vol. 39, *chüan* 468, pp. 13659–62; and two monographs by Kao Yu-kung, "A Study of the Fang La Rebellion," *Harvard Journal of Asiatic Studies*, vol. 24 (1962–63): 17–63; and

"Source Materials on the Fang La Rebellion," *Harvard Journal of Asiatic Studies*, vol. 26 (1966): 211–40. The proximate source of the above four lines is *Shui-hu ch'üan-chuan*, vol. 3, ch. 72, p. 1216, l. 8.

44. This is the slogan adopted by the bandit band in the *Shui-hu chuan* to justify their taking the law into their own hands. It also occurs in the *San-kuo chih t'ung-su yen-i* where, ironically, it is put into the mouth of Ts'ao Ts'ao (155–220), who is popularly regarded as the villain of the story. See *San-kuo chih t'ung-su yen-i*, vol. 1, *chüan* 10, p. 464, l. 18.

45. Lord Meng-ch'ang was the title of T'ien Wen (d. 279 B.C.), a member of the ruling house of the state of Ch'i during the Warring States period (475–221 B.C.) who was famous for his patronage of large numbers of retainers. For his biography, see *Shih-chi*, vol. 7, *chüan* 75, pp. 2351–63; and Yang and Yang, *Records of the Historian*, pp. 76–88.

46. Ch'ai Jung (921–959) was the second to last emperor (r. 954–959) of the Later Chou dynasty (951–960).

47. The proximate source of this quatrain is the corresponding passage in *Shui-hu ch'üan-chuan*, vol. 1, ch. 23, p. 346, l. 2. It also occurs in other works of vernacular literature, such as the anonymous Yüan-Ming tsa-chü drama *P'o feng-shih* (The critique of the poem on the wind), in *Ku-pen Yüan Ming tsa-chü*, vol. 3, scene 3, p. 11a, l. 3; the early vernacular story *Ch'ien-t'ang meng* (The dream in Ch'ien-t'ang), included as part of the front matter in the 1498 edition of the *Hsi-hsiang chi* (The romance of the western chamber), fac. repr. (Taipei: Shih-chieh shu-chü, 1963), p. 3b, ll. 1–2; the early vernacular story *Lo-yang san-kuai chi* (The three monsters of Lo-yang), in *Ch'ing-p'ing shan-t'ang hua-pen*, p. 77, ll. 2–3; the middle-period vernacular story *Ch'en Hsün-chien Mei-ling shih-ch'i chi* (Police chief Ch'en loses his wife in crossing the Mei-ling Range), in ibid., p. 133, ll. 14–15; the sixteenth-century novel by Lo Mao-teng entitled *San-pao t'ai-chien Hsi-yang chi t'ung-su yen-i* (The romance of Eunuch Cheng Ho's expedition to the Western Ocean), author's preface dated 1597, 2 vols. (Shanghai: Shang-hai ku-chi ch'u-pan she, 1985), ch. 10, p. 130, ll. 9–10; and the early seventeenth-century novel by Teng Chih-mo entitled *T'ang-tai Lü Ch'un-yang te-tao Fei-chien chi* (The story of how Lü Tung-pin of the T'ang dynasty obtained the Tao with the aid of his flying sword) (Chien-yang: Ts'ui-ch'ing t'ang, c. 1603), in *Ku-pen hsiao-shuo ts'ung-k'an, ti-shih chi* (Collectanea of rare editions of traditional fiction, tenth series) (Peking: Chung-hua shu-chü, 1990), vol. 5, ch. 7, p. 46b, ll. 6–7.

48. The proximate source of this couplet is the corresponding passage in *Shui-hu ch'üan-chuan*, vol. 1, ch. 23, p. 346, l. 3. It also recurs in ibid., vol. 2, ch. 43, p. 699, l. 10. The ultimate source is the line commentary on the fifth line of the first hexagram in the *I-ching* (Book of changes). See *Chou-i yin-te* (A concordance to the *I-ching*) (Taipei: Chinese Materials and Research Aids Service Center, 1966), p. 2, col. 1, ll. 20–21; and *The I Ching or Book of Changes*, trans. Richard Wilhelm; trans. from the German by Cary F. Baynes, 2 vols. (New York: Pantheon Books, 1961), 1:8.

49. Pien Chuang was a legendary figure from the state of Lu during the Spring and Autumn period (722–481 B.C.) who is alleged to have accounted for the death of two tigers in a single engagement. See *Chan-Kuo Ts'e*, trans. J. I. Crump (Oxford: Oxford University Press, 1970), p. 71; and *Shih-chi*, vol. 7, *chüan* 70, p. 2302, ll. 1–4.

50. Li Ts'un-hsiao (d. 894) is a historical figure. For his biography, see *Chiu Wu-tai shih* (Old history of the Five Dynasties), comp. Hsüeh Chü-cheng (912–981) et al., 6 vols. (Peking: Chung-hua shu-chü, 1976), vol. 3, *chüan* 53, pp. 714–17. He is best known in vernacular literature for his alleged single-handed slaying of a tiger. See, for example, the Ming tsa-chü drama *Yen-men kuan Ts'un-hsiao ta-hu* (Li Ts'un-hsiao slays a tiger at Yen-men Pass), in *Yüan-ch'ü hsüan wai-pien*, vol. 2, scene 2, pp. 559–60.

51. The proximate source of this poem is the corresponding passage in *Shui-hu ch'üan-chuan*, vol. 1, ch. 23, p. 347, ll. 4–10. The same poem, with some textual variants, also occurs in the Ming novel *Ts'an-T'ang Wu-tai shih yen-chuan* (Romance of the late T'ang and Five Dynasties). See the modern reprint entitled *Ts'an-T'ang Wu-tai shih yen-i chuan* (Peking: Pao-wen t'ang shu-tien, 1983), ch. 10, pp. 31–32. In the latter novel the poem is used to describe Li Ts'un-hsiao's tiger-slaying feat.

52. The last three lines of this quatrain are derived from a poem in *Shui-hu ch'üan-chuan*, vol. 1, ch. 23, p. 342, l. 15.

53. This line, with slight textual variation, recurs three times in *Chin P'ing Mei tz'u-hua*, vol. 1, ch. 19, p. 1a, l. 4; vol. 5, ch. 84, p. 10a, l. 10; and vol. 5, ch. 94, p. 1a, l. 4. In the last three cases it occurs in a poem the proximate source of which is *Shui-hu ch'üan-chuan*, vol. 2, ch. 33, p. 513, ll. 3-4. The first two couplets of this poem, including the line in question, and the last two couplets also occur separately in the *Ming-hsin pao-chien*, *chüan* 2, p. 5a, ll. 2–3; and *chüan* 1, p. 3b, ll. 12–13.

54. The last two lines occur, in reverse order, in the *Shen-hsiang ch'üan-pien* (Complete compendium on effective physiognomy), an influential anthology of works on physiognomy compiled by Yüan Chung-ch'e (1376–1458) that was copied in its entirety into the eighteenth-century encyclopedia *Ku-chin t'u-shu chi-ch'eng* (A comprehensive corpus of books and illustrations ancient and modern), presented to the emperor in 1725, where it is located in section 17, *i-shu tien*, *chüan* 631–44. This book is quoted extensively in chapter 29 of the *Chin P'ing Mei*. These two lines are from a work attributed to Hsü Fu (fl. 3d–2d centuries B.C.), a famous physiognomist of the Han dynasty. See ibid., chüan 633, p. 7a, ll. 5–6.

55. The proximate source of the first four lines of this lyric is the *Shui-hu ch'üan-chuan*, vol. 3, ch. 79, p. 1303, l. 3. The source of the last four lines, with minor textual variations, is the second half of a lyric to the same tune by Chu Tun-ju (1081–1159). See *Ch'üan Sung tz'u*, vol. 2, p. 856, lower register, ll. 9–10. The first couplet recurs in the *Chin P'ing Mei tz'u-hua*, vol. 1, ch. 3, p. 8b, l. 11. It also occurs in a variant form in the *Ming-hsin pao-chien*, *chüan* 1, p. 12a, l. 14.

56. As Patrick Hanan has pointed out in his "Sources of the *Chin P'ing Mei*," pp. 34–35, the above six paragraphs are derived from the early vernacular story entitled *Hsiao fu-jen chin-ch'ien tseng nien-shao* (The merchant's wife offers money to a young clerk). See *Ching-shih t'ung-yen* (Common words to warn the world), ed. Feng Meng-lung, first published 1624 (Peking: Tso-chia ch'u-pan she, 1957), *chüan* 16, p. 322, l. 13–p. 323, l. 3; and "The Honest Clerk," in *The Courtesan's Jewel Box*, trans. Yang Xianyi and Gladys Yang (Peking: Foreign Languages Press, 1981), p. 17.

57. The term "golden lotus" was a euphemism commonly employed to designate the feet of women who had been subjected to footbinding. For an informative study of this phenomenon, see Howard S. Levy, *Chinese Footbinding: The History of a Curious Erotic Custom* (New York: Walton Rawls, 1966).

58. The proximate source of this character is probably the figure of the same name who appears in the vernacular story *Hsiao fu-jen chin-ch'ien tseng nien-shao*, p. 223, l. 15, and passim.

59. The proximate source of these lines is the vernacular story *Wen-ching yüan-yang hui*, p. 157, l. 15.

60. The proximate source of these four lines is the vernacular story *Hsiao fu-jen chin-ch'ien tseng nien-shao*, p. 224, l. 16.

61. This simile already occurs in Yüan dynasty tsa-chü drama. See *Yüan-ch'ü hsüan*, 2:472, l. 9; 4:1421, ll. 11–12; and *Yüan-ch'ü hsüan wai-pien*, 1:101, l. 4.

62. The proximate source of this expression is the corresponding passage of the *Shui-hu ch'üan-chuan*, vol. 1, ch. 24, p. 356, l. 6. It also occurs in the Ming dynasty ch'uan-ch'i drama entitled *Yü-huan chi* (The story of the jade ring), which was drawn upon extensively by the author of the *Chin P'ing Mei*. See *Yü-huan chi, Liu-shih chung ch'ü* edition (Taipei: K'ai-ming shu-tien, 1970), scene 16, p. 57, l. 10.

63. The proximate source of this quatrain is the corresponding passage in the *Shui-hu ch'üan-chuan*, vol. 1, ch. 24, p. 356, l. 5.

64. The word that I have rendered as "guitar" is *hu-po-tz'u* in Chinese. It is a transliteration of a foreign term and occurs in Chinese texts in a wide variety of orthographies. The instrument was introduced into China from Central Asia as early as the T'ang dynasty (618–907) and is described in terms that make it sound something like a guitar or banjo. The word that I have rendered as "ukulele" is *ch'a-erh nan* in Chinese; its meaning is uncertain. It may either stand for the name of a tune or be another transliteration of the name of a foreign musical instrument. I have opted for the latter explanation without any particular conviction. The same term recurs in the abbreviated form *ch'a-erh* together with *hu-po-tz'u* in a similar context in chapter 34. In the same chapter the term *hu-po-tz'u* occurs yet again, followed by the term *p'i-p'a*, the name of a well-known musical instrument. This has led me to translate it as I have. See *Chin P'ing Mei tz'u-hua*, vol. 2, ch. 34, p. 6b, l. 11; and p. 13a, l. 11.

65. I have added the information that this new location was on another part of Amethyst Street because the text later describes them as continuing to live on that thoroughfare.

66. The proximate source of this couplet is the corresponding passage in the *Shui-hu ch'üan-chuan*, vol. 1, ch. 24, p. 357, ll. 7–8. It also occurs in the thirteenth-century hsi-wen drama entitled *Chang Hsieh chuang-yüan* (Top graduate Chang Hsieh), which is preserved in the *Yung-lo ta-tien* (Great literary repository of the Yung-lo reign [1403–24]), completed in 1407. See *Yung-lo ta-tien hsi-wen san-chung chiao-chu* (An annotated recension of the three hsi-wen preserved in the *Yung-lo ta-tien*) ed. and annot. Ch'ien Nan-yang (Peking: Chung-hua shu-chü, 1979), p. 67, l. 13.

67. The proximate source of this proverbial saying is the corresponding passage in the *Shui-hu ch'üan-chuan*, vol. 1, ch. 24, p. 358, ll. 2–3. It recurs in the *Chin P'ing Mei tz'u-hua*, vol. 1, ch. 8, p. 10a, ll. 10–11.

68. The proximate source of this couplet is the corresponding passage in the *Shui-hu ch'üan-chuan*, vol. 1, ch. 24, p. 358, l. 3. The first line occurs in the early hsi-wen drama *Chang Hsieh chuang-yüan*, p. 143, l. 12.

69. The proximate source of this quatrain is the corresponding passage in the *Shui-hu ch'üan-chuan*, vol. 1, ch. 24, p. 358, l. 4.

70. The proximate source of this expression is the corresponding passage in the *Shui-hu ch'üan-chuan*, vol. 1, ch. 24, p. 358, l. 11. It also occurs in the *San-kuo chih t'ung-su yen-i*, vol. 2, *chüan* 19, p. 922, l. 18.

71. This couplet recurs in the *Chin P'ing Mei tz'u-hua*, vol. 1, ch. 3, p. 12b, ll. 8–9.

72. The proximate source of this quatrain is the corresponding passage in the *Shui-hu ch'üan-chuan*, vol. 1, ch. 24, p. 359, l. 3.

73. This is a truncated version of an expression that in its full form reads "to discover a piece of gold or a precious stone in the middle of the night." The proximate source is the corresponding passage in the *Shui-hu ch'üan-chuan*, vol. 1, ch. 24, p. 359, l. 8. It also occurs in the early vernacular story entitled *K'an p'i-hsüeh tan-cheng Erh-lang Shen* (Investigation of a leather boot convicts Erh-lang Shen). See *Hsing-shih heng-yen* (Constant words to awaken the world), ed. Feng Meng-lung, first published in 1627, 2 vols. (Hong Kong: Chung-hua shu-chü, 1958), vol. 1, *chüan* 13, p. 254, l. 5; and Lorraine S. Y. Lieu and the editors, trans., "The Boot that Reveals the Culprit," in Ma and Lau, *Traditional Chinese Stories*, p. 516.

74. The proximate source of this expression is the corresponding passage in the *Shui-hu ch'üan-chuan*, vol. 1, ch. 24, p. 359, l. 14. It occurs in the ninth- or tenth-century manuscript from Tun-huang entitled *Yeh Ching-neng shih* (The wizard Yeh Ching-neng). See *Tun-huang pien-wen chi* (Collection of pien-wen from Tun-huang), ed. Wang Chung-min et al., 2 vols. (Peking: Jen-min wen-hsüeh ch'u-pan she, 1984), 1:227, l. 7; and *Ballads and Stories from Tun-huang*, trans. Arthur Waley (London: Allen and Unwin, 1960), p. 143, ll. 15–16. It also recurs in the *Chin P'ing Mei tz'u-hua*, vol. 1, ch. 2, p. 9a, l. 2.

75. The proximate source of this quatrain, with minor textual variants, is the corresponding passage in the *Shui-hu ch'üan-chuan*, vol. 1, ch. 24, p. 359, l. 17.

76. Wang Hui-chih (d. 388) was a famous eccentric, the son of Wang Hsi-chih (321–79), China's best-known calligrapher. According to an anecdote recorded in the *Shih-shuo hsin-yü*, he set out by boat one night during a heavy snowfall to visit his friend Tai K'uei (d. 396), but turned back upon reaching his destination without even going inside. When asked his reason for this behavior, Wang replied, "I originally went on the strength of an impulse, and when the impulse was spent I turned back. Why was it necessary to see Tai?" See Mather, *Shih-shuo Hsin-yü*, ch. 23, item 47, p. 389.

77. Lü Meng-cheng (946–1011) is a historical figure who rose to the position of grand councilor during the early years of the Sung dynasty. For his biography, see *Sung shih*, vol. 26, *chüan* 265, pp. 9145–50; and Franke, *Sung Biographies*, 2:726–28. According to legend he endured dire poverty in his youth and was reduced to living in a dilapidated kiln. This legend provides the theme of the anonymous early Ming ch'uan-ch'i drama *P'o-yao chi* (The dilapidated kiln), several scenes of which treat of the hardships he and his wife endured in their unheated quarters during the snowy season. The proximate source of the above lyric, with some textual variants, is the corresponding passage in the *Shui-hu ch'üan-chuan*, vol. 1, ch. 24, p. 360, ll. 13–14.

78. This expression occurs in a statement attributed to Ch'eng Hao (1032–85), the famous Neo-Confucian philosopher, in a necrology by his brother Ch'eng I (1033–1107) written shortly after his death in 1085. The statement forms part of Ch'eng Hao's assessment of the effect on people's lives of the loss of the true under-

standing of the way after the death of Mencius in 289 B.C. See *Erh-Ch'eng chi* (The collected works of the two Ch'eng brothers), by Ch'eng Hao and Ch'eng I, 4 vols. (Peking: Chung-hua shu-chü, 1981), 2:638, l. 9.

79. The proximate source of this expression is the corresponding passage in the *Shui-hu ch'üan-chuan*, vol. 1, ch. 24, p. 362, l. 4. It was used as early as the twelfth century by the Buddhist monk Fa-ch'üan (1114–69). See *Wu-teng hui-yüan* (The essentials of the five lamps), comp. P'u-chi (1179–1253), 3 vols. (Peking: Chung-hua shu-chü, 1984), vol. 3, *chüan* 20, p. 1358, ll. 12–13.

80. These two expressions are frequently used together to describe a real man. The proximate source is the *Shui-hu ch'üan-chuan*, vol. 1, ch. 24, p. 362, l. 4. They also occur together in Yüan dynasty tsa-chü drama. See *Yüan-ch'ü hsüan*, 4:1561, l. 3; 4:1646, l. 20; and *Yüan-ch'ü hsüan wai-pien*, 1:105, l. 2.

81. The proximate source of this expression is the corresponding passage in the *Shui-hu ch'üan-chuan*, vol. 1, ch. 24, p. 362, l. 5. For another occurrence as early as the twelfth century, see *Tung Chieh-yüan Hsi-hsiang chi*, *chüan* 8, p. 166, l. 3.

82. The proximate source of this expression is the corresponding passage in the *Shui-hu ch'üan-chuan*, vol. 1, ch. 24, p. 362, ll. 5–6. It occurs as early as the eighth century in the *Wu Tzu-hsü pien-wen* (The story of Wu Tzu-hsü), a prosimetric popular account of the career of Wu Tzu-hsü (d. 484 B.C.). See *Tun-huang pien-wen chi*, 1:17, l. 5; and *Tun-huang Popular Narratives*, trans. Victor H. Mair (Cambridge: Cambridge University Press, 1983), p. 145.

83. The proximate source of these two lines is the corresponding passage in the *Shui-hu ch'üan-chuan*, vol. 1, ch. 24, p. 362, l. 6. The same conceit in a slightly different form occurs in the Yüan-Ming hsi-wen drama *Su Wu mu-yang chi* (Su Wu herds sheep), which deals with the story of Su Wu (140–60 B.C.). See *Su Wu mu-yang chi*, item 20 in *Ku-pen hsi-ch'ü ts'ung-k'an, ch'u-chi, chüan* 2, scene 18, p. 11b, ll. 4–5. In this passage the text reads, "I, Su Wu, may recognize you, but my sword will not recognize you."

84. The proximate source of this quatrain is the corresponding passage in the *Shui-hu ch'üan-chuan*, vol. 1, ch. 24, p. 362, l. 9.

85. The proximate source of this idiomatic expression is the corresponding passage in the *Shui-hu ch'üan-chuan*, vol. 1, ch. 24, p. 363, ll. 8–9. It also occurs, in slightly variant form, in Yüan dynasty tsa-chü drama. See *Yüan-ch'ü hsüan*, 3:926, l. 13; and 4:1526, l. 7.

86. The proximate source of this expression is the corresponding passage in the *Shui-hu ch'üan-chuan*, vol. 1, ch. 24, p. 363, l. 9. It also recurs twice, in the same or slightly variant form, in the *Chin P'ing Mei tz'u-hua*, vol. 1, ch. 19, p. 10a, l. 11; and vol. 5, ch. 88, p. 3a, l. 4.

87. The proximate source of this quatrain is the corresponding passage in the *Shui-hu ch'üan-chuan*, vol. 1, ch. 24, p. 363, l. 13.

CHAPTER 2

1. In Chinese popular lore, the Old Man under the Moon is responsible for arranging marriages by tying the feet of the predestined partners together with red cords. The locus classicus for this belief is a T'ang dynasty literary tale by Li Fu-yen (9th century) entitled *Ting-hun tien* (The inn of predestined marriage). See *Hsü*

Hsüan-kuai lu (Continuation of Accounts of mysteries and anomalies), in *Hsüan-kuai lu; Hsü Hsüan-kuai lu* (Accounts of mysteries and anomalies; Continuation of Accounts of mysteries and anomalies), by Niu Seng-ju (779–848) and Li Fu-yen (9th century) (Peking: Chung-hua shu-chü, 1982), pp. 179–81; and "Predestined Marriage," in *Traditional Chinese Tales*, trans. Chi-chen Wang (New York: Columbia University Press, 1944), pp. 104–7.

2. This line, which refers to a character and events that are not introduced until chapter 4, seems anomalous here. Perhaps it is an indication that this poem is borrowed from some unidentified edition of the *Shui-hu chuan* in which the events of chapters 2 to 4 in the *Chin P'ing Mei* occur in one chapter, as they do in chapter 24 of the *Shui-hu ch'üan-chuan*.

3. The Eastern Capital refers to the Northern Sung capital, which was located in what is now the city of K'ai-feng in Honan Province.

4. Chu Mien (1075–1126) is a historical figure. For his biography, see *Sung shih*, vol. 39, *chüan* 470, pp. 13684–86; and Franke, *Sung Biographies*, 1:291–95.

5. The proximate source of this proverbial saying is the corresponding passage in the *Shui-hu ch'üan-chuan*, vol. 1, ch. 24, p. 365, l. 2. It recurs in the *Chin P'ing Mei tz'u-hua*, vol. 4, ch. 71, p. 4a, l. 7, where it is quoted from a tsa-chü drama entitled *Feng-yün hui* (The meeting of wind and cloud), by Lo Kuan-chung (14th century), one of the putative authors of the *Shui-hu chuan*. See *Yüan-ch'ü hsüan wai-pien*, 2:627, ll. 7–8.

6. The proximate source of this proverbial saying is the corresponding passage in the *Shui-hu ch'üan-chuan*, vol. 1, ch. 24, p. 365, l. 3.

7. The proximate source of these five lines is the corresponding passage in the *Shui-hu ch'üan-chuan*, vol. 1, ch. 24, p. 365, l. 5. The first four lines, with minor textual variants, occur together, though in a different order, in Yüan tsa-chü drama. See *Yüan-ch'ü hsüan*, 1:241, ll. 17–18. A variant of the first line occurs independently in ibid., 3:1165, l. 3. A variant of the third and fourth lines occurs independently in the anonymous Yüan-Ming ch'uan-ch'i drama *Pai-t'u chi* (The white rabbit), *Liu-shih chung ch'ü* edition (Taipei: K'ai-ming shu-tien, 1970), scene 7, p. 21, l. 11. A variant of the fifth line also occurs independently in Yüan tsa-chü drama. See *[Chiao-ting] Yüan-k'an tsa-chü san-shih chung* (A collated edition of Thirty tsa-chü dramas printed during the Yüan dynasty), ed. Cheng Ch'ien (Taipei: Shih-chieh shu-chü, 1962), p. 262, l. 11.

8. For an example of the word I have translated as "tick" used in that meaning in Yüan tsa-chü drama, see *Yüan-ch'ü hsüan*, 4:1662, l. 17.

9. The proximate source of this proverbial expression is the corresponding passage in the *Shui-hu ch'üan-chuan*, vol. 1, ch. 24, p. 365, l. 7. For a variant in Yüan tsa-chü drama, see *Yüan-ch'ü hsüan*, 3:947, ll. 10–11. For another variant, see the middle period vernacular story entitled *Jen hsiao-tzu lieh-hsing wei shen* (The apotheosis of Jen the filial son), in *Ku-chin hsiao-shuo*, vol. 2, *chüan* 38, p. 575, l. 7. Further variants recur in the *Chin P'ing Mei tz'u-hua*, vol. 2, ch. 23, p. 8b, l. 7; and vol. 2, ch. 25, p. 5a, ll. 8–9.

10. The proximate source of this expression is the corresponding passage in the *Shui-hu ch'üan-chuan*, vol. 1, ch. 24, p. 365, l. 8. It occurs in a poem by the eleventh-century Buddhist monk Tsung-tse. See *Wu-teng hui-yüan*, vol. 3, *chüan* 16, p. 1071, l. 13. It also occurs in Yüan tsa-chü drama. See *Yüan-ch'ü hsüan*, 3:1287, l. 14.

11. The proximate source of this saying is the corresponding passage in the *Shui-hu ch'üan-chuan*, vol. 1, ch. 24, p. 365, l. 9. A variant form of the same saying occurs as the second half of a couplet meaning "An elder brother is like a father; an elder brother's wife is like a mother" in the anonymous Yüan-Ming ch'uan-ch'i drama entitled *Sha-kou chi* (The stratagem of killing a dog), *Liu-shih chung ch'ü* edition (Taipei: K'ai-ming shu-tien, 1970), scene 6, p. 11, ll. 10–11.

12. The proximate source of this expression is the corresponding passage in the *Shui-hu ch'üan-chuan*, vol. 1, ch. 24, p. 365, l. 10. The same expression occurs in the Yüan-Ming ch'uan-ch'i drama entitled *Chin-yin chi* (The golden seal), by Su Fu-chih (14th century), in *Ku-pen hsi-ch'ü ts'ung-k'an, ch'u-chi*, item 27, *chüan* 2, scene 18, p. 23a, l. 10.

13. The proximate source of this quatrain is the corresponding passage in the *Shui-hu ch'üan-chuan*, vol. 1, ch. 24, p. 365, l. 12.

14. The proximate source of this expression is the corresponding passage in the *Shui-hu ch'üan-chuan*, vol. 1, ch. 24, p. 366, l. 3. The same expression occurs in the *Nü lun-yü* (The female analects), by Sung Jo-shen (d. c. 820), a classic work on female conduct by a consort of Emperor Te-tsung (r. 779–805) of the T'ang dynasty. See *Nü lun-yü*, in *Lü-ch'uang nü-shih* (Female scribes of the green gauze windows), 7 vols., fac. repr. of late Ming edition, in *Ming-Ch'ing shan-pen hsiao-shuo ts'ung-k'an, ch'u-pien*, vol. 1, ch. 7, p. 5a, l. 6.

15. The locus classicus for this simile is the *Chuang-tzu*. See *Chuang-tzu yin-te* (A concordance to Chuang-tzu) (Cambridge: Harvard University Press, 1956), ch. 22, p. 59, l. 39; and *The Complete Works of Chuang Tzu*, trans. Burton Watson (New York: Columbia University Press, 1968), ch. 22, p. 240, ll. 8–9.

16. The proximate source of this proverbial saying is the corresponding passage in the *Shui-hu ch'üan-chuan*, vol. 1, ch. 24, p. 366, l. 12.

17. Ch'en-ch'iao is the name of the town, some miles to the northeast of K'ai-feng, where Chao K'uang-yin (927–76) woke up one day in the year 960 to find that his subordinates had dressed him in imperial robes and subsequently declared himself the founding emperor of the Sung dynasty (r. 960–76).

18. Young Chang refers to the handsome hero of the *Ying-ying chuan* (The story of Ying-ying), by Yüan Chen (775–831), who became the prototype of a romantic young lover in later Chinese literature.

19. P'an Yüeh (247–300) was so famous for his handsome appearance that when he went out in his carriage the women of Lo-yang would throw fruit at him to express their appreciation. See Mather, *Shih-shuo Hsin-yü*, ch. 14, item 7, p. 310.

20. The proximate source of this passage of descriptive parallel prose, with some textual variants, is the *Shui-hu ch'üan-chuan*, vol. 2, ch. 44, p. 723, ll. 3–6. A similar passage occurs in the early vernacular story entitled *Sung Ssu-kung ta-nao Chin-hun Chang* (Sung the Fourth raises hell with Tightwad Chang). See *Ku-chin hsiao-shuo*, vol. 2, *chüan* 36, p. 529, ll. 9–11; and Timothy C. Wong, trans., "Sung the Fourth Raises Hell with Tightwad Chang," in Ma and Lau, *Traditional Chinese Stories*, pp. 538–39.

21. The proximate source of this expression is the corresponding passage in the *Shui-hu ch'üan-chuan*, vol. 1, ch. 24, p. 366, l. 14. Variants of the same expression recur in the *Chin P'ing Mei tz'u-hua*, vol. 1, ch. 12, p. 9b, l. 9; and vol. 3, ch. 54, p. 15a, ll. 1–2.

22. This is a quotation from the *Hsi-hsiang chi*. See *[Chi-p'ing chiao-chu] Hsi-hsiang chi*, play no. 1, scene 1, p. 9, ll. 1–2; and *The Moon and the Zither: The Story of the Western Wing*, by Wang Shifu; trans. Stephen H. West and Wilt L. Idema (Berkeley: University of California Press, 1991), p. 181, ll. 1–2.

23. The proximate source of this quatrain is the corresponding passage in the *Shui-hu ch'üan-chuan*, vol. 1, ch. 24, p. 367, l. 4.

24. King Yama is an Indian god of the dead, introduced into China through Buddhism, who presides over the Hell of Chinese popular religion.

25. The General of the Five Ways is one of the remorseless regents of the Chinese Hell. There is a vivid description of this deity in the eighth-century pien-wen manuscript entitled *Ta Mu-kan-lien ming-chien chiu-mu pien-wen* (Transformation text on Mahāmaudgalyāyana rescuing his mother from the underworld). See *Tun-huang pien-wen chi*, 2:723–24; and Mair, *Tun-huang Popular Narratives*, pp. 97–98.

26. The proximate source of this proverbial couplet is the corresponding passage in the *Shui-hu ch'üan-chuan*, vol. 1, ch. 24, p. 368, l. 2. The second line of the couplet occurs in Yüan tsa-chü drama. See *Yüan-ch'ü hsüan*, 4:1721, l. 1.

27. This line is from a lyric to the tune "Moon on the West River," attributed to Chang Hsiao-hsiang (1132–69) in the early vernacular story *Chang Yü-hu su nü-chen kuan chi*, p. 8b, ll. 2–3.

28. The proximate source of this conceit is the corresponding passage in the *Shui-hu ch'üan-chuan*, vol. 1, ch. 24, p. 369, l. 5. For a variant of the same conceit in Yüan tsa-chü drama, see *Yüan-ch'ü hsüan*, 1:199, ll. 16–17.

29. Lu Chia (c. 228–c. 140 B.C.) is a historical figure who is famous as a rhetorician. For his biography, see *Shih-chi*, vol. 8, *chüan* 97, pp. 2697–2701; and Watson, *Records of the Grand Historian of China*, 1:275–80.

30. Sui Ho (fl. late 3d–early 2d centuries B.C.) is a historical figure who was also famous as a rhetorician. For his biography, see *Shih-chi*, vol. 8, *chüan* 91, pp. 2600–2603; and Watson, *Records of the Grand Historian of China*, 1:198–202.

31. This is an allusion to Su Ch'in (fl. early 3d century B.C.), the archetypical itinerant politician, who is said to have traveled from court to court of the Six States that were left to contend with the state of Ch'in in the late Warring States period, persuading their rulers to undertake a bewildering variety of alliances and counteralliances. His exploits figure prominently in the *Chan-kuo ts'e* (Intrigues of the Warring States). For his biography, which is composed largely of legendary or fictional material, see *Shih-chi*, vol. 7, *chüan* 69, pp. 2241–77.

32. This is an allusion to Li I-chi (d. 203 B.C.), another famous rhetorician. For his biography, see *Shih-chi*, vol. 8, *chüan* 97, pp. 2691–96; and Watson, *Records of the Grand Historian of China*, 1:269–75.

33. The Jade Emperor presides over the pantheon of Chinese popular religion. See Henri Maspero, *Taoism and Chinese Religion*, trans. Frank A. Kierman, Jr. (Amherst: University of Massachusetts Press, 1981), pp. 88–91.

34. The Queen Mother of the West is a matriarchal deity of great antiquity who figures prominently in Chinese popular religion and folklore. See Maspero, *Taoism and Chinese Religion*, pp. 194–96.

35. Devarāja Li, a protective god of Indian origin, is one of the Four Heavenly Kings of Chinese popular religion, often depicted carrying a pagoda in his left hand. See ibid., pp. 126–27.

36. Hārītī is a fertility goddess of Indian origin who figures in Chinese popular religion as Kuei-tzu-mu or Mother of Demons. See ibid., p. 166; and Glen Dudbridge, *The Hsi-yu chi: A Study of Antecedents to the Sixteenth-Century Chinese Novel* (Cambridge: Cambridge University Press, 1970), pp. 16–18.

37. Feng Chih is the protagonist of a ninth-century literary tale entitled *Feng Chih*, by P'ei Hsing (825–80), in which he steadfastly refuses the seductive blandishments of a goddess. His name thus became proverbial for male resistance to sexual temptation. See *P'ei Hsing Ch'uan-ch'i* (P'ei Hsing's *Tales of the marvelous*), ed. and annot. Chou Leng-ch'ieh (Shanghai: Shang-hai ku-chi ch'u-pan she, 1980), pp. 65–69.

38. Ma-ku is a goddess renowned chiefly for her longevity, the earliest reference to whom is found in the *Shen-hsien chuan* (Biographies of divine immortals), by Ko Hung (283–343). For citations of the relevant sources, see *Chung-kuo min-chien chu-shen* (The gods of Chinese folklore), comp. Tsung Li and Liu Ch'ün (Shih-chia chuang: Ho-pei jen-min ch'u-pan she, 1987), pp. 719–24.

39. This line occurs in a song by Chang K'o-chiu (1270–1348). See *Ch'üan Yüan san-ch'ü* (Complete nondramatic song lyrics of the Yüan), comp. Sui Shu-sen, 2 vols. (Peking: Chung-hua shu-chü, 1964), 1:989, ll. 1–2.

40. The Weaving Maid is the star Vega who crosses the Milky Way to meet her lover the Herd Boy, the star Altair, once a year on the night of the seventh day of the seventh month. See Edward H. Schafer, *Pacing the Void: T'ang Approaches to the Stars* (Berkeley: University of California Press, 1977), pp. 143–48. The text of the *Chin P'ing Mei tz'u-hua* actually reads *shu-nü* (chaste maiden), but I have amended it to *chih-nü* (weaving maid) in line with the corresponding passage in the *Shui-hu ch'üan-chuan* and to keep the parallelism with Ch'ang-o in the following couplet.

41. This line occurs in the *Hsi-hsiang chi*. See *[Chi-p'ing chiao-chu] Hsi-hsiang chi*, play no. 3, scene 2, p. 112, ll. 4–5.

42. Ch'ang-o is the goddess of the moon in Chinese folklore. See Maspero, *Taoism and Chinese Religion*, pp. 96–97.

43. The proximate source of this passage of descriptive parallel prose, with some textual variants, is the corresponding passage in the *Shui-hu ch'üan-chuan*, vol. 1, ch. 24, p. 369, ll. 8–12. A similar passage with analogous imagery and some of the same wording occurs in the early vernacular story entitled *Chang Ku-lao chung-kua ch'ü Wen-nü* (Chang Ku-lao plants melons and weds Wen-nü). See *Ku-chin hsiao-shuo*, vol. 2, *chüan* 33, p. 492, ll. 2–4; and Cyril Birch, trans., "The Fairy's Rescue," in his *Stories from a Ming Collection* (London: Bodley Head, 1958), p. 184. For another similar passage, see *Hsiao fu-jen chin-ch'ien tseng nien-shao*, p. 223, ll. 4–5; and "The Honest Clerk" in Yang and Yang, *The Courtesan's Jewel Box*, p. 17.

44. This list of fanciful foodstuffs is difficult to interpret and impossible to translate, but it is obviously intended to be sexually suggestive. I have tried to convey this in my translation. The list ends with the word *ta-la-su*, a transliteration of the Mongol word for liquor. To suggest something of this exotic flavor, I have used the German word for whipped cream and punned "in cider" for "inside her."

45. The proximate source of this proverbial couplet is the corresponding passage in the *Shui-hu ch'üan-chuan*, vol. 1, ch. 24, p. 370, l. 10. It occurs ubiquitously in Chinese vernacular literature. The oldest occurrence I am familiar with is in the early hsi-wen drama *Chang Hsieh chuang-yüan*, p. 152, l. 9.

46. The Chinese text here splits the character for "thief" into its left and right components, which are then used as a slang term for the same word. I have tried to suggest this by punning "proper tea" for "property."

47. This is an allusion to the story told by Sung Yü (3d century B.C.) to King Hsiang of Ch'u (r. 298–265 B.C.) about a tryst between the Goddess of Witch's Mountain and his father King Huai (r. 328–299 B.C.) in the prose preface to the "Kao-t'ang fu" (Rhapsody on Kao-t'ang), traditionally attributed to Sung Yü himself but more probably dating from the first century B.C. In Chinese popular literature the roles played by King Huai and King Hsiang are often confused. For a study and translation of the "Kao-t'ang fu," see Lois Fusek, "The 'Kao-t'ang fu,' " in *Monumenta Serica*, vol. 30 (1972–73): 392–425. The proximate source of this quatrain is the corresponding passage in the *Shui-hu ch'üan-chuan*, vol. 1, ch. 24, p. 371, l. 9.

CHAPTER 3

1. This line occurs in the *Ming-hsin pao-chien, chüan* 2, p. 6b, l. 13; the *Yung-hsi yüeh-fu, ts'e* 18, p. 71b, ll. 1 and 4; the ch'uan-ch'i drama entitled *Hsiu-ju chi* (The embroidered jacket), by Hsü Lin (1462–1538), *Liu-shih chung ch'ü* edition (Taipei: K'ai-ming shu-tien, 1970), scene 10, p. 28, l. 2; and the ch'uan-ch'i drama entitled *Yü-chüeh chi* (The jade thumb-ring), by Cheng Jo-yung (16th century), *Liu-shih chung ch'ü* edition (Taipei: K'ai-ming shu-tien, 1970), scene 34, p. 107, ll. 3–4. A variant occurs in the *Shui-hu ch'üan-chuan*, vol. 1, ch. 21, p. 307, l. 16. It recurs twice in the *Chin P'ing Mei tz'u-hua*, vol. 5, ch. 81, p. 2b, l. 3; and vol. 5, ch. 94, p. 13a, l. 6.

2. This proverbial saying occurs in the same form in the *Yung-hsi yüeh-fu, ts'e* 5, p. 22b, l. 6; and it recurs in the *Chin P'ing Mei tz'u-hua*, vol. 2, ch. 25, p. 11a, l. 8. More common variant forms of the same saying occur in the section entitled "Ching-shih ko-yen" (Aphorisms to warn the world) in the thirteenth-century encyclopedia entitled *Shih-lin kuang-chi* (Expansive gleanings from the forest of affairs), fac. repr. of 14th-century ed. (Peking: Chung-hua shu-chü, 1963), *ts'e* 2, *ch'ien-chi, chüan* 9, p. 9b, l. 5; and the *Ming-hsin pao-chien, chüan* 2, p. 2a, l. 12.

3. A variant of this line occurs in Yüan tsa-chü drama. See *Yüan-ch'ü hsüan*, 3:1109, l. 2.

4. Teng T'ung (2d century B.C.) is a historical figure. He was the male favorite of Emperor Wen (r. 180–157 B.C.) of the Han dynasty, who gave him the right to mint copper coins so that his wealth became proverbial. For his biography, see *Shih-chi*, vol. 10, *chüan* 125, pp. 3192–93; and Watson, *Records of the Grand Historian of China*, 2:462–64.

5. This expression denotes something sharp or dangerous, the nature of which is disguised by a soft exterior. It occurs as early as the anonymous thirteenth-century prosimetric narrative entitled *Liu Chih-yüan chu-kung-tiao* (Medley in various modes on Liu Chih-yüan). See *Liu Chih-yüan chu-kung-tiao [chiao-chu]* (Medley in various modes on Liu Chih-yüan [collated and annotated]), ed. Lan Li-ming (Ch'eng-tu: Pa-Shu shu-she, 1989), part 2, p. 74, l. 3; and *Ballad of the Hidden Dragon (Liu Chih-yüan chu-kung-tiao)*, trans. M. Doleželová-Velingerová and J. I. Crump (Oxford: Oxford University Press, 1971), p. 74, l. 15.

6. The proximate source of this passage about the five prerequisites for seduction is the corresponding passage in the *Shui-hu ch'üan-chuan*, vol. 1, ch. 24, p. 371, ll. 2–4. They are alluded to again in ibid., vol. 2, ch. 45, p. 733, l. 17.

7. The word "turtle" is a slang term for the penis.

8. Chiang Tzu-ya (11th century B.C.), the chief adviser of the founder of the Chou dynasty (1045–256 B.C.), was enfeoffed as Prince of Wu-ch'eng in A.D. 760 and worshipped as the God of War during most of the period from that time until his worship was formally abolished in 1387.

9. Sun Wu (6th century B.C.) is a historical figure who is traditionally credited with the composition of the famous book on the art of war that bears his name. According to the *Shih-chi* he once undertook to drill the palace ladies of the King of Wu in order to demonstrate his mastery of the military arts. When the king's two favorites, who had been designated officers, failed to obey his commands he had them executed as an example of the need for strict military discipline. For his biography, see *Shih-chi*, vol. 7, *chüan* 65, pp. 2161–62; and Yang and Yang, *Records of the Historian*, pp. 28–29.

10. The proximate source of this expression is the corresponding passage in the *Shui-hu ch'üan-chuan*, vol. 1, ch. 24, p. 372, l. 13. A variant occurs in ibid., vol. 1, ch. 24, p. 377, l. 9; and in the *Chin P'ing Mei tz'u-hua*, vol. 1, ch. 3, p. 10a, ll. 8–9.

11. The Ling-yen Pavilion was erected in 643 by Emperor T'ai-tsung (r. 626–49) of the T'ang dynasty as a Hall of Fame for the most meritorious officials of the regime, whose portraits were displayed on its inside walls.

12. The Tung-t'ing Lake referred to here is another name for Lake T'ai-hu in Kiangsu Province, not the more famous Tung-t'ing Lake in Hunan Province. The islands in Lake T'ai-hu were famous for their production of citrus fruits.

13. The proximate source of this proverbial couplet is the corresponding passage in the *Shui-hu ch'üan-chuan*, vol. 1, ch. 24, p. 373, l. 9. A variant form of the same couplet occurs in the ch'uan-ch'i drama entitled *Nan Hsi-hsiang chi* (A southern version of the *Romance of the western chamber*), by Lu Ts'ai (1497–1537), in *Hsi-hsiang hui-pien* (Collected versions of the *Romance of the western chamber*), comp. Huo Sung-lin (Chi-nan: Shan-tung wen-i ch'u-pan she, 1987), *chüan* 1, scene 19, p. 372, l. 22. Another variant recurs in the *Chin P'ing Mei tz'u-hua*, vol. 1, ch. 4, p. 3b, l. 3.

14. See chapter 2, note 47.

15. The proximate source of this quatrain is the corresponding passage in the *Shui-hu ch'üan-chuan*, vol. 1, ch. 24, p. 373, l. 14.

16. In the Chinese lunar calendar an intercalary month was added every so many years to bring the lunar calendar into closer alignment with the solar calendar. It was probably a folk belief that it was lucky to have one's burial garments made up during an intercalary month because it stood outside the regular calendar, so to speak.

17. The proximate source of this proverbial saying is the corresponding passage in the *Shui-hu ch'üan-chuan*, vol. 1, ch. 24, p. 375, l. 5. It occurs in a speech attributed to the Buddhist monk Yüan-ching (12th century). See *Wu-teng hui-yüan*, vol. 3, *chüan* 19, p. 1295, l. 6. It also occurs in the *Ming-hsin pao-chien*, *chüan* 2, p. 7b, l. 14.

18. The proximate source of this quatrain is the corresponding passage in the *Shui-hu ch'üan-chuan*, vol. 1, ch. 24, p. 375, l. 7.

19. In 1391 Chu Yüan-chang (1328–98), the founding emperor (r. 1368–98) of the Ming dynasty, decreed that all the adult males in the empire should wear hair-

nets over their hair and under whatever they wore in the way of headgear. See *Ming shih* (History of the Ming dynasty), comp. Chang T'ing-yü (1672–1755) et al., 28 vols. (Peking: Chung-hua shu-chü, 1974), vol. 6, *chüan* 66, p. 1620, ll. 9–11. The netting was visible over the upper forehead and was held in place in the rear by tightening a cord between two rings. For an illustration, see Chou Hsi-pao, *Chung-kuo ku-tai fu-shih shih* (History of traditional Chinese costume) (Peking: Chung-kuo hsi-chü ch'u-pan she, 1984), p. 411.

20. See chapter 1, note 55.

21. The proximate source of this line is the corresponding passage in the *Shui-hu ch'üan-chuan*, vol. 1, ch. 24, p. 376, l. 15. The same line recurs in ibid., vol. 3, ch. 75, p. 1254, l. 15. For a variant in Yüan tsa-chü drama, see *Yüan-ch'ü hsüan*, 1:340, l. 2.

22. The proximate source of these six lines is the corresponding passage in the *Shui-hu ch'üan-chuan*, vol. 1, ch. 24, p. 377, l. 1. A variant of the first two lines occurs in the *San Sui p'ing-yao chuan*, *chüan* 1, ch. 1, p. 1b, l. 5; and recurs in the *Chin P'ing Mei tz'u-hua*, vol. 1, ch. 7, p. 3b, l. 7. A variant of all six lines recurs in ibid., vol. 4, ch. 69, p. 3b, ll. 6–7.

23. The proximate source of these two lines is the corresponding passage in the *Shui-hu ch'üan-chuan*, vol. 1, ch. 24, p. 377, ll. 1–2. They occur in the earliest extant printed edition (1470s) of the Yüan-Ming ch'uan-ch'i drama *Pai-t'u chi*. See *[Hsin-pien] Liu Chih-yüan huan-hsiang Pai-t'u chi* ([Newly compiled] Liu Chih-yüan's return home: The white rabbit), in *Ming Ch'eng-hua shuo-ch'ang tz'u-hua ts'ung-k'an*, *ts'e* 12, p. 13b, l. 1. They also occur in the early vernacular story entitled *Cheng Chieh-shih li-kung shen-pi kung* (Commissioner Cheng wins merit with his magic bow), in *Hsing-shih heng-yen*, vol. 2, *chüan* 31, p. 656, ll. 4–5.

24. There is a Ming figure of this name who passed the *chin-shih* examination in 1580 and served as prefect of Hu-chou in 1595. He is mentioned in *Wan-li yeh-huo pien, pu-i* (supplement), *chüan* 2, p. 842, ll. 1–2. See Ku Kuo-jui, "*Chin P'ing Mei* chung te san-ko Ming-tai jen" (Three Ming dynasty figures in the *Chin P'ing Mei*), in *Chin P'ing Mei yen-chiu chi* (Collected studies of the *Chin P'ing Mei*), ed. Tu Wei-mo and Liu Hui (Chi-nan: Ch'i-Lu shu-she, 1988), p. 258.

25. The proximate source of this quatrain is the corresponding passage in the *Shui-hu ch'üan-chuan*, vol. 1, ch. 24, p. 377, l. 4.

26. The proximate source of this proverbial couplet is the corresponding passage in the *Shui-hu ch'üan-chuan*, vol. 1, ch. 24, p. 377, l. 7. It also occurs in ibid., vol. 1, ch. 21, p. 306, l. 16. It recurs twice in the *Chin P'ing Mei tz'u-hua*, vol. 1, ch. 14, p. 13a, l. 5; and vol. 5, ch. 82, p. 3a, l. 7.

27. The proximate source of this proverbial saying is the corresponding passage in the *Shui-hu ch'üan-chuan*, vol. 1, ch. 24, p. 377, l. 8. A variant form of the same saying occurs as early as 1098 in a colophon written by Huang T'ing-chien (1045–1105). See *T'ung-su pien* (Compendium of common expressions), comp. Chai Hao (cs 1754) (Taipei: Ta-hua shu-chü, 1977), p. 895, ll. 5–7.

28. This is a quotation, with an insignificant textual variant, from the "Nei-tse" (The pattern of the family) chapter of the *Book of Rites*, which Legge translates, "at the age of seven, boys and girls did not occupy the same mat." See *Li-chi*, ch. 10, p. 58, l. 17; and Legge, *Li Chi*, 1:478. The same quotation also occurs in the *Ming-hsin pao-chien*, *chüan* 1, p. 14b, l. 13.

29. Cho Wen-chün, an attractive young widow, ran away with Ssu-ma Hsiang-ju (179–117 B.C.), who was to become the best-known poet of his day, after hearing him play the *ch'in*, a kind of zither, in her father's home. This is the most famous elopement in Chinese literature. See *Shih-chi*, vol. 9, *chüan* 117, pp. 3000–3001; and Watson, *Records of the Grand Historian of China*, 2:298–300.

30. The proximate source of this quatrain is the corresponding passage in the *Shui-hu ch'üan-chuan*, vol. 1, ch. 24, p. 378, l. 3.

31. I have emended the date from *keng-ch'en* (1100) to *wu-ch'en* (1088) to make it fit the time scheme of the novel, since the seduction of Chin-lien takes place in 1113. Later in the text the year of Wu Yüeh-niang's birth is given correctly as *wu-ch'en* (1088). See *Chin P'ing Mei tz'u-hua*, vol. 2, ch. 39, p. 6a., l. 7; and vol. 3, ch. 46, p. 16a, l. 9.

32. The proximate source of this proverbial couplet is the corresponding passage in the *Shui-hu ch'üan-chuan*, vol. 1, ch. 24, p. 378. l. 10.

33. The proximate source of this expression is the corresponding passage in the *Shui-hu ch'üan-chuan*, vol. 1, ch. 24, p. 378, l. 12. It already occurs in a speech attributed to the Buddhist monk Tao-k'uang (10th century). See *Wu-teng hui-yüan*, vol. 2, *chüan* 8, p. 458, l. 2.

CHAPTER 4

1. King Chou (r. 1086–1045 B.C.) was the "evil last ruler" of the Shang dynasty whose fall was traditionally blamed on his infatuation with his voluptuous and amoral favorite Ta-chi (d. 1045 B.C.).

2. Hsi-shih was a famous beauty who was presented by Kou-chien, the ruler of the state of Yüeh (r. 497–465 B.C.), to Fu-ch'a, the ruler of the state of Wu (r. 495–473 B.C.), in the hope that her beauty would distract him from affairs of state. The plan resulted in the demise of the state of Wu and the suicide of King Fu-ch'a in 473 B.C. The role she plays in Chinese literature is roughly comparable to that of Helen of Troy in the Western tradition.

3. The proximate source of the first six lines of this poem, with some textual variants, is the *Shui-hu ch'üan-chuan*, vol. 1, ch. 24, p. 355, ll. 3–4.

4. The proximate source of this couplet is the corresponding passage in the *Shui-hu ch'üan-chuan*, vol. 1, ch. 24, p. 379, l. 12. It also occurs in the early vernacular story entitled *Pai Niang-tzu yung-chen Lei-feng T'a* (The White Maiden is eternally imprisoned under Thunder Peak Pagoda). See *Ching-shih t'ung-yen*, *chüan* 28, p. 425, l. 3; and Diana Yu, trans., "Eternal Prisoner under the Thunder Peak Pagoda," in Ma and Lau, *Traditional Chinese Stories*, p. 360.

5. The proximate source of this set piece of descriptive parallel prose is the corresponding passage in the *Shui-hu ch'üan-chuan*, vol. 1, ch. 24, pp. 379–80. Very similar passages occur in the early vernacular stories entitled *Chang Yü-hu su nü-chen kuan chi*, p. 17a, l. 8–p. 17b, l. 2; and *Wu-chieh Ch'an-shih ssu Hung-lien chi* (The Ch'an Master Wu-chieh defiles Hung-lien), in *Ch'ing-p'ing shan-t'ang hua-pen*, p. 140, ll. 14–16. Lines 7–14 of this passage, with some textual variation, also recur in the *Shui-hu ch'üan-chuan*, vol. 4, ch. 104, p. 1598, ll. 5–7.

6. The Chinese for this expression consists of four characters that mean "color," "silk," "son," and "woman," respectively, which makes no sense. If the first pair of

graphs are combined into a single character they form the word "utterly," and if the second pair are combined they form the word "wonderful." Thus the four-character expression is slang for "utterly wonderful." Since two words are hidden under what appears at first glance to be four words, I have tried to render something of the cleverness of the original by punning on "too wonderful for words." This example of wordplay is ultimately derived from an anecdote of the third century A.D. recorded in the *Shih-shuo hsin-yü*. See Mather, *Shih-shuo Hsin-yü*, chap. 11, item 3, p. 293. An expanded version of this anecdote is also included in the *San-kuo chih t'ung-su yen-i*, vol. 2, *chüan* 15, pp. 681–82.

7. The proximate source of this formulaic couplet is the corresponding passage in the *Shui-hu ch'üan-chuan*, vol. 1, ch. 24, p. 380, l. 13, where it appears in a slightly variant form. It also recurs in ibid., vol. 3, ch. 80, p. 1329, l. 5; and in the *Chin P'ing Mei tz'u-hua*, vol. 1, ch. 12, p. 14a, ll. 3–4. This couplet is ubiquitous in Chinese vernacular literature. For an early occurrence, see *Chang Hsieh chuang-yüan*, p. 106, l. 4.

8. The proximate source for this expression is the corresponding passage of the *Shui-hu ch'üan-chuan*, vol. 1, ch. 24, p. 380, l. 13. It also occurs in ibid., vol. 1, ch. 21, p. 317, l. 4.

9. "Snowflake" silver was a name used to designate a superior grade of silver, presumably because it was as pure as snow. See Lien-sheng Yang, *Money and Credit in China: A Short History* (Cambridge: Harvard University Press, 1952), p. 46. The image of black eyes lighting up at the sight of white silver occurs in Yüan tsa-chü drama. See *Yüan-ch'ü hsüan*, 3:1115, l. 8; and 4:1418, l. 11. It recurs in the *Chin P'ing Mei tz'u-hua*, vol. 1, ch. 7, p. 4b, l. 5; and vol. 4, ch. 79. p. 26b, l. 1.

10. The last two phrases of this sentence are lifted verbatim from the *Hsi-hsiang chi*. See *[Chi-p'ing chiao-chu] Hsi-hsiang chi*, play no. 3, scene 2, p. 109, l. 5; and West and Idema, *The Moon and the Zither*, p. 292, l. 11.

11. This punning couplet, with some textual variants, is from a lyric by Wen T'ing-yün (c. 812–c. 870). See *Ch'üan T'ang shih*, vol. 9, *chüan* 583, p. 6764, l. 15. It recurs, with variants, in the *Chin P'ing Mei tz'u-hua*, vol. 1. ch. 14, p. 14b, ll. 9–10. The couplet depends for its force on a pun between the word *jen*, meaning "fruit kernel," and the word *jen*, meaning "person," and probably refers to an intricately carved toggle in the shape of a peach stone that can be opened to reveal a miniature couple engaged in copulation. For a photograph of such an object, see Lawrence E. Gichner, *Erotic Aspects of Chinese Culture* (N.p.: Privately published, 1957), p. 32. The same conceit occurs in a lyric by Huang T'ing-chien (1045–1105). See *Ch'üan Sung tz'u*, 1:409, lower register, ll. 15–16.

12. Yen Hui (521–490 B.C.) was the favorite disciple of Confucius (551–479 B.C.). According to a famous passage in Book 6 of the *Lun-yü*, as translated by Arthur Waley, "The Master said, Incomparable indeed was Hui! A handful of rice to eat, a gourdful of water to drink, living in a mean street—others would have found it unendurably depressing, but to Hui's cheerfulness it made no difference at all. Incomparable indeed was Hui!" See Waley, *The Analects of Confucius*, pp. 117–18.

13. Hsü Yu is the name of a legendary recluse, frequently mentioned in the *Chuang-tzu*, to whom Yao is said to have offered to cede the throne without success. According to a story in the *Ch'in-ts'ao* (Zither motifs), usually attributed to Ts'ai Yung (133–92), as quoted in the encyclopedia *T'ai-p'ing yü-lan* (Imperial digest of

the T'ai-p'ing reign period [976–84]), "Hsü Yu lacked any cup or utensil and was accustomed to scooping up water with his hands. Someone presented him with a gourd dipper and when he had finished drinking from it he hung it on a tree. When the wind blew on the tree the gourd moved, making an audible sound. Hsü Yu found this so distracting that he took the gourd and threw it away." See *T'ai-p'ing yü-lan*, comp. Li Fang (925–96) et al., completed in 983, fac. repr. of a Sung edition, 4 vols. (Peking: Chung-hua shu-chü, 1963), vol. 4, *chüan* 762, p. 1b, ll. 11–13.

14. It was customary for mountebanks to peddle their panaceas in gourds, the opaque nature of which prevented the customers from seeing what they were getting. There is a passage of humorous double entendre in one of the versions of the *Nan Hsi-hsiang chi* that throws some light on the last line. See *Nan Hsi-hsiang chi* (A southern version of the *Romance of the western chamber*), usually attributed to Li Jih-hua (fl. early 16th century), *Liu-shih chung ch'ü* edition (Taipei: K'ai-ming shu-tien, 1970), scene 4, p. 8, ll. 1–3.

15. This is a composite work produced by combining parts of two anonymous songs to this tune included in the *Yung-hsi yüeh-fu*. For lines 1–2 and 5–7, see ibid., *ts'e* 17, p. 29b, ll. 6–8; and for lines 3–4, see ibid., *ts'e* 17, p. 29a, ll. 6–7.

16. There are recipes for these breath-sweetening lozenges, the Chinese name for which means "fragrant tea," in *Yin-shan cheng-yao* (Correct essentials of nutrition), by the Mongol physician Hu-ssu-hui (fl. early 14th century), completed in 1330 (Peking: Jen-min wei-sheng ch'u-pan she, 1986), *chüan* 2, p. 59, ll. 3–5; and *Tsun-sheng pa-chien* (Eight disquisitions on nurturing life), by Kao Lien (16th century), author's preface dated 1591 (Ch'eng-tu: Pa-Shu shu-she, 1988), p. 754, ll. 10–13.

17. The proximate source of this proverbial couplet is the corresponding passage in the *Shui-hu ch'üan-chuan*, vol. 1, ch. 24, p. 380, ll. 14–15. It occurs, with an insignificant variant, in a speech attributed to the Buddhist monk Shao-tsung (fl. early 10th century). See *Wu-teng hui-yüan*, vol. 2, *chüan* 9, p. 547, l. 1. It recurs in the *Chin P'ing Mei tz'u-hua*, vol. 5, ch. 85, p. 3a, ll. 5–6.

18. The proximate source of this quatrain is the corresponding passage in the *Shui-hu ch'üan-chuan*, vol. 1, ch. 24, p. 380, l. 16.

19. The proximate source of these two lines, with some textual variation, is the corresponding passage in the *Shui-hu ch'üan-chuan*, vol. 1, ch. 24, p. 381, l. 12. They recur, with insignificant variants, in the *Chin P'ing Mei tz'u-hua*, vol. 5, ch. 90, p. 8a. l. 1.

20. The proximate source of this expression is the corresponding passage in the *Shui-hu ch'üan-chuan*, vol. 1, ch. 24, p. 381, l. 13. A similar saying is attributed to the Buddhist monk Hui-yüan (1103–76). See *Wu-teng hui-yüan*, vol. 3, *chüan* 19, p. 1287, l. 13.

21. The proximate source of this couplet is the corresponding pasage in the *Shui-hu ch'üan-chuan*, vol. 1, ch. 24, p. 382, ll. 3–4. It occurs ubiquitously in Chinese vernacular literature. For an early occurrence, see *Chang Hsieh chuang-yüan*, p. 44, l. 4.

22. The Spirit of the Perilous Paths is a formidable deity, more than ten feet in height, whose effigy, dressed in full battle regalia, is carried at the head of Chinese funeral processions to clear the way for and protect the coffin of the deceased. See *San-chiao yüan-liu sou-shen ta-ch'üan* (Complete compendium on the pantheons of

the three religions), pref. dated 1593, fac. repr. (Taipei: Lien-ching ch'u-pan shih-yeh kung-ssu, 1980), p. 346; and J. J. M. De Groot, *The Religious System of China*, 6 vols. (Taipei: Ch'eng Wen Publishing Company, 1972), 1:161–62.

23. The proximate source of this couplet, with some textual variation, is the corresponding passage of the *Shui-hu ch'üan-chuan*, vol. 1, ch. 24, p. 382, l. 4. A variant of the first line occurs in the anonymous Yüan-Ming ch'uan-ch'i drama entitled *Chao-shih ku-erh chi* (The story of the orphan of Chao). See *Ku-pen hsi-ch'ü ts'ung-k'an, ch'u-chi*, item 16, *chüan* 2, scene 28, p. 8b, l. 5. Variants also occur in the middle-period vernacular stories entitled *Ts'o-jen shih* (The wrongly identified corpse), in *Ch'ing-p'ing shan-t'ang hua-pen*, p. 227, l. 3; and *Jen Hsiao-tzu lieh-hsing wei shen*, p. 584, l. 7.

CHAPTER 5

1. This line occurs in a poem by Ch'ü Yu (1341–1427) included in his *Chien-teng hsin-hua*, the author's preface to which is dated 1378. See ibid., p. 114, l. 9. The same poem is quoted without attribution at the beginning of the middle-period vernacular story entitled *Chieh-chih-erh chi* (The story of the ring). See *Ch'ing-p'ing shan-t'ang hua-pen*, pp. 244–45. Variants of this line occur in the *Yüan-ch'ü hsüan*, 3:974, ll. 15–16; and 3:1276, ll. 19–20; the fourteenth-century ch'uan-ch'i drama entitled *P'i-p'a chi* (The lute), by Kao Ming (d. 1359), ed. Ch'ien Nan-yang (Peking: Chung-hua shu-chü, 1961), scene 21, p. 124, l. 10; see *The Lute: Kao Ming's P'i-p'a chi*, trans. Jean Mulligan (New York: Columbia University Press, 1980), p. 166, l. 12; the middle-period vernacular story entitled *Yüeh-ming Ho-shang tu Liu Ts'ui* (The monk Yüeh-ming converts Liu Ts'ui), in *Ku-chin hsiao-shuo*, vol. 2, *chüan* 29, p. 433, l. 6; the fifteenth-century literary tale *Chung-ch'ing li-chi, chüan* 6, p. 33a, l. 6; and the sixteenth-century collection of court case fiction entitled *Pai-chia kung-an* (A hundred court cases), 1594 ed., fac. repr. in *Ku-pen hsiao-shuo ts'ung-k'an, ti-erh chi* (Collectanea of rare editions of traditional fiction, second series) (Peking: Chung-hua shu-chü, 1990), vol. 4, *chüan* 6, ch. 56, p. 21a, l. 7. Variants of this line recur in the *Chin P'ing Mei tz'u-hua*, vol. 2, ch. 21, p. 1a, l. 4; and vol. 4, ch. 73, p. 14b, l. 3.

2. This couplet also occurs in the middle-period vernacular story entitled *Hsin-ch'iao Shih Han Wu mai ch'un-ch'ing*, p. 77, l. 12.

3. The proximate source of this poem is the *Shui-hu ch'üan-chuan*, vol. 1, ch. 26, p. 405, ll. 3–4. It also occurs, with some textual variants, as the opening poem of the middle-period vernacular story entitled *Jen Hsiao-tzu lieh-hsing wei shen*, p. 571, ll. 2–3.

4. From as early as the twelfth century the word "duck" was slang for "cuckold" in some parts of China. See *Chi-le pien* (Chicken ribs collection), by Chuang Ch'o (c. 1090–c. 1150), pref. dated 1133 (Peking: Chung-hua shu-chü, 1983), *chüan* 2, p. 73, ll. 3–5.

5. This formulaic rhetorical question already occurs in Yüan tsa-chü drama. See, e.g., *Yüan-ch'ü hsüan*, 2:548, l. 6.

6. This formulaic expression already occurs in Yüan tsa-chü drama. See, e.g., *Yüan-ch'ü hsüan*, 2:771, ll. 9 and 15.

7. It was a folk belief that the revenants of persons devoured by tigers remained subject to them and were constrained to assist them in capturing other victims. This

belief is attested as early as the ninth century. See the literary tale by P'ei Hsing (825–80) entitled *Ma Cheng*, in *P'ei Hsing Ch'uan-ch'i*, p. 63, ll. 4–5.

8. The proximate source of the first three lines of this quatrain is the corresponding passage in the *Shui-hu ch'üan-chuan*, vol. 1, ch. 25, p. 395, l. 11. The first line recurs in the *Chin P'ing Mei tz'u-hua*, vol. 1, ch. 12, p. 8a, l. 11.

9. The proximate source of this couplet is the corresponding passage in the *Shui-hu ch'üan-chuan*, vol. 1, ch. 25, p. 396, l. 11. It recurs in the *Chin P'ing Mei tz'u-hua*, vol. 5, ch. 82, p. 10a, l. 2.

10. The proximate source of this couplet is the corresponding passage in the *Shui-hu ch'üan-chuan*, vol. 1, ch. 25, p. 396, l. 13. It also occurs in ibid., vol. 1, ch. 9, p. 143, l. 5; and p. 144, l. 13.

11. The proximate source of this idiom, in a variant form, is the corresponding passage in the *Shui-hu ch'üan-chuan*, vol. 1, ch. 25, p. 396, l. 16. It recurs in a number of variations in the *Chin P'ing Mei tz'u-hua*, vol. 1, ch. 12, p. 8b, ll. 2–3; vol. 1, ch. 18, p. 4a, l. 5; vol. 2, ch. 25, p. 8a, l. 4; and vol. 3, ch. 53, p. 21a, l. 2.

12. The proximate source of the first two of these three lines is the corresponding passage in the *Shui-hu ch'üan-chuan*, vol. 1, ch. 25, p. 396, l. 17. The second and third lines recur together in the *Chin P'ing Mei tz'u-hua*, vol. 5, ch. 82, p. 4a, l. 11.

13. The proximate source of this expression is the corresponding passage in the *Shui-hu ch'üan-chuan*, vol. 1, ch. 25, p. 397, l. 6. It also occurs in *Yüan-ch'ü hsüan*, 4:1401, l. 16.

14. The proximate source of this expression is the corresponding passage in the *Shui-hu ch'üan-chuan*, vol. 1, ch. 25, p. 397, l. 7. According to the *T'ung-su pien*, *chüan* 1, p. 1, ll. 10–11, the ultimate source is a variant of a line in the *Yin-fu ching* (Classic of the harmony of the seen and the unseen), a Taoist work of uncertain date commonly attributed to the mythical Yellow Emperor. See *The Texts of Taoism*, trans. James Legge, 2 vols. (New York: Dover Publications, 1962), 2:260, ll. 14–15.

15. The word that I have translated as "knockabout" literally means "pounder." It was a slang term for "rascal" or "vagabond." I have rendered it as I have to retain something of its literal force.

16. The proximate source of this proverbial couplet is the corresponding passage in the *Shui-hu ch'üan-chuan*, vol. 1, ch. 25, p. 397, l. 11. It recurs, with some variation, in the *Chin P'ing Mei tz'u-hua*, vol. 1, ch. 8, p. 10a, l. 6; and vol. 1 ch. 16, p. 8b, ll. 3–4.

17. The proximate source of this proverbial couplet is the corresponding passage in the *Shui-hu ch'üan-chuan*, vol. 1, ch. 25, p. 397, l. 13. It is ubiquitous in Chinese vernacular literature. Variants occur as early as the Yüan-Ming *ch'uan-ch'i* drama entitled *Yu-kuei chi* (Tale of the secluded chambers), *Liu-shih chung ch'ü* edition (Taipei: K'ai-ming shu-tien, 1970), scene 12, p. 37, l. 4.

18. The proximate source of this formulaic couplet is the corresponding passage in the *Shui-hu ch'üan-chuan*, vol. 1, ch. 25, p. 397, l. 13. This couplet is ubiquitous in Chinese vernacular literature. A variant occurs as early as the T'ang dynasty in a speech attributed to Chang Kuang-sheng just prior to his death in 784. See *Feng-t'ien lu* (Record of [the imperial sojourn in] Feng-t'ien), by Chao Yüan-i (8th century), in *Ts'ung-shu chi-ch'eng*, vol. 3834, *chüan* 4, p. 33, ll. 13–14. It occurs in the same form as in the novel in the speech of a tenth-century Buddhist monk. See *Wu-teng hui-yüan*, vol. 3, *chüan* 16, p. 1093, l. 6. It recurs in the *Chin P'ing Mei tz'u-hua*, vol. 2, ch. 25, p. 7a, l. 3; and vol. 5, ch. 86, p. 7b, l. 1.

19. The proximate source of these two proverbial couplets, with insignificant textual variants, is the corresponding passage in the *Shui-hu ch'üan-chuan*, vol. 1. ch. 25, p. 397, l. 14. They appear ubiquitously in Chinese vernacular literature. The first line occurs as early as the sixth century in a work by Wei Shou (505–72). See *Ch'üan Shang-ku San-tai Ch'in Han San-kuo Liu-ch'ao wen* (Complete prose from High Antiquity, the Three Dynasties, Ch'in, Han, the Three Kingdoms, and the Six Dynasties), comp. Yen K'o-chün (1762–1843), 5 vols. (Peking: Chung-hua shu-chü, 1965), vol. 4, *Ch'üan Pei-Ch'i wen*, (Complete prose of the Northern Ch'i dynasty), *chüan* 4, p. 10a, l. 9. All four lines occur together, with insignificant textual variants, in the *[Hsin-pien] Wu-tai shih p'ing-hua* ([Newly compiled] p'ing-hua on the history of the Five Dynasties), originally published in the fourteenth century (Shanghai: Chung-kuo ku-tien wen-hsüeh ch'u-pan she, 1954), p. 8, ll. 6–7. See also *Hua Kuan So jen-fu chuan* (The story of how Hua Kuan So claimed his patrimony), fac. repr. in *Ming Ch'eng-hua shuo-ch'ang tz'u-hua ts'ung-k'an, ts'e* 1, p. 2a, ll. 8–9; and King, *The Story of Hua Guan Suo*, p. 87, ll. 15–18.

20. The proximate source of this quatrain is the corresponding passage in the *Shui-hu ch'üan-chuan*, vol. 1, ch. 25, p. 397, l. 16. The first two lines are identical, the third is modified, and the fourth is completely different.

21. The proximate source of this idiom is the corresponding passage in the *Shui-hu ch'üan-chuan*, vol. 1, ch. 25, p. 398, l. 8. It occurs in a more common variant form in the *Yüan-ch'ü hsüan*, 1:401, l. 4; and 2:504, l. 10.

22. The proximate source of this idiom is the corresponding passage in the *Shui-hu ch'üan-chuan*, vol. 1, ch. 25, p. 398, ll. 10–11. It occurs in a poem in the *Chin-kang k'o-i* (Liturgical exposition of the *Diamond sutra*), a thirteenth-century Buddhist work. See *[Hsiao-shih] Chin-kang k'o-i [hui-yao chu-chieh]* ([Clearly presented] liturgical exposition of the *Diamond sutra* [with critical commentary]), ed. and annot. Chüeh-lien (16th century), pref. dated 1551, in *[Shinzan] Dai Nihon zokuzōkyō* ([Newly compiled] great Japanese continuation of the Buddhist canon), 100 vols. (Tokyo: Kokusho kankōkai, 1977), 24:725, lower register, l. 4. It also occurs in the early (13th or 14th century) hsi-wen drama entitled *Huan-men tzu-ti ts'o li-shen* (The scion of an official's family opts for the wrong career). See *Yung-lo ta-tien hsi-wen san-chung chiao-chu*, p. 243, l. 11; and *Eight Chinese Plays*, trans. William Dolby (London: Paul Elek, 1978), p. 47, l. 9.

23. This detail, along with several others, the most significant of which is the administration of medicine (poison/aphrodisiac) to an incapacitated victim, foreshadows the death of Hsi-men Ch'ing in chapter 79. There are a number of verbal correspondences.

24. For a succinct discussion of the "three ethereal souls" and the "seven material souls," see Maspero, *Taoism and Chinese Religion*, pp. 266–67. For a description of the City of the Unjustly Dead and the Terrace of Homeward Gazing Spirits, along with the other salient features of the Chinese Hell, see ibid., pp. 176–87.

25. The proximate source of this set piece of descriptive parallel prose, with some textual variants, is the corresponding passage in the *Shui-hu ch'üan-chuan*, vol. 1, ch. 25, p. 399, ll. 7–9. A shorter passage, also describing a poisoning, of which the first two lines are identical and the last two lines similar, occurs in the *Ta-T'ang Ch'in-wang tz'u-hua* (Prosimetric story of the Prince of Ch'in of the Great T'ang), 2 vols., fac. repr. of early 17th-century ed. (Peking: Wen-hsüeh ku-chi k'an-hsing she, 1956), vol. 2, *chüan* 8, ch. 61, p. 43b, ll. 4–5. A couplet expressing the same idea as

the last two lines also occurs in the middle-period vernacular story *Ts'o-jen shih*, p. 221, l. 6.

26. The proximate source of this expression is the corresponding passage in the *Shui-hu ch'üan-chuan*, vol. 1, ch. 25, p. 399, l. 11. See also, *Yüan-ch'ü hsüan*, 2:674, l. 18; *San-kuo chih t'ung-su yen-i, chüan* 10, p. 456, l. 10; and *Hsi-yu chi*, vol. 1, ch. 27, p. 309, ll. 8–9.

27. The proximate source of this disquisition on the varieties of weeping is the corresponding passage in the *Shui-hu ch'üan-chuan*, vol. 1, ch. 25, pp. 399–400. See also, *Hsi-yu chi*, vol. 1, ch. 39, pp. 445–46; and Yu, *The Journey to the West*, 2:214.

28. This is an example of a popular type of Chinese wordplay called *hsieh-hou yü*, literally "left-off end expression," which may be defined as a two-part humorous or allegorical saying, of which the first part, always stated, is descriptive, while the second part, sometimes unstated but always implied, and frequently involving a pun, carries the message. The *Chin P'ing Mei* is a major repository of early examples of this type of wit, and a book-length monograph has been written on the subject in Japanese. See Torii Hisayasu, *Kinpeibai sharekotoba no kenkyū* (A study of proverbial witticisms in the *Chin P'ing Mei*) (Tokyo: Kōseikan, 1972). For a recent study of this variety of Chinese wit in English, see John S. Rohsenow, A *Chinese-English Dictionary of Enigmatic Folk Similes (Xiehouyu)* (Tucson: University of Arizona Press, 1991). A variant of the same play on words occurs in the Yüan-Ming ch'uan-ch'i drama *Sha-kou chi*, scene 6, p. 12, l. 4. Another variant occurs in the *Shih-yü sheng-sou: Chung-yüan shih-yü* (Market argot and slang: The market argot of the Central Plain), published in the Lung-ch'ing reign period (1567–72) and reprinted in *Han-shang huan wen-ts'un* (Literary remains of the Han-shang Studio), by Ch'ien Nan-yang (Shanghai: Shang-hai wen-i ch'u-pan she, 1980), p. 165, upper register, l. 13. It recurs twice in the *Chin P'ing Mei tz'u-hua*, vol. 1, ch. 8, p. 3a, l.9; and vol. 4, ch. 79, p. 4b, ll. 6–7.

29. The "three luminaries" are the sun, moon, and stars. This couplet recurs three times in the *Chin P'ing Mei tz'u-hua*, vol. 3, ch. 60, p. 9a, l. 10; vol. 4, ch. 72, p. 5a, ll. 8–9; and vol. 5, ch. 82, p. 10b, l. 3.

30. This quatrain is made up of two couplets that occur independently in other contexts. The last couplet appears ubiquitously in Chinese vernacular literature. For an early occurrence, see *P'i-p'a chi*, scene 29, p. 166, l. 13. A variant occurs in Chüeh-lien's commentary (pref. dated 1551) to the *Chin-kang k'o-i*. See *[Hsiao-shih] Chin-kang k'o-i [hui-yao chu-chieh]*, p. 731, upper register, ll. 14–15. It recurs twice in the *Chin P'ing Mei tz'u-hua*, vol. 2, ch. 25, p. 6b, ll. 4–5; and vol. 4, ch. 67, p. 19a, l. 1.

CHAPTER 6

1. The expression "catastrophe will arise within the screen-wall of the house" is derived from a famous passage in Book 16 of the *Lun-yü*, which Waley translates, "I am afraid that the troubles of the Chi Family are due not to what is happening in Chuan-yü, but to what is going on behind the screen-wall of his own gate." See Waley, *The Analects of Confucius*, pp. 203–4. This allusion is very apposite to the concerns of the novel, one of the main points of which is that the greatest dangers to the individual, the family, or the state arise from within rather than without. This entire line of poetry occurs in a ballad by the T'ang poet Wang Han (cs 710, d. 726). See *Ch'üan T'ang shih*, vol. 3, *chüan* 156, p. 1603, l. 6.

2. The proximate source of the first seven lines of this poem, with some textual variants, is the *Shui-hu ch'üan-chuan*, vol. 1, ch. 25, p. 393, ll. 3–4. The last line is completely different.

3. The proximate source of this proverbial expression is the corresponding passage in the *Shui-hu ch'üan-chuan*, vol. 1, ch. 25, p. 401, l. 4. It occurs as early as 1137, according to an anecdote recorded in the *Ch'i-tung yeh-yü* (Rustic words of a man from eastern Ch'i), by Chou Mi (1232–98), pref. dated 1291 (Peking: Chung-hua shu-chü, 1983), *chüan* 2, p. 25, ll. 4–5. It occurs in the *Yüan-ch'ü hsüan*, 1:338, l. 15; and the *[Hsin-pien] Liu Chih-yüan huan-hsiang Pai-t'u chi*, p. 2a, l. 8. It recurs in the *Chin P'ing Mei tz'u-hua*, vol. 5, ch. 83, p. 4a, ll. 6–7.

4. These are all technical terms for various parts of the eye employed in traditional Chinese ophthalmology. The proximate source of these three lines, with some textual variants, is the corresponding passage in the *Shui-hu ch'üan-chuan*, vol. 1, ch. 25, p. 401, l. 15. Very similar locutions occur in the early vernacular stories *Chang Ku-lao chung-kua ch'ü Wen-nü*, p. 493, l. 12; see Birch, *Stories from a Ming Collection*, p. 187, ll. 9–10; and *Ts'ui Ya-nei pai-yao chao-yao* (The white falcon of Minister Ts'ui's son embroils him with demons), in *Ching-shih t'ung-yen, chüan* 19, p. 265, l. 11; see *Eight Colloquial Tales of the Sung*, trans. Richard F. S. Yang (Taipei: The China Post, 1972), p. 194, ll. 21–22. The same locution recurs in the *Chin P'ing Mei tz'u-hua*, vol. 4, ch. 63, p. 2b, l. 6.

5. The proximate source of these four lines, with a minor textual variant, is the corresponding passage in the *Shui-hu ch'üan-chuan*, vol. 1, ch. 25, p. 401, l. 16. The same four lines occur in a different order in the early vernacular story entitled *San hsien-shen Pao Lung-t'u tuan-yüan* (After three ghostly manifestations Academician Pao rights an injustice), in *Ching-shih t'ung-yen, chüan* 13, p. 175, ll. 2–3; and *Chinese Literature: Popular Fiction and Drama*, trans. H. C. Chang (Edinburgh: Edinburgh University Press, 1973), p. 194, ll. 12–14. These symptoms of poisoning are compatible with those described in the classic of Chinese forensic medicine, the *Hsi-yüan lu* (The washing away of wrongs), by Sung Tz'u (1186–1249), author's pref. dated 1247 (Peking: Ch'ün-chung ch'u-pan she, 1982), *chüan* 4, pp. 71–72. See *The Washing Away of Wrongs: Forensic Medicine in Thirteenth-Century China*, trans. Brian E. McNight (Ann Arbor: Center for Chinese Studies, University of Michigan, 1981), p. 134.

6. The four-character expression that I have translated "hugger-mugger" literally means "with seven hands and eight feet." It occurs as early as the twelfth century in a speech by the Buddhist monk Te-kuang (1121–1203). See *Wu-teng hui-yüan*, vol. 3, *chüan* 20, p. 1337, l. 12.

7. The proximate source of this four-character expression is the corresponding passage in the *Shui-hu ch'üan-chuan*, vol. 1, ch. 26, p. 407, l. 4. It recurs in ibid., vol. 2, ch. 46, p. 765, l. 15. It also recurs in a variant form in the *Chin P'ing Mei tz'u-hua*, vol. 1, ch. 19, p. 3b, l. 3.

8. The proximate source of this four-character expression is the corresponding passage in the *Shui-hu ch'üan-chuan*, vol. 1, ch. 26, p. 407, l. 4. For occurrences in Yüan tsa-chü drama, see *[Chi-p'ing chiao-chu] Hsi-hsiang chi*, play no. 4, scene 2, p. 148, l. 15; *Yüan-ch'ü hsüan*, 3:1258, l. 4; and *Yüan-ch'ü hsüan wai-pien*, 1:88, l. 2.

9. The first line of this couplet occurs in the *Hsi-hsiang chi*. See *[Chi-p'ing chiao-chu] Hsi-hsiang chi*, play no. 1, scene 2, p. 21, l. 7. Both lines recur together in the *Chin P'ing Mei tz'u-hua*, vol. 5, ch. 82, p. 3b, l. 7.

10. The proximate source of these four lines of narrator's commentary is the corresponding passage in the *Shui-hu ch'üan-chuan*, vol. 1, ch. 26, p. 407, l. 5. The same four lines of commentary recur at a critical juncture in chapter 79 of the *Chin p'ing Mei* just before the death of Hsi-men Ch'ing from sexual exhaustion. See the *Chin P'ing Mei tz'u-hua*, vol. 4, ch. 79, p. 10a, l. 1.

11. The proximate source of this couplet is the corresponding passage in the *Shui-hu ch'üan-chuan*, vol. 1, ch. 26, p. 407, l. 7. The remainder of this lyric, as given in the *Chin P'ing Mei*, is completely different from that in the *Shui-hu chuan*. However, a version that is much closer to that in the *Shui-hu chuan* occurs in the *Chin P'ing Mei tz'u-hua*, vol. 1, ch. 9, p. 1a, ll. 3–6.

12. See chapter 4, note 2.

13. The God of the Eastern Peak is the god of Mount T'ai in Shantung Province, the most important of the five sacred mountains of China. As a terrestrial deputy of the Jade Emperor he presides over life and death in this world and is one of the most important deities in Chinese popular religion. See Maspero, *Taoism and Chinese Religion*, pp. 102–5.

14. These two lines, with insignificant textual variation, recur in the *Chin P'ing Mei tz'u-hua*, vol. 5, ch. 85, p. 7a, l. 9.

15. The term for "old flower" also has the slang sense of "old beggar."

16. This concluding couplet recurs in the *Chin P'ing Mei tz'u-hua*, vol. 2, ch. 27, p. 7a, ll. 1–2.

17. This song, with some textual variation, is included in two sixteenth-century anthologies of popular song lyrics. See *Tz'u-lin chai-yen* (Select flowers from the forest of song), comp. Chang Lu, pref. dated 1525, 2 vols., fac. repr. (Peking: Wen-hsüeh ku-chi k'an-hsing she, 1955), 1:27, ll. 2–5; and *Yung-hsi yüeh-fu, ts'e* 16, p. 23a, l. 8–p. 23b, l. 1.

18. Variants of this four-character expression occur as early as the eleventh century in the lyrics of Liu Yung (cs 1034). See *Ch'üan Sung tz'u*, 1:26, lower register, l. 15; and 1:29, lower register, l. 12. It appears in the form given here in *Tung Chieh-yüan Hsi-hsiang chi, chüan* 5, p. 114, l. 3; *[Chi-p'ing chiao-chu] Hsi-hsiang chi*, play no. 5, scene 3, p. 187, l. 10; *Chien-teng hsin-hua, chüan* 3, p. 79, l. 2; and *San-kuo chih t'ung-su yen-i, chüan* 2, p. 77, l. 6.

19. This was a pastime among foot-fetishists at least as early as the eleventh century. T'ao Tsung-i (c. 1316–c. 1403) in his *Ch'o-keng lu* (Notes recorded during respites from the plow), pref. dated 1366 (Peking: Chung-hua shu-chü, 1980), *chüan* 23, p. 279, ll. 7–10, quotes a poem on this subject by Wang Ts'ai (1078–1118) and mentions that it was a favorite pastime of his contemporary Yang Wei-chen (1296–1370). T'ien I-heng (1524–c. 1574) quotes a lyric on the same subject by Ch'ü Yu (1341–1427), the author of the *Chien-teng hsin-hua*, allegedly written for the delectation of Yang Wei-chen. See his *Liu-ch'ing jih-cha* (Daily jottings worthy of preservation), pref. dated 1572, fac. repr. of 1609 ed. (Shanghai: Shang-hai ku-chi ch'u-pan she, 1985), *chüan* 25, p. 7a, l. 7–p. 7b, l. 5. For three more lyrics on the same subject by a contemporary of the author of the *Chin P'ing Mei*, see Feng Wei-min (1511–80), *Hai-fu shan-t'ang tz'u-kao* (Draft lyrics from Hai-fu shan-t'ang), pref. dated 1566 (Shanghai: Shang-hai ku-chi ch'u-pan she, 1981), *chüan* 3, pp. 158–59; and p. 169, ll. 2–5. The minor historical figure Wang Ts'ai, whose poetic effusion on the "shoe cup" is referred to above, shows up later in the novel as the feckless and dissolute third son of Imperial Commissioner Wang, one of Hsi-men Ch'ing's princi-

pal rivals in the licensed quarter. For his name, see the *Chin P'ing Mei tz'u-hua*, vol. 3, ch. 42, p. 8b. l. 3.

20. This four-character expression occurs in a lyric by Yüan Hao-wen (1190–1257), in *Ch'üan Chin Yüan tz'u*, 1:87, upper register, l. 10; in *[Chi-p'ing chiao-chu] Hsi-hsiang chi*, play no. 2, scene 3, p. 73, l. 14; in *Yüan-ch'ü hsüan*, 3:1095, l. 1; and 4:1421, l. 16; and in the early vernacular story *Pai Niang-tzu yung-chen Lei-feng T'a*, p. 430, l. 7.

21. This four-character expression is ubiquitous in Chinese vernacular literature. See, e.g., *Ch'üan Yüan san-ch'ü*, 1:29, l. 11; and *[Chi-p'ing chiao-chu] Hsi-hsiang chi*, play no. 5, scene 4, p. 200, l. 7.

22. This four-character expression occurs in the innocent sense of "showing off what you can do" in the *San-kuo chih t'ung-su yen-i, chüan* 1, p. 41, l. 3; and in the *San Sui p'ing-yao chuan, chüan* 4, ch. 16, p. 8a, l. 6.

23. "Dipping the candle upside down" is a metaphoric expression for vaginal intercourse with the woman on top of the man. It is mentioned in *San-pao t'ai-chien Hsi-yang chi t'ung-su yen-i*, vol. 1, ch. 32, p. 412, l. 7; and *Jou p'u-t'uan* (The carnal prayer mat), by Li Yü (1610–80), pref. dated 1657, 4 *chüan* (Japanese ed. of 1705), *chüan*, 1, ch. 3, p. 22a, l. 8. See *The Carnal Prayer Mat*, trans. Patrick Hanan (New York: Ballantine Books, 1990), p. 42, l. 13. It recurs in the *Chin P'ing Mei tz'u-hua*, vol. 4, ch. 72, p. 18b, l. 2; and ch. 79, p. 16a, ll. 6–7. The last reference is particularly significant since it is one of the acts that precipitates Hsi-men Ch'ing's death from sexual exhaustion.

24. "Punting the boat by night" is the name of a lyric tune as well as a metaphorical expression for intercourse with the man on top of the woman, with his weight on his knees and wrists, while the woman's legs are raised and knees flexed so that her lover's abdomen rests on the backs of her thighs. For an illustration of this posture, accompanied by a lyric to this tune, see the erotic album *Hua-ying chin-chen* (Variegated positions of the flowery battle) (Hang-chou: Yang-hao chai, c. 1610), fac. repr. in R. H. Van Gulik, *Erotic Colour Prints of the Ming Period with An Essay on Chinese Sex Life from the Han to the Ch'ing Dynasty, B.C. 206–A.D. 1644*, 3 vols. (Tokyo: Privately published in fifty copies, 1951), 3:2a and 2b. The picture is described and the lyric translated in ibid., 1:210.

25. "The butterfly nibbles at the calyx of the flower" is probably a metaphorical reference to cunnilingus. See Van Gulik, *Erotic Colour Prints of the Ming Period*, 1:190–91 and plate XIV.

26. The term "divine turtle" is a standard euphemism for the penis. The expression "silvery stream," the literal meaning of which is "clear stream," in the context of this poem refers unmistakably to semen, but it also puns with another compound that means "copper cash." Taking the pun into consideration, this line could, therefore, be rendered "The eye of the urethra disgorges copper cash, or filthy lucre." This is but one of many hints scattered throughout the novel that the author perceives a symbolic interchangeability between money and semen. In this way the sexual transactions for which the novel is so notorious are symbolically equated with the economic, political, and spiritual transactions that also play such a conspicuous part in the narrative.

27. The verb that I have translated as "left behind" puns with another meaning "to dribble," and thus serves to introduce the subliminal impression that Hsi-men Ch'ing made his departure after having "dribbled a few pieces of loose silver."

For a discussion of the significance of these puns on money and semen, see pp. xxxviii–xl of the introduction.

28. This couplet alludes to a famous story about how two young men, Liu Ch'en and Juan Chao, lost their way in the T'ien-t'ai Mountains and stumbled upon the abode of two immortal maidens with whom they lived for half a year. When they pled to go home their hosts reluctantly allowed them to leave, but when they returned to the mortal world they discovered that seven generations had passed during their absence. The term "Master Liu" became proverbial for an infatuated young lover. See *Yu-ming lu* (Records of the realms of the dead and the living), comp. Liu I-ch'ing (403–44); ed. and annot. Cheng Wan-ch'ing (Peking: Wen-hua i-shu ch'u-pan she, 1988), pp. 1–3; and Cordell D. K. Yee, trans., "Liu Ch'en and Juan Chao," in *Classical Chinese Tales of the Supernatural and the Fantastic*, ed. Karl S. Y. Kao (Bloomington: Indiana University Press, 1985), pp. 137–39.

CHAPTER 7

1. This line occurs in the ch'uan-ch'i drama entitled *Pao-chien chi* by Li K'ai-hsien (1502–68), a source from which the author of the *Chin P'ing Mei* is known to have borrowed heavily. See *Pao-chien chi*, scene 30, p. 56, ll. 22–23.

2. According to a fifteenth-century source, this type of fine cotton fabric was used for the manufacture of the imperial underwear during the Ming dynasty. See the *Shu-yüan tsa-chi* (Random jottings from the bean garden), by Lu Jung (1436–94) (Peking: Chung-hua shu-chü, 1985), *chüan* 1, p. 1, l. 8.

3. For an early occurrence of this idiom, see *Yüan-ch'ü hsüan wai-pien*, 3:986, l. 10. It recurs three times in the *Chin P'ing Mei tz'u-hua*, vol. 2, ch. 34, p. 8b, ll. 3–4; vol. 4, ch. 73, p. 6b, l. 11; and vol. 5, ch. 87, p. 2a, l. 5.

4. This proverbial saying occurs in Yüan tsa-chü drama. See *Yüan-ch'ü hsüan*, 1:375, l. 9.

5. For Chang Liang and Han Hsin, see chapter 1, notes 23 and 15. A variant of this couplet occurs in the Ming dynasty ch'uan-ch'i drama entitled *Yü-ch'u chi* (The jade pestle), pref. dated 1606, in *Ku-pen hsi-ch'ü ts'ung-k'an, ch'u-chi*, item 86, *chüan* 1, scene 18, p. 56b, l. 7.

6. This idiom occurs as early as the twelfth century in a poetical exegesis of the *Diamond Sutra* by the Buddhist monk Tao-ch'uan (fl. 1127–63). See *Chin-kang pan-jo-po-lo-mi ching chu* (Commentary on the *Vajracchedikā prajñāpāramitā sutra*), by Tao-ch'uan, pref. dated 1179, in *[Shinzan] Dai Nihon zokuzōkyō*, vol. 24, *chüan* 2, p. 552, lower register, l. 16.

7. A variant of this couplet occurs in an anonymous early Ming tsa-chü drama entitled *Lung-men yin-hsiu* (The beauty concealed at Lung-men), in *Ku-pen Yüan Ming tsa-chü*, vol. 3, scene 4, p. 10b, ll. 6–7; and *San-pao t'ai-chien Hsi-yang chi t'ung-su yen-i*, vol. 1, ch. 38, p. 491, l. 15. It recurs in the *Chin P'ing Mei tz'u-hua*, vol. 2, ch. 30, p. 10b, l. 11.

8. This couplet is ubiquitous in Chinese vernacular literature. See, e.g., *Chang Hsieh chuang-yüan*, p. 78, ll. 8–9. It recurs, with minor textual variants, in the *Chin P'ing Mei tz'u-hua*, vol. 5, ch. 90, p. 3a, l. 3; and, the first line only, in vol. 5, ch. 98, p. 7a, l. 10.

9. This line, translated literally, means "the holes in the water clock do not retain silk threads." Puns on three of the five characters in the expression make it actually

mean "reveal your words without keeping anything to yourself." The same expression recurs in the *Chin P'ing Mei tz'u-hua*, vol. 5, ch. 85, p. 9a, l. 5.

10. A variant of this proverbial expression occurs in the middle period vernacular story entitled *K'uai-tsui Li Ts'ui-lien chi* (The story of the sharp-tongued Li Ts'ui-lien), in *Ch'ing-p'ing shan-t'ang hua-pen*, p. 58, l. 8. See H. C. Chang, trans., "The Shrew," in his *Chinese Literature: Popular Fiction and Drama*, p. 41, l. 5.

11. This idiom recurs in the *Chin P'ing Mei tz'u-hua*, vol. 5, ch. 89, p. 2a, l. 4.

12. This idiomatic expression is ubiquitous in Chinese vernacular literature. See, e.g., *Yüan-ch'ü hsüan*, 1:278, l. 3; and *Shui-hu ch'üan-chuan*, vol. 1, ch. 26, p. 408, l. 2.

13. Kuan-yin is the Goddess of Mercy of Chinese popular religion. For a definitive account of the hagiography that developed around this figure, see Glen Dudbridge, *The Legend of Miao-shan* (London: Ithaca Press, 1978). Sudhana is the hero of the last book of the *Avatamsaka Sutra*, also known as an independent scripture called *Gandavyūha*, but in Chinese popular religion he has been reduced to the role of an iconographic attendant of Kuan-yin. For those interested in his original story, see *The Flower Ornament Scripture: A Translation of the Avatamsaka Sutra*, vol. 3, *Entry into the Realm of Reality*, trans. Thomas Cleary (Boston: Shambhala, 1987).

14. This was an ancient Chinese game in which the contestants attempted to toss arrows into a narrow-necked vessel. It was considered important enough to have a chapter devoted to it in the Confucian *Book of Rites*. See Legge, *Li Chi*, 1:50–51; and 2:397–401.

15. This four-character expression occurs ubiquitously in Chinese vernacular literature. See, e.g., *Shui-hu ch'üan-chuan*, vol. 1, ch. 14, p. 206, l. 16; and vol. 3, ch. 75, p. 1257, l. 11.

16. The *ch'i-lin* is a mythical Chinese beast, believed to be very auspicious, whose name is often translated, somewhat misleadingly, as unicorn. The *ch'i-lin* in the mandarin square was an insignia of rank that could be worn legally during most of the Ming dynasty only by nobles and, as a special mark of distinction, commanders of the Embroidered-Uniform Guard. Only for a brief period in the early sixteenth century was the right to wear this insignia conferred on certain officials of the fourth and fifth ranks, but this was regarded as anomalous. Needless to say, Meng Yü-lou, whose deceased husband was only a cloth merchant, was not legally entitled to wear such an insignia. This is but one of many examples in the novel of the deliberate flouting of sumptuary regulations. See *Ming shih*, vol. 6, *chüan* 67, pp. 1638–39.

17. Variants of this conventional couplet occur in many other works of Chinese vernacular literature. See, e.g., *Tung Chieh-yüan Hsi-hsiang chi*, *chüan* 5, p. 113, l. 3; *Huan-men tzu-ti ts'o li-shen*, p. 221, l. 7; *Yüan-ch'ü hsüan*, 1:16, l. 12; and *Hsüan-ho i-shih* p. 49, l. 5.

18. A variant form of these four lines recurs in the *Chin P'ing Mei tz'u-hua*, vol. 5, ch. 91, p. 8a, ll. 4–5.

19. This proverbial saying recurs twice, in slightly variant form, in the *Chin P'ing Mei tz'u-hua*, vol. 1, ch. 16, p. 5a, l. 10; and vol. 4, ch. 74, p. 4a, l. 2.

20. The ultimate source of this admonitory couplet is the Confucian classic, the *Book of Rites*. See *Li-chi*, ch. 10, p. 55, l. 2; and Legge, *Li Chi*, 1:455, ll. 6–8. It recurs in the *Chin P'ing Mei tz'u-hua*, vol. 5, ch. 83, p. 3b, ll. 2-3.

21. This proverbial expression recurs twice in the *Chin P'ing Mei tz'u-hua*, vol. 1, ch. 18, p. 6a, l. 11; and vol. 4, ch. 73, p. 9b, l. 5.

22. This four-character idiom recurs in the *Chin P'ing Mei tz'u-hua*, vol. 4, ch. 76, p. 16a, l. 11.

23. This statement is reminiscent of a passage in chapter 12 of the *Hsün-tzu* where he says, "The ruler is the source of order. . . . If the water of the source is clear, the lower reaches of the stream will be clear. If the water of the source is muddy, the lower reaches of the stream will be muddy." See *Hsün-tzu yin-te*, ch. 12, p. 44, l. 15; and introduction, note 65.

24. This conventional four-character expression occurs in Yüan-Ming tsa-chü drama. See *Yüan-ch'ü hsüan wai-pien*, 3:895, l. 20; and *Ming-jen tsa-chü hsüan*, p. 52, l. 11.

25. This four-character expression occurs twice in *[Chi-p'ing chiao-chu] Hsi-hsiang chi*, play no. 4, scene 2, p. 149, l. 6; and play no. 5, scene 1, p. 175, l. 14. It also occurs in *Pao-chien chi*, scene 51, p. 91, l. 4.

26. The expression that I have translated "a sometime thing" comes from chapter 16 of *Chuang-tzu*. See *Chuang-tzu yin-te*, ch. 16, p. 41, ll. 18–19. A. C. Graham translates the passage in question as follows: "A thing which comes to us by chance is a lodger with us, and we who give it lodging can neither ward off its coming nor stop its going away." See *Chuang-tzu: The Seven Inner Chapters and Other Writings from the Book Chuang-tzu*, trans. A. C. Graham (London: Allen and Unwin, 1981), p. 172, ll. 34–36. Variants of this line occur in *Yüan-ch'ü hsüan*, 1:222, l. 9; and *Chin-yin chi, chüan* 2, scene 18, p. 26a, l. 10.

27. Variants of this line occur in *Yüan-ch'ü hsüan*, 2:757, l. 3; and *Yüan-ch'ü hsüan wai-pien*, 1:327, l. 14.

28. The importance of this topical allusion to a contemporary practice for the dating of the *Chin P'ing Mei* was first pointed out by Wu Han in 1933. See Wu Han, "*Chin P'ing Mei* te chu-tso shih-tai chi ch'i she-hui pei-ching" (The date of composition of the *Chin P'ing Mei* and its social background), reprinted in his *Tu-shih cha-chi* (Notes on reading history) (Peking: San-lien shu-tien, 1957), pp. 20–24; and Hanan, "The Text of the *Chin P'ing Mei*," p. 39, n. 45. In his article Wu Han argues that the misappropriation of funds from the Court of the Imperial Stud only became common after 1582 and that the *Chin P'ing Mei* must, therefore, have been written after that date. More recently, however, in 1984 Hsü Shuo-fang published an article in which he cited evidence from the *Ming shih-lu* (Veritable records of the Ming dynasty) showing that this practice had also occurred with some frequency in the period from 1537 to 1541. See Hsü Shuo-fang, "*Chin P'ing Mei* ch'eng-shu hsin-t'an" (A new study of the composition of the *Chin P'ing Mei*), *Chung-hua wen-shih lun-ts'ung* (Collections of essays on Chinese literature and history), no. 3 (1984): 185–87. It would seem, therefore, that this particular piece of evidence as to the terminus post quem for the date of composition of the *Chin P'ing Mei* can no longer be regarded as conclusive.

29. Variants of this expression occur in *Yüan-ch'ü hsüan*, 2:542, l. 18; 2:548, l. 3; 4:1363, l. 16; *Yüan-ch'ü hsüan wai-pien*, 1:329, l. 11; 2:584, l. 18; and *Ming-jen tsa-chü hsüan*, p. 204, l. 15. The same expression recurs in the *Chin P'ing Mei tz'u-hua*, vol. 2, ch. 29, p 11b, l. 3; and ch. 37, p. 7a, ll. 2–3.

30. These two lines are derived from a couplet in a poem by the eighth-century poet Liu Shang. See *Ch'üan T'ang shih*, vol. 5, *chüan* 303, p. 3453, l. 2.

31. The ultimate source of this saying is the *Pai-hu t'ung* (Comprehensive discussions in the White Tiger Hall), a compilation of scholastic opinion dating from

the first century A.D. See the text as reproduced in *Pai-tzu ch'üan-shu* (Complete works of the hundred philosophers), fac. repr., 8 vols. (Hang-chou: Che-chiang jen-min ch'u-pan she, 1984), vol. 6, *chüan* 1, p. 10b, l. 14. The relevant passage has been translated by Tjan Tjoe Som as follows: "When a son is born he is turned towards the inside of the house because it is his duty to remain in the family; when a daughter is born she is turned towards the outside because it is her duty to follow her husband." See *Po Hu T'ung: The Comprehensive Discussions in the White Tiger Hall*, trans. Tjan Tjoe Som, 2 vols. (Leiden: E. J. Brill, 1949), 2:419, ll. 23–27.

32. Variants of this couplet occur in *Yüan-ch'ü hsüan wai-pien*, 2:403, l. 15; and in a song quoted by Li K'ai-hsien (1502–68) in his *Tz'u-nüeh*, p. 287, l. 9. The same couplet recurs in the *Chin P'ing Mei tz'u-hua*, vol. 5, ch. 90, p. 6a, ll. 10–11.

33. A variant of this expression, which means to pretend one thing while doing another, occurs in a song by Feng Wei-min (1511–80). See *Hai-fu shan-t'ang tz'u-kao, chüan* 3, p. 169, l. 9. This expression recurs five times in the *Chin P'ing Mei tz'u-hua*, vol. 1, ch. 13, p. 10b l. 9; vol. 2, ch. 26, p. 9a, l. 6; vol. 3, ch. 58, p. 17b, l. 5; vol. 4, ch. 61, p. 8b, l. 8; and ch. 67, p. 18b, l. 1.

34. The ultimate source of this proverbial expression is a line in the *O-pang kung fu* (Rhapsody on the O-pang Palace) by Tu Mu (803–52). See *Ch'üan T'ang wen*, vol. 16, *chüan* 748, p. 2a, l. 8. It occurs ubiquitously in Chinese vernacular literature. See, e.g., *Shui-hu ch'üan-chuan*, vol. 1, ch. 3, p. 47, l. 5.

35. The literary conceit expressed in these four lines occurs in *Wen-ching yüan-yang hui*, p. 160, l. 2; and *Hsiu-ju chi*, scene 41, p. 110, l. 4. Both of these texts are sources from which the author of the *Chin P'ing Mei* is known to have borrowed extensively.

36. A variant of this expression occurs in a song by Shang Tao (cs 1212). See *Ch'üan Yüan san-ch'ü*, 1:21, l. 10. See also *Yüan-ch'ü hsüan*, 3:925, l. 19; 3:1021, ll. 4–5; *Pao-chien chi*, scene 3, p. 9, l. 16; and *Hai-fu shan-t'ang tz'u-kao, chüan* 1, p. 4, ll. 2–3; and p. 17, l. 5.

37. Lieh-tzu is the name of a shadowy personage who figures prominently in ancient Taoist thought and for whom one of the Taoist classics has been named. See *The Book of Lieh-tzu*, trans. A. C. Graham (London: John Murray, 1960). In the *Chuang-tzu* he is alleged to have been able to ride the wind. See *Chuang-tzu yin-te*, ch. 1, p. 2, ll. 19–20; and Watson, *The Complete Works of Chuang Tzu*, ch. 1, p. 32, ll. 5–7.

38. This quatrain recurs in the *Chin P'ing Mei tz'u-hua*, vol. 5, ch. 97, p. 11b, ll. 2–3.

CHAPTER 8

1. The ultimate source of this formulaic four-character expression is a line repeated three times in the six stanzas of song no. 35 in the *Shih-ching* (The book of songs). In the original context it is part of the plaint of a neglected wife, but it has come to be used to celebrate newlywedded bliss. See *Mao-shih yin-te*, song no. 35, pp. 7–8; and Waley, *The Book of Songs*, pp. 100–101. It occurs ubiquitously in Chinese vernacular literature from as early as the twelfth century. See, e.g., *Tung Chieh-yüan Hsi-hsiang chi, chüan* 5, p. 110, l. 11. It recurs twice in the *Chin P'ing Mei tz'u-hua*, vol. 5, ch. 91, p. 10b, l. 2; and ch. 97, p. 11a, l. 11.

2. The ultimate source of this four-character expression is a speech attributed to Tzu-hsia (b. 507 B.C.), one of the principle disciples of Confucius, in the *Han-shih wai-chuan* (Exoteric anecdotes illustrative of the Han version of the *Book of songs*), an anthology of quotations from earlier works compiled by Han Ying (2d century B.C.). See ibid. in *Ts'ung-shu chi-ch'eng*, 1st series, vol. 525, *chüan* 9, p. 122, l. 8; and *Han Shih Wai Chuan: Han Ying's Illustrations of the Didactic Application of the Classic of Songs*, trans. James Robert Hightower (Cambridge: Harvard University Press, 1952), ch. 9, item 25, p. 314, ll. 7–8. Although it did not originally refer to intimate relations between men and women, it came to do so in the vernacular literature where it occurs ubiquitously in that sense only. See, e.g., *Shui-hu ch'üan-chuan*, vol. 1, ch. 21, p. 307, l. 2; and vol. 2, ch. 45, p. 741, l. 16.

3. Shoes, like coins, can be tossed in the air a prescribed number of times and, depending on whether they land upside down or right side up, used to select one of the sixty-four hexagrams in the *Book of Changes*, which can then be interpreted in connection with a particular question. The hexagram so selected, when the question in mind has to do with love, is called a "love hexagram."

4. This couplet, with some textual variants, is derived from one in a poem by the late eighth-century poet Yü Hu. See *Ch'üan T'ang shih*, vol. 5, *chüan* 310, p. 3498, l. 5.

5. This line refers to a famous story about Chang Ch'ang (d. 51 B.C.), a prominent official of the Former Han dynasty, who is said to have been so uxorious that he painted his wife's eyebrows. When the emperor charged him with this practice he replied, "Your servant has heard that in the intimacies between husband and wife in the privacy of the boudoir more things may occur than the painting of eyebrows." See *Han-shu*, vol. 7, *chüan* 76, p. 3222, ll. 15–16. Variants of this line occur ubiquitously in Chinese vernacular literature. See, e.g., *Tung Chieh-yüan Hsi-hsiang chi*, *chüan* 6, p. 133, l. 1; a song by Kuan Han-ch'ing (13th century), in *Ch'üan Yüan san-ch'ü*, 1:166, ll. 5–6; and *Yüan-ch'ü hsüan*, 1:60, l. 7. It recurs in an anonymous song quoted in the *Chin P'ing Mei tz'u-hua*, vol. 5, ch. 83, p. 1b, ll. 8–9.

6. These two anonymous songs appear, with some textual variants, in the sixteenth-century anthology of short song lyrics entitled *Yüeh-fu ch'ün-chu* (A string of lyric pearls), modern ed. ed. Lu Ch'ien (Shanghai: Shang-wu yin-shu kuan, 1957), *chüan* 1, p. 57, ll. 10–13; and *Yung-hsi yüeh-fu*, *ts'e* 20, p. 7a, ll. 5–10. The versions in the *Chin P'ing Mei tz'u-hua* are closer to those in the *Yung-hsi yüeh-fu* than to those in the *Yüeh-fu ch'ün-chu*.

7. The ultimate source of this proverbial expression is a line in the *Han Fei tzu* (Works of Master Han Fei), by the Legalist philosopher Han Fei (c. 280–233 B.C.). See *Han Fei tzu so-yin* (A concordance to *Han Fei tzu*) (Peking: Chung-hua shu-chü, 1982), ch. 29, p. 783, ll. 3–4; and *The Complete Works of Han Fei Tzu*, trans. W. K. Liao, 2 vols. (London: Arthur Probsthain, 1959), 1:278, ll. 16–17. It also occurs in the *Shui-hu ch'üan-chuan*, vol. 2, ch. 47, p. 783, l. 16.

8. This line, which has become proverbial, first occurs in a poem by Ou-yang Pin (10th century) that is quoted in a work entitled *Hai-wen lu* (Record of startling events), by Li T'ien (cs 992). This work is no longer extant in its complete form, but twenty-one items from it are included in the *Lei-shuo*. See *Lei-shuo*, vol. 2, *chüan* 19, p. 8b, ll. 7–8. This phrase occurs in *Yüan-ch'ü hsüan*, 2:470, l. 9. It recurs in the *Chin P'ing Mei tz'u-hua*, vol. 4, ch. 76, p. 12b, l. 11.

9. Like the two songs quoted above, this anonymous song appears, with some textual variants, in the *Yüeh-fu ch'ün-chu*, p. 57, ll. 8–9; and the *Yung-hsi yüeh-fu, ts'e* 20, p. 7a, ll. 2–4. The version in the *Chin P'ing Mei tz'u-hua* is slightly closer to that in the *Yung-hsi yüeh-fu* than to that in the *Yüeh-fu ch'ün-chu*.

10. Hung-niang is the name of the maidservant who is instrumental in bringing the lovers together in the *Ying-ying chuan* and its chantefable and dramatic derivatives.

11. This anonymous song appears, with some textual variants, in the fourteenth-century anthology of song lyrics entitled *Li-yüan an-shih yüeh-fu hsin-sheng* (Model new song lyrics from the Pear Garden), modern ed. ed. Sui Shu-sen (Peking: Chung-hua shu-chü, 1958), *chüan* 3, p. 115, ll. 11–12; and the *Yung-hsi yüeh-fu, ts'e* 19, p. 25a, ll. 2–4. The version in the *Chin P'ing Mei tz'u-hua* is closer to that in the *Yung-hsi yüeh-fu* than to that in the *Li-yüan an-shih yüeh-fu hsin-sheng*.

12. The "wooden mule," like the "wooden horse" of Europe, was a kind of saw-horse on wheels that miscreants were condemned to ride astride as a form of torture and ignominy. Chinese criminals condemned to execution by slow slicing were made to ride this contrivance on their way to the execution ground.

13. This four-character expression occurs frequently in Chinese vernacular literature. See, e.g., *[Chi-p'ing chiao-chu] Hsi-hsiang chi*, play no. 4, scene 1, p. 142, ll. 11–12; and *Yüan-ch'ü hsüan*, 2:465, l. 13; 2:645, l. 20; and 4:1573, l. 8. It recurs in the *Chin P'ing Mei tz'u-hua*, vol. 4, ch. 61, p. 19b, l. 1; and ch. 79, p. 16a, l. 2.

14. Variants of this formulaic couplet recur four times in the *Chin P'ing Mei tz'u-hua*, vol. 1, ch. 12, p. 6a, ll. 8–9; vol. 2, ch. 38, p. 8b, l. 11; vol. 5, ch. 85, p. 5b, ll. 1–2; and ch. 98, p. 10b, l. 4.

15. A variant of this expression occurs in *Yüan-ch'ü hsüan*, 2:767, l. 14.

16. This couplet is derived from one in a quatrain by the T'ang poet Wang Ya (cs 792, d. 835). See *Ch'üan T'ang shih*, vol. 6, *chüan* 346, p. 3876, l. 16. A variant of the same couplet recurs in the *Chin P'ing Mei tz'u-hua*, vol. 2, ch. 38, p. 8b, ll. 1–2.

17. A variant of this proverbial four-character expression occurs in a speech attributed to Ma Wu (d. A.D. 61) in the *Hou-Han shu*, vol. 1, *chüan* 1a, p. 20, l. 8. There is a story that when Chiang Tzu-ya (11th century B.C.) was a young man, his wife left him because of his poverty, but that when he became, in his old age, the chief adviser of the founder of the Chou dynasty, she sought a reconciliation. He thereupon emptied a jug of water on the ground and asked her to retrieve it, saying, "If you speak of reunion after separation, spilt water can surely never be recovered." See *Yeh-k'o ts'ung-shu* (Collected writings of a rustic sojourner), by Wang Mao (1151–1213) (Peking: Chung-hua shu-chü, 1987), *chüan* 28, p. 327, ll. 4–6. This expression occurs ubiquitously in Chinese vernacular literature. See, e.g., *Wu Tzu-hsü pien-wen*, p. 2, l. 10; *Ta Mu-kan-lien ming-chien chiu-mu pien-wen*, p. 736, l. 6; and *Huan-men tzu-ti ts'o li-shen*, p. 243, l. 11.

18. The source of this four-character expression is a passage in Book 1a.7 of *Mencius*, which Legge translates, "But doing what you do to seek for what you desire is like climbing a tree to seek for fish." See Legge, *The Works of Mencius*, p. 145, ll. 14–15.

19. The Temple of the God of the Sea refers to the story of Wang K'uei (1036–63), who fell in love with a singing girl named Kuei-ying while he was still a student and swore eternal fidelity to her in the Temple of the God of the Sea. In 1061 he took

first place in the metropolitan examinations and married someone more befitting his newly exalted social status. As a result of this betrayal, Kuei-ying committed suicide and her ghost then hounded him to death after lodging a complaint against him in the Temple of the God of the Sea. For a succinct summary of the development of this story and the text of a Ming vernacular version, see Hu Shih-ying, *Hua-pen hsiao-shuo kai-lun* (A comprehensive study of promptbook fiction), 2 vols. (Peking: Chung-hua shu-chü, 1980), 1:332–38.

20. These four anonymous songs appear together in a group of seven songs to this tune in the *Yung-hsi yüeh-fu, ts'e* 15b, pp. 35a–36a. The author has chosen the fifth, second, third, and sixth songs, in that order. Although there is some textual variation, the two versions are very close.

21. Variants of this proverbial saying occur in the *Shui-hu ch'üan-chuan*, vol. 1, ch. 21, p. 307, l. 6; and the middle-period vernacular story *Hsin-ch'iao shih Han Wu mai ch'un-ch'ing*, p. 73, l. 11.

22. These oaths, especially the first, occur frequently in Chinese vernacular literature. See, e.g., *Yüan-ch'ü hsüan*, 1:60, l. 5; and 3:1118, l. 20; *Yüan-ch'ü hsüan wai-pien*, 2:492, l. 7; and *Shui-hu ch'üan-chuan*, vol. 2, ch. 53, p. 876, l. 17. The two oaths recur together in the *Chin P'ing Mei tz'u-hua*, vol. 5, ch. 82, p. 10a, ll. 1–2.

23. For a good picture of what this type of headgear looked like, see the illustration reproduced in Shen Ts'ung-wen, *Chung-kuo ku-tai fu-shih yen-chiu* (A study of traditional Chinese costume) (Hong Kong: Shang-wu yin-shu kuan, 1981), p. 399. According to the recollections of a contemporary of the author of the *Chin P'ing Mei*, in the early years of the Chia-ching reign period (1522–66) only government students eligible to participate in the provincial examinations wore this kind of hat. It was not until the years after 1541 that a few wealthy commoners began to follow suit. See Fan Lien (b. 1540), *Yün-chien chü-mu ch'ao* (Jottings on matters eyewitnessed in Yün-chien), pref. dated 1593, in *Pi-chi hsiao-shuo ta-kuan* (Great collectanea of note-form literature), 17 vols. (Yang-chou: Chiang-su Kuang-ling ku-chi k'o-yin she, 1984), vol. 6, *ts'e* 13, *chüan* 2, p. 1a, ll. 12–13.

24. According to the anonymous Southern Sung (1127–1279) work *Li Shih-shih wai-chuan* (Unofficial biography of Li Shih-shih), in the year 1110 Emperor Hui-tsung (r. 1100–25) proposed this couplet as the subject for a painting competition in the Imperial Academy and presented the winning picture to the famous courtesan Li Shih-shih, with whom he was carrying on a clandestine affair. See ibid., in *T'ang Sung ch'uan-ch'i chi*, pp. 317–18. This couplet appears in many works of Chinese vernacular literature. See, e.g., *Yüan-ch'ü hsüan*, 1:264, ll. 20–21; the early vernacular stories entitled *Hsi-hu san-t'a chi* (The three pagodas at West Lake), in *Ch'ing-p'ing shan-t'ang hua-pen*, p. 29, l. 4; and *Cheng Chieh-shih li-kung shen-pi kung*, p. 657, l. 11; the 1431 manuscript of the anonymous ch'uan-ch'i drama *Chin-ch'ai chi* (The gold hairpin), modern ed. ed. Liu Nien-tzu (Canton: Kuang-tung jen-min ch'u-pan she, 1985), scene 40, p. 67, ll. 7–8; the ch'uan-ch'i drama *Hsiang-nang chi* (The scent bag), by Shao Ts'an (15th century), *Liu-shih chung ch'ü* edition (Taipei: K'ai-ming shu-tien, 1970), scene 10, p. 26, ll. 6–7; the *Shui-hu ch'üan-chuan*, vol. 4, ch. 101, p. 1571, l. 8; and *Ta-T'ang Ch'in-wang tz'u-hua, chüan* 4, p. 1a, ll. 6–7. It recurs in the *Chin P'ing Mei tz'u-hua*, vol. 5, ch. 82, p. 8a, ll. 9–10.

25. Fine folding fans of Szechwan manufacture were made to order for the palace in the latter decades of the Chia-ching reign period (1522–66) and were often be-

stowed upon high officials as marks of imperial favor. See *Wan-li yeh-huo pien*, vol. 3, *chüan* 26, pp. 662–63.

26. Pu Chih-tao is an example of a punning name that suggests the words "do not know." He is one of the group of Hsi-men Ch'ing's boon companions that are introduced in chapter 10, all of whom have punning names of this kind. I have there rendered his name as No-account Pu.

27. Versions of this set-piece of descriptive parallel prose occur, with some textual variants, in the early vernacular story *Sung Ssu-kung ta-nao Chin-hun Chang*, p. 533, ll. 10–11; and the *Shui-hu ch'üan-chuan*, vol. 2, ch. 37, pp. 580–81. Lines 5–8 are derived from ibid., vol. 1, ch. 8, p. 128, l. 17–p. 129, l. 1.

28. Variants of this proverbial expression occur in *Yüan-ch'ü hsüan*, 1:76, l. 8; and in *Hsi-yu chi*, vol. 2, ch. 76, p. 876, l. 14.

29. Variants of this descriptive couplet occur ubiquitously in Chinese vernacular literature. See, e.g., the early vernacular stories *Lo-yang san-kuai chi*, p. 70, l. 15; *Wu-chieh Ch'an-shih ssu Hung-lien chi*, p. 139, l. 14; *Chin-ming ch'ih Wu Ch'ing feng Ai-ai* (Wu Ch'ing meets Ai-ai at Chin-ming Pond), in *Ching-shih t'ung-yen*, *chüan* 30, p. 466, l. 15; *Wan Hsiu-niang ch'ou-pao shan-t'ing-erh* (Wan Hsiu-niang gets her revenge with a toy pavilion), in ibid., *chüan* 37, p. 567, l. 6; and *Lü Tung-pin fei-chien chan Huang-lung* (Lü Tung-pin beheads Huang-lung with his flying sword), in *Hsing-shih heng-yen*, vol. 2, *chüan* 21, p. 464, l. 1; the middle-period vernacular story *Ts'o-jen shih*, p. 229, l. 4; the *Shui-hu ch'üan-chuan*, vol. 2, ch. 31, p. 477, l. 11; and vol. 4, ch. 103, p. 1588, ll. 16–17; and *San Sui p'ing-yao chuan*, *chüan* 3, ch. 13, p. 48a, ll. 7–8. It recurs in the *Chin P'ing Mei tz'u-hua*, vol. 5, ch. 95, p. 5a, l. 7.

30. The proximate source of this quotation is probably the *Shui-hu ch'üan-chuan*, vol. 1, ch. 25, p. 397, ll. 10–11. The ultimate source is a line in the *Book of Rites*. See *Li-chi*, ch. 1a, p. 3, l. 4; and Legge, *Li Chi*, 1:77, ll. 11–12.

31. The *Lotus Sutra* is perhaps the most influential of all Chinese Buddhist texts. For an English translation from the Chinese version of Kumārajīva (fl. 350–410), see *Scripture of the Lotus Blossom of the Fine Dharma*, trans. Leon Hurvitz (New York: Columbia University Press, 1976).

32. This is the popular name of a liturgical work apocryphally attributed to Emperor Wu (r. 502–49) of the Liang dynasty (502–57), a great patron of Buddhism, the correct title of which is *Tz'u-pei tao-ch'ang ch'an-fa* (Compassionate litany of repentance). It is commonly employed in services for the dead.

33. The proximate source of this couplet, with some textual variants, is the *Shui-hu ch'üan-chuan*, vol. 2, ch. 45, p. 735, ll. 2–3. The expression "monkey of the mind and horse of the will" is of Buddhist origin, but has long since been sinicized and incorporated into Chinese popular literature as a nonsectarian term. For a definitive study of the evolution of this expression, see Dudbridge, *The Hsi-yu chi: A Study of Antecedents to the Sixteenth-Century Chinese Novel*, pp. 167–76.

34. The proximate source of this set-piece of descriptive parallel prose, with some textual variants, is the *Shui-hu ch'üan-chuan*, vol. 2, ch. 45, pp. 734–35.

35. This four-character expression literally means "permit a woman to sit in one's lap without becoming disorderly." It is derived from a story about Liu-hsia Hui, a worthy of ancient times, who once allowed an inadequately clothed woman to sit in his lap all night in order to keep her from freezing but did not attempt to take advantage of her. See T'ao Tsung-i, *Ch'o-keng lu*, *chüan* 4, p. 54, l. 1. It occurs in the

anonymous Ming ch'uan-ch'i drama entitled *Ku-ch'eng chi* (The reunion at Ku-ch'eng), in *Ku-pen hsi-ch'ü ts'ung-k'an, ch'u-chi*, item 25, *chüan* 1, scene 11, p. 17b, l. 1. It recurs in the *Chin P'ing Mei tz'u-hua*, vol. 3, ch. 56, p. 11b, l. 1.

36. The proximate source of this four-line diatribe is the *Shui-hu ch'üan-chuan*, vol. 2, ch. 45, p. 734, l. 8. The accusation that Buddhist priests are "sex-starved hungry ghosts" is also quoted in the *Hsi-yu chi*, vol. 1, ch. 23, p. 262, l. 6.

37. Su Shih (1037–1101) is one of the giants of Chinese literature and the greatest of the many great writers of the Northern Sung dynasty, both in prose and in verse. For an excellent survey of his career, see the biographical study by George C. Hatch in Franke, *Sung Biographies*, 3:900–68.

38. The proximate source of these four lines of repartee is the *Shui-hu ch'üan-chuan*, vol. 2, ch. 45, p. 734, ll. 6–7. The ultimate source is an apocryphal work attributed to Su Shih entitled *Wen-ta lu* (A record of repartee), in *Ts'ung-shu chi-ch'eng*, 1st series, vol. 2987, p. 1, l. 12. According to the anecdote recorded there, one day Su Shih was drinking with his friend the Buddhist priest Fo-yin (1032–98) when the latter challenged him to cap a four-line epigram as follows:

> The unstingy are not rich,
> The unrich are not stingy,
> The stingy are most likely to be rich,
> The rich are most likely to be stingy.

Su Shih, realizing that the epigram was directed at him, returned the compliment by replying as quoted in the text. These four lines also occur in the early vernacular story entitled *Fo-yin Shih ssu t'iao Ch'in-niang* (The priest Fo-yin teases Ch'in-niang four times), in *Hsing-shih heng-yen*, vol. 1, *chüan* 12, p. 235, l. 6.

39. The proximate source of this anticlerical disquisition, with considerable textual variation, is the *Shui-hu ch'üan-chuan*, vol. 2, ch. 45, p. 734, ll. 1–6.

40. The proximate source of this quatrain, with some textual variation, is the *Shui-hu ch'üan-chuan*, vol. 2, ch. 45, p. 739, l. 15. A version of the final couplet is quoted as a proverbial saying in *Chi-shan lu* (Record of accumulated good deeds), by Huang Kuang-ta, pref. dated 1178, in *Shuo-fu* (The frontiers of apocrypha), comp. T'ao Tsung-i (c. 1316–c. 1403), 2 vols. (Taipei: Hsin-hsing shu-chü, 1963), vol. 2, *chüan* 64, p. 4a, l. 10.

41. It was an erotic practice in China to burn cone-shaped pellets of dried moxa on various parts of the female body that were regarded as particularly sensitive, including the breasts, the lower abdomen, and the mons veneris, in order to induce an involuntary writhing that was regarded as sexually stimulating to both partners, but primarily the man. The woman's willingness to undergo this painful ordeal in order to increase her partner's pleasure was regarded as a token of affection. For an evocative song on this subject by a contemporary of the author of the *Chin P'ing Mei*, see Feng Wei-min (1511–80), *Hai-fu shan-t'ang tz'u-kao, chüan* 3, p. 157, ll. 9–13.

42. This is a quotation, immediately recognizable to all educated Chinese, from a passage in the first paragraph of Book 1 of the *Lun-yü*, which Waley translates, "That friends should come to one from afar, is this not after all delightful?" See Waley, *The Analects of Confucius*, p. 83, ll. 6–7. This kind of irreverent use of quotations from canonical sources is characteristic of the rhetoric of the *Chin P'ing Mei*.

43. The proximate source of these two lines is the *Shui-hu ch'üan-chuan*, vol. 2, ch. 45, p. 735, l. 2. The ultimate source is a passage in Book 4a.27 of *Mencius*, which Legge translates as follows: "The richest fruit of benevolence is this,—the service of one's parents. The richest fruit of righteousness is this,—the obeying one's elder brothers. . . . The richest fruit of music is this,—the rejoicing in those two things. When they are rejoiced in, they grow. Growing, how can they be repressed? When they come to this state that they cannot be repressed, then unconsciously the feet begin to dance and the hands to move." See Legge, *The Works of Mencius*, pp. 313–14. Here the order of the two clauses is reversed, but they appear in the same order as in the *Chin P'ing Mei* in the so-called Great Preface to the *Book of Songs*, a text of uncertain authorship and date, but of great significance in the history of Chinese literary criticism. Legge translates the relevant passage as follows: "The feelings move inwardly, and are embodied in words. When words are insufficient for them, recourse is had to sighs and exclamations. When sighs and exclamations are insufficient for them, recourse is had to the prolonged utterances of song. When those prolonged utterances of song are insufficient for them, unconsciously the hands begin to move and the feet to dance." See *The She King*, trans. James Legge (Hong Kong: Hong Kong University Press, 1960), prolegomena, p. 34, ll. 5–9. The same two lines recur in the *Chin P'ing Mei tz'u-hua*, vol. 3, ch. 60, p. 4b, l. 10.

44. The word translated here as "top" is the same word translated as "mons" above. See note 41. It should be pointed out that the word "furnace" is also used in Taoist physiological alchemy and in slang to mean "vagina."

45. The ultimate source of this couplet, with some textual variants, is a quatrain by the famous Sung painter Li T'ang (c. 1049–c. 1130). See *Sung-shih chi-shih*, *chüan* 44, p. 1140, l. 7. The whole poem occurs in *Yüan-ch'ü hsüan*, 4:1657, ll. 12–13. The same couplet recurs twice in the *Chin P'ing Mei tz'u-hua*, vol. 4, ch. 65, p. 16b, l. 6; and vol. 5, ch. 94, p. 11a, ll. 10–11.

CHAPTER 9

1. The proximate source of all but the last two lines of this lyric, with some textual variants, is the *Shui-hu ch'üan-chuan*, vol. 1, ch. 26, p. 407, ll. 7–8. The first couplet has already appeared in the *Chin P'ing Mei tz'u-hua*, vol. 1, ch. 6, p. 4a, l. 5. The second to last line occurs in *Yüan-ch'ü hsüan*, 2:820, ll. 6–7; 3:908, l. 10; *Yüan-ch'ü hsüan wai-pien*, 2:450, l. 11; and the *Shui-hu ch'üan-chuan*, vol. 2, ch. 35, p. 545, l. 3.

2. This four-character expression occurs in *[Chi-p'ing chiao-chu] Hsi-hsiang chi*, play no. 5, scene 3, p. 190, l. 12.

3. This proverbial couplet depends for its force on a pun between the word *yüan*, meaning "round," and the word *yüan*, meaning "garden." This couplet recurs in the *Chin P'ing Mei tzu-hua*, vol. 1, ch. 20, p. 3b, l. 2.

4. This formulaic four-character expression occurs ubiquitously in Chinese vernacular literature. See, e.g., *Chang Hsieh chuang-yüan*, p. 215, l. 15; *Huan-men tzu-ti ts'o li-shen*, p. 245, l. 6; *Yüan-ch'ü hsüan*, 3:1243, l. 14; and the *Shui-hu ch'üan-chuan*, vol. 2, ch. 45, p. 741, l. 16.

5. The proximate source of this set piece of descriptive parallel prose is the *Shui-hu ch'üan-chuan*, vol. 1, ch. 24, p. 357, ll. 3–4.

6. These four lines, with some textual variation, recur in the *Chin P'ing Mei tz'u-hua*, vol. 5, ch. 91, p. 4b, ll. 10–11.

7. These four lines, with some textual variants, recur in the *Chin P'ing Mei tz'u-hua*, vol. 4, ch. 77, p. 18a, ll. 3–4.

8. Yang Kuei-fei (719–56), the favorite of Emperor Hsüan-tsung (r. 712–56) of the T'ang dynasty, was said to have performed a dance upon an emerald disk. For a description of her dance in Yüan tsa-chü drama, see *Yüan-ch'ü hsüan*, 1:354–55.

9. This couplet recurs in the *Chin P'ing Mei tz'u-hua*, vol. 2, ch. 23, p. 12a, l. 7.

10. The proximate source of this quatrain is probably the *Shui-hu ch'üan-chuan*, vol. 1, ch. 23, p. 345, l. 2. It recurs twice in the *Chin P'ing Mei tz'u-hua*, vol. 1, ch. 18, p. 11b, ll. 2–3; and ch. 20, p. 7a, ll. 2–3. The second couplet also occurs independently. See *Sha-kou chi*, scene 18, p. 71, l. 4; *Chao-shih ku-erh chi*, *chüan* 1, scene 17, p. 32b, ll. 7–8; *P'o-yao chi*, *chüan* 1, scene 14, p. 41b, ll. 9–10; the anonymous Ming ch'uan-ch'i drama *Hsün-ch'in chi* (The quest for the father), *Liu-shih chung ch'ü* edition (Taipei: K'ai-ming shu-tien, 1970), scene 5, p. 14, l. 11; and scene 31, p. 100, l. 2; the Ming ch'uan-ch'i drama *Shuang-chung chi* (The loyal pair), by Yao Mao-liang (15th century), in *Ku-pen hsi-ch'ü ts'ung-k'an, ch'u-chi*, item 33, *chüan* 1, scene 14, p. 30a, l. 10; *Yü-chüeh chi*, scene 13, p. 42, l. 2; and *Shui-hu ch'üan-chuan*, vol. 3, ch. 61, p. 1025, l. 7.

11. The proximate source of this four-character expression is the corresponding passage in the *Shui-hu ch'üan-chuan*, vol. 1, ch. 26, p. 408, l. 7. It occurs frequently in Chinese vernacular literature. See, e.g., *P'i-p'a chi*, scene 33, p. 184, l. 9. It recurs three times in the *Chin P'ing Mei tz'u-hua*, vol. 3, ch. 59, p. 12b, l. 10; vol. 4, ch. 62, p. 1a, l. 7; and ch. 79, p. 19b, l. 7.

12. The proximate source of this proverbial couplet is the corresponding passage of the *Shui-hu ch'üan-chuan*, vol. 1, ch. 26, p. 408, l. 9. It is ubiquitous in Chinese vernacular literature. See, e.g., *Chang Hsieh chuang-yüan*, p. 152, l. 11; *Yüan-ch'ü hsüan*, 2:434, l. 1; *Pai-t'u chi*, scene 8, p. 25, l. 2; *P'i-p'a chi*, scene 20, p. 119, l. 15; *Ming-hsin pao-chien*, *chüan* 2, p. 1b, l. 2; *Chieh-chih-erh chi*, p. 256, l. 2; *San-kuo chih t'ung-su yen-i*, vol. 1, *chüan* 10, p. 471, ll. 14–15; and *Hsi-yu chi*, vol. 1, ch. 10, p. 104, l. 3. It also recurs in the *Shui-hu ch'üan-chuan*, vol. 4, ch. 101, p. 1573, l. 11; and the *Chin P'ing Mei tz'u-hua*, vol. 5, ch. 81, p. 4b, l. 2.

13. A possible source for this couplet is the second and fourth lines of a quatrain attributed to the Buddhist priest Hsüeh-feng (822–908) in Chüeh-lien's commentary on the *Chin-kang k'o-i*. See *[Hsiao-shih] Chin-kang k'o-i [hui-yao chu-chieh]*, *chüan* 1, p. 657, upper register, ll. 10–11. The same poem is quoted again in ibid., *chüan* 2, p. 673, middle register, ll. 13–14.

14. The proximate source of this proverbial saying is the corresponding passage in the *Shui-hu ch'üan-chuan*, vol. 1, ch. 26, p. 408, l. 10. Variants occur in ibid., vol. 2, ch. 51, p. 842, l. 1; and vol. 4, ch. 102, p. 1581, l. 6; and in *Chin-yin chi*, *chüan* 2, scene 19, p. 29a, l. 1. They also recur in the *Chin P'ing Mei tz'u-hua*, vol. 5, ch. 81, p. 4b, l. 2; and ch. 85, p. 10b, l. 4.

15. The proximate source of this set piece of descriptive parallel prose, with some textual variants, is the corresponding passage in the *Shui-hu ch'üan-chuan*, vol. 1, ch. 26, p. 409, ll. 7–8.

16. The proximate source of these three lines is the corresponding passage in the *Shui-hu ch'üan-chuan*, vol. 1, ch. 26, p. 413, l. 1. Variants of the first two lines occur

in a handbook of rules for administrative practice by Hu T'ai-ch'u (cs 1238), entitled *Chou-lien hsü-lun* (A preliminary discussion of diurnal routine), written 1235, published 1253, in *Shuo-fu*, vol. 2, *chüan* 89, p. 7b, l. 10; *Yüan-ch'ü hsüan*, 1:241, l. 16; 2:650, l. 3; 3:1011, ll. 19–20; and 4:1612, l. 1; and in the early and middle-period vernacular stories *Chien-t'ieh ho-shang*, p. 14, ll. 7–8; and *Jen Hsiao-tzu lieh-hsing wei shen*, p. 581, l. 6. A variant of the second and third lines occurs in *Yüan-ch'ü hsüan*, 3:1163, l. 14; and a variant of all three lines occurs in ibid., 4:1381, l. 10.

17. The proximate source of these four lines is the corresponding passage in the *Shui-hu ch'üan-chuan*, vol. 1, ch. 26, p. 413, l. 7. The same four lines, with minor textual variants, occur in the *Ming-hsin pao-chien*, *chüan* 2, p. 6a, ll. 10–11; *Sha-kou chi*, scene 7, p. 23, l. 10; and *Ta-T'ang Ch'in-wang tz'u-hua*, *chüan* 6, ch. 48, p. 67b, ll. 3–4; and *chüan* 8, ch. 58, p. 19a, ll. 5–6.

18. The first line of this couplet occurs as early as the T'ang dynasty, when it is said to have been a satirical catch-phrase current during the reign of Empress Wu (r. 684–705). See *Ch'ao-yeh ch'ien-tsai* (Comprehensive record of affairs within and without the court) comp. Chang Cho (cs 675) (Peking: Chung-hua shu-chü, 1979), *chüan* 1, p. 12, l. 8; and *Ch'üan T'ang shih*, vol. 12, *chüan* 878, p. 9943, l. 4. The two lines occur together, with some textual variation, in the early vernacular story entitled *Chi Ya-fan chin-man ch'an-huo* (Duty Group Leader Chi's golden eel engenders catastrophe), in *Ching-shih t'ung-yen*, *chüan* 20, p. 278, ll. 4–5. A variant of the same two lines recurs in the *Chin P'ing Mei tz'u-hua*, vol. 4, ch. 76, p. 18a, ll. 4–5.

CHAPTER 10

1. The proximate source of these eight lines of pentasyllabic verse, with some textual variation, is probably the *Shui-hu ch'üan-chuan*, vol. 2, ch. 45, p. 731, ll. 3–4. The same lines, with some textual variants, occur in the *Ming-hsin pao-chien*, *chüan* 2, p. 3b, ll. 9–11, where they are attributed to the Buddhist monk Tao-chi (1148–1209). Another version of the same lines, with some textual variation, occurs in the middle-period vernacular story entitled *Li Yüan Wu-chiang chiu chu-she* (Li Yüan saves a red snake on the Wu River), in *Ch'ing-p'ing shan-t'ang hua-pen*, p. 324, ll. 3–6.

2. A variant of this couplet occurs in *Yüan-ch'ü hsüan*, 4:1507, l. 21. It recurs in the *Chin P'ing Mei tz'u-hua*, vol. 5, ch. 92, p. 8b, ll. 6–7.

3. The proximate source of the name Ch'en Wen-chao is the corresponding passage in the *Shui-hu ch'üan-chuan*, vol. 2, ch. 27, p. 424, l. 11. There are two historical figures from whom the name may have been derived. One is Ch'en Lin (1312–68), usually referred to by his courtesy name as Ch'en Wen-chao, an honest and conscientious official of the Yüan dynasty, who may have been personally acquainted with Lo Kuan-chung, the putative author of the *Shui-hu chuan*, and Kao Ming, the author of the *P'i-p'a chi*. The other is a man of the same name who passed the *chin-shih* examinations in 1514 and was known in his day for his fearless opposition to the corrupt grand secretary Yen Sung (1480–1565). For a discussion of the first possibility and its ramifications, see Wang Li-ch'i, "Lo Kuan-chung yü *San-kuo chih t'ung-su yen-i*" (Lo Kuan-chung and *The romance of the Three Kingdoms*), in *San-kuo yen-i yen-chiu chi* (Collected studies on *The romance of the Three Kingdoms*) (Ch'eng-tu: Ssu-ch'uan sheng She-hui k'o-hsüeh yüan ch'u-pan she, 1983), pp. 240–47. For the

latter identification and a discussion of its possible significance for the date of composition of the *Chin P'ing Mei*, see Liu Chung-kuang, "*Chin P'ing Mei* jen-wu k'ao-lun" (A study of the historical figures in the *Chin P'ing Mei*), in Yeh Kuei-t'ung et al., eds., *Chin P'ing Mei tso-che chih mi* (The riddle of the authorship of the *Chin P'ing Mei*) (N.p.: Ning-hsia jen-min ch'u-pan she, 1988), pp. 152–54.

4. It is reported of Sun K'ang (5th century) that he was so poor as a youth that he pursued his studies at night by the moonlight reflected from the snow. See *Nan shih* (History of the Southern dynasties), comp. Li Yen-shou (7th century), completed in 659, 6 vols. (Peking: Chung-hua shu-chü, 1975), vol. 5, *chüan* 57, p. 1420, ll. 11–12.

5. The Palace of Golden Bells was the name of an audience hall in the imperial palace compound of the T'ang dynasty. It was located next to the Han-lin Academy and was a place where brilliant young scholars from that institution might be summoned for interrogation by the emperor.

6. These are actions reportedly taken by the local populace to show their reluctance to let them go when Hou Pa (d. A.D. 37) and Yao Ch'ung (651–721), two honest and capable officials, were ordered to leave their posts. See *Hou-Han shu*, vol. 4, *chüan* 26, p. 901, l. 12; and *K'ai-yüan T'ien-pao i-shih* (Forgotten events of the K'ai-yüan [713–41] and T'ien-pao [742–56] reign periods), comp. Wang Jen-yü (880–942), in *K'ai-yüan T'ien-pao i-shih shih-chung* (Ten works dealing with forgotten events of the K'ai-yüan and T'ien-pao reign periods), ed. Ting Ju-ming (Shanghai: Shang-hai ku-chi ch'u-pan she, 1985), *chüan* 1, p. 66, ll. 2–3.

7. The proximate source of this set piece of descriptive parallel prose, with a few textual variants, is the corresponding passage in the *Shui-hu ch'üan-chuan*, vol. 2, ch. 27, p. 424, ll. 12–14. The same passage occurs in the *San Sui p'ing-yao chuan*, *chüan* 3, ch. 11, p. 6b, ll. 4–8; and a very similar passage occurs in the *Hsi-yu chi*, vol. 2, ch. 97, p. 1090, ll. 13–14.

8. For this article of the Ming penal code, see *Ming-tai lü-li hui-pien* (Comprehensive edition of the Ming penal code and judicial regulations), comp. Huang Chang-chien, 2 vols. (Taipei: Academia Sinica, 1979), vol. 2, *chüan* 19, p. 807, l. 2.

9. The third year of the Cheng-ho reign period corresponds to the year 1113.

10. I have added Lai-wang's name here because, by his own testimony later in the text, he was one of those who went to the Eastern Capital on this occasion. See *Chin P'ing Mei tz'u-hua*, vol. 2, ch. 25, pp. 6b–7a.

11. This four-character expression recurs in the *Chin P'ing Mei tz'u-hua*, vol. 2, ch. 26, p. 9a, l. 6.

12. This couplet recurs in the *Chin P'ing Mei tz'u-hua*, vol. 2, ch. 26, p. 10a, ll. 9–10.

13. The proximate source of this quatrain, with some textual variants, is the *Shui-hu ch'üan-chuan*, vol. 2, ch. 30, p. 467, l. 2. The same quatrain recurs, with some textual variation, in the *Chin P'ing Mei tz'u-hua* vol. 2, ch. 26, pp. 10a–10b.

14. Hsiang-chou is an ancient name for a region in the far southwest of China located in what are now Kwangsi and Kweichow provinces. For a good discussion of its exotic connotations, see Edward H. Schafer, *The Vermilion Bird: T'ang Images of the South* (Berkeley: University of California Press, 1967), pp. 95–96.

15. Ho-p'u, on the coast of Kwangsi province, has been since classical times the most famous pearl fishery in China. For more information on this subject, see ibid., pp. 160–61.

16. The four-character phrase that I have translated "gray mullet large enough to swallow an official seal" first occurs in a poem by Su Shih (1037–1101). See *Su Shih shih-chi* (Collected poetry of Su Shih), 8 vols. (Peking: Chung-hua shu-chü, 1982), vol. 4, *chüan* 21, p. 1092, l. 3. There was an extended controversy during the Southern Sung dynasty over the interpretation of the phrase and whether or not Su Shih had used it correctly. See *Jung-chai sui-pi* (Miscellaneous notes from the Tolerant Study), by Hung Mai (1123–1202), 2 vols. (Shanghai: Shang-hai ku-chi ch'u-pan she, 1978), vol. 2, collection no. 4, *chüan* 8, pp. 704–5.

17. The ultimate source of these two lines is a rhyming couplet quoted in the *Lo-yang ch'ieh-lan chi* (A record of Buddhist monasteries in Lo-yang), by Yang Hsüan-chih (6th century), completed c. 547. See *Lo-yang ch'ieh-lan chi chiao-chu* (A critical edition of A *record of Buddhist monasteries in Lo-yang*), ed. Fan Hsiang-yung (Shanghai: Ku-tien wen-hsüeh ch'u-pan she, 1958), *chüan* 3, p. 161, l. 6; and *A Record of Buddhist Monasteries in Lo-yang*, trans. Yi-t'ung Wang (Princeton: Princeton University Press, 1984), p. 151.

18. "Phoenix tablets" were round cakes of brick tea of the highest grade embossed with the stamped image of a phoenix and prepared for imperial consumption.

19. See chapter 1, note 45.

20. See note 2 to the prefatory lyrics before chapter 1.

21. This formulaic four-character expression occurs as early as the T'ang dynasty. See *Wei-mo-chieh ching chiang-ching wen* (Sutra lecture on the *Vimalakīrti sutra*), text no. 1, in *Tun-huang pien-wen chi*, 2:541, l. 2. It also occurs in *Pai Niang-tzu yung-chen Lei-feng T'a*, p. 437, l. 6; and *Hsiu-ju chi*, scene 7, p. 17, l. 10.

22. The proximate source of the character Liang Shih-chieh and the information given about him here is the *Shui-hu ch'üan-chuan*, vol. 1, ch. 12, p. 182, ll. 12–13.

23. This date would correspond to February 24, 1111, in the Western calendar. The text actually reads "the third year of the Cheng-ho reign period," which would correspond to the year 1113, but this does not fit the chronology of the novel. I have therefore emended "third" to "first."

24. This raid on Ta-ming Prefecture and the burning of the Blue Cloud Tavern are described in chapter 66 of the *Shui-hu ch'üan-chuan*, but they are there described as taking place on the fifteenth day of the first month of the year 1120, and it is not Li K'uei but Tu Ch'ien and Sung Wan who "slaughter the entire household" of Privy Councilor Liang Shih-chieh. See *Shui-hu ch'üan-chuan*, vol. 3, ch. 66, p. 1128, l. 16.

25. Until quite late in the Ming dynasty the term "Western Ocean" was used to designate the western part of what are now called the South China Sea and the Indian Ocean.

26. There was a tradition that before becoming the founding emperor of the Sung dynasty in 960, Chao K'uang-yin (927–76) formed a club of ten sworn brothers. See, e.g., *Wen-chien chin-lu* (Recent records of things heard and seen), by Wang Kung (1048–c. 1102), fac. repr. of Sung ed. (Peking: Chung-hua shu-chü, 1984), p. 24b, ll. 3–10; and Djang and Djang, *A Compilation of Anecdotes of Sung Personalities*, pp. 8–9. This tradition is also alluded to in Yüan tsa-chü drama. See *Yüan-ch'ü hsüan wai-pien*, 3:981, l. 5. This could be the inspiration for the ironic use of the same theme in the *Chin P'ing Mei*, and is but one of many indications that Hsi-men Ch'ing is intended to play the role of a surrogate emperor.

27. For an early occurrence of this four-character expression, see *Yüan-ch'ü hsüan*, 3:1134, l. 17.

28. This quatrain, with considerable textual variation, occurs in *Chin-yin chi*, *chüan* 1, scene 5, p. 6b, l. 9. A variant of the second couplet recurs in the *Chin P'ing Mei tz'u-hua*, vol. 2, ch. 27, p. 9a, l. 4.

29. The instrument in question is a fipple flute, like a flageolet or recorder, rather than a transverse flute.

30. This four-character expression means either "to refer to something circuitously" or "to promise more than one can deliver," since pointing to the mountain merely indicates the location of the cliff out of which the stone might be quarried from which the promised millstone might be made. Variants of this expression occur in *Yüan-ch'ü hsüan*, 2:491, l. 7; and 4:1416, l. 5; *Ch'üan Yüan san-ch'ü*, 2:1784, l. 12; and *Tz'u-nüeh*, p. 287, l. 6.

31. This couplet recurs twice, with minor textual variation, in the *Chin P'ing Mei tz'u-hua*, vol. 4, ch. 74, p. 2a, ll. 9–10; and vol. 5, ch. 82, p. 6a, ll. 1–2. The first line also recurs in ibid., vol. 3, ch. 51, p. 22a, ll. 6–7.

32. A slightly different version of the same lyric recurs in the *Chin P'ing Mei tz'u-hua*, vol. 1, ch. 17, p. 2a, ll. 8–11.

33. This couplet recurs twice in the *Chin P'ing Mei tz'u-hua*, vol. 3, ch. 59, p. 7b, ll. 10–11; and vol. 5, ch. 97, p. 11a, l. 11.

CHAPTER 11

1. The Cold Food Festival is celebrated 105 days after the winter solstice, and the Lantern Festival on the fifteenth day of the first lunar month. For a succinct description of these festivals, see Tun Li-ch'en (1855–1911), *Annual Customs and Festivals in Peking*, trans. and annot. Derk Bodde (Hong Kong: Hong Kong University Press, 1965), pp. 6–9 and 26–27.

2. This stanza of hexasyllabic doggerel is notable for the ironic deployment of a cliché as the climax, or anticlimax, of every line.

3. For an early occurrence of this four-character expression, see *[Chi-p'ing chiao-chu] Hsi-hsiang chi*, play no. 2, scene 3, p. 73, l. 14; and West and Idema, *The Moon and the Zither*, p. 253, l. 4.

4. This four-character expression recurs in the *Chin P'ing Mei tz'u-hua*, vol. 2, ch. 25, p. 7b, l. 5.

5. The Chinese word for the lugs or handles on basins and jugs is the same as the word for ear. Variants of this expression occur in *Yüan-ch'ü hsüan*, 2:494, l. 12; *Shui-hu ch'üan-chuan*, vol. 3, ch. 78, p. 1298, l. 2; and vol. 4, ch. 99, p. 1556, ll. 15–16. It recurs in the *Chin P'ing Mei tz'u-hua*, vol. 5, ch. 85, p. 4b, l. 2.

6. This expression occurs in an early Ming list of slang terms then in use in the brothels of Nanking. See *Chin-ling liu-yüan shih-yü* (Market argot of the six licensed brothels of Chin-ling), in *Han-shang huan wen-ts'un*, p. 130, l. 8.

7. This expression occurs in *Yüan-ch'ü hsüan*, 1:210, l. 8. It recurs in the *Chin P'ing Mei tz'u-hua*, vol. 4, ch. 62, p. 24b, ll. 5–6.

8. A variant of these two lines recurs in the *Chin P'ing Mei tz'u-hua*, vol. 4, ch. 69, p. 17a, l. 6.

9. This four-character expression occurs in *Yüan-ch'ü hsüan*, 3:1065, l. 21. It recurs in the *Chin P'ing Mei tz'u-hua*, vol. 5, ch. 83, p. 10a, l. 9.

10. This four-character expression occurs as early as the third century. See *San-kuo chih* (History of the Three Kingdoms), comp. Ch'en Shou (233–97), 5 vols. (Peking: Chung-hua shu-chü, 1973), vol. 5, *chüan* 57, p. 1331, l. 11.

11. A variant of these two lines recurs in the *Chin P'ing Mei tz'u-hua*, vol. 4, ch. 75, p. 25a, l. 8.

12. Variants of this expression recur twice in the *Chin P'ing Mei tz'u-hua*, vol. 4, ch. 75, p. 24a, l. 3; and p. 27a, l. 10.

13. It is an ancient Taoist belief that the consumption of grain engenders within the body of every individual the Three Worms, also called the Three Corpses, transcendent spirits that consume his vitality and lead eventually to death. See Maspero, *Taoism and Chinese Religion*, pp. 331–38.

14. The Five Viscera are the lungs, heart, spleen, liver, and kidneys, each of which is presided over by a god of its own.

15. Variants of these two lines recur twice in the *Chin P'ing Mei tz'u-hua*, vol. 3, ch. 59, p. 12a, l. 6; and vol. 4, ch. 75, p. 10b, ll. 9–10.

16. The second couplet of this quatrain occurs ubiquitously in Chinese vernacular literature. See, e.g., *Huan-men tzu-ti ts'o li-shen*, p. 237, l. 1; and *P'i-p'a chi*, p. 103, l. 4. It recurs three times in the *Chin P'ing Mei tz'u-hua*, vol. 3, ch. 56, p. 6b, ll. 4–5; vol. 4, ch. 62, p. 14a, l. 4; and vol. 5, ch. 86, p. 8b, l. 11.

17. This four-character expression occurs in Yüan tsa-chü drama. See *[Chiao-ting] Yüan-k'an tsa-chü san-shih chung*, p. 266, ll. 4–5. It recurs three times in the *Chin P'ing Mei tz'u-hua*, vol. 3, ch. 59, p. 11a, l. 2; vol. 5, ch. 81, p. 8b, l. 8; and ch. 85, p. 10a, l. 2.

18. The following passage about the ten members of Hsi-men Ch'ing's club largely replicates a passage that has already occurred in ch. 10, pp. 200–201. The most likely explanation of this redundancy is that the author had experimented with inserting this material in two different places and had not made up his mind which place to put it before he lost control of the manuscript.

19. This four-character expression occurs ubiquitously in Chinese vernacular literature. See, e.g., *Yüan-ch'ü hsüan*, 1:99, l. 4; *Yüan-ch'ü hsüan wai-pien*, 1:130, ll. 17–18; *Yung-hsi yüeh-fu*, *ts'e* 5, p. 22b, l. 2; and *Pao-chien chi*, scene 26, p. 47, l. 6. It recurs in the *Chin P'ing Mei tz'u-hua*, vol. 2, ch. 35, p. 1a, l. 9.

20. The three-character expression that I have expanded into "talking his way into the brothels in the licensed quarter without purchasing their wares" is defined in *Chin-ling liu-yüan shih-yü*, p. 129, l. 10.

21. Emperor Hsüan-tsung (r. 712–56) of the T'ang dynasty established an institution for training male and female musicians that was located in a part of the palace precincts adjacent to a pear garden. In subsequent times male and female professional actors and musicians came to be conventionally referred to as "children of the Pear Garden."

22. The proximate source of this set piece of descriptive parallel prose, with minor textual variants, is the *Shui-hu ch'üan-chuan*, vol. 2, ch. 51, p. 840, ll. 7–9.

23. Variants of this idiomatic expression occur ubiquitously in Chinese vernacular literature. See, e.g., *Yüan-ch'ü hsüan*, 1:109, l. 3; 2:476, l. 20; and 3:890, l. 21; *Hsün-ch'in chi*, scene 14, p. 46, l. 11; and *Hsiu-ju chi*, scene 19, p. 51, l. 10.

24. A variant of the last line occurs in the *Pao-chien chi*, scene 17, p. 34, l. 21.

25. This song is by T'ang Shih (fl. late 14th–early 15th centuries). See *Ch'üan Yüan san-ch'ü*, 2:1553, ll. 2–3. Versions of the same song also occur in *Yung-hsi*

yüeh-fu, ts'e 18, p. 49a, ll. 6–9; and *Pei-kung tz'u-chi wai-chi* (Supplementary collection to northern-style song lyrics), comp. Ch'en So-wen (d. c. 1604), 3 *chüan*, in *Nan-pei kung tz'u-chi [chiao-pu]* (Southern- and northern-style song lyrics [collated and augmented], comp. Wu Hsiao-ling (Peking: Chung-hua shu-chü, 1961), *chüan* 2, p. 29, ll. 8–9. The version in the *Chin P'ing Mei tz'u-hua* is slightly closer to that in the *Yung-hsi yüeh-fu* than to the other two versions, although the differences are not great.

26. Liu Ling (3rd century) is one of the "Seven Worthies of the Bamboo Grove," a famous coterie of eccentric intellectuals, and is chiefly renowned for his drinking. See Mather, *Shih-shuo Hsin-yü*, pp. 128–30 and 372–74.

27. This poem is by the famous T'ang poet Li Ho (791–817). See *Ch'üan T'ang shih*, vol. 6, *chüan* 393, p. 4434, ll. 7–8; and *The Poems of Li Ho*, trans. J. D. Frodsham (Oxford: Oxford University Press, 1970), p. 239. Versions of the same poem also occur in *Hsüan-ho i-shih*, p. 52, ll. 3–5; *[Hsin-pien] Wu-tai shih p'ing-hua*, p. 18, ll. 2–4; and *Hsi-hu san-t'a chi*, p. 27, ll. 6–7.

28. The locus classicus for this four-character expression is a famous essay by Ou-yang Hsiu (1007–72) entitled *Tsui-weng t'ing chi* (The old drunkard's pavilion), written in 1046. See *Ou-yang Hsiu wen hsüan-tu* (Selected readings in Ou-yang Hsiu's literary prose), ed. Ch'en P'u-ch'ing (Ch'ang-sha: Yüeh-lu shu-she, 1984), p. 274, l. 1; and Ronald C. Egan, *The Literary Works of Ou-yang Hsiu* (Cambridge: Cambridge University Press, 1984), p. 216, l. 33.

29. See chapter 2, note 47.

30. The source of this song, with some textual variation, is scene 6 of the *Yü-huan chi*, where it is sung by the virtuous hero in praise of a courtesan with a heart of gold with whom he is falling in love. See *Yü-huan chi*, scene 6, p. 21, ll. 2–4. In the novel the author uses it ironically by putting it into the mouth of an enterprising young prostitute bent on attracting a rich patron.

31. The proximate source of this quatrain is probably the *Yü-chüeh chi*, scene 22, p. 71, ll. 2–3. It recurs in the *Chin P'ing Mei tz'u-hua*, vol. 4, ch. 76, p. 20b, ll. 1–2.

CHAPTER 12

1. The proximate source of the first and last couplets of this stanza of hexasyllabic verse is probably the *Yü-chüeh chi*, scene 8, p. 25, ll. 10–11. The last line occurs in a tsa-chü drama attributed to Wang Shih-fu (13th century), the author of the *Hsi-hsiang chi*. See *T'ai-ho cheng-yin p'u* (Formulary for the correct sounds of great harmony), comp. Chu Ch'üan (1378–1448), in *Chung-kuo ku-tien hsi-ch'ü lun-chu chi-ch'eng*, 3:177, l. 6. Variants of this line occur in *Yüan-ch'ü hsüan*, 1:378, l. 3; and the Yüan-Ming ch'uan-ch'i drama entitled *Ching-ch'ai chi* (The thorn hairpin), *Liu-shih chung ch'ü* edition (Taipei: K'ai-ming shu-tien, 1970), scene 31, p. 98, l. 11. Variants recur in the *Chin P'ing Mei tz'u-hua*, vol. 3, ch. 43, p. 14b, l. 9; and vol. 5, ch. 86, p. 14a, l. 6.

2. This four-character expression occurs in *Chang Yü-hu su nü-chen kuan chi*, p. 15b, l. 1.

3. The Phoenix Terrace alludes to a story in the *Lieh-hsien chuan* (Biographies of immortals), traditionally attributed to Liu Hsiang (79–8 B.C.), in which Nung-yü, the daughter of Duke Mu of Ch'in (r. 659–621 B.C.), fell in love with and married a

flautist named Hsiao-shih who taught her to play the flute so skillfully that phoenixes came down to roost on their dwelling. The duke consequently built the Phoenix Terrace for them, from which they did not descend for several years, until one day they flew off into the sky with the phoenixes they had attracted by their flute playing. See *Le Lie-sien Tchouan*, trans. Max Kaltenmark (Peking: Université de Paris, Publications du Centre d'études sinologiques de Pékin, 1953), pp. 125–27.

4. This four-character expression occurs in a lyric by Hsin Ch'i-chi (1140–1207) written in the year 1175; see *Ch'üan Sung tz'u*, 3:1870, lower register, l. 5; in a song suite by Kuan Yün-shih (1286–1324); see *Ch'üan Yüan san-ch'ü*, 1:383, l. 8; in *Yüan-ch'ü hsüan*, 2:851, l. 2; in *Chang Yü-hu wu-su nü-chen kuan*, scene 4, p. 624, l. 7; and in the *Shui-hu ch'üan-chuan*, vol. 1, ch. 21, p. 306, l. 13.

5. This formulaic four-character expression is ubiquitous in Chinese vernacular literature. See, e.g., *Yüan-ch'ü hsüan*, 2:500, l. 14; *San-kuo chih t'ung-su yen-i*, vol. 1, *chüan* 6, p. 297, l. 20; and *Shui-hu ch'üan-chuan* vol. 1, ch. 2, p. 30, l. 6.

6. This anonymous song appears in *Yung-hsi yüeh-fu*, *ts'e* 20, pp. 35a–35b. The two versions are identical.

7. This song also appears in *Yung-hsi yüeh-fu*, *ts'e* 20, p. 35b, ll. 7–8. In *Ts'ai-pi ch'ing-tz'u* (Emotive lyrics from variegated brushes), comp. Chang Hsü, pref. dated 1624, fac. repr. in *Shan-pen hsi-ch'ü ts'ung-k'an* (Collectanea of rare editions of works on dramatic prosody), vols. 75–76 (Taipei: Hsüeh-sheng shu-chü, 1987), vol. 76, *chüan* 12, pp. 13a–13b, this song is attributed to the Yüan dynasty lyricist Lu Chih (cs 1268). See *Ch'üan Yüan san-ch'ü*, 1:132, l. 2. The fact that these two songs appear on the recto and verso of the same page in *Yung-hsi yüeh-fu*, and that the versions found there are identical to those in the *Chin P'ing Mei tz'u-hua*, make it the most likely proximate source.

8. A version of this anonymous song, with some textual variation, appears in *Yung-hsi yüeh-fu*, *ts'e* 18, p. 21a, ll. 3–5.

9. The word translated as "covered drain" may also be used to refer to the female pudendum.

10. Sun Ssu-miao (581–682) is a famous figure in the history of Chinese alchemy and medicine who has become a Taoist immortal in the popular tradition. For a classic study of the meager biographical facts pertaining to his career, see Nathan Sivin, *Chinese Alchemy: Preliminary Studies* (Cambridge: Harvard University Press, 1968), pp. 81–144. For his iconographic association with a tiger, see Anne Swann Goodrich, *The Peking Temple of the Eastern Peak* (Nagoya: Monumenta Serica, 1964), pp. 91–92.

11. The expression "to devour people," literally "to devour [people] for nothing," means "to sponge" and puns with Ying Po-chüeh's given name. Shorter versions of this joke appear in two Ming compilations. See *Chieh-yün pien* (An anger-dispelling collection), comp. Lo-t'ien Ta-hsiao sheng allegedly printed in the Chia-ching reign period (1522–66), in *Li-tai hsiao-hua chi hsü-pien* (Continuation of *Jokes of successive ages*), comp. Wang Chen-min and Wang Li-ch'i (Shen-yang: Ch'un-feng wen-i ch'u-pan she, 1985), *chüan* 5, p. 38, ll. 18–20; and *Shih-shang hsiao-t'an* (Jokes currently in vogue), printed in the middle register of *chüan* 1 of *Yao-t'ien yüeh* (The music of Yao's reign), comp. Yin Ch'i-sheng (Chien-yang: Hsiung Jen-huan, late Wan-li [1573–1620]), fac. repr. in *Shan-pen hsi-ch'ü ts'ung-k'an*, vol. 8, *chüan* 1, pp. 31b–32b, middle register.

12. This four-character expression occurs in *Yüan-ch'ü hsüan wai-pien*, 1:67, l. 10; and 2:470, ll. 6–7.

13. The locus classicus for this four-character expression is a speech attributed to Ch'un-yü K'un (4th century B.C.). See *Shih-chi*, vol. 10, *chüan* 126, p. 3199, l. 7; and Yang and Yang, *Records of the Historian*, p. 405, l. 17. It also occurs in the *Hsi-hsiang chi*. See *[Chi-p'ing chiao-chu] Hsi-hsiang chi*, play no. 4, scene 3, p. 160, l. 9; and West and Idema, *The Moon and the Zither*, p. 354, l. 3.

14. For an early occurrence of this fanciful title, together with an explanation of how it was earned, see *Yüan-ch'ü hsüan*, 2:517, ll. 3–5.

15. The expression "Temple of the Five Viscera" is used here as a humorous euphemism for the stomach and digestive system. On the Five Viscera, see chapter 11, note 14.

16. The term *ching-kuang*, which I have translated "Purifying Light," puns with an expression meaning "completely" in the sense of "to polish off completely." There is, of course, no Buddha of this name. But if the character *kuang* is a copyist's error for the character *fan*, which it somewhat resembles graphically, this would produce one form of the name for Śuddhodana, the king of Kapilavastu and father of Śākyamuni Buddha, whose name in its more common orthography could be misunderstood to mean "The Buddha King Who Polishes Off the Food." See William Edward Soothill and Lewis Hodous, A *Dictionary of Chinese Buddhist Terms* (London: Kegan Paul, Trench, Trubner & Co., 1937), p. 358, left column, ll. 14–15; and right column, ll. 26–27.

17. This proverbial couplet occurs in the *Hsi-yu chi*, vol. 1, ch. 10, p. 104, l. 8. It also recurs three times in the *Chin P'ing Mei tz'u-hua*, vol. 2, ch. 23, p. 5a, l. 5; ch. 25, p. 7a, ll. 4–5; and vol. 4, ch. 62, p. 5a, l. 4.

18. For this couplet, which has become proverbial, see *[Chi-p'ing chiao-chu] Hsi-hsiang chi*, play no. 3, scene 2, p. 113, l. 5; and West and Idema, *The Moon and the Zither*, p. 301, ll. 19–21. The second line occurs independently in *Yüan-ch'ü hsüan*, 1:279, l. 14. The couplet recurs in the *Chin P'ing Mei tz'u-hua*, vol. 4, ch. 76, p. 3b, l. 11.

19. This couplet recurs twice in the *Chin P'ing Mei tz'u-hua*, vol. 4, ch. 80, p. 4b, l. 11; and vol. 5, ch. 98, p. 8a, l. 3.

20. The proximate source of this set piece of descriptive parallel prose, with some textual variation, is the *Shui-hu ch'üan-chuan*, vol. 2, ch. 45, p. 739, ll. 9–12. A very similar passage occurs in the unexpurgated edition of the middle-period vernacular story entitled *Yüeh-ming Ho-shang tu Liu Ts'ui* (The Monk Yüeh-ming converts Liu Ts'ui), in *Ku-chin hsiao-shuo*, 2 vols., fac. repr. of original edition published in 1620–24 (Taipei: Shih-chieh shu-chü, 1958), vol. 2, *chüan* 29, p. 5b, ll. 2–6. A slightly different version of the same passage occurs in the retelling of the above story in *San-pao t'ai-chien Hsi-yang chi t'ung-su yen-i*, vol. 2, ch. 92, p. 1186, ll. 2–4. Another close analogue of this passage recurs in the *Chin P'ing Mei tz'u-hua*, vol. 5, ch. 83, p. 9b, ll. 3–8. The ultimate source of the last couplet is probably a quatrain by the Buddhist monk Chih-ts'ung (10th century) that is quoted in the *Shih-erh hsiao-ming lu shih-i* (Addendum to the *Record of courtesans' professional names*), comp. Chang Pang-chi (12th century), in *Pai-hai* (Sea of fiction), comp. Shang Chün (fl. 1593–1619), fac. repr., 5 vols. (Taipei: Hsin-hsing shu-chü, 1968), 2:8a–8b (1233). Other versions of this couplet occur in *Yüan-ch'ü hsüan* 3:1240, l. 6; *Wu-chieh Ch'an-shih*

ssu Hung-lien chi, p. 141, l. 1; *Yüeh-ming Ho-shang tu Liu Ts'ui*, p. 432, l. 9; and *San-pao t'ai-chien Hsi-yang chi t'ung-su yen-i*, vol. 2, ch. 92, p. 1187, l. 10.

21. This four-character expression is ubiquitous in Chinese vernacular literature. See, e.g., *Hsi-yu chi*, vol. 2, ch. 83, p. 950, l. 1.

22. The locus classicus for this proverbial couplet, with some textual variation, is a remonstrance addressed to Liu Pi (213–154 B.C.), the Prince of Wu, by Mei Ch'eng (d. 141 B.C.), who endeavored unsuccessfully to dissuade him from undertaking the disastrous revolt of 155 B.C. See *Han-shu*, vol. 5, *chüan* 51, p. 2360, l. 6. It occurs in the same form as in the novel in *K'an p'i-hsüeh tan-cheng Erh-lang Shen*, p. 248, l. 16. Variants occur in *Ching-ch'ai chi*, scene 46, p. 132, l. 9; *Sha-kou chi*, scene 14, p. 53, l. 10; *Ming-hsin pao-chien, chüan* 1, p. 6a, l. 2; *San-kuo chih t'ung-su yen-i, chüan* 11, p. 519, l. 10; and *Ch'ien-chin chi*, scene 42, p. 134, ll. 9–10. It recurs twice in the *Chin P'ing Mei tz'u-hua*, vol. 4, ch. 69, p. 18b, l. 3; and ch. 77, p. 17a, l. 3.

23. This formulaic couplet occurs ubiquitously in Chinese vernacular literature. See, e.g., *Chang Hsieh chuang-yüan*, p. 3, l. 15; *Ch'i-kuo ch'un-ch'iu p'ing-hua* (The p'ing-hua on the events of the seven states), originally published in 1321–23 (Shanghai: Ku-tien wen-hsüeh ch'u-pan she, 1955), p. 53, l. 5; and p. 75, ll. 12–13; *[Hsin-pien] Wu-tai shih p'ing-hua*, p. 27, l. 14; *Hua Kuan So jen-fu chuan*, p. 7b, l. 9; and *Shui-hu ch'üan-chuan*, vol. 2, ch. 31, p. 485, ll. 3–4.

24. Variants of this formulaic couplet are ubiquitous in Chinese vernacular literature. See, e.g., *Yüan-ch'ü hsüan*, 2:639, ll. 17–18; and p. 745, l. 9; *San-kuo chih t'ung-su yen-i, chüan* 10, p. 456, l. 13; *Shui-hu ch'üan-chuan*, vol. 2, ch. 39, p. 624, l. 14; and *San Sui p'ing-yao chuan, chüan* 1, ch. 5, p. 54a, l. 2.

25. The four-character expression that I have translated "guilty of a clear-cut violation of Heaven's law" occurs in *Pao-chien chi*, scene 14, p. 28, l. 20.

26. This four-character expression recurs in the *Chin P'ing Mei tz'u-hua*, vol. 4, ch. 72, p. 17b, l. 5.

27. The idiomatic expression that I have translated as "preposterous" literally means "a Heaven without a sun." A variant of this expression occurs in *Yüan-ch'ü hsüan*, 4:1523, l. 8.

28. This four-character expression occurs in the long literary tales entitled *Chiao Hung chuan* (The story of Chiao-niang and Fei-hung), by Sung Yüan (14th century), in *Ku-tai wen-yen tuan-p'ien hsiao-shuo hsüan-chu, erh-chi* (An annotated selection of classic literary tales, second collection), ed. Ch'eng Po-ch'üan (Shanghai: Shanghai ku-chi ch'u-pan she, 1984), p. 289, ll. 8–9; and *Huai-ch'un ya-chi, chüan* 10, p. 34a, l. 14, upper register.

29. This four-character expression occurs ubiquitously in Chinese vernacular literature. See, e.g., *Shui-hu ch'üan-chuan*, vol. 2, ch. 51, p. 841, l. 10; and vol. 3, ch. 65, p. 1110, l. 11. It recurs in the *Chin P'ing Mei tz'u-hua*, vol. 4, ch. 62, p. 12a, l. 9.

30. This four-character expression recurs in the *Chin P'ing Mei tz'u-hua*, vol. 4, ch. 76, p. 4b ll. 1–2.

31. This four-character expression recurs in the *Chin P'ing Mei tz'u-hua*, vol. 5, ch. 93, p. 9b, l. 3.

32. This idiomatic four-character expression was in use as early as the time of Chu Hsi (1130–1200). See *Chu-tzu yü-lei*, vol. 1, *chüan* 12, p. 3a, l. 5. It occurs ubiquitously in Chinese vernacular literature. See, e.g., *Yüan-ch'ü hsüan*, 3:1,073, l. 7; and *Hsi-yu chi*, vol. 1, ch. 36, p. 410, l. 5.

33. The ultimate source of this couplet, with minor textual variation, is a poem by Po Chü-i (772–846). See *Ch'üan T'ang shih*, vol. 7, *chüan* 426, p. 4694, l. 7. It has become proverbial and occurs in many works of Chinese vernacular literature. See, e.g., *Chin-yin chi, chüan* 1, scene 8, p. 16b, l. 7; and *San-yüan chi* (Feng Ching [1021–94] wins first place in three examinations), by Shen Shou-hsien (15th century) *Liu-shih chung ch'ü* edition (Taipei: K'ai-ming shu-tien, 1970), scene 3, p. 8, l. 5; and scene 9, p. 22, ll. 6–7. The first line occurs independently in *Pai-t'u chi*, scene 12, p. 40, l. 1. A variant of this couplet also recurs in the *Chin P'ing Mei tz'u-hua*, vol. 2, ch. 38, p. 10b, l. 4.

34. There is a historical figure named Wu K'ai who was a native of Yang-ku district in Shantung province and who passed the *chin-shih* examinations in 1514. See Liu Chung-kuang, "*Chin P'ing Mei* jen-wu k'ao-lun," pp. 158–59.

35. For another occurrence of this idiom by a contemporary of the author of the *Chin P'ing Mei*, see Feng Wei-min, *Hai-fu shan-t'ang tz'u-kao, chüan* 1, p. 36, l. 6.

36. There is a minor character named Chou Hsiu in the *Hsüan-ho i-shih*, the proprietor of a tea shop in the capital who identifies Li Shih-shih, the famous courtesan, to Emperor Hui-tsung, who later rewards him with an official post. See *Hsüan-ho i-shih*, pp. 50 and 63. Although his story does not correspond with that of Commandant Chou Hsiu in the novel, it has been suggested that the author may have chosen his name because it was associated with the illicit sex-life and favoritism of Emperor Hui-tsung. See Liu Chung-kuang, "*Chin P'ing Mei* jen-wu k'ao-lun," pp. 111–12.

37. Fan K'uai (d. 189 B.C.) is a historical figure who is chiefly remembered for barging into a banquet in 206 B.C. at which his master Liu Pang, the founder of the Han dynasty, was in danger of assassination, and thereby saving his life. For his biography, see *Shih-chi*, vol. 8, *chüan* 95, pp. 2651–60. The fullest account of the incident in question has been translated in Watson, *Records of the Grand Historian of China*, 1:49–55. A variant of this proverbial expression occurs in the *Hsüan-ho i-shih*, p. 53, l. 10. Variants recur three times in the *Chin P'ing Mei tz'u-hua*, vol. 1, ch. 17, p. 6b, l. 8; vol. 4, ch. 69, p. 11b, l. 6; and vol. 5, ch. 93, p. 2a, ll. 2–3.

38. Variants of these four lines of proverbial wisdom occur together in the *Ming-hsin pao-chien, chüan* 1, p. 1b, ll. 11–12; the *Shui-hu ch'üan-chuan*, vol. 2, ch. 31, p. 474, l. 6; and the middle-period vernacular stories *Jen Hsiao-tzu lieh-hsing wei shen*, p. 578, l. 13; and *Shen Hsiao-kuan i-niao hai ch'i-ming* (Master Shen's bird destroys seven lives), in *Ku-chin Hsiao-shuo*, vol. 2, *chüan* 26, p. 399, l. 13. For an English translation of this story under the title "The Canary Murders," see Birch, *Stories from a Ming Collection*, pp. 155–71. The passage in question is on p. 167, ll. 19–22.

39. The locus classicus for this expression is the punch line from a famous passage in Book 17 of the *Lun-yü*, which is translated by Arthur Waley as follows: "The Master said, How could one ever possibly serve one's prince alongside of such low-down creatures? Before they have got office, they think about nothing but how to get it; and when they have got it, all they care about is to avoid losing it. And so soon as they see themselves in the slightest danger of losing it, there is no length to which they will not go." See Waley, *The Analects of Confucius*, p. 213.

40. This four-character idiom for a casual sexual liaison recurs three times in the *Chin P'ing Mei tz'u-hua*, vol. 2, ch. 23, p. 8a, ll. 2–3; p. 9b, ll. 7–8; and vol. 5, ch. 99, p. 11b, l. 2.

41. This proverbial couplet is quoted, in exactly the same words, as being current in Nanking in the late sixteenth century. See *K'o-tso chui-yü* (Superfluous words of a sojourner), by Ku Ch'i-yüan (1565–1628), author's colophon dated 1618 (Peking: Chung-hua shu-chü, 1987), *chüan* 1, p. 10, ll. 13–14.

42. A variant of this four-character expression occurs in *San-yüan chi*, scene 20, p. 54, l. 11. Another variant recurs in the *Chin P'ing Mei tz'u-hua*, vol. 5, ch. 92, p. 6a, l. 7.

43. The same two lines recur in the *Chin P'ing Mei tz'u-hua*, vol. 4, ch. 73, p. 7b, l. 11.

44. This formulaic four-character expression occurs in *Yüan-ch'ü hsüan*, 4:1691, ll. 3–4; and *Ch'ien-chin chi*, scene 39, p. 126, ll. 6–7.

45. This four-character expression occurs in the *Hsi-yu chi*, vol. 1, ch. 17, p. 190, l. 5.

46. Variants of this proverbial expression occur as early as the T'ang dynasty in poems by Liu Yü-hsi (772–842) and Tu Hsün-ho (846–907). See *Ch'üan T'ang shih*, vol. 6, *chüan* 365, p. 4112, l. 14; and vol. 10, *chüan* 693, p. 7983, l. 9. It occurs in the same form as in the novel in a statement attributed to Su Shih (1037–1101) in the *Neng-kai chai man-lu* (Random notes from the studio of one capable of correcting his faults), by Wu Tseng (d. c. 1170), 2 vols. (Shanghai: Shang-hai ku-chi ch'u-pan she, 1979), vol. 2, *chüan* 16, p. 474, l. 2. It also occurs in *Yüan-ch'ü hsüan*, 1:171, l. 7; 2:847, l. 15; 2:855, l. 8; and in the *Pao-chien chi*, scene 29, p. 54, ll. 21–22.

47. For an illuminating monograph on this subject, see Ching-lang Hou, "The Chinese Belief in Baleful Stars," in Holmes Welch and Anna Seidel, eds., *Facets of Taoism: Essays in Chinese Religion* (New Haven: Yale University Press, 1979), pp. 193–228.

48. The "eight characters" that determine one's horoscope are the four pairs of characters from the sexagenary cycle that indicate the year, month, day, and hour of one's birth. The several pages that follow are replete with the technical jargon of Chinese astrology, an arcane subject that I cannot pretend to have mastered. I have done my best to make sense out of it, but the reader may be excused if he or she finds it confusing, since the author himself intended it to convey the impression of mumbo-jumbo. Although the jargon employed is authentic, the horoscopes that appear in this and other passages in the novel are calendrically impossible, which suggests that the author did not intend his readers to take them too seriously. On this subject, see Paul Varo Martinson, "*Pao* Order and Redemption: Perspectives on Chinese Religion and Society Based on a Study of the *Chin P'ing Mei*," pp. 346–52. The most informative study of this variety of Chinese fortune-telling in English is Chao Wei-pang, "The Chinese Science of Fate-Calculation," *Folklore Studies*, vol. 5 (1946), pp. 279–315.

49. The method of fortune-telling on the basis of the "eight characters" that determine one's horoscope seems to have been developed during the Sung dynasty. It is traditionally attributed to a shadowy figure named Hsü Tzu-p'ing who is said to have lived during the tenth century and to have been associated with Ch'en T'uan (895–989), the famous Taoist recluse who is also an important figure in the history of Chinese physiognomy. Whatever the actual facts may be, this variety of fortune-telling, which is still practiced at the present time, has come to be called the "Tzu-p'ing School."

50. I have emended the text from *chia-ch'en* (1124) to *chia-wu* (1114) to make it conform to the time scheme of the novel. If this is not a careless mistake on the part of the author, it may be a copyist's error.

CHAPTER 13

1. This line occurs in the *Ming-hsin pao-chien, chüan* 1, p. 11b, l. 5. It is the second line of an eight-line poem that also occurs in the *Chin P'ing Mei tz'u-hua*, vol. 2, ch. 28, p. 1a, ll. 3–6.

2. A variant of this couplet occurs in *Chin-yin chi, chüan* 2, scene 19, p. 28b, l. 11. The second line occurs independently in *Yung-hsi yüeh-fu, ts'e* 5, p. 22a, l. 4; and in the *Chin P'ing Mei tz'u-hua*, vol. 5, ch. 86, p. 11a, l. 2.

3. This eight-line poem recurs, with some textual variation, in the *Chin P'ing Mei tz'u-hua*, vol. 5, ch. 86, p. 1a, ll. 3–6.

4. I have inserted the words "earlier that summer" because the events of the previous chapter took place in the seventh and eighth months of the year 1114 and this must, consequently, represent a flashback, although the text does not say so.

5. This couplet occurs frequently in Chinese vernacular literature. See, e.g., the *Hsüan-ho i-shih*, p. 51, l. 14; and p. 61, l. 4; and the *San-kuo chih t'ung-su yen-i, chüan* 22, p. 1066, l. 5. It recurs in the *Chin P'ing Mei tz'u-hua*, vol. 4, ch. 79, p. 10b, ll. 5–6.

6. This four-character expression is ubiquitous in Chinese vernacular literature. See, e.g., *Yü-huan chi*, scene 14, p. 49, l. 3; *Shui-hu ch'üan-chuan*, vol. 4, ch. 89, p. 1458, l. 9; and ch. 97, p. 1530, l. 4; and *Pao-chien chi*, scene 2, p. 7, l. 3.

7. The number nine is used to designate the unbroken or yang lines in the hexagrams of the *Book of Changes*, so the ninth day of the ninth month is called the Double Yang festival. It was customary on this day for people to go out to the suburbs and climb to some high spot for an outing.

8. This was a drinking game in which a flower was passed from hand to hand to the beat of a drum. Whoever was holding the flower when the drum stopped beating had to drink a cup of wine as a forfeit.

9. In Chinese mythology there is a raven in the sun and a hare in the moon. Hence the words "raven" and "hare" are often used to stand for the sun and moon.

10. Chang Chün-jui and Ts'ui Ying-ying are the hero and heroine of the *Hsi-hsiang chi*. For the climactic scene in which their love affair is consummated, see *[Chi-p'ing chiao-chu] Hsi-hsiang chi*, play no. 4, scene 1, pp. 141–45; and West and Idema, *The Moon and the Zither*, pp. 327–37.

11. It was not Sung Yü but King Huai of Ch'u with whom the Goddess of Witches' Mountain had a tryst, but since it was he who described it he is often mistaken for the protagonist in the popular tradition. See chapter 2, note 47.

12. This four-character expression occurs in a lyric by Li Ch'ing-chao (1084–c. 1151). See *Ch'üan Sung tz'u*, 2:928, upper register, l. 16. It recurs in the *Chin P'ing Mei tz'u-hua*, vol. 4, ch. 72, p. 16a, l. 8; ch. 78, p. 9b, l. 5; and p. 10a, l. 9.

13. The locus classicus for this reference to the "touch of the magic rhinoceros horn" is a line from a poem by Li Shang-yin (c. 813–58). See *Ch'üan T'ang shih*, vol. 8, *chüan* 539, p. 6163, l. 8; and *The Poetry of Li Shang-yin*, trans. James J. Y. Liu (Chicago: University of Chicago Press, 1969), p. 86, ll. 16–17. It was believed that the horn of the "magic rhinoceros" contained a single white strand that ran through it

from the root to the tip. Although in its original context the metaphor referred to psychological communion, it is not hard to see how the image could develop phallic connotations. See, e.g., *[Chi-p'ing chiao-chu] Hsi-hsiang chi*, play no. 3, wedge, p. 99, l. 11; and West and Idema, *The Moon and the Zither*, p. 280, ll. 1–2. This four-character expression recurs twice in the *Chin P'ing Mei tz'u-hua*, vol. 2, ch. 21, p. 3b l. 8; and vol. 4, ch. 68, p. 16a, l. 1.

14. See chapter 8, note 42.

15. This four-character expression occurs three times in *[Chi-p'ing chiao-chu] Hsi-hsiang chi*, play no. 1, scene 3, p. 34, l. 6; play no. 2, scene 4, p. 82, l. 14; and play no. 3, scene 2, p. 113, l. 12.

16. This four-character expression for clandestine love affairs alludes to two episodes described in the *Lieh-hsien chuan* and the *Shih-shuo hsin-yü*. In the first, a certain Cheng Chiao-fu in ancient times attempts unsuccessfully to appropriate the girdle pendants of two river nymphs he encounters on the beach. See Kaltenmark, *Le Lie-sien Tchouan*, pp. 96–101. In the second, Han Shou (d. 291) acquires a rare perfume from Chia Wu (d. 300), the daughter of Chia Ch'ung (217–82), with whom he has been carrying on a clandestine affair. The aura of the perfume about his person leads to the discovery of the affair and the marriage of the lovers. See Mather, *Shih-shuo Hsin-yü*, pp. 487–88. The fact that Han Shou first gains access to Chia Wu by climbing over a wall makes this allusion particularly appropriate to the affair between Hsi-men Ch'ing and Li P'ing-erh. This four-character expression occurs three times in *[Chi-p'ing chiao-chu] Hsi-hsiang chi*, play no. 1, scene 2, p. 16, l. 15; play no. 3, scene 3, p. 126, l. 9; and scene 4, p. 132, l. 6. It recurs in the *Chin P'ing Mei tz'u-hua*, vol. 4, ch. 80, p. 1a, l. 2.

17. These four lines of sententious doggerel occur in the *Ming-hsin pao-chien*, *chüan* 1, p. 6a, ll. 1–2; and in the middle-period vernacular stories *Jen Hsiao-tzu lieh-hsing wei shen*, p. 579, l. 8; and *Ho-t'ung wen-tzu chi* (The story of the contract), in *Ch'ing-p'ing shan-t'ang hua-pen*, p. 33, ll. 3–4.

18. This six-character expression is ubiquitous in Chinese vernacular literature. See, e.g., *Yüan-ch'ü hsüan*, 1:75, l. 7; *Yüan-ch'ü hsüan wai-pien*, 1:145, l. 15; *San-kuo chih t'ung-su yen-i*, vol. 1, *chüan* 2, p. 99, l. 13; *Shui-hu ch'üan-chuan*, vol. 2, ch. 32, p. 507, l. 8; *Hsi-yu chi*, vol. 1, ch. 31, p. 351, l. 5; and *Ming-feng chi*, scene 14, p. 62, l. 3. It recurs in the *Chin P'ing Mei tz'u-hua*, vol. 2, ch. 28, p. 6b, l. 4.

19. Variants of this expression recur in the *Chin P'ing Mei tz'u-hua*, vol. 2, ch. 23, p. 10a, ll. 3–4; and vol. 4, ch. 72, p. 4a, ll. 4–5.

20. This seven-character expression recurs in the *Chin P'ing Mei tz'u-hua*, vol. 4, ch. 61, p. 9b, l. 1.

21. A variant of this proverbial couplet occurs in the *Hsi-yu chi*, vol. 2, ch. 81, p. 922, l. 8. It recurs in the *Chin P'ing Mei tz'u-hua*, vol. 2, ch. 32, p. 8a, l. 2; and ch. 35, p. 12a, l. 2.

22. For Sung Yü see chapter 2, note 47. That he was reputed to be handsome is indicated by two famous works attributed to him entitled *Teng-t'u tzu hao-se fu* (Rhapsody on Master Teng-t'u's lust) and *Feng fu* (Rhapsody on admonishing by indirection). For the texts of these works, see *Sung Yü tz'u-fu i-chieh* (Sung Yü's rhapsodies translated and interpreted), ed. and annot. Chu Pi-lien (Peking: Chung-kuo she-hui k'o-hsüeh ch'u-pan she, 1987), pp. 100–109 and 130–33. For English translations, see *A Hundred and Seventy Chinese Poems*, trans. Arthur Waley (New

York: Alfred A. Knopf, 1919), pp. 43–44; and *The Temple and Other Poems*, trans. Arthur Waley (New York: Alfred A. Knopf, 1923), pp. 25–26.

23. The erotic albums entitled *Feng-liu chüeh-ch'ang* (Summa elegantia), published in 1606, and *Hua-ying chin-chen* (Variegated positions of the flowery battle), published c. 1610, both depict twenty-four positions for sexual intercourse. For descriptions of these albums and a complete annotated translation of the text accompanying the second, see Van Gulik, *Erotic Colour Prints of the Ming Period*, 1:177–185 and 205–27. References to the twenty-four positions recur twice in the *Chin P'ing Mei tz'u-hua*, vol. 4, ch. 78, p. 10a, l. 10; and vol. 5, ch. 83, p. 9a, l. 6.

24. Variants of this couplet occur in the *Shui-hu ch'üan-chuan*, vol. 1, ch. 16, p. 236, ll. 8–9; and vol. 2, ch. 27, p. 428, l. 11; and in *Hsin-ch'iao shih Han Wu mai ch'un-ch'ing*, p. 66, l. 2. It recurs twice in the *Chin P'ing Mei tz'u-hua*, vol. 5, ch. 91, p. 2a, l. 7; and ch. 98, p. 7b, l. 8.

25. Versions of this lyric, with some textual variation, recur twice in the *Chin P'ing Mei tz'u-hua*, vol. 1, ch. 17, p. 1a, ll. 3–5; and vol. 5, ch. 82, p. 1a, ll. 3–6.

CHAPTER 14

1. The first couplet of this poem is probably derived from the first and sixth lines of a poem by Han Wo (844–923). See *Ch'üan T'ang shih*, vol. 10, *chüan* 683, p. 7831, ll. 14–15. Han Wo's poem occurs, without attribution, at the head of the *Wen-ching yüan-yang hui*, p. 154, ll. 8–11. This story is known to have been drawn upon by the author of the *Chin P'ing Mei*.

2. For Ssu-ma Hsiang-ju and Cho Wen-chün see chapter 3, note 29. According to the sixth-century compilation *Hsi-ching tsa-chi* (Miscellanies of the Western Capital), Cho Wen-chün wrote the "Song of White Hair" in protest against her husband Ssu-ma Hsiang-ju's intention of taking a concubine, with the result that he desisted. See ibid., in *Pi-chi hsiao-shuo ta-kuan*, vol. 1, *ts'e* 1, *chüan* 3, p. 3b, l. 5. For the text of the song, see *Hsien-Ch'in Han Wei Chin Nan-pei ch'ao shih*, 1:274, ll. 6–8. For an English translation, see Waley, *A Hundred and Seventy Chinese Poems*, pp. 71–72.

3. Variants of this expression occur in *Yüan-ch'ü hsüan wai-pien*, 1:130, l. 12; and 3:986, l. 3. It recurs in the *Chin P'ing Mei tz'u-hua*, vol. 3, ch. 46, p. 9b, l. 5.

4. This proverbial expression occurs in a set of song lyrics by Li K'ai-hsien (1502–68), the author's preface to which is dated 1544, in *Li K'ai-hsien chi* (The collected works of Li K'ai-hsien), ed. Lu Kung, 3 vols. (Peking: Chung-hua shu-chü, 1959), 3:877, l. 10; in the *Hsi-yu chi*, vol. 1, ch. 31. p. 361, l. 3; and ch. 42, p. 487, l. 13; and is listed as being current in Nanking in the late sixteenth century by Ku Ch'i-yüan (1565–1628), in *K'o-tso chui-yü*, *chüan* 1, p. 10, l. 10. It recurs in the *Chin P'ing Mei tz'u-hua*, vol. 2, ch. 26, p. 4b, l. 1.

5. Variants of this expression occur in the *Hsi-yu chi*, vol. 1, ch. 14, p. 159, l. 12; and vol. 2, ch. 77, p. 879, l. 1; and *San-pao t'ai-chien Hsi-yang chi t'ung-su yen-i*, vol. 1, ch. 23, p. 297, l. 10.

6. Variants of this couplet occur in a quatrain by Jen Ta-chung (11th century); see *Sung-shih chi-shih*, vol. 3, *chüan* 17, p. 448, l. 1; in *Yüan-ch'ü hsüan*, 2:466, l. 17; and 3:1256, l. 16; in *Chin-yin chi*, *chüan* 4, scene 41, p. 19b, ll. 6–7; and in *San-pao t'ai-chien Hsi-yang chi t'ung-su yen-i*, vol. 2, ch. 94, p. 1212, l. 11. The second line

of the couplet also occurs independently in a song lyric by Liu Shih-chung (14th century), see *Ch'üan Yüan san-ch'ü,* 1:651, l. 12; and in *Yü-chüeh chi,* scene 3, p. 5, l. 1.

7. This formulaic couplet recurs twice in the *Chin P'ing Mei tz'u-hua*. vol. 1, ch. 18, p. 1a, l. 8; and vol. 2, ch. 30, p. 2b, ll. 7–8. The first line occurs independently in the early vernacular story entitled *Shih Hung-chao lung-hu chün-ch'en hui* (Shih Hung-chao: The meeting of dragon and tiger, ruler and minister), in *Ku-chin hsiao-shuo,* vol. 1, *chüan* 15, p. 225, l. 11; and recurs in the *Chin P'ing Mei tz'u-hua,* vol. 4, ch. 70, p. 4a, l. 11.

8. Yang Shih (1053–1135) is a historical figure. For his biography, see *Sung shih,* vol. 36, *chüan* 428, pp. 12738–43; and Franke, *Sung Biographies,* 3:1226–30. He was one of the most respected philosophers of the Sung period and played a key role in the so-called orthodox transmission of Neo-Confucian doctrine between the Ch'eng brothers and Chu Hsi. He was also the putative founder of the Tung-lin Academy, which played such a devisive role in late Ming politics. One can only speculate as to why the author of the *Chin P'ing Mei* chose to depict such a paragon of Confucian rectitude in such a questionable light, unless he was himself critical of orthodox Neo-Confucianism or the Tung-lin Academy, or both. It is true that at one time or another Yang Shih accepted the patronage of such dubious historical figures as Ts'ai Ching (1046–1126) and Wang Fu (d. 1126), who are among the villains of the novel, but he later opposed their policies. The most likely explanation is that the author wished to show that the system was so corrupt that even such a paragon of rectitude as Yang Shih could not help being compromised by it. It is perhaps relevant to note that in the early vernacular story *K'an p'i-hsüeh tan-cheng Erh-lang Shen,* pp. 256–57, Yang Shih is also depicted in a somewhat questionable light as a superstitious protégé of Ts'ai Ching and Yang Chien. See Ma and Lau, *Traditional Chinese Stories,* p. 519.

9. The proximate source of this set piece of descriptive parallel prose, with some textual variation, is the *Shui-hu ch'üan-chuan,* vol. 1, ch. 13, p. 194, ll. 12–14.

10. This aphorism occurs in the *Ming-hsin pao-chien, chüan* 2, p. 8a, l. 15; and the *Shui-hu ch'üan-chuan,* vol. 4, ch. 116, p. 1742, l. 14.

11. This five-character expression occurs in a song lyric by Feng Wei-min (1511–80), a contemporary of the author of the *Chin P'ing Mei*. See *Hai-fu shan-t'ang tz'u-kao, chüan* 1, p. 43, ll. 11–12. It recurs in the *Chin P'ing Mei tz'u-hua,* vol. 2, ch. 26, p. 7b, ll. 7–8.

12. A variant of this expression occurs in *Yüan-ch'ü hsüan,* 2:505, l. 12. It recurs, with an insignificant variant, in the *Chin P'ing Mei tz'u-hua,* vol. 2, ch. 25, p. 7a, l. 2.

13. This expression recurs in the *Chin P'ing Mei tz'u-hua,* vol. 5, ch. 86, p. 6a, ll. 10–11.

14. A variant of this couplet occurs in the *Book of Rites*. See *Li-chi,* ch. 10, p. 57, ll. 14–15; and Legge, *Li Chi,* 1:470, ll. 16–17.

15. This four-character expression, which has become proverbial, occurs as early as the sixth century in the *Ch'ien-tzu wen,* p. 523, upper register, l. 11. It is ubiquitous in Chinese vernacular literature. See, e.g., *Yüan-ch'ü hsüan,* 3:922, l. 1; 3:923, l. 1; 3:1169, l. 1; and 4:1678, ll. 3 and 4; *Chien-teng hsin-hua,* p. 81, l. 12; and *Pai Niang-tzu yung-chen Lei-feng T'a,* p. 432, ll. 1–2.

16. This couplet occurs in the *Ming-hsin pao-chien, chüan* 2, p. 2b, ll. 9–10.

17. Tao Chih, or Robber Chih, was a legendary outlaw of ancient times whose feats are referred to in many classical texts. The most famous description of his libertarian point of view is to be found in chapter 29 of *Chuang-tzu*. See *Chuang-tzu yin-te*, pp. 80–82; and Watson, *The Complete Works of Chuang Tzu*, pp. 323–31.

18. The proximate source of the first four lines of this poem, with some textual variation, is the *Shui-hu ch'üan-chuan*, vol. 2, ch. 28, p. 436, l. 3. The first two lines appear to be derived from the opening couplet of a quatrain that occurs in the *Ming-hsin pao-chien, chüan* 1, p. 10a, ll. 5–6; and the early vernacular story entitled *Tsao-chiao Lin Ta-wang chia-hsing* (A feat of impersonation by the King of Tsao-chiao Wood), in *Ching-shih t'ung-yen, chüan* 36, p. 546, l. 2.

19. For a monographic study of this rite, see Michael R. Saso, *Taoism and the Rite of Cosmic Renewal* (N.p.: Washington State University Press, 1972).

20. Yang-kao wine was a famous product of Fen-chou in Shansi Province. A recipe is included in the *Tsun-sheng pa-chien*, p. 729.

21. This four-character expression is ubiquitous in Chinese vernacular literature. See, e.g., *Yüan-ch'ü hsüan*, 2:708, l. 8; 3:956, l. 4; 4:1313, l. 18; and 4:1365, l. 16; and *Pao-chien chi*, scene 15, p. 32, l. 14.

22. A variant of this four-character expression occurs in *Yüan-ch'ü hsüan wai-pien*, 2:417, l. 3. It recurs twice in the *Chin P'ing Mei tz'u-hua*, vol. 2, ch. 34, p. 2a, l. 1; and p. 4a, l. 4.

23. This is an example of the type of Chinese wordplay called *hsieh-hou yü*. See chapter 5, note 28. There is a four-character expression, probably from a children's primer, that means "donkeys and horses are animals." The word for "animals," *ch'u-sheng*, is a synonym compound, the second character of which puns with the word *sheng*, which means "birth." What the Chinese text actually says is "Today is your 'donkeys and horses are ani-'," and since the omitted second half of the word for "animal," which puns with the word for "birth," would immediately come to mind, what the cryptic statement actually means is "Today is your birthday." Since the expression "born under a lucky star" is a cliché in English, I have used a truncated version of it to suggest something of the complexity of the Chinese original.

24. This four-character expression recurs in the *Chin P'ing Mei tz'u-hua*, vol. 2, ch. 30, p. 6a, l. 4.

25. This formulaic seven-character line occurs ubiquitously in Chinese vernacular literature. See, e.g., *San-kuo chih p'ing-hua*, p. 1, l. 13; *Yüan-ch'ü hsüan*, 3:1270, l. 8; and 4:1591, ll. 12–13; *Wan Hsiu-niang ch'ou-pao shan-t'ing-erh*, p. 560, l. 17; and the early vernacular story entitled *Ts'ui Tai-chao sheng-ssu yüan-chia* (Artisan Ts'ui and his ghost wife), in *Ching-shih t'ung-yen, chüan* 8, p. 94, l. 12. For an English translation of the last story, see Conrad Lung, trans., "Artisan Ts'ui and His Ghost Wife," in Ma and Lau, *Traditional Chinese Stories*, pp. 252–63. The line in question is translated on p. 257, left column, l. 4.

26. This four-character expression recurs in the *Chin P'ing Mei tz'u-hua*, vol. 2, ch. 29, p. 3a, l. 11.

27. This four-character expression recurs in the *Chin P'ing Mei tz'u-hua*, vol. 4, ch. 69, p. 8b, ll. 2–3.

28. See chapter 4, note 11.

CHAPTER 15

1. The Verdant Spring Bordello is the name of the establishment where Su Hsiao-ch'ing, the heroine of a famous lost love story, was employed. This story about the love affair of the young scholar, Shuang Chien, and the courtesan, Su Hsiao-ch'ing, was so well known in the Southern Sung, Yüan, and Ming dynasties that the name Verdant Spring Bordello became a generic term for houses of prostitution. On this lost love story, see chapter 7 in J. I. Crump, *Songs from Xanadu: Studies in Mongol-Dynasty Song-Poetry (San-ch'ü)* (Ann Arbor: Center for Chinese Studies, University of Michigan, 1983), pp. 171–89.

2. This line recurs in the *Chin P'ing Mei tz'u-hua*, vol. 3, ch. 42, p. 1a, l. 5.

3. The text reads "Lai-an" here, but I have emended it to "P'ing-an" since Lai-an is not introduced into the household until chapter 20. See the *Chin P'ing Mei tz'u-hua*, vol. 1, ch. 20, p. 12a, ll. 9–10.

4. The preceding two lines occur together in reverse order in *Huai-ch'un ya-chi*, *chüan* 9, p. 17a, l. 11, upper register.

5. The proximate source of the first eight lines of this set piece of descriptive parallel prose, with some textual variation, is the *Shui-hu ch'üan-chuan*, vol. 2, ch. 33, p. 516, ll, 15–16.

6. Meng Chiang is the heroine of one of the best-known Chinese legends, which is more than two thousand years old and exists in innumerable forms. Basically it is the story of a wife whose grief for her dead husband is so great that it causes the wall in which he has been buried to crumble so that she is able to find his bones and take them home for burial. See, e.g., *Meng Chiang nü pien-wen*, in *Tun-huang pien-wen chi*, 1:32–35; and Waley, *Ballads and Stories from Tun-huang*, pp. 145–49.

7. This famous story in which the Buddhist monk Yüeh-ming induces the enlightenment of the courtesan Liu Ts'ui exists in more than one version. See *Yüan-ch'ü hsüan*, 4:1335–52; and the middle-period vernacular story entitled *Yüeh-ming Ho-shang tu Liu Ts'ui* (The Monk Yüeh-ming converts Liu Ts'ui), in *Ku-chin hsiao-shuo*, vol. 2, *chüan* 29, pp. 428–41.

8. Chung K'uei is the principal demon queller of Chinese popular tradition. According to the most common version of the legend, he committed suicide after having been unjustly rejected in the imperial examinations because of the extreme ugliness of his appearance. Later he appeared to the emperor in a dream and demonstrated his prowess at quelling demons, as a result of which he was duly put in charge of that function. In some versions of the story, even after his suicide he arranged the marriage of his younger sister to the benefactor who had paid his way to the capital to take the examinations. For further information on this subject, see Ma Shu-t'ien, *Hua-hsia chu-shen* (The various gods of China) (Peking: Pei-ching Yen-shan ch'u-pan she, 1990), pp. 265–79.

9. Liu Hai is the name of a Taoist immortal in Chinese folklore who is iconographically associated with a three-legged toad and a string of cash. See E. T. C. Werner, *A Dictionary of Chinese Mythology* (New York: The Julian Press, 1961), pp. 255–57.

10. The proximate source of the preceding four lines, with the second and third lines transposed, is the *Shui-hu ch'üan-chuan*, vol. 2, ch. 33, p. 516, l. 16.

11. The Seven Perfected Ones are variously defined sets of Taoist patriarchs, and the Five Ancients are the personifications of the "five phases" or "five planets."

12. Yang Yeh (d. 986) is a historical figure, a famous military commander of the early years of the Sung dynasty. For his biography, see *Sung shih*, vol. 27, *chüan* 272, pp. 9303–6; and Franke, *Sung Biographies*, 3:1246–47. He is chiefly remembered as the patriarch of a legendary family of military heroes whose exploits are celebrated in the *Yang-chia fu shih-tai chung-yung yen-i chih-chuan* (Popular chronicle of the generations of loyal and brave exploits of the Yang household), pref. dated 1606, 2 vols., fac. repr. (Taipei: Kuo-li chung-yang t'u-shu kuan, 1971).

13. Tripitaka is one of the titles of the famous Buddhist monk Hsüan-tsang (602–64) who made a celebrated journey to India in the years 629–45. For an account of the life of the historical figure, see Arthur Waley, *The Real Tripitaka and Other Pieces* (London: Allen and Unwin, 1952), pp. 11–130. He became a legend in his own lifetime and is best known to the general public as the protagonist of the great sixteenth-century novel *Hsi-yu chi* (The journey to the west). For an account of how the legends about this figure developed, see Dudbridge, *The Hsi-yu chi: A Study of Antecedents to the Sixteenth-Century Chinese Novel.*

14. Shih Ch'ung (249–300), whose name has become eponymous for extravagance and ostentation, once constructed a brocaded windbreak fifty li long to outdo his rival in conspicuous consumption, Wang K'ai. See Mather, *Shih-shuo Hsin-yü*, chapter 30, p. 459, item 4.

15. The "jade hare" is a kenning for the moon. This formulaic four-character expression is ubiquitous in Chinese vernacular literature. See, e.g., *Hsüan-ho i-shih*, p. 52, l. 9; *Yüan-ch'ü hsüan wai-pien*, 3:974, l. 10; the *Shui-hu ch'üan-chuan*, vol. 2, ch. 35, p. 557, l. 9; the early vernacular story entitled *I-k'u kuei lai tao-jen ch'u-kuai* (A mangy Taoist exorcises a lair of demons), in *Ching-shih t'ung-yen, chüan* 14, p. 192, l. 1; and Morgan T. Jones, trans., "A Mangy Taoist Exorcises Ghosts," in Ma and Lau, *Traditional Chinese Stories*, p. 395, left column, l. 13.

16. The proximate source of this quatrain is probably the *Yü-chüeh chi*, scene 12, p. 38, ll. 6–7, where it appears in identical form. The first, third, and fourth lines are taken verbatim from the first, seventh, and eighth lines of an eight-line poem by the ninth-century poet Li Shan-fu. See *Ch'üan T'ang shih*, vol. 10, *chüan* 643, p. 7373, ll. 13–14. The first couplet recurs in the *Chin P'ing Mei tz'u-hua*, vol. 5, ch. 90, p. 3a, l. 2.

17. This four-character expression occurs in an ephemeral late Ming compilation entitled *Hsin-ch'i teng-mi: Chiang-hu ch'iao-yü* (Novel and unusual lantern riddles: Witticisms current in the demimonde), reprinted in *Han-shang huan wen-ts'un*, p. 169, upper register, l. 2.

18. This four-character expression occurs in *Yüan-ch'ü hsüan*, 4:1752, l. 10.

19. This song lyric is derived, with some textual variation, from a work by Ch'en To (fl. early 16th century). See his collection of satirical song lyrics entitled *Hua-chi yü-yün* (Superfluous rhymes on humorous subjects), reprinted from a Wan-li [1573–1620] edition, in Lu Kung, *Fang-shu chien-wen lu* (Record of things seen and heard in the search for rare books) (Shanghai: Shang-hai ku-chi ch'u-pan she, 1985), p. 325, ll. 16–18. The expression "tiger's mouth," in addition to its common meaning of "dangerous situation," may also refer to the mouth of the vagina. For evidence of this usage, see *Hsiu-ju chi*, scene 11, p. 29, l. 10; and the *Chin P'ing Mei tz'u-hua*, vol. 2, ch. 32, p. 5a, l. 8; and vol. 3, ch. 52, p. 11a, l. 3.

20. The lyrics to this anonymous song suite may be found in *Tz'u-lin chai-yen*, 2:618–23; and *Yung-hsi yüeh-fu, ts'e* 12, pp. 57a–59a. For a translation of this song

suite, see appendix II, item 1. The same song suite is performed once again in the *Chin P'ing Mei tz'u-hua*, vol. 4, ch. 78, p. 20a, l. 3. The performance of this song suite for the entertainment of Hsi-men Ch'ing and his cronies is significant because it turns out to be a celebration of spring in the capital city and ends with a coda wishing long life to the emperor. It is one of nine such song suites performed in the course of the novel for the benefit of Hsi-men Ch'ing or his wives that are, in fact, addressed to the emperor or express gratitude for imperial favor. This rhetorical device is analogous, on a larger scale of magnitude, to that of the *hsieh-hou yü* in that it employs a partial quotation to suggest a part of the work alluded to that is not quoted directly. It is also no accident that the lyrics about prostitutes, "cribbers," and "ball clubbers" introduced in chapter 12 and this chapter are all to the tune "Imperial Audience." These rhetorical devices are but some among many that suggest, subtly but unmistakably, that the Hsi-men household is intended to be seen as a microcosm of the empire. On this issue, see Carlitz, *The Rhetoric of Chin p'ing mei*, pp. 40–44.

CHAPTER 16

1. This formulaic four-character expression is ubiquitous in Chinese vernacular literature. See, e.g., *Yüan-jen tsa-chü kou-ch'en* (Rescued fragments from tsa-chü drama by Yüan authors), comp. Chao Ching-shen (Shanghai: Shang-hai ku-tien wen-hsüeh ch'u-pan she, 1956), p. 25, l. 4; *P'i-p'a chi*, scene 8, p. 53, l. 5; and *Yüeh-ming Ho-shang tu Liu Ts'ui*, p. 430, l. 6.

2. This four-character expression recurs twice in the *Chin P'ing Mei tz'u-hua*, vol. 3, ch. 42, p. 4a, l. 11; and vol. 5, ch. 93, p. 10a, l. 4.

3. The Chinese game of dominoes is played with thirty-two pieces and is traditionally thought to have been invented during the reign of Emperor Hui-tsung (r. 1100–1125) of the Sung dynasty, the very period in which the story of the *Chin P'ing Mei* is set. The best study of Chinese dominoes in English is Stewart Culin, "Chinese Games with Dice and Dominoes," *Annual Report of the U. S. National Museum, 1893*, pp. 491–537.

4. A variant of this idiomatic expression recurs in the *Chin P'ing Mei tz'u-hua*, vol. 3, ch. 59, p. 7a, ll. 7–8.

5. This proverbial couplet recurs in the *Chin P'ing Mei tz'u-hua*, vol. 4, ch. 74, p. 4a, l. 2.

6. For further information on the "titillating bell," better known by the homophonous name "Burmese bell," and references to other Chinese- and European-language sources on the subject, see R. H. Van Gulik, *Sexual Life in Ancient China: A Preliminary Survey of Chinese Sex and Society from ca. 1500 B.C. till 1644 A.D.* (Leiden: E. J. Brill, 1961), pp. 165–67; and the note to this passage in Lévy, *Fleur en Fiole d'Or*, 1:1137–38, n. 1. There is an elaborate description of the effects on a woman of the use of this sexual implement in the pornographic novel *Hsiu-t'a yeh-shih* (Unofficial history of the embroidered couch), by Lü T'ien-ch'eng (1580–1618), pref. dated 1608, fac. repr. in *Chung-kuo feng-liu hsiao-shuo ts'ung-shu, ti-wu chi* (Collectanea of Chinese erotic fiction, fifth series) Nagoya: Ikemoto Yoshio, 1979), pp. 64–75.

7. Wang-tzu Ch'iao is a legendary Taoist immortal, the son of King Ling (r. 571–545 B.C.) of the Chou dynasty, who is reported to have been fond of playing the

sheng, a type of mouth-organ whose sound was thought to resemble the cry of the phoenix. He became a transcendant who was last seen on the back of a white crane hovering over the summit of a sacred mountain. See Kaltenmark, *Le Lie-sien Tchouan*, pp. 109–114. For an illustrated description of the *sheng*, see Walter Kaufmann, *Musical References in the Chinese Classics* (Detroit: Information Coordinators, Inc., 1976), pp. 158–65.

8. This couplet is derived, with some textual variation, from the final couplet of a quatrain by Kao P'ien (d. 887). See *Ch'üan T'ang shih*, vol. 9, *chüan* 598, p. 6924, l. 2.

9. This four-character expression occurs in the early vernacular story *Chi Ya-fan chin-man ch'an-huo*, p. 277, l. 9. The preceding two lines recur together in the *Chin P'ing Mei tz'u-hua*, vol. 5, ch. 92, p. 13b, l. 2.

10. This four-character expression is ubiquitous in Chinese vernacular literature. See, e.g., *Yüan-ch'ü hsüan wai-pien*, 2:536, l. 9; *San-kuo chih t'ung-su yen-i*, vol. 1, *chüan* 12, p. 548, l. 3; *Shui-hu ch'üan-chuan*, vol. 2, ch. 35, p. 552, l. 16; the early vernacular story entitled *Yang Wen lan-lu hu chuan* (The story of Yang Wen, the road-blocking tiger), in *Ch'ing-p'ing shan-t'ang hua-pen*, p. 170, l. 9; and Peter Li, trans., "Yang Wen, the Road-Blocking Tiger," in Ma and Lau, *Traditional Chinese Stories*, p. 86, left column, l. 18.

11. A variant of this idiomatic expression recurs in the *Chin P'ing Mei tz'u-hua*, vol. 4, ch. 74, p. 3a, l. 10.

12. This proverbial expression occurs in a song lyric by Hsüeh Lun-tao (c. 1531–c. 1600), a contemporary of the author of the *Chin P'ing Mei*. See *Ming-tai ko-ch'ü hsüan* (An anthology of Ming song lyrics), comp. Lu Kung (Shanghai: Shang-hai ku-tien wen-hsüeh ch'u-pan she, 1956), p. 105, l. 25. It recurs in the *Chin P'ing Mei tz'u-hua*, vol. 1, ch. 17, p. 6b, ll. 4–5.

13. This idiomatic expression recurs in the *Chin P'ing Mei tz'u-hua*, vol. 5, ch. 81, p. 7a, l. 2.

14. This is the first line of the *Pai-chia hsing* (Surnames of the hundred families), a list of 438 surnames, including 30 disyllabic surnames, making 472 characters in all, arranged in rhyming four-syllable lines, that has been in common use as a primer since the Northern Sung dynasty. Its first line would have been familiar to anyone who had ever received even the most rudimentary education. See the text of the *Pai-chia hsing* printed at the head of *Pai-chia hsing tz'u-tien* (Encyclopedia of surnames), comp. Mu Liu-sen (Shen-chen: Hai-t'ien ch'u-pan she, 1988), p. 1, l. 1. The same line is quoted to humorous effect in *Yüan-ch'ü hsüan wai-pien*, 1:155, l. 5.

15. On the various customs associated with the Dragon Boat Festival, including the *tsung-tzu*, mentioned two lines below, which are triangular masses of rice wrapped in leaves that are traditionally consumed on this occasion, see Bodde, *Annual Customs and Festivals in Peking*, pp. 42–46; and H. Y. Lowe, *The Adventures of Wu: The Life Cycle of a Peking Man*, 2 vols. (Princeton: Princeton University Press, 1983), 1:141–48.

16. The three characters that, translated literally, mean "Eighteenth Youngster" can be combined to form the common surname "Li." Hence this example of wordplay is an esoteric way of referring to Li Kuei-chieh. Li P'ing-erh, of course, has the same surname.

17. Variants of this proverbial couplet occur in *Yüan-ch'ü hsüan*, 1:110, ll. 9–10; *Sha-kou chi*, scene 3, p. 7, l. 8; scene 27, p. 99, l. 8; and p. 101, l. 1; *Shui-hu ch'üan-*

chuan, vol. 1, ch. 15, p. 217, l. 11; and vol. 4, ch. 113, p. 1699, l. 6; and *San-pao t'ai-chien Hsi-yang chi t'ung-su yen-i*, vol. 1, ch. 48, p. 620, ll. 7–8 and 9–10. Allusion to the first two sources named is especially relevant since they represent two different generic versions of a story that subjects the facile oaths of sworn brothers to satirical exposure.

18. This couplet represents a satirical twist on the wording of the famous "Oath in the Peach Orchard" among Liu Pei (161–223), Kuan Yü (160–219), and Chang Fei (d. 221), in which the second line reads, "We are willing to die together on the same day." See *San-kuo chih p'ing-hua*, p. 12, ll. 11–12; *Hua Kuan So ch'u-shen chuan*, p. 1b, l. 5; and *San-kuo chih t'ung-su yen-i*, vol. 1, *chüan* 1, p. 5, ll. 12–13. In the *Sha-kou chi*, scene 3, p. 7, ll. 6–7, the wording of the original oath is quoted on the same page with the promise to go through fire and water, which makes it the most probable source for this passage in the *Chin P'ing Mei*.

19. Versions of this anonymous song suite are preserved in *Sheng-shih hsin-sheng* (New songs of a surpassing age), pref. dated 1517, fac. repr. (Peking: Wen-hsüeh ku-chi k'an-hsing she, 1955), pp. 513–14; *Tz'u-lin chai-yen*, 1:235–37; and *Yung-hsi yüeh-fu*, *ts'e* 16, pp. 8a–9a. For a translation of this song suite, see appendix II, item 2. The same song suite is performed a second time in the *Chin P'ing Mei tz'u-hua*, vol. 2, ch. 31. p. 15a, l. 5.

20. This formulaic four-character expression is ubiquitous in Chinese vernacular literature. See, e.g., *Yüan-ch'ü hsüan*, 4:1732, l. 5; *Chien-teng hsin-hua*, p. 63, l. 10; and p. 95, l. 5; and *San-kuo chih t'ung-su yen-i*, vol. 2, *chüan* 18, p. 852, l. 15.

21. This couplet occurs in a speech attributed to Wei Chao-shih (fl. mid-6th century) in an anecdote recorded in *Yu-yang tsa-tsu* (Assorted notes from Yu-yang), comp. Tuan Ch'eng-shih (c. 803–863) (Peking: Chung-hua shu-chü, 1981), *ch'ien-chi* (first collection), *chüan* 12, p. 113, l. 3.

22. This line alludes to the story of Lady Li, a favorite consort of Emperor Wu (r. 141–87 B.C.) of the Han dynasty. For her biography, see *Han-shu*, vol. 8, *chüan* 97, pp. 3951–56; and *Courtier and Commoner in Ancient China: Selections from the History of the Former Han by Pan Ku*, trans. Burton Watson (New York: Columbia University Press, 1974), pp. 247–51.

23. As pointed out by André Lévy, *Fleur en Fiole d'Or*, 1:1140, n. 1, this couplet is from a ballad by Liu Hsi-i (fl. early 8th century). See *Ch'üan T'ang shih*, vol. 2, *chüan* 82, p. 885, ll. 12–13. On the vexed question of the dating of Liu Hsi-i's work, I am persuaded by the argument presented in Stephen Owen, *The Great Age of Chinese Poetry: The High T'ang* (New Haven: Yale University Press, 1981), p. 321, n. 14.

24. The last two lines of this quatrain are derived from the final couplet of a lyric by Yen Chi-tao (c. 1031–c. 1106). See *Ch'üan Sung tz'u*, 1:225, lower register, l. 10. The same couplet, in a version closer to its original form, recurs in the *Chin P'ing Mei tz'u-hua*, vol. 1, ch. 20, p. 3b, ll. 5–6.

CHAPTER 17

1. This lyric has already occurred in the *Chin P'ing Mei tz'u-hua*, vol. 1, ch. 13, p. 12b, ll. 3–5; and it recurs in ibid., vol. 5, ch. 82, p. 1a, ll. 3–6. The last couplet is missing in the version found in chapter 17. Assuming this omission to be inadvertent, I have supplied it from the earlier occurrence of the same lyric at the end of chapter 13.

2. The character Ching Chung makes a brief appearance as the military commissioner of Ch'ing-ho in the *Shui-hu ch'üan-chuan*, vol. 3, ch. 78, pp. 1295, 1299, and 1300.

3. Hsi-wen is an early name for the long southern-style drama that is also known as nan-hsi or ch'uan-ch'i. This style of drama first developed in southern Chekiang Province in the twelfth century and became the dominant dramatic genre during the Ming dynasty, eclipsing the shorter tsa-chü form in popularity. See William Dolby, *A History of Chinese Drama* (New York: Barnes and Noble, 1976), ch. 5, pp. 71–101.

4. For an early occurrence of this four-character expression, see *[Chi-p'ing chiao-chu] Hsi-hsiang chi*, play no. 4, scene 1, p. 145, l. 3; and West and Idema, *The Moon and the Zither*, p. 337, l. 1.

5. This lyric is a variant of one that has already occurred in the *Chin P'ing Mei tz'u-hua*, vol. 1, ch. 10, p. 8b, ll. 5–7. For the "magic rhinoceros horn," see chapter 13, note 13.

6. Variants of this idiomatic expression recur three times in the *Chin P'ing Mei tz'u-hua*, vol. 1, ch. 19, p. 6b, l. 5; vol. 4, ch. 64, p. 2b, l. 6; and ch. 77, p. 3a, ll. 3–4.

7. Ch'en Hung (fl. mid-16th century) was the name of a notorious eunuch who served at court during the Lung-ch'ing (1567–72) reign period and is said to have actively encouraged the emperor to engage in dissipation and extravagance. See *Ming shih*, vol. 17, *chüan* 193, p. 5126, ll. 6–8; vol. 19, *chüan* 203, p. 5641, l. 13; *chüan* 220, p. 5800, l. 8; vol. 26, *chüan* 305, p. 7799, ll. 10–11; and p. 7800, l. 6.

8. Wang Fu (1079–1126) is a historical figure. For his biography, see *Sung shih*, vol. 39, *chüan* 470, pp. 13681–84; and Djang and Djang, *A Compilation of Anecdotes of Sung Personalities*, pp. 537–42.

9. A possible source for this name is that of the rich silk merchant in K'ai-feng who figures in the early vernacular story *Hsiao fu-jen chin-ch'ien tseng nien-shao*, p. 222, l. 13; and Yang and Yang, *The Courtesan's Jewel Box*, p. 17, l. 11.

10. This four-character expression occurs in *Chiao Hung chuan*, p. 294, l. 4; and *Hsi-yu chi*, vol. 2, ch. 70, p. 803, l. 7.

11. Yü-wen Hsü-chung (1079–1146) is a historical figure. For his biography, see *Sung shih*, vol. 33, *chüan* 371, pp. 11526–29; and *Chin shih* (History of the Chin dynasty [1115–1234]), comp. T'o-t'o (1313–55) et. al., 8 vols. (Peking: Chung-hua shu-chü, 1975), vol. 6, *chüan* 79, pp. 1791–92.

12. For the proximate source of this sentence, see *Hsüan-ho i-shih*, p. 77, l. 7; and Hennessey, *Proclaiming Harmony*, p. 97, ll. 38–40. The ultimate source is *Sung ta-shih chi chiang-i* (Lectures on the principal events of the Sung dynasty), by Lü Chung (cs 1247), in *Ssu-k'u ch'üan-shu chen-pen, erh-chi* (Rare volumes from the *Complete library of the four treasuries*, second series), vols. 146–47 (Taipei: T'ai-wan Shang-wu yin-shu kuan, 1971), vol. 147, *chüan* 22, p. 10a, l. 8.

13. For the proximate source of this proverbial couplet, see *Hsüan-ho i-shih*, p. 77, l. 8; and Hennessey, *Proclaiming Harmony*, p. 98, ll. 2–3. For the ultimate source of the first line, see *Shan-hai ching chiao-chu* (A critical edition of *The classic of mountains and seas*), ed. and annot. Yüan K'o (Shanghai: Shang-hai ku-chi ch'u-pan she, 1980), *chüan* 5, p. 165, l. 6 and n. 4. For the ultimate source of the second line, see *Huai-nan hung-lieh chi-chieh*, vol. 2, *chüan* 17, p. 16a, l. 2.

14. Pien Ch'üeh is one of the names of a semilegendary physician of ancient times. For his biography, see *Shih-chi*, vol. 9, *chüan* 105, pp. 2785–94.

15. The language of this clause, with one minor variant, occurs in an imperial rescript of the year 1126 demoting T'ung Kuan (1054–1126), the eunuch military commander, from his various high offices. See *Sung tsai-fu pien-nien lu [chiao-pu]* ([Collated and supplemented recension of] A chronological record of the rescripts appointing and demoting the chief ministers of the Sung dynasty), comp. Hsü Tzuming (fl. early 13th century), ed. Wang Jui-lai, 4 vols. (Peking: Chung-hua shu-chü, 1986), vol. 2, *chüan* 13, p. 842, l. 3.

16. Kuo Yao-shih (d. after 1126) is a historical figure. For his biography, see *Sung shih*, vol. 39, *chüan* 472, pp. 13737–40; and *Chin shih*, vol. 6, *chüan* 82, pp. 1833–34.

17. This may be an example of the author's use of the device of deliberate anachronism to remind the informed reader that his attention is not really focused on the time frame in which the story is ostensibly set. In the novel this memorial by Yü-wen Hsü-chung is represented as having been presented to the throne in the fifth month of the year 1115. There is a relatively unknown Sung figure named Chang Ta who died in the defense of T'ai-yüan in 1126. See *Chin-shih*, vol. 6, *chüan* 79, pp. 1787–88. However, Chang Ta is also the name of a much better known regional commander who gained national fame and a posthumous imperial commendation for dying in the defense of Ta-t'ung, not far north of T'ai-yüan, against the invading forces of Altan Khan (1507–82) in the sixth month of the year 1550. Sixteenth-century readers could have been expected to recognize this allusion to a contemporary event. See *Ming shih-lu* (Veritable records of the Ming dynasty), 133 vols., fac. repr. (Taipei: Academia Sinica, 1961–66), vol. 85, *chüan* 361, p. 3a, l. 12–p. 3b, l. 7; *chüan* 362, p. 1a, ll. 7–9; and p. 2a, l. 12–p. 2b, l. 9; *Kuo-ch'üeh* (An evaluation of the events of our dynasty), by T'an Ch'ien (1594–1658), 6 vols. (Peking: Ku-chi ch'u-pan she, 1958), vol. 4, *chüan* 59, p. 3750, ll. 8–15; and Goodrich and Fang, *Dictionary of Ming Biography*, 1:253.

18. For this allegation, made of Ts'ai Ching rather than Wang Fu, see *Sung shih*, vol. 39, *chüan* 472, p. 13727, l. 11.

19. This expression was used by the historical figure Lü Hui (1014–71) in a memorial to the throne impeaching the controversial minister, Wang An-shih (1021–86). See *Sung shih*, vol. 30, *chüan* 321, p. 10429, l. 10. Lü Hui's memorial, including this phrase, is also quoted in *Hsüan-ho i-shih*. See ibid., p. 8, l. 3; and Hennessey, *Proclaiming Harmony*, p. 11, ll. 9–10.

20. The locus classicus for this idiom is the biography of Fan Chü (d. 255 B.C.) in the *Shih-chi*, vol. 7, *chüan* 79, p. 2414, l. 5; and Yang and Yang, *Records of the Historian*, p. 105, ll. 31–32. It also occurs in *Yüan-ch'ü hsüan*, 3:1217, l. 9; and *Ju-i chün chuan*, p. 10a, l. 5.

21. This four-character expression occurs in an imperial rescript of the year 1100 demoting the former grand councilor, Chang Tun (1035–1101). See *Sung tsai-fu pien-nien lu [chiao-pu]*, vol. 2, *chüan* 11, p. 672, ll. 1–2.

22. This language occurs in a memorial impeaching Ts'ai Ching submitted to the throne in 1109 by a student in the National University named Ch'en Ch'ao-lao. See *Sung shih*, vol. 39, *chüan* 472, p. 13725, l. 7. The locus classicus for the above two clauses is a passage in the *Tso-chuan* under the year 608 B.C. See Legge, *The Ch'un Ts'ew with the Tso Chuen*, p. 280, ll. 13–14; and p. 283, left column, ll. 58–60.

23. This four-character expression occurs in a scathing memorial attacking the Chia-ching emperor's failures as a ruler that was submitted to the throne in the sixth

month of 1548 by a member of the Ming royal house named Chu Ch'in-yü. See *Ming shih-lu*, vol. 85, *chüan* 337, p. 4a, l. 3.

24. There was a eunuch of this name who served at court during the reign of the Cheng-te emperor (r. 1505–21). See *Ming shih*, vol. 18, *chüan* 203, p. 5368, l. 8.

25. The text here does not read Hsi-men Ch'ing, but Chia Lien, the name to which Hsi-men Ch'ing's name is altered in chapter 18. See chapter 18, note 13. Since this does not make any sense in terms of the plot, I have amended the text to read Hsi-men Ch'ing.

26. Variants of this couplet occur in the *Hsi-yu chi*, vol. 1, ch. 34, p. 390, l. 17; and vol. 2, ch. 82, p. 941, l. 17. It recurs twice, with some textual variation in the first instance, in the *Chin P'ing Mei tz'u-hua*, vol. 3, ch. 47, p. 7a, ll. 8–9; and ch. 59, p. 10a, ll. 6–7. For the "three bristles and seven apertures of the heart," see *Shih-chi*, vol. 9, *chüan* 105, p. 2818, l. 8. I do not know precisely what the expression "three bristles" is intended to indicate in anatomical terms.

27. This formulaic couplet recurs in the *Chin P'ing Mei tz'u-hua*, vol. 5, ch. 86, p. 9a, ll. 1–2.

28. Variants of this idiomatic expression occur in *Yüan-ch'ü hsüan*, 2:423, l. 18; 2:475, l. 18; and 3:846, l. 15; and *Shui-hu ch'üan-chuan*, vol. 3, ch. 56, p. 942, l. 17; and vol. 4, ch. 104, p. 1598, l. 16.

29. The four-character expression that I have rendered as "beyond the nine heavens" is ubiquitous in Chinese vernacular literature. See, e.g., *[Chi-p'ing chiao-chu] Hsi-hsiang chi*, play no. 4, scene 1, p. 144, l. 11; *Yüan-ch'ü hsüan*, 4:1621, l. 20; *Yüan-ch'ü hsüan wai-pien*, 2:396, l. 13; and *Shui-hu ch'üan-chuan*, vol. 1, ch. 9, p. 134, l. 6.

30. Variants of this formulaic couplet appear ubiquitously in Chinese vernacular literature. See, e.g., *Chao-shih ku-erh chi*, *chüan* 1, scene 14, p. 25b, l. 7; and scene 24, p. 46a, l. 7. A variant of the second line occurs as early as the T'ang dynasty. See *Wu Tzu-hsü pien-wen*, p. 5, ll. 14–15; and p. 9, l. 9.

31. This proverbial couplet occurs in a speech attributed to the Buddhist monk Tsung-ta (fl. 12th century). See *Wu-teng hui-yüan*, vol. 3, *chüan* 16, p. 1081, l. 13. It is ubiquitous in Chinese vernacular literature. See, e.g., *Yu-kuei chi*, scene 7, p. 15, l. 4; *Shui-hu ch'üan-chuan*, vol. 1, ch. 26, p. 410, ll. 10–11; and *Hsi-yu chi*, vol. 2, ch. 56, p. 649, l. 8. It recurs in the *Chin P'ing Mei tz'u-hua*, vol. 2, ch. 29, p. 3b, l. 7; vol. 5, ch. 87, p. 8b, ll. 1–2; and, in a slightly variant form, ch. 88, p. 11a, l. 5.

32. A variant of this idiomatic expression recurs in the *Chin P'ing Mei tz'u-hua*, vol. 4, ch. 69, p. 18a, l. 6.

33. This four-character expression is ubiquitous in Chinese vernacular literature. See, e.g., *Yüan-ch'ü hsüan*, 2:524, l. 1; 3:980, l. 7; and 4:1689, l. 2. It recurs twice in the *Chin P'ing Mei tz'u-hua*, vol. 2, ch. 26, p. 16b, l. 7; and vol. 3, ch. 41, p. 5a, l. 2.

34. Variants of this proverbial couplet appear ubiquitously in Chinese vernacular literature. See, e.g., *Chang Hsieh chuang-yüan*, p. 56, l. 3; *Yüan-ch'ü hsüan*, 1:418, l. 7; *Yüan-ch'ü hsüan wai-pien*, 1:196, l. 12; and the middle-period vernacular story *Ts'o-jen shih*, p. 216, l. 14. It recurs in the *Chin P'ing Mei tz'u-hua*, vol. 3, ch. 51, p. 6b, l. 11.

35. For the translation of this term, see Manfred Porkert, *The Theoretical Foundations of Chinese Medicine* (Cambridge: MIT Press, 1974), p. 218.

36. For this term, see ibid., p. 220.

37. The proximate source of this phrase and several others in the following pages is a literary tale by Chao Pi (fl. early 15th century) entitled *P'eng-lai hsien-sheng chuan* (The story of Mr. P'eng-lai), which contains an analogous plot situation. The

author's postface to the collection in which this tale is found is dated 1428. See *Hsiao-p'in chi*, p. 71, l. 6. The fact that the author of the *Chin P'ing Mei* may have drawn on this tale for this episode was first suggested by Sun K'ai-ti in 1933. See his *Jih-pen Tung-ching so-chien hsiao-shuo shu-mu* (Bibliography of works of Chinese fiction seen in Tokyo, Japan) (Peking: Jen-min wen-hsüeh ch'u-pan she, 1958), p. 118.

38. For this phrase, see *P'eng-lai hsien-sheng chuan*, p. 71, l. 4.

39. This four-character expression occurs in a speech attributed to the Buddhist monk Fa-chen (878–963). See *Ku tsun-su yü-lu* (The recorded sayings of eminent monks of old), comp. Tse Tsang-chu (13th century), in *Hsü Tsang-ching* (Continuation of the Buddhist canon), 150 vols., fac. repr. (Hong Kong: Hsiang-kang ying-yin *Hsü Tsang-ching* wei-yüan hui, 1967), vol. 118, *chüan* 35, p. 306b, upper register, l. 3. It is ubiquitous in Chinese vernacular literature. See, e.g., *Yüan-ch'ü hsüan*, 2:607, l. 5; *Yüan-ch'ü hsüan wai-pien*, 1:236, l. 8; and *Hsi-yu chi*, vol. 2, ch. 97, p. 1093, l. 14. It recurs in the *Chin P'ing Mei tz'u-hua*, vol. 4, ch. 74, p. 18a, l. 10.

40. This four-character expression recurs in the *Chin P'ing Mei tz'u-hua*, vol. 5, ch. 92, p. 14a, l. 9.

41. The source of this sentence is *P'eng-lai hsien-sheng chuan*, p. 72, l. 9.

42. This proverbial expression combines allusions to two famous stories about demonstrations of gratitude. For the first, see *Hsü Ch'i Hsieh chi* (Continuation of *Tales of Ch'i Hsieh*), by Wu Chün (469–520), in Wang Kuo-liang, *Hsü Ch'i Hsieh chi yen-chiu* (A study of *Hsü Ch'i Hsieh chi*) (Taipei: Wen shih che ch'u-pan she, 1987), pp. 26–27; and *The Man Who Sold a Ghost: Chinese Tales of the 3rd–6th Centuries*, trans. Yang Hsien-yi and Gladys Yang (Peking: Foreign Languages Press, 1958), p. 114. For the second, see *The Ch'un Ts'ew with the Tso Chuen*, trans. James Legge (Hong Kong: Hong Kong University Press, 1960), p. 328, par. 4.

43. For this sentence, see *P'eng-lai hsien-sheng chuan*, p. 72, ll. 9–10.

44. Variants of this formulaic couplet are ubiquitous in Chinese vernacular literature. See, e.g., *Yüan-ch'ü hsüan*, 1:234, ll. 4–5; and 3:1001, ll. 18–19; *Shui-hu ch'üan-chuan*, vol. 1, ch. 3, p. 49, l. 6; and *San-yüan chi*, scene 13, p. 35, l. 2.

45. For an early occurrence of this four-character expression, see *Hsüan-ho i-shih*, p. 60, l. 12; and Hennessey, *Proclaiming Harmony*, p. 77, ll. 7–8.

46. This is a variant of a four-character expression that is ubiquitous in Chinese vernacular literature. See, e.g., *[Chi-p'ing chiao-chu] Hsi-hsiang chi*, play no. 1, scene 2, p. 17, l. 8; and West and Idema, *The Moon and the Zither*, p. 185, l. 26.

47. This four-character expression occurs in *Lao-hsüeh An pi-chi* (Miscellaneous notes from an old scholar's retreat) by Lu Yu (1125–1210), Peking: Chung-hua shu-chü, 1979), *chüan* 8, p. 105, l. 2; and in *Pao-chien chi*, scene 51, p. 93, l. 19. It recurs twice in the *Chin P'ing Mei tz'u-hua*, vol. 1, ch. 19, p. 1a, l. 8; and ch. 20, p. 12a, l. 8.

48. This couplet occurs in *Yüan-ch'ü hsüan*, 2:541, ll. 2–3.

CHAPTER 18

1. This line occurs in the *Shen-hsiang ch'üan-pien* in a section entitled *Ta-mo hsiang-yen* (Bodhidharma on physiognomizing eyes), presumably attributed to the famous Buddhist monk Bodhidharma (fl. 470–528), *chüan* 633, p. 40b, l. 1.

2. The proximate source of this poem is the *Shui-hu ch'üan-chuan*, vol. 2, ch. 53, p. 874, ll. 3–4. It also occurs, with some textual variation, in the *Ming-hsin pao-chien*, *chüan* 2, p. 4b, ll. 10–12.

3. This four-character expression is ubiquitous in Chinese vernacular literature. See, e.g., *[Hsin-pien] Wu-tai shih p'ing-hua*, p. 9, l. 1; and p. 169, l. 12; *Yang Wen lan-lu hu chuan*, p. 170, l. 14; *Ts'ui Tai-chao sheng-ssu yüan-chia*, p. 95, l. 2; *Pai Niang-tzu yung-chen Lei-feng T'a*, p. 434, l. 6; *San-kuo chih t'ung-su yen-i*, vol. 2, *chüan* 18, p. 837, l. 12; and *Shui-hu ch'üan-chuan*, vol. 1, ch. 5, p. 81, l. 6.

4. This four-character expression is ubiquitous in Chinese vernacular literature. See, e.g., the song lyric attributed to Shang T'ing (1209–88), in *Ch'üan Yüan san-ch'ü*, 1:63, l. 1; *[Chi-p'ing chiao-chu] Hsi-hsiang chi*, play no. 4, scene 2, p. 148, l. 15; *Yüan-ch'ü hsüan*, 1:387, l. 2; *Ching-ch'ai chi*, scene 33, p. 102, l. 1; *Hsi-yu chi*, vol. 1, ch. 20, p. 223, l. 7; and *San-pao t'ai-chien Hsi-yang chi t'ung-su yen-i*, vol. 1, ch. 36, p. 467, l. 8.

5. This idiomatic expression for rumors recurs three times in the *Chin P'ing Mei tz'u-hua*, vol. 2, ch. 25, p. 11a, l. 3; ch. 26, p. 10b, l. 6; and vol. 5, ch. 91, p. 1a, l. 11.

6. This four-character expression is ubiquitous in Chinese vernacular literature. See, e.g., *Yüan-ch'ü hsüan wai-pien*, 1:67, l. 8; and 1:234, l. 2; *San-yüan chi*, scene 27, p. 74, l. 12; *Ch'ien-chin chi*, scene 26, p. 88, l. 10; *San-kuo chih t'ung-su yen-i*, vol. 1, *chüan* 5, p. 233, l. 23; and *Shui-hu ch'üan-chuan*, vol. 1, ch. 10, p. 151, l. 6.

7. The locus classicus for this four-character expression is the *Hsi-ching fu* (Western metropolis rhapsody), by Chang Heng (78–139). See *Wen-hsüan* (Selections of refined literature), comp. Hsiao T'ung (501–31), 3 vols., fac. repr. (Peking: Chung-hua shu-chü, 1981), vol. 1, *chüan* 2, p. 14b, l. 6; and *Wen xuan or Selections of Refined Literature*, trans. and annot. David R. Knechtges (Princeton: Princeton University Press, 1982), 1:205, l. 13.

8. Ts'ai Yu (1077–1126) is a historical figure. For his biography, see *Sung shih*, vol. 39, *chüan* 472, pp. 13730–32; and Djang and Djang, *A Compilation of Anecdotes of Sung Personalities*, pp. 524–25.

9. During the fifteenth and sixteenth centuries, the expressions "yellow rice" and "white rice" were used as euphemisms for gold and silver. The words "five hundred piculs of white rice," therefore, meant "five hundred taels of silver." See *Chih-shih yü-wen* (Recollections of a well-governed age), by Ch'en Hung-mo (1474–1555), originally completed in 1521 (Peking: Chung-hua shu-chü, 1985), *chüan* 4, pp. 64–65; and Goodrich and Fang, *Dictionary of Ming Biography*, 1:837.

10. Li Pang-yen (d. 1130) is a historical figure. For his biography, see *Sung shih*, vol. 32, *chüan* 352, pp. 11120–21.

11. The locus classicus for this four-character expression, with an insignificant textual variant, is a famous document written by Ch'en Lin (d. 217) in the year 200, entitled *Wei Yüan Shao hsi Yü-chou* (Proclamation to Liu Pei [161–223] on behalf of Yüan Shao [d. 202]). See *Wen-hsüan*, vol. 2, *chüan* 44, p. 5a, ll. 9–10.

12. The ultimate source of this proverbial four-character expression is an apologue in the *Chan-kuo ts'e*. See *Chan-kuo ts'e* (Intrigues of the Warring States), comp. Liu Hsiang (79–8 B.C.), 3 vols. (Shanghai: Shang-hai ku-chi ch'u-pan she, 1985), vol. 2, *chüan* 14, p. 482; and Crump, *Chan-Kuo Ts'e*, p. 225.

13. In cursive script it would not be hard to combine the characters *hsi* and *men* in such a way that they would resemble the character *chia* and to alter the character *ch'ing* so as to make it look like the character *lien*.

14. In Chinese legend, Fu-sang is the name of a mythical tree at the eastern extremity of the world that the sun climbs up as it rises.

15. This formulaic couplet occurs in *Yüan-ch'ü hsüan*, 1:175, l. 16; and *Shui-hu ch'üan-chuan*, vol. 3, ch. 62, p. 1046, ll. 6–7.

16. The probable source of this proverbial quatrain, with some textual variation, is the early vernacular story *Hsiao fu-jen chin-ch'ien tseng nien-shao*, p. 229, l. 6. The second couplet occurs independently in *Chin-ch'ai chi*, scene 67, p. 124, ll. 1–2; *San Sui p'ing-yao chuan*, *chüan* 2, ch. 6, p. 1a, l. 7; and the *Chin P'ing Mei tz'u-hua*, vol. 5, ch. 94, p. 12b, ll. 5–6. The third line occurs independently in a song suite attributed to Kao An-tao (14th century). See *Ch'üan Yüan san-ch'ü*, 2:1110, l. 15. The fourth line occurs independently in *Yüan-ch'ü hsüan*, 4:1679, l. 12.

17. The Ullambana is the Buddhist Festival of All Souls, or Ghost Festival, which is celebrated in China on the fifteenth day of the seventh month. On this day ceremonies are performed by Buddhist and Taoist priests for the purpose of releasing from purgatory the souls of those who have died on land or sea. For a monographic study of the development of this festival, see Stephen F. Teiser, *The Ghost Festival in Medieval China* (Princeton: Princeton University Press, 1988).

18. For a detailed contemporaneous description of this pastime as it was practiced in Peking, see *Wan-shu tsa-chi* (Miscellaneous records concerning the magistracy of Wan-p'ing), by Shen Pang, preface dated 1592 (Peking: Pei-ching ku-chi ch'u-pan-she, 1980), *chüan* 17, pp. 190–91.

19. A variant of this proverbial couplet recurs in the *Chin P'ing Mei tz'u-hua*, vol. 4, ch. 76, p. 4a, l. 10.

20. This formulaic couplet, or slight variants thereof, occurs in *Yüan-ch'ü hsüan*, 3:886, l. 19; and *Yüan-ch'ü hsüan wai-pien*, 1:130, l. 8; and 2:377, l. 1.

21. Variants of this idiomatic expression recur twice in the *Chin P'ing Mei tz'u-hua*, vol. 4, ch. 75, p. 23b, l. 5; and ch. 76, p. 4a, l. 6.

22. This couplet, which has become proverbial, is from a poem by Fang Yüeh (1199–1262). See his *Ch'iu-ya chi* (Autumn cliff collection), in *Ssu-k'u ch'üan-shu chen-pen, san-chi* (Rare volumes from the *Complete library of the four treasuries*, third series), 400 vols. (Taipei: T'ai-wan Shang-wu yin-shu kuan, 1972), vol. 248, *chüan* 4, p. 8a, l. 7. It recurs in the *Chin P'ing Mei tz'u-hua*, vol. 2, ch. 30, p. 9b, l. 7.

23. In attempting to translate the technical jargon of sixteenth-century Chinese dominoes in the passage that follows, I have consulted four extant manuals dating from the fifteenth to the nineteenth centuries. See *Hsüan-ho p'ai-p'u* (A manual for Hsüan-ho [1119–25] dominoes), by Ch'ü Yu (1341–1427), in *Shuo-fu hsü* (*The frontiers of apocrypha* continued), comp. T'ao T'ing (cs 1610), fac. repr. of Ming edition included in *Shuo-fu san-chung* (*The frontiers of apocrypha*: Three recensions), 10 vols. (Shanghai: Shang-hai ku-chi ch'u-pan she, 1988), vol. 10, *chüan* 38, pp. 1a–17a; *P'ai-p'u* (A manual for dominoes), by Ku Ying-hsiang (1483–1565), in *Hsin-shang hsü-pien* (A collectanea on connoisseurship continued), comp. Mao I-hsiang (16th century), Ming ed. in the Gest Collection of the Princeton University Library, *chüan* 9, pp. 1a–31b; *P'ai-t'u* (Illustrated domino combinations), in *San-ts'ai t'u-hui* (Assembled illustrations from the three realms), comp. Wang Ch'i (c. 1535–c. 1614), pref. dated 1609, fac. repr., 6 vols. (Taipei: Ch'eng-wen ch'u-pan she, 1970), vol. 4, *jen-shih* (Human affairs), *chüan* 8, pp. 43a-51b; and *Hsüan-ho p'u ya-p'ai hui-chi* (A manual for Hsüan-ho dominoes with supplementary materials), original compiler's preface dated 1757, redactor's preface dated 1886 (N.p.: Hung-wen chai, 1888). In the first, third, and fourth of these manuals, each combination is designated by a

fanciful name; in the second and third manuals, each combination is assigned a number; and in all four of them, each combination is accompanied by a line of poetry from a T'ang or Sung poet. However, the names, numbers, and lines of poetry assigned to each combination in the various manuals are not always the same, and none of the manuals provides adequate information on the rules of the game to determine precisely how it was played. For these reasons the translation that follows must be regarded as tentative.

24. For illustrations of this combination, see *Hsüan-ho p'ai-p'u*, p. 13b; *P'ai-p'u*, p. 26b; and *P'ai-t'u*, p. 49a. In *Hsüan-ho p'u ya-p'ai hui-chi, chüan* 1, p. 4a, the same name is used to designate the two-domino combination of a double six and a double one.

25. For illustrations of this combination, see *Hsüan-ho p'ai-p'u*, p. 10a; *P'ai-p'u*, p. 16b; *P'ai-t'u*, p. 46b; and *Hsüan-ho p'u ya-p'ai hui-chi, chüan* 1, p. 7a. The name of this combination also occurs in the version of *Nan Hsi-hsiang chi* attributed to Li Jih-hua (fl. early 16th century) in a passage of dialogue that plays on the names of domino combinations, scene 7, p. 21, l. 1.

26. For an illustration of this combination, see *Hsüan-ho p'u ya-p'ai hui-chi, chüan* 1, p. 14b. The name of this combination also occurs in the version of *Nan Hsi-hsiang chi* attributed to Li Jih-hua, scene 7, p. 21, l. 10.

27. Variants of this formulaic couplet recur twice in the *Chin P'ing Mei tz'u-hua*, vol. 5, ch. 93, p. 12a, ll. 4–5; and ch. 94, p. 4a, l. 3.

28. For an illustration of this combination, see *Hsüan-ho p'u ya-p'ai hui-chi, chüan* 1, p. 11b. I have not been able to reconcile the information in the domino manuals with the play described in the novel to my satisfaction, but that is attributable to the fact that I do not understand the rules of the game.

29. This four-character expression occurs in *Ju-i chün chuan*, p. 9a, l. 1. It recurs in the *Chin P'ing Mei tz'u-hua*, vol. 2, ch. 28, p. 1b, l. 1.

30. See *Ju-i chün chuan*, p. 18a, ll. 4–5.

31. See *Ju-i chün chuan*, p. 12b, ll. 6–7.

32. This four-character expression for vaginal intercourse from behind occurs in *San-pao t'ai-chien Hsi-yang chi t'ung-su yen-i*, vol. 1, ch. 32, p. 412, l. 6; and *Jou p'u-t'uan, chüan* 1, ch. 3, p. 22a, l. 7. See Hanan, *The Carnal Prayer Mat*, p. 42, ll. 10–11. A variant of this expression occurs in *Ch'ün-yin lei-hsüan* (An anthology of songs categorized by musical type), comp. Hu Wen-huan (fl. 1592–1617), 4 vols., fac. repr. (Peking: Chung-hua shu-chü, 1980), 3:1863, l. 10. The same expression recurs in the *Chin P'ing Mei tz'u-hua*, vol. 2, ch. 27, p. 5a, l. 3; and, in a variant form, in vol. 4, ch. 72, p. 17b, l. 9; and p. 19b, l. 3.

33. A variant of this expression occurs in a speech attributed to the Buddhist monk Wu-yin (884–960). See *Ching-te ch'uan-teng lu* (The transmission of the lamp compiled in the Ching-te reign period [1004–7]), comp. Tao-yüan (fl. early 11th century), in *Taishō shinshū daizōkyō* (The newly edited great Buddhist canon compiled in the Taishō Reign Period [1912–1926]), 85 vols. (Tokyo: Taishō issaikyō kankōkai, 1922–32), vol. 51, no. 2076, *chüan* 17, p. 343, upper register, l. 7. The same variant also occurs in *Chin-kang pan-jo-po-lo-mi ching chu, chüan* 2, p. 551, middle register, l. 23. The expression occurs in the same form as in the novel in *Shui-hu ch'üan-chuan*, vol. 1, ch. 8, p. 129, ll. 8–9. It recurs in the *Chin P'ing Mei tz'u-hua*, vol. 5, ch. 97, p. 5a, l. 5.

34. Variants of this proverbial expression occur as early as the T'ang dynasty. See *Yen-tzu fu* (Rhapsody on the swallow), in *Tun-huang pien-wen chi*, 1:262, l. 14; and *Ch'a chiu lun* (Debate between tea and wine), in ibid., 1:268, l. 7. It recurs twice in the *Chin P'ing Mei tz'u-hua*, vol. 3, ch. 41, p. 8a, ll. 3–4; and vol. 5, ch. 86, p. 7b, l. 2.

35. This proverbial expression recurs three times, with insignificant textual variants, in the *Chin P'ing Mei tz'u-hua*, vol. 4, ch. 78, p. 26b, l. 5; vol. 5, ch. 86, p. 14b, l. 7; and ch. 87, p. 7a, l. 2.

36. This proverbial couplet recurs in the *Chin P'ing Mei tz'u-hua*, vol. 5, ch. 81, p. 9b, l. 8.

37. This four-character expression occurs in *San-pao t'ai-chien Hsi-yang chi t'ung-su yen-i*, vol. 1, ch. 20, p. 260, l. 2. A variant occurs in *Chien-teng hsin-hua*, *chüan* 3, p. 79, l. 3. Another variant occurs in *Yüan-ch'ü hsüan*, 4:1690, l. 7; *Shui-hu ch'üan-chuan*, vol. 1, ch. 2, p. 17, l. 8; and in the *Chin P'ing Mei tz'u-hua*, vol. 5, ch. 82, p. 8a, l. 3.

38. A variant of this four-character expression occurs in *Yüan-ch'ü hsüan wai-pien*, 1:73, l. 7; and *San-kuo chih t'ung-su yen-i*, vol. 2, *chüan* 13, p. 584, l. 25.

39. This formulaic four-character expression recurs twice in the *Chin P'ing Mei tz'u-hua*, vol. 3, ch. 42, p. 10b, l. 3; and vol. 4, ch. 69, p. 8b, l. 3.

40. The ultimate source of this couplet, with some textual variation, is a quatrain by Lo Yin (833–909). See *Ch'üan T'ang shih*, vol. 10, *chüan* 662, p. 7594, l. 2.

41. This poem recurs as the prefatory poem to chapter 83 in the *Chin P'ing Mei tz'u-hua*, vol. 5, ch. 83, p. 1a, ll. 3–6.

CHAPTER 19

1. The proximate source of this poem, with some textual variation, is the *Shui-hu ch'üan-chuan*, vol. 2, ch. 33, p. 513, ll. 3–4. The first two couplets, with some textual variation, also occur, without attribution, in the *Ming-hsin pao-chien*, *chüan* 2, p. 5a, ll. 2-3; while the last two couplets, with some textual variation, occur elsewhere in the same anthology, attributed to *Lieh-tzu* [*sic*], see ibid., *chüan* 1, p. 3b, ll. 12–13; and in *Pai-t'u chi*, scene 4, p. 8, ll. 10–11. The same poem, in its entirety, recurs in the *Chin P'ing Mei tz'u-hua*, vol. 5, ch. 94, p. 1a, ll. 3–6; while the third and fourth lines recur in ibid., vol. 5, ch. 84, p. 10a, l. 10; and the sixth, seventh, and eighth lines recur in ibid., vol. 4, ch. 61, p. 26a, ll. 7–8.

2. This formulaic four-character expression occurs in *Chien-teng hsin-hua*, *chüan* 3, p. 66, l. 13; *Huai-ch'un ya-chi*, *chüan* 9, p. 24b, l. 16; and *Hsi-yu chi*, vol. 2, ch. 64, p. 731, l. 2. It recurs twice in the *Chin P'ing Mei tz'u-hua*, vol. 2, ch. 36, p. 4b, ll. 8–9; and vol. 3, ch. 48, p. 6a, l. 6.

3. This four-character expression occurs in the anonymous middle-period vernacular story entitled *Tu Li-niang mu-se huan-hun* (Tu Li-niang yearns for love and returns to life), in Hu Shih-ying, *Hua-pen hsiao-shuo kai-lun*, 2:533, l. 24.

4. The ultimate source of this couplet, with considerable textual variation, is a couplet by Wang Lin (fl. 9th century). See *T'ang chih-yen*, *chüan* 13, p. 150, l. 2; and *Ch'üan T'ang shih*, vol. 11, *chüan* 795, p. 8948, l. 6.

5. Bamboos are referred to as "gentlemen" because of an anecdote about the famous eccentric Wang Hui-chih (d. 388), who is said to have remarked, when asked

why he had planted bamboos about his temporary residence, "How could I live a single day without these gentlemen?" See Mather, *Shih-shuo Hsin-yü*, p. 388.

6. Pines are referred to as "grandees" because Ch'in Shih Huang-ti (259–210 B.C.) is said to have sought shelter from a storm under a tree while visiting Mount T'ai in 219 B.C., and to have expressed his gratitude by enfeoffing it as a grandee. See *Shih-chi*, vol. 1, *chüan* 6, p. 242, ll. 8–9; and Yang and Yang, *Records of the Historian*, p. 169, ll. 12–14. Later scholiasts identified the tree in question as a pine. See *I-wen lei-chü* (A categorized chrestomathy of literary excerpts), comp. Ou-yang Hsün (557–641), 2 vols. (Peking: Chung-hua shu-chü, 1965), vol. 2, *chüan* 88, p. 1512, ll. 1–2. The "gentleman" bamboo and "grandee" pine are also paired in a couplet in *Tung Chieh-yüan Hsi-hsiang chi*, *chüan* 1, p. 6, l. 2.

7. This couplet occurs in *Ch'ien-t'ang meng*, p. 1b, ll. 7–8; and, in a slightly variant form, in *Tu Li-niang mu-se huan-hun*, p. 533, ll. 26–27. It recurs in the *Chin P'ing Mei tz'u-hua*, vol. 3, ch. 52, p. 16b, l. 10.

8. This couplet occurs in *Ch'ien-t'ang meng*, p. 2b, l. 8. Variants of the same couplet occur in *Yüan-ch'ü hsüan*, 2:817, ll. 4–5; 3:1043, l. 1; and 3:1235, l. 19. It recurs in the *Chin P'ing Mei tz'u-hua*, vol. 5, ch. 90. p. 2b, ll. 1–2.

9. The expression "batting at the butterflies" has erotic connotations. It is the tune title for a lyric that complements an erotic color print illustrating one of the twenty-four positions for intercourse in the *Hua-ying chin-chen*. See ibid., plate no. 21, recto and verso; and the annotated translation in Van Gulik, *Erotic Colour Prints of the Ming Period*, 3:224–25. As Van Gulik points out, the tune titles for the lyrics that accompany the illustrations in the late Ming erotic albums were chosen for their suggestiveness. This particular lyric also appears in Van Gulik's edition of the *Hsiu-t'a yeh-shih*, although it is not in the only edition accessible to me. See ibid., 3:128–34.

10. This formulaic four-character expression is ubiquitous in Chinese vernacular literature. See, e.g., *Yüan-ch'ü hsüan*, 1:180, l. 13; 2:802, l. 19; and 4:1562, l. 3; and *Yüan-ch'ü hsüan wai-pien*, 2:384, l. 19; and 2:387, l. 10.

11. This couplet recurs, with some textual variation, in the *Chin P'ing Mei tz'u-hua*, vol. 3, ch. 52, p. 19b, ll. 3–4.

12. This formulaic four-character expression occurs in *Yü-ch'iao hsien-hua*, scene 4, p. 11b, l. 12.

13. The ultimate source of this couplet, with considerable textual variation, is a couplet by Hsieh I (d. 1113). See *Sung-shih chi-shih*, vol. 6, *chüan* 33, p. 850, l. 4. It recurs in the *Chin P'ing Mei tz'u-hua*, vol. 5, ch. 82, p. 3b, ll. 5–6.

14. A version of this anonymous song is included in *Yung-hsi yüeh-fu*, *ts'e* 17, p. 43b, ll. 2–5. It recurs in the *Chin P'ing Mei tz'u-hua*, vol. 3, ch. 52, p. 19b, ll. 7–9.

15. For a detailed description, based on primary sources, of the entertainment quarters in the capitals of the Northern and Southern Sung dynasties, see Wilt Idema and Stephen H. West, *Chinese Theater 1100-1450: A Source Book* (Wiesbaden: Franz Steiner Verlag, 1982), pp. 14–29 and 56–83.

16. The locus classicus for the first line of this couplet is a speech by Han Sung in reply to a request from Liu Piao (144–208) in A.D. 199. See *Fu-tzu* (The treatise of Master Fu), by Fu Hsüan (217–78), as quoted in P'ei Sung-chih's (372–451) commentary to the *San-kuo chih*, vol. 1, *chüan* 6, p. 213, l. 4. It also occurs in *Shui-hu ch'üan-chuan*, vol. 1, ch. 15, p. 211, l. 5. The same couplet occurs in a slightly variant

form in *San-pao t'ai-chien Hsi-yang chi t'ung-su yen-i*, vol. 2, ch. 92, p. 1182, ll. 11–12. The first line recurs in a variant form in the *Chin P'ing Mei tz'u-hua*, vol. 5, ch. 88, p. 6a, l. 1.

17. This appears to have been a device attached to the penis in order to titillate the clitoris during intercourse. The same nomenclature occurs in the anonymous Ming drama *Wei Feng-hsiang ku Yü-huan chi* (The old version of Wei Kao [746–806] and the story of the jade ring), item 22 in *Ku-pen hsi-ch'ü ts'ung-k'an, ch'u-chi, chüan* 1, scene 6, p. 11a, l. 8; and the anonymous late Ming ch'uan-ch'i drama entitled *Chin-ch'üeh chi* (The golden sparrow), *Liu-shih chung ch'ü* edition (Taipei: K'ai-ming shu-tien, 1970), scene 13, p. 37, l. 6. It recurs in the *Chin P'ing Mei tz'u-hua*, vol. 4, ch. 79, p. 6a, l. 3. What is probably the same device is referred to as a "Cantonese tickler" in the *Ju-meng lu* (Record of a seeming dream), an anonymous mid-seventeenth-century work on life in the city of K'ai-feng before the Manchu conquest in 1644, where it is said to have been offered for sale along with other paraphernalia for sexual stimulation. See ibid., in *San-i t'ang ts'ung-shu* (Three pleasures studio collectanea), comp. Chang Feng-t'ai, (K'ai-feng: Ho-nan kuan-shu chü, 1926), *ts'e* 48, p. 25b, ll. 7–8.

18. This appears to have been the name of another device similar in function to that described in the previous note.

19. This formulaic four-character expression occurs ubiquitously in Chinese vernacular literature. See, e.g., *Yüan-ch'ü hsüan*, 1:259, l. 7; and *Yüan-ch'ü hsüan wai-pien*, 2:371, l. 20.

20. This idiomatic expression occurs in the *Hsi-yu chi*, vol. 1, ch. 20, p. 224, l. 17. It recurs in the *Chin P'ing Mei tz'u-hua*, vol. 1, ch. 19, p. 9b, l. 3.

21. The best-known occurrence of this expression is in the *Hsi-hsiang chi*. See *[Chi-p'ing chiao-chu] Hsi-hsiang chi*, play no. 4, scene 2, p. 152, l. 5; and West and Idema, *The Moon and the Zither*, p. 346, l. 12. It also occurs in *Yüan-ch'ü hsüan*, 3:1293, l. 5; 4:1431, l. 18; and 4:1522, l. 3; *Yüan-ch'ü hsüan wai-pien*, 2:481, l. 18; and *Yü-ch'iao hsien-hua*, scene 3, p. 8b, l. 6.

22. "Ox-yellow" is the Chinese word for bezoar or *Calculus bovis*, a medication extracted from the gall stones of the ox or buffalo. See Shiu-ying Hu, *An Enumeration of Chinese Materia Medica* (Hong Kong: The Chinese University Press, 1980), p. 76.

23. "Ice-crystals" is the Chinese word for borneol camphor. See ibid., p. 89.

24. This clause echoes an almost identical line in the *Hsi-hsiang chi*. See *[Chi-p'ing chiao-chu] Hsi-hsiang chi*, play no. 3, scene 3, p. 125, l. 8; and West and Idema, *The Moon and the Zither*, p. 311, l. 19.

25. Variants of this proverbial expression recur in the *Chin P'ing Mei tz'u-hua*, vol. 3, ch. 52, p. 5b, ll. 3–4; and vol. 5, ch. 86, p. 10b, l. 9.

26. The locus classicus for this four-character expression is the *San-kuo chih*, vol. 5, *chüan* 57, p. 1337, l. 1. It also occurs in *Yüan-ch'ü hsüan*, 3:1044, l. 5; and 4:1637, l. 20; and the *Shui-hu ch'üan-chuan*, vol. 1, ch. 4, p. 61, l. 4.

27. The Chinese olive, *Canarium album*, is said to have a bitter flavor at first, which develops into a pleasing aftertaste. As early as the tenth century this characteristic of the olive was used as a metaphor for the frank remonstrance that is at first distasteful to the person to whom it is addressed but later turns out to be beneficial. See the poems on this theme by Wang Yü-ch'eng (954–1001) and others in *Ch'üan-*

fang pei-tsu (A comprehensive florilegium on horticulture), comp. Ch'en Ching-i, preface dated 1256, 2 vols. (Peking: Nung-yeh ch'u-pan she, 1982), vol. 2, *chüan* 4, pp. 7b–8b.

28. A variant of this proverbial expression recurs in the *Chin P'ing Mei tz'u-hua*, vol. 4, ch. 72, p. 23a, ll. 5–6; while the first half occurs by itself in vol. 4, ch. 76, p. 5a, l. 6; and the last half in vol. 2, ch, 26, p. 2b, l. 2.

29. A literal translation of this four-character expression would be "the white sun in a blue sky." It is commonly used to refer to something that is obvious for all to see, such as the innocence of someone against whom a crime is committed in broad daylight. It occurs in a letter by Han Yü (768–824). See *Han Ch'ang-li wen-chi chiao-chu* (The prose works of Han Yü with critical annotation), ed. Ma T'ung-po (Shanghai: Ku-tien wen-hsüeh ch'u-pan she, 1957), *chüan* 3, p. 110, l. 1. He seems to have been particularly fond of the expression since it also occurs twice in his poetry. See *Ch'üan T'ang shih*, vol. 5, *chüan* 338, p. 3793, l. 15; and *chüan* 344, p. 3864, l. 7.

30. Very similarly worded formulas for the final clauses of contracts occur in *Yüan-ch'ü hsüan*, 4:1593, ll. 18–19; 4:1645, l. 21; and 4:1650, l. 11.

31. This formulaic four-character expression is ubiquitous in Chinese vernacular literature. See, e.g., *Yüan-ch'ü hsüan*, 1:115, l. 11; *Yüan-ch'ü hsüan wai-pien*, 2:573, l. 6; and *Yung-hsi yüeh-fu, ts'e* 19, p. 33a, l. 8. It recurs in the *Chin P'ing Mei tz'u-hua*, vol. 3, ch. 50, p. 1b, l. 2.

32. This idiomatic expression recurs in the *Chin P'ing Mei tz'u-hua*, vol. 1, ch. 19, p. 15a, l. 4.

33. This formulaic description of a particular way of kneeling recurs three times in the *Chin P'ing Mei tz'u-hua*, vol. 2, ch. 32, p. 5a, l. 5; vol. 4, ch. 68, p. 10a, l. 6; and vol. 5, ch. 95, p. 10b, ll. 4-5.

34. This four-character expression occurs in *Yang Wen lan-lu hu chuan*, p. 178, l. 14.

35. The proximate source of this couplet is probably the *Hsi-hsiang chi*. See *[Chi-p'ing chiao-chu] Hsi-hsiang chi*, play no. 5, scene 3, p. 190, ll. 2–3; and West and Idema, *The Moon and the Zither*, p. 396, ll. 17–19. It recurs in the *Chin P'ing Mei tz'u-hua*, vol. 4, ch. 72, p. 13b, l. 8.

36. This quatrain, with one textual variant, occurs in the *Pai-chia kung-an, chüan* 10, ch. 93, p. 11a, ll. 9–10. Patrick Hanan has demonstrated that this chapter belongs to the earliest of the three strata that make up this work and has speculated that it must have a source, perhaps in some lost vernacular story. See his "*Judge Pao's Hundred Cases* Reconstructed," *Harvard Journal of Asiatic Studies* 40, no. 2 (1980): 313. The second couplet, with the same textual variant, occurs in the *Chung-ch'ing li-chi*, vol. 2, *chüan* 6, p. 28b, l. 16. The last line, with one textual variant, occurs in *Yüan-ch'ü hsüan*, 4:1500, l. 5; and 4:1687, l. 19.

37. This was an ancient Chinese game in which the contestants attempted to toss arrows into a narrow-necked vessel. It was considered important enough to have a chapter devoted to it in the Confucian *Book of Rites*. See Legge, *Li Chi*, 1:50–51; and 2:397–401.

38. This was a vase filled with different kinds of grain, miniature ingots of gold and silver, or other precious objects, carried by the bride when she entered the bridegroom's house. No doubt it was a symbol of fertility. This custom is still observed in

some parts of China. See Lou Tzu-k'uang, *Hun-su chih* (A record of wedding customs) (Taipei: T'ai-wan Shang-wu yin-shu kuan, 1968), pp. 74–75.

39. The Nine Springs is one of many names for the Chinese underworld, or abode of the dead.

40. This idiomatic expression recurs in the *Chin P'ing Mei tz'u-hua*, vol. 4, ch. 72, p. 16b, l. 11.

41. This formulaic couplet occurs in the *Shui-hu ch'üan-chuan*, vol. 1, ch. 25, p. 401, l. 17; the *San Sui p'ing-yao chuan, chüan* 3, ch. 12, p. 32a, l. 7; the early vernacular story *San hsien-shen Pao Lung-t'u tuan-yüan*, p. 175, l. 4; and the two middle-period vernacular stories *Hsin-ch'iao shih Han Wu mai ch'un-ch'ing*, p. 64, l. 5; and *Shen Hsiao-kuan i-niao hai ch'i-ming*, p. 394, l. 13. All of these are works that are known to have been drawn upon by the author of the *Chin P'ing Mei tz'u-hua*.

42. This metaphorical use of the term "paste pot," or "paste bucket," occurs in *Yüan-ch'ü hsüan*, 2:800, l. 21; and *Hsiang-nang yüan* (The tragedy of the scent bag), a tsa-chü drama by Chu Yu-tun (1379–1439), author's preface dated 1433, in *Sheng-Ming tsa-chü, erh-chi* (Tsa-chü dramas of the glorious Ming dynasty, second collection), comp. Shen T'ai (17th century), fac. repr. of 1641 edition (Peking: Chung-kuo hsi-chü ch'u-pan she, 1958), scene 3, p. 19a, l. 1. On the important and prolific fifteenth-century playwright Chu Yu-tun, see the monograph of W. L. Idema, *The Dramatic Oeuvre of Chu Yu-tun (1379–1439)* (Leiden: E. J. Brill, 1985).

43. This formulaic four-character expression occurs in *Chang Yü-hu wu-su nü-chen kuan*, scene 3, p. 620, l. 3. A variant occurs in *Yüan-ch'ü hsüan*, 2:546, l. 17; and another variant recurs in the *Chin P'ing Mei tz'u-hua*, vol. 2, ch. 26, p. 4b, l. 7.

44. This formulaic four-character expression occurs in a song by Wang Yüan-heng (14th century). See *Ch'üan Yüan san-ch'ü*, 2:1379, l. 13. It also occurs in *Yüan-ch'ü hsüan*, 2:480, l. 18; and *Yü-ch'iao hsien-hua*, scene 1, p. 2a, l. 11.

45. This formulaic four-character expression occurs in *Yüan-ch'ü hsüan*, 1:115, l. 15; 1:187, l. 13; and 3:1006, l. 7.

46. This formulaic four-character expression occurs in *Yüan-ch'ü hsüan*, 4:1451, l. 4; and 4:1585, l. 12.

47. This formulaic four-character expression occurs in *Ch'ien-chin chi*, scene 19, p. 61, l. 3; and recurs in the *Chin P'ing Mei tz'u-hua*, vol. 5, ch. 81, p. 9b, ll. 1 and 9; and ch. 90, p. 5a, l. 1. Variants recur in ibid., vol. 2, ch. 33, p. 7b, l. 6; and vol. 5, ch. 81, p. 8b, l. 7.

48. This couplet, which has become proverbial, is from a lyric by Liu Yü-hsi (772–842). See *Ch'üan T'ang shih*, vol. 6, *chüan* 365, p. 4110, l. 12. It depends for its force on a pun between the word *ch'ing*, meaning "clear weather," and the word *ch'ing*, meaning "emotion" or "feeling."

CHAPTER 20

1. The proximate source of the first three couplets of this poem is the *Shui-hu ch'üan-chuan*, vol. 1, ch. 7, p. 110, ll. 3–4. The same poem, except for a change in the last line, recurs in the *Chin P'ing Mei tz'u-hua*, vol. 5, ch. 97, p. 1a, ll. 3–6.

2. This formulaic four-character expression occurs as early as the T'ang dynasty. See *Cho Chi Pu chuan-wen* (Story of the apprehension of Chi Pu), in *Tun-huang*

Pien-wen chi, 1:70, l. 12. It is ubiquitous in Chinese vernacular literature. See, e.g., *Tung Chieh-yüan Hsi-hsiang chi*, *chüan* 6, p. 131, l. 3; *Yüan ch'ü hsüan*, 1:154, l. 10; *San-kuo chih t'ung-su yen-i*, vol. 1, *chüan* 2, p. 79, l. 13; and *Hsi-yu chi*, vol. 1, ch. 33, p. 383, l. 4.

3. This idiomatic expression recurs in the *Chin P'ing Mei tz'u-hua*, vol. 2, ch. 40, p. 6b, l. 5.

4. This humorous expression depends for its force on a pun between the word *ch'ien*, meaning "money" or "cost," and the word *ch'ien*, meaning "tug" or "pull."

5. A variant of this proverbial couplet occurs as early as the tenth century in a speech by the Buddhist monk Wen-i (885–958). See *Ching-te ch'uan-teng lu, chüan* 28, p. 448, lower register, ll. 4–5. It also occurs in the biography of the Buddhist monk Mi-kuang (d. 1155). See *Wu-teng hui-yüan*, vol. 3, *chüan*, 20, p. 1329, l. 2.

6. A variant of this expression occurs in *Liu-ch'ing jih-cha*, vol. 1, *chüan* 3, p. 11a, l. 6, where it is defined as chicanery or hanky-panky. It recurs in the *Chin P'ing Mei tz'u-hua*, vol. 2, ch. 37, p. 11a, l. 11.

7. This formulaic four-character expression recurs in the *Chin P'ing Mei tz'u-hua*, vol. 4, ch. 79, p. 3a, l. 2.

8. This humorous expression depends for its force on a pun between the phrases *hsien ts'ao-hsin*, meaning "salty enough to produce heartburn," and *hsien ts'ao-hsin*, meaning "to meddle in other peoples' business." Presumably the turnip peddler tagged along after the salt vendor on the assumption that his customers would want to salt their radishes, though it was, in fact, none of his business. A variant of the same expression recurs in the *Chin P'ing Mei tz'u-hua*, vol. 2, ch. 30, p. 9a, l. 11.

9. This proverbial expression occurs in the *Hsi-yu chi*, vol. 2, ch. 78, p. 893, l. 12. It recurs in the *Chin P'ing Mei tz'u-hua*, vol. 4, ch. 63, p. 12b, l. 3.

10. This humorous expression depends for its force on a pun between the word *hao*, meaning "vermin," and the word *hao*, meaning "good." In an attempt to render something of this play on words, I have punned "furry pest" with "very best."

11. See chapter 9, note 3.

12. The ultimate source of this couplet, which has become proverbial, is the final couplet of a lyric by Yen Chi-tao (c. 1031–c. 1106). See *Ch'üan Sung tz'u*, 1:225, lower register, l. 10. It has already occurred in a truncated form in the *Chin P'ing Mei tz'u-hua*, vol. 1, ch. 16, p. 12b, l. 10. It also occurs in many other works of Chinese vernacular literature. See, e.g., *Yüan-ch'ü hsüan*, 3:1247, l. 2; *P'i-p'a chi*, scene 36, p. 204, l. 13; *Ching-ch'ai chi*, scene 12, p. 38, l. 7; *Sha-kou chi*, scene 33, p. 116, l. 4; and *Yu-kuei chi*, scene 26, p. 84, l. 12.

13. The proximate source of this anonymous lyric is the early vernacular story *Chien-t'ieh ho-shang*, pp. 8–9. It recurs in the *Chin P'ing Mei tz'u-hua*, vol. 5, ch. 83, p. 8a, ll. 5–8. Nine characters have been lost, or inadvertently omitted, from the middle of the lyric as it occurs here. I have supplied them from an analysis of the context and the other two versions of the text. The last couplet also differs from that in the other two versions.

14. Chin-hua wine was a famous product of Chin-hua prefecture in Chekiang Province that had a nationwide reputation during the sixteenth century. It is mentioned more often than any other type of wine in the *Chin P'ing Mei tz'u-hua*. For a study of the rise and fall of its popularity and how this may be reflected in the novel, see Cheng P'ei-k'ai, "*Chin P'ing Mei tz'u-hua* yü Ming-jen yin-chiu feng-shang" (The

Chin P'ing Mei tz'u-hua and Ming literati tastes in wine drinking), *Chung-wai wen-hsüeh* (Chung-wai literary monthly) 12, 6 (November 1983): 4–44.

15. Variants of this idiomatic expression recur in the *Chin P'ing Mei tz'u-hua*, vol. 2, ch. 35, p. 4a, l. 1; vol. 3, ch. 58, p. 15a, ll. 9–10; and p. 17b, l. 3.

16. The ultimate source of this idiomatic expression is a story in the *Yu-ming lu* in which a new ghost is tricked into turning the millstone and grinding the grain for a family of devoted Buddhists. See ibid., *chüan* 4, pp. 131–32; and Yang and Yang, *The Man Who Sold a Ghost*, pp. 105–6. The same idiom recurs twice in the *Chin P'ing Mei tz'u-hua*, vol. 2, ch. 32, p. 8a, l. 7; and vol. 3, ch. 54. p. 14a, l. 8.

17. This formulaic four-character expression recurs three times in the *Chin P'ing Mei tz'u-hua*, vol. 4, ch. 62, p. 10a, l. 5; ch. 68, p. 4a, l. 10; and ch. 75, p. 30b, l. 9.

18. A variant of this formulaic four-character expression recurs in the *Chin P'ing Mei tz'u-hua*, vol. 4, ch. 67, p. 19a, ll. 5–6.

19. This proverbial couplet occurs in *Yung-hsi yüeh-fu, ts'e* 5, p. 22a, l. 6; and recurs in the *Chin P'ing Mei tz'u-hua*, vol. 4, ch. 72, p. 25a, l. 4.

20. A literal translation of this four-character expression would be "tea and water were exchanged between them." It recurs in the *Chin P'ing Mei tz'u-hua*, vol. 5, ch. 84, p. 9b, l. 8.

21. This idiomatic expression recurs three times in the *Chin P'ing Mei tz'u-hua*, vol. 2, ch. 26, p. 11a, l. 5; vol. 4, ch. 67, p. 15a, l. 9; and vol. 5, ch. 85, p. 5a, l. 2.

22. An orthographic variant of this four-character expression occurs in the *Hsi-yu chi*, vol. 1, ch. 12, p. 128, l. 17. Another orthographic variant also recurs in the *Chin P'ing Mei tz'u-hua*, vol. 4, ch. 72, p. 4a, l. 4.

23. This formulaic four-character expression occurs in *Yüan-ch'ü hsüan*, 3:1118, ll. 3 and 4; and *San-pao t'ai-chien Hsi-yang chi t'ung-su yen-i*, vol. 2, ch. 87, p. 1125, l. 9.

24. This formulaic four-character expression occurs in *K'an p'i-hsüeh tan-cheng Erh-lang Shen*, p. 257, l. 16; and *Shui-hu ch'üan-chuan*, vol. 2, ch. 39, p. 616, l. 7.

25. A variant of this proverbial expression occurs in *Yüan-ch'ü hsüan*, 1:409, l. 1.

26. This term, which I have translated functionally, literally means "not recalled at night." It occurs in *Yüan-ch'ü hsüan*, 3:1294, l. 21; *Yü-huan chi*, scene 32, p. 117, l. 7; and *Hsi-yu chi*, vol. 2, ch. 70, p. 795, l. 10. For a definitive study of this term and its usage in the fifteenth and sixteenth centuries, see Henry Serruys, "Towers in the Northern Frontier Defenses of the Ming," *Ming Studies*, vol. 14 (Spring 1982), pp. 47–53.

27. For a good description of this genre, with illustrative samples, see Stephen H. West, *Vaudeville and Narrative: Aspects of Chin Theater* (Wiesbaden: Franz Steiner Verlag, 1977), pp. 24–43.

28. The song suite from which these passages are quoted is from the concluding scene of an anonymous fifteenth-century ch'uan-ch'i drama entitled *Ts'ai-lou chi* (The gaily colored tower), ed. Huang Shang (Shanghai: Shanghai ku-tien wen-hsüeh ch'u-pan she, 1956), scene 20, p. 69, ll. 3–11. It is also preserved independently in the following anthologies: *Sheng-shih hsin-sheng*, pp. 418–20; *Tz'u-lin chai-yen*, 2:1272–75; *Yung-hsi yüeh-fu, ts'e* 16, pp. 32b–33b; and *Ch'ün-yin lei-hsüan*, 3:1971–73. In the first, second, and fourth of these anthologies, the song suite is identified as being from the *Ts'ai-lou chi*. This play is a revision of the earlier *P'o-yao chi* (The dilapidated kiln) and celebrates the willingness of a prime minister's daughter to endure

exile and poverty in order to remain faithful to her husband, the penniless Lü Meng-cheng (946–1011), a paragon of integrity who later becomes a famous statesman. See chapter 1, note 77. In the *Chin P'ing Mei* this song suite is performed to celebrate the entry of an adulterous concubine, who has despoiled her first and second husbands, caused the death of her second, and driven away her third, into the household of a man whose very name has become a byword for corruption, unscrupulousness, and vulgarity. For an analysis of the ironic significance of this allusion to the *Ts'ai-lou chi*, see Carlitz, *The Rhetoric of Chin p'ing mei*, p. 108. For a translation of this song suite, see appendix II, item 3.

29. This idiomatic expression recurs in the *Chin P'ing Mei tz'u-hua*, vol. 4, ch. 79, p. 11b, ll. 3–4.

30. This formulaic hyperbole recurs in the *Chin P'ing Mei tz'u-hua*, vol. 3, ch. 42, p. 9a, ll. 9–10.

31. This formulaic hyperbole occurs in *San-pao t'ai-chien Hsi-yang chi t'ung-su yen-i*, vol. 1, ch. 48, p. 616, l. 11; and recurs in the *Chin P'ing Mei tz'u-hua*, vol. 5, ch. 91, p. 4b, l. 9.

32. This formulaic four-character expression occurs in the *Shen-hsiang ch'üan-pien, chüan* 633, p. 8b, l. 9.

33. This is the punch line from a famous passage in Book 17 of the *Lun-yü*. See chap. 12, note 39. In the *Hsüan-ho i-shih* there is a description of an imperial entertainment in the year 1120 at which the sycophantic chief minister, Ts'ai Ching, and his fellow officials beg for a glimpse of Emperor Hui-tsung's favorite concubine and the emperor accedes to their request. It is probable that the demand by Ying Po-chüeh and his cronies to be vouchsafed a view of Hsi-men Ch'ing's favorite new concubine, Li P'ing-erh, was inspired by this episode in Sung history. This is one instance of many in which the author of the *Chin P'ing Mei* subtly suggests to the informed reader that the household of Hsi-men Ch'ing is meant to be perceived as a microcosm of the imperial court. See *Hsüan-ho i-shih*, pp. 30–31; and Hennessey, *Proclaiming Harmony*, pp. 42–44.

34. This proverbial couplet occurs in the *T'ai-kung chia-chiao* (Family teachings of T'ai-kung), a collection of moral aphorisms that was in circulation as early as the eighth century. See the text of this work as established in Chou Feng-wu, *Tun-huang hsieh-pen T'ai-kung chia-chiao yen-chiu* (A study of the Tun-huang manuscripts of the *T'ai-kung chia-chiao*) (Taipei: Ming-wen shu-chü, 1986), p. 26, ll. 3–4. For a discussion of this work and the history of its use as a primary school text, see Wang Chung-min, *Tun-huang ku-chi hsü-lu* (Descriptive register of ancient manuscripts from Tun-huang) (Peking: Shang-wu yin-shu kuan, 1958), pp. 219–24. The same saying also occurs in the *Ming-hsin pao-chien, chüan* 2, p. 11a, l. 4, where it is attributed to T'ai-kung.

35. The term "three obediences" is found in the Han dynasty compilation on ritual known as the *I-li* (Book of etiquette and ceremonial), where we are told that before marriage a woman owes obedience to her father, after marriage to her husband, and after his death to her son. See *I-li*, in *Shih-san ching ching-wen*, p. 46, ll. 16–17; and *The I-Li or Book of Etiquette and Ceremonial*, trans. John Steele, 2 vols. (London: Probsthain, 1917), vol. 2, ch. 23, p. 20, ll. 9–13. The term "four virtues" refers to the virtue, speech, carriage, and work deemed to be appropriate for a wife. See *Li-chi*, p. 128, l. 6; and Legge, *Li Chi*, 2:432, ll. 12–14. For a different definition of the term "four virtues," see *Yüan-ch'ü hsüan*, 4:1513, ll. 13–14.

36. This was an appellation given to Ssu-ma Hui (d. 208) who is said to have avoided controversy by assenting indiscriminately to any proposition made to him. See Mather, *Shih-shuo Hsin-yü*, pp. 31–32.

37. This proverbial couplet occurs in a speech attributed to the Buddhist monk Huai-lien (1009–90). See *Wu-teng hui-yüan*, vol. 3, *chüan* 15, p. 1007, l. 13. It is ubiquitous in Chinese vernacular literature. See, e.g., *Shih-lin kuang-chi, ch'ien-chi, chüan* 9, p. 8b, l. 9; *Ming-hsin pao-chien, chüan* 2, p. 13a, ll. 6–7; *Chang Wen-kuei chuan* (The story of Chang Wen-kuei), fac. repr. in *Ming Ch'eng-hua shuo-ch'ang tz'u-hua ts'ung-k'an, ts'e* 7, p. 16b, ll. 6–7; and *Ming-chu chi* (The luminous pearl), by Lu Ts'ai (1497–1537), *Liu-shih chung ch'ü* edition (Taipei: K'ai-ming shu-tien, 1970), scene 31, p. 94, l. 11. It recurs in the *Chin P'ing Mei tz'u-hua*, vol. 4, ch. 72, p. 7a, ll. 1–2.

38. This formulaic four-character expression occurs in the *Shen-hsiang ch'üan-pien, chüan* 631, p. 50a, l. 7.

39. This formulaic four-character expression occurs in the *Hsi-yu chi*, vol. 1, ch. 26, p. 294, l. 7; and recurs in the *Chin P'ing Mei tz'u-hua*, vol. 2, ch. 22, p. 7b, l. 5.

40. A variant of this proverbial couplet recurs in the *Chin P'ing Mei tz'u-hua*, vol. 4, ch. 79, p. 20b, ll. 8–9.

41. A variant of this expression occurs in *Yüan-ch'ü hsüan*, 1:38, l. 16. Variants of these two expressions recur together in the *Chin P'ing Mei tz'u-hua*, vol. 3, ch. 51, p. 1b, l. 10.

42. Han Shou (d. 291), when a young man, secretly made his way into the mansion of his superior, the high official Chia Ch'ung (217–82), to carry on a clandestine affair with his daughter, Chia Wu (d. 300). Later he was discovered because of the lingering odor of a rare perfume that he had acquired from his lover, and the two were married to cover the matter up. See Mather, *Shih-shuo Hsin-yü*, p. 487.

43. The expression "eastern couch" has come to mean "son-in-law" from an anecdote about the famous calligrapher Wang Hsi-chih (309–c. 365), who is said to have impressed his future father-in-law, Ch'ih Chien (269–339), by his nonchalance in lying sprawled on the "eastern couch" when he was being looked over as a prospective son-in-law. See Mather, *Shih-shuo Hsin-yü*, pp. 186–87.

44. This formulaic four-character expression occurs in *Yüan-ch'ü hsüan*, 3:1051, l. 15; and 3:1210, l. 21.

45. Meng Hao-jan (689–740) is a T'ang poet who is famous for, among other things, his love of plum blossoms. *Meng Hao-jan Braves the Snow in Search of Plum Blossoms* is the title of a tsa-chü drama written in 1432 by Chu Yu-tun (1379–1439), the famous playwright and grandson of the founder of the Ming dynasty. See Idema, *The Dramatic Oeuvre of Chu Yu-tun*, pp. 102–5. As in the case of the quotation from the *Ts'ai-lou chi* (see note 28 above), there is an ironic contrast between the lofty refinement of Meng Hao-jan's love of plum blossoms and Hsi-men Ch'ing's purely sensual excursion to the pleasure quarter. See Carlitz, *The Rhetoric of Chin p'ing mei*, pp. 99–101.

46. A variant of this formulaic four-character expression occurs in *Yüan-ch'ü hsüan wai-pien*, 1:22, l. 21.

47. This formulaic four-character expression occurs in the *Shui-hu ch'üan-chuan*, vol. 1, ch. 4, p. 73, l. 11; vol. 2, ch. 34, p. 534, l. 14; and ch. 43, p. 699, l. 2; and recurs in the *Chin P'ing Mei tz'u-hua*, vol. 4, ch. 72, p. 2b, l. 11.

48. This formulaic four-character expression is ubiquitous in Chinese vernacular literature. See, e.g., *Yüan-ch'ü hsüan*, 1:141, l. 8; 2:526, l. 20; and 3:1109, l. 21; *Chien-teng hsin-hua, chüan* 3, p. 75, l. 11; *Hsiang-nang yüan*, scene 1, p. 6a, l. 3; and *Shui-hu ch'üan-chuan*, vol. 3, ch. 69, p. 1172, l. 7.

49. This formulaic four-character expression occurs as early as the eleventh century in a lyric by Su Shih (1037–1101). See *Ch'üan Sung tz'u*, 1:278, lower register, l. 15. It is ubiquitous in Chinese vernacular literature. See, e.g., *[Chi-p'ing chiao-chu] Hsi-hsiang chi*, play no. 1, scene 2, p. 17, l. 15; and *Yüan-ch'ü hsüan*, 3:1109, l. 21; 4:1723, l. 11; and 4:1738, l. 3.

50. The ultimate source of this idiomatic four-character expression is the six-character saying "to hang up a sheep's head, but sell dog meat," which occurs as early as the twelfth century in a speech attributed to the Buddhist monk Ch'ing-man. See *Wu-teng hui-yüan*, vol. 3, *chüan* 16, p. 1073, l. 14. The four-character expression occurs in *Ku-ch'eng chi, chüan* 1, scene 4, p. 5b, l. 6; and *Ch'ün-yin lei-hsüan*, 4:2038, l. 4.

51. The formulaic four-character expression that I have translated "raving like thunder" recurs in the *Chin P'ing Mei tz'u-hua*, vol. 2, ch. 26, p. 14b, l. 2.

52. This quatrain occurs in two anthologies of excerpts from ch'uan-ch'i drama entitled *Yüeh-fu ching-hua* (A florilegium of dramatic literature), comp. Liu Chün-hsi (N.p.: San-huai t'ang, 1600), fac. repr. in *Shan-pen hsi-ch'ü ts'ung-k'an*, 1:79, upper register, ll. 1–3; and *Ta ming-ch'un* (Great bright spring), comp. Ch'eng Wan-li (Chien-yang: Chin K'uei, n.d.), fac. repr. of Wan-li (1573–1620) ed., in *Shan-pen hsi-ch'ü ts'ung-k'an*, 6:200, upper register, ll. 7–10. In both cases the excerpts containing this quatrain appear to be from versions of the *Hsiu-ju chi*, although the standard editions of that play do not contain it.

53. This formulaic four-character expression is quoted by Chu Hsi (1130–1200) as early as the eleventh century. See *Chu-tzu yü-lei*, vol. 2, *chüan* 20, p. 28b, l. 4. It is ubiquitous in Chinese vernacular literature. See, e.g., *Tung Chieh-yüan Hsi-hsiang chi, chüan* 4, p. 94, l. 4; *Yüan-ch'ü hsüan*, 2:484, l. 17; *Yüan-ch'ü hsüan wai-pien*, 1:132, l. 6; and *Su Wu Mu-yang chi, chüan* 1, p. 22b, l. 9.

54. The proximate source of this final quatrain is the *Shui-hu ch'üan-chuan*, vol. 1, ch. 21, p. 310, l. 10. In popular Buddhism there is a special place of torment, called the Tongue-plucking Hell, designated for the punishment of those who have been guilty of slander or misrepresentation.

APPENDIX I

1. Much of the following commentary has already appeared in a slightly different form in Roy, "Selections from *Jin Ping Mei*," pp. 18–24.

2. *Chin P'ing Mei tz'u-hua*, vol. 1, ch. 3, p. 1a, l. 3; vol. 5, ch. 81, p. 2b, l. 3; and ch. 94, p. 13a, l. 6.

3. Mather, *Shih-shuo Hsin-yü*, pp. 199–200.

4. Ibid., p. 433.

5. Watson, *Hsün-tzu*, p. 170.

6. *Chin P'ing Mei tz'u-hua*, vol. 1, ch. 8, p. 7b, ll. 8–9.

7. See *Shih-chi*, vol. 1, *chüan* 7, pp. 333–36; and Watson, *Records of the Grand Historian of China*, 1:70–73.

8. *Hsün-tzu yin-te*, ch. 4, p. 9, ll. 18–19; and Knoblock, *Xunzi*, 1:188, ll. 34–38.

9. Li P'ing-erh's death occurs in chapter 62.

10. This incident occurs in chapter 50.

11. *Chin P'ing Mei tz'u-hua*, vol. 4, ch. 62, p. 25b, ll. 3–6.

12. *Hsün-tzu yin-te*, ch. 12, p. 48, l. 13; and Knoblock, *Xunzi*, 2:189, ll. 1–3.

13. See the biography of Cheng Kuei-fei in Goodrich and Fang, *Dictionary of Ming Biography*, 1:208–11; and Ray Huang, *1587, A Year of No Significance: The Ming Dynasty in Decline* (New Haven: Yale University Press, 1981), pp. 75–103 and passim.

14. This incident occurs in chapter 13.

15. This incident occurs in chapter 1.

16. This incident occurs in chapter 87.

17. This incident occurs in chapter 5.

18. This incident occurs in chapter 59.

19. On Cheng and Wei, see note 2 to the colophon.

20. *Juan Chi chi chiao-chu* (The works of Juan Chi edited and annotated), by Juan Chi (210–63), ed. and annot. Ch'en Po-chün (Peking: Chung-hua shu-chü, 1987), pp. 5–9; and Donald Holzman, *Poetry and Politics: The Life and Works of Juan Chi* (Cambridge; Cambridge University Press, 1978), pp. 40–41.

BIBLIOGRAPHY

PRIMARY SOURCES
(Arranged Alphabetically by Title)

The Analects of Confucius. Translated by Arthur Waley. London: Allen and Unwin, 1949.

Annual Customs and Festivals in Peking. By Tun Li-ch'en (1855–1911); translated and annotated by Derk Bodde. Hong Kong: Hong Kong University Press, 1965.

Ballad of the Hidden Dragon (Liu Chih-yüan chu-kung-tiao). Translated by M. Doleželová-Velingerová and J. I. Crump. Oxford: Oxford University Press, 1971.

Ballads and Stories from Tun-huang. Translated by Arthur Waley. London: Allen and Unwin, 1960.

The Book of Lieh-tzu. Translated by A. C. Graham. London: John Murray, 1960.

The Book of Songs. Translated by Arthur Waley. London: Allen and Unwin, 1954.

The Carnal Prayer Mat. Translated by Patrick Hanan. New York: Ballantine Books, 1990.

Ch'a chiu lun 茶酒論 (Debate between tea and wine). In *Tun-huang pien-wen chi*, 1:267–72.

Chan-kuo ts'e 戰國策 (Intrigues of the Warring States). Compiled by Liu Hsiang 劉向 (79–8 B.C.). 3 vols. Shanghai: Shang-hai ku-chi ch'u-pan she, 1985.

Chan-Kuo Ts'e. Translated by J. I. Crump. Oxford: Oxford University Press, 1970.

Chang Chu-p'o p'i-p'ing Ti-i ch'i-shu Chin P'ing Mei 張竹坡批評第一奇書金瓶梅 (Chang Chu-p'o's commentary on The number one marvelous book *Chin P'ing Mei*). Edited by Wang Ju-mei 王汝梅 et al. 2 vols. Chi-nan: Ch'i-Lu shu-she, 1988.

Chang Hsieh chuang-yüan 張協狀元 (Top graduate Chang Hsieh). In *Yung-lo ta-tien hsi-wen san-chung chiao-chu*, pp. 1–217.

Chang Ku-lao chung-kua ch'ü Wen-nü 張古老種瓜娶文女 (Chang Ku-lao plants melons and weds Wen-nü). In *Ku-chin hsiao-shuo*, vol. 2, *chüan* 33, pp. 487–502.

Chang Wen-kuei chuan 張文貴傳 (The story of Chang Wen-kuei). Fac. repr. In *Ming Ch'eng-hua shuo-ch'ang tz'u-hua ts'ung-k'an, ts'e* 7.

Chang Yü-hu su nü-chen kuan chi 張于湖宿女貞觀記 (Chang Yü-hu spends the night in a Taoist nunnery). In *Yen-chü pi-chi*, vol. 2, *chüan* 6, pp. 6b–24b, lower register.

Chang Yü-hu wu-su nü-chen kuan 張于湖誤宿女眞觀 (Chang Yü-hu mistakenly spends the night in a Taoist nunnery). In *Ming-jen tsa-chü hsüan*, pp. 595–628.

Chao-shih ku-erh chi 趙氏孤兒記 (The story of the orphan of Chao). In *Ku-pen hsi-ch'ü ts'ung-k'an, ch'u-chi*, item 16.

Ch'ao-yeh ch'ien-tsai 朝野僉載 (Comprehensive record of affairs within and without the court). Compiled by Chang Cho 張鷟 (cs 675). Peking: Chung-hua shu-chü, 1979.

Chen Yüeh-o ch'un-feng Ch'ing-shuo t'ang 甄月娥春風慶朔堂 (Chen Yüeh-o: Spring breeze at Ch'ing-shuo Pavilion). By Chu Yu-tun 朱有燉 (1379–1439).

Microfilm copy of the original edition, preface dated 1406, in the Peking Library.

Ch'en Hsün-chien Mei-ling shih-ch'i chi 陳巡檢梅嶺失妻記 (Police Chief Ch'en loses his wife in crossing the Mei-ling Range). In *Ch'ing-p'ing shan-t'ang hua-pen*, pp. 121–36.

Cheng Chieh-shih li-kung shen-pi kung 鄭節使立功神臂弓 (Commissioner Cheng wins merit with his magic bow). In *Hsing-shih heng-yen*, vol. 2, *chüan* 31, pp. 656–73.

Cheng-t'ung Tao-tsang 正統道藏 (The Cheng-t'ung [1436–49] Taoist canon). Shanghai: Shang-wu yin-shu kuan, 1926.

Chi-le pien 雞肋編 (Chicken ribs collection). By Chuang Ch'o 莊綽 (c. 1090–c. 1150). Preface dated 1133. Peking: Chung-hua shu-chü, 1983.

[Chi-p'ing chiao-chu] Hsi-hsiang chi 集評校注西廂記 (The romance of the western chamber [with collected commentary and critical annotation]). Edited and annotated by Wang Chi-ssu 王季思. Shanghai: Shang-hai ku-chi ch'u-pan she, 1987.

Chi-shan lu 積善錄 (Record of accumulated good deeds). By Huang Kuang-ta 黃光大. Preface dated 1178. In *Shuo-fu*, vol. 2, *chüan* 64, pp. 1a–5a.

Chi Ya-fan chin-man ch'an-huo 計押番金鰻產禍 (Duty Group Leader Chi's golden eel engenders catastrophe). In *Ching-shih t'ung-yen, chüan* 20, pp. 274–88.

Ch'i-kuo ch'un-ch'iu p'ing-hua 七國春秋平話 (The p'ing-hua on the events of the seven states). Originally published in 1321–23. Shanghai: Ku-tien wen-hsüeh ch'u-pan she, 1955.

Ch'i-tung yeh-yü 齊東野語 (Rustic words of a man from eastern Ch'i). By Chou Mi 周密 (1232–98). Preface dated 1291. Peking: Chung-hua shu-chü, 1983.

Chiao Hung chuan 嬌紅傳 (The Story of Chiao-niang and Fei-hung). By Sung Yüan 宋遠 (14th century). In *Ku-tai wen-yen tuan-p'ien hsiao-shuo hsüan-chu*, erh-chi, pp. 280–323.

[Chiao-ting] Yüan-k'an tsa-chü san-shih chung 校訂元刊雜劇三十種 (A collated edition of Thirty tsa-chü dramas printed during the Yüan dynasty). Edited by Cheng Ch'ien 鄭騫. Taipei: Shih-chieh shu-chü, 1962.

Chieh-chih-erh chi 戒指兒記 (The story of the ring). In *Ch'ing-p'ing shan-t'ang hua-pen*, pp. 244–71.

Chieh-yün pien 解慍編 (An anger-dispelling collection). Compiled by Lo-t'ien Ta-hsiao sheng 樂天大笑生. Allegedly printed in the Chia-ching reign period (1522–1566). In *Li-tai hsiao-hua chi hsü-pien*, pp. 13–74.

Chien-teng hsin-hua 剪燈新話 (New wick-trimming tales). By Ch'ü Yu 瞿佑 (1341–1427). In *Chien-teng hsin-hua [wai erh-chung]*, pp. 1–119.

Chien-teng hsin-hua [wai erh-chung] 剪燈新話 [外二種] (New wick-trimming tales [plus two other works]). Edited and annotated by Chou I 周夷. Shanghai: Ku-tien wen-hsüeh ch'u-pan she, 1957.

Chien-teng yü-hua 剪燈餘話 (More wick-trimming tales). By Li Ch'ang-ch'i 李昌祺 (1376–1452). Author's preface dated 1420. In *Chien-teng hsin-hua [wai erh-chung]*, pp. 121–312.

Chien-t'ieh ho-shang 簡貼和尚 (The monk's billet-doux). In *Ch'ing-p'ing*

shan-t'ang hua-pen 清平山堂話本, pp. 6–21.
Chien-wen lu 見聞錄 (A record of things seen and heard). By Hu No 胡訥 (fl. late 10th century). In *Lei-shuo*, vol. 2, *chüan* 19, pp. 11a–17a.
Ch'ien-chin chi 千金記 (The thousand pieces of gold). By Shen Ts'ai 沈采 (15th century). *Liu-shih chung ch'ü* edition. Taipei: K'ai-ming shu-tien, 1970.
Ch'ien Kung-liang Ts'e-yü 錢公良測語 (Penetrating aphorisms of Ch'ien Ch'i 錢琦 [1469–1549]). In *Ts'ung-shu chi-ch'eng,* 1st series, vol. 374.
Ch'ien-t'ang meng 錢塘夢 (The dream in Ch'ien-t'ang). Included as part of the front matter in the 1498 edition of the *Hsi-hsiang chi*, pp. 1a–4b.
Ch'ien-tzu wen 千字文 (Thousand-character text). By Chou Hsing-ssu 周興嗣 (d. 521). In *Dai Kan-Wa jiten*, 2:522–23.
Chih-shih yü-wen 治世餘聞 (Recollections of a well-governed age). By Ch'en Hung-mo 陳洪謨 (1474–1555). Originally completed in 1521. Peking: Chung-hua shu-chü, 1985.
Chin-ch'ai chi 金釵記 (The gold hairpin). Manuscript dated 1431. Modern edition edited by Liu Nien-tzu 劉念茲. Canton: Kuang-tung jen-min ch'u-pan she, 1985.
Chin-chien chi 錦箋記 (The brocade note). By Chou Lü-ching 周履靖 (16th century). *Liu-shih chung ch'ü* edition. Taipei: K'ai-ming shu-tien, 1970.
Chin-ch'üeh chi 金雀記 (The golden sparrow). *Liu-shih chung ch'ü* edition. Taipei: K'ai-ming shu-tien, 1970.
Chin-kang k'o-i 金剛科儀. See *[Hsiao-shih] Chin-kang k'o-i [hui-yao chu-chieh]*.
Chin-kang pan-jo-po-lo-mi ching chu 金剛般若波羅蜜經註 (Commentary on the *Vajracchedikā prajñāpāramitā sutra*). By Tao-ch'uan 道川 (fl. 1127–63). Preface dated 1179. In *[Shinzan] Dai Nihon zokuzōkyō*, 24:535–65.
Chin-ling liu-yüan shih-yü 金陵六院市語 (Market argot of the six licensed brothels of Chin-ling). In *Han-shang huan wen-ts'un*, pp. 129–30.
Chin-ming ch'ih Wu Ch'ing feng Ai-ai 金明池吳清逢愛愛 (Wu Ch'ing meets Ai-ai at Chin-ming Pond). In *Ching-shih t'ung-yen*, *chüan* 30, pp. 459–71.
"*Chin P'ing Mei* pa" 金瓶梅跋 (Colophon to the *Chin P'ing Mei*). By Hsieh Chao-che 謝肇淛 (1567–1624). In his *Hsiao-ts'ao chai wen-chi*, *chüan* 24, pp. 30b–31b.
"*Chin P'ing Mei* tu-fa" 金瓶梅讀法 (How to read the *Chin P'ing Mei*). By Chang Chu-p'o 張竹坡 (1670–1698). Included in the prolegomena to his commentary on the novel, in *Chang Chu-p'o p'i-p'ing Ti-i ch'i-shu Chin P'ing Mei*, 1:25–50.
Chin P'ing Mei tz'u-hua 金瓶梅詞話 (Story of the plum in the golden vase). Preface dated 1618. 5 vols., fac. repr. Tokyo: Daian, 1963.
Chin shih 金史 (History of the Chin dynasty [1115–1234]). Compiled by T'o-t'o 脫脫 (1313–55) et. al. 8 vols. Peking: Chung-hua shu-chü, 1975.
Chin shu 晉書 (History of the Chin dynasty [265–420]). Compiled by Fang Hsüan-ling 房玄齡 (578–648) et al. 10 vols. Peking: Chung-hua shu-chü, 1974.
Chin-yin chi 金印記 (The golden seal). By Su Fu-chih 蘇復之 (14th century). In *Ku-pen hsi-ch'ü ts'ung-k'an, ch'u-chi*, item 27.
Ch'in ping liu-kuo p'ing-hua 秦併六國平話 (The p'ing-hua on the annexation of the six states by Ch'in). Originally published in 1321–23. Shanghai: Ku-tien wen-hsüeh ch'u-pan she, 1955.

Chinese Literature: Popular Fiction and Drama. Translated by H. C. Chang. Edinburgh: Edinburgh University Press, 1973.

Chinese Rhyme-Prose: Poems in the Fu Form from the Han and Six Dynasties Periods. Translated by Burton Watson. New York: Columbia University Press, 1971.

Ching-ch'ai chi 荆釵記 (The thorn hairpin). *Liu-shih chung ch'ü* edition. Taipei: K'ai-ming shu-tien, 1970.

Ching-shih t'ung-yen 警世通言 (Common words to warn the world). Edited by Feng Meng-lung 馮夢龍 (1574–1646). First published 1624. Peking: Tso-chia ch'u-pan she, 1957.

Ching-te ch'uan-teng lu 景德傳燈錄 (The transmission of the lamp compiled in the Ching-te reign period [1004–7]). Compiled by Tao-yüan 道原 (fl. early 11th century). In *Taishō shinshū daizōkyō*, vol. 51, no. 2076, pp. 196–467.

Ch'ing-p'ing shan-t'ang hua-pen 清平山堂話本 (Stories printed by the Ch'ing-p'ing Shan-t'ang). Edited by T'an Cheng-pi 譚正璧. Shanghai: Ku-tien wen-hsüeh ch'u-pan she, 1957.

Chiu Wu-tai shih 舊五代史 (Old history of the Five Dynasties). Compiled by Hsüeh Chü-cheng 薛居正 (912–981) et al. 6 vols. Peking: Chung-hua shu-chü, 1976.

Ch'iu-ya chi 秋崖集 (Autumn cliff collection). By Fang Yüeh 方岳 (1199–1262). In *Ssu-k'u ch'üan-shu chen-pen, san-chi*, vols. 248–51.

Cho Chi Pu chuan-wen 捉季布傳文 (Story of the apprehension of Chi Pu). In *Tun-huang pien-wen chi*, 1:51–84.

Ch'o-keng lu 輟耕錄 (Notes recorded during respites from the plow). By T'ao Tsung-i 陶宗儀 (c. 1316–c. 1403). Preface dated 1366. Peking: Chung-hua shu-chü, 1980.

Chou-i yin-te 周易引得 (A concordance to the *I-ching*). Taipei: Chinese Materials and Research Aids Service Center, 1966.

Chou-lien hsü-lun 晝簾緒論 (A preliminary discussion of diurnal routine). By Hu T'ai-ch'u 胡太初 (cs 1238). Written 1235, published 1253. In *Shuo-fu*, vol. 2, *chüan* 89, pp. 1a–18b.

Chu-tzu yü-lei 朱子語類 (Classified sayings of Master Chu). Compiled by Li Ching-te 黎靖德 (13th century). 8 vols. Taipei: Cheng-chung shu-chü, 1982.

Ch'uan-ch'i. See *P'ei Hsing Ch'uan-ch'i*.

Chuang-tzu: The Seven Inner Chapters and Other Writings from the Book Chuang-tzu. Translated by A. C. Graham. London: Allen and Unwin, 1981.

Chuang-tzu yin-te 莊子引得 (A concordance to *Chuang-tzu*). Cambridge: Harvard University Press, 1956.

Ch'ui-chien lu ch'üan-pien 吹劍錄全編 (Record of breathing into a sword-guard, complete edition). By Yü Wen-pao 俞文豹 (fl. c. 1250). Peking: Chung-hua shu-chü, 1959.

The Ch'un Ts'ew with the Tso Chuen. Translated by James Legge. Hong Kong: Hong Kong University Press, 1960.

Chung-ch'ing li-chi 鍾情麗集 (A pleasing tale of passion). In *Yen-chü pi-chi*, vol. 2, *chüan* 6, pp. 1a–40b, and vol. 3, *chüan* 7, pp. 1a–30a, upper register.

Chung-kuo feng-liu hsiao-shuo ts'ung-shu, ti-wu chi 中國風流小說叢書, 第五輯 (Collectanea of Chinese erotic fiction, fifth series). Nagoya: Ikemoto Yoshio, 1979.

Chung-kuo ku-tien hsi-ch'ü lun-chu chi-ch'eng 中國古典戲曲論著集成 (A corpus of critical works on classical Chinese drama). Compiled by Chung-kuo hsi-ch'ü yen-chiu yüan 中國戲曲研究院 (The Chinese Academy of Dramatic Arts). 10 vols. Peking: Chung-kuo hsi-chü ch'u-pan she, 1959.

Chung-kuo min-chien chu-shen 中國民間諸神 (The gods of Chinese folklore). Compiled by Tsung Li 宗力 and Liu Ch'ün 劉群. Shih-chia chuang: Ho-pei jen-min ch'u-pan she, 1987.

Ch'üan Chin Yüan tz'u 全金元詞 (Complete lyrics of the Chin and Yüan dynasties). Compiled by T'ang Kuei-chang 唐圭璋. 2 vols. Peking: Chung-hua shu-chü, 1979.

Ch'üan-fang pei-tsu 全芳備祖 (A comprehensive florilegium on horticulture). Compiled by Ch'en Ching-i 陳景沂. Preface dated 1256. 2 vols. Peking: Nung-yeh ch'u-pan she, 1982.

Ch'üan-Han chih-chuan 全漢志傳 (Chronicle of the entire Han dynasty). 12 *chüan*. Chien-yang: K'o-ch'in chai, 1588. Fac. repr. In *Ku-pen hsiao-shuo ts'ung-k'an, ti-wu chi*, vols. 2–3.

Ch'üan Shang-ku San-tai Ch'in Han San-kuo Liu-ch'ao wen 全上古三代秦漢三國六朝文 (Complete prose from high antiquity, the Three Dynasties, Ch'in, Han, the Three Kingdoms, and the Six Dynasties). Compiled by Yen K'o-chün 嚴可均 (1762–1843). 5 vols. Peking: Chung-hua shu-chü, 1965.

Ch'üan Sung tz'u 全宋詞 (Complete *tz'u* lyrics of the Sung). Compiled by T'ang Kuei-chang 唐圭璋. 5 vols. Hong Kong: Chung-hua shu-chü, 1977.

Ch'üan T'ang shih 全唐詩 (Complete poetry of the T'ang). 12 vols. Peking: Chung-hua shu-chü, 1960.

Ch'üan T'ang wen 全唐文 (Complete prose of the T'ang). 20 vols. Kyoto: Chūbun shuppan-sha, 1976.

Ch'üan Yüan san-ch'ü 全元散曲 (Complete nondramatic song lyrics of the Yüan). Compiled by Sui Shu-sen 隋樹森. 2 vols. Peking: Chung-hua shu-chü, 1964.

Ch'ün-yin lei-hsüan 群音類選 (An anthology of songs categorized by musical type). Compiled by Hu Wen-huan 胡文煥 (fl. 1592–1617). 4 vols., fac. repr. Peking: Chung-hua shu-chü, 1980.

Classical Chinese Tales of the Supernatural and the Fantastic, Edited by Karl S. Y. Kao. Bloomington: Indiana University Press, 1985.

A *Compilation of Anecdotes of Sung Personalities*. Compiled by Ting Ch'uan-ching; translated by Chu Djang and Jane C. Djang. (N.p.: St. John's University Press, 1989.)

The Complete Works of Chuang Tzu. Translated by Burton Watson. New York: Columbia University Press, 1968.

The Complete Works of Han Fei Tzu. Translated by W. K. Liao. 2 vols. London: Arthur Probsthain, 1959.

The Courtesan's Jewel Box. Translated by Yang Xianyi and Gladys Yang. Peking: Foreign Languages Press, 1981.

Courtier and Commoner in Ancient China: Selections from the History of the Former Han by Pan Ku. Translated by Burton Watson. New York: Columbia University Press, 1974.

Dai Kan-Wa jiten 大漢和辭典 (Great Chinese-Japanese dictionary). Compiled by Morohashi Tetsuji 諸橋轍次. 13 vols. Tokyo: Taishūkan shoten, 1960.

Djin Ping Meh: Schlehenblüten in goldener Vase. Translated by Otto and Artur Kibat. 6 vols. Hamburg: Verlag Die Waage, 1967–83.

Eight Chinese Plays. Translated by William Dolby. London: Paul Elek, 1978.

Eight Colloquial Tales of the Sung. Translated by Richard F. S. Yang. Taipei: The China Post, 1972.

Erh-Ch'eng chi 二程集 (The collected works of the two Ch'eng brothers). By Ch'eng Hao 程顥 (1032–85) and Ch'eng I 程頤 (1033–1107). 4 vols. Peking: Chung-hua shu-chü, 1981.

Fan Shih-hu chi 范石湖集 (Collected works of Fan Ch'eng-ta 范成大 [1126–93]). 2 vols. Peking: Chung-hua shu-chü, 1962.

Fei-yen chuan 飛烟傳 (The story of Pu Fei-yen). By Huang-fu Mei 皇甫枚 (fl. early 10th century). In *T'ang Sung ch'uan-ch'i chi*, pp. 160–65.

Feng Chih 封陟. By P'ei Hsing 裴鉶 (825–80). In *P'ei Hsing Ch'uan-ch'i*, pp. 65–69.

Feng-t'ien lu 奉天錄 (Record of [the imperial sojourn in] Feng-t'ien). By Chao Yüan-i 趙元一 (8th century). In *Ts'ung-shu chi-ch'eng*, 1st series, vol. 3834.

Feng-yün hui 風雲會 (The meeting of wind and cloud). By Lo Kuan-chung 羅貫中 (14th century). In *Yüan-ch'ü hsüan wai-pien*, 2:617–32.

Fleur en Fiole d'Or (Jin Ping Mei cihua). Translated by André Lévy. 2 vols. Paris: Gallimard, 1985.

The Flower Ornament Scripture: A Translation of the Avatamsaka Sutra. Vol. 3, *Entry into the Realm of Reality*. Translated by Thomas Cleary. Boston: Shambhala, 1987.

Fo-yin shih ssu t'iao Ch'in-niang 佛印師四調琴娘 (The Priest Fo-yin teases Ch'in-niang four times). In *Hsing-shih heng-yen*, vol. 1, *chüan* 12, pp. 232–40.

The Golden Casket: Chinese Novellas of Two Millennia. Translated by Wolfgang Bauer and Herbert Franke; translated from the German by Christopher Levenson. New York: Harcourt Brace and World, 1964.

The Golden Lotus: A Translation, from the Chinese Original, of the Novel Chin P'ing Mei. Translated by Clement Egerton. 4 vols. London: Routledge & Kegan Paul, 1972.

Hai-fu shan-t'ang tz'u-kao 海浮山堂詞稿 (Draft lyrics from Hai-fu Shan-t'ang). By Feng Wei-min 馮惟敏 (1511–80). Preface dated 1566. Shanghai: Shang-hai ku-chi ch'u-pan she, 1981.

Hai-wen lu 駭聞錄 (Record of startling events). By Li T'ien 李畋 (cs 992). In *Lei-shuo*, vol. 2, *chüan* 19, pp. 3b–11a.

Han Ch'ang-li wen-chi chiao-chu 韓昌黎文集校注 (The prose works of Han Yü 韓愈 [768–824] with critical annotation). Edited by Ma T'ung-po 馬通伯. Shanghai: Ku-tien wen-hsüeh ch'u-pan she, 1957.

Han Fei tzu so-yin 韓非子索引 (A concordance to *Han Fei tzu*). Peking: Chung-hua shu-chü, 1982.

Han-shang huan wen-ts'un 漢上宦文存 (Literary remains of the Han-shang Studio). By Ch'ien Nan-yang 錢南揚. Shanghai: Shang-hai wen-i ch'u-pan she, 1980.

Han-shih wai-chuan 韓詩外傳 (Exoteric anecdotes illustrative of the Han version of the *Book of songs*). Compiled by Han Ying 韓嬰 (2d century B.C.). In *Ts'ung-shu chi-ch'eng*, 1st series, vols. 524–25.

Han Shih Wai Chuan: Han Ying's Illustrations of the Didactic Application of the Classic of Songs. Translated by James Robert Hightower. Cambridge: Harvard University Press, 1952.

Han-shu 漢書 (History of the Former Han dynasty). Compiled by Pan Ku 班固 (32–92). 8 vols. Peking: Chung-hua shu-chü, 1962.

Ho-t'ung wen-tzu chi 合同文字記 (The story of the contract). In *Ch'ing-p'ing shan-t'ang hua-pen*, pp. 33–38.

Hou-Han shu 後漢書 (History of the Later Han dynasty). Compiled by Fan Yeh 范曄 (398–445). 12 vols. Peking: Chung-hua shu-chü, 1965.

Hou-ts'un Ch'ien-chia shih chiao-chu 後村千家詩校注 (Liu K'o-chuang's Poems by a thousand authors edited and annotated). Compiled by Liu K'o-chuang 劉克莊 (1187–1269); edited and annotated by Hu Wen-nung 胡問儂 and Wang Hao-sou 王皓叟. Kuei-yang: Kuei-chou jen-min ch'u-pan she, 1986.

"How to Read the *Chin P'ing Mei*." By Chang Chu-p'o (1670–98). Translated by David T. Roy. In *How to Read the Chinese Novel*, edited by David L. Rolston, pp. 202–43.

How to Read the Chinese Novel. Edited by David L. Rolston. Princeton: Princeton University Press, 1990.

Hsi-ching fu 西京賦 (Western metropolis rhapsody). By Chang Heng 張衡 (78–139). In *Wen-hsüan*, vol. 1, *chüan* 2, pp. 1a–29b.

Hsi-ching tsa-chi 西京雜記 (Miscellanies of the Western capital). Compiled in the sixth century. 6 *chüan*. In *Pi-chi hsiao-shuo ta-kuan*, vol. 1, *ts'e* 1.

Hsi-hsiang chi 西廂記 (The romance of the western chamber). Fac. repr. of 1498 edition. Taipei: Shih-chieh shu-chü, 1963.

Hsi-hsiang hui-pien 西廂匯編 (Collected versions of the *Romance of the western chamber*). Compiled by Huo Sung-lin 霍松林. Chi-nan: Shan-tung wen-i ch'u-pan she, 1987.

Hsi-hu san-t'a chi 西湖三塔記 (The three pagodas at West Lake). In *Ch'ing-p'ing shan-t'ang hua-pen*, pp. 22–32.

Hsi-yu chi 西遊記 (The journey to the west). 2 vols. Peking: Tso-chia ch'u-pan she, 1954.

Hsi-yüan lu 洗冤錄 (The washing away of wrongs). By Sung Tz'u 宋慈 (1186–1249). Author's preface dated 1247. Peking: Ch'ün-chung ch'u-pan she, 1982.

Hsiang-nang chi 香囊記 (The scent bag). By Shao Ts'an 邵璨 (15th century). *Liu-shih chung ch'ü* edition. Taipei: K'ai-ming shu-tien, 1970.

Hsiang-nang yüan 香囊怨 (The tragedy of the scent bag). By Chu Yu-tun 朱有燉 (1379–1439). Author's preface dated 1433. In *Sheng-Ming tsa-chü, erh-chi*.

Hsiao fu-jen chin-ch'ien tseng nien-shao 小夫人金錢贈年少 (The merchant's wife offers money to a young clerk). In *Ching-shih t'ung-yen*, *chüan* 16, pp. 222–33.

Hsiao-p'in chi 效顰集 (Emulative frowns collection). By Chao Pi 趙弼. Author's postface dated 1428. Shanghai: Ku-tien wen-hsüeh ch'u-pan she, 1957.

[Hsiao-shih] Chin-kang k'o-i [hui-yao chu-chieh] [銷釋] 金剛科儀 [會要註解] ([Clearly presented] Liturgical exposition of the *Diamond sutra* [with critical commentary]). Edited and annotated by Chüeh-lien 覺連. Preface dated 1551. In *[Shinzan] Dai Nihon zokuzōkyō* 24:650–756.

Hsiao-ts'ao chai wen-chi 小草齋文集 (Collected prose from the Small Grass Script Studio). By Hsieh Chao-che 謝肇淛 (1567–1624). Preface dated 1626. Original edition in Sonkeikaku Library, Tokyo.

Hsieh hsüeh-shih wen-chi 解學士文集 (Collected works of Academician Hsieh). By Hsieh Chin 解縉 (1369–1415). 10 *chüan*. Preface dated 1562. Microfilm copy in the East Asian Library, University of Chicago.

Hsien-Ch'in Han Wei Chin Nan-pei ch'ao shih 先秦漢魏晉南北朝詩 (Complete poetry of the Pre-Ch'in, Han, Wei, Chin, and Northern and Southern dynasties). Compiled by Lu Ch'in-li 逯欽立. 3 vols. Peking: Chung-hua shu-chü, 1983.

Hsin-ch'i teng-mi: Chiang-hu ch'iao-yü 新奇燈謎江湖俏語 (Novel and unusual lantern riddles: Witticisms current in the demimonde). Compiled in late Ming. In *Han-shang huan wen-ts'un*, pp. 168–74.

Hsin-ch'iao shih Han Wu mai ch'un-ch'ing 新橋市韓五賣春情 (Han Wu-niang sells her charms at New Bridge Market). In *Ku-chin hsiao-shuo*, vol. 1, *chüan* 3, pp. 62–79.

[Hsin-k'o hsiu-hsiang p'i-p'ing] Chin P'ing Mei 新刻繡像批評金瓶梅 ([Newly cut illustrated commentarial edition] of the *Chin P'ing Mei*). 2 vols. Chi-nan: Ch'i-Lu shu-she, 1989.

[Hsin-pien] Liu Chih-yüan huan-hsiang Pai-t'u chi 新編劉知遠還鄉白兔記 ([Newly compiled] Liu Chih-yüan's return home: The white rabbit). In *Ming Ch'eng-hua shuo-ch'ang tz'u-hua ts'ung-k'an, ts'e* 12.

[Hsin-pien] Wu-tai shih p'ing-hua [新編] 五代史平話 ([Newly compiled] p'ing-hua on the history of the Five Dynasties). Originally published in the 14th century. Shanghai: Chung-kuo ku-tien wen-hsüeh ch'u-pan she, 1954.

Hsin-shang hsü-pien 欣賞續編 (A collectanea on connoisseurship continued). Compiled by Mao I-hsiang 茅一相 (16th century). Ming edition in the Gest Collection of the Princeton University Library.

Hsing-shih heng-yen 醒世恆言 (Constant words to awaken the world). Edited by Feng Meng-lung 馮夢龍 (1574–1646). First published in 1627. 2 vols. Hong Kong: Chung-hua shu-chü, 1958.

Hsiu-ju chi 繡襦記 (The embroidered jacket). By Hsü Lin 徐霖 (1462–1538). *Liu-shih chung ch'ü* edition. Taipei: K'ai-ming shu-tien, 1970.

Hsiu-t'a yeh-shih 繡榻野史 (Unofficial history of the embroidered couch). By Lü T'ien-ch'eng 呂天成 (1580–1618). Preface dated 1608. Fac. repr. In *Chung-kuo feng-liu hsiao-shuo ts'ung-shu, ti-wu chi.*

Hsü Ch'i Hsieh chi 續齊諧記 (Continuation of *Tales of Ch'i Hsieh*). By Wu Chün 吳均 (469–520). In Wang Kuo-liang, *Hsü Ch'i Hsieh chi yen-chiu*, pp. 23–64.

Hsü Hsüan-kuai lu 續玄怪錄 (Continuation of *Accounts of mysteries and anomalies*). See *Hsüan-kuai lu; Hsü Hsüan-kuai lu*, pp. 135–98.

Hsü Tsang-ching 續藏經 (Continuation of the Buddhist canon). 150 vols., fac.

repr. Hong Kong: Hsiang-kang ying-yin *Hsü Tsang-ching* wei-yüan hui, 1967.

Hsüan-ho i-shih 宣和遺事 (Forgotten events of the Hsüan-ho reign period [1119–25]). Shanghai: Shang-hai ku-tien wen-hsüeh ch'u-pan she, 1955.

Hsüan-ho p'ai-p'u 宣和牌譜 (A manual for Hsüan-ho [1119–25] dominoes). By Ch'ü Yu 瞿佑 (1341–1427). In *Shuo-fu hsü*, vol. 10, *chüan* 38, pp. 1a–17a.

Hsüan-ho p'u ya-p'ai hui-chi 宣和譜牙牌彙集 (A manual for Hsüan-ho [1119–25] dominoes with supplementary materials). Original compiler's preface dated 1757, redactor's preface dated 1886. N.p.: Hung-wen chai, 1888.

Hsüan-kuai lu; Hsü Hsüan-kuai lu 玄怪錄, 續玄怪錄 (Accounts of mysteries and anomalies; Continuation of *Accounts of mysteries and anomalies*). By Niu Seng-ju 牛僧孺 (779–848) and Li Fu-yen 李復言. (9th century). Peking: Chung-hua shu-chü, 1982.

Hsün-ch'in chi 尋親記 (The quest for the father). *Liu-shih chung ch'ü* edition. Taipei: K'ai-ming shu-tien, 1970.

Hsün Tzu: Basic Writings. Translated by Burton Watson. New York: Columbia University Press, 1963.

Hsün-tzu yin-te 荀子引得 (A concordance to *Hsün-tzu*; Taipei: Chinese Materials and Research Aids Service Center, 1966.

Hua-chi yü-yün 滑稽餘韻 (Superfluous rhymes on humorous subjects). By Ch'en To 陳鐸 (fl. early 16th century). Reprinted from a Wan-li [1573–1620] edition. In Lu Kung, *Fang-shu chien-wen lu*, pp. 317–38.

Hua Kuan So ch'u-shen chuan 花關索出身傳 (The story of how Hua Kuan So got his start in life). Originally published in 1478. Fac. repr. In *Ming Ch'eng-hua shuo-ch'ang tz'u-hua ts'ung-k'an, ts'e* 1.

Hua Kuan So jen-fu chuan 花關索認父傳 (The story of how Hua Kuan So claimed his patrimony). Fac. repr. In *Ming Ch'eng-hua shuo-ch'ang tz'u-hua ts'ung-k'an, ts'e* 1.

Hua-ying chin-chen 花營錦陣 (Variegated positions of the flowery battle). Hang-chou: Yang-hao chai, c. 1610. Fac. repr. in R. H. Van Gulik, *Erotic Colour Prints of the Ming Period*, vol. 3.

Huai-ch'un ya-chi 懷春雅集 (Elegant vignettes of spring yearning). In *Yen-chü pi-chi*, vol. 3. *chüan* 9, pp. 16b–32a, and *chüan* 10, pp. 1a–39b, upper register.

Huai-nan hung-lieh chi-chieh 淮南鴻烈集解 (Collected commentaries on the *Huai-nan tzu*). Edited by Liu Wen-tien 劉文典. 2 vols. Taipei: T'ai-wan Shang-wu yin-shu kuan, 1969.

Huan-hun chi 還魂記 (The return of the soul). Attributed to Hsin-hsin k'o 欣欣客. In *Ku-pen hsi-ch'ü ts'ung-k'an, erh-chi*, item 5.

Huan-men tzu-ti ts'o li-shen 宦門子弟錯立身 (The scion of an official's family opts for the wrong career). In *Yung-lo ta-tien hsi-wen san-chung chiao-chu*, pp. 219–55.

Huan-tai chi 還帶記 (The return of the belts). By Shen Ts'ai 沈采 (15th century). In *Ku-pen hsi-ch'ü ts'ung-k'an, ch'u-chi*, item 32.

Huang-ch'ao pien-nien kang-mu pei-yao 皇朝編年綱目備要 (Chronological outline of the significant events of the imperial [Sung] dynasty). Compiled by Ch'en Chün 陳均 (c. 1165–c. 1236). Preface dated 1229. 2 vols., fac. repr. Taipei: Ch'eng-wen ch'u-pan she, 1966.

Hui-chu lu 揮麈錄 (Records for chowrie waving conversation). By Wang Ming-ch'ing 王明清 (1127–c. 1214). Peking: Chung-hua shu-chü, 1961.

A Hundred and Seventy Chinese Poems. Translated by Arthur Waley. New York: Alfred A. Knopf, 1919.

The I Ching or Book of Changes. Translated by Richard Wilhelm; translated from the German by Cary F. Baynes. 2 vols. New York: Pantheon Books, 1961.

I-k'u kuei lai tao-jen ch'u-kuai 一窟鬼癩道人除怪 (A mangy Taoist exorcises a lair of demons). In *Ching-shih t'ung-yen, chüan* 14, pp. 185–98.

I-li 儀禮 (Book of etiquette and ceremonial). In *Shih-san ching ching-wen*.

The I-Li or Book of Etiquette and Ceremonial. Translated by John Steele. 2 vols. London: Probsthain, 1917.

I-wen lei-chü 藝文類聚 (A categorized chrestomathy of literary excerpts). Compiled by Ou-yang Hsün 歐陽詢 (557–641). 2 vols. Peking: Chung-hua shu-chü, 1965.

Jen hsiao-tzu lieh-hsing wei shen 任孝子烈性為神 (The apotheosis of Jen the filial son). In *Ku-chin hsiao-shuo*, vol. 2, *chüan* 38, pp. 571–86.

Jou p'u-t'uan 肉蒲團 (The carnal prayer mat). By Li Yü 李漁 (1610–80). Preface dated 1657. 4 *chüan*. Japanese edition of 1705.

Journey to the West. Translated by W. J. F. Jenner. 3 vols. Beijing: Foreign Languages Press, 1982–86.

The Journey to the West. Translated by Anthony C. Yu. 4 vols. Chicago: University of Chicago Press, 1977–83.

Ju-i chün chuan 如意君傳 (The tale of Lord As You Like It). Japanese movable type edition, colophon dated 1880.

Ju-meng lu 如夢錄 (Record of a seeming dream). In *San-i t'ang ts'ung-shu, ts'e* 48.

Juan Chi chi chiao-chu 阮籍集校注 (The works of Juan Chi edited and annotated). By Juan Chi 阮籍 (210–63); edited and annotated by Ch'en Po-chün 陳伯君. Peking: Chung-hua shu-chü, 1987.

Jung-chai sui-pi 容齋隨筆 (Miscellaneous notes from the Tolerant Study). By Hung Mai 洪邁 (1123–1202). 2 vols. Shanghai: Shang-hai ku-chi ch'u-pan she, 1978.

K'ai-yüan T'ien-pao i-shih 開元天寶遺事 (Forgotten events of the K'ai-yüan [713–41] and T'ien-pao [742–56] reign periods). Compiled by Wang Jen-yü 王仁裕 (880–942). In *K'ai-yüan T'ien-pao i-shih shih-chung*, pp. 65–109.

K'ai-yüan T'ien-pao i-shih shih-chung 開元天寶遺事十種 (Ten works dealing with forgotten events of the K'ai-yüan [713–741] and T'ien-pao [742–756] reign periods). Edited by Ting Ju-ming 丁如明. Shanghai: Shang-hai ku-chi ch'u-pan she, 1985.

K'an p'i-hsüeh tan-cheng Erh-lang Shen 勘皮靴單證二郎神 (Investigation of a leather boot convicts Erh-lang Shen). In *Hsing-shih heng-yen*, vol. 1, *chüan* 13, pp. 241–63.

Kin Pei Bai 金瓶梅 (Chin P'ing Mei). Translated by Ono Shinobu 小野忍 and Chida Kuichi 千田九一. 3 vols. Tokyo: Heibonsha, 1962.

K'o-tso chui-yü 客座贅語 (Superfluous words of a sojourner). By Ku Ch'i-yüan 顧起元 (1565–1628). Author's colophon dated 1618. Peking: Chung-hua shu-chü, 1987.

Ku-ch'eng chi 古城記 (The reunion at Ku-ch'eng). In *Ku-pen hsi-ch'ü ts'ung-k'an, ch'u-chi*, item 25.

Ku-chin hsiao-shuo 古今小說 (Stories old and new). Edited by Feng Meng-lung 馮夢龍 (1574–1646). 2 vols., fac. repr. of original edition published in 1620–24. Taipei: Shih-chieh shu-chü, 1958.

Ku-chin hsiao-shuo 古今小說 (Stories old and new). Edited by Feng Meng-lung 馮夢龍 (1574–1646). 2 vols. Peking: Jen-min wen-hsüeh ch'u-pan she, 1958.

Ku-chin t'u-shu chi-ch'eng 古今圖書集成 (A comprehensive corpus of books and illustrations ancient and modern), presented to the emperor in 1725. Fac. repr. Taipei: Wen-hsing shu-tien, 1964.

Ku-chin tz'u-hua 古今詞話 (Comments on lyrics ancient and modern). Compiled by Shen Hsiung 沈雄 (17th century). In *Tz'u-hua ts'ung-pien*, 1:727–1051.

Ku-pen hsi-ch'ü ts'ung-k'an, ch'u-chi 古本戲曲叢刊, 初集 (Collectanea of rare editions of traditional drama, first series). Shanghai: Shang-wu yin-shu kuan, 1954.

Ku-pen hsi-ch'ü ts'ung-k'an, erh-chi 古本戲曲叢刊, 二集 (Collectanea of rare editions of traditional drama, second series). Shanghai: Shang-wu yin-shu kuan, 1955.

Ku-pen hsiao-shuo ts'ung-k'an, ti-erh chi 古本小說叢刊, 第二集 (Collectanea of rare editions of traditional fiction, second series). Peking: Chung-hua shu-chü, 1990.

Ku-pen hsiao-shuo ts'ung-k'an, ti-wu chi 古本小說叢刊, 第五集 (Collectanea of rare editions of traditional fiction, fifth series). Peking: Chung-hua shu-chü, 1990.

Ku-pen hsiao-shuo ts'ung-k'an, ti-shih chi 古本小說叢刊, 第十集 (Collectanea of rare editions of traditional fiction, tenth series). Peking: Chung-hua shu-chü, 1990.

Ku-pen Yüan Ming tsa-chü 孤本元明雜劇 (Unique editions of Yüan and Ming tsa-chü drama). Edited by Wang Chi-lieh 王季烈. 4 vols. Peking: Chung-kuo hsi-chü ch'u-pan she, 1958.

Ku-tai wen-yen tuan-p'ien hsiao-shuo hsüan-chu, er-chi 古代文言短篇小說選注, 二集 (An annotated selection of classic literary tales, second collection). Compiled by Ch'eng Po-ch'üan 成柏泉. Shanghai: Shang-hai ku-chi ch'u-pan she, 1984.

Ku tsun-su yü-lu 古尊宿語錄 (The recorded sayings of eminent monks of old). Compiled by Tse Tsang-chu 賾藏主 (13th century). In *Hsü Tsang-ching*, 118:79a–418a.

K'uai-tsui Li Ts'ui-lien chi 快嘴李翠蓮記 (The story of the sharp-tongued Li Ts'ui-lien). In *Ch'ing-p'ing shan-t'ang hua-pen*, pp. 52–67.

Kuo-ch'üeh 國榷 (An evaluation of the events of our dynasty). By T'an Ch'ien 談遷 (1594–1658). 6 vols. Peking: Ku-chi ch'u-pan she, 1958.

Lao-hsüeh An pi-chi 老學菴筆記 (Miscellaneous notes from an Old Scholar's Retreat). By Lu Yu 陸游 (1125–1210). Peking: Chung-hua shu-chü, 1979.

Lei-shuo 類說 (Categorized records). Compiled by Tseng Ts'ao 曾慥 (12th century). 5 vols., fac. repr. Peking: Wen-hsüeh ku-chi k'an-hsing she, 1955.

Li-chi 禮記 (The book of rites). In *Shih-san ching ching-wen*.

Li Chi: Book of Rites. Translated by James Legge. 2 vols. New Hyde Park, N.Y.: University Books, 1967.

Li K'ai-hsien chi 李開先集 (The collected works of Li K'ai-hsien). By Li K'ai-hsien 李開先 (1502–68). Edited by Lu Kung 路工. 3 vols. Peking: Chung-hua shu-chü, 1959.

Li Shih-shih wai-chuan 李師師外傳 (Unofficial biography of Li Shih-shih). In *T'ang Sung ch'uan-ch'i chi*, pp. 313–20.

Li-tai hsiao-hua chi hsü-pien 歷代笑話集續編 (Continuation of *Jokes of successive ages*). Compiled by Wang Chen-min 王貞珉 and Wang Li-ch'i 王利器. Shen-yang: Ch'un-feng wen-i ch'u-pan she, 1985.

Li-tai tz'u-hua 歷代詞話 (Talks on lyrics chronologically arranged). Compiled by Wang I-ch'ing 王弈清 (cs 1691) et al. In *Tz'u-hua ts'ung-pien*, 2:1053–1323.

Li-yüan an-shih yüeh-fu hsin-sheng 梨園按試樂府新聲 (Model new song lyrics from the Pear Garden). Modern edition edited by Sui Shu-sen 隋樹森. Peking: Chung-hua shu-chü, 1958.

Li Yüan Wu-chiang chiu chu-she 李元吳江救朱蛇 (Li Yüan saves a red snake on the Wu River). In *Ch'ing-p'ing shan-t'ang hua-pen*, pp. 324–34.

Le Lie-sien Tchouan. Translated by Max Kaltenmark. Peking: Université de Paris, Publications du Centre d'études sinologiques de Pékin, 1953.

Liu Chih-yüan chu-kung-tiao [chiao-chu] 劉知遠諸宮調 [校注] (Medley in various modes on Liu Chih-yüan [collated and annotated]). Edited by Lan Li-ming 藍立蓂. Ch'eng-tu: Pa-Shu shu-she, 1989.

Liu-ch'ing jih-cha 留青日札 (Daily jottings worthy of preservation). By T'ien I-heng 田藝蘅 (1524–c. 1574). Preface dated 1572. Fac. repr of 1609 edition. Shanghai: Shang-hai ku-chi ch'u-pan she, 1985.

Liu-shih chung ch'ü 六十種曲 (Sixty ch'uan-ch'i dramas). Compiled by Mao Chin 毛晉 (1599–1659). 60 vols. Taipei: K'ai-ming shu-tien, 1970.

Lo-yang ch'ieh-lan chi chiao-chu 洛陽伽藍記校注 (A critical edition of *A record of Buddhist monasteries in Lo-yang*). Edited by Fan Hsiang-yung 范祥雍. Shanghai: Ku-tien wen-hsüeh ch'u-pan she, 1958.

Lo-yang san-kuai chi 洛陽三怪記 (The three monsters of Lo-yang). In *Ch'ing-p'ing shan-t'ang hua-pen*, pp. 67–78.

Lung-men yin-hsiu 龍門隱秀 (The beauty concealed at Lung-men). In *Ku-pen Yüan Ming tsa-chü*, vol. 3.

The Lute: Kao Ming's P'i-p'a chi. Translated by Jean Mulligan. New York: Columbia University Press, 1980.

Lü-ch'uang nü-shih 綠窗女史 (Female scribes of the green gauze windows). 7 vols. Fac. repr. of late Ming edition. In *Ming-Ch'ing shan-pen hsiao-shuo ts'ung-k'an, ch'u-pien*.

Lü Tung-pin fei-chien chan Huang-lung 呂洞賓飛劍斬黃龍 (Lü Tung-pin beheads Huang-lung with his flying sword). In *Hsing-shih heng-yen*, vol. 2, *chüan* 21, pp. 453–66.

Ma Cheng 馬拯. In *P'ei Hsing Ch'uan-ch'i*, pp. 62–64.

The Man Who Sold a Ghost: Chinese Tales of the 3rd–6th Centuries. Translated by Yang Hsien-yi and Gladys Yang. Peking: Foreign Languages Press, 1958.

Mao-shih yin-te 毛詩引得 (Concordance to the Mao version of the *Book of songs*).

Tokyo: Japan Council for East Asian Studies, 1962.

Master Tung's Western Chamber Romance. Translated by Li-li Ch'en. Cambridge: Cambridge University Press, 1976.

Mencius. Translated by D. C. Lau. Baltimore: Penguin Books, 1970.

Meng Chiang nü pien-wen 孟姜女變文 (The story of Meng Chiang). In *Tun-huang pien-wen chi*, 1:32–35.

Meng-tzu yin-te 孟子引得 (A Concordance to *Meng-tzu*). Taipei: Chinese Materials and Research Aids Service Center, 1966.

Ming Ch'eng-hua shuo-ch'ang tz'u-hua ts'ung-k'an 明成化說唱詞話叢刊 (Corpus of prosimetric tz'u-hua narratives published in the Ch'eng-hua reign period [1465–1487] of the Ming dynasty). 12 *ts'e*. Shanghai: Shanghai Museum, 1973.

Ming-Ch'ing shan-pen hsiao-shuo ts'ung-k'an, ch'u-pien 明清善本小說叢刊初編 (Collectanea of rare editions of Ming-Ch'ing fiction, first series). Taipei: T'ien-i ch'u-pan she, 1985.

Ming-chu chi 明珠記 (The luminous pearl). By Lu Ts'ai 陸采 (1497–1537). *Liu-shih chung ch'ü* edition. Taipei: K'ai-ming shu-tien, 1970.

Ming-feng chi 鳴鳳記 (The singing phoenix). *Liu-shih chung ch'ü edition*. Taipei: K'ai-ming shu-tien, 1970.

Ming-ho yü-yin 鳴鶴餘音 (Lingering notes of the calling crane). Compiled by P'eng Chih-chung 彭致中 (14th century). In *Cheng-t'ung Tao-tsang, ts'e* 744–45.

Ming-hsin pao-chien 明心寶鑑 (A precious mirror to illuminate the mind). Microfilm copy of a Ming edition in the East Asian Library, University of Chicago.

Ming-jen tsa-chü hsüan 明人雜劇選 (An anthology of Ming tsa-chü drama). Compiled by Chou I-pai 周貽白. Peking: Jen-min wen-hsüeh ch'u-pan she, 1958.

Ming shih 明史 (History of the Ming dynasty). Compiled by Chang T'ing-yü 張廷玉 (1672–1755) et al. 28 vols. Peking: Chung-hua shu-chü, 1974.

Ming shih-lu 明實錄 (Veritable records of the Ming dynasty). 133 vols., fac. repr. Taipei: Academia Sinica, 1961–66.

Ming-tai ko-ch'ü hsüan 明代歌曲選 (An anthology of Ming song lyrics). Compiled by Lu Kung 路工. Shanghai: Shang-hai ku-tien wen-hsüeh ch'u-pan she, 1956.

Ming-tai lü-li hui-pien 明代律例彙編 (Comprehensive edition of the Ming penal code and judicial regulations). Compiled by Huang Chang-chien 黃彰健. 2 vols. Taipei: Academia Sinica, 1979.

The Moon and the Zither: The Story of the Western Wing. By Wang Shifu; translated by Stephen H. West and Wilt L. Idema. Berkeley: University of California Press, 1991.

Mu-tan t'ing 牡丹亭 (The peony pavilion). By T'ang Hsien-tsu 湯顯祖 (1550–1616); edited and annotated by Hsü Shuo-fang 徐朔方 and Yang Hsiao-mei 楊笑梅. Peking: Chung-hua shu-chü, 1959.

Nan Hsi-hsiang chi 南西廂記 (A southern version of the *Romance of the western chamber*). Usually attributed to Li Jih-hua 李日華 (fl. early 16th century). *Liu-shih chung ch'ü* edition. Taipei: K'ai-ming shu-tien, 1970.

Nan Hsi-hsiang chi 南西廂記 (A southern version of the *Romance of the western chamber*). By Lu Ts'ai 陸采 (1497–1537). In *Hsi-hsiang hui-pien*, pp. 323–416.

Nan-pei kung tz'u-chi [chiao-pu] 南北宮詞紀校補 (Southern- and Northern-style song lyrics [collated and augmented]). Compiled by Wu Hsiao-ling 吳曉鈴. Peking: Chung-hua shu-chü, 1961.

Nan shih 南史 (History of the Southern dynasties). Compiled by Li Yen-shou 李延壽 (7th century). Completed in 659. 6 vols. Peking: Chung-hua shu-chü, 1975.

Neng-kai chai man-lu 能改齋漫錄 (Random notes from the studio of one capable of correcting his faults). By Wu Tseng 吳曾 (d. c. 1170). 2 vols. Shanghai: Shang-hai ku-chi ch'u-pan she, 1979.

Nü lun-yü 女論語 (The female analects). By Sung Jo-shen 宋若莘 (d. c. 820). In *Lü-ch'uang nü-shih*, 1:1a–8b.

Ou-yang Hsiu wen hsüan-tu 歐陽修文選讀 (Selected readings in Ou-yang Hsiu's literary prose). Edited by Ch'en P'u-ch'ing 陳蒲清. Ch'ang-sha: Yüeh-lu shu-she, 1984.

Outlaws of the Marsh. Translated by Sidney Shapiro. 2 vols. Bloomington: Indiana University Press, 1981.

Pai-chia hsing tz'u-tien 百家姓辭典 (Encyclopedia of surnames). Compiled by Mu Liu-sen 穆柳森. Shen-chen: Hai-t'ien ch'u-pan she, 1988.

Pai-chia kung-an 百家公案 (A hundred court cases). 1594 edition. Fac. repr. In *Ku-pen hsiao-shuo ts'ung-k'an, ti-erh chi*, vol. 4.

Pai-ch'uan shu-chih 百川書志 (A catalogue of the hundred streams). By Kao Ju 高儒. Preface dated 1540. Shanghai: Ku-tien wen-hsüeh ch'u-pan she, 1957.

Pai-hai 稗海 (Sea of fiction). Compiled by Shang Chün 商濬 (fl. 1593–1619). 5 vols., fac. repr. Taipei: Hsin-hsing shu-chü, 1968.

Pai-hu t'ung 白虎通 (Comprehensive discussions in the White Tiger Hall). In *Pai-tzu ch'üan-shu*, vol. 6.

Pai Niang-tzu yung-chen Lei-feng T'a 白娘子永鎮雷峰塔 (The white maiden is eternally imprisoned under Thunder Peak Pagoda). In *Ching-shih t'ung-yen*, *chüan* 28, pp. 420–48.

Pai-t'u chi 白兔記 (The white rabbit). *Liu-shih chung ch'ü* edition. Taipei: K'ai-ming shu-tien, 1970.

Pai-tzu ch'üan-shu 百子全書 (Complete works of the hundred philosophers). 8 vols., fac. repr. Hang-chou: Che-chiang jen-min ch'u-pan she, 1984.

P'ai-p'u 牌譜 (A manual for dominoes). By Ku Ying-hsiang 顧應祥 (1483–1565). In *Hsin-shang hsü-pien*, *chüan* 9, pp. 1a–31b.

P'ai-t'u 牌圖 (Illustrated domino combinations). In *San-ts'ai t'u-hui*, vol. 4, *jen-shih* 人事 (Human affairs), *chüan* 8, pp. 43a–51b.

Pao-chien chi 寶劍記 (The story of the precious sword). By Li K'ai-hsien 李開先 (1502–68). In *Shui-hu hsi-ch'ü chi, ti-erh chi*, pp. 1–98.

Pei-ho chi-yü 北河紀餘 (Supplementary account of the northern section of the Grand Canal). By Hsieh Chao-che 謝肇淛 (1567–1624). In *Ssu-k'u ch'üan-shu chen-pen, erh-chi*, vol. 138.

Pei-kung tz'u-chi wai-chi 北宮詞紀外集 (Supplementary collection to northern-style song lyrics). Compiled by Ch'en So-wen 陳所聞 (d. c. 1604). 3 *chüan*. In

Nan-pei kung tz'u-chi [chiao-pu], pp. 1–89.
P'ei Hsing Ch'uan-ch'i 裴鉶傳奇 (P'ei Hsing's [825–80] *Tales of the marvelous*). Edited and annotated by Chou Leng-ch'ieh 周楞伽. Shanghai: Shang-hai ku-chi ch'u-pan she, 1980.
P'eng-lai hsien-sheng chuan 蓬萊先生傳 (The story of Mr. P'eng-lai). In *Hsiao-p'in chi*, pp. 69–76.
The Peony Pavilion. By Tang Xianzu; translated by Cyril Birch. Bloomington: Indiana University Press, 1980.
Pi-chi hsiao-shuo ta-kuan 筆記小說大觀 (Great collectanea of note-form literature). 17 vols. Yang-chou: Chiang-su Kuang-ling ku-chi k'o-yin she, 1984.
P'i-p'a chi 琵琶記 (The lute). By Kao Ming 高明 (d. 1359); edited by Ch'ien Nan-yang 錢南揚. Peking: Chung-hua shu-chü, 1961.
Po Hu T'ung: The Comprehensive Discussions in the White Tiger Hall. Translated by Tjan Tjoe Som. 2 vols. Leiden: E. J. Brill, 1949.
P'o feng-shih 破風詩 (The critique of the poem on the wind). In *Ku-pen Yüan Ming tsa-chü*, vol. 3.
P'o-yao chi 破窰記 (The dilapidated kiln). In *Ku-pen hsi-ch'ü ts'ung-k'an, ch'u-chi*, item 19.
The Poems of Li Ho. Translated by J. D. Frodsham. Oxford: Oxford University Press, 1970.
The Poetry of Li Shang-yin. Translated by James J. Y. Liu. Chicago: University of Chicago Press, 1969.
Proclaiming Harmony. Translated by William O. Hennessey. Ann Arbor: Center for Chinese Studies, University of Michigan, 1981.
A *Record of Buddhist Monasteries in Lo-yang*. Translated by Yi-t'ung Wang. Princeton: Princeton University Press, 1984.
Records of the Grand Historian of China. Translated by Burton Watson. 2 vols. New York: Columbia University Press, 1961.
Records of the Historian. Translated by Yang Hsien-yi and Gladys Yang. Hong Kong: Commercial Press, 1974.
San-chiao yüan-liu sou-shen ta-ch'üan 三教源流搜神大全 (Complete compendium on the pantheons of the three religions). Preface dated 1593. Fac. repr. Taipei: Lien-ching ch'u-pan shih-yeh kung-ssu, 1980.
San hsien-shen Pao Lung-t'u tuan-yüan 三現身包龍圖斷冤 (After three ghostly manifestations Academician Pao rights an injustice). In *Ching-shih t'ung-yen, chüan* 13, pp. 169–84.
San-i t'ang ts'ung-shu 三怡堂叢書 (Three pleasures studio collectanea). Compiled by Chang Feng-t'ai 張鳳臺. K'ai-feng: Ho-nan kuan-shu chü, 1926.
San-kuo chih 三國志 (History of the Three Kingdoms). Compiled by Ch'en Shou 陳壽 (233–97). 5 vols. Peking: Chung-hua shu-chü, 1973.
San-kuo chih p'ing-hua 三國志平話 (The p'ing-hua on the history of the Three Kingdoms). Originally published in 1321–23. Shanghai: Ku-tien wen-hsüeh ch'u-pan she, 1955.
San-kuo chih t'ung-su yen-i 三國志通俗演義 (The romance of the Three Kingdoms). Attributed to Lo Kuan-chung 羅貫中 (14th century). Preface dated 1522. 2 vols. Shanghai: Shang-hai ku-chi ch'u-pan she, 1980.

San-pao t'ai-chien Hsi-yang chi t'ung-su yen-i 三寶太監西洋記通俗演義 (The romance of Eunuch Cheng Ho's expedition to the Western Ocean). By Lo Mao-teng 羅懋登. Author's preface dated 1597. 2 vols. Shanghai: Shang-hai ku-chi ch'u-pan she, 1985.

San Sui p'ing-yao chuan 三遂平妖傳 (The three Sui quash the demons' revolt). Fac. repr. Tokyo: Tenri daigaku shuppan-bu, 1981.

San-ts'ai t'u-hui 三才圖會 (Assembled illustrations from the three realms). Compiled by Wang Ch'i 王圻 (c. 1535–c. 1614). Preface dated 1609. 6 vols., fac. repr. Taipei: Ch'eng-wen ch'u-pan she, 1970.

San-yüan chi 三元記 (Feng Ching 馮京 [1021–94] wins first place in three examinations). By Shen Shou-hsien 沈受先 (15th century). *Liu-shih chung ch'ü* edition. Taipei: K'ai-ming shu-tien, 1970.

Scripture of the Lotus Blossom of the Fine Dharma. Translated by Leon Hurvitz. New York: Columbia University Press, 1976.

Sha-kou chi 殺狗記 (The stratagem of killing a dog). *Liu-shih chung ch'ü* edition. Taipei: K'ai-ming shu-tien, 1970.

Shan-hai ching chiao-chu 山海經校注 (A critical edition of *The classic of mountains and seas*). Edited and annotated by Yüan K'o 袁珂. Shanghai: Shang-hai ku-chi ch'u-pan she, 1980.

Shan-pen hsi-ch'ü ts'ung-k'an 善本戲曲叢刊 (Collectanea of rare editions of works on dramatic prosody). Taipei: Hsüeh-sheng shu-chü, 1984–87.

The She King. Translated by James Legge. Hong Kong: Hong Kong University Press, 1960.

Shen-hsiang ch'üan-pien 神相全編 (Complete compendium on effective physiognomy). Compiled by Yüan Chung-ch'e 袁忠徹 (1376–1458). In *Ku-chin t'u-shu chi-ch'eng*, section 17, *i-shu tien* 藝術典, *chüan* 631–44.

Shen Hsiao-kuan i-niao hai ch'i-ming 沈小官一鳥害七命 (Master Shen's bird destroys seven lives). In *Ku-chin hsiao-shuo*, vol. 2, *chüan* 26, pp. 391–403.

Sheng-Ming tsa-chü, erh-chi 盛明雜劇, 二集 (Tsa-chü dramas of the glorious Ming dynasty, second collection). Compiled by Shen T'ai 沈泰 (17th century). Fac. repr. of 1641 edition. Peking: Chung-kuo hsi-chü ch'u-pan she, 1958.

Sheng-shih hsin-sheng 盛世新聲 (New songs of a surpassing age). Preface dated 1517. Fac. repr. Peking: Wen-hsüeh ku-chi k'an-hsing she, 1955.

Shih-chi 史記 (Records of the historian). By Ssu-ma Ch'ien 司馬遷 (145–c. 90 B.C.). 10 vols. Peking: Chung-hua shu-chü, 1972.

Shih-erh hsiao-ming lu shih-i 侍兒小名錄拾遺 (Addendum to the *Record of courtesans' professional names*). Compiled by Chang Pang-chi 張邦幾 (12th century). In *Pai-hai*, vol. 2, pp. 1a–9a (1230–34).

Shih Hung-chao lung-hu chün-ch'en hui 史弘肇龍虎君臣會 (Shih Hung-chao: The meeting of dragon and tiger, ruler and minister). In *Ku-chin hsiao-shuo*, vol. 1, *chüan* 15, pp. 212–38.

Shih-lin kuang-chi 事林廣記 (Expansive gleanings from the forest of affairs). Fac. repr. of 14th-century edition. Peking: Chung-hua shu-chü, 1963.

Shih-san ching ching-wen 十三經經文 (The texts of the thirteen classics). Taipei: K'ai-ming shu-tien, 1955.

Shih-shang hsiao-t'an 時尚笑談 (Jokes currently in vogue). Printed in the middle register of *Yao-t'ien yüeh, chüan* 1, pp. 1b–48b.

Shih-shuo Hsin-yü: A New Account of Tales of the World. By Liu I-ch'ing; translated by Richard B. Mather. Minneapolis: University of Minnesota Press, 1976.

Shih-shuo hsin-yü chiao-chien 世說新語校箋 (A critical edition of the *Shih-shuo hsin-yü*). Edited by Yang Yung 楊勇. Hong Kong: Ta-chung shu-chü, 1969.

Shih-yü sheng-sou: Chung-yüan shih-yü 市語聲嗽中原市語 (Market argot and slang: The market argot of the Central Plain). Published in the Lung-ch'ing reign period (1567–72). In *Han-shang huan wen-ts'un*, pp. 165–68.

[Shinzan] Dai Nihon zokuzōkyō 新纂大日本續藏經 ([Newly compiled] great Japanese continuation of the Buddhist canon). 100 vols. Tokyo: Kokusho kankōkai, 1977.

The Shoo King or The Book of Historical Documents. Translated by James Legge. Hong Kong: Hong Kong University Press, 1960.

Shu-yüan tsa-chi 菽園雜記 (Random jottings from the bean garden). By Lu Jung 陸容 (1436–94). Peking: Chung-hua shu-chü, 1985.

Shuang-chung chi 雙忠記 (The loyal pair). By Yao Mao-liang 姚茂良 (15th century). In *Ku-pen hsi-ch'ü ts'ung-k'an, ch'u-chi*, item 33.

Shui-hu ch'üan-chuan 水滸全傳 (Variorum edition of the *Outlaws of the Marsh*). Edited by Cheng Chen-to 鄭振鐸 et al. 4 vols. Hong Kong: Chung-hua shu-chü, 1958.

Shui-hu hsi-ch'ü chi, ti-erh chi 水滸戲曲集, 第二輯 (Corpus of drama dealing with the *Shui-hu* cycle, second series). Edited by Fu Hsi-hua 傅惜華. Shanghai: Ku-tien wen-hsüeh ch'u-pan she, 1958.

Shuo-fu 說郛 (The frontiers of apocrypha). Compiled by T'ao Tsung-i 陶宗儀 (c. 1316–c. 1403). 2 vols. Taipei: Hsin-hsing shu-chü, 1963.

Shuo-fu hsü 說郛續 (*The frontiers of apocrypha* continued). Compiled by T'ao T'ing 陶珽 (cs 1610). Fac. repr. of Ming edition. In *Shuo-fu san-chung*, vols. 9–10.

Shuo-fu san-chung 說郛三種 (*The frontiers of apocrypha*: Three recensions). 10 vols. Shanghai: Shang-hai ku-chi ch'u-pan she, 1988.

Ssu-k'u ch'üan-shu chen-pen, erh-chi 四庫全書珍本, 二輯 (Rare volumes from the *Complete library of the four treasuries*, second series). 400 vols. Taipei: T'ai-wan Shang-wu yin-shu kuan, 1971.

Ssu-k'u ch'üan-shu chen-pen, san-chi 四庫全書珍本, 三輯 (Rare volumes from the *Complete library of the four treasuries*, third series). 400 vols. Taipei: T'ai-wan Shang-wu yin-shu kuan, 1972.

Ssu-shu chang-chü chi-chu 四書章句集注 (Collected commentary on the paragraphed and punctuated text of the *Four books*). By Chu Hsi 朱熹 (1130–1200). Peking: Chung-hua shu-chü, 1983.

Stories from a Ming Collection. Translated by Cyril Birch. London: Bodley Head, 1958.

The Story of Hua Guan Suo.Translated by Gail Oman King. Tempe, Ariz.: Center for Asian Studies, Arizona State University, 1989.

The Story of the Stone. By Cao Xueqin; translated by David Hawkes and John Minford. 5 vols. Harmondsworth: Penguin Books, 1973–86.

Su Shih shih-chi 蘇軾詩集 (Collected poetry of Su Shih). By Su Shih 蘇軾

(1037–1101). 8 vols. Peking: Chung-hua shu-chü, 1982.
Su Wu mu-yang chi 蘇武牧羊記 (Su Wu herds sheep). In *Ku-pen hsi-ch'ü ts'ung-k'an, ch'u-chi*, item 20.
Sung shih 宋史 (History of the Sung dynasty). Compiled by T'o-t'o 脫脫 (1313–1355) et al. 40 vols. Peking: Chung-hua shu-chü, 1977.
Sung-shih chi-shih 宋詩紀事 (Recorded occasions in Sung poetry). Compiled by Li O 厲鶚 (1692–1752) and Ma Yüeh-kuan 馬曰琯 (1688–1755). 14 vols. Shanghai: Shang-wu yin-shu kuan, 1937.
Sung Ssu-kung ta-nao Chin-hun Chang 宋四公大鬧禁魂張 (Sung the Fourth raises hell with Tightwad Chang). In *Ku-chin hsiao-shuo*, vol. 2, *chüan* 36, pp. 525–50.
Sung ta-shih chi chiang-i 宋大事記講義 (Lectures on the principal events of the Sung dynasty). By Lü Chung 呂中 (cs 1247). In *Ssu-k'u ch'üan-shu chen-pen, erh-chi*, vols. 146–47.
Sung tsai-fu pien-nien lu [chiao-pu] 宋宰輔編年錄 [校補] ([Collated and supplemented recension of] a chronological record of the rescripts appointing and demoting the chief ministers of the Sung dynasty). Compiled by Hsü Tzu-ming 徐自明 (fl. early 13th century); edited by Wang Jui-lai 王瑞來. 4 vols. Peking: Chung-hua shu-chü, 1986.
Sung Yü tz'u-fu i-chieh 宋玉辭賦譯解 (Sung Yü's rhapsodies translated and interpreted). Edited and annotated by Chu Pi-lien 朱碧蓮. Peking: Chung-kuo she-hui k'o-hsüeh ch'u-pan she, 1987.
Ta ming-ch'un 大明春 (Great bright spring). Compiled by Ch'eng Wan-li 程萬里. Chien-yang: Chin K'uei, n.d. Fac. repr. of Wan-li (1573–1620) edition. In *Shan-pen hsi-ch'ü ts'ung-k'an*, vol. 6.
Ta Mu-kan-lien ming-chien chiu-mu pien-wen 大目乾連冥間救母變文 (Transformation text on Mahāmaudgalyāyana rescuing his mother from the underworld). In *Tun-huang pien-wen chi*, 2:714–55.
Ta-T'ang Ch'in-wang tz'u-hua 大唐秦王詞話 (Prosimetric story of the Prince of Ch'in of the Great T'ang). 2 vols. Fac. repr. of early 17th-century edition. Peking: Wen-hsüeh ku-chi k'an-hsing she, 1956.
Taishō shinshū daizōkyō 大正新修大藏經 (The newly edited great Buddhist canon compiled in the Taishō reign period [1912–26]). 85 vols. Tokyo: Taishō issaikyō kankōkai, 1922–32.
T'ai-ho cheng-yin p'u 太和正音譜 (Formulary for the correct sounds of great harmony). Compiled by Chu Ch'üan 朱權 (1378–1448). In *Chung-kuo ku-tien hsi-ch'ü lun-chu chi-ch'eng*, 3:1–231.
T'ai-kung chia-chiao 太公家教 (Family teachings of T'ai-kung). In Chou Feng-wu, *Tun-huang hsieh-pen T'ai-kung chia-chiao yen-chiu*, pp. 9–28.
T'ai-p'ing yü-lan 太平御覽 (Imperial digest of the T'ai-p'ing reign period [976–984]). Compiled by Li Fang 李昉 (925–96) et al. Completed in 983. Fac. repr. of a Sung edition. 4 vols. Peking: Chung-hua shu-chü, 1960.
T'ang chih-yen 唐摭言 (A gleaning of T'ang anecdotes). By Wang Ting-pao 王定保 (870–c. 954). Shanghai: Ku-tien wen-hsüeh ch'u-pan she, 1957.
T'ang Po-hu ch'üan-chi 唐伯虎全集 (Complete works of T'ang Yin 唐寅 [1470–1524]). Taipei: Tung-fang shu-tien, 1956.

T'ang Sung ch'uan-ch'i chi 唐宋傳奇集 (An anthology of literary tales from the T'ang and Sung dynasties). Edited by Lu Hsün 魯迅. Peking: Wen-hsüeh ku-chi k'an-hsing she, 1958.

T'ang-tai Lü Ch'un-yang te-tao Fei-chien chi 唐代呂純陽得道飛劍記 (The story of how Lü Tung-pin of the T'ang dynasty obtained the Tao with the aid of his flying sword). By Teng Chih-mo 鄧志謨. Chien-yang: Ts'ui-ch'ing t'ang, c. 1603. Fac. repr. In *Ku-pen hsiao-shuo ts'ung-k'an, ti-shih chi*, vol. 5.

T'ao Yüan-ming: His Works and Their Meaning. By A. R. Davis. 2 vols. Cambridge: Cambridge University Press, 1983.

The Temple and Other Poems. Translated by Arthur Waley. New York: Alfred A. Knopf, 1923.

The Texts of Taoism. Translated by James Legge. 2 vols. New York: Dover Publications, 1962.

Ting-hun tien 定婚店 (The inn of predestined marriage). By Li Fu-yen 李復言 (9th century). In *Hsüan-kuai lu; Hsü Hsüan-kuai lu*, pp. 179–81.

Traditional Chinese Stories: Themes and Variations. Edited by Y. W. Ma and Joseph S. M. Lau. New York: Columbia University Press, 1978.

Traditional Chinese Tales. Translated by Chi-chen Wang. New York: Columbia University Press, 1944.

Ts'ai-lou chi 彩樓記 (The gaily-colored tower). Edited by Huang Shang 黃裳. Shanghai: Shang-hai ku-tien wen-hsüeh ch'u-pan she, 1956.

Ts'ai-pi ch'ing-tz'u 彩筆情詞 (Emotive lyrics from variegated brushes). Compiled by Chang Hsü 張栩. Preface dated 1624. Fac. repr. In *Shan-pen hsi-ch'ü ts'ung-k'an*, vols. 75–76.

Ts'an-T'ang Wu-tai shih yen-i chuan 殘唐五代史演義傳 (Romance of the late T'ang and Five Dynasties). Peking: Pao-wen t'ang shu-tien, 1983.

Tsao-chiao Lin Ta-wang chia-hsing 皁角林大王假形 (A feat of impersonation by the King of Tsao-chiao Wood). In *Ching-shih t'ung-yen, chüan* 36, pp. 546–55.

Ts'o-jen shih 錯認屍 (The wrongly identified corpse). In *Ch'ing-p'ing shan-t'ang hua-pen*, pp. 212–35.

Ts'ui Tai-chao sheng-ssu yüan-chia 崔待詔生死冤家 (Artisan Ts'ui and his ghost wife). In *Ching-shih t'ung-yen, chüan* 8, pp. 90–104.

Ts'ui Ya-nei pai-yao chao-yao 崔衙內白鷂招妖 (The white falcon of Minister Ts'ui's son embroils him with demons). In *Ching-shih t'ung-yen, chüan* 19, pp. 261–73.

Tsun-sheng pa-chien 遵生八箋 (Eight disquisitions on nurturing life). By Kao Lien 高濂 (16th century). Author's preface dated 1591. Ch'eng-tu: Pa-Shu shu-she, 1988.

Ts'ung-shu chi-ch'eng 叢書集成 (A corpus of works from collectanea). 1st series. Shanghai: Shang-wu yin-shu kuan, 1935–37.

Tu Li-niang mu-se huan-hun 杜麗娘慕色還魂 (Tu Li-niang yearns for love and returns to life). In Hu Shih-ying, *Hua-pen hsiao-shuo kai-lun*, 2:533–37.

Tun-huang pien-wen chi 敦煌變文集 (Collection of pien-wen from Tun-huang). Edited by Wang Chung-min 王重民 et al. 2 vols. Peking: Jen-min wen-hsüeh ch'u-pan she, 1984.

Tun-huang Popular Narratives. Translated by Victor H. Mair. Cambridge: Cambridge University Press, 1983.

Tung Chieh-yüan Hsi-hsiang chi 董解元西廂記 (Master Tung's Western chamber romance). Edited and annotated by Ling Ching-yen 凌景埏. Peking: Jen-min wen-hsüeh ch'u-pan she, 1962.

T'ung-su pien 通俗編 (Compendium of common expressions). Compiled by Chai Hao 翟灝 (cs 1754). Taipei: Ta-hua shu-chü, 1977.

Tz'u-hua ts'ung-pien 詞話叢編 (A collectanea of talks on lyrics). Compiled by T'ang Kuei-chang 唐圭璋. 5 vols. Peking: Chung-hua shu-chü, 1986.

Tz'u-lin chai-yen 詞林摘艷 (Select flowers from the forest of song). Compiled by Chang Lu 張祿. Preface dated 1525. 2 vols., fac. repr. Peking: Wen-hsüeh ku-chi k'an-hsing she, 1955.

Tz'u-nüeh 詞謔 (Pleasantries on lyrical verse). By Li K'ai-hsien 李開先 (1502–68). In *Chung-kuo ku-tien hsi-ch'ü lun-chu chi-ch'eng*, 3:257–418.

Wan Hsiu-niang ch'ou-pao shan-t'ing-erh 萬秀娘仇報山亭兒 (Wan Hsiu-niang gets her revenge with a toy pavilion). In *Ching-shih t'ung-yen, chüan* 37, pp. 556–71.

Wan-li ti-ch'ao 萬曆邸鈔 (Transcriptions from gazettes of the Wan-li period [1573–1620]). 3 vols., fac. repr. Taipei: Cheng-chung shu-chü, 1969.

Wan-li yeh-huo pien 萬曆野獲編 (Private gleanings of the Wan-li reign period [1573–1620]). By Shen Te-fu 沈德符 (1578–1642). Author's preface dated 1619. 3 vols. Peking: Chung-hua shu-chü, 1980.

Wan-shu tsa-chi 宛署雜記 (Miscellaneous records concerning the magistracy of Wan-p'ing). By Shen Pang 沈榜. Preface dated 1592. Peking: Pei-ching ku-chi ch'u-pan-she, 1980.

The Washing Away of Wrongs: Forensic Medicine in Thirteenth-Century China. Translated by Brian E. McNight. Ann Arbor: Center for Chinese Studies, University of Michigan, 1981.

Wei Feng-hsiang ku Yü-huan chi 韋鳳翔古玉環記 (The old version of Wei Kao 韋皋 [746–806] and the story of the jade ring). In *Ku-pen hsi-ch'ü ts'ung-k'an, ch'u-chi*, item 22.

Wei-mo-chieh ching chiang-ching wen 維摩詰經講經文 (Sutra lecture on the *Vimalakīrti sutra*), text no. 1. In *Tun-huang pien-wen chi*, 2:517–61.

Wei shu 魏書 (History of the Northern Wei dynasty). Compiled by Wei Shou 魏收 (505–72). 8 vols. Peking: Chung-hua shu-chü, 1974.

Wei Yüan Shao hsi Yü-chou 爲袁紹檄豫州 (Proclamation to Liu Pei 劉備 [161–223] on behalf of Yüan Shao 袁紹 [d. 202]). By Ch'en Lin 陳琳 (d. 217). In *Wen-hsüan*, vol. 2, *chüan* 44, pp. 3b–10a.

Wen-chien chin-lu 聞見近錄 (Recent records of things heard and seen). By Wang Kung 王鞏 (1048–c. 1102). Fac. repr. of Sung edition. Peking: Chung-hua shu-chü, 1984.

Wen-ching yüan-yang hui 刎頸鴛鴦會 (The fatal rendezvous). In *Ch'ing-p'ing shan-t'ang hua-pen*, pp. 154–69.

Wen-hsüan 文選 (Selections of refined literature). Compiled by Hsiao T'ung 蕭統 (501–31). 3 vols., fac. repr. Peking: Chung-hua shu-chü, 1981.

Wen-ta lu 問答錄 (A record of repartee). Attributed to Su Shih 蘇軾 (1037–1101). In *Ts'ung-shu chi-ch'eng*, 1st series, vol. 2987.

Wen xuan or Selections of Refined Literature. Translated and annotated by David R. Knechtges. Vol. 1. Princeton: Princeton University Press, 1982.

The Works of Hsüntze. Translated by Homer H. Dubs. London: Arthur Probsthain, 1928.

The Works of Mencius. Translated by James Legge. Hong Kong: Hong Kong University Press, 1960.

Wu-chieh Ch'an-shih ssu Hung-lien chi 五戒禪師私紅蓮記 (The Ch'an Master Wu-chieh defiles Hung-lien). In *Ch'ing-p'ing shan-t'ang hua-pen*, pp. 136–54.

Wu-teng hui-yüan 五燈會元 (The essentials of the five lamps). Compiled by P'u-chi 普濟 (1179–1253). 3 vols. Peking: Chung-hua shu-chü, 1984.

Wu Tzu-hsü pien-wen 伍子胥變文 (The story of Wu Tzu-hsü). In *Tun-huang pien-wen chi*, 1:1–31.

Xunzi: A Translation and Study of the Complete Works. Translated by John Knoblock. 2 vols. Stanford: Stanford University Press, 1988–90.

Yang-chia fu shih-tai chung-yung yen-i chih-chuan 楊家府世代忠勇演義志傳 (Popular chronicle of the generations of loyal and brave exploits of the Yang household). Preface dated 1606. 2 vols., fac. repr. Taipei: Kuo-li chung-yang t'u-shu kuan, 1971.

Yang Wen lan-lu hu chuan 楊溫攔路虎傳 (The story of Yang Wen, the road-blocking tiger). In *Ch'ing-p'ing shan-t'ang hua-pen*, pp. 169–86.

Yao-t'ien yüeh 堯天樂 (The music of Yao's reign). Compiled by Yin Ch'i-sheng 殷啓聖. Chien-yang: Hsiung Jen-huan, late Wan-li [1573–1620]. Fac. repr. In *Shan-pen hsi-ch'ü ts'ung-k'an*, vol. 8.

Yeh Ching-neng shih 葉淨能詩 (The wizard Yeh Ching-neng). In *Tun-huang pien-wen chi*, 1:216–29.

Yeh-k'o ts'ung-shu 野客叢書 (Collected writings of a rustic sojourner). By Wang Mao 王楙 (1151–1213). Peking: Chung-hua shu-chü, 1987.

Yen-chü pi-chi 燕居筆記 (A miscellany for leisured hours). Edited by Lin Chin-yang 林近陽 (fl. early 17th century). 3 vols., fac. repr. of Ming edition. In *Ming-Ch'ing shan-pen hsiao-shuo ts'ung-k'an, ch'u-pien*.

Yen-men kuan Ts'un-hsiao ta-hu 雁門關存孝打虎 (Li Ts'un-hsiao slays a tiger at Yen-men Pass). In *Yüan-ch'ü hsüan wai-pien*, 2:554–67.

Yen-tzu fu 鷰子賦 (Rhapsody on the swallow). In *Tun-huang pien-wen chi*, 1:262–66.

Yin-shan cheng-yao 飲膳正要 (Correct essentials of nutrition). By Hu-ssu-hui 忽思慧 (fl. early 14th century). Completed in 1330. Peking: Jen-min wei-sheng ch'u-pan she, 1986.

Ying-ying chuan 鶯鶯傳 (The story of Ying-ying). By Yüan Chen 元稹 (775–831). In *T'ang Sung ch'uan-ch'i chi*, pp. 127–36.

Yu-kuei chi 幽閨記 (Tale of the secluded chambers). *Liu-shih chung ch'ü* edition. Taipei: K'ai-ming shu-tien, 1970.

Yu-ming lu 幽明錄 (Records of the realms of the dead and the living). Compiled by Liu I-ch'ing 劉義慶 (403–444); edited and annotated by Cheng Wan-ch'ing 鄭晚晴. Peking: Wen-hua i-shu ch'u-pan she, 1988.

Yu-yang tsa-tsu 酉陽雜俎 (Assorted notes from Yu-yang). Compiled by Tuan Ch'eng-shih 段成式 (803–63). Peking: Chung-hua shu-chü, 1981.

Yung-hsi yüeh-fu 雍熙樂府 (Songs of a harmonious era). Preface dated 1566, 20 *ts'e*, fac. repr. Shanghai: Shang-wu yin-shu kuan, 1934.

Yung-lo ta-tien hsi-wen san-chung chiao-chu 永樂大典戲文三種校注 (An annotated recension of the three hsi-wen preserved in the *Yung-lo ta-tien*). Edited and annotated by Ch'ien Nan-yang 錢南揚. Peking: Chung-hua shu-chü, 1979.

Yü-ch'iao hsien-hua 漁樵閑話 (A casual dialogue between a fisherman and a woodcutter). In *Ku-pen Yüan Ming tsa-chü*, vol. 4.

Yü-ching t'ai 玉鏡臺 (The jade mirror stand). By Chu Ting 朱鼎 (16th century). *Liu-shih chung ch'ü* edition. Taipei: K'ai-ming shu-tien, 1970.

Yü-ch'u chi 玉杵記 (The jade pestle). Preface dated 1606. In *Ku-pen hsi-ch'ü ts'ung-k'an, ch'u-chi*, item 86.

Yü-chüeh chi 玉玦記 (The jade thumb-ring). By Cheng Jo-yung 鄭若庸 (16th century). *Liu-shih chung ch'ü* edition. Taipei: K'ai-ming shu-tien, 1970.

Yü-huan chi 玉環記 (The story of the jade ring). *Liu-shih chung ch'ü* edition. Taipei: K'ai-ming shu-tien, 1970.

Yüan-ch'ü hsüan 元曲選 (An anthology of Yüan tsa-chü drama). Compiled by Tsang Mao-hsün 臧懋循 (1550–1620). 4 vols. Peking: Chung-hua shu-chü, 1979.

Yüan-ch'ü hsüan wai-pien 元曲選外編 (A supplementary anthology of Yüan tsa-chü drama). Compiled by Sui Shu-sen 隋樹森. 3 vols. Peking: Chung-hua shu-chü, 1961.

Yüan-jen tsa-chü kou-ch'en 元人雜劇鈎沈 (Rescued fragments from tsa-chü drama by Yüan authors). Compiled by Chao Ching-shen 趙景深. Shanghai: Shang-hai ku-tien wen-hsüeh ch'u-pan she, 1956.

Yüan-shan t'ang ch'ü-p'in 遠山堂曲品 (The Yüan-shan T'ang critical classification of ch'uan-ch'i dramas). By Ch'i Piao-chia 祁彪佳 (1602–1645). In *Chung-kuo ku-tien hsi-ch'ü lun-chu chi-ch'eng*, 6:1–133.

Yüeh-fu ching-hua 樂府菁華 (A florilegium of dramatic literature). Compiled by Liu Chün-hsi 劉君錫. N.p.: San-huai t'ang, 1600. Fac. repr. In *Shan-pen hsi-ch'ü ts'ung-k'an*, vol. 1.

Yüeh-fu ch'ün-chu 樂府群珠 (A string of lyric pearls). Modern edition edited by Lu Ch'ien 盧前. Shanghai: Shang-wu yin-shu kuan, 1957.

Yüeh-ming Ho-shang tu Liu Ts'ui 月明和尚度柳翠 (The Monk Yüeh-ming converts Liu Ts'ui). In *Ku-chin hsiao-shuo*. Fac. repr. of original edition published in 1620–24, vol. 2, *chüan* 29, pp. 1a–18a.

Yüeh-ming Ho-shang tu Liu Ts'ui 月明和尚度柳翠 (The Monk Yüeh-ming converts Liu Ts'ui). In *Ku-chin hsiao-shuo*, vol. 2, *chüan* 29, pp. 428–41.

Yün-chien chü-mu ch'ao 雲間據目抄 (Jottings on matters eye-witnessed in Yün-chien). By Fan Lien 范濂 (b. 1540). Preface dated 1593. In *Pi-chi hsiao-shuo ta-kuan*, vol. 6, *ts'e* 13.

SECONDARY SOURCES
(Arranged Alphabetically by Author)

Appel, Alfred, Jr. "Introduction." in Nabokov, *The Annotated Lolita*, pp. xvii–lxvii.

Bakhtin, M. M. *The Dialogic Imagination: Four Essays*. Edited and translated by

Caryl Emerson and Michael Holquist. Austin: University of Texas Press, 1981.
Birch, Cyril. "Some Concerns and Methods of the Ming *Ch'uan-ch'i* Drama." In Birch, *Studies in Chinese Literary Genres*. pp. 229–37.
————, ed. *Studies in Chinese Literary Genres*. Berkeley: University of California Press, 1974.
Booth, Wayne. *The Rhetoric of Fiction*. Chicago: University of Chicago Press, 1961.
Boyd, Brian. *Vladimir Nabokov: The Russian Years*. Princeton: Princeton University Press, 1990.
Carlitz, Katherine. "The Conclusion of the Jin Ping Mei." *Ming Studies*, 10 (Spring 1980): 23–29.
————. "Puns and Puzzles in the *Chin P'ing Mei*: A Look at Chapter 27." *T'oung Pao* 67, 3–5 (1981): 216–39.
————. *The Rhetoric of Chin p'ing mei*. Bloomington: Indiana University Press, 1986.
————. "The Role of Drama in the *Chin P'ing Mei*: The Relationship between Fiction and Drama as a Guide to the Viewpoint of a Sixteenth-Century Chinese Novel." Ph.D. dissertation, University of Chicago, 1978.
Chan, Hok-lam, and Wm. Theodore de Bary, eds. *Yüan Thought: Chinese Thought and Religion Under the Mongols*. New York: Columbia University Press, 1982.
Chao Wei-pang. "The Chinese Science of Fate-Calculation." *Folklore Studies* 5 (1946): 279–315.
Cheng P'ei-k'ai 鄭培凱. "*Chin P'ing Mei tz'u-hua* yü Ming-jen yin-chiu feng-shang" 金瓶梅詞話與明人飲酒風尚 (The *Chin P'ing Mei tz'u-hua* and Ming literati tastes in wine drinking). *Chung-wai wen-hsüeh* 中外文學 (Chung-wai literary monthly) 12, 6 (November 1983): 4–44.
Chou Feng-wu 周鳳五. *Tun-huang hsieh-pen T'ai-kung chia-chiao yen-chiu* 敦煌寫本太公家教研究 (A study of the Tun-huang manuscripts of the *T'ai-kung chia-chiao*). Taipei: Ming-wen shu-chü, 1986.
Chou Hsi-pao 周錫保. *Chung-kuo ku-tai fu-shih shih* 中國古代服飾史 (History of traditional Chinese costume). Peking: Chung-kuo hsi-chü ch'u-pan she, 1984.
Chu, Hung-lam. "The Authorship of the Story *Chung-ch'ing li-chi*." *Asia Major*, third series, 1, 1 (January 1988): 71–82.
Chung-hua wen-shih lun-ts'ung 中華文史論叢 (Collections of essays on Chinese literature and history). Shanghai: Shang-hai ku-chi ch'u-pan she.
Crump, J. I. *Songs from Xanadu: Studies in Mongol-Dynasty Song-Poetry (San-ch'ü)*. Ann Arbor: Center for Chinese Studies, University of Michigan, 1983.
Culin, Stewart. "Chinese Games with Dice and Dominoes." *Annual Report of the U. S. National Museum, 1893*, pp. 491–537.
de Bary, Wm. Theodore. "Individualism and Humanitarianism in Late Ming Thought." In de Bary, *Self and Society in Ming Thought*, pp. 145–247.
————, ed. *Self and Society in Ming Thought*. New York: Columbia University Press, 1970.
De Groot, J. J. M. *The Religious System of China*. 6 vols. Taipei: Ch'eng Wen

Publishing Company, 1972.
Dickens, Charles. *Bleak House*. Baltimore: Penguin Books, 1975.
Dolby, William. *A History of Chinese Drama*. New York: Barnes and Noble, 1976.
Dudbridge, Glen. *The Hsi-yu chi: A Study of Antecedents to the Sixteenth-Century Chinese Novel*. Cambridge: Cambridge University Press, 1970.
————. *The Legend of Miao-shan*. London: Ithaca Press, 1978.
Egan, Ronald C. *The Literary Works of Ou-yang Hsiu*. Cambridge: Cambridge University Press, 1984.
Ellmann, Richard. *James Joyce*. New York: Oxford University Press, 1982.
Fairbank, John K., ed. *Chinese Thought and Institutions*. Chicago: University of Chicago Press, 1957.
Franke, Herbert, ed. *Sung Biographies*. 4 vols. Wiesbaden: Franz Steiner Verlag, 1976.
Freud, Sigmund. *Civilization and Its Discontents*. Translated by Joan Riviere. New York: Doubleday Anchor Books, n.d.
Fusek, Lois. "The 'Kao-t'ang fu.'" *Monumenta Serica*, 30 (1972–73): 392–425.
Gichner, Lawrence E. *Erotic Aspects of Chinese Culture*. N.p.: Privately published, 1957.
Goodrich, Anne Swann. *The Peking Temple of the Eastern Peak*. Nagoya: Monumenta Serica, 1964.
Goodrich, L. Carrington, and Chaoying Fang, eds. *Dictionary of Ming Biography*. 2 vols. New York: Columbia University Press, 1976.
Grant, Douglas, and Millar Maclure, eds. *The Far East: China and Japan*. Toronto: University of Toronto Press, 1961.
Hanan, Patrick. *The Chinese Vernacular Story*. Cambridge: Harvard University Press, 1981.
————. "The Early Chinese Short Story: A Critical Theory in Outline." *Harvard Journal of Asiatic Studies*, 27 (1967): 168–207; also in Birch, *Studies in Chinese Literary Genres*, pp. 299–338.
————. "Judge Pao's Hundred Cases Reconstructed." *Harvard Journal of Asiatic Studies*, 40, 2 (1980): 301–23.
————. "A Landmark of the Chinese Novel." In Grant and Maclure, *The Far East: China and Japan*, pp. 325–35.
————. "Sources of the *Chin P'ing Mei*." *Asia Major*, n.s. 10, 1 (1963): 23–67.
————. "The Text of the *Chin P'ing Mei*." *Asia Major*, n.s. 9, 1 (1962): 1–57.
Hatch, George C. "Su Shih." In Franke, *Sung Biographies*, 3: 900–68.
Hawkes, David, "Introduction." In *The Story of the Stone*, 1:14–46.
Hervouet, Yves, ed. *Études d'Histoire et de Littérature Chinoises Offertes au Professeur Jaroslav Průšek*. Paris: Presses Universitaires de France, 1976.
Hightower, James R. "Yüan Chen and 'The Story of Ying-ying.'" *Harvard Journal of Asiatic Studies*, 33 (1973): 90–123.
Holzman, Donald. *Poetry and Politics: The Life and Works of Juan Chi*. Cambridge: Cambridge University Press, 1978.
Hou, Ching-lang. "The Chinese Belief in Baleful Stars." In Welch and Seidel, *Facets of Taoism: Essays in Chinese Religion*, pp. 193–228.
Hsia, C. T. "*Chin P'ing Mei*." In Hsia, *The Classic Chinese Novel*, pp. 165–202.

———. *The Classic Chinese Novel*. New York: Columbia University Press, 1968.

Hsü Shuo-fang 徐朔方. "*Chin P'ing Mei* ch'eng-shu hsin-t'an" 金瓶梅成書新探 (A new study of the composition of the *Chin P'ing Mei*). *Chung-hua wen-shih lun-ts'ung*, no. 3 (1984): 159–98.

Hu Shih-ying 胡士瑩. *Hua-pen hsiao-shuo kai-lun* 話本小說概論 (A comprehensive study of promptbook fiction). 2 vols. Peking: Chung-hua shu-chü, 1980.

Hu, Shiu-ying. *An Enumeration of Chinese Materia Medica*. Hong Kong: The Chinese University Press, 1980.

Huang, Ray. *1587, A Year of No Significance: The Ming Dynasty in Decline*. New Haven: Yale University Press, 1981.

Idema, W. L. *The Dramatic Oeuvre of Chu Yu-tun (1379–1439)*. Leiden: E. J. Brill, 1985.

———. "Zhu Youdun's Dramatic Prefaces and Traditional Fiction." *Ming Studies*, 10 (Spring 1980): 17–21.

———, and Stephen H. West. *Chinese Theater 1100–1450: A Source Book*. Wiesbaden: Franz Steiner Verlag, 1982.

Irwin, Richard Gregg. *The Evolution of a Chinese Novel: Shui-hu-chuan*. Cambridge: Harvard University Press, 1966.

James, Henry. *The Figure in the Carpet and Other Stories*. New York: Penguin Books, 1986.

Kahn, Harold L. *Monarchy in the Emperor's Eyes: Image and Reality in the Ch'ien-lung Reign*. Cambridge: Harvard University Press, 1971.

Kao Yu-kung. "A Study of the Fang La Rebellion." *Harvard Journal of Asiatic Studies*, 24 (1962–63): 17–63.

———. "Source Materials on the Fang La Rebellion." *Harvard Journal of Asiatic Studies*, 26 (1966): 211–40.

Kaufmann, Walter. *Musical References in the Chinese Classics*. Detroit: Information Coordinators, Inc., 1976.

Knechtges, David R. *The Han Rhapsody: A Study of the Fu of Yang Hsiung*. Cambridge: Cambridge University Press, 1976.

Ku Kuo-jui 顧國瑞. "*Chin P'ing Mei* chung te san-ko Ming-tai jen" 金瓶梅中的三個明代人 (Three Ming dynasty figures in the *Chin P'ing Mei*). In Tu Weimo and Liu Hui. *Chin P'ing Mei yen-chiu chi*, pp. 245–58.

Lévy, André. "About the Date of the First Printed Edition of the *Chin P'ing Mei*." *Chinese Literature: Essays, Articles, Reviews* 1, 1 (January 1979): 43–47.

———. *Études sur le Conte et le Roman Chinois*. Paris: École Française d'Extrême-Orient, 1971.

———. "Introduction." In *Fleur en Fiole d'Or (Jin Ping Mei cihua)*, 1:xxxvii–lxxi.

Levy, Howard S. *Chinese Footbinding: The History of a Curious Erotic Custom*. New York: Walton Rawls, 1966.

Liu Chung-kuang 劉中光. "*Chin P'ing Mei* jen-wu k'ao-lun" 金瓶梅人物考論 (A study of the historical figures in the *Chin P'ing Mei*). In Yeh Kuei-t'ung et al., *Chin P'ing Mei tso-che chih mi*, pp. 105–224.

Lou Tzu-k'uang 婁子匡. *Hun-su chih* 婚俗志 (A record of wedding customs). Taipei: T'ai-wan Shang-wu yin-shu kuan, 1968.

Lowe, H. Y. *The Adventures of Wu: The Life Cycle of a Peking Man*. 2 vols. Princeton: Princeton University Press, 1983.

Lu Kung 路工. *Fang-shu chien-wen lu* 訪書見聞錄 (Record of things seen and heard in the search for rare books). Shanghai: Shang-hai ku-chi ch'u-pan she, 1985.

Ma Shu-t'ien 馬書田. *Hua-hsia chu-shen* 華夏諸神 (The various gods of China). Peking: Pei-ching Yen-shan ch'u-pan she, 1990.

Ma Tai-loi 馬泰來. "Hsieh Chao-che te '*Chin P'ing Mei* pa'" 謝肇淛的金瓶梅跋 (Hsieh Chao-che's "Colophon to the *Chin P'ing Mei*"). *Chung-hua wen-shih lun-ts'ung*, no. 4 (1980): 299–305.

————. "Ma-ch'eng Liu-chia ho *Chin P'ing Mei*" 麻城劉家和金瓶梅 (The Liu Family of Ma-ch'eng and the *Chin P'ing Mei*). *Chung-hua wen-shih lun-ts'ung*, no. 1 (1982): 111–20.

Malmqvist, Göran, "The *Cherng Shiang* Ballad of the *Shyun Tzyy*." *Bulletin of the Museum of Far Eastern Antiquities*, 45 (1973): 63–89.

Martinson, Paul Varo. "The *Chin P'ing Mei* as Wisdom Literature: A Methodological Essay." *Ming Studies*, 5 (Fall 1977): 44–56.

————. "*Pao* Order and Redemption: Perspectives on Chinese Religion and Society Based on a Study of the *Chin P'ing Mei*." Ph.D. dissertation, University of Chicago, 1973.

Miller, J. Hillis. "Introduction." In Dickens, *Bleak House*, pp. 11–34.

Maspero, Henri. *Taoism and Chinese Religion*. Translated by Frank A. Kierman, Jr. Amherst: University of Massachusetts Press, 1981.

Nabokov, Vladimir. *The Annotated Lolita*. Edited and annotated by Alfred Appel, Jr. New York: Vintage Books, 1991.

Needham, Joseph, and Lu Gwei-djen. *Science and Civilisation in China*. Vol. 5, part V. *Spagyrical Discovery and Invention: Physiological Alchemy*. Cambridge: Cambridge University Press, 1983.

Owen, Stephen. *The Great Age of Chinese Poetry: The High T'ang*. New Haven: Yale University Press, 1981.

Plaks, Andrew H., ed. *Chinese Narrative: Critical and Theoretical Essays*. Princeton: Princeton University Press, 1977.

————. "The Chongzhen Commentary on the *Jin Ping Mei*: Gems amidst the Dross." *Chinese Literature: Essays, Articles, Reviews*, 8, 1 and 2 (July 1986): 19–30.

————. *The Four Masterworks of the Ming Novel*. Princeton: Princeton University Press, 1987.

————. "Neo-Confucian Issues in Ming-Ch'ing Fiction." Princeton University, 1977. Manuscript.

————. "*Shui-hu chuan* and the Sixteenth Century Novel Form: An Interpretive Reappraisal." *Chinese Literature: Essays, Articles, Reviews*, 2, 1 (1980): 3–53.

Porkert, Manfred. *The Theoretical Foundations of Chinese Medicine*. Cambridge: MIT Press, 1974.

Proceedings of the International Conference on Sinology, Section on Literature,

August, 1980. Taipei: Academia Sinica, 1981.
Rohsenow, John S. *A Chinese-English Dictionary of Enigmatic Folk Similes (Xiehouyu)*. Tucson: University of Arizona Press, 1991.
Rolston, David L. "Intertextuality in Chinese Full-length Fiction." In Rolston, "Theory and Practice: Fiction Criticism, and the Writing of the *Ju-lin wai-shih*." 2:270–424.
———. "Nonrealistic Uses of Oral Performing Literature in Traditional Chinese Fiction: The Model of the *Jin Ping Mei cihua* and Its Influence." University of Michigan, 1991. Manuscript.
———. "Theory and Practice: Fiction Criticism, and the Writing of the *Ju-lin wai-shih*." 4 vols. Ph.D. dissertation, University of Chicago, 1988.
Roy, David T. "The Case for T'ang Hsien-tsu's Authorship of the *Jin Ping Mei*." *Chinese Literature: Essays, Articles, Reviews*, 8, 1 and 2 (July 1986): 31–62.
———. "Chang Chu-p'o's Commentary on the *Chin P'ing Mei*." In Plaks, *Chinese Narrative: Critical and Theoretical Essays*, pp. 115–23.
———. "A Confucian Interpretation of the *Chin P'ing Mei*." In *Proceedings of the International Conference on Sinology, Section on Literature, August, 1980*, pp. 39–61.
———, trans. "Selections from *Jin Ping Mei*." *Renditions*, 24 (Autumn 1985): 13–62.
Rushton, Peter. "The Daoist's Mirror: Reflections on the Neo-Confucian Reader and the Rhetoric of *Jin Ping Mei*." *Chinese Literature: Essays, Articles, Reviews*, 8, 1 and 2 (July 1986): 63–81.
———. "The Narrative Form of Chin P'ing Mei." Ph.D. dissertation, Stanford University, 1978.
San-kuo yen-i yen-chiu chi 三國演義硏究集 (Collected studies on *The romance of the Three Kingdoms*. Ch'eng-tu: Ssu-ch'uan sheng She-hui k'o-hsüeh yüan ch'u-pan she, 1983.
Saso, Michael R. *Taoism and the Rite of Cosmic Renewal*. N.p.: Washington State University Press, 1972.
Satyendra, Indira. "Metaphors of the Body: The Sexual Economy of the *Chin P'ing Mei tz'u-hua*." Paper presented at the Annual Meeting of the Association for Asian Studies, New Orleans, April, 1991.
———. "Toward a Poetics of the Chinese Novel: A Study of the Prefatory Poems in the *Chin P'ing Mei tz'u-hua*." Ph.D. dissertation, University of Chicago, 1989.
Schafer, Edward H. *Pacing the Void: T'ang Approaches to the Stars*. Berkeley: University of California Press, 1977.
———. *The Vermilion Bird: T'ang Images of the South*. Berkeley: University of California Press, 1967.
Scholes, Robert. *Elements of Fiction*. New York: Oxford University Press, 1967.
Scott, Mary Elizabeth. "Azure from Indigo: *Hong lou meng*'s Debt to *Jin Ping Mei*." Ph.D. dissertation, Princeton University, 1989.
Serruys, Henry. "Towers in the Northern Frontier Defenses of the Ming." *Ming Studies*, 14 (Spring 1982): 8–76.

Shen Ts'ung-wen 沈從文. *Chung-kuo ku-tai fu-shih yen-chiu* 中國古代服飾研究 (A study of traditional Chinese costume). Hong Kong: Shang-wu yin-shu kuan, 1981.

Sivin, Nathan. *Chinese Alchemy: Preliminary Studies*. Cambridge: Harvard University Press, 1968.

Soothill, William Edward, and Lewis Hodous. *A Dictionary of Chinese Buddhist Terms*. London: Kegan Paul, Trench, Trubner & Co., 1937.

Sun K'ai-ti 孫楷第. *Jih-pen Tung-ching so-chien hsiao-shuo shu-mu* 日本東京所見小說書目 (Bibliography of works of Chinese fiction seen in Tokyo, Japan). Peking: Jen-min wen-hsüeh ch'u-pan she, 1958.

Teiser, Stephen F. *The Ghost Festival in Medieval China*. Princeton: Princeton University Press, 1988.

Torii Hisayasu 鳥居久靖. *Kinpeibai sharekotoba no kenkyū* 金瓶梅しやれことばの研究 (A study of proverbial witticisms in the *Chin P'ing Mei*). Tokyo: Kōseikan, 1972.

Tu Kuo-hsiang 杜國庠. "Lun Hsün-tzu te 'Ch'eng-hsiang p'ien'" 論荀子的成相篇 (On Hsün-tzu's 'Ch'eng-hsiang' chapter). In his *Tu Kuo-hsiang wen-chi*, pp. 158–83.

————. *Tu Kuo-hsiang wen-chi* 杜國庠文集 (Collected essays of Tu Kuo-hsiang). Peking: Jen-min ch'u-pan she, 1962.

Tu Wei-mo 杜維沫 and Liu Hui 劉輝, eds. *Chin P'ing Mei yen-chiu chi* 金瓶梅研究集 (Collected studies of the *Chin P'ing Mei*). Chi-nan: Ch'i-Lu shu-she, 1988.

Van Gulik, R. H. *Erotic Colour Prints of the Ming Period with An Essay on Chinese Sex Life from the Han to the Ch'ing Dynasty,* B.C. *206–*A.D. *1644*. 3 vols. Tokyo: Privately published in fifty copies, 1951.

————. *Sexual Life in Ancient China: A Preliminary Survey of Chinese Sex and Society from ca. 1500* B.C. *till 1644* A.D. Leiden: E. J. Brill, 1961.

Waley, Arthur. *The Real Tripitaka and Other Pieces*. London: Allen and Unwin, 1952.

Wang Chung-min 王重民. *Tun-huang ku-chi hsü-lu* 敦煌古籍敘錄 (Descriptive register of ancient manuscripts from Tun-huang). Peking: Shang-wu yin-shu kuan, 1958.

Wang, John C. Y. "The Cyclical View of Life and Meaning in the Traditional Chinese Novel." In Hervouet, *Études d'Histoire et de Littérature Chinoises Offertes au Professeur Jaroslav Průšek*, pp. 275–301.

Wang Kuo-liang 王國良. *Hsü Ch'i Hsieh chi yen-chiu* 續齊諧記研究 (A study of *Hsü Ch'i Hsieh chi*). Taipei: Wen shih che ch'u-pan she, 1987.

Wang Li-ch'i 王利器. "Lo Kuan-chung yü *San-kuo chih t'ung-su yen-i*" 羅貫中與三國志通俗演義 (Lo Kuan-chung and *The romance of the Three Kingdoms*). In *San-kuo yen-i yen-chiu chi*, pp. 240–65.

Watt, Ian. *The Rise of the Novel*. Berkeley: University of California Press, 1957.

Wei Tzu-yün 魏子雲. *Chin P'ing Mei t'an-yüan* 金瓶梅探源 (The origins of the *Chin P'ing Mei*). Taipei: Chü-liu t'u-shu kung-ssu, 1979.

Welch, Holmes, and Anna Seidel, eds. *Facets of Taoism: Essays in Chinese Religion*. New Haven: Yale University Press, 1979.

Werner, E. T. C. *A Dictionary of Chinese Mythology*. New York: The Julian Press, 1961.

West, Stephen H. *Vaudeville and Narrative: Aspects of Chin Theater*. Wiesbaden: Franz Steiner Verlag, 1977.

Wilhelm, Hellmut. "The Scholar's Frustration: Notes on a Type of Fu." In Fairbank, *Chinese Thought and Institutions*, pp. 310–19.

Wright, Arthur F., ed. *The Confucian Persuasion*. Stanford: Stanford University Press, 1960.

————. "Sui Yang-ti: Personality and Stereotype." In Wright, *The Confucian Persuasion*, pp. 47–76.

Wu Han 吳晗, "*Chin P'ing Mei* te chu-tso shih-tai chi ch'i she-hui pei-ching." 金瓶梅的著作時代及其社會背景 (The date of composition of the *Chin P'ing Mei* and its social background). In Wu Han, *Tu-shih cha-chi*, pp. 1–38.

————. *Tu-shih cha-chi* 讀史劄記 (Notes on reading history). Peking: San-lien shu-tien, 1957.

Wu Hsiao-ling 吳曉鈴. "*Chin P'ing Mei tz'u-hua* li te Ch'ing-ho chi i Chia-ching shih-ch'i te Pei-ching wei mo-hsing ch'u-t'an" 金瓶梅詞話裡的清河即以嘉靖時期的北京爲模型初探 (A preliminary study of the fact that Ch'ing-ho in the *Chin P'ing Mei tz'u-hua* is modeled on the Peking of the Chia-ching reign period). *Chung-wai wen-hsüeh* 中外文學 (Chung-wai literary monthly), 18, 2 (July 1989): 107–22.

Yang, Lien-sheng. *Money and Credit in China: A Short History*. Cambridge: Harvard University Press, 1952.

Yeh Kuei-t'ung 葉桂桐 et al., eds. *Chin P'ing Mei tso-che chih mi* 金瓶梅作者之謎 (The riddle of the authorship of the *Chin P'ing Mei*). N.p.: Ning-hsia jen-min ch'u-pan she, 1988.

Yü, Chün-fang. "Chung-feng Ming-pen and Ch'an Buddhism in the Yüan." In Chan and de Bary, *Yüan Thought: Chinese Thought and Religion Under the Mongols*, pp. 419–77.

REFERENCE WORKS FOR THE STUDY OF THE *CHIN P'ING MEI*

(Arranged Alphabetically by Author)

Chou Chün-t'ao 周鈞韜. *Chin P'ing Mei su-ts'ai lai-yüan* 金瓶梅素材來源 (Sources of the *Chin P'ing Mei*). Cheng-chou: Chung-chou ku-chi ch'u-pan she, 1991.

————, ed. *Chin P'ing Mei tzu-liao hsü-pien: 1919–1949* 金瓶梅資料續編: 1919–1949 (Supplementary compilation of materials on the *Chin P'ing Mei*: 1919–1949). Peking: Pei-ching ta-hsüeh ch'u-pan she, 1990.

Chu I-hsüan 朱一玄, ed. *Chin P'ing Mei tzu-liao hui-pien* 金瓶梅資料匯編 (Collected material on the *Chin P'ing Mei*). Tientsin: Nan-k'ai ta-hsüeh ch'u-pan she, 1985.

Fang Ming 方銘, ed. *Chin P'ing Mei tzu-liao hui-lu* 金瓶梅資料匯錄 (Collected material on the *Chin P'ing Mei*). Ho-fei: Huang-shan shu-she, 1986.

Feng Yüan-chün 馮沅君. "*Chin P'ing Mei tz'u-hua* chung te wen-hsüeh shih-liao"

金瓶梅詞話中的文學史料 (Materials for literary history in the *Chin P'ing Mei tz'u-hua*). In her *Ku-chü shuo-hui* 古劇說彙 (Studies of old drama). Peking: Tso-chia ch'u-pan she, 1956, pp. 180–229.

Hou Chung-i 侯忠義 and Wang Ju-mei 王汝梅, eds. *Chin P'ing Mei tzu-liao hui-pien* 金瓶梅資料匯編 (Collected material on the *Chin P'ing Mei*). Peking: Pei-ching ta-hsüeh ch'u-pan she, 1985.

Hu Wen-pin 胡文彬. *Chin P'ing Mei shu-lu* 金瓶梅書錄 (Bibliography of the *Chin P'ing Mei*). Shen-yang: Liao-ning jen-min ch'u-pan she, 1986.

Huang Lin 黃霖 et al., eds. *Chin P'ing Mei ta tz'u-tien* 金瓶梅大辭典 (Great dictionary of the *Chin P'ing Mei*). Ch'eng-tu: Pa-Shu shu-she, 1991.

————, ed. *Chin P'ing Mei tzu-liao hui-pien* 金瓶梅資料彙編 (Collected material on the *Chin P'ing Mei*). Peking: Chung-hua shu-chü, 1987.

Kinpeibai shiwa goi sakuin 金瓶梅詞話語彙索引 (Index to the vocabulary of the *Chin P'ing Mei tz'u-hua*). Nagoya: Saika shorin, 1972.

Li Pu-ch'ing 李布青. *Chin P'ing Mei li-yü su-yen* 金瓶梅俚語俗諺 (Vernacular expressions and proverbial sayings in the *Chin P'ing Mei*). Peking: Pao-wen t'ang shu-tien, 1988.

Li Shen 李申. *Chin P'ing Mei fang-yen su-yü hui-shih* 金瓶梅方言俗語匯釋 (Assembled glosses on the dialectal and idiomatic expressions in the *Chin P'ing Mei*). Peking: Pei-ching shih-fan hsüeh-yüan ch'u-pan she, 1992.

Lu Ko 魯歌 and Ma Cheng 馬征. *Chin P'ing Mei jen-wu ta-ch'üan* 金瓶梅人物大全 (Great compendium of the characters in the *Chin P'ing Mei*). Ch'ang-ch'un: Chi-lin wen-shih ch'u-pan she, 1991.

Pai Wei-kuo 白維國. *Chin P'ing Mei tz'u-tien* 金瓶梅詞典 (Dictionary of the *Chin P'ing Mei*). Peking: Chung-hua shu-chü, 1991.

Sun Hsün 孫遜 et al., eds. *Chin P'ing Mei chien-shang tz'u-tien* 金瓶梅鑑賞辭典 (Dictionary for the appreciation of the *Chin P'ing Mei*). Shanghai: Shang-hai ku-chi ch'u-pan she, 1990.

Ts'ai Tun-yung 蔡敦勇. *Chin P'ing Mei chü-ch'ü p'in-t'an* 金瓶梅劇曲品探 (A critical evaluation of the drama and song quoted in the *Chin P'ing Mei*). Nanking: Chiang-su wen-i ch'u-pan she, 1989.

Wang Li-ch'i 王利器 et al., eds. *Chin P'ing Mei tz'u-tien* 金瓶梅詞典 (Dictionary of the *Chin P'ing Mei*). Ch'ang-ch'un: Chi-lin wen-shih ch'u-pan she, 1988.

Wei Tzu-yün 魏子雲. *Chin P'ing Mei tz'u-hua chu-shih* 金瓶梅詞話註釋 (Glosses on the *Chin P'ing Mei tz'u-hua*). 3 vols. Taipei: Tseng ni chih wen-hua shih-yeh yu-hsien kung-ssu, 1981.

Yao Ling-hsi 姚靈犀. *P'ing-wai chih-yen* 瓶外卮言 (Flowing words outside the vase). Tientsin: T'ien-chin shu-chü, 1940.

INDEX